THE REVENGE

Shirley Conran is the bestselling author of *Lace* and *Super-woman*. She is the mother of designers Sebastian Conran and Jasper Conran. She now divides her time between France and London and has been inspired by her research into Victorian theatre and the birth of the movies in America to write this richly detailed historical novel about two women's lives.

SHIRLEY CONRAN

THE REVENGE

PAN BOOKS

First published 1998 by Macmillan

This edition published 1999 by Pan Books
an imprint of Macmillan Publishers Ltd
25 Eccleston Place, London SW1W 9NF
Basingstoke and Oxford
www.macmillan.co.uk

Associated companies throughout the world

ISBN 0 330 34657 1

7 9 8 6

A CIP catalogue record for this book is available from
the British Library.

Typeset by SetSystems Ltd, Saffron Walden, Essex
Printed and bound in Great Britain by
Mackays of Chatham plc, Chatham, Kent

This book is for Anne Sibbald
with love and thanks

Boiling point . . . the temperature at which the vapour pressure of a liquid equals the external pressure.

– Collins English Dictionary

Chapter One

Whether it was due to God, Fate, Chance or part of some unfathomable cosmic design, Mimi later realized that one small unexpected incident – a broken bootlace – had casually twisted and redirected her destiny. Had her boot-lace not broken, she would probably have started her career as a scullery maid, and finished it as a parlourmaid.

Instead, when she sheltered from the rough April wind in the Railway Refreshment Room at Crewe station, Mimi proved her own equation: chance + choice = fate. Waiting impatiently for the next train to London, she listened to carousing soldiers, tunics unbuttoned, sing in a corner. Hanging on the wall above the small group of soldiers, a gilt-framed mezzotint of a grim-faced woman hung crookedly against the yellowing, smoke-stained walls; the disapproving eye of Queen Victoria – who had died three months before – still gazed severely down at her brave boys, patiently waiting at a provincial station to do their duty and die for their country.

> 'Rule, Britannia! Britannia rules the waves!
> Britons never, never shall be bleeding slaves!'

The stout woman serving behind the food counter

glanced at the soldiers, sneezed, wiped her nose on the back of her hand, then rubbed her hand clean on her grubby white apron. Those poor sods, in the red tunics, waiting for the London train would soon be bleeding themselves, if not corpses, for they were travelling to the Boer War, in South Africa.

Standing in a nimbus of steam, she turned her attention back to the hungry straggle of travellers at the far side of the glass-fronted counter. The tea-urn had broken and she wielded an enormous white teapot like a garden hose, pouring continually along rows of chipped mugs, trailing brown liquid between each one. As she looked up to hand over the first, filled mug, she glanced sharply at the waiting mob; that whey-faced girl looked as if she was about to faint. More trouble.

Standing in the steamy warmth, Mimi Quinn wriggled her toes inside the unyielding cheap leather of her new black boots. Thirteen years old and small for her age, she gazed longingly at the counter, topped with thick plates piled high with succulent ham sandwiches and shiny currant buns. She felt giddy because it was long after midday, and she had not eaten since breakfast – a slice of bread thinly coated with dripping. She could not really afford it, but a hot cup of tea and a sticky cinnamon bun would be a fine way to celebrate her new, frightening freedom! She pulled her darned Paisley shawl closer round her skinny shoulders, and squeezed the comforting coins knotted in her red-spotted handkerchief. Still she could not believe that she had finally escaped. She had dreamed of this so many times but now, having success-fully snatched her opportunity, she *still* seemed to be dreaming. She half expected to feel a cruel, heavy hand drop on her shoulder, and end her dash for freedom. But as she patiently waited for her tea and sticky bun she timorously allowed hope to rise in her heart; and slowly this tremulous note of hope grew into a mighty, orchestrated burst of joy as, for the first time, she felt free. She felt dazed, exultant disbelief, found it hard to believe that she had been so swiftly shoved into action.

There had been no time to think.

She had scampered fast up the cobbled alley, past the pub on the corner, then ran, hell for leather, to the tram stop, where workmen had almost finished erecting the overhead wires to electrify the horse-drawn trams. The bus conductor had grumbled as he dug in his black leather satchel but found no change for a crown. So he allowed the youngster to travel free, provided she sat upstairs in the open air.

As she jumped off the tram, Mimi, unaccustomed to wearing boots, staggered and wrenched her left ankle. She regained her balance but found she had broken her boot-lace, so was forced to sit on the stone kerb, unthread the entire lace, knot and rethread it, before running on towards the station. There a cocky young ticket-office clerk removed a pencil from his ear and gave a waspish smile. 'Pity. Ya just missed the direct London train. Now ya'll have to catch the slow 'un and change at Crewe.'

In the warmth of the refreshment room, two infantry soldiers joined the little crowd before the food counter; the Tommies were self-consciously smart in red tunics, tight black trousers and pillbox hats with a liquorice-black strap under the chin. The chunkier of the two nudged his companion, then both turned to stare at Mimi's small-featured, snub-nosed face: her tangled hair – dirty, but thick and glossy as a golden fox – was held back from her face by a green tartan ribbon; she had the milky skin of a redhead, and a long, graceful neck; her vivid green eyes were bright, sharp and intelligent.

Outside the refreshment room, the distant wail of a steam engine grew louder and louder until, with a whiff of soot and cinders, and an agonizing screech that sounded like two mating dinosaurs, a powerful black engine thundered up to the platform and with a shriek of brakes drew to a halt. Sedate passengers wearing dark cloaks and overcoats slowly climbed down; they carefully avoided a little group dressed in crumpled clothes more colourfully flamboyant than those of other travellers. As this noisy bunch tumbled into the refreshment room everyone turned to stare, for they seemed somehow different to everyone else. Could they be foreigners? . . . No, they all chattered loudly in English.

The five men of the party looked scruffy and yet carried themselves as if they were important. Their womenfolk had unnaturally bold eyes with stiff black lashes, unnaturally red mouths and unnaturally pink cheeks; a couple of them laughed affectionately as they unwound the woollen scarves of two medium-sized children, wiped their snotty little noses and promised them candy-sticks if they behaved themselves.

Mimi wondered if this group was one large family, for they shared an easy familiarity as they noisily settled round a circular corner table beyond the dying coals of the fire. Although they all shared a certain chirpy, self-satisfied awareness, there was no family resemblance; but clearly this little group was accustomed to attracting attention. The adults dumped their luggage and their bursting brown-paper parcels and watched the children feed seed to an unenthusiastic canary in a gilt cage. A stout woman in a grubby pink velvet bonnet called, 'Get us some Guinness, Joe, I'm parched.' A portly, cheerful-looking man with a brown bowler hat tipped to the back of his head obediently pushed back his chair.

'I'll help you get the drinks, Joe,' offered a lanky, ginger-haired lad in a velvet-collared green overcoat that was far too large for him. As he stood up, he noticed Mimi's stare, and winked at her. Mimi blushed and jerked her face away. As she finally reached the front of the food counter, struggling to keep her place, the ginger-haired lad slid in behind her. 'Cor, what a mob! We'll be lucky if we're served before our train leaves.' He lengthened his vowels and shortened his word endings in the soft, soothing voice of a Yorkshireman.

Mimi twisted her head to look up at his freckled, triangular face. Again, the lad winked. Again, Mimi blushed. To hide her confusion, she blurted out, 'You're an uppity lad.'

'Yes, I *am* an ooppity lood.' He gently mimicked her flat, softly mooing Liverpool accent.

'Cheeky, too!' But Mimi was curious. Hesitantly, she asked, 'Are you lot all one family?'

Cocking his head to one side, the lad considered her question. 'In a way, but not the way you mean. We're the Jenkins Theatrical Touring Company, and we work the provinces.' He jerked his thin face towards the stout man in the brown bowler who stood at the bar. 'That's our guv'nor, Jolly Joe Jenkins.'

Mimi's eyes shone. '*You're actors!*'

'No, we tour music halls. Much better pay on the halls than in legit.'

'What's legit?'

'The legitimate theatre – as if everyone in music hall

was illegitimate!' He pulled a theatrically guilty face. 'Ooops! Pardon *me*, Vicar.'

'That's even better!' Mimi had never been in a music hall, but everyone in Britain knew about them. Over a hundred years before, canny tavern landlords had noticed that they sold more ale if there was a sing-song, so they provided free entertainment to promote profitable bonhomie. Then they built a stage for the performers at one end of their supper rooms. Now the variety shows had pushed the bars to the very back of the hall, and music-hall stars had become the popular folk heroes of the day: everyone loved their raffish, carefree zest for life as much as their performances. Apart from pubs, the halls were one of the few places where the poor could go for a bit of cheerful company, light and warmth on a cold winter's night – often the only way they could briefly escape a home which might be one bleak, freezing vermin-infested slum room housing an entire family.

The ginger lad pulled a crumpled paper from his pocket and thrust it into Mimi's hand. Laboriously, she read the handbill.

JOLLY JOE JENKINS PRESENTS ... Jemima Jenkins with her two trained French poodles ... clog dancers ... jugglers ... singers Mavis and Samuel Potts ... trick cyclist ... acrobats ... contortionist ... ventriloquist ... and many comic sketches.

The lad explained, 'We all do at least six different jobs. Joe is our MC and lead comic. I'm Baz Baker – juggler, trick cyclist, clog dancer, singer. Little Daisy – that pouter pigeon in the green bonnet – used to be our tightrope walker 'til she got arthritis, so now she's Wardrobe.'

Mimi looked dubiously at Little Daisy, surely too heavy for any rope to have held her weight. 'What does the pretty one do?' She pointed to a girl so lovely that she might have just stepped out of a calendar picture: she had pulled off her gloves and was blowing on her hands to warm them. She looked at Mimi with large black-fringed violet eyes on either side of a small straight nose, slightly tilted at the tip; the short upper lip above her mouth was that of a china cupid; she hadn't yet put up the thick fair hair that fell on either side of her creamy oval face with the innocent stare of a golden, unattainable angel.

'Betsy? Can't act, got a thin voice, but she don't need more than that face, do she? And she ain't a bad dancer, you should see her cancan – real French style with saucy splits at the finish . . . That's Betsy's ma sitting beside her, the one with the daffodil yellow wig and half a pound of paint on her face; thinks her kiddy's going to be a second Lillie Langtry, guards Betsy like a chick from the foxes.' Baz winked suggestively. Mimi knew that Miss Langtry, famous beauty and long-time mistress of the new king, Edward VII, had recently retired from the stage with a fortune of two million pounds.

Baz spoke so loudly that everyone around him turned to gaze at his mobile face and listen to his patter, but Mimi noticed his grubby adolescent paw swiftly snake out and snatch a ham sandwich from the glass counter.

With equally surprising speed, the fat woman with the teapot leaned forward and grabbed his thin wrist. 'Got you, my lad!' she shrieked. 'See that, folks? I'm sick of you thieving bastards! Someone call a copper!'

Baz Baker tried to tug his grubby wrist away, but the triumphant fat woman grasped it tight with her left hand, while her forgotten right hand continued to pour tea over the penny buns. The crowd around the counter immediately took sides. The soldiers urged the fat woman to let the poor little sod go, while more upright citizens demanded constables and jail.

When Mimi saw the frightened look of surprise in Baz's eyes she realized that this was not the first time he had nicked food, merely the first time that he had been caught. She hesitated, then cried indignantly, 'He *wasn't* stealing. I asked him to get me a sandwich! A girl could starve to death – waiting to be served here!' Mimi held up a silver crown. 'Look, here's me money! I was about to pay you for it.'

The angry woman looked suspiciously at her. 'Where did a girl like you get a silver crown?' she shrieked. 'I bet you two young 'uns work together – *thieving*!'

'I never saw this lad before in me life,' Mimi snapped, 'and me mam gave me her savings to get to London and buy me uniform, for I'm off to work in service! So you'll look right daft if you call a copper! Now – do you want it or not?' The silver coin shone temptingly in her outstretched palm.

Jolly Joe pushed his way through the little crowd and flipped a silver sixpence on the tea-puddled counter. 'Take her money, miss, and forget the misunderstanding.' In order to pick up his tip, the fat woman would have to release the lad's wrist.

'Misunderstanding my arse,' she muttered, but grabbed the silver tanner, for the girl *had* been waiting in front of the boy, she *was* offering to pay, and a copper would say there was no case, although everyone knew that the little bastard had meant to nick that sandwich.

Joe threw an *I'll deal with you later* look at Baz, now massaging his wrist, then turned to Mimi with theatrical politeness. 'My dear young lady, may I invite you to join us at our humble repast?'

Delighted, Mimi followed Joe to the corner table, where everyone around it was indignantly protesting that Baz had *not* nicked the bleeding ham sandwich, which now lay in the dirty sawdust before the counter, trodden to pulp by the waiting crowd.

Joe plonked an armful of bottles on the table. 'That's the last time I'm saving your backside, Baz. You're lucky this little lady is such a good actress, and had her wits about her.'

Everybody burst out laughing. Little Daisy pulled out a pocket knife and divided a couple of pork pies; stout Mrs Jenkins produced cheese sandwiches and iced buns; Betsy leaned across to Mimi and offered her an orange; Baz slapped two purple-wrapped bars of chocolate on the table.

'I wonder if Baz paid for them bars of chocolate?' Little Daisy hissed in Mimi's ear.

'What are you girls whispering about?' Jolly Joe called jovially.

'This young lady asked what life was like on the road,' Little Daisy immediately lied.

Jolly Joe said in a resonant voice that did not expect contradiction, 'It's a *good* life! It pays well and there's always a demand — because people'll always pay for their pleasure, won't they?'

His troupe nodded dutifully.

Jolly Joe looked speculatively at Mimi. She would be pretty enough, once she'd been cleaned up, and put on a bit of weight. And a girl didn't need much more than that, for what he had in mind. Swiftly, Jolly Joe caught the eye of Baz, then slightly jerked his head towards Mimi.

Baz nodded.

His eyes now on Mimi, Jolly Joe waved one hand, like God showing off his new world. 'We tour around the country like the idle rich, and we always have good company on our travels. If we don't like one town, why, we'll be moving to another next Sunday! We're free all day while the rest of the world is working its arse off! In the evening, we each do our little turn, then have a bit of a party afterwards! It's a *grand* life!' No need to mention that because they travelled constantly most performers had few friends outside the theatre, or that their demanding life left little energy or time for outside interests.

Looking at Mimi's animated, pretty face, the rest of the troupe sensed that Joe was fishing and required their support, so they nodded hard. They knew that Baz had been without a stooge for over a month, since Nelly stayed behind in Hereford to marry the stage-door keeper of the Kemble.

'Sure, it's a glamorous life on the road,' Baz confirmed, then muttered under his breath, 'If a person's willing to work like a dray horse for about the same pay.'

Hesitantly, Mimi asked Jolly Joe, 'How does a person . . . get on the stage?'

Betsy's beautiful face suddenly became animated. 'First you train. *I* went to the Ada Jarrett School of Drama for two years – but there's plenty of teachers for elocution, singing and voice projection, dancing, and such.'

Baz nodded. 'Once you've trained, you join a good company, to get experience: somewhere like the Theatre Royal, Margate'll take you for six months, if you pay twenty-five quid.'

Daisy chipped in, 'After that, you work in panto at Christmas – nothing better to help you get used to an audience . . . see them as friends, nothing to be frightened of.' No need to mention the constant hope and rejection, the alarmingly addictive and giddy elation of having enthralled a good audience or the energy-sucking, instant gloom of a lethargic audience.

Mimi was clearly depressed by these impossible suggestions.

'Of course, if you can't *afford* to train . . . you could just . . . string along with us . . .' Jolly Joe carefully trailed his bait. 'Naturally, you couldn't expect to get paid until you was performing – but you'd get your board and keep.'

Mimi pulled her shawl more tightly around her shoulders.

Everyone waited.

She stammered, 'But what could I *do*?'

'Baz'll teach you whatever you need to know, ducky,' Jolly Joe offered. 'And you can give Daisy a hand in Wardrobe.'

'I can wash well, sir, for me mam works in a laundry,' Mimi said eagerly, 'but I can't sew or make clothes.'

'You'll soon pick it up,' Jolly Joe said serenely.

If Daisy taught her to sew, mend and pack, Mimi thought, then even if life in the theatre didn't work out quite so jolly as it sounded, she might have a better chance as a lady's maid.

Baz leaned forward. 'There's only a couple of things you need to know about life on stage. One, never be late. Two, never be tired. The public loves energy, see? Good spirits is contagious.'

Mrs Joe beamed benevolently from beneath her pink bonnet. 'And there's another big advantage to this business, dearie – you ain't never friendless, you ain't never alone. Wherever you go, you'll find other friendly stage folk with the same interests.' No need to mention that the warm family feeling of the theatre, so enticingly dangled to his little fish by Jolly Joe, was due to the fact that performers sought out their own kind – other addicts who understood their need – and closed ranks to outsiders who did not understand and often disapproved of a performer's rackety life and problems.

Jolly Joe nodded. 'The performer's motto is the same as the Frog's: Liberty, Equality, Fraternity, but our band of brothers spreads *all around the world* from digs in Brixton to backstage on Broadway; from the ... er ... Trocadero in Paris to some fuzzy-wuzzy show in Timbuktu.'

Mimi listened excitedly as Joe deftly painted theatrical life as one big adventure for one happy family group. He knew that the more she believed this, the lower the salary she would eventually accept from him. No need to mention that at any given moment in the British theatre only about 20 per cent of actors had jobs, so the remaining 80 per cent were out of work. Having made his pitch, he immediately buried his nose in the pink pages of *Sporting Life* as if he had lost interest. He knew that he had caught his little fish.

Mimi remembered being jostled in the station crowds that morning, as she waited to purchase her ticket. Suddenly she had felt as if she trembled on the crumbling edge of a black void, felt a nameless dread, felt completely alone in an unfriendly world, and already homesick for her mam and the little 'uns.

Now she started to tremble with excitement as she considered taking this gamble on an exciting life of travel and friendship, rather than a drab existence as a domestic drudge in London. She forgot her mother's careful plan for her future, and instead felt a wild urge to get on the wrong train and go with this group of strangers to whatever unsuitable place they were travelling towards. She need not then feel anxious about the dreaded possibility of not finding work before her money ran out. She need not buy a hat, supplicate an agency, or stand in line, like a slave at auction, to offer herself as a scullery maid – for now a job was being *offered* to her!

She was not being reckless or impulsive, she was being sensible, Mimi told herself, as she leaned across to Joe, and timidly whispered, 'If I change me ticket, can I join you lot?'

* * *

The train to Scotland pulled away from the platform. From the bench on which Mimi sat, invasive bristles of cheap, plush bench scratched her legs through her serge skirt; from behind her boots rose an odour of old orange peel and cheap cigarette ends. Nevertheless, she looked delightedly from the grimy window as the unheated train bisected the suburbs of Crewe and rushed northwards along the backbone of Britain, through green fields and forests, villages and dark-red towns, acres of factory chimneys that belched black smoke to stain the sky.

Before that morning, Mimi had never travelled on *any* vehicle; now she swayed with dreamy delight to the soothing, *tiddley-tum* rhythm of the iron wheels, and relaxed. Now he couldn't trace her, he couldn't catch her, he couldn't stop her: she was safe, she need never feel afraid again. Whatever lay ahead, nothing could be worse than what she had left behind.

Jolly Joe sat next to Baz, in the coveted window seat; his wife was opposite, next to Betsy and her mother. Mimi sat with her back to the engine, wedged between Daisy and Baz, who balanced his canary cage on his knees. He grinned at Mimi. 'A body can always afford to feed a canary – and I ain't got much else to carry around with me.' He did not add that the cheerful yellow bird was his much-loved, much-needed companion and the only permanent thing in his life. Because performers never knew where they would be next month, whether penniless, or ill amongst strangers, their life was as tough emotionally as it was physically, and so most of them lived in a permanent state of anxiety and insecurity, carefully repressed by simulated gaiety.

The group talked loudly and incessantly: the men talked of sport: boxers, horses, dogs. With varying degrees of envious admiration, the women gossiped about the three actresses who still dominated the world stage: Sarah Bernhardt, Eleanora Duse and Ellen Terry. For years these international stars had been bigger box-office draws than any male. As it was still considered daring for a woman to become a nurse, going on the stage was definitely not respectable – unless you were a star, when you could do as you pleased.

'You can get away with anything, if you're rich and famous,' Mrs Joe sighed enviously.

Little Daisy nodded. 'Just look at Ellen Terry, still a blinking symbol of girlish purity after having them two illegitimate kiddies!'

Mimi's shocked eyes opened wide.

'It's disgusting!' Betsy's mother gave her verdict.

The performers passed around bottled stout, threw oranges to each other, read aloud bits from the latest copy of *The Stage*, pointed to cows in fields, told anecdotes with much dramatic in-ton-a-tion, and shrieked with laughter.

Other travellers poked their heads in through the open window, then swiftly withdrew and hurried on to quieter carriages with more space on the luggage racks.

Jolly Joe's troupe carried their belongings in wicker skips the size of professional laundry baskets; these travelled with their scenery, props and the two poodles in the guard's van. Supposedly, each entertainer carried only a small case containing overnight things plus make-up box, but the luggage rack opposite Mimi was piled to the roof with a collapsible canvas bath, a wicker food hamper, two Gladstone bags, a hatbox and an assortment of large, lumpy brown-paper parcels.

Seeing Mimi stare upwards, plump little Daisy poked a friendly elbow into her ribs. 'It's the packing that puts most people off the Perfeshun. If you can organize your packing for a tour, then you can organize anything, run the blooming country! ... Marie Lloyd even travels with a collapsible billiard table: that way, she meets men.'

'*I* don't want to meet men,' Mimi said abruptly.

Daisy stared at her with the street-sharp brown eyes of a Cockney survivor. The whole troupe respected Daisy's powers of intuition. She had begged Baz's ma not to hop on them new-fangled 'buses. She had been right about not leaving that Leeds landlord with the Potts boy and she had been spot on the nail when she said of their new manager, 'I don't trust that bugger; his eyes remind me of me Uncle Arthur.' Two weeks later, the manager disappeared with the cash box and they never got paid that week. Because of Daisy's expertise, Jolly Joe had quietly asked her to find out about Mimi's background. He wanted to make certain that she wasn't running away from home, because he could expect trouble with the law for abducting a minor.

Daisy had a sympathetic manner and a crooked little mouth that turned up on one side in an understanding grin. Mimi readily told her about her mam, then added that her pa, a shipwright, was dead. Joe overheard, and was reassured.

Daisy continued to probe. 'Mimi, that's an odd moniker.'

'I was christened Thenia, but mam said me first words were "mimimimimi". So that's what she called me.'

'Thenia! That's even *odder*!'

'It's American,' Mimi proudly explained. 'My gran was a Yankee from Boston.' Thenia Crane had died in 1895, when Mimi was only seven years old, but she remembered the shrunken old woman. She had worked as a barmaid in Boston's dock area until 1850, when she fell for Ezekiel Crane, third mate in the *Cultivator*, which sailed from Liverpool carrying Irish immigrants fleeing the potato famine and returned from Boston with cargoes of timber. Mimi's mam had told her that Granny Thenia had once had amber eyes, high cheekbones and thick red hair that hung to her hips – she had been beautiful: child-sized and slender, with a small waist, even after she had given birth to eleven babies.

'So you're from a Liverpool family?' Daisy's detective work was interrupted by Mrs Jenkins, who suggested a sing-song. So they all belted out 'Goodbye Dolly Gray' then 'Tarrara *boom*-de-ay', after which Betsy gave them 'Only a Bird in a Gilded Cage', which she sang with much emotion, eyeing Baz's canary. Baz then bawled 'Burling-ton Bertie' which Daisy explained was a Vesta Tilley number ... '*Never* heard of Vesta Tilley? Britain's most famous male impersonator?'

As an encore, Baz sang, 'Will you be my bundle of trouble?' with naughty innuendo.

Daisy laughed. 'Naughty Baz is the one who's a bundle of trouble. In one part of his act, he slips on a banana skin, waves his arms like windmills, then somehow manages to get back his balance – and he's just like that off stage! Always getting into scrapes. He's quick-witted, so he always gets out of them. But don't let Baz get *you* into trouble.'

Mimi gave Daisy a cold look and drew away from her. 'Nobody's going to get *me* into trouble.'

Daisy giggled, and whispered, 'I didn't mean put you in the family way, ducky. Baz likes the boys, so there ain't no risk of that.'

The only person who did not sing on the journey was Mrs Bridges, or Vi, as Jolly Joe called her, only to be corrected with 'Vio*let*' by Mrs Bridges in a flat-vowelled nasal whine, overlaid by gentility. After that, Jolly Joe referred to Mrs Bridges as 'Violate', to her unconcealed irritation.

Daisy whispered to Mimi, 'Vi wants nothing to do with the troupe, she reckons we're beneath her. Vi makes all Betsy's clothes but she won't lift a bloody finger to help me in Wardrobe. She devotes her bleeding life to Betsy.'

'Lucky Betsy.' Mimi sounded wistful.

'No! Vi never gives that poor girl a moment's peace! Betsy's just fourteen, but already she's scared stiff of losing her looks.' She explained that when Betsy went to bed she wore gloves over creamed hands; her face was nightly painted with calamine lotion to prevent spots, her golden hair pulled up in rag twists that kept her awake. During the day, her feet were jammed into pinching boots, and her hands forced into gloves a size too small, because a lady always had small hands and feet. Her skin was never allowed in the sun, so she always wore a wide-brimmed hat.

After the train passed Manchester, Mrs Bridges went to sleep with her head on her daughter's shoulder, bonnet crooked. Betsy immediately pulled a cheap magazine from her reticule and buried her pretty little nose in *Eve's Own*. Since the Company had been on the move before dawn, they were all eventually lulled to sleep by the rhythm of the wheels. Jolly Joe snored lightly. Daisy's head lolled against Mimi's shoulder.

Only Mimi could not doze off like the others, for too much had happened to her since she woke that morning, and her mind was awhirl with exhilaration and astonishment to find herself in show business. Unaware that she had just met the person who would enrich her exciting new life, and also the person who would twist it into a tortured knot, she smiled at the canary. She was now determined to forget the past, to pretend it had never happened, to wipe the shame and the guilt from her memory.

* * *

Since her birth, Mimi's home had been a 'back-to-back' in an alley of Liverpool slum houses; one room deep, each house had a similar one stuck to the rear of it. There was no yard, and only one small front window through which a little light entered the room from the narrow cobbled alley outside. A communal water tap was fixed to one wall of the alley; on either side of it was a stinking privy, two to serve the entire alley, over which hung a depressed air of poverty and brutality, even in summer when, despite the lethargy and squalor, children played hopscotch on the cobblestones and women sat on doorsteps to feed babies at their breasts.

The houses stank as badly as the occupants; rats moved freely through the buildings, nipping at the toes and fingers of sleepers, biting the faces of babies, who slept in an empty dresser drawer until they were old enough to share the family bed without being smothered. Any epidemic, however mild, brought death to the alley.

Dirty water and chamber-pot slops were thrown into the open central drain, and drunks pissed into it as they staggered homeward at night from the pub on the corner, the Black Bull. The dark silence was broken, not by barking dogs – nobody could afford to feed a dog – but by drunken shouts and terrified screams. The inhabitants of this alley did not live, they existed.

Two other families also dwelled in the house occupied by the Quinns; one family in the cellar and one on the floor above, so there was little privacy and constant noise. The colour of burnt porridge, sagging, scabrous ceilings flaked onto bare, rotting floorboards. Vermin clustered in the damp, bulging plaster walls, in the straw mattresses, in the filthy hair of every inhabitant.

There was little furniture in Mimi's home: a black iron bedstead in the corner, with one castor missing; a shaky wooden table covered with yellowed newspaper; an old wicker armchair and a rotting cupboard for pots, pans and candle stubs. A black cauldron stood on the hearth; on the chimney shelf above was a chipped blue enamel teapot, a candlestick and an out-of-date calendar with a coloured picture of a bluebell-filled wood: Mimi's mam liked to look at it and dream.

Alf Quinn worked – when he could – at the Albert

Dock as a matey, one of the shipwrights who carried out all structural repairs on ships in dry dock. The Muster bell sounded at six in the morning, when workmen clocked into the Dockyard at the big gates; the first Brow count of the day was taken, as each man entered the ship upon which he was working: his departure time was also recorded by time clock. Shipwright Quinn earned twenty-three shillings a week, of which ten shillings were handed to his wife for food, six shillings for rent, a shilling each for the clothing club and for fuel. Alf kept the remaining crown – five shillings. Mrs Quinn's laundry wages of ten shillings a week provided the additional money needed to feed – just – her children.

As long as Mimi could remember, like many other men in the alley, her pa had been drunk or hung-over. Threatened into submission by his unpredictable rages, Alf Quinn's terrified family lived on twenty-four-hour-alert for his next explosion, for the next beating. Ashamed of his savage attacks, they kept them secret, as did many similarly placed women and children of the alley.

Normally Mam left home before dawn, for she worked at a laundry, six days a week. Mimi prepared breakfast (tin mugs of tea, thick bread spread with thin dripping) for young Frank, Hetty and her pa. On Sunday the laundry shut, so Mam cooked, cleaned and mended, while her man stayed in bed and nursed his sore head until the Black Bull opened.

* * *

As the northbound train sped on through field and forest, towns and tunnels, Mimi found it hard to believe that only a few hours had passed since that morning, when her pa had left for the pub, as usual. Mam had pinned shawls round the little 'uns and pushed them out to play in the alley, although a cold wind was blowing: she had then turned to look sadly at her puzzled daughter. Once, Mrs Quinn thought, she had also possessed that same thick red hair and pale, smooth skin, but now her face was gaunt from anxiety, overwork and birthing seven children, four of whom had died before they could talk. Now, her withered face was surrounded by thin wisps of ginger-grey hair, her sunken cheeks, her dry, pinched mouth, her blackened or missing teeth proof of malnourishment and ill-treatment: she was thirty-four years old. But seemingly undefeated by their bitter experiences, her eyes were still the same clear, piercing green as those of her daughter, just as trusting and hopeful.

Mimi stared back, puzzled.

Mam said in a low, urgent voice, 'You started to bleed last week.'

'Mam, you told me that's what happens when a girl grows up. You said I wasn't going to die, that I mustn't worry . . .'

'What I didn't tell you was the bleeding means you can have a baby, love. So that means you must leave. I'll put up with a lot to see us fed, but not that.' Mam spoke stiffly and swiftly, as if following a course of pre-determined action that she dreaded, but was bent on pursuing.

Mimi hesitated, then pointed out, 'Hetty's only eight years old.'

'So were you,' her mam said shortly; she moved to the bedstead where the reeking blankets were still flung back, as her pa had left them. Her bare feet were thrust into worn, wooden clogs; over a ragged flannel skirt darkened by grease, she wore a much-patched grey man's shirt.

From beneath the bed her mam pulled out a pair of new black boots and a faded red Paisley shawl. She beckoned Mimi over, sat her on the edge of the bed, pulled off her dirty wooden clogs and eased the new boots on her daughter's grubby bare feet: they were a little tight, but Mimi gazed proudly at them. Mam then tied her hair back with a new green tartan ribbon, carefully wrapped the Paisley shawl around her daughter's shoulders, felt for her daughter's hand, and wrapped it around a knotted red handkerchief.

'There's a bit of real soap and two silver crowns in that kerchief.' Mam spoke rapidly again, as if rehearsed. 'Catch the horse tram to the railway station and get a third-class ticket to London. Pay a penny for the Ladies' Room and clean yourself up – they got water taps in them places. Soon as you get to London, buy a hat: a girl's got to look respectable if she wants a situation. Then catch a bus to Baker Street and ask for Massey's Employment Agency, where they placed your Aunt Gert.'

Mrs Quinn hugged her astonished daughter. 'Try to get a job as a laundry maid.' If Mimi started off as a laundry maid, she'd maybe rise to second lady's maid (if the establishment was a big one) and finally might reach the position of lady's maid to the mistress.

'Be sure to ask for *any* job in a place with a big staff – for you'll not get ahead as the maid-of-all-work,' Mam warned. 'You'll be paid next to nothing, but you'll have a roof over your head, and you'll be fed.' Children even younger than thirteen were employed in domestic service, as scullery maids, boot boys and tweenies; some earned as much as nine pounds a year; but for that money Mrs Quinn knew that Mimi would be expected to work from five in the morning to ten at night. She would be free on Thursday afternoon, but expected to return before supper-time.

'When you're situated, the housekeeper'll give you an advance of pay to buy your uniform – don't pay more than a shilling for stockings or four shillings for a cotton dress!' Mam tried to sound cheerful. 'Remember to be nice to the lady's maid – do *anything* you can to help her, then you'll learn from her, like Gert did.' Aunt Gert, now a lady's maid in Edinburgh, was the family's success story, although her success had meant that now she wanted no contact with her family. But if Gert could manage it from a Liverpool slum, why then surely Mimi could.

Mimi unknotted the handkerchief and saw two silver coins. She breathed, 'Mam, where did you get all this money?'

'Uncle,' Ma replied, using the euphemism for a pawn shop.

'But you ain't got nothing left to pawn except...' Mimi grabbed Mam's left hand. It was sinewy and raw-knuckled, with broken, split nails, and fingertips permanently wizened by immersion in water.

Mimi looked for what her mam most treasured, what most women in their alley did not possess: a gold wedding ring, sign of respectability, sign that once she had been loved. It was missing from her mam's thin finger.

Mam snatched her hand away. 'Be off, fast as you can, love. And when you get to London, *don't* write home – I'd get a black eye every time you sent a postcard. Just run to that agency. I don't want you sleeping rough in a park for longer than you need. *And don't talk to any men.* If they talk to you – just move away without looking at 'em.'

'You don't have to tell me about men, Mam,' Mimi said bitterly.

Her mother's hasty and casual revelation that she had known of Mimi's suffering had come almost as a physical blow to her daughter. For five years her beloved mam had known of her torture, yet had done nothing to stop it. Her mam had shut her eyes to what was going on. Whatever her reasons, she must have guessed at her daughter's mental anguish. Mam had done nothing to save her. Mimi felt betrayed.

'Why didn't you stop him, Mam?'

'And have him beat me near to death? Then find another woman? He don't have to go no further than the Black Bull. Then we'd a been destitute.' She looked bitter. 'I'm just glad your gran died afore he started on you.'

Mother and daughter stared at each other, until the older woman added helplessly, 'I didn't have much choice, Mimi. We needed his money for food and rent. If you stay, you'll have his baby. If you go, he'll start on Hetty. What would *you* do, Mimi, if you was me?'

* * *

Mimi's nightmare had started on a cold November night when the rain was pissing down outside, and her heavily pregnant mam had hurried along the alley to help Ma Jones, whose new baby was dying of the croup.

In the light of the candle flickering above the empty grate Mimi was already shivering in bed with Frank and Hetty when her pa had called her over to his wicker armchair. As usual, Mimi smelt sour beer on his breath, stale sweat, the doggy odour of his matted, unwashed hair, and the greasy stench of his clothes.

He caught her by her thin waist, pulled her onto his lap and started to tickle her. Mimi wriggled and giggled, afraid to laugh aloud, lest she wake the little 'uns. Her pa tickled her under her chin, in her scrawny armpits, and flickered his fingers across her skinny ribs, like the man at the Black Bull played the upright piano. Then, breathing hoarsely, he slipped his hand up her ragged skirt and pushed at her flesh with his index finger.

'Stop, Pa, you're hurting me!' Mimi gasped in pain.

He took no notice but carried her to the bed, threw her upon the end, pulled up her ragged skirt, and hurled his heavy sweaty body upon hers. Trembling and fearful, Mimi was pinned to the bed by his legs and could hardly breathe. Besides, her pa had brutally beaten her many times in the past, and now hissed a threat of further walloping if she resisted. He rubbed his body against hers, fumbled for his trouser buttons. Roughly, he jerked her knees apart.

Mimi started to sob. Tears ran down her face onto the dirty bedding. She jerked her head away to avoid his beery breath, felt his stubble scrape her face as his repeated attempts at penetration caused her worse pain than any beating. The weight of her father's body forced the air from her lungs. The pain worsened.

Realizing that the little 'uns were awake and silently terrified, she tried to stifle her sobs. But she couldn't stop the scream that tore from her mouth as her flesh tore, when he finally rammed himself into her.

Pa slammed a calloused, filthy hand over her mouth, looked into her terrified eyes as if he saw nothing and then thrust harder. Every time he jerked his body towards hers, her pain worsened. This was a far worse punishment than she had ever before experienced. But what had she done? *Why* was she being punished in this unexpected way? Why was her own Pa whispering filth in her ear as he apparently tried to tear her in two? Mimi wondered whether she was dying, whether he was murdering her.

At last Pa grunted, shuddered and lay still. When he finally rolled off her, Mimi waited, trembling silently, not daring to move.

Is this what other pas did to their little girls? Did their mams know? Of course her mam would never have let Pa hurt Mimi so, no matter how naughty she'd been – and of course that was why her pa had waited until her mam was out: undoubtedly her pa would punish her even more cruelly, should she complain to Mam.

Instinctively, Mimi knew that if her mam were aware of what had just happened, she would fly at her pa and a horrible fight would follow; maybe he'd blacken Mam's eye again, or worse: when he'd broke Mam's arm she hadn't been able to work at the laundry for weeks, so they had eaten even less than usual.

Mimi put her hand down to her still-shaking thighs. She felt a sticky, trickling fluid: now she understood why her mam went to the water bucket after he'd lain upon *her* in the night. Poor Mam.

Pa pulled himself up to sit on the side of the bed. He buttoned himself. Then he leaned over Mimi, still lying spreadeagled on her back, and grunted, 'This is *our* secret, Mimi, do ye hear? Do ye promise? If ye don't, if ye tell your mam – I'll up and leave the lot of you!'

Mimi knew that this was the ever-present, unspoken threat that controlled them all. Without Pa, they wouldn't be able to pay the rent, they'd be put out in the street – she, Frank, Hetty and her mam. In the storybook at school, a papa was supposed to love you and look after you, but in real life her pa was a tyrant who held his family completely in his power. Without fear or remorse, Alf Quinn could do as he pleased to his family, provided he did it in his own home, and didn't kill anyone. The police could not stop him: an Englishman's home was his castle, and the man within it was king of the castle. Every male and his woman in their alley knew that.

Stammering, Mimi promised to say nothing to anyone. In doing so, she acquired an added burden of guilt, for although she would not lie directly to her mam she was about to deceive her.

After Pa had left, slamming the front door, Mimi slowly edged off the bed. She crouched by the little 'uns and whispered, 'Don't worry. He's gone to the Bull. He won't touch you . . . But don't tell our mam, see?'

Mimi heard two frightened whispers of assent. She then crept to the water bucket that stood by the hearth. Still trembling, she reached for the slimy flannel with which Mam washed their scrawny little bodies every Saturday night.

Mimi scrubbed hard at her body, trying to wash away her humiliation. Dazed and bewildered, she dried herself on her skirt, blew out the candle, felt her way to the bed, and buried herself beneath the grey blankets, too weary and shocked to sob further, wondering only when the pain down there would stop, let her sleep . . . and forget.

* * *

Alf Quinn deliberately shut his ears to his daughter's whimpers and pleading; he shut his eyes to her tears and terror. He easily persuaded himself that his little daughter wanted sex as much as he did: that's why she didn't make no fuss – she liked it. They all did. Sex was enjoyable for him, so it must be enjoyable for her. And so, as far as he was concerned, *she* was just as responsible as he for their illicit coupling.

Besides, who better than her pa to teach his daughter about sex, show her the ropes before some other man did? No other man had that right, for she was *his* daughter! And it was a daughter's duty to obey her father, without any fuss. And it was better that he did it with his daughter, rather than go with some poxy tart. Keep it in the family. Keep himself clean for his wife.

* * *

Mimi's mam, who worked long hours in the laundry, always returned home long after her pa. On the following evening, as soon as he had returned from work, her pa had pushed the little 'uns out into the street, although it was raining, and then he did it again.

Mimi then realized that she had *not* somehow imagined it and she could *not* forget it – for it was *not* going to stop.

Every time her father raped her, she tried to block out the horror of what she endured. As soon as she felt herself in danger, she mentally detached herself from her body, floated up to the ceiling and pretended to be watching someone else on the bed down below. After Pa had finished, she always tried to pretend that it had not happened, but paradoxically lived in dread of the next time – for now she knew there would always be one.

Usually he did not undress, but merely undid his buttons. Mimi had never seen her pa naked, only the glistening pale thing rearing out of the hairy dark gap.

She always felt relief when she heard her father's grunt of release, then felt his sticky fluid slowly drain out of her body, dribble down between her legs. She did not understand what pleasure he could possibly derive from using her body like the cracked chamber-pot beneath the bed. Sometimes, when he did it, her revulsion made her retch, whereupon he walloped the side of her head, where no bruise could be seen.

She never again mentioned the matter to the little 'uns as she endured her pa's abuse for the remaining five years of her childhood.

Every time her body was violated, Mimi's burden of fierce resentment and stifled anger grew more intolerable. There was no one in whom she could confide. She was in awe of the stern-faced harassed teacher who unsuccessfully tried to keep fifty slum children quiet. Not even the threat of the often-administered cane could totally control these pinch-faced tough little gutter-rats.

There was another, more powerful reason why she dared not confide in an adult. Surely such a horrible punishment wouldn't be administered by God if she didn't deserve it? So she must, in some inexplicable way, be *very bad*. If she complained, she might be further punished. In this way, her sexual abuse left her bewildered and anxious, with a permanent sense of unspecified dread and pending doom.

Whenever she consciously caught herself thinking about her father's terrible treatment, Mimi pushed the nasty visions out of her mind and slammed the door. She knew that one of these days she would be able to pretend that none of it had ever happened. And nobody else in her new life knew about it.

* * *

And, after all, it hadn't harmed her – she was out of harm's way now, off on a steam train, so he'd never be able to dirty her again. If it had harmed her, she would have cried, wouldn't she? But after the first time there had never been no tears although the little 'uns at the other end of the bed always snivelled after it happened. Mimi had never once been able to cry, in fact she never felt anything once he'd left for the Black Bull: she had always felt as cold and hard as a block of ice, not like a real person at all.

Like the Ice Maiden whose feelings were frozen, Mimi's inability to release her tangled, painful feelings in a flood of tears, combined with her inability to confide in anyone, meant she had buried in her unconscious all the pain, fear, bewilderment and outrage that was her experience of sexual union. The only way she had been able to cope with those years of quivering submission and carefully concealed anger was by not coping with it, which was why she had tried so hard to bury those horrible memories and pretend to herself that she had never suffered longterm harm during those years of ordeal.

She was too young to understand that she had been irreparably damaged in a way that she would never be capable of understanding, for she could never know what it was to think and feel as a normal young woman naturally would.

* * *

As the train thundered towards Carlisle, Jolly Joe opened his eyes, yawned and pulled a crumpled paper bag out of his pocket. 'Cheer up, Mimi, you've a face as long as a fiddle. Have a bit of fudge.'

Mimi jumped, and wrenched her thoughts back to the present. She remembered the promise she had made to herself on the windy top of the tram after leaving home:

she was going to do her best to forget – for whatever the unknown future held in store for her, it could never be as bad as the past. Now she would make her fortune on the stage, then go back and rescue Mam and the little 'uns. One day her pa would get back from work to find that dark, stinking hole empty, and serve him right.

This new confidence dissolved like morning mist in sunlight, as Mimi suddenly wondered how Jolly Joe and Baz could be so confident that she would be a success, standing up there, on stage, before all those people.

Chapter Two

6.30 p.m., Thursday 30 May 1901

'Which of you tarts has nicked me best pink garters?' yelled Mrs Potts with frustration. Her remark was greeted by a chorus of loud boo-hoos from the other occupants of the small, stuffy ladies' dressing room at the Theatre Royal, Wigan.

'Blast! I've laddered me new tights,' hollered Maisie, the acrobat, thin as a curtain rod, 'real silk, cost thirty bob a pair!'

'Who's swiped me red cancan chemise?' yelled Mimi.

'I'm *mending* yer red chemise, Mimi.' Daisy spoke despite lips clamped round a cheap cigarette.

The hefty Lancastrian call-boy (who looked more like a farmhand) had just banged on the door and hollered to remind the occupants that it was half an hour before curtain up. The ladies' dressing room was in its usual state of confusion as latecomers flung off their street clothes; other women, colour sticks in hand, were already seated before the Bench – a long shelf beneath a mirror – to peer at crudely coloured faces beneath hair hidden under a wide headband or twisted up in a turban; crumpled kimonos covered their naked flesh and undergarments.

Betsy, seated before the Bench, winked at Mimi's

reflection in the mirror and slyly pulled back her pink net skirt from her knees. Mimi glimpsed silk rosettes on a pair of pink garters and burst out laughing. Betsy would never dare try such a naughty trick if her ma was here. Mrs Bridges behaved as if she was a royal nanny. When the overexcited Betsy came off stage she was immediately wrapped in a shawl and handed a mug of warm milk, both of which brought her back to earth: she hated returning to a drab, normal life in the chilly wings; she infinitely preferred the magical intensity of the make-believe world on stage. Betsy hated hot milk, but obediently drank it, for she always obeyed her mother, who also told her what to think, what to say, what to do and what not to do. Sometimes for days Mrs Bridges would not speak to her cherished child and locked her alone in the bedroom back at digs whenever she was off stage, until a tearful Betsy had promised, on her honour, to behave like a little lady in future.

Unsurprisingly, Betsy could not stand being alone (she unconsciously related it to punishment) and she would never take responsibility for any wrongdoing, however minor or accidental. Kind-hearted Mimi, who didn't care a tinker's cuss for Mrs Bridges, often took the blame for Betsy's minor misdemeanours. So she would chirrup off-hand apologies: 'Sorry about that spilt powder, Mrs B., me hand was shaking with stage fright . . . Sorry I tore the frill off the back of Betsy's skirt, Mrs B., I stepped on it accidental like, running downstairs behind her.' Furthermore, Mimi knew that already *she* was a part of this glamorous world, to which Mrs Bridges so obviously longed to belong, and never would.

After listening to Mimi's lying confessions, Betsy always flashed her a fervent look of gratitude that sometimes made her wonder what the devil a *mother* could do to frighten a girl so.

'Hurry up with that chemise, Daisy,' Mimi urged, as she sponged her arms and hands with wet-white, mixed that morning. Barefoot and naked to the waist, she wore only a pair of drawers, an undergarment that consisted of a three-inch waistband fastened by a drawstring at the back from which were suspended two lace-trimmed white cotton cylinders that fell just below her knee. This ingenious contraption had been invented to simplify the sanitary arrangements of a woman who needed both her arms to lift her heavy skirts before squatting on a chamber pot, or sitting on the privy; it was this garment that thrilled the audience of a row of Parisian cancan dancers, at that shocking moment when each one clutched an ankle, held it high above her head and hopped around in circles. Needless to say, such foreign antics were not allowed in respectable British music halls.

Mimi started to slap wet-white on her shoulders and the tops of her tiny breasts. Happily she sniffed the now-familiar odour of sweat, cardboard, hot greasepaint and sweetly scented face powder. After six weeks on tour, she now knew the hard reality of backstage life: scrimping landladies, travelling with your own mousetraps, the general discomfort (sometimes squalor) of digs, plus the feeling of never being settled, never belonging. Mimi also knew that, just as all theatre people belonged to one big family, they also quarrelled, argued, bitched and moaned like one big family.

Nevertheless, Mimi woke every morning to a thrill of excitement and expectation. She now ate three meals a day, with an apple or a bar of candy between them; much to Betsy's envy she did not put on weight. Betsy had been laced into whalebone corsets at the age of twelve. Her tendency to put on weight meant she was not allowed to eat cake or chocolate. If she developed even a tiny pimple, her mother threatened to wallop whoever had given her contraband chocolate.

Mimi also experienced the heady sensuality of wearing pretty clothes, as she stood nightly in the seductive warmth of the footlights, the focus of hundreds of eyes; she always tumbled off stage with adrenalin tingling through her body as she heard the thrilling sound of applause – approval. If such addictive excitement (which lasted for at least two hours and made sleep difficult) resulted from being the lowly assistant who handed Baz his props, what would it be like when she danced well enough to be his partner? Or perhaps one day have her *own* act?

On stage every morning, Baz, agile as an acrobat, taught her dancing steps; she had a good sense of rhythm, was nimble, and could already perform an adequate soft-shoe-shuffle – although she would never attain Betsy's skilled fouettés, jetés, and entrechats, as taught at the Ada Jarrett School of Drama. The only other things Mimi needed – according to Baz – were perseverance and patience, as she waited for the lucky break that all performers secretly believe is theirs by right.

In the stuffy ladies' dressing room, she glanced sideways at Betsy. Calm and unhurried as she held her worn beige stick of Leichner No. 5, Betsy leaned back as far as possible from the mirror, to judge the effect from the back of the pit. From the neat array of colours laid on the towel before her she pulled forward the pan in which she had melted her hot-black; she dipped in a matchstick and applied a bead of black to every third eyelash, then added a blob of red at her inner eyes, to make them seem wider apart.

'Like me to treat you at the whelk stall after the show?' Mimi offered. Betsy adored shellfish, and luckily so did her mother.

'Umm ... umm ... wait a minute ...' Self-absorbed, Betsy was carefully colouring her cheeks.

'Betsy, you're not bloody listening!' Mimi stamped her bare feet.

'Er ... umm ... yes, I am,' murmured Betsy, as she leaned towards the mirror, as she smoothed an eyebrow with her left hand and then leaned back from the mirror with an air of concentration such as might be worn by Fabergé as he gazed at a half-finished Easter egg for the Tsarina.

'Betsy!'

'Umm, what is it?' Still gazing at her face, Betsy absent-mindedly dropped her empty powder box into one of the thimble-shaped metal waste bins that stood under the Bench.

Mimi banged her bum on the chair. *'What did I just say?'*

Betsy jumped, looked flustered, then triumphantly remembered, 'You're not bloody listening.'

Mimi burst into laughter. 'Useless to talk to you when you're sitting before a mirror. Vain as a peacock, you are!'

Betsy tried to look injured but started to giggle. 'Pea-*hen*, if you please!'

Mimi grinned, then tipped her chair back and yelled impatiently, 'I need that chemise *fast*, Daisy, or I'll cause a riot out front!'

Daisy balanced her cigarette on the edge of the Bench, bent to bite the red thread, and threw the red taffeta chemise to Mimi, who thrust up one hand and caught it in mid-air.

'Tell Daisy it's dangerous to smoke in the dressing room,' Betsy whispered to Mimi. Both girls knew there was always danger of a fire in a theatre, which was why all British theatres were obliged to have a fireman on duty, twenty-four hours a day. Every theatre was subject to stringent fire regulations and fire precautions: a framed set of these regulations hung in every dressing room, where nobody read them.

'Mimi, for God's sake tell Daisy to snuff her ciggie!'

'Betsy, *you* tell Daisy,' Mimi said amiably. 'Do your own dirty work for a change.' Mimi liked Daisy, who had always worked on the halls, and stoically bore the arthritic pain that had stiffened her joints and wrecked her career as a wirewalker. However, nothing could keep Daisy from the Perfeshun: she had simply changed jobs. Every afternoon, Mimi worked with Daisy in the wardrobe room, where they mended whatever had been torn on the previous night, then sponged and pressed the costumes. She had trusted Daisy since the morning after she joined the Company, when she had anxiously confided to her that Jolly Joe had stealthily pinched her thigh throughout the tram journey to their digs; she showed Daisy the line of bruises – the colour of the bloom on a plum – which proved her claim. As she exposed her skinny thigh, Mimi again nervously wondered whether she had jumped out of the frying pan – into the fire.

Small, chubby Daisy turned doe-brown eyes on the young recruit. 'Gawd bless you, gel, *that's* nothing new! A girl can't advance herself on stage without a few pinches, or more! Top comedian always gets first choice of the chorus line-up, it's a music-hall tradition.'

Mimi sniffed. 'Well, *my* tradition is a hatpin where it hurts!'

'Want to lose your new job?' Daisy asked sharply. 'Want to be a skivvy or a shop girl or a whore?' They both knew that these were Mimi's only alternative employments.

Mimi's doleful face suddenly looked hopeful. 'How about if I pretend to be sweet on Baz?'

Daisy laughed. '*That* won't work with Jolly Joe! I told you, Baz is a fairy – Lor', where was you brought up? – a pansy, a nancy boy ... one of them Oscar Wilde types. Tell you what, when Mrs Joe comes in for her costume, I'll rub embrocation in them bruises, and you can snivel a bit. She ain't stupid, and she knows Joe's slightly given to fornication, especially when he's had a couple ... Start blubbing, I can hear them poodles yapping!'

Mrs Joe's lips tightened at the sight of the bruises. Jolly Joe had never pinched Mimi again.

Now, from a corner of the dressing room, Maisie yelled, 'Daisy, be a sport. Lend me a pair of tights.'

'You should always have a spare pair, luv,' Daisy reproached, as she hobbled to the skip in the corner.

'I'll never have enough to buy me boarding house if I buy spares of everything,' Maisie said defensively. Her plan was to retire with her stage partner and offstage lover, a silent Dane, pale as a peeled potato, called Gustav. As she was only twenty-six nobody listened seriously to her talk of retirement, and there were similar jeers of 'Pigs might fly!' when Mimi declared that *her* ambition was to own her own theatre.

Half-serious, Mimi retorted, 'If you don't have a target, you ain't going to hit it.'

'A girl can dream, can't she?' Maisie nodded. Both girls

believed in the tangible security of bricks and mortar, which would mean that they would never again be penniless, frightened victims of fate, but in control of their own destinies.

Betsy leaned across the Bench to Mimi. 'Daisy just lit up another one!'

'Shut up, Betsy, this ain't San Francisco,' Mimi yawned. San Francisco theatre fires were those most frequently reported in the newspapers; it sometimes seemed as if those theatres went up in flames as fast as they were built. Every performer knew the dangers of a theatre fire and nervously crossed their fingers as they whispered the news to each other.

'Did you read about the Blackpool Empress?'

'Sixty burned to a crisp, ain't it awful?'

'Somebody tripped on the gallery stairs and they all fell over each other.'

'Not so bad as that dump in Exeter. A hundred and fifty poor souls dead, I read . . .'

'Mimi, will you lace me stays?' Betsy pleaded.

Mimi was briskly stuffing socks down the side of her own stays, to further thrust up what little bust she had. 'Can't you see I'm busy, Betsy? Ask a blooming dresser.' The theatre employed a couple of dressers, tipped by visiting performers every week.

'They're both still off with scarlet fever.'

'Where's your ma, then?' Mimi was now dabbing colour on her mouth.

'Bilious attack. Ate too much fried fish last night. She's gone to lie down in our digs.'

Usually it was impossible to keep Betsy's mother out of the dressing room; she had been stage-struck since her first visit to the theatre, a musical comedy – *Floradora* –

on her two-day honeymoon at Southend. So even before she was conceived, Betsy's career had been decided. Mrs Bridges' theatrical ambition had been thrust upon her chubby baby's shoulders from the moment of her birth. She still made all Betsy's clothes – far too elaborate and adult in style – and each night her beautiful daughter dutifully acted out her mother's fantasy: being the dazzling centre of attention.

Trained like a Guardsman but indulged in all other ways, in the eyes of her adoring mother Betsy could do no wrong – unless her mother said so. She owed her caryatid posture to her mother's insistence that every morning she walk downstairs to breakfast with a book balanced on her head. As a result, she moved stiffly and self-consciously, in a manner that matched her drilled obedience. Unlike Mimi – who always stood in the wings to study the timing of the comics – she had no sense of humour *or* timing, but her mother could not see this flaw in her passport to fame and success.

Betsy whined theatrically, 'I can't lace me stays by meself.'

'OK, Betsy, I'll do you when I've finished me hair.' As she relented, Mimi picked up her curling tongs from the gas ring; soon her pert little face was framed by a frizz of tiny red curls.

She leaned forward and peered critically in the mirror: she already realized that the world belonged to beautiful women, and she was not one of them, despite her tilted green eyes and the red-gold hair that rippled down past her waist. Her cheeky, street-urchin liveliness did not fit current beauty fashions ... a pity that she looked so young, but not young enough for a child act ... If she put on enough make-up with enough care she could make herself look older and reasonably pretty, but she didn't have the patience, and she didn't want to look like all the other girls. Of course neither they nor she could compete with Betsy, at whom she now glanced as she hairpinned her kiss-curls into place. Betsy's profile looked like that of a goddess stamped on some ancient golden Greek coin. No wonder all the other women were jealous of her: even the amiable Daisy was a little sour.

However, Mimi felt no envy, but only admiration. Partly because of this, the two girls had quickly become friendly. Apart from the tired, hopeless love of her mam, and the clinging affection of the little 'uns, this was Mimi's first relationship that had not been overcast by anxiety. She now had a girl-friend – someone of her own age, someone to whom her frozen little heart could warm; someone in whom she could confide, someone with whom she could walk arm in arm, giggle and chat, and wonder, in whispers, what *exactly* Baz and his friends did when they were alone.

A sudden scream rang from the back of the dressing room, followed by the scrape of chairs being hurriedly pulled back and then overturned, as women scrambled away from the Bench. Mimi and Betsy turned their heads to see flames flickering up from one of the metal waste bins on the floor. Betsy, nearest to the door, darted towards it, followed by a small stampede of women who knew the ease with which a fire could start in a theatre: backstage, a blaze could flare up from one carelessly discarded match among the paints and glues in the scenery shop; from inflammable timber stored in the workshop; from furniture, thousands of odd articles – property (props) – and particularly from clothes, *especially* in the dressing rooms if net skirts or sleeves accidentally flicked over the naked flame of the gas jets used to heat hair tongs and flat irons.

Betsy twisted the doorknob and pushed at the door, which did not budge. Frantically, she rattled the knob and beat her hands on the wooden panels. 'The door won't open!' she cried. 'We're trapped!'

'Maybe it's locked from outside,' yelled Daisy from the rear.

'Help! Help!' screamed Maisie, which set off the rest, for they all knew you could burn to death in less than a minute.

'My children! My children!' hollered Mrs Potts, trying to elbow her way to the front of the heaving bunch of women, all fighting to get to the door.

'Stop your shoving, bitch!'

'Get the fire brigade!'

'Break the bloody door down!'

The frantic group swayed. Through the shrill screams of 'Gawd Almighty,' and 'Get us *out*!' the women suddenly heard the slow, deep voice of the burly call-boy. 'Now all you ladies stand well back! I'll put me shoulder to the door! I'll smash her in!'

The women heard what sounded like an ox hit the door. Slowly, it heaved open. All the females shoving against it fell backwards on those behind them. The frightened women disentangled themselves and scrambled to their feet. Facing them in the doorway (and blocking the exit) was the large, solid figure of the call-boy. 'Where's fire, then?' he demanded.

The women turned to point behind them ... and gasped.

There was no fire. By a smoking metal waste bin stood a grinning Mimi, arms akimbo – 'When I saw the bin was aflame, I shoved another on top of it,' she explained, 'that put it out, quick enough.'

No longer frightened, the women became indignant to excuse their hysteria.

'Who first called fire?'

'That stupid stuck-up Betsy!'

'Why wouldn't the bloody door open?'

The call-boy obligingly explained. 'Nowt wrong with bloody door! The young leddy were *pushing* door, not pulling her.' Now the focus of attention, he added, 'All I had to do to door wer turn handle and door opened. 'Twas hard work heaving against you lot.' An oafish black-toothed grin.

All heads swivelled indignantly to stare at Betsy, who slowly turned as red as her rouge pot. She couldn't hide behind her mother's skirts because her mother wasn't there. Oh, it wasn't *only* her fault. If they hadn't all shoved her against the door until a person couldn't breathe, she would have quickly corrected her understandable mistake.

'Frightened us all for nothing!'

'Bitch!'

'Cow!'

Realizing that they now had a scapegoat for their panic, the women looked contemptuously at Betsy, and threateningly moved towards her.

At this point Daisy, using a towel to protect her hands, gingerly pulled the top waste bin away from the bottom waste bin into which she peered. She then drew out a still-smoking pair of blackened hair-curling tongs. With triumphant defiance Daisy also glared at Betsy. 'Now you can *all* see as it wasn't started by my ciggie! The hot tongs fell in the bin among the curl papers!'

Seeking to dispel the lynch-mob atmosphere, Mimi

pushed through to Betsy's side and loudly asked their bovine rescuer, 'How long before we're on?'

'Ten.'

This immediately distracted the performers, who darted back, each to her place at the Bench.

'Mimi, I can't go on unlaced!' Betsy whispered urgently.

'Gawd, Betsy, I'll lace you when I've got me hat properly crooked.' Mimi carefully skewed a final hatpin into the nosegay of violets tilted over her left eye, then stood up, turned to Betsy's proffered frilly rear and violently yanked the corset laces. Betsy squawked, and both girls giggled.

As Mimi finished tying the laces of Betsy's stays, the call-boy stuck his head around the door. 'Everything all right in here now?' He ducked a powder puff thrown at him and grinned at cries of 'Get out!' and 'Peeping Tom!'

'You was happy enough to see me at the quarter. Overture and beginners, please.'

Friday 31 May 1901

On the following morning Mimi hurried, late, to the theatre, for the dratted landlady had forgotten to call her early, as requested. You were expected to find your own theatrical digs, and you paid for them. Often there was a list of available places pinned up in the theatre, but it wasn't always possible to book in advance. Unless you'd been there before, or had a tip-off from another performer, digs were a lucky dip or a gamble, depending on your temperament.

Mimi had already discovered that the best landladies

were ex-theatricals who understood the importance of punctuality, who didn't mind a bit of noise and who enjoyed a sing-song around a kitchen table littered with beer bottles. In digs, you got undercooked porridge for breakfast and a hot evening meal (boiled meat and vegetables with steamed suet pudding or rice afterwards) but after the performance you had to get back fast, because the landlady was always impatient to get to bed – unless she was an old pro.

Whether or not she was an old-timer, there was always a smell of cabbage in the hall and the faint odour of cat's piss everywhere else. Beds and greasy armchairs always sagged in bedrooms that were slightly smelly and unclean with a floor invariably covered by cold green or brown linoleum. However, Mimi never complained like the rest of the troupe, for all digs were luxurious compared to the home she had so recently left.

She still found it difficult to believe how much her life had improved in only six weeks: it seemed such a short time since Daisy had scrubbed the new girl in a tin bath, then rubbed Keating's flea powder over every inch of her skinny little body. Flesh tingling, she felt that she had sloughed off her old skin to match her new clean personality in this exciting new world, where she would find frivolity, fun, play and laughter, none of which she had known in childhood. Eager and hopeful, she now enjoyed the present and dared to plan her future, which she determinedly painted only in cheerful colours.

Within a few weeks the troupe had become her family and the theatre had become her home, her playroom, her love and her life. Mimi noticed that theatre life provided the entire troupe with a sense of security and closeness that the outside world denied them. She quickly understood that this was why performers formed one huge clan with its own language, jokes, habits and haunts. The theatre was like a secret society to which they all belonged and in which they all felt safe and united: none of the endless backstage jealousies or squabbles could threaten the all-enveloping, invisible, invincible solidarity. They all talked only of the theatre because they weren't really interested in anything or anyone outside it.

At first she had found it hard to believe that theatre people, who had so few possessions, could be so generous and high-spirited; that people who appeared to be so childishly jealous and vain could also be so strongly supportive and loyal; or that people who appeared so disinclined to effort could work so hard when necessary. She had quickly discovered that there were other, darker reasons for the acting profession's camaraderie, described so eloquently by Jolly Joe in the Crewe Railway Refreshment Room.

Nevertheless, she was still dizzily delighted to belong to this enticing, tawdry world of make-believe and make-do. Although only a small part of Baz's act, she was a necessary part. Baz was always in authority (for he was three years older than her, male, and owner of the act) but she was happily aware of the rough affection that he felt for her. Perhaps their friendship was close because both youngsters were alone in the world. Baz's mother had been killed in a Cardiff road accident, three years earlier: jumped off a horseless 'bus before it stopped, and been crushed to death by the horseless carriage behind. Baz had never known his father, an ignorance Mimi envied, for in her nightmares her pa lurked outside the stage door, waiting in the dark. After the performance she would sometimes sense a heavy hand on her shoulder and her heart would sink to her boots; in similar nightmares, she would jerk awake, sweating and trembling with fright.

* * *

Rain started as she turned right into the alley behind the Theatre Royal, and again she cursed her landlady; her new fondant-green spring coat was drenched by the time she darted through the stage door. Feeling like an old pro, Mimi hurried past the stage-door keeper; nose buried in the *Greyhound News*, he sat in his snug little hutch, always the warmest part of the unheated building. No matter how grand the theatre, Mimi now knew that backstage was always cold and draughty, especially in winter when actors wore coats, hats, mufflers and sometimes gloves to rehearse.

Mimi paused at the noticeboard to check the call sheets and see there were no messages for her before she scampered down the high narrow white-tiled corridor; as she did so, she heard footsteps clatter down invisible stairs, the laughter and voices of invisible people. Backstage was always a rabbit warren leading to dressing rooms, prop rooms, storerooms, workshops for scenery painting and carpentry; the small smelly dressing rooms were always down in the basement or at the top of the building, reached by steep corkscrewing cast-iron staircases: all empty dressing rooms smelled of Crowe's face cream, stale tobacco, stale beer, and the sweetish odour of dust and face powder.

* * *

After the rehearsal, Jessie, the Company manager, hurriedly set up a folding card table on stage and dragged two chairs behind it. Although only twenty-one, Jessie was a calm, comfortable creature, with a determined chin, large tortoiseshell-framed spectacles and floppy brown hair yanked back in a bun at the base of her neck. Jessie kept track of the Company's money, added up the takings and prepared the wages that Jolly Joe doled out on stage every Friday at midday. Sitting behind the collapsible card table, Jolly Joe handed over the little buff envelope, then Jessie gave each performer the pen to sign the receipt book. If you missed a show you didn't get paid, and there were fines for bad behaviour, as was customary in the Business.

Mimi skipped off stage with her envelope and waited for Betsy to join her. Briefly she remembered how surprised she had been to find that the height of the theatre backstage was as vast as the auditorium; at the front of this huge black space was the stage, like a shoebox in an empty wardrobe.

Betsy joined her friend. 'Come up to the dressing room, Mimi, I've got something to show you.'

'Don't mind if I do. It's still raining, so I'll share your brolly. I'll have enough saved to buy me own next week.'

Once in the deserted dressing room, trembling with anticipation, Betsy pointed to the Bench, on which lay a long, thin elegantly wrapped parcel; she hopped excitedly from one foot to the other as Mimi carefully unwrapped the glossy mauve paper (to use again), opened the dark green box within and drew out a crimson silk umbrella, the china handle splattered with hand-painted rosebuds.

'I knew you didn't have a brolly,' Betsy explained, then humbly added, 'And you was such a good pal yesterday.' She looked embarrassed. After the false-alarm fire the other occupants of the dressing room had refused to talk to her, although many a sarcastic remark had been addressed to the ceiling about stupid cows that lost their heads and nearly gave a person a bloody heart attack.

Mimi hugged her friend. 'They only act up so because they was scared to death.'

'No, I deserved it.' Betsy spoke her rehearsed words with as much difficulty as if she were regurgitating swallowed string. 'It was *me* what made 'em frightened. But how can I tell 'em I'm sorry when they won't speak to me?'

'You could buy one of them gigantic boxes of chocolates with a bow on top. I'll pass 'em round this evening; I'll say, "Betsy says she's sorry," then shove them tempting violet creams right under their noses. A girl can't take a choccy if she's treating you like something the cat brought in ... Let's see if between us we got enough money for ...' Mimi stared at Betsy then said sharply, 'How did you get the spondulicks for a genuine Finnigan's umbrella?' Mrs B. hardly allowed Betsy any money, all the cash went on her back.

Betsy hung her head. 'I've managed to put a few sovereigns that Ma don't know about. I keep 'em knotted in an old stocking pushed in the toe of me winter boots.'

Mimi carefully placed the crimson umbrella on the Bench then hugged her friend again. 'No need to look so guilty, Betsy. *You* earned the money, didn'cha?' Normally Mimi never said a word against Mrs B. but now she gently reproved her friend, 'You shouldn't let your ma boss you around *all* the time.' It was the general view that the unpleasant aspects of Betsy's character stemmed from being overburdened and overpushed (the whole troupe knew that overencouragement could be destructive) and being controlled like a blooming marionette on strings.

'Come to think of it, where *is* your ma?' Mimi asked. 'How did you manage to give her the slip?'

'Ma's still laid low. Says never again will she mix fried fish, pickles and port wine.' Betsy looked thrilled by this medical bulletin. 'Listen, Mimi, that brolly ain't all I planned for you! Sit down at the Bench, my girl!'

Quivering with excitement, she opened the little wicker basket that she had brought with her and drew out her black japanned box of colours, two clean towels and her imitation-leather jewel box. 'Tell you what I'm going to do for you, Mimi? I'm going to make you look like a royal princess!' As she pulled a face, Betsy chided her, 'You need to take more trouble with your appearance. You're quite a pretty little thing when you make a bit of an effort!'

Mimi sat down, resigned, as Betsy carefully laid out her colours on one towel and tucked the other around Mimi's neck. Mimi loathed wearing greasepaint, whereas Betsy said it made *her* feel a different person, why, you could be anyone you chose!

During the following half-hour Mimi tried to be patient but she wriggled, fidgeted, sighed and was clearly restless as Betsy rubbed the colour sticks on the back of her hand until they almost disappeared, then subtly applied them to Mimi's face. However, when finally she peered in the looking glass at Betsy's careful work, she certainly *did* look different. Betsy had pinned her fox-red hair up in curls, snipped a little fringe at the front and then tonged it so it frizzed up quite like Queen Alexandra.

Betsy opened her jewel box and stood behind Mimi; head thrown back, with eyes half-closed, she considered Mimi's reflection; lovingly, she pinned her best diamanté stars in Mini's crisp red curls, then stood back triumphant.

Mimi clapped her applause. 'Indeed I *do* look a treat, to be sure!' Although delighted with the result of Betsy's artful work, she had no intention of getting out of bed half an hour earlier every day in order to look ravishing for Baz. Still, it was ever so thoughtful of Betsy to make such a fuss of her appearance. She understood that Betsy had been taught that this was the way you showed your love for a person.

'See how big your eyes look now? Like a maharajah's emeralds,' Betsy enthused and added in a hoity-toity accent, 'Dearest, you look like a sweetly pretty little doll.'

'Bloody Cinderella ready for the ball!' Mimi grinned with delight. She jumped up, grabbed Betsy's waist and twirled her round the dressing room in a spirited polka until they were both out of breath, too dizzy to continue and laughing fit to burst.

Betsy peered out of the window. 'It's stopped raining! Let's go down to the whelk stall, my treat!' She was having such a happy day. Sedate Betsy loved being alone with Mimi; she loved the way that high-spirited Mimi could coax her into gaiety, make her forget to act like a lady and *not care*! Betsy did so wish that she had Mimi's sparky disposition, her mischievous little redheaded friend fairly quivered with life! Mimi had such guts and go! Betsy wistfully admired her daring and bravado, her little-drummer-boy-on-the-battlefield defiant courage. How she wished that *she* had the gumption to do as she pleased and say what she thought! As she had never known the occasional plunge into loneliness that is the price of freedom, such independence seemed a totally admirable state.

'Whelks it is, then,' Mimi warbled, 'that stallkeeper won't recognize me.' She twirled with delight and curtsied to herself in the looking glass to show Betsy that she was thrilled with the result of her careful work.

Arm in arm, the girls clattered down the stairs and skipped out of the stage door. As they pranced down the alley, Mimi twirled her crimson umbrella and shrieked, 'I'm Burlington Bertie, I rise at ten thirty and stroll down the Strand like a toff . . .'

When the girls reached the High Street they turned left towards the whelk stall. A strong, chill wind was blowing, so although the downpour had ceased there were few people on the street and little traffic on the road: a horse-drawn brewer's dray and two whistling boys on bicycles. The pavements were still gleaming wet and trickles of water dribbled from the convex cobbled road into the dark muddy rivulets that flowed along the gutter.

Larking about, doing the occasional dance step together, the girls continued to squeal and tease each other, happy as kittens in a basket, which is why Mimi, nearest the road, did not notice a hansom cab coming up behind her, the horse moving much too fast and too near the kerb.

As Betsy's head was turned towards Mimi, on the boundary of her peripheral vision she sensed the danger and yanked her friend back, so that Mimi's new coat should not be splashed by muddy water thrown up by the wheels of the hansom.

Not expecting Betsy's sudden jerk, Mimi lost her balance, struggled to regain it on the slippery kerb, almost succeeded, then was drenched to the waist by the slosh of water thrown up by the nearest cab wheel. Jeered at by the driver, she was distracted, lost her balance and tumbled into the muddy gutter.

Betsy stared horrified, not at the danger of Mimi being run over but by the state of her new coat.

To add to Mimi's problems a sudden high gust of wind threatened to blow away her big-brimmed hat. Instinctively, she put up her muddy hands to clutch it; as she did so, she unwittingly covered her newly painted face with mud.

Suddenly Betsy started to giggle.

From the gutter where she sat with her boots apart, her hat askew above her blackened face, Mimi scowled, 'It ain't nothing to laugh about, Betsy! Help me up!'

But Betsy was now helpless with laughter. She pointed a shaking finger at Mimi. 'Oh ... oh dear ... Oh, I'm going to wet meself, I swear it! ... Oh ... Oh ... Sorry, luv, I can't help meself!'

'What's so bloody funny?' yelled Mimi, outraged. She wiped the back of her hand across her face, which smeared more mud.

Betsy was bent over with one leg knotted around the other. 'Oh ... oh ... What's so funny? ... You don't look like a sweetly pretty doll now, dearest ... You look like a dear little ... g–g–golliwog!'

Reluctantly, Mimi grinned then she, too, caught the giggles in the way that only young girls can, powered by no reason other than youthful exuberance and *joie de vivre*.

With tears rolling down her cheeks, Betsy bent to pull her friend to safety. She pulled too hard, and Mimi came up from the gutter like a champagne cork from its bottle, banging into Betsy, covering her, too, with mud. Betsy was too high to care. Clutching each other around the waist, they both staggered away from the kerb and leaned against the nearest shop window where they laughed until their ribs ached. Whenever one girl nearly managed to control herself, she caught the other's eye – and they were both off again. Mimi then caught sight of herself reflected in the shop window and once again screamed with mirth. A nattily dressed gent in black poked his head out of the door and crossly asked them to kindly move on, as they were probably turning away passing trade. This started them off again, and when Mimi noticed that the shop was a funeral parlour she too found it necessary to wind one leg around the other.

Finally, arms around each other's waists, new spring coats now filthy, they staggered along the pavement like a couple of dirty drunks, still unable to control the painful, happy, carefree laughter of girlhood.

Monday 3 June 1901. Queen's Theatre, Worcester

Down in the pit, the pianist retied his muffler and wondered what had happened to summer as he rattled 'Daisy, Daisy' on the upright piano. On stage, Baz was still rehearsing his new bicycle trick, for he had not yet perfected his timing.

Mimi, growing bored, asked, 'OK if I sing, Baz?' She started to hum along with the piano. Then she sang, using a posh accent and plumping out her vowels as if she had a hot chestnut in her mouth: the entire troupe could similarly adopt a toff's accent.

> 'Daisy, Daisy, give me your answer do,
> 'I'm half crazy over the love of you . . .'

Jolly Joe, discussing a safety curtain problem with the front of house manager, looked up in surprise, then listened carefully. Mimi had a surprisingly strong voice, a slightly hoarse contralto with excellent projection; although the middle register was a little vague, her top notes were firm and warm, while the throb of her low notes raised the hairs on the back of his neck.

When Mimi had finished her song he called up, 'You shouldn't be teaching her to dance, Baz, you should be teaching her to *sing*!'

For the rest of the rehearsal hour Baz sulked in the stalls, next to Jolly Joe. Over and over again, Mimi was made to sing 'Two Lovely Black Eyes' and 'The Man Who Broke The Bank in Monte Carlo', the only songs for which the pianist had sheet music.

'Sing from yer diaphragm,' Jolly Joe called up encouragingly, 'then sing from below yer belly button. Then sing from the bottom of yer gut!' He turned to Baz. 'You hear that earthy warmth, that smoky-low sound? That gal's got a darky's voice. Not a very big range, them darky voices, but like a lot of things in life, it's how it's used that counts.' He winked suggestively.

'Maybe she should take proper lessons,' Baz suggested, thinking that would free the stage for him.

'Nah, a singing teacher can ruin a good voice . . . How? By trying to get a natural singer to perform in a different way, that's how! Lots of them great female singers never had a single singing lesson!' Jolly Joe jerked his head towards the stage. 'All that little gal needs to do is learn to project her voice to the back of the gallery. So tomorrow, Baz, you sit up in the back of the gods while she keeps singing, until you can hear her clearly. After that she can pitch the mood of her song to you. All she needs is practice, until her voice obeys her.'

Anxious to know whether he was losing his assistant, and furious at suddenly becoming the coach for someone else's act, Baz asked, sulkily, 'Where are you going to put her, Guv'nor?'

'Mimi stays with you, but when she's ready, she can sing The King – solo.' Every night at the end of the performance the entire company lined up to sing 'God Save the King', the obligatory end to a British evening at the theatre.

When told this news, Mimi forgot her fatigue; instead, she felt simultaneous excitement and terror.

* * *

That night, after the show ended, Mimi quickly wiped off her colours, pulled her coat over her stage costume and (as she often did if the night were not too cold) ran around to the front of the theatre to watch the audience leave. This was breaking with stage tradition, but she did it anyway. She was still fascinated by the transformation of the black, terrifying monster that they had to placate every night into a stream of ordinary, amiable people, shuffling out of the theatre. First out of the side doors came the hooting, scuffling boys from the gallery, then the sweet-hearts holding hands, then the mothers pulling sleepy children home as fast as possible. Married couples often dawdled outside to eat a snack; near the brilliantly lit theatre entrances, there was generally a whelk stall and a baked-potato man, who sold his edible hand-warmers from a blackened metal drum of coals that glowed upon his barrow. Further along the road some fried-fish-shop owner would be shovelling sliced potatoes into boiling fat, while everywhere pub doors beckoned.

The crowd always dispersed with surprising speed. After ten minutes the illuminated canopy above the main entrance dimmed, flickered and then went out. The doors closed with a clang, before being bolted. The show was over.

Like every other young performer, Mimi allowed herself the luxury of dreaming that one day *her* name would be on the lips of an appreciative audience, as they streamed out of the theatre.

Monday 24 June 1901. Palace Theatre, Marlborough

For two weeks Mimi practised her singing every morning, while Baz sat in the back of the gallery, making rude trombone noises if he couldn't hear every word. Finally, Jolly Joe had pinned a postcard to the stage door notice-board, on which his scrawl announced that Mimi would sing the King solo tonight. Squawks of astonishment, indignation and curiosity immediately followed. Emotionally, the theatre was a world of eggshell-brittle egomania and topsy-turvy emotions: disclosures of secret love affairs or a rumoured assignment of some juicy part were instantly followed by tantrums, hysterics or implacable enmity; bitchy repartee and sour comment in turn prompted further rivalry and jealousy. All of these now surfaced.

Prudently, Mimi stayed away from the theatre for the whole day, then arrived in the ladies' dressing room with scant time to change. For Baz's act she wore a white frilled calf-length dress with pink sash and a wide-brimmed hat dripping with pink ostrich feathers. For her solo, Jolly Joe had told her to remove her sash and hat and, instead, wear a simple wreath of artificial white flowers, plus a long white cotton-velour cloak stitched by Daisy.

'I'll look about ten years old,' she objected.

'No lip from you, my girl. And I'll be at the back of the gallery when you sing – so make sure I can hear you, loud and clear.'

That night, after the last act, the scowling cast hurriedly lined up on stage, then switched on brilliant, artificial smiles for the finale. The sparse orchestra – piano, fiddle, trumpet and drums – started the overture. Auditorium seats banged as the entire audience obediently shuffled to its feet, prepared to demonstrate its loyalty by standing to attention. Mimi nervously took a step forward, as instructed, then decided what the hell, and firmly took a further step towards the footlights.

As soon as she sang her first notes she stopped trembling, for there was too much to think about. Her voice was loud, clear and thrilling; by the end of her third line, the audience had stopped shuffling and was listening with surprise, for they couldn't see where that big, rich voice came from.

As Mimi crashed into her final lines, '*Long to reign ooooooover us . . .*', she flung wide her arms, and the audience saw that her white velvet cloak was lined with the red, white and blue of a Union Jack.

Several hundred spines shivered as Mimi's dark-treacle voice sonorously hollered the final words, 'Goooood save *the* King!' The new King was far more popular than the Old Widow, his grim-faced, gloomy mother.

When Mimi finished singing her loyal paean, the theatre was silent.

Oh my Gawd, she thought miserably.

A burst of applause then swept over the footlights towards the girl in white. The audience's patriotism had been thoroughly roused by Mimi's jingoistic singing; they stamped and cheered and roared their approval, while the rest of the cast continued to stand behind her and grin glassily.

'The sly little *bitch*,' Mrs Bridges, in the wings, whispered to herself.

Smiling, Mimi flung wide both arms to acknowledge the thrilling waves of sound that swept up from the dark to enfold her; the approval coming from behind the gas jets of the footlights was meant *for her alone*! Her childish face flushed with delight as, for the first time, she felt truly loved; exultation flooded her trembling body. Mimi felt wrapped by the warm wings of invisible angels, through which nothing could penetrate to harm her.

As she floated from the stage and into the wings, Jolly Joe whispered, 'From now on you get paid three pound a week – to include your shoes and tights, of course.'

In one month, Mimi would earn what would take a skivvy more than a year in service! It was a fortune, she gloated, as she dashed up the circular iron stairs to the dressing room. Tonight, she had unbounded energy. She would never need to sleep again! . . .

Mimi opened the dressing room to an outwardly warm chorus of, 'Well done!' Betsy threw her arms around Mimi's shoulders and hugged her.

As Betsy hugged, Mrs Bridges groped for a bottle of smelling salts, and daintily waved it under her nose, as if suddenly she had been taken poorly. When Daisy carefully removed the white velour cloak from Mimi's shoulders, she whispered, 'Watch out for that Mrs Bridges. She'd like to put a banana skin under your boot, and no mistake about it!'

* * *

Violet Bridges possessed a mercilessly destructive tongue, and was as helpless as a scorpion to suppress her nature. Compulsively, she disrupted contentment and happiness with sour, self-righteous vindictiveness. She simply could not help herself; she would smile, intending to charm, but poison would coat her tongue. 'Pretty hair – pity it's so thin' . . . 'Pretty mouth – pity about the teeth.' She lost one friend after another until she found herself alone.

That night, as the Bridges left the stage door, she hissed to her daughter, 'You realize you ain't *never* going to get a chance to shine with *that* young madam standing in your way!'

'Don't be daft, Ma, there's plenty of room on the bill, and I'm glad for Mimi.' Betsy's mother did not yet know what her daughter was planning with Mimi, or that Mimi's triumph of tonight could only improve their chances.

'Just you *wait* – you'll see her spleen!' Mrs Bridges predicted venomously, as they hurried homewards, under the gas lamps.

'Mimi ain't got no spleen, Ma,' Betsy pleaded.

'Mimi would kick you in the gutter and then walk over you, just to save her slippers! *Don't you trust her!*'

'You're not being fair, Ma! Any one of us would have grabbed that end spot if Joe had offered it.'

'If you don't watch out, that bitch'll *grab your Chance* when it comes along!'

This warning hit home. Like every other performer, Betsy longed for her Chance, and knew that when Fate offered it she had to take it: she must let nothing stand in her way. For years she had worked hard and practised her dancing in every spare moment, so that one day she would appear at the Gaiety Theatre: Gaiety Girls made brilliant marriages, to peers or millionaires, sometimes both.

For years she had also subtly been made to feel that it was her responsibility to compensate her mother for her father's bad behaviour. Mr Bridges had *not* been a banker who died, as Mrs Bridges told everyone, but a bank clerk, who after eleven years of scolding and watching half his pay packet go on ballet lessons for the kiddie, had fled from his wife into the busty embrace of a cheerful young barmaid. Upon being 'widowed', Mrs Bridges had immediately put Betsy into Ada Jarrett's School of Drama, the fees of which she paid by working as a waitress in Gunter's Tea Room, in Mayfair: she could have earned more money elsewhere, but Gunter's was where the gentry took their tea.

After two years Betsy was selected for a Christmas season in panto – the children's chorus of *Sleeping Beauty* – and was then paraded before an experienced theatrical agent, who quickly realized that although the youngster had a wonderful face and was a promising dancer for her age, she had a thin soprano voice and no acting talent. So he suggested that she join a touring concert party, to gain experience: he might be able to get her into the Jenkins troupe, who worked the provincial circuits. She could try for the Gaiety Chorus when she was sixteen – the minimum age. He then had a quiet word with Mrs Bridges about the dangers and temptations of life on the road. 'It'd be a pity if she was . . . spoiled . . . before she became a Gaiety Girl, if you see what I mean.' Mrs Bridges understood perfectly: she already accompanied Betsy wherever she went, and had forbidden her to talk to men.

Betsy also understood perfectly. She and her mother were truly devoted to, as well as dependent upon, each other. She knew the sacrifices her ma had made for her, and that it was her responsibility to make those sacrifices worthwhile. It was her job to hook a rich man who could keep them both in comfort for the rest of their lives.

In order to do that, she had to guard her face, her figure and her virginity, for a rich man did not want to go where others had been before. By trusting her mother's painfully acquired knowledge of the world, she would be guided to a brilliant and successful marriage, the components of which were money, status and power; these guaranteed a woman's security – especially if provided by a mature man, for then she would have little to fear from a younger woman, as time went by. Beauty faded: this was her constant fear, and would be until she felt a wedding ring slip on her finger. Each morning when the alarm clock shrilled she was aware that she had become one day older and one day less eligible; consequently, she felt permanently insecure, seeing the world as a hostile place, full of traps and betrayal.

* * *

After Mimi's debut, back in the chill discomfort of their sparsely furnished bedroom, Mrs Bridges yanked off her shawl in ominous silence, then unwound numerous lilac and mauve chiffon scarves: she always dressed in fluttery clothes, for despite her tough carapace she saw herself as a vulnerable, frail bundle of winsome femininity; she lived in a romantic, make-believe world, and surrounded herself with such props as lavender water and touches of lace at wrist and throat in order to make bearable a life that she felt had treated her unfairly, and passed her by – which was why all her hopes for the future were focused on her daughter.

Mrs Bridges' ominous silence continued as she undressed: after unbuttoning her boots, she pulled her voluminous cream flannel nightgown over her street clothes, which she then discarded. Her nightgown bulged and shook like two making love in a tent for one, as her blouse was removed, then her skirt; each petticoat fell then to the floor, followed by her bloomers. After much under-nightie agitation she shook her mighty hips and her pale-pink whalebone stays fell to the floor, after which she gave a great sigh of satisfaction as she scratched her stomach.

She climbed into bed and blew out the candle without another word to Betsy, turning her back on her daughter, crouched under the same blankets. Betsy must be made to remember her mother's warning words; that little scheming Mimi would grab a blind man's cane.

Thursday 5 September 1901. The Regent Theatre, Preston

By September Baz had lost his assistant and also his coveted spot: although he was still billed above her, Mimi now finished the first half. Sentimental audiences warmed to her urchin charm and chirpy confidence as much as to her voice, which steadily improved: it could reverberate sadly or softly lilt with a sad, poignant sound; Jolly Joe described it as 'a voice with a tear in it'. Mimi introduced each song in her new genteel stage accent, though off stage she still spoke with her own hoarse lilting Liverpool accent.

One evening in early September Jolly Joe got a tip-off from the box office that Mr C. B. Cochran had reserved four seats in the stalls for the following night. Cockie – as everyone called him – was one of the new impresarios who specialized in spectaculars, but presented all forms of entertainment, from classical drama to musical comedy and ballet, from boxing bouts to midget shows, or anything else that people might pay to gawp at; he had a reputation for spotting new talent.

Although Jolly Joe confided this information to his wife alone, within half an hour Maisie had burst into the ladies' dressing room with the news.

Everyone started to talk at once, except Mrs Bridges who simply flashed a meaningful glare at Betsy: this was Her Chance.

As Mimi leaned towards the mirror to apply her colours, she could almost feel Mrs Bridges' loathing: everyone in the dressing room knew that with Mimi ending the first half, no one else stood a chance of discovery.

Vexed, she thought, Blast! Why couldn't Cockie have waited a bit longer? For she had secretly planned with Betsy to quit Jolly Joe and try their luck in London with a Bridges Sisters song-and-dance act; they planned to present this to Betsy's agent in October, when the Jenkins Theatrical Touring Company was playing the Chelmsford Hippodrome, which was close enough to London for a train trip there and back before the evening performance.

* * *

Like most females in the Company, Mimi spent the next afternoon resting in bed, in order to look her best for the evening performance; because of her excitement, she found it difficult to get to sleep. When she woke up, she saw that it was already six o'clock. Blast! The others would have left already for the theatre.

She jumped from her bed and hurriedly started to dress, but she could not find her expensive new purple boots, purchased especially for that evening. She groped on top of the wardrobe and dived in the dust beneath the bed, but realized that she must have left them in the theatre dressing room, in which case she'd be lucky if she ever saw them again.

She cursed under her breath; she would now be seriously late. She tugged on her old black boots, flung a scarf around her neck, skewered her best purple velvet hat on her head, glanced at the window and saw it was drizzling, so grabbed her brolly, and yanked at the doorknob.

The door refused to open.

Mimi looked up and checked that she had pulled back the bolt – keys weren't provided because departing theatricals always forgot to leave them with the landlady. All keys hung on a wooden board inside the kitchen; any room that wasn't paid for was locked by the landlady, who then hid the key. But Mimi had paid her full rent for two weeks in advance!

Again, she carefully turned the doorknob, then tugged it sharply backwards, but still her bedroom door would not open. On hands and knees she looked through the draughty gap beneath it. She could see nothing, except the green linoleum on the stairs outside. Either the door had stuck or it had been locked from the outside. Her yells were met with silence. No doubt her landlady was ensconced in some nearby pub.

She rushed to the window, heaved it up and poked her head out. The tall, thin, brick lodging house was crammed into a narrow street of identical buildings. It had rained during the afternoon, and the autumnal weather was damp and depressing, so all residents were snug inside their homes, either preparing or eating the evening meal. Four floors below, Mimi could see the empty, muddy backyards, battlefields and courting grounds for cats.

She slammed the window shut, ran back to the door of the room and tugged again; frustrated, she kicked it, but only succeeded in hurting her toes. She darted back to the window, threw it up, and shouted for help until her voice was hoarse.

Nobody seemed to notice; if they did, then nobody cared.

Frantic, Mimi wondered if anyone from the theatre might come to look for her. But if Jolly Joe did send a messenger boy the lad would merely knock at the front door, and there was clearly nobody in the house to open it. In any case, it was more likely that by the time they realized she hadn't turned up, the rest of the Company would be too anxious about their own performance to come searching for her.

Mimi unpinned her hat and threw it on the bed. She then twisted her body out of the window, shivered in the damp air, and gazed up at the roof, two floors above, but there was no way for her to reach it, and the dripping windows above were all closed.

The only way out was down. She looked speculatively at the muddy surface of the garden, four floors below. If she made a rope by knotting her two sheets together it would not be long enough to reach the ground.

But if she didn't get out, she could not perform for Cockie.

Sitting on the wet window sill, with her legs dangling inside her room, she leaned as far as she dared to the left of her window, trying to grasp a drainpipe, but it was a good twelve inches beyond her reach. If she *could* reach it, would it bear her weight? It certainly looked solid.

Ten minutes later, she had knotted and reknotted her two bed sheets into a sling. The heavy iron bed legs were fitted with castors, so it was not difficult to tug the bed over to the window, slip the sling around the leg nearest to it, then pull the other end of the sling under her armpits. The most difficult part of the manoeuvre would be when she climbed out of the window, feet first, and then slowly trusted her weight to the knotted sheets.

She knelt on the damp paint-flaked window sill, anxious not to make a false move, but knowing that the longer she waited, the more frightened she would become.

Slowly, she eased her body out of the window until she lay with her stomach on the sill, her rear facing the sky, and her legs dangling towards the ground. Still grasping the bottom of the frame, she eased her body further over the slimy sill, until the nasty moment when she was obliged to . . . drop.

She found herself dangling forty feet above the ground.

Trembling with fear, Mimi rocked her legs slightly to the right, then slightly to the left; her plan was to swing slowly like a pendulum, in an increasingly wide arc, until her feet reached the drainpipe.

After what seemed like hours, her right boot touched the drainpipe. On her next swing to the right, she parted her feet, hoping to hook it with her right toe, but she missed.

As she swung again against the wet brick, she suddenly felt the loop of sheeting sag. She screamed. But she dropped only six inches lower, and found herself still dangling against the slippery brickwork: she realized that her weight must have pulled the bed leg up against the wall, inside her room.

Suppose the entire bed leg was pulled up, and the sling slipped off it?

Trembling and sweating, she hurriedly tried again.

This time she tucked her feet firmly around the drain-pipe, although the top part of her body still hung in the sling.

Slowly she eased her right arm free, leaving her trembling left arm hooked inside the cotton sheeting. She realized that her next movement would be the most dangerous, when her trembling right hand reached across the bricks towards the drainpipe.

Eventually she touched it and carefully hooked her arm around it.

Holding her breath, Mimi slowly pulled herself over until she was able to relinquish the sling and cling to the pipe with both arms as well as both feet. Slowly, painfully, an inch at a time, she slid down. She passed the third-floor window. Then the second-floor window. Soon she would be safe!

Suddenly the bottom part of the pipe flew away from the wall. She lost her grip and plunged to the garden below.

* * *

'Don't you *never* do such a damfool thing again,' Jolly Joe said sternly the following morning as he sat at Mimi's bedside in the Royal Victoria Hospital.

Despite a sprained left ankle and fractured left wrist, Mimi had managed to haul herself to the unlocked back door, let herself into the house and drag herself to the front door. A neighbour ran for a cab, which took Mimi to the theatre.

When Joe saw the ashen-faced Mimi hobble in, he told the stage-door keeper to whistle for a cab and get the girl to a doctor. In the casualty department of the Royal Victoria Hospital a doctor had bandaged her foot, set her wrist in plaster and told her what a foolish girl she was, for she might easily have killed herself.

Lying in the white-ribbed hospital bed, Mimi sniffed at the musty bronze chrysanthemums brought by Joe. Sadly she asked, 'What did Cockie think of the show?'

'Wrong bloke, same name.' Joe shrugged.

Realizing that she had risked her life for nothing, Mimi burst into tears.

Joe leaned forward and patted her shoulder. 'That's show business, duckie. Cheer up! You didn't miss a thing.'

Mimi continued to sob into her chrysanthemums, until eventually she snuffled, 'I still don't understand what happened to my bedroom door.'

'I can guess,' said Joe sourly. 'Somebody dropped a pound note in the hall, knowing your landlady would pick it up and head straight for the pub. That somebody then nipped into the kitchen, unhooked your key from the board, crept up and locked your door from the outside, and returned the key to its hook in the kitchen. Today, your landlady's got a killer of a hangover, can't remember a thing, and wouldn't admit it if she did.'

'But *who* would want to do such a thing?'

'Wake up, Mimi! Anyone who wanted you out of the way last night! Anyone who didn't want Cockie to see your act!' Joe looked at her with commiseration. 'How many of our lot are staying at your digs?'

command. 'Betsy and her ma. Maisie and Gustav. The Potts family.'

'I bet it's Betsy or her ma – for a penny that old bitch would have your guts for garters!'

'Betsy's my *best friend*!' Mimi said indignantly. 'She'd *never* do a thing like that!' Betsy was her future partner, her trusted confidante, a mixture of mother and sister.

Jolly Joe wrinkled his forehead. 'Whether Betsy did it or not, you'll never prove it either way.' He wagged his forefinger at Mimi. 'In future, my gel, you see she don't get the chance. Never underestimate professional jealousy, my gel ... By the way, what happened to them purple boots you told me was missing?'

Slowly Mimi said, 'Betsy found them downstairs, under the kitchen table.'

'Ha! What were they doing *there*? They was probably sneaked out of your room well beforehand, by someone who wanted you to be searching for them, in too much of a tizzy to notice any noise, when she locked the door.'

'How can you *know* it was Betsy? It might have been Gustav! Why on earth should only *Betsy* be jealous of *me*?'

'Your voice'll last a damned sight longer than her face.' Again Joe patted Mimi's shoulder. 'Performers are delicate creatures, and some of 'em can be monsters – especially the jealous ones. A jealous person don't have much regard for herself, thinks she's not up to scratch, see? Now that can make a woman spiteful and destructive. That sort of hatred – nothing personal, mind – can smash your career afore it starts, if you don't watch out for it. Under that simpering Goody-Two-Shoes act, Betsy's as tough and ambitious as her ma: she'll stop at nothing to get what she wants. She's a spoilt little tart, and she's jealous of you, and them's two facts.'

'No, she *ain't*!'

'Look, I *know* Betsy did it,' Joe said firmly.

'How do you *know*, Joe?'

Jolly Joe sighed. 'The Potts boy saw Betsy go into the kitchen, just afore they left for the theatre.'

'That don't mean Betsy locked me in the bedroom! Maybe she wanted a drink of water – *if* the Potts boy really saw her. I never yet knew a snotty little boy as wasn't a born liar.'

Jolly Joe sighed again. 'Everyone who tries that locked-door trick thinks it's a new idea.'

Silently determined not to believe him, Mimi said defiantly, 'Betsy's me best friend.' She meant that Betsy loved her. How could a man understand what *that* meant?

Chapter Three

The orchestra was tuning up. Peering through the peep-hole in the curtain, Mimi could not see the puffed-out cheeks of the trumpeters or the drummers thudding their sticks on stretched vellum, or the plinking fingers and swaying arms of the violinists, but she had a good view of the pompous, all-important conductor: until he lifted his baton, no musician would play a note, and no performer would sing one.

On stage, Betsy idly swung a white-booted foot as she sat on a flower-decked swing that hung from the flies. 'What's the house like tonight, Mimi?'

'It's a good house,' Mimi reported; this was not unusual on a Friday night, for people had just been paid their wages. Although the curtain did not go up until nine o'clock, the theatre had been open since six; people used that extra time for conviviality, and the management made a lot of wet money in the pit and dress circle saloons, where prostitutes encouraged the punters to drink.

For the past two weeks the Bridges Sisters' song-and-dance act had opened the first part of the show at the Angel Music Hall. Mimi always modulated her voice in their duets, so that she did not overpower Betsy's frail soprano; Betsy always saved the difficult dance steps for her solos: their act was as successfully interdependent as their offstage relationship so the two seventeen-year-olds were enjoying life. They had money to spend, they wore party frocks every night, they savoured each moment of applause: what more could a girl want?

Beyond the gas mantles of the footlights, Mimi could see that the big black auditorium was crammed with pale faces: bowler hats in the pit and the starched shirt-fronts and sleek heads of West End toffs slumming in the front rows of the stalls. In the gods, high above them, apprentices and workmen leaned over the balcony, whistling and cheering. Young coster lads, who spent their days hawking goods from street barrows, joked noisily with black-faced sweeps and white-faced dustmen. Orange peel and nutshells were amiably thrown, brown bottles of porter passed from hand to hand; the ham-sandwich men and the pigs'-trotter women moved along the aisles, selling their wares from trays suspended from their necks. Until the gods settled down, you hadn't a hope of hearing the orchestra.

Women in the audience had removed bonnets, shawls and coats, for warmth from the gas lamps and closely packed humanity heated the auditorium. But backstage was as draughty as ever, thought Mimi as she sneezed. Blast! She must have caught a cold that morning, hurrying through slushy streets after last night's snowstorm. However, she would soon warm up in the footlights, even if the audience didn't.

In London, you didn't feel greeted by the warmth from the punters and you got less applause than you did in the provinces. Otherwise the audiences were just as predictably unpredictable: nobody could explain why – wherever you played – Thursday's audience reacted differently to that of Wednesday, but they always reacted as one animal, and every night it was a different animal, with a changed personality ... which you could sometimes sense just before the curtain went up. Tonight they seem a jolly lot, Mimi thought as the house lights dimmed.

'You girls ready? We're about to go up,' the stage manager hissed from the wings.

'Who do he think he is, the blooming Tsar of Russia?' Betsy grumbled, as she smoothed her skirts for the last time. Both girls wore identical dresses of mauve taffeta, tightly sashed at the waist; a bunch of violets nestled in each corsage; their perky little pancake hats were tied with mauve satin chin-strings; their gloves, boots and tights were white. As she moved behind Betsy's swing, Mimi wished that Mrs Bridges did not stitch their bodices so tight, for this accentuated Mimi's still-flat chest, although it firmly pushed Betsy's balcony up on display.

Slowly, silently, the curtain rose. There was a sudden hush in the auditorium.

Mimi gave Betsy's backside a mighty push and Betsy flew forward towards the audience, kicking up one leg, to show the frills of her petticoats as she swung out beyond the proscenium arch, preparing to kick her slipper in the audience: it was always returned later, by some hopeful stage door johnny, for these fellows who hung around the performers' entrance took any opportunity to strike up an acquaintance with a pretty actress.

Betsy started to sing.

> 'Wouldn't you like to swing with me?
> Wouldn't you like to push my swing?
> Wouldn't you like to spoon with me?
> Wouldn't that be a thrilling thing ... ?'

Even in the gentlemen's clubs of London, all men knew the indecent version of this song, which was what was exciting the punters tonight.

* * *

When the pair returned to the sweaty dressing room Mrs Bridges quickly unhooked Betsy's costume (the Bridges Sisters were to appear as Spanish dancers in the second half) and anxiously asked Betsy yet again what she thought her chances were.

That morning, in a crowded agent's waiting room, the Bridges Sisters had waited to audition for the chorus of the New Gaiety. They had sat amongst many other brightly smiling beautifully dressed seventeen-year-olds, all wearing their best feathered hats, all carrying their crimping irons and little bottles of purple meths, in case it rained and they had to curl their hair again. All the hopefuls carefully wore a carelessly confident air to hide fear or desperation; all joined in the chat, spiked with gossip, malice and exaggeration, as frivolously delicious as a meringue. Lies about past or future work were politely accepted (although they fooled nobody) but everyone present understood that such fibs covered up the fibber's ever-present anxiety.

'But you must have *some* idea whether they liked you or not,' Mrs Bridges persisted.

'Ma, they just said, "Thank you, next please," as usual.'

You would think Mrs Bridges imagined *she* was about to strut her stuff before the footlights, Mimi muttered to herself as she stuck her foot on a chair to unlace her boot. Mrs Bridges did not know that each girl had secretly promised the other that both or neither would kick in the Gaiety chorus, although it wouldn't be the end of the world if only Betsy was accepted – as was likely – for Mimi was reasonably confident of getting a solo spot as a singer.

Two sumptuous bouquets of hothouse flowers stood on Betsy's place on the Bench: Betsy's mother allowed her to accept such tributes from stage door johnnies because flowers did not compromise a girl's reputation, as a piece of jewellery might.

'Pity there ain't no flowers for you, Mimi,' Mrs Bridges commiserated, with a false smile.

'I don't want no flowers, nor no johnnies,' Mimi growled. She never accepted an invitation and always asked the stage-door keeper whether all the johnnies had left before she ventured out into the alley.

'You'll never get married if you don't make an effort to be pleasant to the gentlemen,' huffed Mrs Bridges.

'Well, snap my garters! I saw what marriage did for my mam, and them other women in our alley. I ain't *never* going to get married.'

'Then you'll need a nest egg,' Mrs Bridges pointed out. 'But you'll never build one up if you don't go out with the johnnies.'

Mimi's other neighbour, Lily, who had recently been given a coveted diamond bracelet, giggled, 'You don't have to go all the way, Mimi, they'll settle for a bit of slap-and-tickle. And an evening at Romano's ain't so painful.' In the mirror, she winked at Mimi.

'Diamond bracelets ain't no nest egg,' Mimi sniffed. 'Diamond bracelets end up in a pawn shop, then they're gone. What *I* want is solid bricks and mortar: you ain't tempted to sell the odd brick to Uncle, when you need to raise a couple of bob.'

'You mean like Maisie's boarding house?' Betsy asked.

To everyone's surprise, Maisie had managed to get a gentleman friend (who knew nothing of the Great Dane) to purchase for her a house in Pimlico, which now had a brass sign over the bell that read THEATRICAL BOARDING HOUSE. This was a respectable establishment, with bobble-edged maroon plush curtains and tablecovers, red Turkey carpets, and ferns and aspidistras on lurid china columns.

'I can't blackmail me lover if I ain't intending to have one,' Mimi pointed out.

' 'Twasn't blackmail. He just wanted to . . . look after Maisie.'

'Only after Gustav followed him home, found out where he lived, and threatened to tell his missus.' Mimi pulled a horrified-wife face.

Betsy giggled. Mrs Bridges gave a genteel burp. 'Oops, pardon. It's my delicate stomach.'

'Ma, I warned you not to have chocolate creams after them herrings and pickled onions,' Betsy said mildly. 'Why not cross to the pub for something to settle your stomach? I'll join you, soon as the show's over.'

Mrs Bridges looked grateful for the suggestion; she was partial to a sip or two – not more, mind – of medicinal brandy to warm her up on a cold winter's night, especially before returning to their digs in an unheated tram. She flung her feather boa around her neck, straightened her hat brim, and headed for the ladies' bar at the Pig and Whistle.

As Mimi swiftly unpinned her mauve taffeta hat, she listened to the gossip and complaints of the girls around her. Careless Doreen in Wardrobe had used a too-hot iron on a skirt and burned it; Doreen had forgotten to clean Lily's blouse; Doreen had absent-mindedly handed Dora's dress to a larger girl, who had burst the seams.

Mimi's faded pink tights needed redying, but getting the colour correct was tricky: if Doreen left them in the dye bath too long, they would end up blood red. Mimi turned to Betsy. 'After the curtain, I'm going to dye me tights in Wardrobe. Anything I can do for you?'

'Um-hmmm,' Betsy said absent-mindedly: she was trying out her new eye colour.

'Betsy, you're not bloody listening!' Mimi was laughingly exasperated. 'I said I'm going up to Wardrobe.'

'Do you think this sea blue on the outer lids will make my eyes look bigger?' Self-absorbed, Betsy leaned back and threw an artificially bright smile at her reflection, to judge the effect from the back of the pit.

'Betsy! Do you want me to dye your tights?'

Betsy turned, so that she could see her face three-quarter view as she murmured, 'No thanks, Ma does mine.'

'See you later, then. At the Pig and Whistle?'

'Umm.'

Mimi shrugged on her heavy purple winter coat, for it would be freezing cold up in the unheated laundry.

She stuck her head round the door of Wardrobe. 'All right if I dye me tights tonight, Doreen?'

'If you're quick, ducky.' Bespectacled Doreen nodded as she bent over the long counter just inside the door, concentrating on the cardboard crown she was touching up with gold paint. 'Drat it, I forgot the bottom of that crown was wet, now I'll have to do it again . . . Blast! Now I've got gold paint on me apron!'

Clothes were handed out over Doreen's long counter and examined on it when they were returned; behind the counter lay the magical kingdom over which Doreen queened it. To the left of the entrance was a high window, beneath which two seamstresses frantically pedalled sewing machines during the day. To the right of the entrance, shelves were stacked with boxes of accessories: gloves and tights of every colour, brilliantly coloured glass jewels, pounds of enormous fake pearls. Above them stood hats, wigs and pasteboard tiaras, all covered by glass domes. Beyond these, rows of clothes hung from wheeled racks.

Mimi slipped around the counter, pushed her way through the crowded clothes racks and opened the door to the rear laundry. In the small room stood a large central wooden table, beyond which were several ginger-stained ceramic sinks below a window set high in the white-tiled wall. On the left of the sinks was a smaller wooden table upon which stood gas rings, a stack of dye pans and a litter of tea packets, milk bottles, cake tins and newspapers. Overhead, clothes dried on wooden battens, pulled by ropes up to ceiling height.

Mimi struck a match, lit the gas jet on the wall, lit a gas ring, closed the laundry door to keep inside what little heat the gas provided, picked up a pan, and briskly sprinkled burgundy dye powder into it.

* * *

Twenty minutes later, Doreen yawned, stretched, and forgetting that Mimi was in the back laundry buttoned her coat around her heavy body, pulled on her galoshes, then left Wardrobe. In the passage, she carefully shut and locked the door: if any clothes were stolen, she was fined, and theatricals were a light-fingered lot, so she was always careful, even if she was only going along the passage to have a widdle.

Doreen stuck her head round the door of the ladies' dressing room and saw Betsy, still trying out her new colours; she was the only person in the room.

'Feel like a Guinness?' Doreen asked.

'Not for me, but if you're going across to the Pig and Whistle, tell my ma I'll be over soon.'

'Hurry up. You're the last one, and I can't lock this dressing room until you've left it. So I'll be back in twenty minutes.'

* * *

In the laundry, Mimi lifted her elbows and twisted the water from her freshly dyed tights; she lowered a dryer, draped her tights over the wooden slats and heaved on the rope that raised it back to ceiling height: they'd be dry by morning.

She whistled as she washed her hands: hopeless to get the dye off, she looked as if she'd just knifed somebody. She turned off the gas lamp, yanked open the dividing door to the next room, and saw that the lights were out in Wardrobe.

'Doreen?' she called sharply.

No answer.

'Well, snap my garters, if she ain't a careless cow!' Mimi muttered as she turned back in the laundry, groped her way around the central table, felt for the matches, and relit the gas lamp. She then checked the little silver fob watch pinned inside her coat. Eleven fifteen. Doreen was probably locking up the dressing rooms. Or she'd nipped out to the pub for a quick 'un. Not a bad idea.

Mimi left the laundry door open so that light shone directly into Wardrobe; she pushed her way through the clothes racks to the door and twisted the doorknob. The door would not open: she rattled and turned it repeatedly, with no result.

Suddenly she realized that if Doreen *had* left for the night, then she might have to spend the night in Wardrobe. Blast!

Still, things could be worse: she wouldn't need to climb down a wet drainpipe, there was plenty of fabric with which to make a makeshift bed: Scottish chieftain plaids, dozens of shawls, ermine-trimmed crimson velvet trains.

No! There was no need for her to spend the night in a nest of cheap cotton velvet, because Betsy knew she was dying her tights. Betsy would soon come looking for her. She had merely to wait.

In the unheated room, she shivered, then sneezed. She'd better get back in the laundry and make a cup of hot tea.

* * *

With satisfaction, Betsy peered at her long black lower eyelashes as she snapped shut the child's paintbox which had provided them. Briskly she creamed her face clean, then looked around the dressing room. Mimi's coat was not hanging from her peg; maybe she'd gone round to the front to watch the audience leave, the naughty girl, and would join them at the pub later. Betsy glanced at her watch. Heavens, she had no idea it was so late. Ma would be waiting, might even be a bit tipsy. She'd better hurry.

At the stage door, Betsy passed the fireman, about to start his first night patrol.

'Night, miss. Everyone left up there?'

'Yes, I'm the last one out. If Doreen comes back, tell her I locked up our dressing room for her.'

'She'll see the key on the hook, miss.'

'Of course.' Betsy opened the stage-door keeper's

cubicle, and hung the ladies' dressing room key on the board inside, next to the Wardrobe key. Then she skipped off to the Pig and Whistle.

* * *

The paint store was in the basement, below the stage, next to the scenery store and carpentry shop: Fireman Heath reached it at 11.40 p.m., and recorded this on one of the automatic clocks he punched in various parts of the premises, to prove the time of his visit.

He opened the door to the paint store.

Whoosh! The fireman staggered back as a six-foot wall of orangē and yellow flames leaped hungrily towards him. He turned and tore towards the fire alarm, up by the stage door. Behind him, flames swept outward and upwards, through the open door, and along the passage.

The Angel Music Hall had been built on a corner of Islington High Street and Fern Lane. Just before Fireman Heath reached the fire alarm a policeman, walking his beat in Fern Lane, noticed a red glow under a side door. As he stared, smoke curled round its edges.

He immediately ran towards the High Street, where he hailed a cab and, shouting an order, leaped in. The tired old nag clopped off as fast as she could, slipping occasionally on the wet cobbles, as she headed for the Islington fire station, less than half a mile distant.

Once the alarm was given, the firemen dashed to their posts. Horses were swiftly harnessed. *Crack* went the whips, and sparks flew from the cobbles as the engines dashed around the corner and broke into a gallop. As they charged through the night, the firemen clinging to the sides of their engines yelled, 'Hi! Hi! Hi!' to signal their approach. Swiftly, the fire engines passed all other vehicles and many surprised pedestrians, returning home from a night out.

The theatre fireman dashed forward as soon as he heard the screech of braking wheels. Even in the short space of time between the raising of the first alarm and the arrival of the first engines the flames had spread alarmingly.

As firemen jumped down from their engines great columns of fire leaped up into the sky; blazing flames were mirrored in the windows of surrounding buildings, transforming the surrounding darkness. Everywhere seemed aflame.

Despite the late hour, crowds of people stood to watch this unexpected excitement, held back by policemen. There was a storm of shouting, as tipsy passers-by offered advice or inaccurate information. The police found it difficult to keep the narrow side streets free from spectators, who kept edging forward to watch the free show.

By twenty minutes past midnight, thirteen red engines with extending ladders and horse-escapes were grouped around the theatre. Each fireman (and there were now over a hundred present) knew his priority: to rescue the living, to stop the fire spreading, to rescue any valuable property within, and then to extinguish the fire.

Although the fire had now spread over the entire back of the theatre at ground level, many firemen entered to see if they could remove anything flammable. However, they found it impossible to fight their way through the flames to the scene dock at the back of the stage, where most of the lath-and-canvas scenery was stored.

* * *

Upstairs, on the floor of the laundry room, Mimi dozed in a nest of velvet Venetian Renaissance cloaks, until she was awakened by strange noises from the street. She sneezed, groped for her handkerchief, blew her nose, and then became aware of a strange noise *inside* the theatre: it was like applause, but at a faster tempo.

Mimi jerked her head up and sniffed. Despite her cold, she could smell smoke. She opened her eyes, then quickly scrambled to her feet, as she looked up at the small window above the sinks, where the glass panes were a flickering orange, lit from outside. The entire laundry was brightly illuminated by this exterior, ruddy glow.

The theatre was on fire!

She dashed into the other room, also lit by the exterior glare.

Terrified, she pushed through the racks of clothes towards the exit. To her horror, beyond Doreen's counter, she saw oily black smoke outline the door to the corridor. She dashed forward to open it, but although the brass handle turned, the door refused to budge. Remembering Betsy's stupid mistake, she slowly and carefully turned the knob clockwise and pulled hard. The black, oily smoke made her cough and gasp for breath as she turned the doorknob anticlockwise and tried again: the door was immovable. It was locked.

Remembering her Preston escape from a locked room, she decided to try to open the big window.

Crack! Crack! Crack! The glass domes that covered the wigs and hats exploded in the heat behind her, as she climbed onto one of the sewing-machine tables and attempted, without success, to push it open. Looking up, she saw the dangling, frayed rope of a broken sash cord: no wonder the window frame would not budge! Looking down, she saw that the stage door alley – sixty feet below – was deserted.

Where was the theatre fireman? There was *always* a fireman on duty at night! Wasn't the bloody fireman supposed to check that the building was empty? *Where was he?*

* * *

Within an hour of the first lick of fire, nothing could stop the flames. When they reached the roof, and the sharp wind fanned them, the huddle of spectators heard a roar, like an express train crashing through a tunnel. Above the crackle and roar of the flames, a thunderous rumbling was heard.

'Roof's falling in, Chief!' a blackened fireman yelled, as he ran from the building, followed by other firefighters.

The onlookers heard a mighty crash, followed by an eerie whistling sound as the rest of the theatre roof fell in. The flames and sparks shot up even higher; more belching black smoke rose steadily from the tangled mess of girders, broken brick walls and other debris.

Nothing could save the theatre now.

* * *

Inside the burning building Mimi heard the eerie whistling sound and shuddered. She remembered newspaper reports of the awful fire at the Alhambra Theatre in Leicester Square, only eighteen months before. She had read that twenty fire engines were on the scene, in no time. *Why weren't any fire engines here to save her?*

Despite shaking with fear, she forced herself to remember theatre fire drill. Smoke was the greatest danger, because you could not avoid being poisoned by the fumes; useless to wrap yourself in wet material, for the intense heat of the fire dried the stuff in seconds. Keep your face close to the ground, because smoke and heat rose, so there might be a couple of inches of clear air at ground level . . . If she broke these small glass window panes, she would be able to breathe fresh air. She had seen axes somewhere . . . with the suits of armour!

Mimi jumped down, and ran to the armoury rail, beside which spears and axes lolled in an umbrella rack.

Mimi snatched an axe. She immediately realized that it was made of rubber. Weeping tears of fury, she hurled the axe at the window: it rebounded from the window frame and fell to the floor.

Grabbing a Roman spear, she realized that it was a disguised broom handle. She ran to the big window and banged it against the glass panes; as they smashed, she felt more hopeful, for a freezing wind rushed into the wardrobe room, now starting to fill with smoke.

She climbed on a sewing machine table, and started to smash the glass panes high above her.

* * *

'Person reported, Chief,' shouted a black-faced fireman. 'Upper window at rear of building. Theatre fireman reports it's the wardrobe room.'

'Slip the Escape!' bellowed the Chief. 'Get jets set in!' Wearily, he rubbed his soot-blackened face, for he knew there was little hope. A fire crew rushed down Fern Lane to the stage door alley. White canvas hoses snaked across the cobbles, as the escape crew pitched the ladder up towards the window, where the face had been seen.

* * *

Mimi heard a blinding flash, felt searing heat on the left side of her face, then saw that the door to the passage had crashed into the room, where it lay burning fiercely. Beyond it she could see yellow-orange flames that growled and roared towards her. She fiercely turned up her collar, wrapped a wet shawl around her head and instinctively protected her face with her arms and hands, now covered by silvery knight's gauntlet-gloves. Coughing badly, she backed away from the flames.

There was nothing more she could do. She only had a few minutes to live before an agonizing death. And she was alone.

Don't give up!

The window was the only way out.

She dashed forward, again jumping up on a sewing-machine table. Again she tried to heave up the smouldering window frame. As she pushed, it burst into flames, and an agonizing pain shot through her hands as she fell backwards, to the floor.

She tore away what remained of the gauntlets, then staggered to her feet, backing away from the window.

* * *

Outside, the fireman's fifty-foot ladder failed to extend to the seventh-floor window.

'Can't reach the person, sir! We'll have to try from inside.'

* * *

Doreen's counter, facing the door to the passage, had now caught fire. Flames were nearing Mimi, leaping and dancing towards her, all shades of oranges and lemons: delicate, flickering, menacing.

She started to cough even more heavily as the smoke thickened. What an awful way to die! To be burnt to a

crisp like a piece of blackened toast. To die just because
your tights had faded!

* * *

'Chief, one of them new engines just arrived, from Regent
Street Fire Station.'

The Chief ran up Fern Lane to the High Street, where,
to his relief, he saw one of the latest motor-pump Merry-
weather escape units; he knew it had a jack-knifed
sixty-foot escape ladder, plus nearly two hundred feet of
canvas hose.

* * *

Mimi shouted to God for a quick death. If He, in whom
she did not believe, wanted her to die – if it was her turn
– then please would He get it over quickly? She was
exhausted by her coughing. She wanted to sleep. She had
had enough, couldn't God realize that?

She was trapped with her back against the small area of
relatively unheated whitewashed brick wall opposite the
blazing window. But she was not alone.

Before fire had consumed the basement the resident
rats had prudently retreated to the front of the theatre;
when the firemen broke in, they streaked out. Others, on
the upper floors, had run to the roof, where they were
burned to death when it crashed in. A few were still
lurking in small areas in the middle of the theatre, and
three of them scuttled out of holes and cracks into Wardrobe. One by one, these terrified creatures seeking refuge
from the heat retreated to the least hot part of the
floorboards, which happened to be where the equally
terrified Mimi stood.

She sensed rather than saw the swift brown blur at her

feet, then felt a rat scrabble over her right boot. She felt her stomach shrivel and her bowels contract. Of course she screamed, but nobody heard and the rat took no notice.

Eventually Mimi forced herself to stop gazing downward in sick horror and once more look up in desperation at the ceiling, wondering fearfully which part was going to come crashing down next.

Gradually the floorboards grew so hot that she could feel the heat through the soles of her boots. She suddenly realized that she was in equal danger from the floor catching fire or collapsing. Suppose they gave way, and she fell into a lake of flames, engulfed in hell on earth? She jerked with fright and in doing so trod on the tail of a rat. In a frantic bid for safety it jumped up her long thick navy serge skirt and managed to cling to the laces of her left boot, just below the frill of her drawers. She felt she could bear no more: never in her most threatening nightmares had she known such terror.

The terrified rat then leaped upwards. Instinctively Mimi pressed her knees together. Squashed by her thighs, the panic-stricken rat bit with sharp little teeth, again and again, in a desperate effort to escape. Mimi screamed, inhaled smoke and choked. She felt searing heat in her right foot; she smelled roasting flesh, realized her foot was burning. She coughed and screamed, but instinctively held her arms up to protect her face; as she did so she felt as if burning daggers were piercing her hands, her feet, her legs. She smelled singeing hair before she collapsed to the floorboards, still holding her arms before her face. The rat eventually struggled free of her skirts, leaving a bloody trail. Mimi lay gasping and choking.

Suddenly she became blearily aware that something

had changed. She lifted her head slightly, to peek beyond her arms, up at the big burning window. As she did so, a jet of water crashed through it, hurling her head back to the floor, and soaking her entire body.

Dazed, disbelieving, she saw a moving dark shape silhouetted against the window. She glimpsed a flash of brass . . . it was a helmet! A fireman!

The burly black figure smashed with his axe, again and again, until the blazing window frame fell into the room. The fireman hurled himself towards Mimi, threw her over his left shoulder, shouting, 'Hang on, miss.' He stamped back to the black gap in the wall, and the blissfully damp night air beyond it.

Mimi, only half-conscious and in agonizing pain, felt a springing, jerking motion as the fireman moved, fast but carefully, down the ladder. Spectators below gawped upwards in horror as they watched the fireman back down the long ladder, a dripping, dark burden on his back.

Mimi was shivering, and her teeth were chattering, from cold and shock. She would like to go to sleep, if nobody minded . . . again she smelled the roast-pork odour of burnt flesh . . . someone was sobbing . . . then roaring, merciful blackness closed around her.

* * *

By 1.30 a.m., about two hours after the fire had broken out, the firemen at last gained control of the flames.

By 3.30 a.m., the fire had been virtually extinguished, although firemen continued to direct water on smouldering wreckage to cool it and so prevent the fire from breaking out again.

At dawn, the Chief inspected what remained of the blackened building. The front part of the theatre was intact, and the auditorium – apart from being blackened by smoke – was undamaged by fire, thanks to the fireproof curtain. However, what the fire had not destroyed the firemen had ruined with their hoses, or smashed with their axes, as they hacked through whatever stood in their way, to search for survivors and prevent the blaze from spreading.

As well as the roof, the rear of the building had been completely destroyed, including workshops, scenery and property stores, dressing rooms, Wardrobe and passages. Except for a few blackened timbers, the stage was open to the sky. All the complicated machinery for the raising and lowering of scenery was a mass of black, twisted metal.

Fire Chief Archer sniffed the nauseous smell of damp, charred wood and smouldering rubble. Wearily, he ordered his exhausted men back to his fire station, where they would be cleaned up by their wives.

The cause of the fire at the Angel Music Hall was never discovered: in fact, a bucket of rags soaked in linseed oil had combusted in the paint store.

* * *

Three days later, Mimi became aware of the sounds of sobbing. She sniffed antiseptic. She opened her eyes with difficulty because the lids felt glued together. Beyond the white triangle of a nurse's headdress she glimpsed Betsy's tear-smeared face at the end of a white metal bed, then she again lost consciousness.

* * *

'There *isn't* a mirror in the ward,' the chubby young nurse insisted unconvincingly. Burn victims were not allowed mirrors. She added, 'But there's nothing wrong with your face, and your hair will grow again. You'll soon recover, dearie.' Her face contradicted her words.

* * *

Two weeks later, Fred Jennings, the theatre fireman who had been on duty the night of the fire, stood at the end of Mimi's hospital bed; he clutched a brown bowler hat in one hand and a drooping bunch of late snowdrops in the other. He was shocked by Mimi's appearance. Most of her hair had been burned and what remained had been cropped short: on the bandaged side of her face a burn ran from the top of her forehead to her ear. She was lucky to have been protected by her thick serge coat and boots, but Fred Jennings knew the girl had second-degree burns on her back, and third-degree burns on her arms, feet and legs; the worst burns were on her upper calves, her knees and her hands. The poor kiddie was lucky none of them rat bites had turned septic. The nurse had told him.

Mimi, still in great pain, knew that she was lucky to have survived. Although she was not supposed to watch when her dressings were changed – an agonizing procedure – through half-closed eyes she saw her still-raw, red, open flesh, and the charred, blistered tissue; she saw glistening, crusted scabs, and the yellow and black contusions that seemed to cover the rest of her body.

Fred shuffled forward and laid the limp snowdrops on Mimi's bedside locker. 'If only them flames had started a bit later, miss!' he said sadly, 'I always check Wardrobe within twenty minutes of starting my night patrol, so I would have found you locked inside.'

'Fred, it ain't your fault,' Mimi whispered.

'I don't blame myself, miss. I know I done nothing

wrong.' One of the reasons that Fred had come to visit Mimi was to tell her something, because he did not want to be blamed in any way – by Mimi or anyone else – for not rescuing her. Fred had acted correctly, but unfortunately on false information. Earnestly, he explained, 'I could have got you out, miss, if I'd knowed as you was there. The fire didn't start upstairs, it started in the basement, so there would of been plenty of time to get you out afore it took hold upstairs.'

Mimi looked up, puzzled. 'Then why didn't you?'

'That friend of yours, miss, the one with the lovely face, she told me there wasn't no performers left upstairs. She told me everyone had left.'

'*What?*' Mimi couldn't believe that she had suffered all that terror and these terrible injuries – because Betsy had lied to the theatre fireman, had told him that she had left the building!

After Fred's departure, her resentment started to simmer. Encumbered by bandages and unable to move, she lay for hour after hour in her hospital bed, wondering how her best friend could have done such a cruel thing.

* * *

At Betsy's next appearance, Mimi lifted her bandaged arms and screamed, 'Get out of here!'

Astonished, Betsy stared at her. 'What's wrong?'

'I *know*, Betsy, I *know*! *You* told the theatre fireman I'd left the building! And *that's* why I was trapped in them flames! He could have got me out, easy, if he'd knowed I was upstairs.' Clumsily, Mimi held out her bandaged arms. 'Betsy, look at me! When they change me dressings, I don't see white arms and legs, I see blackened flesh, blood and pus. And now *I know that's your fault, Betsy!*'

'You can't blame me for that fire!' Betsy immediately looked defensive and frightened. 'It *weren't* my fault, Mimi! Why not blame Doreen for locking you up in the first place?'

'Doreen's not my best friend! I thought *you* were! I thought *you* cared for me! But *you* told Doreen I'd left the theatre!'

'Because I truly thought you had!' snivelled Betsy. 'I can't remember exactly what happened, but Doreen said as everyone had gone ... and your coat wasn't on your dressing-room hook!'

'Because I'd gone up to the bloody laundry, where there's no heat, and it's always bloody freezing! I *told* you!'

'Well, I forgot! You can't blame me for forgetting one little thing!'

'Yes, I can! I blame you for being so wrapped up in yourself! For being so bloody careless! Because that's why *this* happened to me!' Again, Mimi slowly and clumsily thrust her bandaged arms towards her. '*Look at me!* Me body's burned to bits, God knows what me face is like under the bandages, me career's down the drain – and all because *you* said I'd left the theatre – when I hadn't!'

'That ain't fair!'

'No, it *ain't* fair! It ain't fair on *me*! Because it's *your* bleeding fault I was nearly burned alive, and I ain't going to let you wriggle out of that!'

Mimi had never dared show her anger to her terrifying father, responsible for the indignation and humiliation, rage and self-imposed guilt that had weighed down her heart since she was eight years old. But Mimi was not frightened of Betsy, so there was no psychological block to prevent her voicing her anger at the damage her friend had done to her. Once the floodgates of her anger had been opened, many years' accumulation of rage burst from her undammed heart as she unwittingly offloaded it on Betsy's shoulders.

The chubby young nurse rushed down the ward to Mimi's bed. 'All this noise! You're disturbing the other patients!' She turned to Betsy. 'I think you'd better leave, miss.'

As Betsy trailed down the ward between two rows of white iron beds to the door, she wept tears of self-pity into her handkerchief. 'It ain't *fair*! It ain't *not* fair! It *wasn't* my fault! *I* didn't start the dratted fire!'

Nothing was *ever* Betsy's fault: she could never bear to be in the wrong, or take responsibility for any unfortunate action – so she always twisted logic in order to blame somebody else ... She hadn't meant to do it ... She didn't realize ... Nobody warned her ... Somebody should have done something ... Nobody could have expected ... It wasn't Betsy's fault that Mimi had decided to dye her tights that night ... and Doreen shouldn't have locked Wardrobe without checking that the laundry room was empty! By denying her guilt, however, Betsy merely pushed it below the surface of consciousness, where it would continue to torment her.

Mimi felt a similarly urgent need to blame somebody else for her mutilated body. She did not want to feel that her life had been wrecked because she decided to dye her tights. She violently resented this second damaging card that Fate had dealt her.

In the years ahead, Mimi would continue to dump all the sorrows and injustices of her childhood on Betsy. And to excuse it, she would unknowingly exaggerate Betsy's responsibility for her burns: little by little, day by day, Mimi would monsterize Betsy.

* * *

'How did you get here?' Mimi stared at the pale triangular face of Baz, who stood at the end of her bed, wearing a natty ginger-checked bookie's suit and a canary waistcoat; he hugged a small wicker hamper.

'It weren't front page news in *The Stage* but we got tomtom drums in the Business. Word gets around fast.' He opened the wicker basket. 'One bottle of bubbly, one glass – that's from Joe. Them grapes are from his missus. Daisy sent the rose water, and the daffs are from Jessie.'

For the next ten minutes he chatted frantically, to hide his shock upon seeing the extent of Mimi's injuries.

'Where are you all playing?' Mimi asked weakly.

'Finished at Bournemouth last night, open at the Hove Lyceum tomorrow. The Guv'nor ain't got time to come here himself, so he sent me to tell you you're not to worry, he's paying your hospital bill. You can pay him back when it suits you.'

Mimi knew that in the Business 'when it suits you' meant 'never'. Her eyes watered.

'Hey, I ain't come here to make you blub!' Baz added carefully, 'Jolly Joe says he'd be glad to have you back. We can cover your arms and legs.'

'What about me face?'

Baz hesitated. 'The nurse told me that'll clear up. And if it don't, you can cover it with paint and dress your hair over it – a good dresser will fix that.' He dared not mention blackface.

Mimi burst into angry tears. 'So that's it! *That's* me

destiny – Number Three tours hiding me face until I die! While Betsy's kicking her bloody heels up in the Gaiety chorus, without a care in the world! – although what's happened to me is all *her* fault.'

'I heard as nobody in the Angel Company would speak to Betsy after the fire,' Baz said quietly, 'especially after she tried to blame Doreen. Like I said, word gets around.'

Through tears Mimi yelled her frustration. 'I'm going to get my own back on Betsy, if it takes a lifetime.'

Baz cocked his head on one side. 'Ain't you got better things to do in your life than waste time on revenge?'

'*What* better things? I'm scarred for life, so I can't do me job, and I ain't got so much as a shilling! So what *can* I do?'

Baz pulled a grape from the bunch in the basket; with a flourish, he popped it in his mouth, then grinned. 'I got an idea.'

Chapter Four

On the evening after Mimi left hospital Baz took her to the London Hippodrome, where Vesta Tilley, the outstanding male impersonator of her day, topped the bill. Now in her early forties, Tilley could stamp like a Guardsman or strut like an officer; taps were fixed to the heels and toes of her shoes, so that they clicked audibly when she turned sharply, in a military manner; her immaculately cut suits were stitched in Savile Row and much copied by provincial would-be men-about-town.

Once seated in the pit, Baz told Mimi that Joe wanted her to attend every performance until the end of the week, and that Daisy had already started to plan her costumes. Carefully he added, 'You're lucky you got your voice back after that smoke. Your body and legs'll be completely covered by men's clothes, and you'll always wear gloves.'

Mimi thought about this possible new career for several minutes, then objected, 'I don't want to copy someone else.'

'Tilley didn't *invent* the male impersonator,' Baz pointed out; secretly he hoped that by copying someone with such swaggering bravado, Mimi would regain her own lost self-confidence.

He added, 'That's only the way you *start*, Mimi. By the time you finish rehearsing, you'll have developed your own style: and *nobody* can beat your voice.'

Mimi gave a small smile of satisfaction. Effortlessly, she could once again throw her dark, hot-honey voice to the furthest, highest corner of a theatre; she could sound mischievous or romantic; in the middle of a comic song she could suddenly switch to a pathos that hushed the house; she always, instantly, communicated her mood to her audience.

'No harm in giving it a go,' she eventually agreed, cautiously. Once again, it was not difficult for her to make an important decision, for she had nothing to lose. And she'd always wanted to see Tilley.

* * *

Mimi was fascinated by the neat-featured, elegant Vesta Tilley's performance; Mimi bounced up and down on her seat, for she couldn't clap because both hands were still bandaged. Tilley had been a totally convincing 'male' – although she made no attempt to sing like a man – and she had a magnetic presence: that indefinable extra-some-thing-special called star quality. Mimi's spine tingled, and she shivered with excitement.

'Oh, Baz, I couldn't do anything like *that*!'

'No – *you'll* do something different. Now don't get cold feet on me! You got as much guts as Tilley, ain't yer?'

Mimi still looked uncertain.

* * *

Once she returned to the stage, Mimi gradually recovered her self-confidence. Eventually she once more crackled with energy. Finally, one evening, she relaxed and her charisma returned. 'Her star quality's still there,' noted Jolly Joe, relieved. After that, Mimi enjoyed her quick changes as she metamorphosed from an obsequiously flirtatious chauffeur in cap and leggings to a bawdy sailor, a toff in blazer and flannels, a drunken reveller in a top hat, or a huntsman in his pink coat. She could quickly switch from a posh accent to a slow Somerset burr, Welsh, Scottish or Irish voice. Her favourite role was that of a spunky little drummer-boy, bravely marching into battle although his knees were knocking with fear. Apart from him, she avoided soldier songs such as 'Goodbye Dolly Gray', because these were associated with Vesta Tilley, as much as 'I'm Burlington Bertie' and 'Champagne Charlie is me Name'.

Audiences loved Mimi's frankness and lack of pretence, her sharp, tart, street-urchin repartee and impish sense of humour. A pretty girl who could be a clown was a rarity, and Mimi could also be a tomboy without being coarse. She was witty and sometimes slightly improper, but she was never lewd or vulgar, and did not offend the women in her audiences. Baz had taught her to look innocently upwards when speaking a blue line, to emphasize the double meaning; alternatively, she gave an exaggerated, conspiratorial wink. Often, her songs had a simple chorus, heralded by a thwack on the bass drum and a suggestive raspberry-tootle on the French horn, after which the audience always joined in the chorus.

Naturally, Mimi did not *really* try to impersonate a male – but that was the joke. To the huge delight of the mostly male audience, Mimi proved, with her every movement, that it was *not* possible for a woman to be a man.

* * *

Baz had not only rescued Mimi's career with his clever idea, he had improved it. When performing solo, Mimi quickly became far more successful than she had been as half of a simpering Singing Sisters act, and she preferred her new male roles. Jolly Joe was delighted by his investment, although he quickly realized that he would not long be able to keep her on Number Three tours.

* * *

Six months later, Mimi acquired a London booking agent and left Joe's troupe. Within three years, she was playing twice nightly, plus a couple of matinées, at the London Coliseum: in theatrical terms, this was the equivalent of playing a two a day at Broadway's Palace Theatre, and meant that she could now appear at top theatres anywhere in the English-speaking world.

Once back on stage, Mimi again felt safe and loved; off stage she also appeared to be enjoying her new success.

Little Daisy – now Mimi's dresser – never tried to belittle the puckered glistening scar that ran down the left side of her forehead to her ear. Daisy had once soothingly said, 'Nobody notices that any more,' whereupon Mimi had erupted, 'We paint it out, and we powder on top, but what other woman wears greasepaint off stage? Don't try to tell me that nobody notices! We've grown me fringe and looped me hair forward over me ears but don't you ever try to kid me that nobody notices! I notice!'

She had eventually come to terms with her disfigurement by telling herself that some girls had ugly noses or teeth and they couldn't do a darn thing about it; at least she could disguise her scars and act as if they didn't exist. However, this pretence was fragile and always fractured if she caught someone staring in fascinated horror. So she took pains to see that nobody ever did.

Only Daisy was allowed to see Mimi when her face was unpainted. After a performance Baz had once burst into her dressing room without knocking; Mimi jumped up and turned away from him with shoulders hunched up; her left hand flew up to cover her scar as she screamed, '*Get out!* And don't *never* come in without bloody knocking!' It had taken Daisy two hours to calm her down.

Daisy knew that there were also invisible scars; her new boss never went out to supper with any of the johnnies that waited at the stage door or sent her a bouquet with a note tucked in it. Daisy guessed that to avoid the embarrassment and humiliation of seeing a man shocked by the sight of her face and body, Mimi took care to see that no man ever got the chance. At any mention of Betsy her mouth tightened and her body visibly tensed.

Saturday 25 May 1907. The Coliseum Theatre, London

On the evening before Mimi's twentieth birthday, Daisy had laid out the towels and tub of cold cream on the bench in her little private dressing room.

'Good house tonight, Daisy!' Mimi skipped in and threw her policeman's helmet on a hatstand knob; she was – as always – exhilarated after her act. Tonight, her comic songs had gone down particularly well, especially 'Bill Bailey!'. She had not waited long for the amused and happy hum, which then broke into quiet guffaws followed by a wave of titters, and then a roar of delight. Mimi loved hearing laughter even more than she loved applause, because when she made people laugh, she felt that she was part of their happy warmth.

She had finished her act with 'Sweet Adeline', for she liked to end with a sad number that hushed the house: she loved that still moment when you could hear a pin drop and knew she'd got 'em in the palm of her hand! At that thrilling, heady second of power, she felt almost as if she was physically attached to the audience by an invisible umbilical cord, so aware was she of her public's emotion.

As Mimi threw herself onto her chair before the Bench, Daisy handed her the glass of champagne and Guinness which she drank every night after her performance. She then carefully peeled off Mimi's gloves; three years after the fire, this was still a delicate process, which always reminded Mimi of her disfigurement: the skin on her calves and hands had been burned down to the underlying muscle, and the scar tissue was reddish-purple, puckered and ugly.

Suddenly Mimi shuddered violently, then slumped in her chair, as if all the energy had been syphoned from her body.

'Another bad turn?' Daisy asked quietly.

'Yes,' Mimi admitted, 'and one as I came off stage. Suddenly, I was back there – choking and gasping, with them terrifying flames licking nearer and nearer! I could hear that hungry roar in me ears ... When it happens, Daisy, *I am there again*!' She buried her head in her twisted hands. 'I never know when I'm going to get one of these bloody nightmares – daymares, I call 'em, for when I'm back in that fire, it's *real* to me, not just a memory. I'm terrified: I can't move. It's me real life that seems only a dream.' Mimi flung her head back in despair. 'And the worst part is, I feel *so alone*! Just as I did at the time.' She looked at Daisy, and for the first time voiced her worst fear. 'Sometimes I wonder if I'm going out of me mind . . .'

'Course you ain't.' Daisy comforted Mimi as she hugged her. As Mimi's snuffles faded, Daisy poured them both another Black Velvet.

In the mirror Mimi looked at her cheeks, streaked with tears and eyeblack; automatically, wearily, she prepared to wipe off her colours.

Daisy now took the opportunity to say what she had tried to tell Mimi for months, although Mimi always snapped at her when she mentioned it. 'It's only natural . . . I had . . . er . . . a cousin who felt the same way when it happened to her . . . One day them daymares will stop, you'll see! But them horrible memories ain't going to fade until you let 'em *all* go.'

'What the 'ell do you mean?' Mimi slowly unpinned her wig; then ran her hands through her hair, to shake it out.

'You got to forget about Betsy,' Daisy said quietly, as she took the wig. 'When you're thinking of Betsy, your face goes tight and your mouth turns down, real ugly. You've got better things to do than waste your time and energy planning some daft revenge on Betsy. Besides, you've *got* your revenge: you're finishing the first half at the Coliseum, while Betsy's still a hoofer in the Gaiety chorus.'

Mimi pinned a band round her head to keep her hair off her face. As she slathered on cold cream, she quietly said, 'How *can* I forget, Daisy, when I go through that fire *again*, and *again*?' Almost as exhausting as the nightmares

– 104 –

were the rage and resentment that surfaced when they woke her.

'Them nasty visions'll stop if you leave 'em alone,' Daisy said firmly. 'Painful memories fade with time, if you let 'em lie still, instead of giving 'em a good shake every morning.'

'It ain't so damned easy as you think.' Mimi wearily wiped her face. She felt swamped by anger whenever, accidentally, she glimpsed her injuries: *Mimi* didn't deserve to be punished because *Betsy* had been careless.

'I understand, all right,' Daisy said. 'It always helps if you can blame another body for your troubles. If this theatre's half-empty, then the manager barks at his assistant, she snaps at the office boy, and *he* kicks the cat.'

Mimi picked up a towel and wiped the colours from her face. 'Sorry, Daisy, but I can't alter what's happened, or how I feel about it.'

Daisy pursed her lips. 'You can't undo the past, but you *can* put it behind you. Can't you just wipe that dratted Betsy off your mind, like you're wiping them colours off your face? Because you'll stay upset until you do. I've been your dresser now for three years, and all that time I've seen you brooding. You're destroying your own peace of mind, and that's not Betsy's fault – it's *yours*!'

'I can't help remembering what she did!' Mimi twisted her chair, and angrily threw her hairbrush across the room.

'And every time you do, you grow more bitter.'

Projecting disapproval, Daisy hobbled across the dressing room and picked the hairbrush up from the floor. 'Bitterness rusts the soul, my girl.'

'You been listening to them soapbox preachers at Hyde Park Corner?'

'Yours ain't the only sob story, Mimi.' Quietly she drained the dregs of her Black Velvet, then set her empty glass on the counter. 'What makes you think *I* ain't suffered? I watched me mother starve in front of me eyes, after scarlet fever wiped out her other five kiddies. And after I trained as a wire artiste, early arthritis stopped me earning good money. At least *you're* getting well paid.'

'Yes, but the money's come too late to do what I really wanted,' Mimi muttered. She had returned to Liverpool to rescue her mother and the little 'uns. Her heart had suddenly started to thump, as she had hurried up the alley, late on a Sunday morning, when she knew her mam would be at home and *he* would be at the pub. There was no answer when she knocked at the door. Finally a neighbour looked out. 'No use banging. She was took with meningitis two years ago, *and* the little girl – died afore the week was out. Then Alf left with the boy, dunno where. Canada, someone said . . .' The woman then peered closer at Mimi's face. Pale with shock, she had said, 'If it ain't Mimi! I ain't never seen you in fancy clothes! You on the streets now, dearie? It ain't no use crying, dearie, you ain't the only one Death touches, not in this alley.'

In meaningful silence, Daisy brushed Mimi's hair, until Mimi sighed. 'I give in. What do you want me to do, Daisy?'

'Try reading this.' Daisy whipped a slim maroon book from the pocket of her flowered pinafore, and slid it onto the Bench. 'It's one of them little Hope Strong books about forgiveness: such a comfort.'

Mimi flipped open the book at random and read, 'Simply confront those who have hurt you . . . Dig deep and you will find the strength you need for forgiveness . . .'

As Daisy brushed, Mimi read a few pages, then looked up, perplexed and annoyed. 'Daisy, this makes it sound too damned easy! When I dig deep, Daisy, I only find more pain!' Hope Strong did not seem to understand the problem of *wanting* to forgive, but being unable to do so.

Sunday 26 May 1907. Green Park, Piccadilly, London

Late on the afternoon of Mimi's twentieth birthday, she strolled arm in arm with Baz through sunny Green Park. Mimi wore a pink taffeta dress with a bustle, and a toque of pink rosebuds, copied from a photograph of Princess May in the *Illustrated London News*. Baz looked just as smart, a pink carnation in the buttonhole of his natty dark suit, a black bowler tilted over one eye and a white silk evening scarf thrown casually around his neck, just like a toff. Baz now did a supper act at a London restaurant; he'd taken it because he was sick of grubby train journeys and wanted to wake up in the same bed for a bit.

Earlier that afternoon, the two friends had travelled to Victoria (the tram had swayed like Queen Alexandra might after Christmas dinner: slightly tipsy but still majestic), where they watched an American moving picture – *The Great Train Robbery*. Mimi had clung to Baz's arm, nearly sick with excitement; on seaside piers she had peered into flickering picture machines, but this new bioscope beat them all! As an additional birthday treat, Baz was later taking her to meet his special friend at the newly opened Ritz Hotel; then they were all going to the Royal Variety Show, at the rebuilt Alhambra Theatre in Leicester Square.

The whole world seemed to be enjoying the sunshine and spicy hint of sex within the Park gates. After a few beers with steak-and-kidney pudding in some Soho pub, off-duty footmen now lay sleeping under elm trees; under-housemaids in their Sunday best sat gossiping in deckchairs, as they watched the swells stroll by. Baz automatically noticed which toff eyed the loitering rent boys, ready to follow one of them to some tavern back room or a private molly club, which was safer. Baz had good reason to know that for many policemen the hunting of homosexuals had almost become a sport; thousands were arrested every year, and often severely injured, 'as a result of resisting police arrest'.

If caught by the police, there was only one way for a homosexual to avoid prosecution: to marry. It was generally considered impossible for a married man to be a pervert. Without legal threat, some guiltily tried to repress or disguise their instincts by marrying; others projected their unconscious, vindictive fury onto those who did not hide their inclinations, whom they hounded.

Which was why Baz glared at a group of uniformed policemen, conferring beneath an ancient elm. He growled, 'Although it's buggery that's illegal, lots of nellies ain't buggers. They're slicklegs or mouthers, or they use their hands, like the rest of the world. There ain't no reason for them bluebottle bullies to hunt *all* of us, like foxes.'

Mimi, who hated talk of sex, swiftly changed the subject. 'Let's go to the bandstand, Baz. It's the Grenadier Guards this afternoon.' The two friends drifted over the grass towards Buckingham Palace.

'Well, snap my garters!' Mimi pointed a white kid finger as suddenly, running fast and frightened as a disturbed hare, a ragamuffin dashed from a laurel thicket ahead; the youth was bareheaded and wore no shirt beneath his shabby dark jacket.

Baz pushed his bowler to the back of his head. 'Strike me pink if that ain't . . .' He stopped, put two fingers to his mouth, whistled hard, then hollered, '*Ned!*'

The runner jerked his head round, then swerved towards Baz, stumbling as he approached.

Swiftly Baz unwound his white silk scarf. 'Take his arm,' he urged Mimi, 'and laugh as hard as you can.'

As the frightened, sweating lad reached him, Baz jammed his bowler hat on the youth's head, twisted the white silk scarf round his neck, and swiftly buttoned his jacket.

'Keep yer chin down,' Baz urged the newcomer, as the laughing Mimi linked arms with the sweating, trembling lad, whose panting now also appeared to be laughter.

'Keep on course, don't hurry,' Baz muttered, through his chuckles.

Ahead, two blue-uniformed policemen burst from the laurel thicket, charged forward, then stopped. They ran a few steps to the left and paused. They ran a few steps to the right, then paused again. They questioned a passer-by, who shook his head. Not one person in the crowded park offered any information, although many had seen what had happened.

Mimi suddenly shrieked with genuine laughter; her face reddened, tears of mirth ran down her cheeks and she clutched her sides.

'Don't overdo it,' Baz warned.

'Can't help it, Baz. Them peelers . . . they're acting just like them cops we saw in that moving picture show this afternoon.'

'It ain't so funny when a pack of 'em's hunting *you* with them truncheons,' Baz growled.

* * *

After the trio passed through the black-curlicued park gates into busy Piccadilly, Ned stopped. As he wiped the sweat from his face on his trembling sleeve, Mimi saw that he was well muscled, with curly brown hair, a short, wide nose, big brown eyes and a thick, strong neck.

Mimi slipped him a sovereign and a free pass for Monday's show, always a quiet night. Baz said he could keep the white silk muffler, advised him to visit the Turkish Baths in Jermyn Street for a quick clean-up, and muttered something else that Mimi could not hear. Ned awkwardly mumbled his thanks, then hurried off towards Piccadilly Circus.

'Good-looking lad,' Mimi commented, as she and Baz strolled beneath the arched colonnade of the Ritz.

'Fancy Ned, do you? I expect he'll come backstage after the show tomorrow.'

'You know I ain't got time for spooning, Baz. It's just that Ned didn't look . . . like a buttercup.'

'We ain't all girlies, you know. You only get them buttercups and daisies at the molly clubs, or below stairs in service. If you was to walk in St James's Park or the Covent Garden piazzas, you'd see strapping soldiers, tough navvies, engineers, doctors, city gents . . . even policemen! People got this idea that big athletic men *couldn't possibly* be fairies!' Baz had switched to a posh class accent. '*Not* people one knows socially!' He reverted to his normal voice and smiled grimly. 'But we ain't *all* that easy to spot.'

Mimi acted as if self-assured and at ease, but she suddenly felt a nervous little nobody as she and Baz walked along the wide red-carpeted corridor towards the Ritz tearoom. She was glad they'd made fools of those peelers but she also realized that she could no longer afford to get involved in Baz's scrapes; she was becoming known, she couldn't risk getting her name in some newspaper scandal: like Daisy said, she should curb her reckless streak. Look before you leap. Thought before action.

The two friends entered a big glass-roofed tearoom, hung with chandeliers and lined by elegant mirrors. Against the rear wall, in a fountain flanked by ferns, a plump golden nude, attended by overweight cupids, dipped her golden toe in genuine water, ignored by fashionably dressed women perched on little gold chairs, who talked in low voices to well-groomed, attentive men in stiffly starched shirts: female nudity was permissible if it was Art.

The large tearoom was full, for this was the middle of the three-month London Season, a gathering of the elite, who had been stuck on their estates all winter with only dull neighbours for company: now they could again get together at their convenience and bore whom they pleased.

As Mimi and Baz entered the tearoom a tall, dark man stood up, hesitated, then bowed to them. Mimi immediately realized why Baz was now a supper act in London. *He* was a real looker, she thought, with them dark blue eyes, an excellent example of what Baz had earlier described: no one would ever suspect this well-built, handsome member of a famous theatrical family, who owned a string of provincial theatres, plus several in

London; no one would *ever* guess that Toby Fane was one of them.

* * *

Later that evening, at the Alhambra entrance, commissioners whistled shrilly, ragged urchins jumped to steady some horse's head and footmen beckoned their coachmen forward. Under the harshly unbecoming new electric lights, Mimi enjoyed being part of the fashionable audience. Around her, men in evening dress and opera hats escorted women in taffeta cloaks over low-necked satin and lace gowns, who sparkled with jewellery as they waited for a hansom, a four-wheeler or their private carriage to draw up.

At that evening's Royal Command Variety Performance, these privileged people had watched the best entertainers and singers in Britain. The exuberant Hetty King – not much older than Mimi – had sung 'All the Nice Girls Love a Sailor'; under a vast feathered hat Marie Lloyd had belted out 'I'm One of the Ruins Cromwell Knocked About a Bit'; Harry Tate had performed his celebrated motoring sketch, at the end of which his vehicle fell apart. The theatre had become an electrical power-house as the artist's energy bounced back from the audience, and out to them again. Even *this* sophisticated crowd was still elated and excited, thought Mimi, as she waited for their cab.

As soon as the cab creaked off Mimi clapped her white-gloved hands together. 'Tell you what, boys! I'll treat us all to a slap-up supper and a bottle of bubbly at the Savoy!' She had seen the Savoy Grill dinners advertised at five shillings a head, which she could easily afford.

Sitting opposite her, Toby flashed a look of consternation at Baz. 'I've already booked a private room at the Cavendish,' he said, then added hastily, 'but of course, we can go wherever you prefer, Miss Quinn.'

Of course. Toby couldn't be seen openly with Baz in some where as popular as the Savoy. After a quiet supper at the Cavendish, Mimi knew that she would be handed into a pre-paid cab, which would take her back to her digs.

Swiftly Mimi said, 'What a treat! I *love* the Cavendish.' This was true. The Cavendish was owned by a pretty cook called Rosa Lewis, who had appeared recently from nowhere, then mysteriously acquired a hotel in Jermyn Street, reputedly purchased for her by the King: so Rosa Lewis was Maisie's patron saint. A quiet hotel, the Cavendish was built around a courtyard and furnished like an English country mansion, with chintz curtains, flounced, fat armchairs, brass beds and discreet service. Assignations passed unnoticed: if Lord A reserved a bedroom, nobody noticed if it was later entered by Lady B – or Lord B.

Dinner at the Cavendish was delicious: vichyssoise, followed by oysters, then roasted pigeons – one each, served with an assortment of vegetables so small and perfect that the carrots and potatoes looked like dolls' house food. The pudding that followed was meringue glacé, and compote of chestnuts, topped with squiggles of whipped cream. Mimi had never smelled anything like the subsequent runny French cheese – downright rude, it was.

Toby carefully included her in all conversation, which was of course about the Business.

'Does your family own any music halls?' Mimi asked, at one point.

'No, although I've several times suggested that our

smallest theatre – the Minerva – might be tried out as a music hall. You see, it's very small, so plays are difficult to stage there.'

Mimi gave Baz a swift comprehending look: one way to leap to the top of the bill, overnight.

Toby continued, 'My father still only sees me as his youngest son. Sometimes I wonder if he's noticed I've left school!' Although he laughed, he clearly found this irksome. 'I've had lots of exciting ideas, but they didn't interest my father.' He added regretfully, 'He's one of the old-school actor-managers: strictly legitimate.'

'Pity,' Mimi said equally regretfully: she might have hitched a ride on Baz's coat-tails.

11 p.m., Thursday 30 May 1907. The Coliseum Theatre

'Come in.' Mimi pulled off her wig and leaned forward, about to wipe off her colours. To her surprise, reflected in the dressing-room mirror, she saw the well-muscled body and strong bull-like face of Ned, the lad she and Baz had saved in Green Park. He had come backstage to thank her after the show last Monday, but Mimi had thought that was the last she'd see of him.

'Sorry to bother you. Couldn't think of no one else.' Ned spoke in a Cockney twang, as, nervously, he fingered his white silk scarf.

'What's up?' Mimi swung her chair round to face him, pulling her silk kimono closer to her body: although not cold, she sensed danger.

'Baz and Toby was arrested in Green Park, just after dusk. I saw it happen, then I followed 'em to the police station.'

'*How could they be so bloody stupid?*'

'Mimi, ain't you ever been in love? Done daft things?'

'No,' Mimi said shortly. 'Give me five minutes, Ned. Get a cab. See you at the end of the stage door alley.'

* * *

Hurriedly, Mimi finished buttoning her navy coat; she pinned on a pretty toque smothered by primroses, peered in the mirror, then unpinned the toque and crammed on her wide-brimmed navy street hat. When in trouble with the Law, play respectable.

As she clattered down the theatre stairs, another thought struck her. She dashed back upstairs to Wardrobe, and emerged two minutes later, wearing a large fake diamond ring on the third finger of her left hand, over her glove.

* * *

The interior of Green Park Police Station was bleak: walls were covered by tiles the colour of strong tea, the floor-boards were bare. As Mimi stood before the high counter, upon which a large charge book stood open, she hoped she looked demure and respectable.

'What can I do for you, miss?' asked the whiskered sergeant on duty.

'I am Miss Baker. I have been informed that my brother, Basil, and my fiancé, Mr Tobias Fane, have been detained by you. I would like to see them.' Mimi spoke quietly, in a well-modulated toff's voice that wouldn't have fooled a toff but was good enough to be met with instant servile respect from the sergeant.

After some muttered discussion with two other constables, Mimi was escorted down dark winding stone stairs.

She kept close behind the peeler with his lantern as they moved along a cold stone passage lined with black metal doors, before one of which the policeman stopped. He slid back a little metal panel at face level, and held up his lamp.

Mimi heard a scrabbling behind the door. Baz's pale triangular face appeared behind the bars of the aperture.

Mimi gasped and put her left hand to her mouth, ostentatiously waggling the ring finger. 'Basil! What are you doing here? Mummy will be *horrified*! What *has* happened? What have you *done*? Why won't they tell me? And I hear *Toby's* here as well ... And it's only a month to our *wedding*!'

Baz looked suitably distraught. 'Please don't let Mummy know.' He spoke as if someone were pinching his nostrils together. 'Tell Daddy we was ... *were* ... um ... taking a short cut through the Park, from Aunt Jane's place in Belgrave Square to Toby's club in Pall Mall. Then a bunch of fellows set upon us. It was dark and we thought they were footpads out to rob us, so we fought back. But they overpowered us, then dragged us to Piccadilly, where we saw that they was ... were ... policemen. They slammed us into a police van and brought us to this ... um ... wretched place.'

''E didn't talk so posh when 'e was brought in,' observed the constable.

'I expect he didn't want you to know who he was,' Mimi said, with quiet dignity.

Toby sat on the straw-scattered floor in the adjoining cell; his dark hair was tousled, his face was dirty, his left cheek was streaked with dried blood, his dark-blue eyes looked mutinous yet frightened, as he scrambled to his feet and peered out at Mimi.

'Toby, you poor, poor darling! I hope that nasty cut heals before our wedding next month! Basil said you were taking a short cut through the park from Aunt Jane's in Belgrave Square . . .'

When Mimi had finished, Toby muttered, 'Thank God you're here! Get hold of my father as fast as you can – he'll be at his set in Albany, off Piccadilly. Ask for Sir Octavius Fane and tell him to get here quickly with Bennett, that's our family lawyer.'

Mimi made little kissing sounds and leaned forward. '*Of course*, my darling . . . Yes, I'll go straight to Sir Octavius.'

Back at the sergeant's desk, Mimi twisted her engagement ring ostentatiously around her white-gloved finger. 'I shall return as quickly as possible, Sergeant, with my future father-in-law, Sir Octavius Fane, and our family lawyer . . . This is clearly a case of mistaken identity.'

Outside the police station, Mimi hailed a cab. 'Git to Albany, opposite Fortnum & Mason, in Piccadilly. Sixpence extra if you're quick.'

* * *

Sir Octavius, who had just returned from one of his theatres, was sipping a rum toddy in a dark-green Regency-striped study, hung with framed antique playbills. Lady Fane was at a spa, taking a cure for her rheumatism. His manservant had gone to bed.

When he answered the door bell, Sir Octavius was astonished to see the porter, accompanied by a young redheaded female. She gasped, 'I've come about Toby.'

Quickly Sir Octavius pulled her inside. 'Where's Toby? What's happened?'

'Toby's been arrested in Green Park.'

'Oh God, I've dreaded this! Where is he now? And who are *you*?'

Mimi sat primly on an uncomfortable Regency chair, while Sir Octavius paced his study. He avoided looking at her as he listened to her story.

Once tall, dark, slim and vain, Sir Octavius was now thin, stooped, grey and still vain. His pale, heavily lined face had a tight, mean mouth and watery blue eyes; his sparse grey hair was speckled with dandruff. 'I cannot believe that a son of *mine* . . . the wretched *disgrace* . . . my *poor* dear wife . . . !'

Mimi stared at him. She had never heard a person speak like that off stage – like he was reading from a book.

Sir Octavius pulled a gold watch from his waistcoat pocket. 'After midnight. Bennett won't like this.' He sighed, sat at the spindly Sheraton desk, dipped a quill in the silver ink pot, scribbled a note, picked up the internal telephone to the porter's lodge, and arranged for the note to be delivered immediately.

Mimi said, 'While we're waiting—'

Sir Octavius interrupted, 'There is no need for you to wait, young woman. I shall arrange for a cab to take you home.'

'If it's all the same to you, I'm staying till I see Baz outside them bars,' Mimi said firmly.

'Then this young person really *is* your brother?'

'No, but he's my friend.' Mimi looked steadily at Sir Octavius.

Evenutally Sir Octavius said, as if he smelled something unpleasant, 'I expect Bennett can act for both of them.'

'I expect he can,' Mimi said grimly. She sat while Sir

Octavius again paced the room, silently remembering the terrible scandal caused in '95 by Oscar Wilde's liaison with Lord Alfred Douglas. Lord Arthur Somerset had also been driven into exile after what had been reported in *The Times* as 'hideous, loathsome and horrible conduct with a postal messenger'. Then there had been that Conservative MP, accused of indecency with a soldier in a London park; although acquitted with the help of character witnesses, he had later fled abroad rather than face another similar charge.

For a moment Sir Octavius pictured the library at the Garrick Club, on the day that his fellow members read in their newspapers of Toby's misconduct. He shivered as he imagined the commiserating pats on the back. 'Sorry to hear about your son . . .' 'Such a pity about your boy . . .' Nobody would actually mention the word *degenerate*, of course.

'Before yer lawyer gets here,' Mimi offered, 'I've an idea that might get Toby off the hook.'

'How could *you* possibly help?'

'What if I was to be really married?'

Sir Octavius stopped in mid-stride, and swivelled to face Mimi. 'How much do you expect me to pay you to marry my son?' he asked contemptuously.

Mimi was astonished. 'I was trying to help . . .' She felt burning resentment rise as she stared at the disdainful face of the old actor. Once again, she seemed to have been convicted in her absence of a serious crime – only this old geezer wasn't her pa, so she wasn't scared of him, no matter how he glared at her, the old ham. She'd give him a bit of his own medicine!

Mimi glared up at Sir Octavius, and threw back her head with the same contemptuous stare. This silly old sausage didn't realize they had been talking at cross-purposes. The stupid geezer didn't realize that Mimi had offered to marry *Baz*, which would let Baz off the hook – which would *also* let Toby-blooming-Fane off the hook!

Then she realized exactly what Sir Octavius had said. The old boy was actually willing for her to *marry Toby*! Clearly, he thought it was now merely a question of bargaining over the price. And clearly he wasn't thinking so much of saving his son, as saving his own pride, and the bleeding family honour!

Suddenly Mimi had another cheeky idea that might also kill several birds with one stone, in fact it might bring down the entire flock of pigeons in Trafalgar Square.

Mimi had remembered that when Toby, she and Baz had dined at the Cavendish, Toby had mentioned that he'd asked his pa to convert that little theatre to a music hall, but the snobbish old streak of vinegar wouldn't hear of it. Toby had said that his old man still thought of him as a schoolboy, and then had added regretfully that this was a pity, because he 'had a lot of exciting ideas'.

Mimi then remembered Maisie and her boarding house, Rosa Lewis and her hotel.

She thought: Why not? I've nothing to lose by asking. And if I manage to pull it off, then Toby would get what he wants, and Baz and I will get a crack at top billing!

So she said demurely to Sir Octavius, 'Since you put it that way . . . don't you own that little theatre in the Strand, the Minerva?'

'My wife does, yes,' Sir Octavius sounded guarded.

'Well, that's my price . . .'

'*Never!* This is blackmail!'

'No, it ain't.' Mimi knew that she stood no chance of getting the theatre for herself, for the Fanes could easily buy a much cheaper bride for their son. 'I don't want a penny for myself, but I want that little theatre given to Toby, as a wedding gift.'

'*Unthinkable!*'

'That's my only offer,' Mimi said politely.

'And this is my only refusal! ... I expect you would like to leave now?'

'No. I'm going to stick around till Baz is sprung.' Sir Octavius did not dare call a porter to throw her out.

In silence, they waited for the lawyer, their thoughts running in very different directions. The more Mimi thought of her reckless, spur-of-the-moment suggestion, the more alluring it seemed. Should she and Toby marry, they would be obliged to live in the same house, if he were to be really safe from the law, but obviously they could come to some suitable domestic arrangement, like lots of other people. They could do a deal about the theatre. Perhaps, if Toby turned the Minerva into a little music hall, the other acts could change, but Mimi would always be top of the bill, with a star on her dressing room door. That was her price. Why *not*? ... No more touring, no more mousetraps, no more beds with sagging springs ...

Meanwhile, Sir Octavius gloomily wondered where he had gone wrong. Of course the theatre was full of moral degenerates of a certain type, but as a child and as a youth Toby had been *specifically* kept away from them. Sir Octavius remembered that when he had found the fifteen-year-old Toby reading *The Picture of Dorian Gray*, by Oscar Wilde, he had immediately taken it from him and struck him across the face with it, slowly opened it and spat theatrically upon each page as he tore it out and threw it on the coal fire. As the last page had flared up, he had turned malevolent eyes on his terrified son and said hoarsely, 'If *ever* again I catch you reading such filth, I will strangle you with my bare hands.' He had stamped out of the room, leaving Toby white-faced, stunned, unable to move.

* * *

Mr Bennett duly arrived; he had clearly dressed in haste, but his pince-nez were clamped firmly on his parrot nose, he clutched his briefcase, and was clearly prepared for any emergency that might await.

'Would you mind moving to the hall, young woman, while we talk privately?' Sir Octavius asked Mimi, in a glacial tone.

Banished to the hall, Mimi immediately put her ear to the door of the study. She could not always hear what Sir Octavius said, but she clearly heard the lawyer's grave, booming replies.

'If Sir Octavius will remember . . . not as if this were the first time . . . social ostracism . . . a marriage would undoubtedly help . . . take time for me to find a suitable young lady . . . Naturally, she would require a substantial lump sum . . . That young person in the hall? . . . You're *sure* she requires no payment? . . . Permit me to contradict you, dear sir: what is *most* important, is that the young person is immediately available . . . But if he were to be married then there would be no scandal . . . Then let us all proceed to the police station . . . no doubt a generous payment to the Police Widows and Orphans Fund . . . no, not a cheque, the sergeant will prefer a cash payment, some of which will undoubtedly reach the Fund.'

'*I'm damned if I will!*'

'You'll be doomed if you don't, my dear sir . . .'

Half an hour later, Sir Octavius had reluctantly agreed in principle to Mimi's proposition.

With a grin, Mimi removed her ear from the keyhole, stood up, and carefully adjusted her hat brim.

* * *

'Thank Gawd *that's* over! You're a peach, Mimi!' Baz collapsed into a corner of the cab. It was two o'clock in the morning.

'It ain't over yet!' Mimi said drily. 'I really *am* going to marry Toby.'

Baz sat up sharply. He scratched his freckled nose and then relaxed against the horsehair seat. 'So you'll be our cover, that ain't a bad idea . . . Hey, where does this cabby think he's going? This ain't the way to Brixton!'

'We're going to the Strand first,' Mimi said firmly, 'to look at me husband's theatre.'

* * *

Clouds drifted across the moon. All day, office workers and crowds of sightseers jammed the Strand, dodging the red double-decker horse buses and the stream of traffic, but at this time of night the wide road was empty. Halfway between Trafalgar Square and the Savoy Hotel, Baz and Mimi stood on the pavement and gazed across the deserted street at the pale stone version of a little Greek temple, with MINERVA THEATRE carved on the pediment that hid the roof from the street; the name was repeated in gold on the canopy over the door.

The pretty little theatre had been built in 1870 for the stage-struck daughter of Mr Enoch Walter, who had invented the invisible zip-fastener and acquired a fortune. Miss Bluebell Walter danced a little, sang songs, recited poems and monologues written by herself and occasionally presented a melodrama, with Bluebell Walter in the lead. By 1880, Miss Walter had tired of the stage, and the theatre had been sold to Octavius Fane.

Mimi gazed at the pale temple across the street, not yet daring to believe that both this theatre, and the security it would bring, were almost within her grasp, for even a small London theatre provided a good income. However, it did not occur to her to ask Toby Fane for a legal and binding agreement in the form of a marriage settlement, so that she would control the theatre during his life and own it upon his death. Such prudent considerations rarely occurred to reckless young persons, aged twenty, as Mr Bennett realized.

6 p.m., Saturday 22 June 1907

Seated at one of the little round tables in the Ritz tearoom, Toby leaned towards Mimi. She now noticed his resemblance to Sir Octavius, who seemed like a faded, crumpled photograph of his tall, good-looking son. Again she thought what a corker Toby was: his thick black hair and bright blue eyes had already attracted discreet sideways glances from other ladies in the tearoom.

Toby looked embarrassed. 'Mimi, are you sure you understand that this can *never* be a *real* marriage?'

'That's what I like about it,' Mimi said firmly. She, who distrusted, was terrified of men, now had her security without having to sleep with one.

'You understand that I shall never change? You don't secretly hope I will?' Toby asked. 'You see, I know I was born this way, just as you were born the way you are: so I shall never change.'

'I understand that. I've known Baz a long time. Live and let live is my motto. I expect we'll get along nicely: it'll be much the same for me as living in digs, with only one other lodger.'

'No,' Toby said. 'It's going to be much better for you than that.' He reached inside his jacket, produced a large buff envelope tied with peppermint-pink tape, and gravely handed it to her. 'This is your wedding present, from me.'

Mimi picked up an elaborate little silver cake-knife, slit open the envelope, and pulled out a battered sheaf of grubby documents. 'What the 'ell's this, Toby?'

'The deeds to a house in Fitzroy Square, near Regent's Park. If you look at the back page, you will see that it now belongs to you. I've purchased it on a mortgage; I'll meet the payments from the theatre receipts.'

Mimi quickly shuffled through the tattered pages, and on the last one she saw her own name entered as the new owner. She looked up, eyes glistening. 'But I never asked for this! You needn't . . .'

Toby had alarmed her, with his gentle speech, and his generosity. Suppose she *did* grow to love him?

No, she'd never allow that to happen to her. Love was a trap. Love allowed a man to manipulate you. To love was to risk deception and shame, pain and humiliation. Mimi had had enough of those. Her personal life insurance policy was to trust nobody, which ruled out love.

Toby glanced up at the wall clock. 'I'd better get to the theatre.' He was playing the detective's best friend, Lord Harry Hartfield, in *The Perfect Murder* at the

Majestic. Toby was a good enough actor, but not good enough for lead parts: he invariably played the hero's best friend, always Mercutio, never Romeo; always Enobarbus, never Antony. The Fane family had long realized that Toby would never be a star like his sister, the well-known tragedienne, Cassandra Fane, or his adored older brother, the celebrated Shakespearean actor, Orlando Fane, who had died of typhoid at the age of thirty-four.

Tuesday 25 June 1907

Three weeks after the banns were first published, Mimi walked up the aisle of St James's Church in Piccadilly on the arm of Baz. As she gazed unseeingly at the altar (exquisitely carved by Grinling Gibbons), she was scarcely aware of the romantic effect she created: she wore a small wreath of orange blossom over a simple high-necked gown of ivory silk with a straight skirt that swept up at the back into a small bustle.

The following evening, Mimi sat in her dressing room after the show (neither the bride nor the groom had missed a performance) and once again looked with pleasure at the society column in *The Times*. The top announcement read:

The marriage took place quietly yesterday at St James's Church, Piccadilly, of Thenia, daughter of the late Mr and Mrs Albert Quinn of Liverpool, and Tobias, son of Sir Octavius and Lady Fane of the Laurels, Bradshaw, Essex, and of Albany, Piccadilly, London.

Gaily Mimi said, 'Wish me mam could see her name in the newspaper.'

'It's just as well she don't know what you married.' Daisy gloomily handed a glass of Black Velvet to the bride.

Mimi looked up icily. 'Both Toby and I are getting what we want, and we ain't got no illusions about each other: that seems a damned good basis for a marriage.'

'Is that what you call it? Sounds more like a business deal to me.'

'It's that as well,' Mimi said, with satisfaction.

'It don't seem natural to me!'

Suddenly quiet, Mimi said, 'I ain't sure I know what's natural.'

'You never let any man near enough to find out!'

'That's my choice,' Mimi pointed out shortly. How could she explain to Daisy that she had lost her sense of herself as a woman? The outside of her body was now as disgustingly repulsive as the inside, down below. Mimi tried not to touch, look at or think of her private parts and was going to make damn sure that no man ever got near them again. Only the previous week when a man had attempted to kiss her hand outside the stage door she had frozen then screamed at the top of her lungs to get his bloody hands off! She had turned to Daisy and said, 'Now maybe that bastard'll understand I don't want no man in my bed.'

Now Daisy said, 'You Ice Maidens change your tune when you meet Mr Right and then you ain't frightened of the personal side.'

'For God's sake, Daisy, for the last time, can't you understand that I don't want a man and I never shall! If you'd been through what I have, you'd feel the same!

Now switch off your bloody intuition and stop moping. At last everything in my life is coming up roses! There's nothing to worry about!'

Daisy did not look convinced.

Chapter Five

Mimi looked anxiously at Toby as the train rushed northwards, drawing nearer every minute to Bradshaw, the Essex town closest to the Fane family home. 'They'll all be toffs, Toby. I'll feel out of place.' She was as nervous as any bride on her first visit to her mother-in-law's home, for Lady Fane had been taking the Cure at Baden-Baden when Toby and That Person had decided to marry, and both she and Mimi had avoided meeting, before and since.

'No, you won't feel strange.' Toby again smiled reassurance. 'My parents'll behave as if there's nothing odd about our marriage; anyone who hints otherwise will get an icy stare of incomprehension from my mother.' Because of his mother's fierce sense of family pride, he knew that she would protect and defend Mimi in all social situations, now that Mimi – for better, for worse – was a Fane.

'Families make me nervous,' said Mimi, meaning fathers.

So that's it, thought Toby. They had only once discussed Mimi's background and that had been indirectly. He said, 'Some psychologists believe that childhood involves the full range of human potential, from good to evil.'

'Why?' Mimi muttered, looking hard at the floor.

'They think the steel cobweb of family life is Nature's training ground for real life in the real world.'

'*Why?*' Mimi asked again, fiercely.

'The theory is that once you've emerged from it, you can endure anything.'

Mimi gave a short laugh. 'Then perhaps I was lucky, but it didn't seem so.'

Toby thought of his own outwardly comfortable childhood and sighed. Not for the first time he wondered: When was that picture-book golden age of the fully functioning Happy Family, that cosy blood-bond group whose values were so frequently and wistfully referred to by campaigning politicians? The Happy Family that lived in a home so sacred that a British policeman was lawfully bound to stop at the front door, beyond which Father was God, a dominant position that often led at best to petty tyranny ('Chew each mouthful twenty-three times and be grateful!') and at worst to neglect or the cruel and systematic abuse of mind and body (sometimes both) in mental persecution, bullying, violence, rape, incest and even death.

He leaned across the compartment and patted Mimi's gloved hand. 'It's only an overnight stay. If you find it difficult to play the devoted bride, just think of your new home, then smile at me,' he suggested.

Mimi cheered up immediately. 'I won't find that difficult.' He had given her a generous cheque for a hundred pounds to furnish their five-floor cream-fronted town house in Fitzroy Square. Mimi (who had never before purchased even a chair) felt inadequate as soon as the curtain maker had asked what pelmets madam required. After Toby had explained what a pelmet was, Mimi quickly asked him to help her. Equally quickly, she found that he had extravagant decorating ideas: their dining-room walls were covered with apricot silk, a foil to Mimi's golden-red hair; a four-poster bed in rose-patterned chintz was chosen for her bedroom, because it would be so pretty in summer and cosy in winter; for his bedroom, on the floor above, Toby picked a crimson taffeta four-poster.

After one trip to Waring & Gillow the entire cheque had been spent, although the house was not yet half-furnished. Surprisingly Sir Octavius provided additional funds: Toby was his only surviving son, and appearances had to be kept up.

With mischievous glee, Mimi chose her cook and housemaid from Massey's Employment Agency, in Baker Street, to which her mother had directed her all those years before. She then left her servants to their own devices, with disastrous results: on the day that breakfast was not served until noon because Cook was drunk and the housemaid had not yet returned from an unscheduled night out, Toby quietly took over the reins of the house-hold rather than live in chaos.

Sometimes Mimi's untidiness exasperated her husband ('Lor', Toby, give over! Nobody never *taught* me to be tidy!'), but Toby appreciated her ebullient, generous nature as much as her tart tongue and often she caught him looking at her with indulgent affection. Mimi simi-larly appreciated his amiability, good manners, patience, and fussy attention to comfort.

Mimi enjoyed Toby's company, and saw more of him than she expected; they rarely met after six in the eve-ning, but always breakfasted together, in her bedroom. Within a month of their marriage, she felt that she had known him for years; Baz was their most frequent visitor; when they all spent an evening together, Mimi went first up to bed.

* * *

As the hansom carriage turned into a gravelled drive, Mimi first saw The Laurels. Toby's family home was a rambling Regency house of no architectural merit, set in a gently undulating landscape surrounded by woodland. To Mimi it was as awe-inspiring as a palace. As their carriage approached the grass roundabout before the columns of the entrance, Mimi nervously clutched Toby's sleeve. 'I won't know what to say! I won't know what knife and fork to use!'

'If you don't say anything, Mimi, then no one can criticize you. At meals, use the outside cutlery and work inward: refuse anything that looks difficult to eat. Don't let anyone see you're nervous. Don't be intimidated by the butler – ignore him. Never mention sex, religion or politics, because those topics start argument. There's nothing else to worry about. We'll be shown to adjoining rooms, then my mother will take you around the rose garden, after which my father will show you the family portraits. Just keep smiling.'

Mimi sniffed. She knew that she could never transmogrify into a toff and that if she tried to she would be treated with quiet contempt, or jeered at behind her back. So she had decided to remain what she was: a cleaned-up Liverpool guttersnipe. Whether or not she was accepted, it would be as herself, with no airs or graces.

On cue, the front door was flung wide and Toby's parents appeared to welcome them; Sir Octavius bowed to kiss Mimi's gloved hand, threw his head back and declaimed, 'Welcome, dear child, a thousand times welcome!'

Sir Octavius was almost as thin as his wife, but moved with measured tread and shoulders thrown back, as if on stage; his boyish charm was eerie in that wrinkled face: Dorian Gray in reverse.

Mimi was glad that Toby looked like his father, not his mother: chinless and long-nosed, thin and grey, Lady Fane bent in the middle like a poplar tree in a gale, although she was not as frail as she appeared. Demure in public, she carefully played the self-effacing wife of a great man, but her inquisitive little eyes missed nothing; it was she who had provided the foresight, finance and ferocious ambition that initially had been responsible for the success of the present generation of Fanes.

As Toby had predicted, his shrewd mother now behaved as if her son had married a royal princess. Toby knew that the alternative – to recognize her son's marriage as a misalliance – would mean even greater loss of face, so instead, Lady Fane played her part as if she were some well-bred duchess whose son had married a Gaiety Girl: it was unfortunate, but they must all make the best of it.

Lady Fane admired Mimi's pink costume (although privately she thought it *most* unsuitable for travel), asked for Mimi's opinions, laughed at Mimi's timid jokes, and was volubly concerned about her comfort. Would Mimi prefer a bedroom that faced west? At what hour did she require a maid to dress her hair? At what time did she require breakfast to be served? In her bedroom? The bathroom – a recent installation – was used by the gentlemen in the morning and by the ladies after tea, unless Mimi wished to make alternative arrangements. Would she care to see the rose garden?

By the end of her father-in-law's tour of the picture gallery Mimi had warmed to him a little, for the old boy was so endearingly theatrical that she felt on stage and secure, as he gestured gracefully to each portrait, throwing her a smile over his shoulder, flashing unnaturally white false teeth as he held his pose. Sir Octavius clearly forgot that he was no longer in his twenties and the long sideways glance from half-closed eyes, which once had been heart-stopping, was now faintly embarrassing. He was as transparent as a little boy in his vanity and fake humility ('Of course one must not forget the Barrymores . . .') and Mimi was unable to get a word in, as he endlessly recited the family triumphs.

After an hour, Mimi felt as if a year of history lessons had been crammed into her at the speed a Strasbourg goose was fed. She had learned that actors, originally considered immoral, were despised and refused Christian burial (even Molière had to be buried at night, in unconsecrated ground), until as late as 1900 in France! Only when Queen Victoria – who enjoyed an evening out at the theatre – knighted Henry Irving did acting become respectable. Now, ha ha, society hostesses relied on thespian guests from the theatre to enliven their parties, and aristocrats had started to marry showgirls: suddenly the stage had become the only route by which a pretty woman could jump from the very bottom rung, right to the top of the social ladder.

At this point of Sir Octavius's monologue Mimi looked sharply at her host, but clearly he intended merely to explain the rise and importance of the nineteenth-century actresses, actors and – on top of the theatrical pyramid – actor-managers, such as himself.

Having been forced to submit during her childhood,

the energetic, independent Mimi was determined never to be submissive to anyone, but she did not forget the pretence of meekness that she had learnt under her pa: she had learnt to lie low. So she listened attentively as Sir Octavius explained how an inexperienced, inefficient actor-manager could lose a packet if he couldn't deal with the complexities and day-to-day crises of the theatre. (Wheezy chuckle.)

The Fane acting dynasty had started humbly in the sixteenth century. According to family legend, Barnabus Fane, a strolling player, joined the London acting company which, in 1576, opened the first fixed British theatre, in Shoreditch. Within a hundred years, the British stage had been well sprinkled with Fanes; Fanny Fane played in David Garrick's company at Drury Lane; Augustus Fane toured with Edmund Keane; and Theodore Fane (who had sired Sir Octavius) managed to flirt with Ellen Terry under Sir Henry Irving's large nose.

Lady Fane had equally impressive theatrical antecedents: born in New York, she was a direct descendant of the British actor-manager Louis Hallam, who had brought the British travelling repertory system to America when his troupe of players landed at Williamsburg, Virginia, in 1752. After a tough two years touring the East Coast (the Puritan Churches were vigorously opposed to play-acting), Louis Hallam had sailed to Jamaica, where his seventeen-year-old nephew married Cassandra, the beautiful daughter of a rum-sozzled innkeeper, rumoured – with *no* justification – to have ... ahem ... black blood. Cassandra Fane later eloped with the captain of a cotton trader, abandoning her eighteen-month-old son, Marmaduke, who in 1798 helped to build and launch New York's Park Theatre.

Sixty-two years later, the eighteen-year-old bespectacled

long-nosed Ada Hallam (granddaughter of Marmaduke) saw the Fane Shakespearean Company – direct from London – perform *Romeo and Juliet*. Naturally, the established actors kept the juicy parts to themselves, so a teenage Fane daughter played the Old Nurse while her mother played Juliet; young Octavius Fane played a dashing Mercutio, while his father played Romeo. Ada watched the eighteen-year-old Mercutio hold his poses with grace; his declamation thrilled her, his projection was perfection. As soon as the curtain descended on the pot-bellied corpse of Romeo and his stout Juliet, Ada whipped off her spectacles and hurried to the pass door that led backstage.

A month later, Octavius married Ada, or perhaps it was the other way around. Certainly it was she who made their decisions, after they sailed back to London and settled on Chelsea Embankment in a house purchased from her dowry, which later also paid for a short lease of the Lyric Theatre, Hammersmith.

Naturally, Octavius acted all male leading roles in their productions, and Ada saw that star status was his alone. She also ensured that Octavius learned every aspect of what would later be known as direction: the choice of play, actors, music, theatre lighting, scenery and costumes.

She was far from idle: she worked sixteen hours a day to master every aspect of theatrical management, from keeping the accounts to booking the tour theatres. By the turn of the century, she had also borne nine children and negotiated the purchase of four London theatres, plus a string of provincial ones. Octavius, by then fifty-eight years old, was acknowledged as one of Britain's leading actor-managers, and in 1901 had been knighted by Queen

Victoria: bossy, frugal, ambitious Ada had become Lady Fane.

Mimi knew that only three of Ada's nine children had survived infancy; Toby had been the slightly embarrassing surprise of Ada's fortieth year; by the time he arrived, Lady Fane had many other responsibilities and interests, so her last child (born delicate) was virtually raised by a nanny, and then a tutor.

At the age of ten, the introverted, quiet Toby had contracted tuberculosis, so was dispatched to the Lake District with his tutor as was the custom of that time, until he either died or recovered. After eighteen months, Toby, by then a reclusive bookworm, was pronounced fit; he travelled back to Chelsea, where his mother seemed to notice his return little more than she had his absence. Orlando, her elder son, was the adored child-prodigy, apple of her eye. But he died of typhoid, after a private command performance in Her Majesty's presence, at Windsor Castle, where the drains were disgusting.

As Sir Octavius escorted Mimi from the portrait gallery, Mimi realized how sad and disappointed Toby's parents must be; despite their determined fecundity, their only daughter Cassandra, although married, was childless at the age of forty-five. Toby was a mere twenty-seven, but clearly the Fane dynasty would stop with his generation.

On the paved garden terrace, footmen in dark-green livery with yellow-striped waistcoats poured vintage Krug for Lady Fane's luncheon guests; these had been carefully chosen to spread fast, through all branches of the theatrical grapevine, their approving opinions of the little trollop that Toby had married. Everyone in the business would soon hear how witty, how pretty, how deliciously droll Toby's tiny smokescreen was.

The frothy gossip was as quick and witty as it was malicious: every pretty leading actress in London was promiscuous, every ugly one was temperamental; successful actors were mere matinée idols, all playwrights were obstinate neurotics. Not that different from dressing-room chat, thought Mimi, relaxing as she was introduced to a pudding-faced and bespectacled Miss Lilian Baylis.

'How de do, dear,' she said to Mimi in a pronounced Cockney accent. The left side of her mouth was slightly lifted, and appeared paralysed, but did not much affect her speech. Despite the sunny July day, Miss Baylis was draped in dark brown garments, which seemed flung upon her as if overnight on a comfortably upholstered bedroom chair.

'How's yerself?' Mimi relaxed, feeling suddenly at ease with this Church worker, or governess, or whatever she was.

'I hear you're a singer, dear,' Miss Baylis said, a glint in her eye. 'I come from a musical family meself. Used to tour South Africa in a bullock cart with our act. The Gypsy Revellers we were called, us nine children plus Ma and Pa. Then Pa was taken ill in Johannesburg, so I went out and taught dancing to the miners.'

'Do you still teach?' Mimi asked.

'Gracious me, no, dear. I help me Aunt Emma with her charitable work.'

Aha, so she had been right, Mimi thought, but then Miss Baylis added, 'I'm a theatre manager, been it since 1898.' She went on to explain that her aunt owned a temperance concert hall. Young Lilian had decided that more souls would be saved from the demon drink and fill the theatre if the programmes were less dull. 'So I asked the Governors to develop our musical concerts into grand opera.'

'You must be very musical,' Mimi said politely, thinking 'very ambitious'.

'Not really, dear, but I wanted The Best for my *audiences*. We already had an amateur chorus of students and shop assistants, although of course they could only work in the evenings, to help entertain the unfortunate.'

Mimi thought that this didn't sound like The Best, but within a few minutes surprised herself by agreeing to become a patron of the Royal Victoria Hall, at the cost of a guinea a year.

The forceful Lilian Baylis immediately repaid this favour by introducing Mimi to the famous impresario Mr Cochran. Cockie was not the dazzling figure that Mimi had expected; in fact he looked a bit like Jolly Joe: short and chunky, with shrewd eyes set in a benevolent red face edged by thinning white hair; clearly tough and optimistic; clearly restless and authoritative.

Cockie knew why Mimi wore gloves and a high neckline, although it was a warm day. As he admired courage and always enjoyed a pretty face, he eventually murmured suavely, 'Let me know if I can ever help you,' and Mimi's knees trembled with excitement.

Suddenly, Toby lifted his head. 'What's that noise?' The little group on the terrace looked curiously towards a distant point where the gravel drive emerged from the woods and led towards the house.

The staccato noise grew louder. It sounded like a thousand tin cans rattling together.

'It's an automobilist!' Toby cried, as from the trees burst a green and brass machine, travelling at great speed, and trailing smoke.

Admiring murmurs. Automobilists were considered daring, dashing creatures. The machine drew steadily nearer, until the watchers on the terrace could clearly see the two acetylene headlamps, the black rear hood (folded back like a baby carriage) and the driver's face, hidden by goggles and a peaked cap.

'It's a new Peugeot!' Toby exclaimed.

'It's Tudor Perkins, at last!' murmured Lady Fane, conscious that luncheon had already been held up for ten minutes.

'I'll meet him, Mama.' Toby ran round the building to the front door as the dusty green automobile reached the grass roundabout but failed to slow down.

'Can't stop her – the gear's stuck!' the muffled automobilist shouted to Toby, as the machine flashed past him.

'I'll have to drive until the petrol runs out,' the figure shouted again, as he flashed past Toby for the second time, charging through his own stinking exhaust fumes. Faintly, Toby heard the words, 'Please don't wait luncheon on my account.'

'Serves the damned fool right for driving a foreign machine,' sniffed Sir Octavius, as he shepherded his hungry guests towards the dining room.

Luncheon started with a serious discussion of Irish Home Rule, and Christabel Pankhurst's latest suffragette outrage, but – as at all theatrical gatherings, whatever their size – the talk drifted, waspishly fast, to the Business: the recent strike of music-hall performers demanding higher pay; the sensational success of Florenz Ziegfeld's first revue, *The Follies of 1907*. The dazzlers of earlier days. As lamb cutlets were served, Mimi heard Sir Octavius boom,

'Best advice I ever had was from Ellen Terry. She said, "Always remember to act in your pauses, my boy."'

As he spoke, the tall figure of Tudor Perkins, in cream flannels and a striped maroon blazer, staggered dizzily into the dining room. 'So terribly sorry, Lady Fane, couldn't shift her out of gear. Apparently the brake cord thing has snapped.'

'Why didn't you disconnect the ignition?' Toby asked curiously.

Tudor stared at him and burst into laughter. 'Didn't think of it, dear chap.'

When Tudor smiled his eyebrows shot up, his forehead wrinkled and he looked disarmingly gleeful. Another looker, thought Mimi as she studied the lean face, high cheekbones, dark-lashed, sleepy brown eyes and chestnut hair of Lady Fane's young protégé: a perfect juvenile lead – if he could act, and if he had the push.

Tudor was amiable, and well mannered, but Mimi immediately noticed that he lacked the aggressive thrust and ambition which she sensed in almost everyone else sitting around the lace-covered dining table. After lunch Lady Fane relaxed slightly. Her new daughter-in-law was not, after all, a social disaster. In fact she had impressive insouciance for one so young: her droll, bold humour was not offensive and her pithy, accurate remarks pleasantly punctured the inflated egos of Fane rivals who had not been invited. Mimi had given a good performance.

Toby was relieved and pleased that Mimi had behaved with such deceptive demureness. What little she said had been quietly intelligent: it was sharp of her not to attempt to change her soft Liverpool accent. Mimi had not attempted to pretend that she was what she was not, so she would be categorized as an entertaining, slightly eccentric but attractive young woman, and therefore acceptable anywhere in British society, even were the King to be present – *particularly* if His Majesty were present, for pretty women who could entertain him were constantly sought by anxious hostesses.

* * *

Lady Fane's guests returned to London by the late afternoon train, so only the family gathered for the evening meal; nevertheless, the table was laid with Brussels lace on cloth of gold, which glistened subtly beneath the light of the candelabra. With satisfaction, Mimi thought: Well-heeled is a nice change from down-at-heel. Suddenly she felt a stab of pain, as she caught herself thinking, Pity Mam can't be here, with the little 'uns, all of us living it up together! Mimi immediately remembered that she would never see them again, something she only allowed herself to think about when in bed, in the dark. Quickly, she bent her head over her crested plate, to hide the tears welling in her eyes.

* * *

Long after the Fane family had retired to their bedrooms, Mimi felt her shoulder shaken.

'*Wake up, Mimi!*'

Mimi slowly opened her eyes. Illuminated by the flickering light of the candle he held was Toby's anxious face.

'*What's up?*' Mimi jerked upright in bed.

The figure in blue-striped pyjamas held a cautionary finger to his mouth. 'Shhhh! You were having a nightmare!

Making an awful noise! I was afraid you'd wake the whole house.'

'Sorry, I don't often have nightmares,' Mimi lied.

'Yes, you do! I've often heard you yelling and sobbing in your sleep.'

'Must have been indigestion,' Mimi said defensively. She felt ashamed of her childish nightmares, in which she was always in the dark, always conscious of looming danger . . . although she never knew what or where the threat was. Mimi always opened her mouth to scream for help . . . but no sound ever came . . . She was unable to run, for her feet were sunk in mud . . . So, helpless, Mimi waited in the dark, to be consumed by the invisible, enormous, terrifying Thing that she could hear crashing towards her . . .

'I want you to see a doctor about these nightmares,' Toby said firmly, 'because that's not all that's wrong, is it? There are mornings when you wake depressed, for no reason you can tell me; mornings when you burst into tears and won't say why; when you're tense, on edge, irritable.'

'Women's problems,' said Mimi briskly.

Toby sat on the edge of her bed. 'Don't be afraid to tell me, Foxtop. Are these nightmares about . . . your father?' Mimi had eventually confessed all to Toby.

'They certainly ain't!' About that, Mimi had adopted the emotional armour of an Amazon. Consciously she had determined to erase her father from her memory. Furiously she denied to herself that those brutal experiences had affected her in any way, except that she didn't fancy sex – and plenty of women didn't.

'Then are your nightmares about that fire?' Toby persisted.

'Of course they are!' Mimi buried her face in scarred hands. 'Night after night, I go through the bloody thing, again and again. Dr Higgins gave me a bottle of laudanum for nights, but that don't stop them daymares. I can't do anything about 'em! They sneak into me mind when I'm thinking about nothing in particular – brushing me teeth, or walking along the street – and then I'm *back there in the flames*! I *feel* the same terror and panic.'

She looked up, despondent. 'When I come out of it, me whole body's shaking, but at least I'm back in the real world. All of a sudden, I'll feel exhausted and drained.' She started to cry. 'I get this sinking, shrivelled feeling in me stomach, then I find meself full of rage.' She muttered through her tears, 'Betsy never would admit it was her fault, you know.'

'Foxtop, believe me, I *know* it can be hard for *anyone* to accept responsibility for one casual, careless moment of forgetfulness – especially when it's had such a disastrous effect on somebody else.' Toby patted her shoulder with rough affection, as if Mimi was his younger sister. 'But Betsy didn't do it deliberately, after all.'

'That's what I can't forgive,' Mimi sobbed, 'Betsy's carelessness wrecked my life, and then she tried to blame Doreen! *She wouldn't admit she done it! That's* what I can't forgive.'

'Mimi, you have to look forward now: get on with your life. You can't wipe out your past – we all have to carry it with us – but if you also carry hatred and bitterness, *that* load'll weigh you down.'

'One day, please God, I'll get the chance to make Betsy feel as she made me feel – *still* makes me feel!'

Toby felt helpless against this fierce persistence: for

once, he wished he knew more about women. 'I sense that's not all, Mimi. There's something else bothering you, isn't there?'

Mimi was silent, then started to sob into her hands. 'Yes. *I miss her!*'

Toby immediately understood. 'Of course you miss her. You lost your best friend. You can't stop loving someone because that person behaves badly, even though you feel betrayed and angry.' He put the silver candle holder on the bedside table and hugged Mimi's thin shoulders.

'I'm angry because Betsy *won't leave me alone*! I can't get the dratted woman out of me *own head*!' Mimi hissed. 'Suddenly, in the middle of a lovely day ... *she* flashes into my mind, and there I am, tense and bitter, with the day ruined!' Tearful green eyes looked up at Toby. 'Some day, *somehow*, I'm going to get me own back on her – and perhaps *then* these thoughts'll stop, and I'll get a bit of peace.'

Toby remembered an anthropologist's lantern-slide lecture at the Reform Club. To submit meant to be despised by your enemies and yourself, hence an eye for an eye and a tooth for a tooth. Alternatively, many primitives atoned with payments of goods and money. Payback restored the wronged one's dignity, status and self-esteem; without atonement, a thirst for revenge could develop into a zigzag of destruction between two people, two families, two nations.

Toby rubbed his tired eyes. 'Forget revenge, Mimi. Whatever you do to hurt Betsy, you'll *never* feel that you've got even.' Again, he put his arms around her and added gently, 'Because your body's scarred, there's no reason why your mind should be, Foxtop. The worst thing about revenge is that you risk starting a spiral of violence that might finally destroy *you*!'

'But what can I do about all this?'

'If you won't go to the doctor again, you might try talking to a priest: they're supposed to understand the destructive fears of human beings . . .'

'You reckon our local vicar can handle that load?'

'No harm in talking to him.'

Silence.

With resignation Mimi said, 'If you want me to, then I'll try it.'

* * *

Breakfast at The Laurels was a buffet: on the dining-room sideboard stood three large covered silver dishes which contained fried eggs, scrambled eggs, kidneys, bacon, sausages, kedgeree, mushrooms, tomatoes and sliced sauté potatoes. There was a silver coffee pot and two silver teapots, for Indian and China tea.

Nobody ever spoke at breakfast, for the vintage port drunk by the gentlemen after dinner often left them with sore heads on the following morning. So Toby whispered as he stared at Mimi's piled plate, 'You've got a good appetite, Mimi.'

'I ain't eaten proper since yesterday morning. But I *do* know how to use a knife and fork for a fry-up.'

Mimi, who had only been in a church the once, when she married, felt slightly apologetic as she tiptoed into the shadowed, peaceful interior of St John's, Portland Place. After peering into every hallowed corner, she eventually spotted a large man in white dog collar and black robes. He was studying a ledger, in a side room that looked like any other shabby office, except that the shelves were stacked with disintegrating prayer books.

'Are you the vicar, mister? Got five minutes to spare? Monday *is* your slack day, ain't it?'

The vicar, a well-built chap who had played rugby for his college, looked at Mimi's distressed, white face, offered her a chair and asked how he could help.

Slowly, stumbling, contradicting and repeating herself, Mimi told the stranger in black about the fire, about Betsy's responsibility for her entrapment, her own subsequent nightmares and terrifying flashbacks during the day.

Equally slowly, but with more clarity, the vicar explained, 'We're all born with emotions, and no relationship is free from occasional hurt or anger. However, it's self-destructive to let your anger overwhelm your other emotions. So if you're asking me how to free yourself from your anger, the way to do it is both simple and difficult: you must forgive your friend.'

Mimi's green eyes widened in furious surprise. 'Why should *I* forgive *her*? She ain't even admitted it's her fault!'

'If you wait for this lady's apology, you might wait for ever,' the vicar pointed out. 'You might condemn yourself to a life sentence of unresolved bitterness. And in that time, your anger might grow until it overshadows your entire life – unforgiving people never realize that they're damaging themselves.'

Shaking with indignation, Mimi tugged off her gloves, and thrust forward her damaged hands. Bitterly, she asked, 'Why should *I* be punished *even more*? I'm the *innocent* party!'

'Then you are the one with the power – the power to forgive,' the vicar said firmly.

'But I *can't* forgive her . . . I've tried!'

'It doesn't matter if you can't forgive, so long as you truly try. That's what matters to God.'

'God knows I've tried! If trying gets results, then why can't I *forget*?'

The vicar slowly leaned back in his chair and put the tips of his fingers together. 'You can never forget until you truly forgive. Forced forgiveness never works, for resentment continues to fester below the surface. Perhaps you might attempt to understand *why* your friend behaved as she did. Understanding how something happened is the beginning of forgiveness.'

Mimi stood up. 'I hoped you'd help me to find peace of mind. I didn't expect to be treated as if me troubles was me own fault!'

'Of course this sad affair isn't your fault. But only *you* can free yourself of your demons.'

Mimi left, unconvinced. She had expected better from a bloke who'd been to university.

Mimi had not yet told Toby of her plan to make the Minerva a small music hall, starring herself. Prudently, she had decided to wait until six months after he had taken over management of the theatre. But in November, only two months distant, the Minerva lease would expire: their little theatre would be untenanted and free.

Because they both performed at the same time, Mimi rarely visited Toby's dressing room; but late one September afternoon the upholsterer needed a quick decision about chair covers, so before going to work she took a cab to the Duchess Theatre, where she asked the driver to wait for her.

Toby's dressing-room door was locked. When Mimi put her ear to the keyhole, she heard the sound of vomiting.

Hissing through the keyhole, Mimi eventually persuaded Toby to unlock the door. She found him grey-faced and gaunt beneath his suntan greasepaint; his hands were trembling, his knees shook.

'I'll send my cab for a doctor,' Mimi said swiftly. 'Where's your bloody dresser?'

'Don't get a doctor. And don't blame Ernie. I told him to get out of the way. He knows this happens every night. I'm used to it – it's simply stage fright.' Before every performance, Toby trembled in the wings, feeling naked and defenceless, dreading audience disapproval: every night he hovered between this terror and bravery. Eventually, because come what might the show must go on, Toby always summoned up his courage – and strode on stage.

Mimi ran to the water jug. She knew there was even more anxiety in the legitimate theatre than in music hall.

The high-voltage tension attached to performing a play as a group was not so marked on the halls, where either you could do your act or you couldn't. She had been told that most actors were half-paralysed with nerves before making their first entrance, but she had never personally experienced this.

Carefully, Mimi sponged Toby's face. '*You're telling me this happens every night, Toby?* Why the hell do you keep doing it?'

'Same reason as everyone else,' Toby laughed shakily, 'I'm so frightened that I want to die before I go on, but afterwards, there's that elation!'

'But is acting really worth this torture?'

Toby looked sadly defiant. 'What would my parents say if I didn't act?'

Mimi silently decided to find out.

Sunday 22 September 1907. Fitzroy Square

The black-uniformed maid carefully drew aside the heavy rose-printed bedroom curtains, which allowed the mild autumn sunshine to filter into Mimi's bedroom from Fitzroy Square.

As Mimi sleepily sat up and stretched, the maid moved to the bed, smoothed the cover, plumped up Mimi's four frilled pillows and carefully placed the breakfast tray before her mistress. With a happy sigh, Mimi started her breakfast – a grilled kipper, which she ate with her favourite glass of stout mixed with champagne: Toby had nicknamed her the Girl with the Black Velvet Voice. This was the moment of the day that Mimi most enjoyed, as she surveyed the delicate Wedgwood china and the silver coffee pot then remembered the chipped enamel mug of tea and slice of bread and dripping that she had eaten for breakfast when a child – if she was lucky.

There was plenty of similar poverty in London's East End but that was a long way from the elegantly bohemian Fitzroy Square. Mimi now saw London from a different viewpoint: the city had a special aura; it was the home of Royalty, the political and financial centre of the nation; London had beautiful buildings, and parks, and plenty of entertainment: museums, concerts, theatre galore, great parties. If Mimi wished to escape the noisy excitement and bustle of the traffic-laden streets, she could simply stroll up the street to leafy Regent's Park.

Now Mimi no longer travelled by horse bus but raised her hand and a cab stopped. When Mimi shopped at the big stores, such as nearby Debenham & Freebody, or Marshal & Snelgrove, she merely signed the bill, where-upon her purchases were delivered to her home: she never carried a parcel. Mimi, who could never stick to a budget, never knew how much she was going to spend when she went shopping; she loved grandly telling a store assistant to put everything on her account, knowing that the bills would not arrive until the end of the month, when some-how Toby would pay them. Mimi, who had had hardly any schooling, knew only simple arithmetic. She never opened her own bank statements, and threw her hands up in theatrical horror if asked to read any sort of financial document: she left all that to Toby.

Increasingly, she found it hard to leave her home comfort for the small hotels and tiring routine of a tour, even though she now did only Number Ones to the biggest towns, and always had her own dressing room.

A knock on her bedroom door was followed by Toby,

arrived for his usual breakfast cup of black coffee. As he fitted his lean body into a rose-splattered armchair, he surveyed the room with indulgent amusement. Life in the theatre had conditioned Mimi to be disciplined and punctual – but she was incurably untidy. She never unpacked her suitcase when travelling but left it open on the bedroom floor, dived into it for whatever she needed, and excused this habit by explaining that in this way she never left anything behind.

At home, Mimi liked to live comfortably surrounded by a litter of her possessions; she rarely threw away anything – not even parcel string – for it might come in useful, some time. The disorder in her bedroom reflected her untidy, generous, open-handed attitude to life. Beneath the rose-tinted lampshade on her bedside table stood a china cupid, a travelling clock, glass jars of peppermints, rose-petal jelly from Fortnums, rose and jasmine scent from Floris; opened letters fanned upon a scatter of periodicals. On the bed, newspapers and bills were scattered around, while a white Persian cat curled at the foot; its mate yawned in a big basket by the open log fire, next to which Toby sat, looking unusually grave.

From beneath the canopy of old-rose silk, draped from the ceiling behind her tumbled lace pillows, Mimi looked sharply at Toby. 'What's up, love?'

He waved a bank statement. 'The Minerva rent is late, as usual, which means my mortgage payments on this place are going to be late again. It's too bad! Pierson has been playing to full houses.'

'*You* know the landlord always gets paid last,' Mimi yawned, without much concern.

Carefully Toby said, 'When Pierson's lease runs out at the end of November, he wants to book the Minerva for a

Christmas panto.' He looked speculatively at Mimi. He had it in mind to grant the lease, but only with a special condition.

Mimi looked up, scenting her chance. '*I've* always wanted to play panto.'

Toby quickly said, 'Then I'll tell Pierson. He'll probably jump at the chance.' He was surprised and relieved that there had been no need to persuade Mimi to take this first step; he was convinced she could be an even greater success in the legitimate theatre, and panto would be the easiest step upwards for her, nepotism or not.

Simultaneously, Mimi jumped at her chance to stop Toby acting and start him in management. Quickly, she suggested, 'Why not stage the panto ourselves? Why rent your theatre to somebody else, to make money for *him*? Why shouldn't *you* present a panto? Then, if we have a hit you might follow it with a straight play – maybe a Sherlock Holmes: surely by now you know all there is to know about detective drama?'

Events were moving faster than Toby had expected. He warned, 'Steady, Foxtop. First I'll need to find a backer.'

'Sir Octopus is a backer, ain't he?'

'He only finances drama in his own theatres.'

'You're his only son,' Mimi pointed out. 'Ask Sir Octopus nicely and if that don't work, put a bit of pressure on him: threaten to leave the stage and run a gambling club, or something.'

Toby was shocked. 'I will do no such thing.'

'Then I will,' Mimi said firmly. Sir Octavius had warmed towards her, for he admired Mimi's stage success and her cheeky bravado; also, to his relief, his son's unconventional household arrangement seemed to serve its purpose admirably: the Fane name was no longer in danger. Sir Octavius had relaxed.

Mimi immediately scribbled an invitation for her father-in-law to take tea with her, and sent it with the bootboy to Albany.

On the following afternoon, in her gilt-and-plum drawing room, Mimi pitched her pantomime proposition to Sir Octavius.

The watery blue eyes brightened at the mention of pantomime. Mimi then listened patiently to a short history lesson . . . an offshoot of *commedia dell'arte*, with Harlequin and Columbine as performed by Italian travelling players of the sixteenth century . . . For modern Christmas pantomime, the hero-pursues-heroine plot was now interspersed with fairy-tale sub-plots, music-hall turns, vaudeville songs and satire. Splendid! Splendid! 'And which is your pantomime to be, Mimi? *Red Riding Hood*? *Aladdin*? *Babes in the Wood*?'

'*Cinderella*,' Mimi said firmly, for she felt she had much in common with that heroine.

'An excellent choice. If you feel the stage is big enough.'

'So you'll do it?'

'I might. Indeed I might.'

He threw her a roguish smile and for one numbing moment, Mimi wondered if Sir Octopus thought she had invited *him* to play the Prince.

'Of course, I need to speak to her ladyship. But why not? Young Toby must start in management at some point.'

Mimi, who had not expected her task to be so easy, gleefully thought: No more touring.

* * *

Lady Fane also had one proviso: a part for young Tudor Perkins, whose mother was her close friend.

Toby had intended to ask Baz (who would had been perfect) to play Buttons. Politely, he argued with his mother. 'Tudor hasn't had enough experience, Mama, and there isn't a suitable part for such a good-looking juvenile lead.'

'But you have not yet cast Buttons, I believe? ... That's settled then, my dearest.' Lady Fane interpreted the Golden Rule, correctly, as meaning that she who has the gold makes the rules.

Chapter Six

One of Toby's problems was to find a Cinderella smaller than Mimi. Secure in her role as Prince Charming, Mimi now realized how depressing it was for a director to reject, reject and reject again these hopeful performers, as every morning they auditioned on the empty stage. They also had innumerable meetings with author, set designer, wig maker and costumier in the small, overcrowded offices at the back of the Minerva, where battered grey metal filing cabinets bulged with details of artists; schedules and timetables covered the walls and three middle-aged secretaries administered author royalties, contracts and wages.

The first read-through was held at 10 a.m. on a minimally lit stage, before a backdrop of autumnal Scottish mountains rearing out of mist. *Bonny Prince Charlie* was currently playing at the Minerva, so the dressing rooms were occupied by the Bonny Prince and his adversaries. As there was no heating, the actors on stage wore overcoats, mufflers, gloves and hats as they sat in a circle of battered bentwood chairs, clutching scripts and making nervously brittle conversation.

Soon the sand-filled fire buckets that had been dragged on stage were littered with cigarette stubs. The cast read their parts with minimal energy; nobody would learn a part by heart until told to by the producer, for there would be many changes before the final version was decided. As the actors mumbled through the read-through, Toby's assistant timed the run with a stopwatch. It overran by twenty-seven minutes. Not bad.

* * *

In the chorus dressing room of the Gaiety, Betsy threw down the *Evening Gazette* and burst into jealous tears. 'Mimi's got her name in the papers again, *real* big this time, Ma!'

'Yes, and we all know how she did it. I wouldn't have you stoop, dear.' Mrs Bridges put down the costume she was mending, delicately picked up the newspaper, then sniffed, 'It's only an advert.' Not even to herself would she admit her disappointment.

'But she's billed above the title,' wept Betsy, 'and I'm still only a chorus girl.'

The half-dressed Chorine, sitting next to Betsy at the Bench, put down her stub of No. 5 and stared through black-beaded eyelashes. 'And what's *wrong* with being in the Gaiety chorus, Miss Hoity-Toity?'

'Common as dirt,' sniffed Mrs Bridges to the ceiling.

'Time you got out, Mrs B.,' snapped Chorine. 'You know as you ain't allowed backstage during the performance.'

'It ain't *fair*,' sobbed Betsy. Her exquisite face had many times attracted attention, and she was frequently asked to audition; Betsy was not temperamental, but she was so self-conscious, so drilled in exhibiting her beauty to the best advantage, that her movements were mechanical, and she was unable to forget herself in portraying another character. On stage she moved stiffly, like a marionette, head held high as if balancing an invisible book on it, and inevitably drew the swift, sing-song response, 'Thank you. Next, please.'

Off stage, Mrs Bridges had been equally, silently disappointed by lack of tangible result. Betsy had many would-be admirers, but none of them were thought good enough by Mrs Bridges to play the fairy-tale part she had sketched out for them in her plot of her daughter's life. Mrs Bridges would not consider a moneyed gentleman without a title, and the titled stage door johnnies who took a shine to Betsy were invariably penniless younger sons.

She refused to admit that her daughter might have more success if allowed out on her own: a girl raised decent should *always* be chaperoned. However, the occasional threesome supper was never a success: Betsy sat stiffly at the restaurant table, as staid and anxious as her mother. So once Betsy's face became familiar to her suitors, there was nothing left to intrigue or surprise them: Betsy did not have Mimi's spontaneous charm, and familiarity bred boredom.

Betsy remained depressed by Mimi's success: on the following morning, in their Lambeth bedroom with walls patterned by autumn leaves, she and her mother dressed in doleful silence, one on either side of the double bed.

Suddenly, Betsy burst into tears. 'Ma, what's *wrong* with me? I've had masses of auditions but never landed a good part. I've had plenty of beaux I like, but not one of them is good enough for *you*, Ma!' She glared at the heavy red-bound copy of *Burke's Peerage*, which lay on the chest of drawers; Mrs Bridges never travelled without this tome, in which she checked all of Betsy's admirers.

Betsy ran over to the book, which listed all the eligible young men to whom she would never be married; defiantly, she grabbed it, turned, and hurled it at her mother's head.

Mrs Bridges dodged the heavy volume before it crashed to the floor. Such ill-treatment of her reference book, as precious to her as the Bible, released all her disappointment and fury. Red-faced and angry, Mrs Bridges, for the first time, fired a stream of accusations at her daughter. 'After all I've done for you . . . Worked my fingers to the bone to put you through stage school . . . Scrimped for your finery . . . Sacrificed myself . . . To think that my only child . . . Selfish . . . Ungrateful . . .' She then collapsed on the bed and howled noisily into the fat fingers that she claimed to have worked to the bone.

Betsy was instantly remorseful. She rushed to her mother and hugged her, for what she said *was all true*! Her mother *had* sacrificed herself, and devoted her life to Betsy, who had not yet repaid her mother with the success due to her. Betsy did not realize that it was her mother's wheedling and threatening that gave her an unattractive, visibly-desperate need to succeed, for success was the only way in which she could repay her mother's unremitting devotion. She failed to see the clinging and devouring woman from whom her suffocated husband had finally escaped.

On the floor below, the landlady stood on a chair and banged the ceiling with her broomstick. 'Less noise up there! This is a boarding house, not a bawdy house!'

* * *

Five days after Toby had warned the cast that he wanted them all off-book at the next rehearsal, the first dress rehearsal of *Cinderella* was held. Toby and his small group of production people huddled around the centre of row G in the stalls, where Toby bent his long legs almost up to his chin, and propped his feet on the tip-up seats before him. It was his job to give support and confidence to his team by listening carefully to their questions, suggesting solutions, and being quietly firm when authority was necessary. He also constantly dictated notes of criticism to his assistant, which would be handed over later, privately, to the artist concerned.

The rehearsal lasted fifteen hours; the assistant stage manager trotted out repeatedly for fried-egg sandwiches, bacon sandwiches and meat pies: endlessly, he produced mugs of tea and coffee, and jugs of stout for the Ugly Sisters, Vaselina and Coldcrema.

Tudor's performance exasperated Toby. When Tudor leapt on stage with graceful agility, Toby patiently called up, 'No! No, Buttons! As I've told you before, I want *verve* and *bounce*! Buttons is a cheeky young Cockney lad, not a damned ballet dancer!'

Toby jumped on stage to demonstrate what he required. But five minutes later, he again called up, 'Buttons, *don't* open the invitation while Cinderella is speaking or you'll upstage her ... And if you come in early, you kill her laugh line ... Now I want to run through the ball scene again and improve Prince Charming's exit ... Let's take it from the top, Prince Charming. Everyone else, take ten.' The cast obediently shuffled off stage for a ten-minute break in which to bitch about Tudor and speculate as to why he'd got the part. Theatre people could be rapier-fast and comically cruel with their tongues, so were more likely to have violently venomous rows than a group of architects, bricklayers or poultry pluckers. There was

always much to be comic about: rumoured sexual performance or otherwise, religion, politics, hobbies, age, shape,
clothes, spouses and children. Any minority group was
particularly likely to cause uproar, particularly homosexuals, who were often oversensitively prone to imagine
hostility, as Toby well understood. He knew that the
entire cast would be making who-does-what-and-with-
what-and-to-whom jokes about his relationship with
Tudor, but there was nothing that he could do except
ignore it.

By three o'clock in the morning the actors were
exhausted and so difficult to manage that sometimes Toby
despaired at the missed cues, the muddled lines, and the
general air of harassment and irritation.

'Where's Vaselina's mirror?'

'The Robber Baron's using it – half his beard's just
fallen off.'

'Have those bloody glass slippers been delivered yet?'

'Gamba promised to have them here by teatime.'

'*Teatime!* It's past bloody midnight! Use her street shoe
... Christ almighty, where's the page's tasselled cushion
for the glass slipper?'

When the rehearsal ended, the exasperated Toby
addressed the cast. 'I know that everyone's trying hard,
and we're all tired, but not *once* today has this production
constantly kept in rhythm! In particular, when Buttons
forgets his words or stumbles, then the rest of the cast
lose their concentration while they're waiting for Buttons
to work out where he is ...'

Tudor looked apologetic. 'Frightfully sorry, everyone,
it really is decent of you all to put up with me.'

Afterwards, Toby muttered wearily to Mimi, 'I hope
I'm not being too hard on them.'

'Course not. And they can't complain you don't know what you want.'

'Yes – perhaps for the very first time in my life ... Do you mind running through your scenes with Buttons early tomorrow morning? We've simply got to get him into shape. Tudor's hopelessly miscast, and he doesn't even *look* the part.'

Mimi agreed. 'He should be playing a toff with a tennis racket in *Charley's Aunt*, or flirting with the ingénue in some drawing-room comedy. But we're stuck with him, dearie. It ain't the hand that rocks the cradle as rules the world, but the hand that holds the purse.'

* * *

The full dress rehearsal was held two days before Christmas. A table had been set up in the middle of the stalls, behind which sat Toby, the electrician, the costumier, the stage manager and all their assistants. Waiting in the wings, Mimi (wearing a white satin coat, knee breeches and ostrich-plumed tricorn hat) peeked through the flats at the interior of the theatre. The house lights were still on, and the auditorium of the Minerva looked very pretty: it was painted in cream, pale blue and gilt, with dark-blue plush, tip-up seats and a dark-blue velvet stage curtain, as heavily encrusted with gold braid as an Admiral of the Fleet.

When the house lights went down, only the faint light from the orchestra pit remained. Backstage, the actors waited, tense, agitated, sweating, or else frozen solid and incapable of thought. Vaselina complained that he couldn't move his arms in his costume; Coldcrema growled that he couldn't turn his head in his wig. Someone snapped, 'No one will notice the difference.'

The full dress rehearsal lasted nine hours, during which there were several long pauses due to lighting problems. As usual, the rehearsal took far longer than anticipated. Everything that could seemed destined to go wrong. Weary, silent actors sat in their dressing rooms and stared at half-empty cups of cold tea and curling, half-eaten sandwiches as they waited for a set to be changed, or for electricians to stop tinkering with the lights.

Toby remained calm, knowing that panic was the main cause of high tension at dress rehearsal. Outbursts of temper and complaints were to be expected. Most members of the cast were miserably jealous of other actors' parts and performances; they all knew that talent and ambition were not enough to get ahead in the theatre: connections, tenacity, ruthlessness and luck were just as important. This generated much tension among actors anxious not to miss perhaps the only Big Chance of their career.

As the day dragged on, the actors grew more tired and dispirited, and began to complain about each other.

'Buttons *still* isn't picking up his bloody cues.'

'Cinderella won't look me in the eye, she's cheating to the audience. I can't kiss the back of her bloody head!'

Cinderella suggested what Prince Charming might kiss instead. Toby threw her a warning look.

Finally Coldcrema roared, 'If Vaselina tries to upstage me *once* more, I'll shove his ugly bum down in the orchestra pit!'

After the rehearsal finished, everyone around the table in the stalls continued in earnest discussion. Eventually, Toby asked for certain scenes to be repeated. After that, he called the entire cast on stage, and gave them his final advice. '. . . Above all, *please* will everyone remember that panto is very formalized and traditional, with a definite rhythm to the whole production. So for Heaven's sake *keep to the beat*, or the audience won't laugh, and then you'll lose your nerve and go too fast – and *then* we'll lose that vital rhythm. That's all. Thank you.'

* * *

Cinderella opened, according to pantomime tradition, on Boxing Night. There was a cheerful air of anticipation in the lobby of the Minerva and a far noisier, cheerful hum in the auditorium, which contained many overexcited children. As usual, the gallery had filled first, followed below by the upper circle, where heads hung over the front rail, to spot the celebrities below. The dress circle was well behaved, but the people in the stalls were restless: First-Nighters twittered and coughed; critics who had been persuaded to attend by Sir Octavius (who had called in every outstanding favour) shifted in their seats, yawned and wondered what they were doing at a bloody pantomime.

Backstage, the atmosphere was less relaxed. Toby knew that on a First Night everyone on stage felt exposed to frustration, ridicule and humiliation. Some actors needed silence in order to concentrate, others talked feverishly to everyone in sight, in order to distract themselves from their tension. Cinderella was humming into a flat, which reflected the sound so that the whole of her face vibrated and relaxed. Dandini, who had overstrained her voice, and could not speak above a whisper, gargled every five minutes. Mimi was going up and down the scale, to warm up her voice.

To her surprise, Mimi found herself more anxious for Toby's success than for her own. She was actually enjoying her first stage part in this highly stylized, magical madness; clearly a panto was far more fun, and less demanding, than a straight play. Of course, as Mimi was in the enviable position of being married to the theatre owner and producer, she possessed a sense of security that the rest of the cast didn't share.

In the wings, the stage manager was unsuccessfully trying to hush a bunch of stage mothers holding shawls for their talented tots. A sequin-scattered fairy whined, 'Me wings feel loose.'

Toby seemed calm. He knew that as soon as the actors had appeared on stage they would relax and start to enjoy the evening.

The curtain was ten minutes late going up, because Prince Charming's crown had disappeared, then an elf's mother fainted by the prompt corner.

Although exhausted, Toby dealt with each crisis as it occurred. 'Someone pull that woman away from the prompt corner and give her a slug of brandy . . .'

He turned his attention back to the stage. 'We're going up in five minutes. Mimi, you'll just have to wear that white ostrich-feather hat until they find your crown.'

Out front, the lights dimmed, the conductor lifted his arms, the curtain rose soundlessly, and for everyone in the theatre, the evening had started.

* * *

The audience clapped, cheered and whistled as the curtain finally descended on the glittering, newly wed Cinderella and Prince Charming.

Mimi and Toby took their separate curtain calls, both knowing that they had also successfully taken a step in a new direction.

In her box, calm and tough, Lady Fane announced imperiously to her husband, 'Buttons must be replaced *immediately*. I can't imagine why Toby chose Tudor, he's hopelessly miscast.'

* * *

In their dressing rooms, flushed with success, actors now received compliments and kisses from their friends, then they departed, in small groups, to celebrate in nearby pubs. The principal performers left for Romano's, where their ostentatious entry would be clapped by other diners, and the maître d'hôtel would (equally ostentatiously) rush forward with a bottle of (non-vintage) complimentary house champagne.

In the Minerva, the fire curtain was lowered, the exit doors clanged shut, the lights were switched off. The theatre was silent for the night.

Wednesday 1 January 1908. Fitzroy Square

At noon on New Year's Day, Mimi opened one eye, shuddered, and hastily closed it again. After the curtain had fallen on *Cinderella*, to celebrate the New Year the young Fanes, plus a group of friends (which did not include Baz, playing Puss in *Dick Whittington* in Edinburgh), had attended the Chelsea Arts Ball – with every famous and infamous Bohemian in London, it seemed: painters, sculptors, models, writers, poets and musicians – mostly wearing fancy dress – had drunk champagne and danced rowdily until dawn. Mimi vaguely remembered performing a violent and erratic paso doble with the bear-sized, bearded Augustus John, whose guests were all dressed as gypsies: and that was her last memory of her evening.

Cautiously, she again opened her eye. In the dark, shadowy warmth of her bedroom, she could see that the fire still smouldered in the grate, and the curtains had not been completely pulled together. She could distinguish the familiar shapes of her furniture. Lazily, she listened to street sounds float up from the square outside: clopping, snuffling horses; the creak of wooden wheels; the piercing whistle of a delivery boy.

And a soft snore.

Mimi jerked her head to the right. Lying next to her was the dark outline of a recumbent body.

She felt instant repugnance, then realized that it was only Toby. He had probably helped her up to bed, lain down to chat about the ball, then dozed off.

Slowly and painfully she lifted her head. In the half-light she saw striped breeches, sashes, shirts and swashbuckling thigh-boots scattered over the Turkey carpet; her unlaced pink stays had been flung on a chair, over the back of which were draped her frilled white bloomers.

Mimi put her hand to her breast and realized that she was naked.

Cautiously, Mimi trailed her hand towards the neighbouring body and gently touched – warm, naked flesh! She yanked back her hand, as if stung by a nettle. 'Toby,' she hissed.

Mimi heard a yawn, then a groan.

Slowly Toby turned towards her, and muttered, 'That was a good party, Baz.'

'I *ain't* Baz, you fool!'

Sharply, Toby sat up, groaned, and promptly fell back against his pillow. 'What the deuce? ... Good heavens, how did I get *here*? ... I can't remember a thing...'

'Neither can I.'

Mimi could sense Toby cautiously feel his body; she heard a groan when he realized that he was naked.

Slowly, Toby lifted his head, and observed the chaos of disordered clothes, flung everywhere. His head slumped back on the pillow. He groaned again.

'We was both a bit tiddly,' Mimi offered.

'Slightly squiffy,' Toby agreed.

After a strained pause, Toby asked tentatively, 'We didn't, did we?'

'It feels to me as if we did, dearie.'

'Oh, crikey! I'm most awfully sorry, Mimi!' Toby carefully sat up in bed and grabbed the edge of the sheet, to cover his naked chest.

'Takes two,' Mimi sighed, glad that she couldn't remember a thing, astonished that she had obviously been a willing partner.

Toby put one long leg out of bed; he grabbed the pink silk coverlet and wrapped it round his loins.

Mimi giggled. 'You look like the Sheikh of Araby, dearie.'

Toby tottered around the room, holding his sarong together with one hand, while with the other he groped for his scattered clothes.

As he stood by the door, Toby looked towards her. 'So *dreadfully* sorry ... I mean, *deeply* grateful ... I mean ... Oh, hell!'

'I know what you're thinking, Toby. Wotcha going to say to Baz?'

'Exactly.' Toby looked harassed. 'I simply don't know what Baz will say.' He shuddered.

'What Baz don't know won't hurt him, so let's just forget it ever happened – *not* that we know that anything *did* happen, remember!'

Toby looked hopeful, but still guilty. 'Supposing Baz found out?'

'How? I ain't going to tell him.' Mimi regarded that relationship as none of her business. She added, 'Now hop off to your own bedroom, Toby, before Rose brings in me breakfast tray: I got me reputation to consider.'

Tuesday 7 April 1908. Paris

'April in Paris!' Excitedly, Mimi fumbled with the unaccustomed handle, flung open the long windows and gazed down from her pretty bedroom, papered in blue-and-cream *toile de Jouy*, with curtains to match. Below her, bay trees in neat white tubs lined the central courtyard of the Ritz Hotel, where beautifully turned out women, in huge feathered hats, sipped morning coffee or early aperitifs with their top-hatted escorts.

Gazing down into the charming courtyard, Mimi could hardly believe that she had spent four days in Paris, the epitome of luxury, frivolity and naughtiness! When rich Britishers tired of the country house parties at which they hunted, shot, fished, ate enormous meals and conducted discreet liaisons after lights out, they fought off boredom by taking a trip to the French metropolis, where amusement was taken very seriously.

Toby had taken Mimi and Baz to Paris for a week, to

celebrate the end of the pantomime season and Toby's first successful production at the Minerva. They had travelled from Victoria in a train with a restaurant car that smelt of rich food and good cigars; each elegantly appointed table had a rose-silk shaded electric lamp, and a silver vase of carnations. As the lemon syllabub was served, Baz had leaned forward, lifted his glass of champagne, winked at Mimi and said, 'Here's remembering the Railway Refreshment Room at Crewe!'

'I'd rather drink to your first memories of Paris,' Toby had smiled.

Now, as Mimi leaned out of her bedroom window, and gazed into the Ritz courtyard below, she understood why Toby had said that everyone remembers the first trip to Paris, because it always seems a little dreamlike and no matter what you expect – Paris is always unexpected – and better.

Mimi had sensed the excitement in the air – so different to sedate and pompous London – as soon as she descended from the train at the Gare du Nord: in Paris, people clearly seemed determined to enjoy themselves.

She had not changed her first impression. She had found Paris as charming and frivolous as a wedding cake in the spring air, with a pale-blue, boundless sky that stretched above tall dove-grey buildings lining wide and splendid boulevards, sprinkled with frothy blossom from rows of chestnut trees. Napoleon's administrator, Baron Haussmann, had torn down much of the dirty old city to create this new clean cream Paris, with splendid green parks, gardens, and wide boulevards lined by 30,000 gas lamps.

The dazzled Mimi loved to ride in an open carriage – a fiacre – up the Boulevard de la Madeleine, which was always crammed with horse buses, carriages and smart new automobiles. After shopping in the splendid emporium of the Galleries Lafayette, Mimi had returned to the Place Vendôme laden with boxes of delicately coloured suede gloves, silk stockings, fragile underwear and six frivolously irresistible new hats. She tried to absorb all the strange new sights that she saw from their carriage: the concierges that guarded every building, the ragged women who cleaned them; the open-air boulevard cafés, where cocky young men sipped aperitifs and eyed the passing girls; the elegant *haut monde* in their smart clothes; the extravagant *courtisanes* and *grandes cocottes* who paraded for all to admire in beautifully turned-out carriages that trotted down the Bois de Boulogne, where working families ate Sunday picnics on the grass, and young lovers floated in punts on the River Seine.

At night, Paris also seemed to have a special glow that owed nothing to the many white globes of the gas-lit street lamps, beneath which people strolled, eyed each other flirtatiously or sat contentedly in open-air restaurants, watching everyone else.

Mimi loved everything about Paris, even the smells: the odours of rich food that swept from open restaurant doors, the beguiling perfumes that every smartly dressed woman seemed to wear, the strange tang of garlic and the harsh, pungent odour of cheap cigarettes.

* * *

Mimi sat in the stalls at the Folies-Bergère, the world's most famous revue and already synonymous with French naughtiness. Enthusiastically, Mimi applauded Mistinguett, the current star, and as much a symbol of Paris as the Eiffel Tower. Her gurgling French accent with its back-throated r's matched her effervescent personality; she also had sensational legs which she displayed with disdainful panache. Mimi gasped at the finale, when Mistinguett, escorted by two dozen top-hatted nancy boys, slowly descended an ornate curving staircase: she wore a six-foot-wide pink ostrich-feather hat and trailed a matching twenty-foot feathered train.

After the show, the three Britishers strolled through the delightful Winter Gardens, which were crammed with young men-about-town meeting their *copains* and showing off their female companions. Suddenly, an American voice hailed Toby.

Toby turned towards a small, portly parrot-nosed man who wore white tie and tails, and waved confidently from the middle of a smartly dressed group.

'Mr Ziegfeld, what a pleasant surprise,' Toby said in a voice beneath which Mimi detected no pleasure at all.

Mimi was delighted to meet the famous American showman, for she knew that many famous foreign artistes appeared in the New York Ziegfeld Follies. Mr Ziegfeld signed only the best talent, and he combed the world for it, determined that each of his productions would be more lush than the last. He spent lavishly. Waving aside Toby's polite objections, Ziegfeld swept the Britishers into his entourage. 'No, no, pal, *you* must come with *me* to Maxim's, I've gotten into the habit of booking a permanent table there when I'm in Paris . . . Saw your pa only last week, Toby, when Dan Leno gave a dinner party for me at the Savoy . . .'

Five minutes later the British trio was speeding along the boulevards in one of Mr Ziegfeld's entourage of spotless navy-blue Hispano-Suizas.

At Maxim's, Mimi sat between Mr Ziegfeld and Toby on the maroon plush banquette. Mr Ziegfeld then decided what everyone was going to eat for supper, after which he turned his attention to Mimi. 'Wasn't that Mistinguett just great? Tried to get her to New York, but she's afraid they won't understand her. Holy smoke, it wouldn't matter if she sang in Swahili, the guys'd just goggle at those gams, pay big bucks to see 'em a second time.'

Mr Ziegfeld then told Mimi that he had already caught her act in London, the previous year, and liked it, but judged it far too British-flavoured for American audiences to understand. He asked if Mimi had ever thought of doing a straight singing act.

Mimi smiled and shook her head: to sing 'straight' she would need to wear costumes that revealed her arms, legs and back.

Guessing her thoughts, Toby whispered to Mimi, 'Don't worry about the costumes. We'll find a way round it. I think you *should* sing for him. He'll be in London next week. We could invite him to dinner?'

Mimi whispered back, 'No, I don't want Ziegfeld interested in me when he can't sign me up.'

'Why shouldn't he sign you up? Wouldn't you like to appear in New York?'

Mimi hesitated for a moment, looked sideways at Toby, and slowly shook her head. 'Not just at the minute, dearie because . . . You see . . . I'm pregnant.'

Toby turned white. He shot a worried glance towards the other end of the table, where Baz was eagerly in conversation. Toby relaxed, and turned back to Mimi. 'Foxtop, that's a joke in rather poor taste, don't you think?'

'It ain't a joke,' Mimi said quietly. She had not meant

to tell him until they returned to London, but it had been on her mind for weeks and now ... she had suddenly heard herself telling Toby: it had just popped out.

'Are you *sure*?' Toby hissed in her ear.

'If it ain't that, it's a record-breaking early menopause,' Mimi whispered back.

'Oh, Great Scott! ... You're truly *not* joking, Mimi?'

'Cross me heart.' She looked regretfully at Toby's horrified face. 'Remember New Year's Eve?'

'Ssssh!' Toby looked nervously towards Baz, then whispered to Mimi, 'We'll talk about this later. Thank God we're in Paris.'

'There ain't nothing to talk about, I've told you all there is to tell.' Although Toby's reaction was exactly what Mimi had expected, it was not what she had hoped for. She turned her back to him and talked to Mr Ziegfeld.

Mimi got on well with Mr Ziegfeld, who knew that she had pulled herself up by her bootstraps from the gutter. He was intrigued by her impudent street-urchin personality, and her straightforward unpretentiousness; she treated everyone, including waiters, in the same friendly, effervescent manner, and clearly enjoyed shocking the pompous with her exuberance.

After the hors d'oeuvres were served Mimi did not get much chance to talk, for Mr Ziegfeld told her of his trip. Every big producer knew – and had probably seen – all the hits in New York, London, Paris and Vienna. Mr Ziegfeld had already visited Britain. After Paris, he would travel to Berlin, Vienna and Rome, before returning to London to catch the ship back to New York. He travelled with a retinue of valet, maid, two secretaries, his own bookie, and always a beautiful companion ... 'Sometimes my wife.' Mimi politely treated this last titbit of information as a joke.

'Did you see anybody interesting in London?' Mimi asked, although she knew that if Ziegfeld had signed anyone important he was unlikely to tell her about it.

'There's always a lot to see in London,' Mr Ziegfeld said smoothly. 'I've finished auditioning there, except for a minor singing spot, but I've already heard the gal and I'll probably sign her on my way back. She's a beautiful creature in the line-up at the Gaiety . . . Betty something . . .'

'Betsy Bridges?'

'Yeah, that's her.'

Mimi controlled her shaking voice and carefully said, 'We were once . . . briefly . . . in the same company . . . Tell me, you did say you had *heard* Miss Bridges *sing*?'

'Yeah. Thin soprano, but that face is spectacular.' Ziegfeld then leaned across Mimi and asked Toby what his next production was going to be.

'A detective drama, *The Mystery of Fernhurst Grange*, and after that we plan another straight play, starring Mimi.' Toby looked sideways at his scowling wife, then hastily added, 'But that's not definite.'

* * *

On the following morning, Mimi, in her lace bedjacket, leaned back against frilled pillows; as she dipped her croissant into a bowl of *café au lait*, she once more assured Toby that she had not been joking: indeed, she was pregnant.

Mimi was annoyed that he appeared harassed. 'Any other bloke would be delighted! Your old man'll be tickled pink – especially if it's a boy!' She looked up and glared. 'But all *you* can think about – *don't* deny it – is how you're going to explain this to Baz!' She pushed her tray aside. 'And don't think for *one minute* that I'll consider getting rid of it!' She looked up, pleading. 'Toby, this is something I ain't never expected in my life – never dared hope for it. But now it's happened, you'd better get used to it – for *I'm* looking forward to having me own baby!'

'Of course I'm happy for you, Mimi.' But Toby looked even more anxious. 'However, I'll not deny that I have mixed feelings about the . . . er . . . happy event.'

'Then don't tell Baz till we get back to London,' Mimi advised. 'Or it'll spoil our trip.'

'Good idea. I won't . . . You look a little pale,' Toby noticed, 'don't tell me *this* time that it's just your monthly.'

'It's nothing,' Mimi said hurriedly, but she had spent a restless night, trying to calm herself, trying to doze off, trying to think only of her dear little baby. However, all she could think of was that cursed Betsy, who now again popped unbidden into her mind to spoil her Paris trip – Betsy, the toast of New York. She stared into the dark night, but all she could see was Betsy, Queen of Broadway, with her lily-white hands and her long, graceful legs, happily acknowledging the applause from a full house of cheering Yankees.

Just before she rang her bedside bell for breakfast, she decided what to do about Betsy. She asked to see the agenda that Toby had so carefully prepared for his Paris trip. She studied it, then looked up winningly. 'Toby, I can see you've put a lot of thought behind this, but I want to see *real* Paris life, not only the showy stuff on display for tourists!' She flung her arms out, theatrically. 'I want to see the man-in-la-rue's Paris, the little music halls and cellar-clubs.'

Toby was surprised. What was the point of coming to Paris to see third-class shows that they wouldn't bother to visit in Britain?

'You really mean it?' He was hesitant.

'Yes.' Mimi was firm. 'I got a craving to see the rough side of the city.'

* * *

With good nature, Toby cancelled his tables at the Café de la Paix, the Café Riche in the Boulevard des Italiens and the Café Viennois, patronized by the King of Belgium, also his reservations at the Bal du Moulin Rouge, Le Ciel, L'Enfer and all the other frivolous, fashionable, late-evening entertainments that he had planned they should visit.

Instead, they visited the old Quartier St-Germain, on the Rive Gauche, the dives of the Latin Quarter, where bohemian students and artists sat in cheap cafés, quietly reading *Le Petit Parisien*, or nursing their hangovers as they argued fiercely about which way the world should be run.

One evening the three Britishers found themselves in the middle of an open-air ball, held in a street near the Place Pigalle, where workmen and their girls danced to an accordion, as rough red wine or absinthe quenched their thirst and fired their lust. Prodded by Mimi, Toby and Baz danced with little hat-trimmers and *midinettes*, who slaved fourteen hours a day in miserable sweatshops to make exquisite clothes for rich women, but who now forgot their exhaustion over a glass of wine and a rousing polka.

Visiting the new Bal Tabourin for the first time, Mimi saw *real* French cancan: plump thighs shook above black stockings in a crotch-revealing split of lace. The trio then took a cab to Les Halles, the great central market of Paris that operated throughout the night. Here, after hours spent dancing, well-heeled revellers often patronized the shabby little restaurants to taste the famous piquant onion soup, the breakfast of the porters who carried on their backs the boxes of fruits and vegetables, the baskets of glittering fish, the cadavers of stiff, gutted pigs and cows, which were later bartered to provide the following day's food for the huge, sprawling city.

The next morning, Mimi suggested to Toby that they extend their visit for a second week, for there was *so much* to see in Paris.

* * *

Surprisingly, on the following Friday night, Mimi found what she was looking for, in a working-man's bar buried deep in the medieval labyrinth of the Montagne-Ste-Geneviève. It was really only a cellar in which local workmen drank, but Toby heard that a new young singer had appeared there the previous week; she was thought to be a runaway from Lyons, and sang under the name Zilda.

Eyed suspiciously by the locals, the British trio, conspicuously clean, sat in the light of guttering candles stuck in empty wine bottles on up-ended barrels. A mournful little man squeezed popular French songs from his accordion.

Suddenly, a girl was pushed through a dirty bead curtain hanging before a side door: Zilda, who could not have been older than sixteen, wore a clinging black bathing-belle costume, and stood defiantly, hands on hips and legs apart. Loudly and appreciatively, the audience eyed her figure and excellent legs; her sulky white face was surrounded by short, sleek, black hair, her eyes were outlined by kohl, her lips painted scarlet. Black, white, and that gash of scarlet were very effective, Mimi noted.

In the young girl's face, her stance, her defiant attitude, Mimi also sensed barely concealed fury. Zilda projected a tigerish quality, you felt she knew how to fight tooth and nail. Whatever dreadful things this girl had experienced, she was a defiant survivor of the streets. Beneath her fighting spirit, only Mimi sensed a forlorn loneliness.

The girl glared at the noisy men as if daring them to touch or insult her, then, ignoring them, she started to sing. Gradually, they quieted as they listened to the throbbing pathos of a voice that unaccountably moved them: nobody knew better than Mimi that this was all that mattered. Zilda's voice was rough and untrained, her singing style was simple; but it was also nostalgic and achingly erotic.

When Zilda finished her song (about the loneliness of a country girl in the city) there was a roar of applause, then shouted lewd suggestions. Still scowling, the girl sang a second song about a little mermaid; slowly, sensuously, she mimed swimming strokes, moving each shoulder forward in turn, with provocatively covert invitation.

When she had finished her song, while the men were still roaring applause, Zilda nodded curtly, disappeared through a side door, and gave them no encore.

The three Britishers tried to go backstage, but were

politely refused admittance through the dirty beaded curtain. 'Must be a real hell-hole back there,' Mimi muttered. 'Doesn't matter. Ziegfeld will know how to reach her.'

'Is that what this week has been about?' Toby demanded. 'Why the deuce should *you* scout for Ziegfeld?'

Midday, Wednesday 15 April 1908. The Ritz, Paris

Even in the hushed Ritz, Mimi could hear the noon hooter that announced the French lunch hour. Sitting up against the brass bedhead, the remains of her breakfast on the tray in front of her, Mimi glared at Toby, already smartly dressed, in stiff white collar and pale-grey suit with a pearl tiepin stuck in his oyster silk cravat.

Toby, accustomed to Mimi's mutinous glare, ignored it, rested his suede-gloved hands on his silver-knotted walking stick, and repeated his question. 'Once more, *will* you agree to forget about that singer?'

'You're too late,' Mimi said sulkily, 'I've already sent a note to Mr Ziegfeld in Rome. Gave it to a page-boy, half an hour ago.'

Vexed, Toby muttered, 'I should have suspected you'd be up to mischief when I heard Ziegfeld enthusing about Betsy at Maxim's.'

Mimi pouted. 'Don't be horrid, Toby. Not when I'm feeling queasy, 'cause of the baby.'

'If you're feeling queasy, it's because of that vile wine we drank in that cheap dive last night!'

Mimi scowled again. 'Whatever the reason, I don't feel in the mood for being ticked off by you!'

Frustrated, Toby banged his cane on the floor. 'I'm genuinely fond of you, Mimi, and I have a high regard for your intelligence. However, I'm disappointed that you will not admit – even to yourself – that you are hell-bent on revenge!'

'I merely dropped a line to Mr Ziegfeld . . .'

'You have been *deliberately* seeking someone in Paris who will interest Ziegfeld more than Betsy!'

Mimi sniffed. 'Oh, very well, have it your own way! I ain't going to let you make me feel guilty, so you can stop trying!'

'I'm not trying to make you feel guilty. *Qui s'excuse, s'accuse*,* as they say here! You *already* feel guilty – with good reason! I'm not convinced that Betsy deliberately meant to harm you. But *you* have just deliberately tried to harm her.'

This silenced Mimi, for she knew it to be true.

Seeing that Mimi, at last, was listening to him, Toby lowered his voice. 'Foxtop, please be sensible. Betsy's bound to hear about this, and then she'll be out for *your* blood! . . . You know what the theatre's like!'

Slowly, Mimi nodded.

'Don't make unnecessary enemies. It can only hurt you.'

'Betsy can't hurt *me*.' Mimi sniffed. Mimi was a star. Mimi was married. Mimi had a lovely home. Mimi was going to have a baby. Mimi was *safe*, which was more than Betsy could say.

Toby looked pleadingly at her, 'Yes, Foxtop, she *can* hurt you. So please stop this *now*.'

Mimi grinned. 'Don't worry, Toby. I've evened the score, so I ain't worried no more. Now I've put all that behind me, I slept like a baby last night.'

* He who excuses himself, accuses himself.

'*You* might have done – but Betsy won't, and her mother won't! Revenge easily escalates. Sicilian vendettas start over some minor grievance, then a hundred years later – after two families have been decimated – none of them can remember what started the violence in the first place!'

'Don't worry, Toby. After all, we ain't Sicilian peasants.'

* * *

Two nights after the three friends returned to London Mimi was woken by a crash from the floor above. She jumped from her bed, fumbled for her bedside candle and matches, then prudently decided not to leave her room, for she could now hear angry voices upstairs. Instead, she tiptoed to the door, and quietly opened it an inch.

Overhead, she heard Baz's angry voice. 'I thought I could trust you!'

Toby broke in. 'So you can, but—'

'Two can play at that game, you know!'

'No, Baz, *no*! . . . It only happened once—'

'That's what they all say!'

'But neither of us meant it. And we were so tipsy that neither of us can remember it!'

'That's *also* what they all say!'

'Honestly, we didn't intend to deceive you – and we *haven't* deceived you.'

'You can't expect *me* to believe that neither you nor Mimi had anything to do with this blooming bun in her oven!'

Mimi could hear the hurt that lay behind Baz's angry voice.

'Baz, *please* don't go!'

Mimi withdrew quickly as she heard an upstairs door slam. Somebody stamped down the stairs. The front door crashed shut.

Prudently, she jumped back into bed, blew out the candle and pulled the eiderdown over her head. It was really none of her business. This was between Baz and Toby. It would all blow over in a couple of weeks. Baz would just have to get used to the idea ... She wished she didn't feel so sorry for him.

Friday 1 May 1908. Betsy's digs, Lambeth

'You're as good as that bitch any day! *Better!*' In their Lambeth bedroom, Mrs Bridges loyally but unsuccessfully tried to comfort Betsy, who lay face down on the bed, and howled, 'She's got a husband and a home *and* her own bloody theatre! She's a star and I'm still in the chorus! Explain *that* to me, Ma!' Betsy sat up and waved away the little brown bottle of MacKenzie's smelling salts offered by her mother. She rummaged under her pillow and produced a crumpled letter. She swung her feet to the floor.

Seated on the edge of the bed, Betsy continued to drop tears on the letter. 'I *know* as Mr Ziegfeld was really interested in me – otherwise why would he have asked me for a *second* audition? So that dressing room gossip must be true!' She peered through her reddened eyes at the letter. 'Mr Ziegfeld cancelled my audition yesterday – and you've seen this morning's *Gazette*!' Betsy snatched up the crumpled newspaper and read aloud, in a deliberately snobbish voice, ' "The famous impresario Mr Florenz Ziegfeld sailed yesterday for New York in the SS *Moravia*, accompanied by a retinue that includes his new French discovery, Mademoiselle Zilda, whom Mr Ziegfeld confidently predicts will be the next Mistinguett." ' Another tear splashed on the letter. 'Oh, Ma, what's to become of me? I'm twenty-one years old and *nothing's* happened yet!'

Mrs Bridges, hair still in curlers and hairnet, shuffled in worn slippers and Jaeger dressing gown to Betsy's side; gently she stroked Betsy's dishevelled fair hair. 'Don't blame yourself, dearie. It's all *her* fault! That little bitch is just as jealous of you as all the rest.'

Betsy stopped sobbing and looked up, puzzled. 'No, Ma. Mimi ain't *never* been jealous of me.'

'Course she is! Why else should she wreck your chance of a trip to New York? It's thanks to *her* that you missed your Big Chance!'

Betsy nodded slowly, relieved to be able to blame her failure on somebody else. Mollified, she dried her eyes. She picked up the *Gazette*, and again looked at the list of people who had sailed to New York on the previous day. Thoughtfully she said, 'Ma, maybe I'd stand more of a chance if we went somewhere new, where the agents aren't sick of seeing me; somewhere as I'd be a fresh face. Ma, when my contract ends in December, why *don't* we sail to New York . . . by ourselves?'

Mrs Bridges looked up sharply, as she realized that Betsy was serious. She considered the idea. 'We've got enough saved . . . You've never had any trouble landing a job . . . There's certainly nothing to hold us *here* . . . *Why not?*' She added, grimly, 'But I'll not forget what that bitch done to you! One day we'll get our own back on her, you'll see.'

Betsy cheered up at this thought. 'Yes, some day I'm going to show Mimi she ain't . . . *isn't* . . . going to stand in my way – *and* I'll make her sorry that she did!'

Chapter Seven

Sunday 20 September 1908. Fitzroy Square

Baz continued to visit Fitzroy Square during Mimi's pregnancy, but their relationship had subtly changed; he no saw longer her as his pal and his alibi, and she was aware of his new guardedness that hid pain and jealousy.

After his initial astonishment, Toby became increasingly intrigued by the thought of being a father – especially when he saw how delighted his parents were. Upon hearing of his news, Sir Octavius had whispered triumphantly to this wife, 'I *told* you that marriage would cure him!'

As each month passed, Toby became more solicitous of Mimi; she teased that he treated her as if she were as fragile as the china cupid on her bedside table. He refused to allow her on stage, she was to take no chances with their precious child; she was to cease wearing stays; she was to get up late in the morning; she was to stroll slowly through the park, to rest in the afternoon, and go to bed early.

'Might as well move into a convent,' Mimi grumbled, but not forcefully, for she felt nauseated and tired throughout her pregnancy.

Conveniently, she went into labour just after breakfast, on a tranquil, golden September Sunday, when Toby had no evening show at the Minerva, where *The Mystery of Fernhurst Grange* continued to play to full houses.

Mimi's first intimation of birth was a slight cramping sensation in her stomach. Why did everyone make such a fuss about this pain? It excited her, she was looking forward to this momentous event, and also to not feeling nauseous for the first time in nine months.

She retired to the pretty lace serenity of her bedroom, and asked Daisy to bring her a glass of champagne and send a message to the doctor. After Daisy had hobbled off, Mimi told Toby to stop twittering round her, like an old mother hen; oh, all right, she wouldn't have any champagne.

When the doctor appeared, he said it would be at least twenty-four hours before anything happened but, nevertheless, he would alert the midwife. After he had left, because Mimi felt perfectly well, she pulled on a cinnamon silk negligée and descended to the dining room for the midday meal.

As Toby carved the roast leg of lamb, Mimi suddenly felt as if iron hands were trying to twist her stomach in two. Gasping for breath, fists clenched, she bent over the table, her face white, perspiration on her forehead. With panic in her voice, she muttered, 'I wish I'd never started this.' Her body now felt so puny and defenceless, while the hard bulge of the baby seemed so ominously large.

Toby dropped the carving knife, dashed to Mimi's side, carefully picked her up, and carried her up the stairs. Mimi's waters broke just before she reached her bed.

Toby hollered for Daisy, who was in the kitchen. Excited, Daisy ordered the cook to boil plenty of hot water, Madam had started.

Toby hailed a cab, and headed for the doctor's Harley Street house, only a few minutes distant. Unfortunately the doctor was attending another birth in Baker Street, but when Toby returned to Fitzroy Square he was informed by the excited housemaid that the midwife and her girl had already arrived. He hurried upstairs.

Briskly in charge of Mimi's bedroom, the midwife, built like a boxer, with a large apron draped over her nurse's uniform, had no intention of allowing a husband into her delivery room: the study was where he belonged, with a decanter of port, nothing stronger, mind. She rolled up her sleeves, pulled back the bedclothes, pushed up Mimi's nightgown and started her examination. Stretched on the bed, Mimi howled and clutched the brass bars of her bedhead, then yanked her knees up on either side of her stomach, as pain shot up through her body.

The midwife calmly held both hands on either side of Mimi's stomach to feel her contraction, then bent down and peered closely at her cervix. 'Half a crown size, we shouldn't have long to wait.' She settled herself into a fireside armchair and asked Daisy for a nice strong cup of tea.

From time to time, Mimi gasped, 'Where's that bloody doctor?'

The midwife wiped Mimi's face, dabbed eau de Cologne on her hands and forehead. 'He'll come as soon as he can, madam, but you're as safe with me as you are with him: I've been bringing babies into this world for nigh on thirty years.'

At last her pattern of pain changed.

'Not long now,' said the midwife brightly.

'You've been saying that for ten bloody hours,' gasped Mimi, wondering if this pain would ever end. Surely this could not be normal? No wonder so many women died in childbirth! Briefly she wondered whether *she* would die. She didn't really care.

'Push, madam, *push*! I can see the top of baby's head! ... You're nearly there, madam ... Push when I tell you and *only* then ... We don't want baby to come out too fast, do we?'

Mimi summoned up the last of her will-power to pant between contractions, as ordered, and push only when the midwife allowed her to do so. With a final mighty effort she felt a slithering sensation ... and then relief, for her baby entered the world.

The midwife had been correctly cautious, for Mimi's baby was born with the umbilical cord wrapped around his neck, and a too-fast delivery might have strangled him at birth. Quickly the midwife disentangled, tied, and cut it, before turning away to attend to the baby. With a glass tube she sucked the mucus from his mouth, then lightly slapped the child's sticky little buttocks; after he gave a frail cry, she handed the wriggling body to her girl, to wash.

The midwife leaned over Mimi and smiled. 'You have a beautiful boy, madam.'

'Never again,' muttered the exhausted Mimi.

The midwife smiled indulgently. 'That's what they all say, madam.'

Sunday 4 October 1908. Fitzroy Square

Two weeks after the birth of her son, Mimi had an unexpected visitor: Jessie Allen, former manager of the Jenkins Theatrical Touring Company. Mimi looked up as her visitor poked her head around the door. Instinctively, her hand flew up to conceal the scar on the left of her face and surreptitiously pull her hair down to cover it. She was delighted to see Jessie's unremarkable square-jawed face, her hair pulled back in a bun beneath an umber felt hat decorated with pheasant feathers. As Jessie entered the bedroom, Mimi saw that she also carried a shawl-wrapped baby.

'Snap!' beamed Jessie and the corners of her brown eyes crinkled behind gold-rimmed spectacles.

'You too, Jessie! *When?* . . . Don't talk too loud, Max is asleep, at last, thank Gawd.' Mimi nodded towards the bottom of her bed, where an elaborate primrose organdie-draped cradle looked a cross between a tent and a ball gown.

'Twenty-five inches long and eight pounds, at birth,' Mimi said proudly. 'Toby named him after his pal, Max Beerbohm.'

Jessie shuddered. 'Don't remind me. My Felicity will be two months old next Tuesday.' She handed her chubby infant to Mimi, who stared into extraordinary eyes: the clear crystalline blue reminded her of a sunny sky after a snow storm.

'Them eyes are going to crack a few hearts, Jessie.'

'That's what my Tom says.' Jessie settled in a rosebud-smothered bedside chair. 'He says he's sorry not to see you, but he's busy packing up, after the end of our summer season.' She had married the lead comic in a concert party that performed on the pier at Southend-on-Sea. As amiable as he was unambitious, Tom did panto in winter, and in between he took anything he could get, mostly Number Three tours.

As well as her father's beautiful eyes, Jessie's daughter

had also inherited his Scandinavian-blond colouring. Luckily, the little kid doesn't take after her mam, thought Mimi, although she hoped that Felicity had inherited Jessie's good heart.

'I was sorry to hear about Jolly Joe,' Mimi said, sadly.

'Poor old thing. Choked on a fish bone, gone in two minutes. I hear the Company disbanded.' They exchanged more cheerful news of other old friends, until Jessie asked, carefully casual, 'How's Baz doing?'

'Got a supper act at the Clarence Hotel.'

'Baz must have been surprised when you had the baby.' Jessie prodded again.

Mimi winked. 'Don't pass it on, but Toby only managed it the once. We'd both had a drop too much. Couldn't neither of us remember anything afterwards. But there's no doubt who Max's dad is – he's got a real Toby jug.' Max had been born with dark hair, blue eyes, and the Fane features. When first he held his perfect, helpless son in his arms, Toby had felt an unexpected thrill of love, pride and protection. After Max's birth, Mimi's attitude towards Toby had become similarly tender, indulgent, almost maternal. Lady Fane, who noticed this, was able to relax: Toby really *was* cured.

Jessie giggled. 'Who would've thought you'd end up with all this?' She waved her arm around Mimi's untidy rose-patterned bedroom, as a starched, uniformed maid entered labouring beneath the weight of a silver tea tray. After the maid had left, Jessie said wistfully, 'It must be fun to be rich, Mimi.' She accepted a china cup wreathed with strawberries, and added sadly, 'You've no need to worry about hard times.'

'Sometimes *I* still find it hard to believe,' Mimi said almost apologetically, knowing that Jessie still led a hand-to-mouth existence, with no home of her own and few possessions.

Jessie's thoughts were much the same, until she remembered what it was like to wake every morning, snuggled in Tom's muscular arms; until she remembered how she enjoyed waking her man by gently blowing on the golden down of his forearm, or by stroking her hands along his warm, strong back. Tom had not managed it only the once: they enjoyed a passionate, erotic marriage.

A wail erupted from the crib at the end of the bed. Instantly, Mimi was as alert as a cat. From the moment when she first held him in her arms, Mimi had known that her son was, and always would be, the only man in her life.

Sunday 4 April 1909. The Plaza Hotel, New York

Once a month, on a Sunday afternoon, Mrs Bridges and Betsy caught the horse bus up Sixth Avenue, to take afternoon tea in the Palm Court lounge of the opulent Plaza Hotel. Mrs Bridges hoped that one day Betsy might take such splendid gentility for granted. In the meantime, the Bridges pretended that they already belonged in such surroundings, as they stepped slowly up the crimson carpet of the wide entrance steps, saluted by the uniformed commissionaire.

The mirrored white-and-gold lounge was encircled by marble columns and tall palm trees; a faintly moustachioed lady in black trilled a harp, accompanied by a pianist with centre-parted hair in evening dress. The Bridges always lingered as long as they dared over a single pot of tea, waving aside the tiny, expensive, triangular sandwiches and ornate creations on the pastry trolley, but they always left a generous tip to ensure a welcome from the waiter on their next visit.

One Sunday in early April they were rising reluctantly to leave when the murmur of the conversation in the Palm Court rose an octave, and was immediately followed by an expectant hush.

Like everyone else, Mrs Bridges and Betsy turned their heads towards the entrance from the hotel lobby, where four overdressed, very pretty young ladies stood beside two men. Betsy stiffened as she recognized the parrot nose and imperious voice of Mr Ziegfeld, laughing with his companion, a big, dark man in his late thirties. The entire room surreptitiously watched as this little party was ushered to the best table, where French champagne was quickly produced and caviar served with a flourish.

Betsy's violet eyes focused on the companion; he had a powerful chest and grey eyes that stared sharply from beneath thick black brows; a crooked nose was set in an amiable, battered face above a straight and ruthless mouth.

'Looks Irish, might well be a prizefighter,' Mrs Bridges sniffed: clearly not a gentleman.

Betsy beckoned a waiter and flashed him a black-fringed glance; in her soft, whispering, little-girl lisp, she asked, 'Could you tell me the name of that gentleman with Mr Ziegfeld?'

The waiter tingled from his Macassar-oiled hair to the darned toes of his socks. 'I'll check at the reception desk, miss.' He returned, to report that the gentleman was a Mr J. O'Brien, owner of a West Coast chain of theatres; Mr O'Brien had spent a week in the Vanderbilt Suite, but was checking out that evening.

Mrs Bridges immediately changed her attitude. 'Why

don't you walk slowly past Mr O'Brien?' she suggested to Betsy. 'Or perhaps I should tip the reception clerk to tell us where his suite is, and then you might knock on the door by mistake, and in that way strike up an acquaintance.' Her standards of masculine eligibility and female chastity had lowered at the same rate as their savings had dwindled.

'Ma, I don't want to be thrown out of the Plaza by a couple of house detectives,' Betsy objected. 'And do you imagine those four young madams will let him out of their sight for one instant?'

That night, Betsy lay in bed and wondered what it would feel like to be whirled around in a waltz by the muscular arms of Mr J. O'Brien. What would it be like to drift with him to a moonlit balcony, to feel those strong arms pull her close to him, feel that hard, straight mouth on hers . . . ? Overexcited by these frustrated sexual yearnings, Betsy did not fall asleep until dawn.

The reality of the Bridges' life in New York was very different to their teatime dreams at the Plaza, and some aspects of it had been an unpleasant shock to both women, who had sailed towards a New Future with unrealistically high hopes and overestimated job vacancy reports, correlated on the Business grapevine.

When their ship had docked in New York Harbour, after a rough trip from Southampton, the first thing that impressed the Bridges was the bitter cold. It had stopped snowing, but as they waited on deck to disembark the freezing, howling January wind tore inside their buttoned-up coats – even sneaked beneath their underclothes – and immediately chilled them to the bone: they had never known such numbingly cold weather in England.

'Looking for a porter, sister, or just surprised to find

the streets ain't paved with gold?' an amiable porter asked Mrs Bridges, having looked her over and decided that she could afford to pay him. Few could, off the immigrant boats from Europe. Many newcomers could afford to travel no further, so had crowded into the Lower East Side slums, which now contained half a million Jewish immigrants alone; they had travelled steerage across the Atlantic, hoping for a better life, but found only poorly paid work in badly lit sweatshops; they lived in over-crowded, unhygienic, disease-ridden tenements, their exteriors zigzagged by blackened fire escapes.

A porter, who addressed her as 'sister', and behaved as if he were her equal – the cheek! Mrs Bridges pointed her nose a little further towards heaven as he amiably located their trunks and heaved them to a cab, which Mrs Bridges then directed to a rooming house on West Thirty-Seventh Street. She had been told that Ma Jackson would house and feed them, for seven dollars a week each.

As the cab creaked away from the pier, both women looked out excitedly at the city. Many buildings were still in the process of construction: there seemed to be a dusty, dirty building site on every block. Of course they had seen newspaper illustrations of New York skyscrapers, but were not prepared for the experience of driving between them as they reared up to the sky on either side of straight streets that seemed to go on for ever. It felt like being at the bottom of a gorge! Mrs Bridges said it made her feel dizzy just to look up.

As soon as they arrived at Ma Jackson's rooming house the Bridges felt at home, for as they unstrapped their trunks in a third-floor back bedroom they could hear an unseen piano tinkle, a guitar twang and voices trilling scales as invisible people repeatedly rehearsed the popular tunes of the day. The new boarders would not be so pleased when they realized that from early morning until well into the night they would hear similar music, the shuffle and tap of some hoofer's routine, or the booming voice of an unseen actor rehearsing his lines.

After meals, which everyone ate in the big kitchen, the boarders entertained each other. The younger ones performed long dramatic speeches from some part they hoped one day to play: the singers made the overhead oil lamp tremble with the strength of their delivery, and the dancers twirled in tap routines around the kitchen table.

As Betsy was not allowed out in the evenings without her mother, and as they could rarely afford to take themselves out on the town, the Bridges much appreciated this cheerful home entertainment. Quickly they learned the language differences and Betsy learned to pronounce useful local Yiddish words such as *schlep*, *schlock*, and *shmuck*.

After unpacking, the Bridges had planned to spend a few days familiarizing themselves with the city, 'getting the lie of the land and making a few important contacts', as Mrs Bridges put it. They had not realized that New York City was built on Manhattan Island so that almost every cross street ended in a view of the sea. Surrounded by water and the Atlantic Ocean beyond its southern tip, Manhattan Island was always windy and vigorous, and seemed to impart this vigour to its inhabitants. The Bridges soon found that everyone – labourers on building sites, corner grocery store owners, drivers of horse-drawn drays, and department store assistants – all had confident plans to make their fortunes, for there was an exultant, tinglish atmosphere in the city which made people feel that not even the sky was their limit: that with hard work and talent, *any* person could get anywhere, and do anything, in this new city of endless possibility.

For their first week, everything in the noisy city that was new to them excited the two Britishers, and Betsy's mother lost her scolding air, becoming almost girlish as they explored the different areas of Manhattan.

Mrs Bridges didn't much care for pretty bohemian Greenwich Village: she didn't understand how educated people like writers and artists could live with such disregard for dust and grime. But she loved the strange bright pink and emerald colours of China Town ('so *very* foreign'), while Betsy preferred the noisy joviality and mouth-watering cookpot smells of Little Italy; they both felt a little alarmed when first they found themselves in the crowded streets of the Lower East Side, nervously edging their way between pushcart pedlars shouting their wares to Greeks, Poles, Egyptians and Arabs, all hustling for a living.

Yet only a short streetcar ride from this alarming yet exciting noisy oriental-bazaar jumble of strange languages, clothes and faces were the glamorous midtown department stores around which the Bridges strolled, pretending to be purchasers, for they could spare no money from their savings.

Both the Bridges also enjoyed the unaccustomed food of New York; in particular, although it triggered her heartburn, Mrs Bridges could not resist the piquant German–Jewish food: pickled herrings, chopped chicken livers, hot pastrami on rye bread, and a combination of smoked salmon and cream cheese on a bun that she learned to call 'lox 'n' bagel'. Betsy loved the street-corner pickle stands and ice cream carts, and the coffee shops that served sugary doughnuts, marshmallow pie and her top favourite: cheesecake.

Most of the town seemed as lively as a circus, especially the area around Fourteenth Street, which swarmed with sailors looking for adventure in saloons where pianos banged and gaudy women beckoned; here, penny arcades lured with peephole machines, automatic strength-testers, fortune-tellers, and other fascinating fairground machines that harvested a steady stream of coins for the arcade owners.

After their week of sightseeing, during which the Bridges had made no contact more important than Ma Jackson's other boarders and the doormen at the Plaza, they confidently went in search of a job. Each winter morning they set out with baked potatoes in their muffs, to keep their hands warm; later, they ate them for lunch; sometimes they also purchased cheap, delicious titbits from one of the little wheeled carts that stood on street corners, and sold eat-in-the-hand food to New Yorkers, who always seemed to be in a hurry, clearly too busy to stop for a meal.

By the end of their second week in New York both mother and daughter were silently anxious, for Betsy had found it impossible to get work in a vaudeville theatre, the closest thing to a British music hall. The standards of singing and dancing needed for chorus work in New York were far higher than those to which she had been accustomed; good singers and dancers were two a penny on Broadway; and there were far more pretty girls in New York than there were in London. In America, no girl wanted to do domestic work, every pretty girl wanted to go on the stage; and she didn't just stay at home and dream about it. Betsy was astonished by the pep and gumption of the American girls she met at auditions, who were far more enterprising and energetic than the European girls she knew, except for Mimi, of course.

Although she would never admit it, Betsy still caught herself wistfully wishing that she could tell Mimi about the odd things in this strange whirlwind of a city and she longed to unburden her worried little family wage earner's heart to the only person she had ever been able to: she couldn't possibly give her mother the heebie-jeebies, her heart was bad enough already.

Betsy now visited agents alone, to save the second streetcar or subway ticket. Although polished daily, her boots soon grew dusty as she covered block after block of city sidewalks, walking from agent to agent, without success. Every evening, Mrs Bridges comforted Betsy and every morning she spurred on her dispirited daughter, often by shrewdly reminding her of Mimi's perfidy. The Bridges had arrived in New York to find that Ziegfeld's new discovery, Zilda, was the toast of New York: Americans were mesmerized by her shapely legs, entranced by her clear singing voice and throaty French accent, intrigued by her surly personality. One mention of Mimi's sabotage always hardened Betsy's resolve. She was damned if she was going to let Mimi wreck her life! She would show her! One day, she would not only drink tea at the Plaza – she would live there!

Each woman kept up the other's spirits, and on the rare occasions when both grew despondent about the future Mrs Bridges (who knew the importance of keeping up Betsy's morale) firmly took her daughter out on the spree, to a nickelodeon. (Surprisingly, Betsy's mother had become an instant nickelodeon fanatic.) These opened at midday, closed late at night and charged a nickel for admission to the cheap, respectable moving pictures. Like their audiences, the nickelodeon proprietors were often Jewish immigrants so they understood the hopes and fears of the city poor, and realized why the long lines of people waited shivering in the cold to enter their house of dreams. Seated in some dark, stuffy, peanut-shell-strewn converted small shop the Bridges forgot their own anxieties as they watched a terrified eyeball-rolling heroine bound to the rail tracks as the express train approached. The Bridges never realized that they were helping to make economic history.

* * *

Eventually Betsy tried to get straight work in the legitimate theatre, so she joined the actors who did the round of agents and talked in self-confident voices about past and future contracts; but performers were normally engaged late in the summer or early in the fall. She was told by another young would-be actress, Elsie Emerald (christened Elsie Kleinhopf), whose grandmother had been in vaudeville, that until recently most American towns had a theatre with a resident company of actors and a repertoire of plays. In addition, many touring companies had taken their productions from one town to the next. But Broadway producers with a hit now sent duplicate companies on the road, cunningly advertised as 'direct from New York'. 'So everyone wants to see the latest Broadway winners and it's goodbye to the local stock company: we haven't had one in Cleveland for years!'

'What difference does it make?' Betsy was puzzled.

Elsie explained that without them, theatre managers throughout the USA were forced to book their shows from New York through a booking agent – 'Who's supposed to plan an acting company's season with as little travel as possible.' Inevitably the smartest booking agents had developed into producers, then, 'Six of these guys formed the Syndicate. They figure they don't risk nothing if they don't put on nothing that ain't been seen before, so you got a choice of costume romances, melodrama, musical comedy or revue spectaculars. You won't see nothing else.' Elsie further explained that the Syndicate was powerful enough to make all those who opposed it wish that they hadn't. 'If stars hold out for a high salary, they find no theatre'll book 'em. If an owner turns down the Syndicate deal, a new theatre will be opened nearby, to put him out of business. The Syndicate controls the entire profession from the top jobs to the bottom ones. That's why we're finding it tough, honey.' Betsy was silent. She had not realized that without powerful contacts it was almost impossible for an unknown outsider to break into American show business.

'Don't look so glum, honey,' Elsie advised her. 'How about we share a chocolate milk shake before our next call?'

Monday 12 April 1909

Late on a sunny morning in mid-April, Betsy and Elsie were sharing a cherry soda in the automat on Forty-Second Street – a favourite resting place for actors making the rounds – when Elsie suggested that they both try for work at the Biograph: the going rate for movie performers was five dollars a day, and as the films were silent there were no lines to learn.

Betsy hesitated. 'I'll lose standing as an actress with theatre people if they see me in a movie.' She knew how the live theatre was contemptuous of the 'flicks', an upstart profession that did not need actors with an actor's greatest asset – his voice.

'Nobody's going to spot you, Betsy, and the money sure is worth it,' Elsie persuaded her. So the two girls caught a streetcar, then walked to 11 East Fourteenth Street, where Biograph had opened a new studio. As they approached the terraced, pinkish-brown stone house, the girls could see that it seethed with activity, as people ran up and down the entrance steps and shirtsleeved men in aprons carried furniture and equipment in or out of the building. When the girls had climbed those steps to the front door, they read a sign: NO VACANCIES FOR ACTORS UNTIL TOMORROW.

On the following day, the two girls returned at seven in the morning. Betsy wore her best clothes: a pale-green linen coat with cream stockings, shoes and a wide-brimmed cream hat. She was anxious to make the best possible impression, for the Bridges had nearly exhausted their savings, and when that point was reached both women would have to try for waitress work.

Outside the Biograph a little group of actors who also hoped for extra work was already clustered around the bottom of the steps, waiting for the executives to arrive. Half an hour later, when it started to rain hard, the actors were allowed to huddle in the front entrance hall, where they listened to the clatter of typewriters and the shrill of telephone bells. Betsy's girl-friend whispered that the doors in the entrance hall led to the front offices. Scripts were studied in the story department; the publicity office wrote the weekly bulletins of new movie releases; in the accounts department bookkeepers wore green eye-shades as they compiled the cost of each movie.

Eventually the door to the tiny casting office was opened. The casting director sat behind a table piled with photographs and typed details of actors; shirtsleeves rolled up, a pencil stuck behind his ear, he scrutinized each actor in turn, then laconically said either, 'OK,' or 'Sorry.' He okayed Betsy and Elsie, told them to keep their own clothes on and get upstairs to the studio on the first floor. Elsie explained to Betsy that movies were shot on the three upper floors, while the dressing room and the props room were in the basement.

At the next floor the two girls entered a chaotic studio, once a ballroom; propped against the walls inside were folded flats, rolled-up carpets, and clusters of arc lights on tall black metal tripods. Because it contained so many lamps the room was very hot; like the nickelodeons, it stank of stale cigarettes, peanuts and perspiration.

Just inside the door was a roll-top desk in front of which the movie director assigned roles to the actors. Betsy and her friend were told to sit at one of the tables in the far end of the room, which had been made to look like the corner of a New York café, with red-checked tablecloths and dark bentwood chairs.

The two girls clattered down to the basement, where Elsie taught Betsy to put on greasepaint so that she made her face very light and her mouth very dark, in order for her face to register in long shot. There was no Wardrobe mistress, so each actor who had been told to change chose his or her own clothes to suit the part, digging from trunks of crumpled hired costumes; they changed in crowded cubicle dressing rooms that stank of chemicals, also stored in the basement. At midday, costume trunks would be closed, Elsie whispered, and the tops used as tables, from which the cast ate their lunch. If a scene ended late, they might not eat their midday meal until the end of the afternoon in which case the workday would probably stretch to midnight, or later.

The director – a commanding, lean man – instructed the cast on set, then rehearsed the scene. Betsy and Elsie simply sat at a table and pretended to talk. The lights were adjusted, the cameraman carefully watched the rehearsal.

Suddenly, the central door of the café burst open. A little street urchin on roller skates entered, clutching a leg of lamb. The lad was pursued by a white-aproned storekeeper; every time the storekeeper nearly grabbed the skilful skater, the boy neatly dodged to escape, whereupon the storekeeper fell into somebody's soup, or knocked the dishes off the table, or fell into some lady's lap, at which she pretended to scream. Eventually, the storekeeper hit the urchin over the head with a chair; as he missed the boy, the chair smashed to pieces on a bowler-hatted man, who then slid – seemingly unconscious – beneath his table. The roller skater then escaped by jumping clean through the non-existent restaurant window, leaving the café in chaos.

As arrogantly authoritative as he was painstaking, the director worked his cast and technicians as hard as he drove himself. After further long and careful rehearsals, a large window in a frame was fitted in the back of the café, and the scene was finally shot in a few minutes.

The director blew a whistle. The unconscious bowler-hatted man briskly scrambled to his feet, and everyone looked expectantly at the director, who laconically said,

'That's OK!' Someone shouted, 'Strike!' and the shirt-sleeved men in aprons appeared to remove the scenery. The actors all wandered to the other end of the room where they smoked and chatted as the restaurant props were removed, and the far end of the ballroom swiftly turned into the cubicled changing room of a swimming pool for the next shot.

'Why wasn't the boy hurt when he jumped through the window?' Betsy asked Elsie, who laughed, 'The glass window was made of sugar sheet, and the chair used to wallop that guy was made of light yucca wood.'

'Who *is* the boy? What's the story of this movie?'

'Oh, the usual sort of thing. *I* don't know,' Elsie shrugged. 'Only the director has the script and it's always under his arm: we do what he tells us. These stories are always simple so they can be understood by immigrants who can't speak English properly, and be sold abroad.'

All the frantic action had taken place to hectic jazz music, played very fast and loudly, on an upright piano just off the set. Elsie told Betsy that suitable music was always played on a movie set, to create the mood of the scene and make the actors feel excited, miserable, terrified or amorous, whichever emotion was required: some stars liked loud jazz to wake them up, some liked violins to make them feel smoochy for a love scene.

After the next scene had been shot, the extras were dismissed for the day. As Betsy left the studio the director, who was also responsible for finding interesting new types, hurried over and asked for her address and telephone number. He wanted to test her on the following Monday. He told her to ask for Mr Griffith.

Suddenly, Elsie was no longer so friendly and informative.

As the two girls left for the day, they stopped at the downstairs office, where each was given a little brown envelope with her name on it. Betsy's envelope contained three dollars. Betsy couldn't believe it! Three dollars for working only two hours! For doing nothing!

Suddenly, Betsy changed her attitude to the movies.

* * *

The next morning the studio telephoned Betsy at Ma Jackson's place, not to test her, but to ask her to get there on the double, to be in another scene. Betsy was to wear the same outfit that she had worn on the previous day, the pea-soup coat with the pale hat.

When Betsy arrived in the ballroom she saw that the far end had been altered again, to look like a bakery: cakes and biscuits were laid in rows upon a counter. She was told to stand in front of the counter, buy a cake from the salesgirl, and then walk out of the shop door, just before the lead actress walked in through it.

Once again Mr Griffith rehearsed his actors in every movement and expression. Once again they were as obedient as puppets, except for Miss Pickford, the leading lady, a sixteen-year-old Canadian stage actress; the Biograph hoped that her dimpled smile, golden ringlets and combination of innocent, childlike charm and adult potential would replace Florence Lawrence, the world's first movie star, who had recently been lured away by a rival studio.

Betsy watched and listened as the tiny leading lady twisted a golden ringlet round her finger and argued with Mr Griffith about the expression that she should wear on her face as she entered the shop. Eventually, the leading lady said – quite loudly and clearly – that she resented Mr

Griffith's patronizing attitude towards her, and she would like to remind him that she had been a stage success on Broadway.

Actors on the set held their breath, for they realized that the girl was also silently reminding Mr Griffith that *he* had *not* been a success as an actor, on stage.

Eventually, Mr Griffith nonchalantly shrugged his lean shoulders, and said, 'OK, Miss Pickford, do it your way – and then we'll do it my way.'

After that, the director rehearsed the golden-ringleted girl again and again and again – far more than was necessary, Betsy suspected.

* * *

On Wednesday, the Biograph again telephoned and asked Betsy to appear after lunch dressed for a dinner scene in a society mansion. Thankful that she had been in Ma Jackson's kitchen to take the call, and wondering whether she might now be given a small part, Betsy quickly changed into a mauve taffeta evening frock, pinned up her hair, and ran for the subway.

When she arrived she was told to sit at a little table in the background, and pretend to talk to the man sitting opposite her. It was sadly clear to her that once again she was merely part of the background scenery, but she firmly reminded herself that she had not yet had her test. Disappointed, she collected her pay envelope and stood on the wide steps which led down to the sidewalk. When she felt a tap on her shoulder, she turned, and vaguely recognized a man she had heard called Mack. As big as a bear, with unusually long arms and a good-natured grin, Mack pushed back the brim of his hat, took the cigar out of his mouth, spat on the step, and slowly surveyed Betsy from the top of her head to her toes.

Outraged, Betsy immediately ran down the steps, away from this impudent man.

Mack clattered down the steps behind her, and caught up with Betsy on the sidewalk. 'I wasn't making a pass at you, young lady,' he explained, 'I also act here, and I want to give you a bit of advice. Almost all movie audiences are poor so they always sympathize with the ill-treated little maid or the penniless orphan girl, not the society debutante you played this afternoon. So after you're tested next week, try to get the badly-treated-girl parts, because that'll build up your audience popularity.'

'Thank you,' said Betsy icily. Upon reaching the street corner, she crossed the road to avoid her follower. She had no intention of playing a servant.

* * *

Before Betsy was tested, Mr Griffith carefully explained the difference between stage acting and movie acting. Stage actors expressed emotion through dialogue, and emphasized these emotions; in silent pictures, it was essential for Betsy to convey the emotion in the first few seconds of a scene, and to do this with her whole body: she had to behave in an unnatural way on set, in order to look natural on screen.

Betsy was nervous about personally receiving instructions from Mr Griffith, an aloof, self-assured man, who, Elsie had said, rarely mixed with the rest of the staff. Elsie had also told her that Mr Griffith worked seven days a week, every hour when not asleep. He spent his evenings and Sundays editing his work, reading future scenarios, or prowling round the streets of New York or sitting in nickelodeons to check out the competition. There was room for little else in his life – except sex. Elsie had warned Betsy that Mr Griffith took advantage of every girl who wanted to advance her career.

Like everyone else at the Biograph, Betsy now knew that Mr Griffith was obsessed by two female types: the saintly wife-and-mother, and the golden-haired virgin in the power of some bestial male sadist. Although Betsy was possibly the only virgin at the Biograph, she did not look one; she certainly had the angelic face that Mr Griffith liked for his virgins, but she was tall and well developed, with a splendid bust and hips, so she did not project his vulnerable child-woman as well as Mary Pickford; neither did she have the sweetness, charm and spunk of Pickford, or the pep and exuberance expected of a Biograph leading lady.

There was (as always) an additional problem. When working as an extra, she had moved naturally, but now, when attention was focused on her, she immediately became self-conscious and stiff. Although she obeyed Mr Griffith's direction, she moved from one pose to the next with no fluidity, as if she had been wound up by a key in her back. When asked to express emotion, she adopted one of her stock expressions: she raised her eyebrows, puckered her mouth, ducked her chin and looked upwards to indicate surprise; to indicate sorrow, she rolled her eyes upwards and opened her mouth, with her head hanging on one side. 'Like Christ on the cross,' muttered Billy, the cameraman.

Nevertheless, Billy agreed that Betsy's small-featured, exquisite face could be shot from any angle, and that certainly she was patient: she could stand without moving until they got exactly the right lighting on her face; in a few experimental close-ups, her pathetically glistening eyes and tremulous lips were sensationally effective.

Eventually Mr Griffith decided that Betsy was useless for comedy but could be used in drama, and should be shot as often as possible in close-up.

She was delighted with the ladylike parts she now received. She earned $35 a week – sometimes more, if there was a rush to finish a movie, and she worked six days a week. Every time Betsy's pay was increased, every time she was given a larger part, Mrs Bridges referred with smug satisfaction to Mimi, as in, 'You see, you done it, my girl, in spite of that bitch!' or, 'I hope they're showing your films in England, dear, so that bitch sees your beautiful face up on the silver screen.'

'That still won't make up for what she done to me, Ma,' Betsy once muttered sadly. She did not like to admit to herself that she still missed Mimi, the only girl who had never been jealous of her, whom she had considered as close as a sister. She still felt indignant about having the blame for Mimi's burns dumped on her alone although she also felt oddly guilty, which exasperated her.

'Don't you worry. She'll get what she deserves – and I hope I have a hand in it!' Mrs Bridges said, with grim satisfaction.

* * *

Once she became accustomed to the camera, and without a theatre audience to distract her, Betsy relaxed, improved, and then received bigger parts: eventually her pay was increased to $100 a week, which was three times more than she had been earning in the Gaiety chorus.

Now she was relieved and happy. She no longer felt

she was letting down her ma, and she enjoyed the playful atmosphere of the studio as much as the excitement and energy of teamwork. And despite her virginity, Betsy enjoyed the flirtation between takes; she treated the entire male sex with a warm indulgence – except for that impertinent Mack Sennett, who always hung around the studios, even when he wasn't needed to act. Non-stop, he peppered the director and technicians with questions about lighting, filming and editing methods.

* * *

The Biograph Company continued to work throughout muggy July and August, when the town was so humid that most of the theatres had closed down, for most of their patrons had fled the steaming city to spend the summer in seaside or mountain resorts; those who stayed did not want to spend an evening enclosed in a hot, stuffy theatre. Actors often followed their audiences to the country or the sea, where they played in small theatres, in summer stock companies which opened only during the summer holiday season.

The Bridges found the New York summer hotter than any they had experienced: the humidity made it exhausting to draw each moist breath, and Mrs Bridges complained that it was like trying to breathe in hot fog, it was that difficult to suck any air into your lungs. Betsy tried to shower as often as possible, for an hour after putting on a clean cotton blouse it would be drenched with sweat, while beneath her corsets her underwear was already unpleasantly damp by midday. She knew that everyone in the city felt listless, too exhausted to do anything that was not essential. She had seen slum inhabitants spend enervating summer evenings slowly fanning themselves on the dirty fire escapes, and often they slept on flat roofs. During the day, Betsy sometimes stopped to watch children dance in fountains of water that spurted from street fire hydrants; cops in hot dark uniforms clearly remembered their own childhoods and looked the other way as heat bounced relentlessly off the sidewalk and back in their faces.

Chapter Eight

Sunday 30 October 1910

Betsy and her mother were laughing with excitement as with the rest of Biograph's troupe they climbed onto the train to travel west, a trip of several uncomfortable days: Mr Griffith was taking his team to California to avoid the freezing winds and snows of a New York winter and benefit from the advantages recently discovered by a handful of movie-making pioneers. Betsy had heard that the climate was sunny all year round, which meant it was always possible to shoot outdoors in a wonderful variety of scenic locations: sea, desert, mountains, forest, farmland. And land was cheap.

Almost as soon as the train steamed out of the station, Mrs Bridges exclaimed, 'Well, I never!' She leaned forward, handed Betsy the *New York Post*, and stabbed her finger at an item headed ZILDA QUITS. Despite her wild success in Mr Ziegfeld's Follies, Zilda had become homesick, and no matter how much Mr Ziegfeld had offered her she had said firmly that no sum of money could compensate for the loss of *la belle France*, to which she had returned – now a national heroine, and clearly about to make a fortune from singing throbbing songs about what hell it was to be poor.

Twenty-three-year-old Betsy bit her lips to suppress

angry tears at the memory of Mimi's sabotage, and the subsequent anxiety of their first months in New York.

* * *

Upon arrival at the Santa Fe terminal, Betsy and her mother climbed down from the train into blinding sunshine, and were then shepherded to a waiting studio bus. As they bumped along the rough road the Bridges inhaled warm, dry air fragrant with jasmine, eucalyptus and geraniums; bougainvillaea, poinsettias and roses grew wild beside the roadside.

Clearly accustomed to the questions of new arrivals, the cheerful bus driver yelled to his passengers that Mexico lay to the south, to the north were the Santa Monica Mountains, to the west the Pacific Ocean (which they could not yet see from the bus), while to the east loomed the snow-capped San Gabriel Mountains. Their destination was built on high ground that caught the sea breeze; it was eight miles from Los Angeles, and twelve miles from the Pacific Ocean; the horseshoe of foothills to the east kept away both cold winter storms and hot desert winds. As the driver called out this helpful geographical detail, his passengers could feel on their faces a warm, dry breeze wafted from the desert, around the edges of which, he informed them, valleys were crammed with vineyards and orange, lemon and grapefruit orchards.

'Paradise,' sighed the Bridges, and everyone else, thinking of the bitter New York winter that they had escaped.

As the bus arrived at the straggling village of Hollywood, Betsy stuck her head out of the window. Eagerly, she stared at tall palm trees, bungalows in pink or tan stucco, shirtless whistling boys on bicycles. Some of the people strolling along the sidewalks wore thick yellow greasepaint and strange costumes: Red Indians in head-dresses stood on the street corner chatting with biblically clad men who waved cigarettes; Pilgrim Fathers chewed gum; from one studio, a crowd of pigtailed Orientals in traditional black pyjamas and brilliantly embroidered satin tops poured out to snatch a quick lunch.

Mr Griffith and his stars had been booked into the Hollywood Hotel, which had an elegant cool veranda lined by scarlet geraniums. The rest of the Biograph outfit were allocated to rooming houses, also with deep shaded porches. Everyone in the Company immediately rushed out to buy sunglasses from Hollywood's only drugstore.

'You sure I don't look a fool?' Mrs Bridges asked doubtfully, peering in the drugstore window at the twin black circles above her nose.

'Course not, Ma. Look over there, even Mack Sennett's wearing 'em.' On the street corner, Mr Sennett, pretending to be blind, was shuffling along with his arms groping before him, hollering, 'Who stole my stick?'

Among the many changes since Betsy joined the Biograph Company was the status of Mr Mack Sennett, who was now directing. He was a careful director; his cast always had fun and worked well together, with none of the tension on Mr Griffith's productions. Mack was ill educated and lacked what Mrs Bridges called 'polish', but he was highly intelligent, amusing and had packed a peculiar assortment of experience into his thirty-odd years: he had started work as a labourer; he had been a boxing trainer, and after that a chorus boy on Broadway. In 1908 he had joined the Biograph as an extra, and was quickly promoted to star parts.

The other major change had been the disappearance of

Mary Pickford, lured away by the IMP Company, for an astounding $175 a week salary. Betsy had not been asked to replace Pickford as she had hoped; instead, a young fifteen-year-old extra, Mabel Normand, had been chosen. Disappointed, Betsy was sure that *she* would have been just as good acting the poor-but-good-girls who always triumphed over seducers with centre partings in well-oiled black hair. And Betsy had *more* 'personality', the motion-picture euphemism for big breasts. Mabel was a likeable character so despite Betsy's initial jealousy they quickly became friendly. Mack Sennett instantly fell in love with Mabel, who had a lovely figure, big brown eyes, and an instinctive sense of comedy. She told Betsy that Mack's secret ambition was some day to direct his own pictures, in which Mabel would star. Mabel laughed.

* * *

Betsy quickly discovered that filming on the West Coast was totally different from New York. The movie factories, euphemistically called 'studios', worked their contracted actors like slaves; the day after a movie finished another one started. If a studio fell behind its shooting schedule it lost money, so actors were forced to endure gruelling conditions (twenty-four hours non-stop was not unusual) and studio doctors provided drugs to wake them up at five in the morning and knock them out again when they were too exhausted to sleep. Provided an actor was willing to accept these conditions – and Betsy was – then working on the West Coast had many compensations.

Here the studio was open to the sky, with only one area covered by canvas, to provide shade: everyone crowded into this space at noon, when they ate sandwiches from their lunch boxes, and drank coffee made on a little kerosene stove. The Biograph outfit filmed in sunshine, sometimes sixteen hours a day; work stopped on the open stage as soon as the sun went behind a cloud. On the rare dull days, the cast didn't bother to show up at the studio. When they wanted to find a new location, the entire company piled into studio automobiles and buses and drove until they found a suitable spot, where they all jumped out and checked their costumes. The crew followed the cast in trucks which contained the fold-up canvas chairs, the director's megaphone, and all the camera and shooting paraphernalia. Rehearsals were then watched by the cameraman, who shot the scene, and then off they drove again, to look for the next setting.

Betsy was still directed by Mr Griffith, who dominated his sets and liked to act out every part himself in rehearsal. As aloof and authoritative as ever, he always wore a tropical pith helmet or an elegant Panama hat, with laced boots and jodhpurs. The crew dressed in open-necked shirts and blue jeans, with boots and leather leggings in the desert regions: they had to protect their legs from cacti and rattlesnakes, and their necks from the sun so they turned their flat caps backwards, or else wore wide-brimmed cowboy hats, pulled well down.

To underline Mr Griffith's rapier dominance, he often deliberately stirred up jealousy among his actors, perhaps by asking several girls to try a leading role when he had already decided who should get it. When – as invariably happened – Mabel was chosen rather than Betsy, Mrs Bridges would quickly comfort her daughter. 'Remember where we was – were – two years ago? You can't go up in just a day, any more than Rome did.' She would firmly resurrect Betsy's optimism and determination by prophesying that soon her little girl would be a star, and *that* would put Mimi's nose permanently out of joint.

Saturday 25 May 1912. Greenwich Village, New York

Shortly after the Company returned to Manhattan for the spring, Mabel Normand and Betsy were waiting in the East 11th Street studio for the lights to be finally adjusted on a streetcar set. Casually, Mabel asked, 'Like to have supper with me and Mack, next Saturday evening?'

Betsy hesitated. 'Are you also asking . . . I mean, I don't like to leave my ma alone on a Saturday night . . .'

The still inviolate twenty-five-year-old Betsy continued to be guarded like a Spanish infanta by Mrs Bridges, who managed to combine the anxious attention of a mother hen with an inexorable eagle's eye. Betsy had been drilled not to throw herself away on some handsome young rapscallion with no sense of duty or responsibility, but that did not stop her flirting delicately with any such young man who appeared at the East 11th Street studio and sensed that dormant passion lay below her icy aloofness.

Only at night, just before drifting to sleep, did Betsy imagine herself in the right arms . . . a tall, well-built, rich and handsome man of good family . . . perhaps a stock-broker or banker. Almost everything about this vision was clear: his strong but sensitive hands, his long legs, lean hips and muscular chest; his polished manner, the manly passion which he always restrained because of his respect for her. Only his face was blurred and indistinct.

'On set, everyone,' bellowed the director's assistant.

As they took their places in a fake streetcar interior,

Betsy looked into Mabel's persuasive, brown eyes, then shook her head. 'Mabel, you know Ma doesn't like me to go out alone with men.'

'It's not men, honest. Only the three of us – you, Mack and me,' Mabel urged. 'And there's a special reason – it's a secret, and only Mack can tell you. But I *promise* that you won't be left alone for a single second, and Mack and I will *both* see you home in a cab.'

Still hesitant, but intrigued, Betsy consulted her mother, who had met and liked Mack, and knew he was sweet on Mabel, so safe. So on the following Saturday evening, Betsy stepped down into an inexpensive basement Italian restaurant that reminded her of her first Biograph set: momentarily, she half-expected to see a boy on roller skates burst in, swinging a leg of lamb.

After finishing their first bottle of Chianti, Mack pushed aside the guttering candle, leaned across the red-checked tablecloth, and solemnly asked Betsy to swear secrecy: it took a few minutes to convince her that this wasn't another of his larks.

He then announced, triumphantly, 'I'm going to start my *own* movie production company in LA – got the backing from a couple of my bookmakers! Several guys at the Biograph are going to come along with me. How about joining us?'

Betsy was silent, knowing that it was unwise to leave a good weekly paycheque for an unknown, non-existent company.

Mabel leaned forward. 'Aw, come on, Betsy. Think what fun it will be in that great California weather all the time, instead of being fried or frozen here in New York! 'Sides, aren't you sick of being pushed around and sneered at by Mr Griffith?'

Betsy thought: If Mabel leaves, then I *know* Mr Griffith will pass over me again, and discover some new star.

She stared across the table at Mack's equally persuasive grin. 'Is this serious? You really do have the financing, and everything?'

'I've even got the studio! I swear it's all fixed! We open in August, our first release goes out end of September: after that, we release a movie every week.' Winningly Mack made his pitch. 'I'd like to use you in bigger roles, Betsy. You're *perfect* for what I have in mind – and I'd like to use you as you are: you don't need to act, just be yourself. You'd still play society parts, but bigger ones. And I'd like to try you in comedy.'

Betsy looked puzzled. 'But Mr Griffith didn't think . . .'

'No, he didn't think,' Mack Sennett grinned.

* * *

The new production company, Keystone, stood next to a field of clover; the large, sprawling shed with big slanting glass roof looked like a factory, except that in front of it a large sign announced MACK SENNETT STUDIOS. Just inside the building was a tiny office permanently jammed with people lying in their attempts to see producers, and being similarly lied to by the man behind the desk, who had been instructed to keep them all out.

Once settled in California, Sennett *did* produce a new frenzied comedy each week. There was never a single script at Keystone – because the company made up the story as they went along. Stunt men, gag men, comics and actors – all constantly thought of new ideas, and bounced them off each other before pitching them to the director.

In his last year at Biograph, Mack had been quietly considering the comic possibilities of cops. So Keystone pictures often featured clumsy, crazily incompetent policemen. Betsy was furiously indignant when she discovered – too late to return to New York – that her role in these haywire comedies was that of a stooge! But eventually, coaxed by Mabel, she agreed to try what Sennett wished.

To Mack's delight – and Betsy's chagrin – movie audiences roared with laughter when the stuck-up elaborately dressed society dame received a custard pie in her haughty kisser. It had been shrewd of him to realize that Betsy's genuine outraged dignity and fury would be far more effective than that assumed by any other actress.

Neat, tidy, decorous Betsy *loathed* working on the Keystone comedy pictures: she hated unsuccessfully dodging custard pies, plates and cups; she hated tripping over things; she hated being kicked in the behind; and she hated having her skirts fly up above her ears. The work messed up her clothes and made her look ridiculous. Furthermore, she despised the vulgarity of the banana-peel, funny-fat-man world of slapstick comedy. But everyone else sure thought the comedies were funny: strangers now stopped her on the street to praise her, and ask her to sign their autograph books. Betsy still longed to be a real actress, like Mary Pickford, but she also loved feeling a genuine success, at last.

When Betsy's salary was raised to $125 a week the Bridges moved out of their rooming house and into Court Constant, a double row of bungalows built in a garden near the Studio; considered a respectable place for single actresses and other women involved in the movie business, it was a friendly little community where the women drifted in and out of each other's bungalows to gossip, drink coffee or cocktails, or sunbathe together on the communal lawns.

On Sundays Mrs Bridges liked to mix with the British Colony, a far-flung corner of the British Empire that desperately tried to remain For Ever England. British actors, hired to play stereotyped British aristocrats, lived their parts twenty-four hours a day. Mrs Bridges adored their tea parties: she was very partial to cucumber sandwiches, although they were inclined to make her tummy act up, and she enjoyed refinement: a genteel hand covered each Bridges belch, she crooked her little finger when she lifted her teacup, never blew on her cuppa to cool it and never sipped tea from her saucer when in company. However, no one had informed her that it was frowned upon to slurp tea through a sugar cube.

Best of all, and what made tea parties feel *completely* genteel, were the Britishers' Sunday cricket matches. Mrs Bridges loved to watch the players, dressed in white flannels and striped schoolboy caps; her suede gloves gently applauded every sixer to the boundary and after the match clutched a refined glass of sweet sherry while thirsty players glugged Scotch-and-splash or gin and tonic. What Hollywood perceived as the stiff, snob attitude of the unrelaxed Britishers was really expatriate shyness and homesickness. Pale mauve Judas trees, magnolias in bloom, pink and white oleander bushes, glossy green banana trees did not compensate for their self-imposed exile, but merely reminded them sadly that they were *not* in Tunbridge Wells.

Sunday 15 March 1914

One cloudy afternoon when they couldn't shoot, and Mrs Bridges was laid low with a bout of cucumber-sandwich gastritis, Mabel Normand, in her new red Pierce-Arrow, drove a bunch of actresses to a tea dance (the latest thing) at the newly built Beverly Hills Hotel, a T-shaped pink stucco building that stood in a wilderness of scrub where two canyon riverbeds met. The hotel was considered a folly, for it looked like a lonely, abandoned real-estate project: just beyond it the sidewalks stopped abruptly in open fields and coyotes howled in the nearby hills. However, as the hotel was quiet and secluded, a girl could let her hair down without being reported.

Betsy returned to her table after a dance to find an unknown young man waiting for her; he looked a bit like the Prince of Wales, an open-faced, tousle-headed, blond young man with neat little features, and a friendly grin. The young man handed her a delicate lace handkerchief. 'I believe you dropped this, miss.'

'I believe I did,' lied Betsy.

'Would you, perhaps, do me the honour...' And off whirled Betsy to dance a sensual tango in his arms.

Mesmerized by Betsy's kitten-that-swallowed-the-cream expression, the young man could only stammer platitudes as he stared at black-lashed violet eyes above the little nose and delicately sculpted mouth; adoringly, he listened to her soft, little-girl whisper and her cute British accent; daringly, he stroked the waves of fair hair at the back of her head. They danced for hours, entwined in each other's arms.

True to her upbringing, and despite her flirtatious

glances and formalized writhing, Betsy behaved with demure propriety, but as her partner sinuously bent forward over her he sensed that beneath her porcelain exterior was a lonely creature who longed for affection, if not erotic adventure.

Sadly, Daniel Bloom was not a rich broker or a banker, but a lowly cameraman at Planet Productions; Betsy knew that her mother would consider him scandalously ineligible and hesitated to tell her the true identity of the sender of the enormous bouquets that now arrived at her dressing room, accompanied by cards which announced that the flowers had been sent with the compliments of Mr Konrad Fisher of Planet Productions.

Two weeks after Daniel and Betsy met, Mabel, in her red automobile, collected her friend from Court Constant. A mile down the road, Betsy once again transferred into Daniel's battered blue roadster, which leaped forwards towards Santa Monica beach, turned north up the coast, and beyond Malibu. The ostensible object of this assignation was to take some different beach photographs of Betsy – romantic rather than cute – which Daniel then proposed to show to his uncles, Konrad and Solomon Fisher who, Daniel said, owned Planet Studios.

Naturally Betsy – after four years in the movie business – checked on what he said; somewhat to her surprise, the Fisher brothers did indeed own Planet: but were they Daniel's uncles? She forgot her cynical scepticism as the roadster rattled along the little coastal road, the sun shone benignly on the dancing waves below, to their left; Betsy's hair blew wildly in the salty ocean breeze, but for once she did not care: she and Daniel were young and in love.

After Daniel had parked, the couple set out for the beach, down the narrow path on the wooden palisade.

Daniel carried his camera, tripod, and case of precious glass negatives; Betsy carried her make-up case and twenty yards of delicate peach chiffon.

When they arrived, Daniel set up his camera, while Betsy found a large rock at the back of the beach; behind this she combed the tangles from her hair, then undressed; she folded her clothes neatly, carefully wound the peach chiffon around her body, pinned it to look more modest than it first appeared and checked her face in the mirror of her powder compact; she then walked towards the water, carefully carrying the ends of the chiffon lengths in both hands, so they did not drag on the sand. Because the tide was out, the ground was damp beneath her naked toes; she squealed with childish pleasure as she watched the froth of the warm Pacific gush over her bare feet.

Daniel had asked Betsy to walk away, then turn and run towards him, along the edge of the shore. He wanted to see her long, loose hair and the two scarves of chiffon flying out behind her, as the incoming surf splashed picturesquely. Betsy was aware that this seemingly simple shot would take hours to perfect, for they had to wait for an appropriate wave, then Daniel needed to keep her in focus while she ran, and finally, he had to catch her face in as good a pose as her body. But Betsy knew that the end result would be stunning, so again and again she walked down the beach, then ran up it towards Daniel, waiting to smile until he shouted, *'Now!'*

After about two hours of running across wet sand, Betsy was less enthusiastic and longing for a break. Once more, she walked slowly away from Daniel, then turned, and took a deep breath before running back up . . . As she did so she glanced up and noticed two dark uniformed highway patrolmen, scrambling down the narrow path towards them. The ends of chiffon flew up behind her as, again, she ran towards Daniel.

One cop called brusquely, 'Stop that, buster! We've had complaints from people on the highway. They told us you was cavorting naked, down here on the beach.'

Betsy felt an angry, mortified flush creep up her neck.

Daniel said, 'Officer, you can see for yourself that's not true.'

'Taking nude shots in a public venue is an offence against public decency,' the second patrolman threatened.

'But we aren't, and we haven't been,' Betsy indignantly objected.

Daniel threw her a warning look: he hoped that Betsy would keep silent, for whatever she said would be wrongly interpreted: he realized that either the two patrolmen resented being on duty and wished they were out of uniform and having fun on the beach, or they were bully boys, looking for trouble.

'We've only *your* word that you ain't been offending public decency.' The first patrolman stood, hands on hips. 'You mean to tell me that these folks on the highway was lying?'

'You'd better scram, before we haul you in,' his companion menaced.

Daniel wondered whether to wave a ten-buck note, or whether that might make things worse. He decided not to risk it but quietly said, 'Go dress, Betsy.'

Humiliated and ashamed, Betsy scuttled to the rocks where her clothes lay.

'OK, buster, let's have your negatives.'

Daniel handed over the black-framed stack of glass

negatives. The patrolman threw them on the beach, and stamped on them with his boots, smashing every one, before kicking them into the sand.

Daniel realized that he was being deliberately provoked, but said nothing.

'Now get the hell out of here!' ordered the first cop.

'Pick up all that garbage first.' The second pointed to the smashed negatives, now partly buried by sand. 'It's an offence to leave litter on a public beach.'

Daniel quietly picked up the shards, then joined Betsy at the back of the beach. In silence, they walked up the narrow path. In silence, they climbed in the blue roadster, which Daniel drove back towards Santa Monica. Betsy put her head in her hands and started to sob. 'I've never felt so humiliated in my entire life!'

Daniel pulled over and put his arms around her. 'Don't let those stinking sons-of-bitches spoil our day together,' he whispered angrily. He gently kissed the top of her silky hair, tilted her chin towards his mouth and licked away her tears. He murmured soothing words of comfort in her ears until her sobs ceased, and she gasped for a different reason: the spark that both had long felt between them, now ignited, spread through both their bodies, faster than a forest fire, until, incensed for being condemned when innocent, Betsy whispered, 'Let's go somewhere . . . private.'

On a moth-eaten car rug spread on the scrubland behind the Beverley Hills Hotel, Daniel's skilfully erotic touch roused the pagan part of Betsy's nature that had for many years been carefully suppressed. Now uninhibited, Betsy experienced her own sexuality, as the wild side of her nature surfaced: her body felt abandoned, totally out of control; her brain seemed frozen while her flesh felt on fire; she no longer cared that her hair was mussed.

Astonished to discover that Betsy was a virgin, Daniel was a tender, considerate and imaginative lover. Once more, he guided Betsy to the peak of her passion: again she felt as if she were riding on the crest of a great Pacific wave . . . pausing . . . then crashing, foam-flecked, on some silent shore . . . before slowly, softly, gently, being sucked back into the depths of a great ocean. Cut! Cut!

* * *

A month after this momentous event Mrs Bridges appeared unexpectedly in Betsy's dressing room two minutes before Daniel burst in with a bunch of violets (to match Betsy's eyes).

Upon seeing Mrs Bridges, with extraordinary presence of mind Daniel bowed and presented the violets to her. To Betsy's surprise, Mrs Bridges smiled graciously as she accepted. Before half an hour had passed it was clear that her eagle-fierce protectiveness had been breached by the considerate young man. To Betsy's astonishment, her mother invited Daniel to supper.

He turned up with two large cellophane boxes, each containing a small orchid. For the entire evening he questioned Mrs Bridges about her life in Britain, and listened with rapt attention to her romantically exaggerated descriptions of British thee-ah-tah life.

After his departure (promptly on the stroke of ten o'clock), Mrs Bridges turned to her daughter. 'That nice young man is the only person I've met in this place who can talk about something other than motion pictures! No wonder his ma is so fond of him.'

Daniel had explained that his mother, an invalid, lived in San Francisco: heart trouble. As he was her only son, Daniel tried to visit her as often as possible. He had even promised not to marry until she . . . passed on. Mrs Bridges was as touched by Daniel's filial devotion as she was impressed by his refined speech: so well-spoken, no swear words. 'Ay can't abide bed lengwij,' she had explained in her genteel voice. Daniel had nodded in agreement.

Thursday 4 June 1914

Daniel and Betsy bumped in the blue roadster up a dirt track north of Hollywood Boulevard to Planet Studios, which consisted of three barns and two street scenes on the back lot: one a contemporary American city street, the other a cowboy town, both backless. As Daniel escorted her to the gloomy baronial dark-panelled office of the Fisher brothers, Betsy felt ashamed of her previous cynical doubts.

Planet had three female and three male stars; all production revolved around these six actors, others were hired from casting offices when required. Their angel-faced blonde Pickford lookalike was currently suffering from septicaemia after an abortion, and the Studio doctor had simply shrugged his shoulders when the Fisher brothers demanded to know when she would be fit to work again. The Fishers – who had seen Betsy's slapstick work for Keystone – took one look at her exquisite face, checked out her real age (as was usual, she had clipped five years off), gave her a test, then offered her a six-month contract at $150 a week. Betsy signed with Planet two days before an obscure Austrian archduke was assassinated in Bosnia by a rebellious student. Who could have realized that his pistol shot would start a worldwide war?

Friday 26 June 1914

Being under contract meant that Betsy had also to be available for any bit part or extra work – even as stand-in for some other female star. But never again would a custard pie be thrown in her face. At last she had achieved star status, of a lowly sort. Planet was not a leading studio, and she was not one of their leading actors, but as Daniel exultantly pointed out, it sure was a leg-up.

Betsy felt she was now well on her way to stardom and tried hard; she was still shy at story sessions and stiff in rehearsals, but once the camera started to roll she relaxed and responded. She was careful to avoid any trouble with her fellow stars: the dark-haired vamp, the lesbian tom-boy comedienne, the cowboy lead, the sophisticated man-about-town or the balding actor with a pencil-line moustache who played villains, fathers and scheming industrialists.

Betsy was considered to have a good eye for fashion, so she was allowed to decide what costumes she needed. Anything necessary for her work that she didn't already own (she spent much of her salary on clothes) was provided by the Studio. The head of Wardrobe took Betsy to the best stores in town, where they chose her stockings, silk lingerie, satin slippers, dresses, coats, purses dyed to match, and large-brimmed picture hats loaded with flowers and ribbons. They carried away none of these purchases, and paid not a cent: everything was delivered to the Studio, and the bill – signed by the head of Wardrobe –

was sent straight to the accounts department. Betsy considered this the ideal way to shop.

When the clothes arrived, she immediately tried on everything again. She loved the newly invented brassieres and the pliant rubber girdles that had replaced whalebone-stiffened corsets. She enjoyed the free movement of a waist no longer nipped in but ignored. She would stroke the soft, supple gauzes and sensual chiffons that had replaced stiff tailored fabrics, and gaze admiringly in the mirror at the bandeaux and turbans that covered her newly bobbed hair. Happily she dabbed rice-powder on her nose and ringed her violet eyes with kohl to make them look even larger, then sprayed herself with some exotic fragrance labelled 'Forbidden Fruit' or 'Evening in Paris', rather than the lavender water and eau de Cologne purchased by Mrs Bridges.

For important publicity appearances – perhaps a premiere or some big party – Wardrobe provided her with a suitably glamorous gown of silk, satin or taffeta trimmed with rhinestones. Her escort (always an actor nominated by the Studio) arrived in a Studio limousine to collect her from Court Constant; he always wore white tie and tails, with a white silk muffler flung around his throat; he carried a top hat, which he donned as soon as he spotted a press camera.

Despite the angry remonstrations of his brother Sol (responsible for finance), Konrad Fisher (production and direction) indulged his stars: the women received flowers every week and, for a particularly good performance, a girl might be presented with a fur evening wrap, a male actor might get a gleaming silver roadster.

To avoid production hold-ups, the Fisher brothers also solved all the personal problems of their actors. Studio doctors provided clap cures and discreet abortions; debts were swiftly settled and deducted from future salary with equal speed. Planet stars therefore grew to depend on the Studio, a psychological advantage to the Fishers. As the brothers knew all the guilty secrets of all their actors, they could quietly blackmail them to do exactly what the Studio required, for it was vitally important that there should be minimal scandal in Hollywood; because of powerful religious organizations and similarly influential women's organizations which could boycott a star, movie or even a studio, scandal was the Achilles' heel of the brilliantly successful new motion-picture industry.

So studio publicity departments had to work hard to ensure that all movie people in the spotlight were seen to lead bland, happy, innocent lives that were acceptable to all fans and self-appointed public guardians of morality. If married stars did not have children, they were told to adopt a couple. Nothing socially unacceptable was allowed to surface: no drinking or drug addiction, no adultery, impotence, venereal diseases or sexual orgies. Homosexual scandals were especially forbidden: officially there were no bisexuals, lesbians or nancy boys in Hollywood, for every actor knew that adverse public opinion could end even a star career overnight: the morality clause in all contracts ensured immediate termination.

Betsy knew that the publicity department at Planet used influence, blackmail and hush-money to persuade police and journalists to 'forget' any detrimental incidents. Thousands of dollars were quietly paid into the right pockets, for the most expensive thing you could buy in Hollywood was silence: avoiding a scandal that would wreck an expensively built-up career or movie was worth any price to a studio. Few stars who incurred such costs realized that every penny was deducted by the studio from their future salaries.

Mrs Bridges smugly thought that Betsy, who neither drank alcohol nor smoked, was safe from such nasty, sordid problems. Although studio hours were exhausting, Mrs Bridges was always waiting at the end of Betsy's working day with a soothing drink of hot milk and honey; often, Betsy was kept in bed all day on Sunday, resting with the blinds down. Mrs Bridges was determined that her daughter should not become one of them nervy Hollywood wrecks.

Betsy's first movies for Planet were easy-to-shoot, unsophisticated adventures, with titles such as *Oasis of Love*, *Desert Passion* or *Fire and Ice*. Each week Betsy was obliged to describe the new plot of her next movie to the excited Mrs Bridges. 'I'm a shy young governess who falls in love with her pupil's father, but just as we are about to marry I discover he already has a mad wife locked in the attic. Luckily, she sets the house ablaze and kills herself.'

Mrs Bridges wondered doubtfully, 'Isn't that *Jane Eyre*?'

'No, her name is Loretta.'

Occasionally Mrs Bridges was more insistent, as when Betsy explained, 'This week I'm Joan of Arc and I lead the French army to throw the British out of France. Then I marry the French King and become the Queen of France . . .'

'But surely St Joan was burnt to death at the stake?' puzzled Mrs Bridges. 'She *didn't* marry the King!'

Serenely Betsy said, 'She does in the movie.'

After six months, Betsy's subsequent contract was negotiated by her newly acquired agent, who would receive 25
per cent of Betsy's $500 a week salary. For the next four
years Betsy's contract would be renewed every year, with
an increase of salary; she was then optioned to Planet for
a further three years.

In their bungalow at Court Constant, Betsy and her
mother hugged each other and sobbed with relief, for both
felt that they could finally relax: Betsy now had an assured
future, both financially and career-wise. Betsy Bridges was
going places!

Betsy now felt that she had finally justified her
mother's faith in her, and repaid her for all her effort and
sacrifices. However, there was one further factor to be
considered. Betsy's agent had firmly advised her that to
refuse a director's or producer's advances would jeopardize
her career. Betsy's mother soon put a stop to that. 'My
Betsy was raised as a lady,' she said firmly, 'and everyone
at Planet Studios had better understand it, or they'll have
me to deal with.'

Betsy was promptly named the Ice Queen, and was left
out of the jollity when some of the company went on
weekends to Laguna or La Jolla for beach parties, drinking
and a little lechery, and gossip.

Despite her soft spot for Daniel, Mrs Bridges had
become uneasy because of his reluctance to introduce
Betsy to his mother. The Los Angeles area was now full
of parasitical rascals and buccaneers, ready to fleece anyone. These conmen were smooth-talking persuaders,
seemingly masterful extroverts who promised, 'Leave

everything to me and just sign here, baby.' Every girl had to watch her step, and so did every girl's mother.

Betsy, still besotted, threw a tantrum when her mother started to hint that perhaps it was time to look elsewhere, bearing in mind that Betsy was almost twenty-eight: she hesitated to say 'nearly thirty', words as inexorably cruel as the midnight chimes to Cinderella.

'The studio publicity sheets say I'm twenty-two, and I'm earning a fortune! Mind your own business, Ma!'

Mrs Bridges did not mind her own business. She hired a private detective, who easily tracked Daniel to the San Francisco Bay area, where he discovered morose Mrs Daniel Bloom, living in Sausalito with her two young sons. A photograph of the gravestone of Daniel's mother was included with the detective's report.

Exposed (not for the first time) as a two-timing rat, Daniel Bloom started to look around for another girl, which he did with some reluctance, for although Betsy wasn't the world's best lay, she sure was the prettiest.

Disbelieving, Betsy couldn't believe that Daniel's love for her did not exist and probably never had. Her heart really did feel ... not broken but brutally bruised, as if laid out defenceless on a butcher's block and then swiftly battered flat with a wooden mallet. At first she was too dazed to weep but later her eyes simply flooded. At first ma was sympathetic with brandy (medicinal) in hot milk but then she turned anxious because by morning Betsy's face had to be in good nick for the studio. So she applied cold compresses for the rest of the night. Betsy lay with her head on a towel and iced water trickling into her ears. She caught herself wistfully wishing that Mimi were there because she could always be straight with her, whereas she couldn't with her ma. Thank Heaven they had always been careful. Thank Heaven her mother had never found out.

Still in love, she found it almost impossible to believe in Daniel's deception. She had finally given her carefully guarded treasure to him – and she had fallen for the same stupid trick as any one of the dumb heroines in one of her own movies! She was shocked, dazed and bitterly disappointed. Daniel had lied to her, he had cheated on her as well as his wife. Well, Betsy would never let *that* happen again! She would *never again* make herself vulnerable to a man. She would *never again* be a fool for love, and so risk losing everything before she got her hands on it.

London, 1914–1916

In wartime London Mimi had had more serious problems. In 1914, when Britain declared war on Germany, Toby had instantly volunteered for the Artists' Rifles, but had failed his army medical because of his childhood tuberculosis. So instead he volunteered to be a Special Constable, and every night after the Minerva's final curtain he paraded the Embankment, from Blackfriars to Westminster.

After an exhausting day's work at the theatre, his nights in blacked-out London were now equally tiring, especially if the maroons banged warning of an impending German Zeppelin airship attack. When there was a bad bombing raid, the incandescent scene above the River Thames dissolved his weariness, as guiltily he thought that not even Max Reinhardt could rival such a spectacle.

Mimi had abandoned her promising career as a musical comedy actress after the start of the war, and returned to male impersonation. 'It's what I like best,' she told Toby over her breakfast tray, on the morning after she opened in *Fun Time* at the Minerva. 'I ain't an actress and I don't want to be. My heart ain't in it. I might have moaned a bit about touring, but I love being an impersonator: it's a release. As soon as I'm in front of them lights, I get a little kick. I feel I can do anything I like and get away with it, I feel like a child in me own playroom. I'm making up for the one I never had.'

'Clearly you're just the stuff to give the troops,' Toby agreed, unsurprised, as he remarked the cheers, whistles and stamping when Mimi had skipped off stage the night before.

As the Fane household staff at Fitzroy Square had either been called up for the army or directed to work in munitions factories, the Fanes moved into the Savoy Hotel, which had an air-raid shelter in the basement for Max, cared for by Daisy since a series of starched, formal nannies had either been dismissed or had left in a huff, saying that if they weren't allowed to discipline that child, they couldn't be held responsible. (Naturally, after the front door had slammed upon the final nanny, an angelically contrite Max had been forgiven by his mother for upsetting that rough creature.)

Daisy, who sympathized with the departing nanny (she had slid into her bed to find it also occupied by a live frog), had cautioned Mimi, 'Watch out, my girl, you're spoiling Max. That lad can wind you round his little finger, and if you forgive him for every naughty thing he does, he'll never learn his limits.' She gave a mighty sniff. 'That kid's got too much charm and not enough discipline, and that's a recipe for trouble.'

Mimi said defensively, 'He didn't mean any *real* harm, did you, ducky?'

Six-year-old Max solemnly shook his head; he had Toby's blue eyes, black brows, and full, wide, mouth below a slightly crooked nose, broken by a cricket ball in the park. Tall for his age, his thin Fane body bent in the middle, and at school he was constantly told to pull his shoulders back and stand up straight, like a man, or he'd never make a soldier. Mimi hoped not.

Although the Minerva was close to the Savoy Hotel, sometimes the maroons would bang when the Fanes were en route to the theatre, and then they would rush into the nearest shelter, dodging from that to another, until they reached the stage door. The Minerva performed intimate revue to packed houses, for London theatres were filled with soldiers on leave, the walking wounded, and other people who wanted to forget the war for an hour or two.

At the outbreak of war, there had been immediate national jingoistic indignation. All combatants of what came to be called the Great War had at first confidently assumed that the war would be over in a few months. The warring nations had then realized the horrific, muddy reality of trench warfare in France and Belgium, as each side in turn hurled their troops through shell-pitted no man's land, to be mown down relentlessly by enemy machine-guns.

After Tom Allen was killed by shrapnel, during a heavy bombardment at the beginning of the Battle of Ypres in April 1915, Jessie worked as a nursing auxiliary at Charing Cross Hospital, where train after train of wounded soldiers arrived from France and Belgium.

Five months after Tom's death, Baz was killed in

Flanders, during the autumn offensive on the Western Front. Baz, who was part of an infantry assault on the German mines, was bayoneted in the back during fierce hand-to-hand fighting: two days later, the position he helped to gain was retaken by the enemy.

When Toby, still in his dark Special Constable's uniform, appeared at dawn in Mimi's bedroom with a telegram in his hand (Baz had given Toby's name as a next of kin), Mimi looked at Toby's white, silent face and knew immediately that Baz was dead. She felt as if all the breath had been suddenly sucked from her body: Baz was the friend of Mimi's youth. He had been her teasing, tomboy companion, and her sufficiently patient, sufficiently impatient teacher, when she first trod the boards. He had cared about her and worried about her enough to invent a new career for her, and then gently push her into it.

Toby clung to Mimi, eventually sobbed his sorrow on her shoulders. Three hours later, she handed him a large whisky and hot water, then sat by his bedside until he fell asleep. After that dawn, the no man's land that had once delineated their respective privacy almost faded away. The death of Baz brought Mimi and Toby emotionally closer because in different ways they had both loved Baz and nobody else could understand how either felt about their loss. Toby became more demonstrative towards Mimi: sometimes poor old Toby needed a cuddle, Mimi realized. Toby now spent as much time as he could with his son, as if he realized that every carefree minute of a loving relationship was precious.

For Max's eighth birthday Toby managed to purchase a third-hand Pollock's model theatre. Everything in Britain was in short supply in 1916, especially toys, so this magnificent gift, painted cream and gold, with crimson velvet curtains, immediately became Max's most precious possession. On Sunday afternoons he and his father sat on Max's bedroom floor and invented plots for the cardboard cut-out characters that they then pushed on stage with wire, for their audience of Mimi and Daisy to applaud.

Sometimes a group of Max's schoolboy chums, looking tidier and more subdued than usual, would appear at the Savoy on Saturday afternoon, while Mimi played a matinée. After a sparse wartime tea (even thinner sandwiches than in peacetime), Toby would take over from Daisy as the boys, having devised some simple plot and using impromptu dialogue, pushed lead figures around the stage (second-hand lead soldiers, repainted by Max as blackamoors or Zulus or wizards). Often Jessie's daughter, Felicity, was left by her harassed, overworked mother in the comfortable Fane nursery, and often she was allowed to take some minor female part; she was treated by Max and his friends with the mild contempt deserved by a girl who couldn't climb trees, cried if she was hurt, and didn't want to practise bayonet-charging with broom handles.

Felicity was a small, scrawny child with unfashionably fine straight flaxen hair and a solemn little face, dominated by large blue crystalline eyes. Much to the annoyance of the young schoolboy performers – who spoke jerkily and gave equal emphasis to each word – the despised Felicity easily invented dialogue, which she spoke naturally and clearly, with an intuitive sense of rhythm. Although it was difficult to condescend to their star performer, the nasty little boys managed to do so. If Daisy returned early from her afternoon off she consoled Felicity with peppermint lumps and hugs, and sniffed that little boys were made of snakes and snails and puppy-dog tails. Jessie comforted Felicity by telling her that stars must expect jealousy and popularity was theirs only when they were needed.

The widowed Jessie and her daughter now lived in Maisie's boarding house, where they managed to survive on Maisie's generosity (bills, when rendered, were very low), Jessie's meagre earnings as a nursing auxiliary, her even more meagre widow's pension, and a weekly contribution from Toby, who also offered to set her up in business as a theatrical agent, when the war ended.

Toby's generous offer had been made only after prompting by Mimi, who had enthusiastically described Jessie's calm efficiency when she was Jolly Joe Jenkins' manager. It had been Jessie's job to organize the entire Company on trains and off them, in theatres and out of them. Jessie had planned all the advance bookings, ensured that handbills were properly printed, and organized urchins to distribute them in each town, before the Company performed there. If Jessie could do that, she was certainly capable of doing anything managerial in the theatre; when the war ended, some shrewd chappie with a bit of spare dosh would do well to set her up as an agent. Certainly the poor woman now needed to settle down in one spot so that little orphan, Felicity, could get a proper education.

Thursday 20 September 1917. London

On Max's ninth birthday he was taken for the first time to see the evening theatre performance of a proper play. (Previously he had only been allowed to attend Christmas pantomimes in the afternoon, for Toby had firmly insisted that wriggling young children distracted a serious audience.) As the house lights dimmed, Toby again assured him, in a whisper, that *Romeo and Juliet* was not just a soppy love story, as rumoured by his school chums.

The footlights glowed and the heavy gold-braided curtains silently rose. Shining from the darkness, the brilliantly illuminated stage revealed a Renaissance market place, where men in coloured tights laughed, joked and strutted like peacocks; the dazzle of the footlights emphasized their colourful romantic costumes, and the actors seemed magical creatures from another world.

'It's just like a pantomime, Daddy!' Max marvelled.

The sets were equally astonishing: real ivy climbed the walls, real autumn leaves were scattered below the balcony upon which Juliet appeared, shining star-bright, in a nightgown of unsuitable silver lamé fashioned from some pre-war costume. In the ball scene Della Robbia-inspired swags of leaves and fruit hung between marble columns. Despite Toby's briefing, Max did not understand the plot but he found the onstage fights thrilling, the murders and poisoning dramatically real.

When the curtain finally descended, his stage-struck eyes were as bright as if he had a fever: he had just realized that, in the theatre, it was possible to make the invented world of his imagination come alive *proper-size*! He immediately decided that one day he would stand where Romeo stood, in dazzling light, listening to a storm of appreciative applause, a hero.

As the house lights went up, and he slowly returned to reality, he turned, puzzled, to Toby. 'Daddy, what was that family feud *about*?'

Toby laughed. 'Nobody knows.'

'But there must have been some dreadful reason for them to have hated each other so?'

'Not necessarily,' Toby said quietly.

* * *

Max did not care so passionately for the cinema: the crude, flickering pictures lacked the depth, colour, immediacy and glamour of the stage. However, one Saturday afternoon, a school friend's mother took him with a group of other boys to see a double feature: Charlie Chaplin in *The Vagabond*, followed by Betsy Bridges in *Desert Passion*.

Upon returning to the Savoy, Max burst into the sitting room of his parents' suite, where they were quietly listening to Gilbert & Sullivan tunes on their new wind-up gramophone. Max started to talk excitedly about the beautiful star, Betsy Bridges.

Mimi turned white.

To Max's astonishment, Toby stood up, pushed his son to his bedroom, closed the door, then quietly told Max never again to mention that woman's name in front of his mother, because the carelessness of Betsy Bridges had been responsible for his mother's injuries. Max longed to know how, but did not dare ask.

Later that evening, as they hurried along the Strand to the Minerva, Toby quietly said, 'Forget it, Foxtop.'

Still vexed and tight-lipped, Mimi muttered, 'I'm so cross I could spit! To think that *my* son has a crush on that cow!'

Toby put one arm around her, and hugged her shoulders. 'Surely you're not silly enough to be jealous of a schoolboy's infatuation for some woman he's never met, a woman who's old enough to be his mother?'

Mimi pressed her lips together even more tightly, and pulled her fur muff to her chest.

'Can't you forget what happened all those years ago, Foxtop? Can't you stop making yourself unhappy? Can't you *try* to forgive, Mimi?'

'It seems not,' Mimi growled.

Toby continued persuasively, 'You can't alter the past, Mimi, but you can try to improve the present. Perhaps one day you'll feel like doing Betsy a *good* turn.'

Mimi's face flushed red. She stopped abruptly, pulled her hands from her fur muff, peeled off her short white gloves. She thrust one horribly scarred hand towards Toby and with the other she yanked back her fringe from the left side of her face which revealed the puckered patch of shiny skin, the colour of yellowing ivory, that ran from her forehead to her ear.

'*Never!*'

Chapter Nine

By 1918, nearly all motion-picture production had moved from the East Coast to Hollywood and the movie industry had become notorious for its Byzantine intrigues and ruthless in-fighting, especially among immigrants who had learned as starved and stunted children in East European ghettos that only the toughest street-fighters survive. More and more small movie businesses were squeezed to bankruptcy, bought out, or forcibly merged with one of the majors. Eventually, only a handful of megalomaniac studio heads were left to rule their new empires: the small fry had been eaten alive and a few sharks ruled the pool. This handful of survivors ganged together to protect their mutual interests and ruthlessly control every aspect of the entire industry and all employed in it. With their invisible, invincible weapon of fear, studio heads kept the Talent (creative people) under their control by blacklisting anyone who didn't obey them, who argued or was otherwise 'difficult'.

As the big studios knocked out their competition, people at all levels of the Industry were laid off; everyone else grew nervous, especially the actors, who always lived amidst anxiety. The ever-present possibility of no work, with no cash put by for a rainy day, loomed over every well-groomed head, however successful, for studios expected their stars to spend every nickel of their salary on photogenic luxury homes (with enormous maintenance bills) in order to project a glamorous, successful image of the Industry.

The rainy day arrived in 1918 when the worldwide outbreak of influenza reached America, killing thousands of people each week. The public avoided places where they might pick up the virus. Overnight, movie theatres were almost empty, box-office takings plunged, the Industry panicked, and every studio ruthlessly cut back expenditure. Even the irrepressible Mabel Normand felt bad luck was lurking around the corner, as she gloomily told Betsy in a gossipy retreat to the ladies' cloakroom during a Sunday tea dance at the swanky Alexandria Hotel.

Betsy did not find it hard to believe that this living legend was depressed and scared, for she suspected that at heart Mabel was a frightened little creature, not the self-confident comedienne that her public adored, the beauty who broke men's hearts.

'But you've got nothing to worry about, Mabel, you could always marry Mack,' she suggested, mischievously. Mabel's stormy love affair with Mack was frequently ruptured, and even movie magazines had lost count of the number of times that Mabel had broken their engagement – generally because of Mack's wandering eye.

'Or Mr Goldwyn,' Betsy added, naughtily. Sam Goldwyn was married, but for over a year he had been clearly crazy about Mabel. Sometimes she appeared with Goldwyn at public functions (to irritate Mack) but she always managed to dodge private encounters. Her unavailability only made her more desirable: the more dates she cancelled – often at the last minute – the more besotted he became.

Mabel giggled, then suddenly adopted the cocky stance and truculent expression of the powerful little producer; as she strutted round the cloakroom, biting her lipstick as a cigar, Betsy laughed so hard that she dropped her powder puff, and groped on the floor for it.

Sharp-eyed Mabel hiked up her skirt and adjusted her garters. 'You still having trouble with your eyes, Betsy?'

Betsy sighed, 'I had a worse time last spring.'

'I know what it's like,' Mabel sympathized. 'You do take after take in front of those damn lights – and then some guy from publicity runs right up to you, yells, "Hold it for a still!" and flashes his damned camera right into your eyes. It's like looking straight into the sun.'

'Don't I know it!' Betsy checked her hair in the mirror. 'I was off shooting for two days last week alone. D'you put castor oil in your eyes, or tea leaves on the lids?'

Mabel fluffed up her hair. 'I lie down, and the studio doctor covers my eyes with slices of cucumber, and slices of potato, then he bandages my eyes. I'm supposed to wear dark glasses whenever I can.'

'When I have a bad bout, flashes of bright light wake me in the middle of the night. But the studio doctor says it'll pass in time.'

Mabel snorted. 'Studio doctors are paid to keep us working!'

Betsy did not know that the previous week – after her mother had persuaded her to consult a private doctor for a second opinion – Mrs Bridges had been quietly told that if Betsy did not stop filming, within a year, she might well be permanently blind. Frightened, Mrs

Bridges had not yet found the strength to tell this to her daughter.

* * *

Three days after the Alexandria tea dance, Betsy received a late-night telephone call from Flora, one of the stenographers in Mr Solomon Fisher's office; prudently, Betsy gave her little-worn discarded clothes to this girl, who overheard much interesting information.

Flora whispered nervously, 'Mr Solomon is negotiating with Harry Warner.'

'A buyout?'

'Sounds like it.' Flora added quickly, 'Mr Solomon and Mr Conrad reviewed all contracts over last weekend. They ain't planning to renew any of 'em.'

This was the news that Betsy had dreaded, for her contract expired just before the end of the year, and it was up to Planet whether or not to pick up the further three-year option. Because she cleaned her face only with olive oil (which she then wiped off) there was still not a line or a wrinkle on her beautiful face. But Betsy knew that soon she would be too old for close-ups.

After talking to Flora, Betsy was unable to sleep. As usual, she staggered out of bed for her 5 a.m. call, with a feeling of foreboding that stayed with her all day. She finished work early that evening and went straight home, in her elegant chauffeur-driven white Twin-Six Packard.

The chauffeur jumped from the car to open the elaborate wrought-iron gates of Betsy's low Spanish-style house with fountain playing in the forecourt, elaborate garden and view of distant mountains. This was normally the moment of her day that she most enjoyed, but that evening she felt only panic as – once again – she calculated the total cost of the chauffeur, the gardeners, the cook, the maids and the damned butler.

As she stepped inside the oval marble hall, Betsy fell into her mother's arms and broke into sobs. Mrs Bridges quickly led her to her bedroom, listened carefully to Betsy's fears, then patted her hand. 'It's time you were married, dearest,' she said firmly.

'Ma, you never let a man get near me!' Betsy wept, conveniently forgetting all the lies she had told successfully in order to be alone with Daniel Bloom.

'You're just as choosy as I am, my girl! But now it's time we found the right man ... an older man, so you'll have nothing to fear from a younger woman, later on.'

Unaware of the doctor's pessimistic prognosis concerning her eyes, Betsy was surprised by her mother's swift decision; for some time she had secretly wondered whether Mrs Bridges really preferred her daughter single so she wouldn't lose both her luxurious home and her constant companion. Hollywood, a town devoted to youth and work, was not a kind place in which a middle-aged woman might happily live alone.

After hours of discussion and much crossing out, Mrs Bridges compiled a shortlist. Betsy looked at the three names, and slowly shook her head. 'It's no use, Ma, none of those studio heads'll marry a shiksa. And I don't fancy any of them ... I mean, I'd have to ... marriage is very *personal*, Ma.'

As she spoke, Betsy remembered the older man she *had* once fancied, the man she had briefly glimpsed with Mr Ziegfeld at the Plaza, when the Bridges had first arrived in New York.

* * *

Eventually, through a man in the Planet publicity department, who knew a reporter on the *San Francisco Chronicle*,
Betsy discovered quite a lot about Mr J. O'Brien, who co-
owned a string of West Coast picture palaces, and was
called Black Jack by his pals, among whom were most of
the powerful men in Hollywood.

The publicity man had quickly cottoned on to Betsy's
casual interest. 'Not a chance, Miss Bridges, this guy plays
the field, hires Tiller Girls by the dozen.' He cheekily
advised her, 'Believe me, you'd be wasting your time.'

Betsy gave a glacial smile: she'd show him.

* * *

Betsy and her mother were repeatedly frustrated in their
attempts to meet Black Jack; San Francisco was hundreds
of miles to the north, and the Bridges knew nobody in
that city. When Black Jack visited Hollywood, he moved
amongst the studio bosses and their families, who never
invited actors to their homes, but only other film-makers,
producers and directors. Actors were considered unstable:
after a few drinks, an actor might ask an important guest
for some favour – a part, a credit, a raise – and so ruin the
atmosphere. Besides, female stars made the moguls' wives
jealous, and male stars tended to flirt with them, which
other female guests resented.

Eventually Mrs Bridges came to an arrangement with a
reception clerk at the Alexandria Hotel, where Black Jack
always stayed. For fifty dollars – an enormous bribe – she
would be informed when he next arrived.

Two months later, Mr J. O'Brien again booked his
usual suite. Betsy was working during the day, but the
Bridges spent all their spare time either lingering in the
dining room of the Alexandria, drinking endless cups of

coffee in the lounge, or hanging around the lobby, lavishly decorated with marble columns, oriental rugs and crystal chandeliers. However, on the few occasions when they glimpsed Black Jack he was always part of a group, either hurrying out of the front entrance or hurrying from it, up to his suite.

These few glimpses excited Betsy more than she cared to admit. At forty-two, Black Jack projected more sexual excitement than most men of twenty; he also had an air of tranquil assurance that only the very rich or improvident possess, plus the careless aura of a reckless past.

Sunday 14 April 1918. Hollywood

On a balmy, April Sunday morning, the Bridges were invited to a cricket match, arranged by middle-aged, beetle-browed British actor, C. Aubrey Smith. Such invitations were prized, for unlike most Britishers in Hollywood, Mr Smith was a genuine gentleman, educated at Cambridge University, and a former member of the All England cricket team.

Unfortunately, Mrs Bridges woke that morning feeling queasy, an unmistakable sign of a bilious attack. Betsy dosed her mother with salts, but it was clear that she would be unable to attend the cricket match. Betsy – bored by cricket – offered to stay at home but her mother refused to consider this: you never know who you might meet at Aubrey's. Betsy had better wear her new white crêpe and pearls.

By early afternoon Mrs Bridges felt sufficiently recovered to take a walk, which always shook her liver down nicely. Despite its international reputation, there were no restaurants and only two small drugstores on Hollywood Boulevard, a drowsy street of little stores, shingled houses, dusty pepper trees and palms; the only public transport was a trolley that banged eight miles from Laurel Canyon to the heart of Los Angeles. She decided to stroll to the nearest drugstore, buy another box of liver salts and a bottle of syrup of figs: Betsy was as regular as clockwork, but Mrs Bridges needed a nightly dose.

Having organized her afternoon, she smoothed on her new bronze-silk frock, a genuine copy of a Poiret; it was high-waisted with a tasselled sash and daring, ankle-length hemline to the hobble skirt. She rolled on her stockings and secured them with an elastic garter above each plump knee. She carefully pinned on her wide-brimmed straw hat, then set off on foot towards Hollywood Boulevard.

Having purchased her necessities, Mrs Bridges left the corner drugstore and was about to cross the almost deserted street when, to her left, she saw a cream and silver open roadster; it was waiting at the intersection for two old folk to cross. Seated alone in the roadster's driving seat was a man Mrs Bridges immediately recognized: she stared in disbelief at the battered face of Black Jack, his dark hair ruffled by the soft, warm breeze.

As the low chassis and long bonnet of the rakish Delage slid forward, Mrs Bridges – with the swift, unthinking heroism that was winning medals in the war – closed her eyes, thought of Betsy, and stepped off the sidewalk, directly into the path of the oncoming automobile.

She heard a squeal of brakes, a screech of tyres, then a furious yell, as the Delage stalled.

Mrs Bridges then collapsed on the dusty street, having genuinely fainted from fear.

'*What the hell do you think you're doing?*' Black Jack

roared, as he jumped from the roadster. He strode to the crumpled bronze heap, and wondered what was wrong – he hadn't even hit this dame. He dragged her to the sidewalk, then ran into the drugstore for help.

'Why, it's Mrs Bridges,' said the surprised druggist upon reaching the sidewalk. 'She just purchased her medication from me.' He checked that none of Mrs Bridges' bones had been broken, and held smelling salts under her nose until she jerked her head away from the ammoniac smell.

Mrs Bridges opened her eyes to see Black Jack's concerned face only a few inches from her own. She felt light-headed. She gasped, 'Dearie me! I *am* so sorry! I *do* apologize. It was entirely my fault. I suddenly came over dizzy.'

Black Jack (who had already decided to contact his lawyer pronto, lest there be some trumped-up claim for damages) realized that this woman was British, and she was no spring chicken; but she refused his offer to take her to see a doctor, adding weakly, 'I feel as fit as a fiddle.'

As the two men helped Mrs Bridges to her feet, she carefully exclaimed, 'Oh, now I shall be late! My daughter will worry!' Tears of genuine anxiety rose to her eyes: could she effect a meeting?

Black Jack (who could still remember his mam's soft lap and warm encircling arms) had a sentimental Irish regard for mothers. 'Don't worry, ma'am,' he gallantly offered, 'I'll drive you to your daughter.' Mrs Bridges almost fainted again, from relief.

* * *

As willow bat thwacked worn leather ball to delicately gloved applause, Betsy started to worry. Twice during the past hour she had telephoned home, to be told by the butler that Mrs Bridges had not yet returned from her walk. Where could she be?

Suddenly, all spectators heard a throaty roar. All heads turned to see the wickedly exciting cream-and-silver Delage pull up near the cricket pavilion. Mrs Bridges, carefully helped out by Black Jack, made the only Big Entrance of her life.

Betsy jumped up from her wicker chair and hurried towards the dumpy bronze figure. 'I've been so worried, Mother.' (Mrs Bridges had not been called 'Ma' in public since the first cricket match.)

Wearing a white crêpe frock with a big pleated-organdie collar, she looked as fragile and mouth-watering as a meringue as she turned her black-lashed violet eyes towards the man silhouetted against the afternoon sun. 'Thank you so much for bringing my mother...' Her voice trailed to silence as she stared with disbelief at the sunburned, craggy face of Black Jack. Betsy's eyes turned to her mother, and saw her serene expression of self-congratulation.

Black Jack stared at Betsy's angelic face and golden hair beneath a wide-brimmed hat that looked like an upturned bowl of white roses. Pressed to stay for afternoon tea and watch the cricket, the mesmerized Black Jack did so.

As he observed the other spectators – dressed as if for a royal garden party – sipping tea and nibbling doll's-house food, Black Jack felt a strange sense of having arrived at a destination that he had never set out to reach: something in his lace-curtain, Irish background sensed this was a genuinely genteel occasion. He was shrewd enough not to ask anyone to explain what the hell the rules of cricket were, and spent the rest of the afternoon at Betsy's side, clapping when everyone else did.

The match resulted in a draw (God knows why, puzzled Black Jack), after which the benevolent, monocled Aubrey Smith, speaking as through a mouth of cotton wool, admired Mr O'Brien's splendid machine: a pre-war Delage was rare on the West Coast. Mr Smith then whispered roguishly, man-to-man, 'In France they say that one owns a Rolls, one drives a Hispano, and one presents a Delage to one's mistress.'

'I haven't got a mistress,' said Black Jack, deliberately loudly. Betsy blushed.

At the end of the afternoon Black Jack offered to give Betsy a lift home, in his two-seater; there was a rumble seat in the back, so she seated four.

'No thank you, Mr O'Brien, we have our chauffeur here.' Betsy was already following her battle plan, hopefully laid out weeks beforehand by Bridges United.

'Then may I call on you tomorrow? To check on your ma's health?'

'Certainly. Mother will be delighted to see you at teatime.'

When Black Jack called with two large Dolly-Varden gilt baskets of violently pink roses, Betsy was at the studio. After tea, as she escorted him to the front door, Mrs Bridges suggested that perhaps Mr O'Brien would care to call on the following Sunday afternoon. Black Jack mentally cancelled plans to return to San Francisco.

He checked up on Betsy. The Ice Queen was considered hoity-toity, a snob; she was guarded like an Easter chick by the old hen of a mother. Cynical and suspicious, Black Jack found it hard to believe that here in the heart of Hollywood was a graceful beauty with a spotless reputation, a genuine class act. Nevertheless, his information double-checked correct. When Black Jack attended the next tedious Sunday cricket match, the British colony – who noticed Mrs Bridges' hopeful, animated face – quickly realized what was going on, and wordlessly rose in support. As if the Bridges were Queen Mary and the Princess Royal, they murmured loudly to themselves, 'Such devotion...' 'So fond of her dear mother...' 'Deuced pretty gal, what?...' 'If only I were younger...' 'Damned fine filly...' Nobody actually said, 'Good breeding stock there,' but the words hung unspoken in the air.

Betsy already knew that every young glamour puss on the West Coast wanted to get her hooks into Black Jack. Predatory women in Hollywood did not bother to target movie stars: they were merely handsome puppets, manipulated by and at the mercy of the men who held the reins of real power in Hollywood. But in a town that seethed and bubbled with sexuality Betsy knew that for a powerful man any sex could be had at any time for any price, while in San Francisco Black Jack had his pick of those damned Tiller Girls, as well as the other beauties of that city. So how could Betsy make this man her lawful wedded husband? How could she bewitch him to the point of an honest proposal?

Betsy planned to use Mabel Normand's successful strategy with Mr Goldwyn: unavailability.

For once, Betsy did not find demure behaviour easy, because whenever Black Jack appeared, she felt a tingling of excitement, an earthy lust beneath the hips and the sharp, focused attention of a lioness on the scent.

However, Betsy was an actress.

Although Mrs Bridges was never far away, sometimes Betsy and Black Jack found themselves alone for a tantalizing half-hour. Betsy said little, but listened, apparently enraptured, and kept her wide-open, black-fringed, violet eyes firmly upon Black Jack's face. Solemnly she nodded from time to time. Encouraged, Black Jack detailed further excitingly complicated business transactions which Betsy did not understand; eyes obediently shone, and an enthralled little smile curved her open lips. However, when Betsy eventually coaxed from her suitor the story of his early life, she found that it genuinely moved her heart, excited and intrigued her.

The elder son of a Belfast butcher's assistant, Jack O'Brien was six years old in 1882 when his mother died of puerperal fever, a few days after giving birth to his younger brother, Sean. The two boys had endured a harsh childhood – although there was always bread to eat and bones to boil for broth – until their father died from tuberculosis, leaving twelve-year-old Jack, a big, strongly-built lad, to look after his sickly little brother.

Luckily, Jack already had a job in a rag-and-bone yard, where he sorted the garbage from the carts into different piles, for reuse. On a chilly November morning in 1890, fourteen-year-old Jack felt something crackle in the sleeve of a greasy overcoat that he was about to throw into the pile of black rags, to be recycled as shoddy cloth. In a secret pocket sewn into the lining of the coat sleeve were folded four white five-pound notes. Quickly, he shoved the money into his boot. At midday, trembling with fear and excitement, he walked out of the rag-and-bone yard for the last time.

On the following night, for £4 apiece, Jack and eight-year-old Sean caught the steamer from Belfast to Liverpool. On Thursday 26 November 1890 the two boys sailed steerage from Liverpool on a schooner bound for St John,

Canada. Jack suspected that Sean would not be passed as fit by the immigration authorities so had decided that both boys should jump ship on the night of arrival. They crept ashore and hid behind a stack of barrels on the quay until the *Lady Jane* left harbour. As soon as it was daylight, they set out to trudge through snow, to the United States border, over sixty miles away.

After midday, the brothers stopped at every shack or farm they thought likely to let them sleep in a barn or outhouse; often the women of the house would take pity on them, and give them a bite to eat, although they were never allowed in the house, for they were too dirty. Illegally, at night, Jack and Sean finally staggered through a wood to cross the US border into Maine. At the next house that fed them scraps, they were advised to head further south, to Boston: that was where the Irish went to find work. It took the boys six weeks to reach Boston, and by the time their leaking boots dragged into the city they were almost penniless.

In Boston the O'Brien boys were immediately made to feel at home. To avoid starvation after the Irish potato famine of 1845, nearly two million people had emigrated to the United States, many to Boston. Most of the 'Micks' arrived with no money, trade or skills, so could only find ill-paid jobs as factory workers or labourers, employed by New England Protestants, who looked down on them: Catholics and failures – the scum of the earth. But the optimistic Irish had a grand advantage over other European immigrants: the Micks spoke English.

Tuberculosis, smallpox and cholera infested the Boston slums. In May, Sean died of pneumonia. Stoically, Jack buried his brother, and looked for a job with better prospects than the factory where he packed boots. After swearing he was sixteen, he was hired as a navvy in one of the tough gangs of Irishmen laying railroad tracks across the Midwest. He was tall, tough, and could be blunt to the point of rudeness, but he also had plenty of Irish charm and was popular in his gang. Because of his wild, black-Irish colouring, his buddies called him Black Jack.

When he was twenty Black Jack and three buddies quit their back-breaking jobs, and hopefully joined the excited gold-rush to Klondike Creek, in the Yukon, where rowdy camps were full of superstitious gamblers. Black Jack made sure that his was a name respected and feared, for in the tough and ruthless Klondike camps only fear guaranteed survival.

Two years later he left the Klondike, bound for Seattle, with a very small bag of gold nuggets strapped to his stomach to pay for his next stake.

In Seattle, having noticed the huge sums that Klondike miners were willing to pay for raunchy entertainment, he purchased a rundown vaudeville theatre, which he repainted bright vermilion; he hired a troupe of dancers, then a handful of urchins to scatter the dockyard saloons with leaflets that promised, 'The prettiest girls on the West Coast at the Mercury Burlesque Theatre'.

The Mercury reopened with a bill to suit a mining camp: comedy, songs with rousing choruses and saucy dancers who displayed as much as was legally permissible of their plump selves. Jack announced the acts in a soothing brogue, contradicted by the watching look in his sharp grey eyes; with tough aggression, the six-foot, powerfully built Black Jack and his two burly bouncers kept the audience in order. The Mercury was soon playing to full all-male houses. Black Jack's show business career had started.

* * *

Black Jack's fascination and lust for Betsy combined with sexual frustration to develop a powerful longing that he had never before felt for a dame, and which – somewhat incredulously – he decided must be love. As he allowed this strange new emotion to grow he found that suddenly the world seemed a more friendly and optimistic place; Black Jack wanted everyone around him to share his expansive and relaxed happiness: he felt a benevolent affection for his fellow creatures. Dimly, he realized that this was a dangerous state of mind for a businessman.

Eventually, the frustrated Black Jack arranged that Betsy be invited to one of the Saturday dinners given by his friend C.B. at the Paradise Ranch. C.B.'s invitation could mention that there would be plenty of other people to chaperone her, and her mother would pointedly not be invited. Black Jack would certainly look after Betsy correctly, but he also planned to take her in his arms in some dark, romantic spot and then see whether the Ice Queen melted. What did he have to lose?

He found out on the following Sunday morning when Betsy, deliciously cool in butter-coloured voile with a matching stiffened-organdie picture hat, sat sipping lemonade on her shaded terrace. With a cautious smile, Black Jack handed her an envelope.

As soon as Betsy read her invitation, her face turned an unbecoming dark pink. She jumped to her feet. 'How *dare* you, Mr O'Brien! Do you think I don't know what goes on at Paradise Ranch? *Everyone* in the Industry knows that

Mrs De Mille is never present! And with good reason . . . *What* sort of a girl do you think I am?' Her lips started to quiver. 'This invitation makes it very clear what sort of girl you think I am – the sort of cheap girl that can be bought for a ruby bracelet!'

She ran into the house, hurried up to her bedroom, and rang to ask the butler to show Mr O'Brien out – immediately.

Betsy then burst into tears of rage and indignation. This time she was not acting.

* * *

Black Jack capitulated. His engagement gift to Betsy was a diamond tiara. He also purchased from Planet (at a large profit to them) the remainder of Betsy's contract and their option, so to Betsy's relief she was saved from the humiliation of not having the contract renewed.

Equally relieved, Mrs Bridges realized that now there was no need to break to Betsy the disastrous prognosis concerning her eyes. Neither was there any need to mention it to dearest Jack: no doubt the problem would clear up now that her triumphant daughter no longer needed to face the studio lights. If it didn't, then dearest Jack would have to deal with it.

At Betsy's somewhat embarrassed request, Mr Solomon Fisher easily arranged for the date on Betsy's birth certificate and passport to be altered from 1887 to 1892. No problem. It was his wedding gift. Now she owed him one big favour.

Saturday 14 June 1918. Hollywood

The whole of the British Colony turned out for Betsy's church wedding. In tiara and simple high-necked ivory-silk dress, with a long train, the bride walked down the aisle to exultant peals from the organ that exactly matched her mood. Mrs Bridges triumphantly watched her dazzling daughter and thought, with satisfaction, that Betsy now held a position of social influence in California similar to that of the Fanes in Britain. For a moment, she wished that spiteful little bitch Mimi could see that Betsy now had a rich and powerful husband – a *real* man – which was more than Mimi could say about that pathetic nancy boy *she* had married.

* * *

Photographers and reporters crowded the station platform as the new Mrs O'Brien waved graciously from the red-carpeted steps of the Super Chief. Briefly, with satisfaction, Betsy remembered the dusty, crowded train that had first brought her to the West Coast, eight years before. For their honeymoon trip, Black Jack had reserved two drawing rooms and two bedrooms with berths that were almost-full-width beds; polished mahogany glowed, brass shone, crimson brocade was inviting; in both drawing rooms, white antimacassars had been placed on top of the seats, so that the Macassar oil which sleeked a gentleman's hair did not stain the upholstery.

* * *

Half an hour after the train steamed out of the station, Black Jack discovered that Betsy was not a virgin. Black

Jack went berserk. He lifted an empty champagne bottle by the neck and threatened her, before hurling it from the window.

He felt betrayed, he felt cheated. He slapped her around the face and tore the shreds of her cream chiffon nightgown from her body, before roughly finishing what he had started out to do.

As her husband moved his body from hers, Betsy could feel her eye painfully start to swell. Clutching the remaining shreds of the nightgown to her body, she whimpered, 'You're not a virgin, are you? *So why should I be?*'

'You know damn well it's different for men,' growled Black Jack. 'You fooled me! You led me to believe I was getting a pure, decent woman, not some used Hollywood whore!'

Enraged, Betsy sat up and glared at her husband. 'I don't regret a thing,' she shouted, with invention born of fury, fear and desperation. 'I was engaged to a wonderful fellow, a *real* gentleman! We decided not to marry until he came back from the war, for he didn't want me maybe tied to a maimed cripple . . . But my brave . . . er . . . Basil . . . was killed fighting in France – which is more than *you* did!' Wet, violet eyes looked reproachfully at Black Jack. 'After that, I never wanted to touch another man . . . until I met you.'

Surprisingly, Black Jack believed this tale, perhaps because he had no pleasant alternative. Horrified by his lack of control, his lack of compassion, his vile behaviour to his sweet angel, he ordered more champagne and a raw steak to apply to his wife's eye. He told her that he was truly sorry and to prove it, handed her a sumptuous red-leather Cartier box, in which lay a diamond bracelet that matched her tiara.

Unusually, Black Jack drank far too much that night, and the following morning found him groaning on his berth. Betsy lovingly prepared her bridegroom's Alka Seltzer, then rang for his beer chaser and shot of rye as she prepared to make the best of things. Daniel Bloom had been a considerate lover who enjoyed arousing Betsy's uninhibited response. Black Jack was clearly what was known in dressing-room parlance as an in-and-outer. Like most such men he was convinced that he was God's gift to women, for clearly no woman had ever disillusioned the powerful, generous, unforgiving Black Jack. However, her bridegroom was a sensual man; he enjoyed cuddling and kissing Betsy, and occasionally handed her another red Cartier box.

The luxurious train provided passengers with a non-stop, rattling good party. They had nothing else to do for five days except gossip, flirt, make love (many a secret rendezvous had been prearranged), drink in the comfortable bar car, or eat in the dining car, which served gourmet food or sent it along to your drawing room.

At Chicago the O'Briens changed trains. At New York, a chauffeured limousine was waiting to purr off with the O'Briens to the Alfred Vanderbilt suite at the Plaza.

Betsy now saw New York from a very different viewpoint.

Every morning, after Black Jack left for business meetings, beribboned great baskets of flowers were delivered to their suite: lilies, carnations, roses – anything she wanted. Black Jack amiably encouraged Betsy to spend lavishly at the smart department stores where previously she had been unable to afford a pair of silk stockings.

At midday, the honeymoon couple ate gourmet French food at Delmonico, the lavish Café Lafayette or the elegant Café des Artistes where, surrounded by sinuous, art-nouveau decor, they dined on the best food in New York. They sat in the best theatre seats to watch every good show on Broadway. After each show, Black Jack showed off his bride in some smart hotel restaurant, such as the Grill at the Claridge, The Astor at the Waldorf or the romantic Oak Room at the Plaza, where oak panelling with fluted columns surrounded murals of mythical German castles.

Like his bride, Black Jack remembered his first trip to New York. A year after opening his first vaudeville theatre he could afford to travel first class to New York, on the railroad that he had helped to build. He had booked a suite at the Waldorf, for you couldn't take a girl up to your bedroom, but you could take her up to your suite. Dazzled by the life and energy of Manhattan, he had seen every vaudeville and burlesque show on Broadway; he was particularly fascinated by the Tiller Girls: a row of precision dancers imported from Britain, they were all of equal height, and had been rigorously drilled to tap-dance and high kick. He immediately sought out John Tiller's New York agent and hired a troupe of fifteen girls. He then returned to Seattle and purchased his second dilapidated theatre, nearer to the docks, where Black Jack's Tiller Girls had been an overnight sensation. Naturally Jack had his pick of the ponies, as the chorus girls were called.

By 1904, Black Jack had been based in San Francisco and his Mercury Company owned twenty-two burlesque theatres along the West Coast, between Santa Barbara and the Canadian border. He had the reputation of a gutter Macbeth who ruthlessly grasped opportunities under hazardous conditions, without conscience or remorse. The following year, in settlement of a debt, he accidentally acquired his first nickelodeon. Quickly, he discovered that his little fleapit was a cash cow; he immediately raised a loan on his other properties with which to purchase a chain of seventeen nickelodeons.

In 1909, on one of his regular visits to New York City, he was surprised and impressed by the huge audience which filled the newly built, extravagant City Theatre cinema palace; immediately understanding that people would rather pay to see a movie in a palace than a fleapit, by the following evening he had commissioned cinema architect Thomas Lamb to build his first 2,000-seat picture palace in San Francisco.

That had been the year in which Black Jack was first described as a tycoon and first stayed in the Vanderbilt suite at the Plaza, which he new occupied with his bride.

On Sunday afternoons, when there were no crowds of workers, Betsy liked her tycoon husband to take her in a horse-drawn cab and clop slowly along Fifth Avenue, which was lined by stately mansions with imposing front entrances and delicate, wrought-iron railings. On the Upper East Side of Central Park, from swank apartment buildings built of pinkish-brown stone, exquisitely dressed women emerged under awnings that stretched above the sidewalk to protect them from the weather; uniformed doormen helped them into their carriages. To Betsy, who well remembered strolling here on Sunday afternoons, as she daydreamed with her mother, the uptown sky turned clearer and more hopeful, the air more exhilarating ... although of course, despite the crossing sweepers, it still smelt of horse dung.

Black Jack never understood why Betsy so enjoyed taking tea in the Palm Court at the Plaza and refused to go elsewhere.

Tuesday 14 May 1918. London

One May morning in 1918, Toby was peremptorily telephoned by Mimi's friend, Lilian Baylis, who summoned him to her office, saying that she had a good thing for him – come round to the Vic immediately. She then rang off.

Although Lilian was fourteen years older than Mimi, they shared a similar determination and defiance towards the world; they both moved among toffs without pretending to be other than their slightly eccentric selves; neither woman cared much what other people thought of her, but each had a mutual respect and affection for the other: they were both enthusiastic and affectionate, shrewd and sharp; both had succeeded despite heavy odds against them, and they recognized each other as survivors: they shared an undiscussed alliance, as do comrades after battle. ('Lilian gets things done,' Mimi approved, when she opened her purse to help.)

Six years earlier, Lilian's Aunt Emma had died, in July. By December, Lilian had obtained a theatre licence ('What a coincidence,' Mimi had said to her, deadpan). Just before the outbreak of war, although completely untrained and without financial backing, ill-educated and not particularly interested in the arts, Lilian had assembled the Old Vic Shakespeare Company and presented her first, full season of good, classical entertainment at prices which the young and working classes could afford.

Despite the war, the Old Vic had triumphantly stayed open. If there was an air raid then Lilian went before the curtain and bellowed to the audience, 'Don't let Kaiser

Bill interfere with our evening! If you want to leave, go now – but the rest of us are staying!'

* * *

An hour after her telephone call, Toby entered Lilian's dark, gloomy office at the Old Vic. The benevolently autocratic Lilian was stolidly seated like an empress on an old ribbed Hamlet chair that looked like the upturned entwined fingers of a pair of hands. Behind her was a battered roll-top desk, above which hung a crucifix and below which shaggy little dogs yapped noisily around their mistress's long skirts. (Mimi had complained to Toby, 'I never know which end I'm patting, until it nips me.')

Lilian looked over her thin silver-rimmed spectacles at Toby and observed by way of greeting, 'Disappointing war news, ain't it?' After the Americans had joined them in battle, the Allies had confidently expected to win the war immediately.

She added in her pronounced Cockney accent, 'I'm told that taxes are to be increased in the next Budget, dear.'

'You're a real ray of sunshine, Lilian.' Toby shook off a little dog that had started to make love to his left leg.

Lilian removed her spectacles, rubbed the sides of her nose and smirked at Toby with the ill-concealed joy of a messenger bearing good news. 'Old Horatio Kemble came to see me yesterday, dear. He needs money – fast, the old bounder. Wanted to know if I'd like to buy the King William.'

The King William Theatre, considered the most beautiful in London, was the last theatre to be owned by the Kemble family. During the previous year, Zeppelin raiders had bombed London, killed hundreds of civilians, demolished many buildings and badly damaged others, including the King William Theatre, which had caught fire.

'But the King William is a wreck, the roof's fallen in!' Toby exclaimed.

'Of course the King William's a wreck, dear. That's why Horace is willing to sell it dirt cheap!' Lilian pointed out. 'Although I don't know why he thought *I* could lay me hands on that sort of money, as I told him straight.'

'You could try God,' Toby half-jokingly suggested. When short of money, Lilian knelt in her office and prayed aloud for God's help: to listen to her prayer was like hearing half of a telephone call to a tight-fisted financier, briskly requesting further funds, and peremptorily explaining why.

Lilian shook her head. 'Not at the moment. I've got me hands full with the Vic, dear. Why don't *you* buy the King William?'

Toby considered. If repaired, the King William would undoubtedly be the prize jewel in the crown of the Fane theatre chain. Slowly, he nodded. 'I'm sure my father might consider . . .'

'*Don't* hand it over to your pa, Toby! Be a man! Buy it yourself!' Lilian was comfortably tactless and unapologetic ('Lilian says what she thinks,' approved Mimi), but she had a soft spot for the kind and thoughtful Toby, and privately considered that he had been squashed beneath his domineering mother's thumb. Of course she guessed young Toby was a nancy boy, but there was no reason why Toby should be a *hen-pecked* nancy boy.

'Buy the King William myself?' Toby was astonished. 'Where would *I* find the money?'

Finding money was Lilian's speciality. 'Borrow on the

Minerva,' she said briskly. 'Try Barclays Bank. Argue with 'em if they turn you down, I always do.' Lilian had terrible rows with people ('She won't be trodden on,' affirmed Mimi).

'Surely no bank would lend money during a war to repair a bombed theatre that is bringing in no income?'

'If they won't, you try Sidney Silver – he's a private financier, used to call 'emselves moneylenders. He's helped me a couple of times. He'll charge you high interest of course, dear, but as soon as this war's over, people'll long for a bit of fun, dear. Sidney knows it's a safe bet to invest in entertainment, my boy, no matter which side wins the war!'

Citing the bad war news, six banks turned down Toby's request, so eventually he approached Lilian's money-lender. To Toby's surprise – and mild panic – Sidney Silver cautiously agreed to advance the necessary money for the purchase and repairs of the King William, against security of the deeds of both the King William and the Minerva, on a fifty-year mortgage at a fixed 8 per cent interest, considered extortionate by normal banking stand-ards at the time.

Sunday 14 July 1918. London

On a warm evening in mid-July, Toby interrupted Mimi's recitation of the latest London gossip (the young Prince of Wales had fallen in love with a married woman whom he had met during an air raid, in a shelter off Berkeley Square).

'Foxtop, there's a cab waiting outside,' Toby an-nounced with the complacent air of a conjurer reaching into his top hat to grasp the white rabbit's ears. He helped the intrigued Mimi into a lilac summer cloak, and hurried her into the cab.

When their cab took a right turn off the Haymarket into King William Square, Mimi – craning from the window – could see a square lined by Regency houses with cream-stucco façades, fronted by black iron railings to prevent passers-by from falling into the basement areas. Black railings also guarded the neglected, overgrown garden at the centre of the square, where soot-covered rhododendron bushes smothered straggling roses. At the far end of the garden, Mimi saw the forlorn boarded windows above the flaking Corinthian columns of the King William Theatre's wide porch.

Puzzled, Mimi watched Toby produce a key, unlock the dirty black door of the theatre, then beckon her in. Mimi pulled her lilac cloak around her to protect her from the dust and dirt, and shivered as they entered the foreboding gloom of the theatre. As Toby switched on his firefighter's torch, Mimi heard him say gleefully, 'I'm the new owner, Foxtop. I signed the deeds yesterday!'

Mimi gasped with pleasure, threw her arms around Toby's neck, and hugged him. Together they entered the auditorium.

'Does Sir Octopus know?' Mimi asked, standing by the stall seats.

'I think he was rather pleased,' Toby said smugly. Sir Octavius had been agreeably surprised to hear of Toby's audacious action.

While they explored the rest of the auditorium, Toby told Mimi what he knew of its history. All the great nineteenth-century actor-managers had played on the boards of the King William; in addition to this impressive list of credits, the King William also had a ghost. Mimi had already heard of the Grey Lady, often seen by actors when rehearsing – with the house lights on: she was the ghost of Cornelia Cole, an ageing leading lady, who in 1842 had forgotten her lines three nights in a row, and subsequently hurled herself from the roof. Occasionally – sometimes in mid-performance – the Grey Lady opened a door at the back of the Gallery.

From the side of the Royal Circle Mimi gazed up at the jagged holes where the auditorium yawned open to the sky. A sparrow flew in and she noted the pale encrustations of bird droppings that dripped from the forlorn, dangling remains of the glass chandeliers.

Mimi pushed a tip-up seat; rusted, it did not budge; her finger sank into the rotten plush. The auditorium seats exuded a damp stench and the entire building stank of mildew. On either side of the blackened proscenium arch, once-crimson velvet curtains hung, dark and dirty. On the scabrous, surrounded walls, Mimi could still see that beneath the grime, large near-naked ladies were energetically pursued by satyrs, while angels serenely played harps in a high wind which artistically revealed plump breasts beneath their drapery.

'This is the worst part,' Toby said apologetically. 'The back and the front of the theatre are pretty well sound.'

'It's bloody *marvellous*!' shouted Mimi. Again she threw her arms around Toby, then clutched his arm as she gazed around the auditorium, seeing it not as it was, but as it would be. 'Toby, let's put on detectives and drawing room comedies with small casts. The public'll want a few safe thrills and laughs after we've kicked the Kaiser back to Prussia.'

Toby was delighted by Mimi's enthusiasm, for she had

seemed depressed, after recently reading in *The Stage* of ex-Gaiety-Girl Betsy Bridges' splendid marriage. But surely, Toby reasoned, now that the Fanes owned the most beautiful theatre in London, Mimi could forget her old grudge against Betsy.

Sunday 21 July 1918. New York

After spending over a month in now-sweltering New York, where Black Jack had combined business with honeymoon, the O'Briens returned by train to the West Coast. Before they left from Grand Central, Black Jack purchased a selection of magazines and newspapers, including the foreign edition of *Variety* magazine.

That night, before she drowsily fell to sleep, Betsy smiled to herself: for a girl with little acting ability, her achievements had been impressive, and now she could relax. She no longer needed eye-opener pills: she could sleep until ten in the morning, or longer. Partly as a result of her gratitude, and partly because she had lost her awe of Black Jack, Betsy now saw him as a great, big, protective, cuddly bear. In fact, to her surprise, she had fallen in love with her husband.

The following morning, as they ate breakfast on the train, Betsy gasped and looked vexed.

Opposite her, Black Jack looked up from yesterday's *Wall Street Journal*. 'What's the matter, honey?'

'Oh, it's nothing. More coffee?' Betsy bit her lip.

Black Jack stretched forward, took *Variety* from his wife's hand, and read that Mr Tobias Fane, of the famous British theatrical family, had just purchased the King William Theatre, considered the most beautiful in Britain.

Black Jack, who now knew the story of Mimi's interference with Mr Ziegfeld, leaned forward and patted Betsy's knee. 'Honey, we have a *string* of theatres.'

'I know. It's not that.' Betsy turned and stared, unseeingly, at the passing scenery. She was remembering her mother's comforting prophecy, 'One day that bitch will get what she deserves! One day *you'll* get the chance to put the boot in, Betsy, just as she did to you!'

But Mimi was not getting what she deserved!

Black Jack could see that although she sought to disguise it, Betsy was clearly upset. After being carved up by many rivals and two partners, Black Jack had painfully and expensively learned to be devious, to play his cards close to his chest, and to trust nobody. He never forgot a good turn or a bad one; he was as ruthless as he was unforgiving, and never showed any vulnerability; he believed in two-eyes-for-an-eye and a complete set of dentures for a tooth: this was justice as he had seen it successfully exercised by his friends, his enemies, and the Hollywood movie moguls.

Black Jack said thoughtfully, 'Maybe this new theatre of theirs will give *you* your chance for revenge, Betsy.' His sharp, grey eyes narrowed. 'But not yet. Let these goddamned Fanes spend some money on it first – bring it up to scratch. Then you can pounce, if that's what you want.' He leaned back and smiled comfortingly at his beautiful bride.

Chapter Ten

Max's school career started scandalously. Originally, he had been put down for Eton, but after Mimi and Toby first escorted him to that ancient and elitist school within a stone's throw of Windsor Castle they received a stream of homesick letters from their twelve-year-old son, who had been thoroughly spoilt by Mimi, and was accustomed to doing exactly as he pleased. Although Max had his own study – as did all the boys – the ancient buildings of Eton were far more austere than his home, and the Boys' Maid complained to his Dame that Max was the untidiest boy in the House. Max hated the uncomfortable uniform of top hat, swallow-tailed morning suit and stiff, high collar; he never bothered to tie his tie neatly and complained that every morning he felt as if he was dressing for a wedding.

After his first fortnight, Max was supposed to understand the school's puzzling, private language; he was supposed never to be late – although there was hardly time to get from one Division to the next – or to break any other of the bewildering rules that he rarely understood. He was also expected to remember seemingly stupid things, such as the initials of all twenty-six Housemasters and the different colours of all twenty-six Houses as well as those of the various sporting teams. Max constantly forgot to perform traditional rites, such as capping: all new boys had to raise their top hats to Senior boys, Beaks and members of Pop, an exclusive boys' society; if a new boy failed to do so, he was flogged or given moss-picking. By the end of the first month, Max felt that he had weeded almost the entire School Yard, and his backside was sore with beatings. As a junior, Max was also expected to run errands and shop for Senior boys at the holler of, 'Boy up!' from some senior in the House Library.

One evening when he was feeling particularly unhappy he was unexpectedly pushed by a waiting Senior boy back into the privy he had just left. Terrified, he turned and faced his aggressor, instinctively jerked up his knee into the older boy's groin, then managed to dodge under his arm and escape, to agonizing howls. Terrified of retaliation, Max dashed back to his study, grabbed his money, slowly sauntered out of the gates, quickly caught a train from Windsor to London, and was back at Fitzroy Square before anyone at Eton had noticed that he was missing.

Mimi had been miserably lonely without her son, but her moroseness was replaced by joy when, unexpected, he appeared. She refused to be parted from him: Max was going to stay at home, where his mam could see he was treated proper. Toby tried to argue with Mimi that Eton offered the best education in Britain, and Max would have run into similar problems at any boarding school in Britain.

'Then he ain't going to boarding school,' decided Mimi. 'He'll go to a London day school, where I can keep him under me eye.'

So Max attended Westminster School, attached to the Abbey since medieval times. He was still obliged to wear a top hat and a high, stiff collar that chafed his neck, but he liked his new school, where pupils had special permission to sit in one of the Galleries of the nearby House of Commons and listen to the speeches of Members of Parliament, whom Toby dismissed as a bunch of old hams with no idea of rhetorical delivery. Easily the best thing about being back in London was that Max could now occasionally go to the theatre in the evening, sitting in the cheap seats of the Gallery, although this meant setting his alarm clock for five o'clock in the morning, in order to do his homework before school.

It wasn't long before Max started to be teased at school by older boys, who had heard rumours that Fane's pater was a nellie, a nancy boy, a pansy, an Oscar Wilde type. The puzzled Max approached his father, for he did not see how it could apply to him. 'Because you're married,' Max pointed out, 'and anyone can see I'm clearly *your* son.' He glanced at the mirror above the fireplace in Toby's study: there could be no doubt about his paternity, he reaffirmed, staring at his wild, black hair and black-lashed, dark-blue eyes. When younger, Max's face had even more resembled that of Toby, but now his features had lost their earlier delicacy, and his face was rougher and stronger than that of his father.

The moment had come, Toby thought, with resignation.

He explained to his son that bisexuality had been commonly accepted amongst the civilized ancients of Greece and Rome, although some religions now considered such practices a sin, and some doctors an illness. Whatever the reason, a passionate longing for love with a person of the same sex was a physical and emotional need for some people. God had made each person the way he was, and for that person to be *truthfully* different was impossible.

Max looked at his father and understood what had not been mentioned; red-faced and near to tears, he rushed from the room.

Max never again discussed homosexuality with his father. Uneasily, Toby watched his son consciously adopt the attitude of a traditionally masculine man, sometimes overemphatically so; all boys were taught that sissy feelings such as gentleness, sensitivity, kindness or creativity were neither admitted or permitted, even to oneself. For some months Max conspicuously avoided his father, who eventually explained the reason for this to the puzzled Mimi.

Two minutes later, she bounded into Max's bedroom and angrily boxed his ears. She enumerated his father's many virtues, and ended her tirade by calling him an ungrateful little brat. She added, '*Your* pa is *my* best friend; he's always stuck up for me, and he's always behaved like a gentleman. He ain't never let me down, nor nobody else. *I* love him and you'd better remember he's *my* husband as well as your pa, you spoilt little sod!' She stormed out, banging the door behind her, and spent the rest of the day locked in her bedroom.

Mimi had fiercely and continually repressed her memories of her own father and had now convinced herself that all those dreadful experiences had never really happened. However, the will is less powerful than people like to believe, so although she had pushed them out of her conscious mind, those repressed memories lurked unconfronted just below the surface of her unconscious and were still a powerful influence on her behaviour. Unsummoned and unwelcome, these frightening recollections now surfaced to be contrasted with Toby's generous loving kindness towards his child.

Astonished by such a critical outburst from his doting mother, Max outwardly dropped his disdainful attitude and, in time, seemed to accept his father as he was. Clearly, in many ways Toby was an admirable parent. Max was the only boy in his form who came under no parental pressure to perform well; he was a lazy pupil, but he had an excellent memory, which enabled him to swot before examinations and pass them with distinction. Toby did not care what Max chose as a career, so long as he was happy – although Mimi liked the idea of her son becoming a respectable doctor or lawyer, with a university degree, one of them black gowns and the flat black hat, with a tassel. Toby hoped that Max would try for a history scholarship at Oxford, but he did not push him towards this goal.

Saturday 16 June 1923

However, one early June afternoon, in 1923, just before his fifteenth birthday, Max secretly nipped round to the Old Vic, and in Miss Baylis's study he confessed to her what he dared not tell his parents.

There was silence in the small dark office. Sitting on her Hamlet chair, Miss Baylis looked shrewdly at him through steel-framed spectacles. Standing before her – he had not been invited to sit – Max could smell the strong odour of fried onions and sausages that exuded from her drab clothes: as usual, Miss Baylis had cooked her midday meal in the wings, in a frying pan over a gas ring.

Max planned to start the conversation in an adult

manner, as he had often heard his father's friends do. Nervously, he said, 'How's Baylis, Miss Business?'

'Could be worse, dear. Of course, money's always a problem. The *King Lear* costumes cost over ten pounds . . .' Miss Baylis frowned, 'I still can't understand why my People didn't come to see our *Lear*, they've plenty of tragedy in their own lives, of *course* they'd have understood it . . . You seen it, dear? . . . Here's a comp, the matinée starts in twenty minutes.'

'Thuh . . . huh . . . thank you, Miss Baylis.' Max took the complimentary pass, and nearly turned to escape, but he knew that he was lucky to be in a position to talk to Miss Baylis.

'Well, what is it, dear?' Miss Baylis asked, a trifle impatiently.

Max's words tumbled over each other; he forgot his carefully rehearsed, man-of-the-world speech, and spoke defensively, so showing the weaknesses of his argument. 'I'm old enough to know what I want . . . I'm old enough to make up my own mind . . . Why should *I* go to university just because *they* didn't? . . . If it's such hell, why do *they* do it?'

'If you're trying to tell me that you want to be an actor,' Miss Baylis said sternly, 'you'll have to improve your delivery, dear.'

Max felt relief and his knees stopped trembling. She *had* understood. Miss Baylis sighed and said it was in his blood she supposed, then suggested he apply for the two-year course at the Royal Academy of Dramatic Art, because the Vic couldn't afford to use amateurs . . . except as unpaid extras, of course.

* * *

No matter how late he left the theatre, Toby always returned to it at nine o'clock on the following morning, impeccably dressed in a dark suit, grey hat, spats and kid gloves; his silk handkerchief, tie and socks were of dove grey or burgundy, and a white carnation was always tucked in his buttonhole.

Once in his office Toby's secretary took his silver-topped walking stick and hat. The dingy walls were covered by a yellowing collection of old posters, several new ones and many effusively signed photographs. Taking up half the room stood a flat-topped walnut desk before which wallowed a luxuriously upholstered green velvet armchair – for stars – that could be hastily exchanged for the battered stenographer's bentwood chair against the wall – for reprimands. From the adjacent offices rose a constant clatter of sound: telephones shrilled like upstart ingenues; imperturbable typewriters zipped along; the lulling murmur of female voices was occasionally interrupted by the staccato click of high heels crossing linoleum.

Every morning when Toby sat at his desk he faced a miniature Swiss Alp of envelopes. Some of the letters requested or confirmed bookings, others contained cheques in advance payment, contracts, programme and poster layouts from the printer for correction, the stage manager's daily report; notes from importuning agents or actors and, of course, bills. This white avalanche was never completely shovelled away because there were five postal deliveries daily. Furthermore, Toby was constantly distracted by the peremptory ring of his telephone, or the insistent presence of his secretary, a flat-chested, grey-bunned woman whom you might mistake for a librarian and who possessed the secretary's primary qualification of being able to look anyone in the eye and calmly lie. Despite her attempts to protect Toby, others constantly interrupted him to discuss matters that concerned the internal running of the theatre. Cleaners, usherettes, bartenders, members of the orchestra needed to be engaged, reprimanded, warned and finally fired, a job that Toby hated: he then had to interview replacements. Carpets needed patching, seats mending, uniforms had to be purchased, altered to fit, maintained. The bar stocks of food and drink had to be purchased, checked in and checked against pilferage. Any pause in his day was filled by agents, actors seeking an interview – even when there were no vacancies – or drama critics seeking free tickets and juicy gossip.

One summer morning Toby's staccato office was interrupted by a welcome visitor for a change.

'Why, Lilian.' Toby beamed his delight as he quickly replaced the old bentwood chair with the green velvet one.

'I'll get straight to the point, Toby, and then I'll get straight back to the Vic. Your Max's been accepted by RADA. Now, you're not going to stand in that dear boy's way, are you?'

Max endured some half-hearted argument from his parents, but soon they became resigned to what they now told each other they should have known was inevitable.

Naturally, Max knew that having been brought up in a theatre family was not nearly enough reason to assume that he would be a good actor: familiarity did not breed technical skills. He knew that in order to be an actor, you had to do more than stand in front of the footlights, feel the emotion that your part required, remember your words and project them clearly, but he had not realized exactly how hard he would need to work at RADA. He endured the elocution and deportment classes, and enjoyed the fencing and dancing classes, but undoubtedly his favourite was the Shakespeare class, filled as it was with emotional and dramatic opportunities to overact. There were ten female students to every male – considered by Max an agreeable ratio – and all competed for the male leads (always far better than female parts, with a few notable exceptions, such as Lady Macbeth and Cleopatra). However, each pupil was required to play different parts in each scene.

Slowly Max began to understand the alertness and judgement that an actor needed. Slowly, he learned to establish a rapport with the other actors, to understand that his first loyalty should be to the play, and to see his part as only a *part* of the whole play – a point which all students immediately forgot in real life, as soon as they landed their first two-line role.

Every evening, Max now hurried over Waterloo Bridge to the shabby side of the River Thames, where the old Vic Theatre allowed the RADA student to walk on in crowd scenes – without payment, as Miss Baylis had warned. Here, he saw that performing the same part, night after night, need never be as monotonous as it seemed to outsiders, for the circumstances were always subtly different, so were the performances of the other actors, and so was the audience: therefore the play never *was* the same because the performance was a completely different experience every night; an actor had to keep alert – far more than most people were in real life.

Among the young actors whose careers Lilian Baylis was responsible for starting was Max's former childhood friend, Felicity Allen, who had been working as an apprentice at the Vic since she was fourteen years old. Felicity had grown into a tall, slim young woman, with long straight white-blonde hair, fair as the down on a thistle top; her horizontal blonde eyebrows almost met above eyes so light and brilliant that they shimmered like light blue glass marbles in the sun. Felicity – now nicknamed Fizz – was popular with the rest of the cast, whereas Max was conspicuously left alone: no one wanted to be accused of sucking up to a young Fane. Max had not cared for this subtle reversal of power.

In 1925 Max left RADA, having failed to shine in the end-of-year shows. Mimi comforted her depressed son by reminding him that he *had* been chosen to play the male lead, Heathcliff, in *Wuthering Heights*, the end-of-term play, and that he had been much applauded. The part had suited Max not only because he was tall, lean and dark as a gypsy, but because beneath his good-mannered exterior he also had a wild streak, and like Heathcliff, the undisciplined Max could not disguise his emotions. So he had enjoyed striding round the stage, being moody and mysterious, tossing back his long wig of unruly raven hair and glowering at the rest of the cast.

* * *

Seated in a plum-velvet buttoned chair, the pear-shaped Lilian Baylis sipped a cup of tea in Mimi's drawing room, where the walls were covered in dusky pink *moiré* taffeta and the windows draped with cream lace; the fitted crimson carpet had been left over from the King William refit, after the war. Lilian looked down at the cheque Mimi had just handed her. Immediately realizing that it would pay for a new set of lights, Lilian slowly nodded. 'OK, Mimi, I'll give him a try-out. But I'm not promising anything more.'

After Max auditioned for the Old Vic (Prince Hal's St Crispin's Day speech) he had rushed home triumphantly to tell his parents that he had been appointed second assistant stage manager, with the promise of small stage parts later!

Upon hearing Max's good news, Sir Octavius had sent his grandson a letter, in which he warned him not to expect the theatre to be a bed of roses, but a bed of thorns: because he came from a famous acting family, more would be expected of him than of others, and he would be shown no mercy by his fellow actors. If successful, he could expect constant accusations of nepotism, and praise only from sycophants who hoped for furtherance in their careers from his family. So his older and, he trusted, wiser grandfather advised him to be courteous to all men and intimate with none: theatrical intimacy bred disturbing jealousies. Therefore it was in his best interest that he expect no engagements from his loving grandfather, who hoped with all his heart that Max would merit the family reputation and add to its lustre in the great profession to which they all belonged.

A fiver would have been more useful than a paper lecture, Max thought. He was earning a pittance at the Vic. But Max loved being there. He enjoyed the constant rush of putting on a new play every three weeks, and loved every minute of the rehearsal period, whether or not he was acting. His passionate interest in every detail, his suggestions, criticism and general well-meant interference often earned him a sharp suggestion from the director that he mind his own damned business. Despite such rebukes,

Max continued to enjoy the camaraderie of rehearsals and the hurried pub lunches – a sausage roll or ham sandwich with a glass of bitter – during which everyone praised the director's concept only to criticize it at the First Night.

After their short lunch-break, the Company fled back from the pub to the Vic to continue work until four in the afternoon, when there was a break until the evening performance. During this break, actors were supposed to rest, but, in fact, they learned their speeches for the next play, heard each others' lines, or were fitted for costumes and wigs.

Max had plenty of work as second assistant stage manager: as well as being general dogsbody to the ASM, he held the prompt book, gave cues, checked actors' entrances, and was responsible for everything on the props table – where all props were laid out and checked, both before and after the play.

Naturally, in a company where everyone was over-worked, he also understudied and took very small parts, so rehearsals, evening performances and matinées consumed his entire day – slavery, with no result, that he could see: impatiently, he longed for tangible fame, his name painted high on the boards above some Shaftesbury Avenue theatre.

Despite Max's training at RADA, he made the usual beginner's mistakes: he forgot what to do, or he did it wrong. The worst moment of his life to date had been the night when he was late on stage, something an actor only does once in his life. The call-boy had burst into the Green Room, where Max was idly pencilling a crossword puzzle, and shouted, 'Max you ass, the others are ad-libbing to cover you – get on stage!'

Shortly after this shaming incident, Max wandered into

Samuel French's bookshop, where he picked up Stanislav-sky's *My Life in Art*; therein the great Russian teacher explained his system of instructing an actor to create a character from *within* that character. When acting a cripple, instead of merely watching a cripple and copying his limp (creating from *without*) a Stanislavsky-trained actor sought to discover *why* the cripple limped, how long he had limped, what he felt about it, and how the limp had affected the rest of his life and his relationships. In order to do this, a pupil studied psychology and social history, also using his intuition and imagination to create a back-ground for his character, to discover and share his thoughts, ambition and motivation.

When Max burst into his father's study to tell him of Stanislavsky's principles, Toby looked up from his desk and listened. Toby then said, 'But a good actor knows instinctively.' He walked across to the bookcase and pulled down a green volume. 'Listen to what Henry Irving wrote.' He read, ' "What is the art of acting? To fathom the depths of a character, to trace his latent motives ... to comprehend the thoughts that are hidden under the words, and thus possess one's self of the actual mind of the individual man." '

Nevertheless, Stanislavsky's book had immediately changed Max's attitude to acting: instead of rushing over Waterloo Bridge ten minutes before curtain up, he arrived at the Vic two hours beforehand, took a thoughtful hour to apply his make-up as a Roman centurion or an Eliza-bethan courtier, and then sat silently in a corner of the men's dressing room, concentrating on 'becoming' his two-line part as he remembered the words of Sir Octavius: 'No such thing as a *small* part, my boy.'

Sunday 12 April, 1925. The Laurels, Bradshaw, Essex

As Lilian Baylis had predicted, British theatres had been packed since the Armistice, by people desperately longing to forget the horrors of war and return to normality. Unfortunately, many returning heroes then had to endure the horrors of peace in a world that had completely changed since they bravely marched away from it. Just as the pre-war balance of political power in Europe had vanished, so had the pre-war economic stability. In Britain alone, two million men were unemployed. Most people were poor and many were starving.

Nevertheless, at her country house in Essex, Lady Fane still employed a butler, a cook, a housekeeper, three liveried footmen, three maids in the kitchen, three in the pantry, three housemaids and a houseboy to clean boots and knives, in addition to the outdoor staff. So, on a warm Sunday in mid-April, Mimi was surprised to see no sign of a servant, or of the afternoon tea, now overdue on the terrace where Lady Fane moved among small groups of her luncheon guests who waited thirstily for their Lapsang Souchong and chocolate cake, before leaving to catch the train back to London.

Now eighty-five, Lady Fane daily grew thinner and more fragile, while her skin became more transparent, like some yellowing, skeletal, autumn leaf. When her mother-in-law threw her an appealing look, Mimi nodded and obediently skipped off to find out why afternoon tea had not yet been served.

Instead of ringing the drawing-room bell, Mimi, in white chiffon with white stockings and white lace cloche hat, headed straight to the kitchen quarters. As soon as she pushed open the green baize door at the end of the corridor, she heard the staccato howl of 'Tiger Rag', realized why tea was late, and smiled.

Traditionally, the housekeeper and butler had Sunday afternoon off, but the rest of the staff were clearly enjoying the impromptu dance: in the centre of the large kitchen, also used as the staff sitting room, stood a long scrubbed wooden table, upon which were scattered Max's ragtime records and a gramophone being wound up by a shirtsleeved footman as he jerked his foot to the energizing, syncopated rhythm of a Dixieland dance band. Two parlourmaids were shimmying together; the scullery maid was prancing with the second footman; sixteen-year-old Max was energetically cavorting with an upstairs maid; the houseboy, clutching the back of a wooden chair for support, tried to imitate Max's frenetic steps.

Mimi gazed fondly at her son. As he kicked his heels backwards, wriggled his hips, energetically shook his entire body to the music, Max projected an energy that attracted people: they sensed that something exciting was about to happen (whether or not it was) and they wanted to be part of it. His youth and intensity sometimes made older people feel overwhelmed, sucked dry of energy. His dark good looks, and the ease with which he manipulated both of his doting parents, had already given Max a permanent sense of entitlement to whatever he wanted in life. Often the world demands too much of a man, but Max already expected too much of the world.

Mimi tapped the houseboy's shoulder, took his hands and danced with him, joining in the high jinks until the record ended. As, laughing, they all gasped for breath, Mimi asked, 'What's happened to tea?'

Everybody froze. 'Oh my Gawd,' groaned the second footman.

The staff scurried to fetch tea trays, kettles and the rest of the elaborate paraphernalia needed to serve tea on the terrace. The chief culprit smiled at his mother as he carefully packed all his gramophone records back in their case.

After Mimi and Max left Lady Fane's kitchen and returned to the terrace, Mimi airily explained. 'Tea will be served a bit late on account of the milk went sour.'

Toby moved closer to Mimi. 'I wouldn't have called this weather thunderous enough for the milk to sour,' he whispered to her, and they both smiled. Max noticed his parents share a secret joke, and stiffened. Max no longer allowed his father to hug him and was still uneasy with Toby, Mimi noticed sadly. She had hoped all that would have been forgotten after he left school.

Lady Fane tottered up to her only grandson. 'Darling Max, do please go and entertain those young ladies.' Max obediently sauntered towards a gaggle of giggling girls at the end of the terrace: they all wore pastel-coloured sleeveless frocks with no waistline, long ropes of pearls and hats like helmets, pulled low to cover bobbed hair.

Fondly, Lady Fane listened to the squeals of delight as he reached the girls, then turned to Lilian with a worried face, 'What can one expect but degeneracy if gels try to look like boys?'

'Women got used to comfortable clothes when they was doing men's work in the war,' Lilian replied; nothing was going to make *her* wear laced-up corsets again.

'But these gels show such a shocking amount of leg! They paint their faces *outside* the theatre and dance

unchaperoned to that *shocking* music!' Lady Fane was refer-
ring to the shamelessly erotic throb of jazz.

'And we can't stop them, dear.' Lilian winked at Mimi.

This has been one of the old girl's most successful
luncheon parties, thought Mimi as she surveyed the crowd
of guests, now overspilling the terrace onto the lawn.
Nearly everyone was an actor or a peripheral – an agent or
designer – and they were all hard at it, talking about
themselves in order to convince themselves of whatever
they were saying, each guest his own best audience. Some
acted humble, some acted charming, some acted listening.
Mimi watched Toby dutifully move among his mother's
guests, kissing a cheek, laughing at a joke, trying not to
linger too long with some man in whom he shouldn't show
too much interest. Mimi thought, he mustn't monopolize
Noël, it'd be giving the game away.

The young, newly successful Noël Coward was sharp
and shrewd, with a quick wit and tart tongue. Despite his
talent, hard work and determination to succeed he had
not been an overnight success, but had managed to live
in a style far beyond his income by what Mimi called
'high-class bumming': top society hostesses offered him
delicious food, drink and pampered weekends in the
country, in return for which, literally and cheerfully, Noël
sang for his supper.

He now lifted a languid hand. Mimi waved back then
continued to listen idly to snatches of show business
gossip.

'. . . What can you expect with a live horse on stage?
And the *stench*! . . .'

'. . . So she held up the jewelled casket and flubbed,
"'Twas King Charles gave me this *pox!*" . . .'

'BBC radio broadcasts will mean the death of the music

hall. Who'll go out and pay money to hear Gertie Gitana or Harry Lauder when they could simply sit by their fire, turn a switch and be entertained, free? . . .'

'. . . Gladys was emoting full strength, centre stage, when her knickers dropped to her ankles and we *all* corpsed . . .'

'. . . forgot his umbrella! . . .'

'. . . forgot his sword! . . .'

'. . . forgot his revolver! . . .'

It was just as well that Mimi was standing too far away to hear what Fizz was telling her mother. Jessie Allen – now an established theatrical agent – was listening to the latest gossip among the Old Vic girls about Max, now known as the Watercress Man. When Jessie, mystified, had first asked for an explanation, Fizz had pointed to the instructions on the packet of watercress which Jessie grew in her kitchen window box. 'For really good results,' Jessie had read, 'spread the seed lavishly.'

Guiltily, Jessie waved a grey suede glove, and in return Mimi waved a white one, then told herself that she shouldn't go and gossip with Jessie, she had better do her duty, for a show business party is rarely held only for pleasure. Mimi moved purposefully towards a trio of businessmen who were quietly discussing the success of the brutally efficient Mussolini and his equally aggressive German counterpart, Adolf Hitler. Mimi rushed up to this little group with as much enthusiastic delight as if they had been the Prince of Wales, Rudolph Valentino and young Gary Cooper. Hopefully, these three portly gentlemen were future backers for the King William, where Toby now successfully presented medium-brow drawing-room comedies, detective dramas and family musicals that could not get into Drury Lane. All King William presentations sold on the reputation of the last one; they always had the same audiences, and could rely on a big and regular trade of visitors from the provinces.

At all levels of society, the theatre was still an important part of British social life: new shows were eagerly discussed, the appearances and idiosyncrasies of actors and actresses carefully copied. As the popularity of music hall faded, the little Minerva had switched to intimate revue, which was cheap to mount and ideal for small theatres. It relied for effect on surprise and speed, a mixture of witty, satirical sketches, catchy songs and a small but erotic chorus of minimally dressed dancers who performed before some simple, uncluttered setting, often just a black velvet curtain. Most had archly suggestive two-word titles such as *Yes, Please!* or *Why Not?* and starred still-inexpensive pretty, promising newcomers, such as exuberant Bea Lillie or naughty Gertie Lawrence.

Mimi, now thirty-seven, was relieved that she had decided not to be an actress, for now she would be worrying about ageing. Besides, there were dozens of actresses, but few male impersonators, and none with her wonderful voice. She had updated her act, now impersonating real people: her favourite was the debonair musical comedy star, Jack Buchanan; dressed in top hat and tails, Mimi's favourite trick was to hold her top hat behind her back as she walked to stage left, then flip it high up in the air, turn swiftly and nonchalantly catch it, as she walked to stage right. She also impersonated film stars, leading politicians and other famous personalities of the day: anyone but Charlie Chaplin, done to death by other impersonators.

When all Lady Fane's guests had finally departed,

Mimi returned to the terrace, pulled off her constricting little cream helmet, and ran her gloved hands vigorously through her hair. As she did so, Tudor Perkins sauntered out of the drawing room.

After his brief appearance as Buttons in *Cinderella*, Tudor had persisted in a theatrical career, and trained at the Birmingham Rep. He had an excellent voice, deep and mellow as a cello, and an elegantly haughty profile. Toby thought that Tudor might successfully have played aristocratic villains, had he not clearly found himself unconvincing as a cad. He was one of those intelligent but limited actors, with sufficient self-confidence but little acting ability, who can only play themselves.

During the Great War, Tudor had left Birmingham to serve with the Guards in Egypt, then in France; he had been bayoneted in the left arm shortly before the British broke through the last defences of the Hindenburg Line in September 1918, just before the war ended. Since his medical discharge, he had stayed with Maisie, who, during the war, after a bad series of Zeppelin raids, had cheaply purchased two neighbouring houses in Earls Court Square. The large brass plate to one side of the main entrance, engraved in elegant Marina script, read THE EARLS COURT THEATRICAL HOTEL. Tudor, who occupied a small attic bedroom, was never presented with a bill, Maisie had confided to Mimi.

Mimi watched Tudor saunter along the now-deserted terrace that separated house from garden. He loped past small round lace-covered tables surrounded by empty little gilt ballroom chairs; he stopped at a table that had not yet been cleared by the servants, picked up an egg sandwich and threw crumbs down on the lawn, where house martins swooped to snatch them up. Then Tudor walked, smiling, towards Mimi, who wondered what could be done about him.

Mimi knew that many actors hide from the world in the skin of the character they play on stage but the intelligent and self-confident Tudor could only play debonair chaps in drawing-room comedy. Everyone in the Business liked Tudor and wanted to help him, but he had the acting ability of a marionette and on wet days, his injured arm was sometimes so painful that he could do nothing at all.

Where could Tudor avoid the rain, and find work?

A grim smile slowly spread over Mimi's face as she suddenly remembered that Betsy Bridge's acting ability was equally non-existent.

Mimi ran towards Tudor, and took both his hands; excitedly, she cried, 'I've got it! I *know* what you should do, Tudor! *Go to Hollywood!*'

Tudor looked to Mimi with a delighted smile, which quickly faded. 'Darling, it's a jolly decent idea – but I can't possibly afford the blinking fare.'

'*I* can!' Mimi remembered Jolly Joe's generosity when she had been burned. She added, 'Pay me back when you can.'

Excited and hopeful at last, Tudor leaned down and gratefully kissed Mimi on the cheek. 'Darling, you're a real old trouper, it's a devilish *brilliant* idea!' He added, 'Could you possibly give me any introductions, old girl? Do you by any chance know Ronald Coleman . . . or Betsy Bridges?'

Chapter Eleven

Just before his marriage, Black Jack had decided to base his still expanding business in Hollywood. He had known continual success since 1910, when he had sold his nickelodeons and burlesque theatres and persuaded a small group of business friends that cinema palaces in downtown districts were a safe investment: eventually he had raised enough money to finance fifty West Coast picture palaces, in which he treated his customers 'as plush as a theatre audience'. Black Jack knew that the way to get asses on seats was to lure them into the cunningly lit gold-painted hall of some Egyptian temple or Moorish palace for only a dime. Now a similarly sumptuous fantasy was purchased for his bride.

The elegant English-manor-type house was in Hancock Park (an area settled by the original Los Angeles Land Grantees), where the old-money families lived. The O'Brien mansion was surrounded by acres of lawn, a rose-wound pergola that led to a flower garden, a tennis court and two swimming pools (one for the kids), surrounded by palms and banana trees; it was staffed by an English butler, chauffeur and housekeeper, a French chef, Mexican domestics and Japanese gardeners.

Black Jack wished that his old mam could see the style

in which he now lived, for she had longed for refinement; in their slum lodging her most precious possession had been a tattered lace tablecloth, only used at Christmas. When Black Jack walked into the auditorium of one of his new sumptuously kitsch movie theatres, he always saw it through the astonished and delighted eyes of his mother. Black Jack knew that his mam would also have been delighted by his bride, for Betsy was a class act: she looked great in her diamond tiara when they threw a lunch party, and she knew stuff like the difference between the big-grained grey squashy Beluga caviar and the smaller black-grained Sevruga.

Black Jack liked being admired, liked being well fed in luxurious but cosy surroundings, with every possible physical comfort. To his surprise, he also enjoyed returning home at night to a stable, predictable base, and relished the calm atmosphere of domesticity and security. Betsy's sedate presence calmed his restless soul, and gave him peace of mind.

Black Jack enjoyed his wife's elegance, and was delighted when his pals compared her to Gladys Cooper (also a former chorus girl), a classic English-rose beauty, the favourite Postcard Girl of British troops in the Great War. Betsy hated being compared to anyone else – even Gladys Cooper – but she loved being encouraged to buy pretty clothes and her dressing room was quickly filled with garments of supple French jersey, sensuous crêpe de Chine, Jap silk, georgette crêpe and erotically flimsy voile; drawers were crammed with daringly sleeveless bathing suits, delicate lingerie stitched by Spanish nuns, fine silk stockings and beaded evening bags. A special cedarwood cupboard kept bugs from her coats of mink and Manchurian wolf, her capes of silver fox and marabou, and her ostrich boas, most of which were unworn, because the West Coast weather was always so warm.

However, no matter how carefully Betsy chose her husband's clothes, Black Jack always looked as if he could never be bothered to tame them: his necktie was never straight, he scorned cuff links and rolled up his shirt-sleeves when he yanked off his jacket; when he wore an elegant overcoat, he turned up the collar and he pushed his black Homburg to the back of his head, which made him look even taller and gave him a raffish air.

For about a year after their marriage, the O'Briens had rarely attended Hollywood parties; instead of going out on the town, they often stayed at home and danced together to the music of a phonograph, repeatedly wound up by the butler, who also placed the needle on the revolving black disc. As he and Betsy tangoed with elegance in their candlelit lounge Black Jack occasionally caught himself nostalgically remembering nights spent making whoopee in Maude's House, but quickly reminded himself that he was now a happily married man.

In return for his lavish expenditure, Black Jack expected his wife to run a trouble-free home, to dress well and learn to handle money; he was a generous husband, but insisted that Betsy stay within her budget and keep detailed records of what she spent. He also impressed upon her the importance of being a lavish hostess.

'See, Betsy, if you got plenty of money to splash around, everyone thinks business must be doing well so you got no credit problems.' He added, 'And get to know the wives real well.'

'Which wives?'

'The wives of the studio bosses, they're the only ones that matter.'

Betsy did not looked pleased: before becoming rich and successful, most studio bosses had married a duplicate of the devoted, self-sacrificing mother left behind in some Polish or Russian ghetto. The wife was expected to provide sons and emotional security, for home was the only place where a movie tycoon felt secure enough to relax his guard, although now he had no time to be a good father or husband.

'They're so *dull*, Jack,' Betsy objected.

'They'll show you the ropes, honey, teach you how to do it. After all, you're married to a successful guy and I want everyone to know it.'

Betsy was silent. She knew that once a studio boss had made it his wife was supposed instantly to transform herself into a refined symbol of his success. She also knew that the wives who were unable to do this were swiftly replaced.

So she palled up to the wives, who quickly taught her the responsibilities of a Hollywood hostess: where to shop for flowers and food, how to give a dinner party at an hour's notice; she kept a menus book which listed all guests and the meals she served them, so they were never offered the same dish twice. The butler dutifully recorded what each guest ordered to drink, so that a returning visitor had his favourite cocktail thrust into his hand as soon as he stepped across the entrance, regardless of what he actually felt like drinking at that moment.

The O'Briens knew everyone of any consequence in town: Mary and Doug, Norma and Irving, Charlie and his young girl of the week, but Black Jack had insisted that Betsy stop seeing Mabel Normand. After yet another major row with Mack in 1918 Mabel had signed a five-year contract with Sam Goldwyn. Separated from Mack

Sennett for the first time in seven years, insecure and unsure of herself, Mabel took drugs to relax and feel in control of herself; she showed up late for work or disappeared for days at a time, while her wild, all-night parties had become notorious. Reluctantly, Betsy eventually obeyed her husband.

At Betsy's big parties the women wore splendid gowns and jewels and the men always wore white tuxedos. White-gloved male servants served French champagne in crystal glasses; each course appeared on silver dishes; one concoction was always served aflame with brandy and there was a choice of three elaborate desserts. After a lavish meal, the women twittered upstairs to repaint their red mouths, then descended to drink coffee and discuss children, clothes and scandal before the men returned and they all went to the projection room to nibble Belgian chocolates and gaze up at some new movie, not yet released. The men smoked cigars on the terrace and talked briefly of sport and other people's gambling losses (nearly all the studio bosses gambled heavily) before discussing business. The perennial argument at Black Jack's gatherings was whether the industry had over-expanded. Sure, America was movie-mad, hence the nationwide picture palace building boom, but Black Jack had calculated that there were *already* too many movie houses for the number of potential movie-goers, and knew that after every boom comes a bust.

After a successful party, Betsy often felt too elated to sleep. Black Jack would wake with a hangover at dawn and glance from his bathroom window to see her drifting in a flimsy negligée among the dark cypresses and mauve-tinted trees of their garden. He did not know that at these moments Betsy exultantly reminded herself that now she was up at dawn only if she chose to be, now she was never too exhausted to eat in the evening and she never had those blinding headaches after a day spent under Klieg lights.

Betsy's first child, Stella (*Never mind, a boy next time*) was born on 29th January 1920, a national day of mourning, for it marked the start of alcohol prohibition throughout the USA.

In 1921, Betsy's second child, Tessa, was born. (*Another girl, pity.*) As soon as she could say, 'Dad, Dad,' Betsy's British nanny pinned up on the nursery wall a list of words which the little girls were never to use: 'dough, scram, sucker, dame, ain't, you betcha', and similar picturesque colloquialisms which, of course, the children could not read. The list was intended covertly to admonish their parents.

Betsy now had not only the wealth that her mother had trained her to hunger for, but also the affection, husband, children and sedate domestic life that *she* had always longed for. Black Jack was an affectionate husband, a sensual man who liked lots of physical contact and enjoyed sex with his wife and cuddling his babies; he also felt a rough affection for Mrs Bridges, so after the birth of his second daughter he suggested that Grandma move into their mansion: the old girl was clearly lonely, and Black Jack knew he could rely on her to see that there would be no cloud on his domestic horizon.

During Betsy's second pregnancy, despite her golden hair and unobtainable-angel face, Black Jack had quietly fallen into the habit of being unfaithful: he saw no reason not to be. Although her husband was discreet, Betsy was quickly and gleefully informed; bitterly hurt, all her insecurities resurfaced.

How she wished that she could cry on Mimi's shoulder, knowing that she would understand what her mother did not: that the solid foundation of her life had suddenly cracked wide, and upon being forced to face her husband's treachery, Betsy could not control her painful emotion, her feelings of bewilderment, anxiety and hurt pride. Her mother was concerned only to keep up external appearances and hang on to the good provider. Mrs Bridges repeatedly told Betsy that she must do as other wives did: disappear when not required, suffer humiliation in silence, turn a blind eye in public, weep in private and find an outside interest. Mrs Bridges warned her daughter not to be so stupid as to take a lover, for Black Jack's masculinity would not tolerate that, and Betsy would risk divorce. 'So long as you behave,' she reassured her, 'he'll never divorce you – because of the children.' Betsy wept even harder.

However, in the back of her mind she had always realized that Black Jack would never be able to settle down with only one woman. A few movie tycoons, such as Louis B. Mayer, Harry Warner, and Carl Laemmle doted on their wives, but sex was a potent symbol of power in Hollywood, so many movie bosses were systematically and flagrantly unfaithful. Because of their aggressively hidden but permanent insecurity, they needed constant flattery to reassure themselves – the sort of adulatory flattery that was not part of a normal marriage. They kept flashy mistresses – often more than one – and call-girls or starlets were regularly summoned to their office executive suites. Naturally, they expected their head secretaries to see that no rumours reached their wives.

Monday 1 June 1925. Hollywood

When Tudor climbed down from the Super Chief at the Santa Fe terminal, he stepped into a glorious, sunny day and smiled with delight, as he saw orange trees growing beyond the rail tracks; he peered north at the distant mountains crouching north of Hollywood, then turned his head to the south, where metal scaffolding towers (oil wells) were scattered across the landscape. As Tudor's cab hurled between trucks, roadsters and jalopies, he gazed out at low factories, ugly little stores, bars, gas stations, and mile after mile of telephone wires.

When his cab reached town, Tudor immediately noticed that it was different from any other place he had visited. Hollywood felt eerily unreal: apart from the hair colouring, nearly all the women were smart, pretty and oddly similar, with cupid-bow mouths, spit-curls, thin, pencilled eyebrows and bosoms bursting from low-cut dresses. Men swaggered in big-checked suits and bright shirts: clearly, everyone was desperate to be noticed. Tudor was more impressed by their sauntering, free-and-easy attitude, which contrasted strongly with the hurrying crowds of sophisticates in New York, who clearly took for granted such new devices as automobiles and radios. Both towns were very different to all those he had seen in staid old Britain.

After his cab dropped Tudor at the low pink pile of Beverly Hills Hotel, he checked into the cheapest room. Without waiting to unpack, he looked at Mimi's list of introductions. Whom should he phone first, Ronald Coleman or Aubrey Smith?

* * *

Welcomed by the British Colony, Tudor was a great social hit in Hollywood. He looked what he was – a man who had known horrifying wartime experiences, but had not been soured by them; in Hollywood there were few war heroes, and no modest ones. Hardly any men had Tudor's beautiful manners or amiable disposition: he was never irritable, always even-tempered and charming. He was also a good guest. Tudor had been raised to look after women, to carefully dance with wallflowers and chaperones as if he were enjoying himself. He was always well groomed and well dressed in the type of clothes that Edward, Prince of Wales, had popularized since the war: casual sports jackets; loose, wide-shouldered, wide-legged, narrow-hipped suits; broad-knotted neckties and a wristwatch, rather than a watch and chain. Tudor's muscular, lean figure looked equally manly in shortsleeved polo sweaters or soft shirts. Consequently, Tudor spent his first fortnight in a mad social whirl. Saturday night was especially lively, when at least twenty-five big parties were given in Hollywood, often with a live band and catered buffet in some peppermint-pink striped marquee, especially erected behind the host's lavish house.

Studio heads rarely appeared at these extravaganzas. Tudor was told that apart from a few dignified charity functions held in some imposing hotel ballroom, the movie moguls rarely appeared in public, and when they did, they rarely mixed with each other; each preferred to preside at his studio's table where he received appropriate non-stop deference and congratulations on his latest business move.

'Hear you got the Majestic chain at last, Jack.'

'Yeah—' Short chuckle. 'Those schmucks can't argue now.'

Studio heads increasingly used their muscle to force out unaffiliated exhibitors, for by owning all the movie theatres they would control the entire Industry. Everyone in the Business knew that a handful of moguls would soon decide among themselves what pictures were shown and where; audiences would be forced to watch whatever the studios produced at whatever price the studios named.

Sunday 14 June 1925. Hollywood

Tudor was eventually introduced to Mrs Jack O'Brien by Aubrey Smith. From beneath a hat that looked like an inverted pink cabbage, Betsy's black-lashed, violet eyes looked up demurely, but no fashionably bandaging underwear could disguise the voluptuous curves beneath Betsy's dusky-pink silk frock.

Equally intrigued, Betsy stared back at Tudor's attractively cadaverous face, at the brown hair that peaked on his forehead above dark, sleepy eyes with long, dark lashes and high cheekbones. Betsy smiled. 'Has *everybody* told you that they love your British accent?'

'Everybody. Constantly.' Tudor's reticence disappeared when he smiled: his eyebrows lifted and his forehead wrinkled as his face slowly broke into a lazy, conspiratorial grin.

'What are you doing in Hollywood?' Betsy asked, with equal predictability.

'I seem to have achieved my ambition.'

'Which is?'

'To live in the sun and wear silk shirts.'

'You must be an actor,' laughed Betsy.

Fascinated by Betsy's beauty, and drawn to the indefinable, underlying sadness that he sensed beneath it, Tudor briefly remembered Mimi's terse description of Betsy ('I knew her, slightly. A spoilt, jealous, two-faced bitch'). Like most people, Tudor was unaware of the depth of animosity that existed between Mimi and this beautiful creature, although when he mentioned Mimi's name he saw the friendliness in Betsy's violet eyes swiftly replaced by a wary, guarded alertness. Tudor hastily redirected his conversation to a less controversial subject.

Saturday 27 June 1925. Hollywood

Two weeks later Tudor, wearing a vanilla linen suit and beige silk Charvet shirt, arrived for cocktails at Betsy's mansion, now furnished in a style that was part ancient Egypt, part modern Hollywood. Betsy's walls and drapes were beige; her bird's-eye maple furniture was liner-lounge sleek; all rugs and upholstery were geometrically patterned in pale chic colours – donkey beige, mouseback grey, dead rose-petal. At this time, Black Jack was often away on business. He had sold his shares in the Golden Gate Picture Palaces, and was now investing the proceeds in a series of California land purchases, buying on the outskirts of San Diego, San Francisco, and Santa Barbara; he had also just acquired a thousand acres of land south of Culver City. Black Jack also invested money in restaurants, and several Ford dealerships, but he put no money in the stock market. He told Betsy that the market was now full of damned idiots who had borrowed money to invest, which artificially drove prices up, so that stock became overvalued.

No sooner had Betsy's butler handed Tudor a Martini

and disappeared than he reappeared in the sitting room to announce in a sonorous voice that madam's crates had just arrived from Paris.

Betsy gave a happy gasp of delight and ordered them to be sent up to her dressing room and broken open immediately. Excited, she asked Tudor whether he would mind if they took their drinks upstairs, in order to watch the unpacking, for she did not know what had been dispatched: she had placed her order by simply sending a banker's draft to Mlle Chanel, who knew what suited her clients.

In Betsy's beige-carpeted dressing room all walls, closets, doors and ceiling were covered by mirror. A second cocktail in his hand, the bemused Tudor watched Betsy's personal maid shake her new clothes free from a sea of white tissue paper. Outfit after outfit appeared: navy, black and cream jersey suits; frocks in cream, apricot and beige silk, some decorated with Cubist motifs. Matching cloche hats were pulled from liquorice-black hatboxes.

In the midst of the unpacking, Betsy's mother appeared. Mrs Bridges' hair was now pulled back in a greying bun at the back of her neck; she wore a dove-grey dress with a modesty vest of cream lace: cunningly, she had transformed herself into the typical movie-Irish-grandmother that brought out Black Jack's protective instinct, as no attractive woman could.

Betsy turned from the mirror, dropped the apricot georgette shift she was holding to her shoulders, and dashed to hug her mother; after that first year of marriage, often spent apart from her, Betsy loved living once more with her mother, as again they laughed and chatted or talked casually together about fashion and feelings, carpets and cookery. Above all, the two women's common interest was Betsy's three children (at last a boy, Nicholas, had been born in early 1924). Mrs Bridges now felt that she had helped her daughter to achieve happiness, so the neurotically ambitious mother had dissolved as she relaxed into her new role of devoted grandmother.

Equally devoted to her children, Betsy was determined to see that they had the Golden Childhood of which her overburdened, eight-year-old self had dreamed when chewing overcooked, over-salted cabbage at some digs dining table after walking back from the theatre in the rain, worried only, as the family wage earner, that she hadn't caught a cold because her boots had been soaked.

Two little girls now dashed into Betsy's dressing room, followed by a uniformed nurse who carried a bewildered-looking baby in white lace. To Tudor, the room suddenly seemed full of tissue paper, clothes, maids, nannies and children. Sipping his Martini, he turned and bumped into himself, in a mirror. As he rubbed his sore forehead, he was butted in the back of his knees by Betsy's youngest daughter, who laughed with delight as he brushed spilled gin from his vanilla linen suit.

From the entrance hall below came the bull-like roar, '*Where is everyone?*' followed by the slam of a door.

The entire dressing room froze, as if an invisible movie reel had broken.

Two squeals of, 'Dad!' 'Pop!' rang out as both little girls dodged past all adult feet, and rushed downstairs to greet their father. The smallest girl was the first to reach Black Jack for she flung her agile little body over the chrome banister rail of the new circular staircase, then swiftly slid down to the hall, where Black Jack called, 'Yippee!' and caught her frilly little bottom in his arms. Tess was blue-eyed and dark, with black eyelashes as long as those of a giraffe; full of bubbly fun, she had clearly inherited her father's Irish fizz.

Five-year-old Stella followed more cautiously, one stair at a time; she had inherited Black Jack's big-boned, tall build and had large hands and feet, a pale skin, and a slow, hesitant voice. No fizz.

Black Jack noisily hugged his daughters. Obviously, Tess was Black Jack's favourite child and she loved having his full, indulgent attention as she smiled an impudent, conspiratorial smile, wriggled in his arms and covered his battered nose with kisses. Tess's flirtatious relationship with her father was that of daddy's little princess, and any sexual undertones to their relationship would have been indignantly denied by Black Jack.

Betsy eagerly followed her daughters down the circular staircase. She loved her husband dearly, except in the one place where love was demonstrated and celebrated: bed. For years, Betsy had faked orgasm, partly in order to be considerate, partly to avoid argument as to whether she was frigid; on the few occasions when Betsy had not faked, she sensed that Jack regarded the situation as a challenge, so thrust grimly on and on as if trying to start an imperturbably obstinate motorbike, until Betsy decided what the hell, and faked it again, anyway.

When Tudor was introduced to Black Jack, he winced as the large, tough hand grasped his, then politely refused another cocktail, which was nevertheless thrust into his hand by the larger, tougher one.

Tudor then agreed that little Nick looked exactly like his father, although privately he thought him indistinguishable from any other toddler. As the women disappeared with the children to the nursery, he accepted his fourth Martini and wobbled out on the terrace with his host.

With hooded grey eyes from beneath heavy black brows, Black Jack looked at his wife's new friend long and carefully, as if he were a casting director. Slowly, seriously, he nodded, 'Betsy needs an escort when I'm away on business. You'll do. A penniless actor would be crazy to screw up a potentially great contact by screwing his host's wife, don't you agree?'

Tudor spluttered into his Martini glass, for once speechless. Eventually he attempted to redirect the conversation as he stuttered, 'Your wife is a charming, *married* woman – with a son and two beautiful little daughters to look after . . . I wouldn't be surprised if they grew up to be movie stars, like their mother . . .' Tudor's light laugh trailed away . . .

Black Jack frowned; he did not intend his daughters to be actresses for the same reason that a whorehouse madam doesn't want her daughter to be a whore. Black Jack had observed the harsh, insecure life of female movie stars – outwardly glamorous and successful but inwardly a constant turmoil of anxiety about their looks and box-office pulling power: Black Jack did not want to see that nervous vulnerability in his own daughters. He was equally determined that his daughters should not marry actors; he never even considered the possibility that his son might become one.

* * *

Betsy had whiled away her pregnancies – and found the outside interest so wisely recommended by her mother – by becoming a leading patron of the Brentwood Players

Little Theater. Uneducated and with no background of culture, Black Jack nevertheless respected it and approved of Betsy's new, classy interest, so long as nobody expected *him* to wear a stiff shirt and listen to some guy play a violin or watch some show by Ibsen where everyone jawed and nobody high-kicked.

As a leading patron and source of funds for the Brentwood Players, Betsy regularly attended First Nights and enjoyed making an entrance. Betsy entered a room full of people with her head held high and a smile on her lips: in the doorway, she froze, willing everyone to notice her, after which she confidently glided forward.

Tudor, who had hoped in Hollywood to get larger parts than the ghost in *Hamlet*, had so far only been able to get a little work as an extra (he was always the stuffed-shirt escort of some society dame). He was therefore nearly always free to escort Betsy to the Brentwood Players productions, and proved an ideal companion, ever mindful of Black Jack's warning.

The Brentwood Players were part of the thousand-strong Little Theater movement that offered experimental alternative entertainment to Broadway-fuelled pap. An amateur theatre club in some small hall hired professionals as soon as they could afford it – starting with a director for Chekhov, Strindberg and Shaw, or new plays written by American authors who had no chance of getting on Broadway if their plays featured marital infidelity, sexual deviation or the greedy selfishness of a capitalist society. Always written in earthy vernacular, such plays exposed the violent fraudulent relationships of family life; the indifference and horrific inhumanity of big-city life; the petty vindictiveness of small-town life (so very different from Norman Rockwell's charming paintings); and other problems that the nation would rather ignore. Grimly, the new, young playwrights also exposed the four main myths of the American Dream as pitched by Hollywood: that unyielding puritanical morality and hard work always lead to success; that money brings happiness, fulfilment and respect; that marriage and motherhood make every woman happy; and that the family unit is the basis of a happy society.

Hollywood took absolutely no notice and continued to check the grosses.

Tudor, theatre-trained, soon started to appear on the other side of the stage of the Brentwood Players theatre; he could not expect payment in the amateur productions, but he loved once again to perform to live audiences, once again to get an immediate reaction to his work, once again to hear the gloriously addictive, anxiety-lulling sound of applause. On stage, Tudor felt as if he belonged there in his own right, whereas he felt unaccountably unfaithful to Mimi when he escorted Betsy.

Chapter Twelve

For six months, Max's promised 'small stage parts' proved little more than walk-ons: the medieval soldier who staggered on stage to cry, 'Alas the battle is lost and Richard fled . . .' or one of Falstaff's drinking companions with a few no-longer-funny Elizabethan jokes. Unlike wine, humour aged badly, Toby consoled his son.

In contrast, Fizz had quickly wheedled her way on stage, was now an accepted member of the Company, and was sometimes given quite meaty parts: her biggest had been Jessica in *The Merchant of Venice*.

Max felt unaccountably put out: all his life he had patronized Fizz, but now he felt like a new boy at school who arrives to find his younger cousin already in a higher class. Naughty Fizz enjoyed this new role reversal, enjoyed watching Max check that the three caskets and all the other props were on the Props table. It had been a long while since Fizz counted her lines – as Max still did.

Fizz had progressed quickly because she had a face of great mobility, while her voice was high, clear and true. She never wasted time discussing Stanislavsky, motivation or inner orientation, but she always arrived at the first reading having done her homework, knowing the historical context and having imagined what it must feel like to be a hunchback or a milkmaid or a princess. Without the benefit of theory, education or much training, Fizz simply walked on stage – and the audience never once took their eyes off her: the other actors might just as well have disappeared.

Despite this, she was popular with her fellow actors; she had a contagious sense of fun and loved to make people laugh. Because she turned everything into a joke, Fizz did not always notice potentially dangerous situations. However, when treated unjustly, her fierce temper was quickly roused, although it was just as quickly subdued and always followed by a flood of charming contrition that invited forgiveness. Fizz never minded apologizing to anyone she had wounded, for she had a soft heart, and could not bear to see anyone cry.

Max and Fizz had quickly clashed offstage, for the Watercress Man frequently prompted babbling brooks of tears amongst the young female members of the Vic, who fell for the practised wicked grin and carefully piratical charm of the tall, lean newcomer. Fizz was equally flirtatious with everyone, but was too occupied by her acting to handle the sort of multiple relationships which Max juggled so easily, and Fizz had no need to prove to herself or anyone else that she was attractive to the opposite sex.

* * *

In March 1926 the seventeen-year-old Max was given his first 'proper' part, in *Romeo and Juliet*; he was to be Count Paris, the dull bridegroom chosen for Juliet by her parents. Max's joy was dampened when he heard that Fizz was to play Juliet. Noticing the miasma of resentment that hung above the younger members of her troupe, Miss Baylis had snapped, 'Actresses always complain they never get a chance to play Juliet before they're too old for the part. That's why we're trying out Fizz.'

However resentful, everyone had to admit that Fizz was physically perfect for Juliet: she had a fine-boned build, with small, high breasts and narrow hips above subtly curved slim legs; her arms were graceful and expressive, her small hands were unusually narrow and had been compared by Toby to the plaster cast of Mrs Patrick Campbell's hand in the Garrick Club. Fizz's fragile appearance contradicted her physical toughness: except for a few childhood complaints, she had never known a day's illness. She ate like a horse, never took any exercise, and never put on an ounce of extra weight.

The first read-through was held in the Vic's dusty old saloon bar at the back of the Dress Circle: above the balding crimson-plush bench seating, walls were covered by flaking gilded mirrors. The room, which smelled of stale cigars, quickly filled with actors who bent over their tattered green-bound parts or muttered their lines, while awaiting the producer.

When he appeared, the producer briefly explained his concept of the play and gave the reasons for his cuts. Most Shakespearean productions were cut, in order to shorten them, to minimize costs, and to give emphasis where a director decided he wanted it, which partly explained why each Shakespearean performance was a different experience, sometimes almost a different play. The first reading began with much mumbling and stumbling, the minimum of emotion and frequent, exasperated cries of 'Sorry'. From time to time, the producer suggested an alternative interpretation.

Later they started 'moving' the play on stage; all movements and groupings were planned and noted ('blocked') by the director's assistant. Carefully the cast kept to the chalk marks drawn over the dusty stage which marked their entrances and exits. The actors paced themselves to conserve their energy, but they were all quickly off the book. Slowly, the different aspects of the play came together, and started to form a cohesive performance.

Max enjoyed every minute of rehearsals, particularly the dress rehearsal, for he knew that however well an actor knows his lines, he never knows his part until he has rehearsed it on stage with his fellow actors, complete with moves, business, furniture and props. The stage was in a permanent state of chaos: the backdrop collapsed in Act One; half of the new lights failed in Act Two; and the final problem was the slow collapse of Juliet's tomb, as she lay gracefully dead upon it, at which Juliet resurrected herself with a screech.

Thursday 8 April 1926

As leading lady, Fizz was allowed to dress in Miss Baylis's tiny office, where a faint whiff of liver and onions lingered from Miss Baylis's midday meal. There was no dressing-room space whatsoever at the Vic, and the rest of the female cast had to dress in the saloon bar running up behind the Dress Circle to change from court attire into nuns' habits, and then run back again. All the men dressed in one of the top boxes, with the red velvet curtains drawn together to conceal the jostling naked bodies.

Fizz laid her make-up towel on the roll-top desk, set out her greasepaint on her towel and sat on the Hamlet chair. The second-best part of her day was when, as now, she looked in her mirror, started to apply her make-up . . .

and slowly saw someone else's face appear before her, as she thought, with growing delight, 'I know this woman. I know how she thinks, speaks and moves. I know her secrets and her ambitions. I know her true self, that she hides from the world; I know the masks she whips on to play each of her different parts in life.'

Keeping this recognition in her mind, on stage, Fizz always felt a gleeful sense of freedom, for her make-up acted as invisible protection from self-consciousness: *Fizz* could not be held morally responsible for the behaviour of her onstage character! Consequently, she felt as uninhibited as, when fifteen years old, she had first travelled alone to France, a foreign country where nothing of her past was known, and so she was freed from it.

As she pinned on the pearl-stranded Juliet cap, Fizz looked forward to her favourite moment of the day: the moment when she first became aware of the delicate stillness which tells an actor that his or her imagination has meshed with that of the entire audience.

From high up in the buzzing auditorium, Max peeped through a chink in the red-velvet curtains of the box where the actors were dressing. Below, he saw his parents with Jessie Allen – proud mother of the star – take their central seats in the stalls. As they did so, Max suddenly felt the vertiginous thrill of a First Night. However well-rehearsed an actor is, what brings out the best in him (adrenalin tingling) is a live audience who have paid for their seats. Admittedly, he had a small part, but it *was* a Shakespearean part. For the first time he felt that he was part of the real theatre, working as a real professional actor, and feeling slightly guilty because he was getting paid (albeit a pittance) for having such fun.

As the audience settled, Max's stomach stirred, flut-

tered, then contracted. Suddenly acting did not seem such
fun. Suppose he forgot his lines and dried? Suppose he
corpsed – giggled hysterically in some serious scene? He
gulped as he quickly pushed his way through the tangle
of half-naked bodies towards the door at the back of the
box, hoping that he would be sick quickly.

* * *

Fizz played fourteen-year-old Juliet as a gauche, gawky,
painfully self-conscious adolescent who did not understand – and was fearful of – her body's new, remorseless
sexual urge. Fizz's greatest gift was her female empathy:
she understood exactly how Juliet felt, and therefore so
did every female in her audience. Fizz delicately projected
submission and dejection, nervous apprehension, fierce
protectiveness, exultant happiness, bitterness and sorrow.
As she did so, every woman in the audience felt once
again the anxiety, oversensitivity and painful self-
consciousness that she, too, had felt as a young girl.

* * *

In the *Sunday Times*, James Agate wrote, 'Felicity Allen,
an enchanting, flowerlike Juliet, projected an astonishing
range of emotions; her moonbeam-elusive spontaneity
made up for those moments where her lack of experience
showed.'

The *Observer* was even more enthusiastic. 'What is it
that this Juliet projects? Star Quality. No one can exactly
describe this magic potion composed of charisma and stage
presence, plus sexual attraction. Few actors are born with
this gift, for, like charm in a woman, star quality cannot
be acquired. It is a magnetic strength that has nothing to
do with age or beauty: one recognizes it instantly, no

matter how young the actor, because one *cannot take one's eyes off that actor.'*

Sitting up in bed, Fizz threw aside the newspapers. *She* knew what star quality was: an energy that an actor projected to other people. It drained some stars, who then needed to rest and recharge their batteries, but it re-energized other actors, who remained on a high and could not sleep after a successful performance. She had not slept all night, but nevertheless this morning felt as if she could dance around the world.

Jessie entered with a breakfast tray, and surveyed the patchwork counterpane strewn with newspapers. She said quietly, almost sadly, *'Do* remember, darling, that star quality isn't enough to succeed in the Business. You also need the tenacity of a bull terrier and a crocodile's hide.'

'Rubbish, Mummy.' Fizz walloped the top from her boiled egg with exultant energy.

Jessie persisted, 'Never forget that actors are insecure, and insecure people are jealous because they're terrified of losing what they have. But some people are envious; *they not only want what you have, but they don't want* you *to have it.* They're the dangerous ones, my darling.'

Fizz ignored her mother, and once again read her reviews. She did not notice that no critic had written one word about Count Paris.

* * *

Backstage, before the next performance, Fizz was uneasily conscious of the unspoken yearning, sorrow, even bitterness of other young members of the company: as her mother had warned her, the green-eyed monster of jealousy was the reverse of the coin of success. She thought that she even saw a hint of malachite in Max's eyes.

* * *

After the end of the run, Sir Octavius Fane sent a note to Lilian Baylis in which he congratulated her on *Romeo and Juliet*, and asked her to take tea with him at Albany.

A few days later, in Sir Octavius's green-striped sitting room, Miss Baylis finished a chocolate eclair then quickly came to the point. 'I know why you asked me here, Octavius; Max has your looks and they send shivers down the spine of all them gallery girls. But to be honest with you, his acting don't live up to his face.'

Reluctantly, Max's grandfather nodded in agreement.

After Miss Baylis had departed Sir Octavius wrote another note, in which he invited his grandson to dine at the Garrick, the stuffy London club to which stuffy distinguished actors belonged.

Here, after an excellent dinner, Sir Octavius leaned over the port towards Max, and said, far be it for him to interfere, but Max had now been a year at the Vic, and might well do a stint with a touring company before he was much older . . . Nothing like six months on the road to get some management experience under your belt, for everything went wrong all the time: scenery didn't arrive . . . The skips were mislaid by the railway companies . . . Some member of the cast always dropped out, and then it was up to everyone else to see that the show went on without a visible hitch . . . Yes, touring really taught you the importance of pulling together, which was the rock-solid base of their beloved profession . . .

Max's face had brightened at the words 'management

experience'. He reminded himself that Sir Octavius had once been one of Britain's most famous actor-managers, that he owned a chain of theatres, and that Max was his only grandson.

Sir Octavius allowed a waiter to refill his glass, and then outlined his plan: the previous week, he had fortuitously run across his chum Digby Marshall, one of the last of the old-school actor-managers, a fine fellow – although possibly a little too fond of his brandy wine – with an excellent company of actors . . . and touring experience was what Max needed.

Max's face brightened further. A touring company took a West End hit with a replica cast to a different town each week, moving on a specific circuit for as long as six months.

'But with no experience, you could hardly expect to start in a Number One touring company . . .'

Max's face fell. A Number One tour covered the bigger cities like Manchester and Glasgow; a Number Two meant towns like Wolverhampton and Huddersfield; a Number Three was small towns and the cheapest digs in Hartlepool or Wigan.

Hesitantly, he asked, 'Wouldn't I get better experience in a good rep company?' Scattered throughout Britain were small repertory theatres with a resident theatre company that produced a different play each week. Frequent changes of bill meant the strain of rehearsing one play while acting another and preparing for a third, plus an exhausting First Night every single week.

More confidently, Max continued, 'Daddy says rep forces your memory, your versatility and your self-confidence.' This from continually dealing with sudden crises onstage.

Sir Octavius cleared his throat. 'I own a chain of provincial theatres,' he pointed out, '*I* require you to tour, dear boy. And when you return, we shall together visit Bennett and Hopson, my lawyers.'

What could be clearer than that, Max wondered? The old boy had practically told him he could expect to inherit the Fane theatrical chain.

With a smile, he accepted another glass of port.

* * *

For his appointment with Sir Digby Marshall, Max arrived well before time; he then sat for hours in the crowded waiting room, and endured the misery of watching other actors and actresses whisk through the frosted glass door of Sir Digby's office. By the time Max heard an imperious secretarial voice call, 'Mr Fane, please,' he was drenched with sweat and apprehension.

In a small room that looked down on the traffic of Charing Cross Road, behind an enormous desk varnished a nasty, glistening yellow, sat a stout man wearing a monocle. Sir Digby was bouncy and affable, with bulging eyes and stomach, a florid complexion (due, perhaps, to the brandy wine) and a pink carnation in his buttonhole. When circumstances required it, Sir Digby had the vocal delivery of a regimental sergeant major that could make his entire company shiver in its shoes, but he switched on his Grand Old Man charm to talk with Max – to be more precise, talk *at* Max.

After a brief and hurried interview, Max was casually told that as assistant stage manager and general under-study, his pay would be thirty shillings a week (which he dared not query) and so Max assumed that he had been hired. He did not realize that the two old boys had pre-arranged the matter over lunch at the Garrick, when Sir Octavius had cautioned Sir Digby, 'Must warn you, my grandson's a good lad but he's been thoroughly spoilt. I'm sorry to say he's an arrogant, conceited, ambitious young puppy.'

Sir Digby had given a wolfish grin as he swirled an excellent Napoleon brandy around his balloon glass. 'By the time the lad gets back, he'll only be ambitious,' he promised.

* * *

Marshall Productions opened successfully in Wolverhampton with *Charley's Aunt*. Max, wearing straw boater, striped blazer and cream flannel trousers, played an Oxford undergraduate. His many other duties seemed to include being Sir Digby's dogsbody. By the end of his first month Max woefully realized how unpleasant and uncomfortable it was to tour, rather than living and performing in one town. Instead of sleeping in his cosy bedroom, he spent the night in some small, uncomfortable room with a cold linoleum floor and a grubby rayon eiderdown upon a sagging bed; the rickety dressing table always had an oval mirror that obstinately swung forward, so that you could never see yourself in it.

Being on tour was also a constant personal strain. An ever-present cloud of insecurity, anxiety and stress hung above every actor's head, for as well as the thrill and enchantment of the theatre they all shared unmentioned fears of a possible future that contained no work, no money, failure. The so-called 'personality problems' that therefore developed in the company were intensified by the unrestful feeling of being always about to be on the move.

By the end of the first week, several of the cast were not speaking to each other. But at any hint of serious trouble, Sir Digby would deal with the matter at the next rehearsal, when his love–hate relationship with his troupe became as apparent as the fact that both his iron hands were clad in metal gauntlets. The stout little man would glare slowly at each member of the entire company, then fix his furious, bulging eyes upon the principal offender and roar, 'I wish to see only *smiles* in this company! Is that *quite*, *quite* clear? *SMILES!*'

After a surprisingly short time on the road Max learned to adapt, compromise and soothe. He also learned to simultaneously handle several crises, ranging from the non-appearance of scenery to the disappearance of the ingénue after a backstreet abortion which had led to septicaemia. On one occasion, Max was standing near Sir Digby at the stage door, when the manager came hurrying up. 'Guv'nor, the costumes have gone to Birmingham on the wrong train. But this theatre has some old Scottish costumes with kilts and tartans that we can use.'

Sir Digby turned to Max. 'One university town is much like another. Kindly inform the company immediately that we are staging the Oxford scenes in Edinburgh.'

Max became accustomed to breaking news of such changes. Like a call-boy, he would poke his head around the door to the actresses' dressing room, whereupon a row of females in kimonos, with their hair twisted up in towels, would turn to stare at him, listen, then grumble. Max would then saunter into the actors' dressing room, close the door, lean against it with his legs crossed and announce the bad news to a group of men in long johns or baggy boxer shorts, socks and suspenders; their dark silk dressing gowns had scarves or towels draped around their shoulders to avoid greasepaint stains. Here, Max's announcements were always greeted with loud and violent curses.

At the end of his third month in the company, Max went to a morning meeting with Sir Digby; he intended to ask if he might possibly be given a small salary rise, as originally he had not been told that he would have to pay for his own railway tickets. He gazed around Sir Digby's grubby dressing room. Cream-painted brick walls, dusty electrical wiring and plumbing pipes running upwards and across the stained ceiling, from which dangled light bulbs sheathed in grey inverted bluebells of frosted glass. In one corner of the room stood a wicker skip and several good quality battered suitcases; in the other corner was a rickety old dressing table. When on tour, Sir Digby used his dressing room as his office, so a small table had been dragged to the centre of the room: it was heaped with papers, behind which Sir Digby sat, wearing a violet dressing gown.

Before Max could open his mouth Sir Digby raised helpless hands to Heaven, then gestured to the mass of opened beige envelopes before him. 'Bills! Bills! Bills! Painters, property makers, dressers, bookkeepers, carpenters, rope-makers, canvas suppliers, printers for handbills, playwright, agents, secretaries . . . plus my own hotel costs, laundry and florists!' Sir Digby looked up as if personally appealing to God. 'Why should *I* have to pay for scraps to feed the ratters? Why can't the damned cats catch their own food?'

Throwing Max a complicit look, as if he was the only person in the entire Company who could understand his troubles, slowly Sir Digby shook his head. 'Dear boy, *little* do the public realize the expense, let alone the work and worry, the risk to health and pocket that is necessary to provide them with a few hours of pleasure!' Sir Digby sighed heavily, leaned back, pulled his gold watch from his pocket, then jumped to his feet. 'Forgive me, dear boy, I'm late for my next appointment and must change! I have *so* enjoyed our little chat.'

After five months on the road, Max realized the shrewdness of his grandfather's advice. Apart from the strain of feeling rootless, his ASM job, and running the additional errands demanded nonstop by Sir Digby, it was tiring to play the same part, to the same standard of freshness, eight times a week, matinées on Thursday and Saturday, for an actor had disappeared: appendicitis. Nightly, Max was now forced to control his tiredness and boredom, to resist the temptation to play practical jokes on his fellow actors, which might make them giggle but always ruined the atmosphere.

Just before the end of the run, the porous-nosed Sir Digby once more called Max to his dressing room. Again, he was seated at a small central table behind a chaotic pile of opened envelopes, but today he waved an egg-yolk-yellow one as Max walked into the room. 'A great opportunity for you, my boy! A grrrrreat opportunity.'

Sir Digby's telegram was from Basil Dean, who had been unexpectedly deprived of his assistant, now ill in hospital. Could Sir Digby recommend any promising and reliable young man, instantly available? Sir Digby, who knew that Max did not intend to join him on a second tour, had suggested young Fane. Same salary. No acting. Only two days after finishing the *Charley's Aunt* tour, Max would be expected to report to the Liverpool Rep. Max knew that Mr Dean – an actor, then Sir Herbert Beerbohm Tree's stage manager before forming his own company in

1919 – was astonishingly inventive; he produced new plays, new ideas, new production techniques, new young actors. Reluctantly recognized as a genius, actors longed to work for him.

Without hesitation, Max accepted, as he knew his grandfather would wish. Assistant to the producer. Wow! Mr Dean was supposed to be an absolute bastard, but then many actors seemed so to describe their producers.

* * *

The Last Night party of *Charley's Aunt* was held at Preston; after the last curtain call, everyone sped to a private upstairs room that had been booked at the Nag's Head, the pub nearest the theatre.

Not until four in the morning was the energy suddenly sucked out of the party. In a blue mist of tobacco smoke, most people yawned, stretched and slipped away, leaving only a few chorus boys ogling each other in dark corners. The gramophone had run down and nobody could be bothered to wind it up. All bottles were empty. The show was over.

* * *

On the following morning, despite their hangovers, the entire cast seemed cheerful; they were looking forward to returning home. When Max turned up, the stage-door keeper looked at him oddly and asked him to go immediately to Sir Digby's dressing room.

Sir Digby stood before the slot-metered gas fire.

'Come in, Max, sit down, me boy.' Sir Digby gave an uneasy smile and held out both his hands: in one was half a tumbler of neat whisky, in the other was a copy of the *Daily Telegraph*, folded back at the obituary page. Max stared at a large photograph of his grandfather, above a list of his achievements. On the previous day, while eating a steak-and-kidney pudding in the Garrick dining room, Sir Octavius had suffered a fatal heart attack.

* * *

Upon Max's subdued return to London, he found that Toby had left for Essex to comfort his mother. Mimi crossly told her son that apparently Sir Octopus had left his whole blooming fortune to his wife, with a list of disbursements to be made at Lady Fane's discretion – which meant that nobody else would get a blooming penny. It was Mimi's opinion that the old girl had old Octopus right under her thumb until the moment he died.

The manly Max burst into tears.

Only the next day did he remember his grandfather's half-promise. Blast! However, it wasn't the end of the world. At least the old boy had *meant* to change his will . . . hadn't he? Max wondered, as he emptied some of his dirty clothes into the laundry basket and threw the rest on the bathroom floor.

As he repacked his suitcase, he told himself that at least the old boy would have been pleased that his grandson was to do a stint with the Liverpool Rep, with Basil Dean. Max expected to learn a great deal from such a gifted man. He was confident that he was now an efficient ASM, which was, after all, why Mr Dean had hired him – unseen – on Sir Digby's recommendation: he looked forward to being Mr Dean's assistant.

* * *

By the end of his second day in Liverpool, Max had noticed that the cast were clearly terrified of their producer: should the tall and solidly built Mr Dean appear unexpectedly, all conversation (however innocent) ceased abruptly and the Company instantly became wary, as if on red alert. Although Mr Dean was invariably at his ease, his mere appearance could raise the stress level of his cast, with tension that was almost visible, and did not dissolve until he was known to have disappeared for the day. When he did, the actors never mentioned Mr Dean. They discussed the play and (endlessly) their own parts, but the words 'Basil Dean' were never mentioned – it was as if the very syllables might suddenly summon up the man himself, in a cloud of sulphurous smoke.

After Max had worked two weeks for him, Basil Dean announced that he was delighted by Max's efficiency; Max now discovered the reality that lay behind Dean's reputation. Every rumour Max had heard was justified: Bastard Basil – as he was called behind his back – was exacting in his requirements, expected instant obedience, and allowed no argument. He was as clever, as articulate and as demoralizing as he was critical. He had a probing instinct for a person's weaknesses, which he then probed savagely, until all his victim's self-confidence had bled away: although as incisive as a brain surgeon, Mr Dean's cuts were rarely meant to heal, but often to destroy. More terrifying than his words were Mr Dean's ominous silences, after some quivering actor had finally sensed his director's displeasure, but not the reason for it. Often, at this point, an actor stumbled, then dried. Mr Dean would take a deep breath, then quietly and skilfully insert his verbal scalpel.

Mr Dean vented his splenetic bad temper most on the obviously frightened members of his cast. Peevish and disdainful, he would harshly, accurately, contemptuously summarize each actor's inadequacies, pausing occasionally to ask the actor if he did not agree.

Two weeks after Max had joined the Company, the cast waited on stage in the sparsely lit theatre for the morning rehearsal of *Macbeth* to begin. When Mr Dean stalked in, it was clear that the actors could expect trouble, and it did not take one of Macbeth's witches to predict that they were in for an unpleasant morning.

For the first two hours of rehearsal, however hard the demoralized actors tried, their efforts could never please the bad-tempered Mr Dean. Naturally, as they were unable to concentrate on their parts, nobody performed well, but the perspiring actors continued to struggle through the play until they reached Lady Macbeth's sleepwalking scene, where she dreamily reproaches her husband: 'Fie, my Lord, fie, a soldier and afeared? ... Yet who would have thought the old man to have had so much blood in him?'

Mr Dean interrupted politely, 'Could Lady Macbeth perhaps *attempt* to indicate disgust as she metaphorically tries to wash the invisible blood of her victims from her guilty hands? Her present efforts indicate that she is merely rinsing Pear's toilet soap from her hands, after her normal morning ablutions.'

After Lady Macbeth stumbled once again through her speech, Mr Dean fell into one of his menacing silences. Each terrified actor on stage waited for the axe to fall on *his* neck, but could do nothing until it did.

Mr Dean suddenly decided to make a scapegoat of the actor who played the part of Lady Macbeth's doctor. An old character actor, trained in the declamatory tradition of the 1890s, Ernie Saville tended to overact. Now he tried hard to follow Mr Dean's direction, as, to protect his sleepwalking patient, he turned to the Old Nurse and ordered her out of earshot with the words, '*Go to! Go to! You have known what you should not!*'

Suddenly old Ernie realized that the producer had decided to pick on him for his morning's sarcastic pleasure. He immediately lost his footing, missed his cue, stuttered, stumbled and trembled in his black gown with his quill pen shaking in his hand. Sixteen times, the Doctor was made to turn to the Old Nurse and order her away, giving the single line.

Finally, Mr Dean looked up from his seat in the stalls and smiled, 'Good Doctor, I really *do* believe that you cannot *understand* where you are at fault! Is that so?'

Relief flooded the Doctor's face. 'I must admit, Mr Dean—'

The producer interrupted him. 'Then I shall ask *all* the other ladies and gentlemen of the cast to join me in the stalls, so they may watch your subtle performance. I shall then ask *each* onlooker to tell the rest of us whether, and if so how, your performance might be improved . . . You will then see' – gentle smile – 'that no personal animosity lies behind my criticism.'

Uneasy but obedient, the actors shuffled off stage and took their places in the front row of the stalls of the darkened theatre. They sat in silence, for they all knew that Mr Dean was correct. Old Ernie had never had much talent, and was now as frightened of losing his memory as he was of ending up destitute.

'*Please* start,' Mr Dean called up politely to the three actors on stage, 'we're all *dying* to watch your performance, Doctor.' His upward glance was as calm and deadly as a tiger waiting to pounce.

The Doctor moistened his lips with his tongue, then

bravely started again, but he was now so agitated that he either overacted (at which Dean sneered that he was a ham) or he stammered, mumbled and generally flubbed his lines, whereupon Mr Dean pleasantly, quietly, and very clearly called him an unprofessional has-been.

After twenty minutes of persecution, the Doctor's wig was awry, his hands were shaking, his face was pale with agitation and he was close to tears as – yet again – he obediently repeated, 'Go to! Go to! You have known what you should *not*!'

'Stop *mumbling*, Doctor!' Mr Dean called up. 'You sound as if you're saying "Goat! Goat!" *You* are the goat, sir! Let's try it again. Please cue him, Lady Macbeth.'

There was a slight stir in the stalls as Max's seat banged up. He scrambled on stage. Astonished, the actors seated below stared up at him. One or two nervous coughs were heard.

Standing astride, his hands on his hips, Max glared down at his boss. 'Mr Dean, we all know that you're a successful, brilliant producer, but you're a *failure* as a human being!'

There was a gasp of horror from the little audience.

'You are also a sadistic bully,' Max called down. 'We have all witnessed you slash Ernie's self-confidence as swiftly and expertly as a butcher slices liver.'

Mr Dean leaned back in his seat and looked up with seemingly polite interest.

Max continued angrily, 'Mr Dean, you have publicly ridiculed not only Ernie the actor, but Ernie the man, and you have forced everyone else in the cast to watch your disgusting performance. Look at Ernie's face, it's grey with fright!' Max walked upstage to the Doctor and placed one hand supportively on the shoulder of the trembling old actor, who could not believe his eyes or ears.

Feeling the silent approval of the rest of the cast, Max strode to the front of the stage, and shouted, 'Take *another* look at Ernie, every one of you! Could you blame him if he put his head in a gas oven tonight? . . . And if he did, how would you feel tomorrow morning about *your* part in it? Because *not one of you stood up for Ernie.*' Max shook both fists at his silent audience. 'I hope you're all ashamed of your cowardice! And as for you Mr Dean, you are like a school bully who frightens away the other children, so that he can enjoy kicking the youngest, weakest one in the playground.'

Mr Dean slowly rose from his seat and fixed glacial eyes on him. Seated on either side of their director, his actors shrank lower in their seats. From the darkness, Mr Dean called calmly up to the stage, 'You are fired, Mr Fane. Please leave the theatre immediately. If you have not left this theatre within five minutes, I shall have you thrown out by the stage hands.'

Max took two steps forward and glared downwards. 'Your words are proof, Mr Dean, that you can't take even a mild dose of the public humiliation that you have just heaped on poor Ernie.' Max took a deep breath, then added, 'I have no wish to work for a swine like you, and I'm sorry for those who are obliged to, or starve: I can think of no other reason to endure your unending malice and cruelty.'

Mr Dean disdainfully ignored Max. 'Cast dismissed for luncheon,' he said quietly.

In silence, the actors picked up their belongings, and hurried backstage.

* * *

As Max walked towards the stage door, trying to saunter as if unconcerned, a few courageous members of the Company shook his hand and wished him luck. One muttered, 'At least you didn't end up like Basil's last assistant. After only one week with the Company, *he* collapsed with an attack of neurasthenia – he's still in the Liverpool Infirmary, under sedation.'

Max did not realize that he and all the other watching actors in the stalls would quickly spread the word that Max Fane had publicly stood up to Bastard Basil.

In ten minutes, he had established a reputation that was simultaneously enviable and a fearful example of how not to behave if you wanted to keep your job; for no producer could afford such a potentially disruptive influence in his Company. Max had just scuppered his career as an actor.

Saturday 12 March 1927

Mimi did not care for a busy social life; she never turned up at luncheon parties, tea parties or Sunday dinner parties, unless she was giving them. Mimi never spent the afternoon shopping or visiting art galleries; whenever she was not at the theatre she pottered around her pretty, warm, clean home. It gave her great pleasure to compare her present to her past and sometimes she muttered a litany – occasionally she sang it and her exultant words vibrated through the house:

> 'With a little bit of luck, perhaps,
> No more travel with me own mousetraps
> To set under some saggy bed,

But a real down pillow for my weary head.
No more cabbage smells in strange halls
Or cracked chamber pots when Nature calls.
No more running out of coins for the gas
On a cold winter's night for this lucky lass.'

On the Saturday of his unexpected return from Liverpool, Max unlocked the front door of his London home, knowing that his mother would be at home. From the basement he heard her husky, velvet voice blast out, 'Shine on, Harvest Moon'. Mimi often sang old music-hall songs, so Max had heard them all his life: 'You Made Me Love You', gently hummed as Mimi moved around the house, or 'How'd You Like To Spoon With Me?' suddenly erupting, full-strength, when she took a bath.

Feeling as if he had been let out of school, Max leaped up the stairs, two at a time, passing etchings of long-dead actors as he ran towards his bathroom. As he reached the last flight of stairs to the top floor, he noticed a geometrically patterned orange garment flung over the top banisters. He then saw that the ceiling trapdoor, which led to the attic, was open; beneath it, a ladder was propped against the wall.

As Max reached the top of the stairs, a dusty beige dress box was flung down from the attic. He paused abruptly.

From the black hole above, two feet in filthy white tennis socks appeared at the top of the ladder: very slowly, two slim, tanned legs started to descend, followed by a shapely behind, not quite covered by peach crêpe de Chine underwear; a small waist then appeared, above which fell a shining length of Scandinavian-fair hair.

Max suddenly remembered upon whom he had seen that geometrically patterned orange frock. He grinned. Impulsively, he crept swiftly and silently forward. As the rounded little rump slowly descended the ladder, Max sharply pinched it.

Fizz gave a startled squawk, missed her footing and fell to the floor.

Furious, she yelled up at Max, 'I might have known it was you, you bloody *blockhead*! I might have broken a leg!' Fizz's temper could suddenly explode, like a box of fireworks into which someone has flung a match.

'But you *didn't* break a leg,' Max pointed out, unperturbed.

'You are *unbelievably* arrogant,' hollered Fizz, who remembered as she gazed at him, how very good-looking the Watercress Man was: forks fell to the floor in restaurants when he entered, as women goggled at his wide cheekbones and square jaw; the rugged toughness of his broken nose (a cricket ball) seemed only to add to his appeal.

But not to Fizz; she scrambled to her feet, quickly jumped forward and gave Max a strong push.

Taken by surprise and pushed off-balance, Max crashed backwards, down the stairs.

Fizz's hand flew to her mouth.

From below, Mimi's singing stopped abruptly. She bellowed up, 'Wot the 'ell was that noise?'

'Nothing, Mummy. I just missed my footing,' Max shouted back.

Like most large male adolescents, her son bounced around his home like an overgrown puppy in a doll's house, so Mimi was unsurprised.

Max slowly scrambled to his feet, clearly unhurt but rubbing one elbow. 'Sorry, I shouldn't have done that. But what were you doing up in our attic?'

Fizz angrily flounced towards her orange frock, wriggled into it, and jammed on her shoes. 'I asked Mimi if I could borrow one of her old Edwardian gad-about-town costumes, for a fancy dress party. And what are *you* doing here? I heard you'd joined the Liverpool Rep.'

'I just quit.'

Tartly, Fizz imitated a herald playing a trumpet, then stuck her tongue out at Max.

Max asked hesitantly, 'D'you think I might get something at the Vic, while I'm waiting for my agent to negotiate the lead in *Hamlet* at the Haymarket?'

Fizz picked up the dusty cardboard box and brushed past the Watercress Man. 'If you come *anywhere* near the Vic – just remember to keep you hands off *me*!'

Chapter Thirteen

Every time he bounced upstairs to his bedroom, Max remembered those long, slim legs slowly descending the ladder from the attic. He told himself to stop that! Plenty of other girls had legs, and Fizz was practically his sister; both eighteen, they had known each other all their lives. An emotional involvement would only lead to trouble when he broke it off, for then Fizz would complain to her mother, who would come round to see *his* mother . . . No, Fizz was definitely forbidden territory.

Nevertheless, two days later, he found himself in a flower shop paying for a clump of narcissi growing in a flowerpot hidden in an upended wide-brimmed straw hat, tied with green ribbons.

Fizz didn't even thank him.

What other people would call infatuation Max had always labelled love. Every time he 'fell in love', he knew that it was the real thing, a feeling of conviction that had swamped him nineteen times since his fourteenth birthday. Max loved falling in love: he loved the tingling thrill as he stared at a girl and saw her blush in response; without some dizzying, elevating passion, he tended to feel low and flat – or else he simply felt restless.

Fizz did not sleep around, but flirtation was second

nature to her. This infuriated the watching, suddenly possessive Max. Instead of waiting to be adored, he now found himself adoring someone else. He also loved this new excitement of adoration; he had never felt so elated and . . . well . . . fizzy.

Depending on the emptiness of Max's pocket, flowers continued to arrive for Fizz; towards the end of the month, some were picked from Mimi's vases, some pinched from the formal flower beds of Regent's Park. Every morning for a week, a special messenger handed Fizz a Shakespeare sonnet. Letters tumbled through the Allens' letter box, and finally so did a pillowcase with *I Love You* scrawled on it in dripping purple paint. But it was the ginger kitten with the beige satin bow round its neck that finally (slightly) breached Fizz's heart. Once the castle walls started to crumble, then the battle of passion was all but won, Max reckoned, when she agreed to have lunch with him.

In an Italian restaurant in Charlotte Street they looked with surprise across plates of spaghetti, and both suddenly felt the thrill of the forbidden as they stared at each other.

Max praised everything Fizz wore and every feature on her face. She graciously acknowledged these tributes, and asked him what his tour had been like. As she listened to his tales, she briefly remembered the drudgery of the Number Threes of her childhood: she remembered her mother's early mornings spent darning tights, dabbing underarm sweat marks from her clothes, and washing her kimono wraps. Max finished an account of his Liverpool sojourn with a description of his row with Basil Dean; at the memory he laughed hard but Fizz looked thoughtful, for she immediately realized the professional implications of his actions.

Max was again playing small parts at the Vic, which had replaced its tatty stage curtains with splendid new crimson ones, paid for by Mimi. (Lilian had warned, 'I'm not helping him for new tabs, dear, but for friendship ... However, I can only go so far, Mimi, for my audience must have the best.')

* * *

Suddenly both Max and Fizz had ten times more energy, seemed to need no sleep, and radiated shafts of happiness as bright as the light of the rising sun. Max now saw Fizz, Life, the World, the Universe through his new pair of magenta-coloured spectacles.

Fizz wondered how she had ever managed to play Juliet before she fell in love with Max and truly, truly realized the wondrous depths and passions of *real* love.

These and similar thoughts occupied their minds when absent from each other, and dominated their conversation when they were together. Fizz and Max sat in penny-hired pale-green deckchairs in Green Park, talking endlessly of their love, as they ate apples for lunch; sometimes, they sailed on the River Thames in the dinghy which Max kept at Richmond, where he raced with the Sailing Club. Sometimes they danced to the gramophone that thumped in Mimi's drawing room: 'I Wish I Could Shimmy Like My Sister Kate', the 'Charleston' or the 'Black Bottom'. Leaving the music playing at full blast, they often sneaked up to Max's bedroom for a quick cuddle. It was because the Watercress Man did not press Fizz to proceed sexually beyond a certain socially acceptable point (under blouse to waist, but not below), that Max realized – to his astonishment – how serious and (*could* it be?) honourable were his intentions towards her.

Lack of money severely restricted his courtship, until the morning when, unexpectedly, he received a gift from Heaven: Max stared disbelievingly at the cheque for £100 that Lady Fane had sent him with a note which said, grudgingly, that his grandfather would have wished to leave Max something. Now that Max had money to splash, as if from a conjuror's hat he produced new treats all through April. Fizz felt as if every other day was Christmas as they breakfasted at the Ritz and lunched in Green Park, but this time from a Fortnum & Mason picnic hamper of delicious food, Irish damask napkins and two crystal flutes for the champagne. One morning, Fizz was woken by a small girl dressed as a daffodil, singing, 'Isn't it a lovely day?' on the Allen doorstep. It seemed as if it always was, as they tootled off to Ascot in Max's little green Morgan sports car (to buy it Max had sold his grandfather's eighteenth-birthday gift – a Cartier wristwatch). Together they watched car races at Brooklands, and enjoyed the parties of the London Season, now in full swing.

They ate at glamorous restaurants – Boulestin and the Café Royal – where Fizz knew that she should politely choose the cheapest dishes, but didn't. Once, Max took her to the Colony nightclub, where the Prince of Wales was dancing with his tiny vivacious mistress, her short dark hair pulled behind her ear by a diamond clip.

As dawn yawned, the steamed-up windows of the little green Morgan often hid two sleepy, but still passionate people.

'No, you *mustn't* . . .'

'. . . Yes, I *must* . . .'

'. . . *Max!*'

'... I can't stand this much longer, *feel* what I feel for you, Fizz.'

'... *No, Max!*'

'... Oh, darling, let's get married ...'

'... *Oh, Max!*'

* * *

As soon as Max and Fizz told their parents that they were going to marry, so much disapproval was showered like confetti upon the young couple that they considered eloping. But they couldn't simply not turn up at the Vic. And both their mothers would cry if they missed the wedding. Besides, you had to give three weeks' notice to get married at a Register Office, and local newspapers always checked the lists: the Fane name would instantly be picked up, and their secret made public before they could marry.

Max and Fizz both felt resentful and indignant: how *dare* any stupid oldie obscure their happiness by dreary talk of pennies and pensions; how dare the dusties link sex with security, matrimony with mortgages, pleasure with prams?

Besides, daringly modern, Max and Fizz had already decided that they would not require a pram. The child of actors, Fizz remembered that children were an added stress to dreary touring: confined to digs, constantly admonished to *ssshhh!*, and inexorably pursued by school inspectors. She knew what a burden she had been to her mother, left almost penniless after her father's death. Fizz wanted no such constraints: she wanted no children. Max accepted that this was her condition of marriage, that Fizz felt her life already overfull, that she wanted to devote what little time acting left her to the delicious prospect of being with him and looking after him. Max was a romantic lover, and he wanted only his wonderful, perfect Fizz *always* to be perfectly happy, he shouted to her above the wind, as they drove to Essex on a warm spring day.

Fizz knew Lady Fane quite well, but upon meeting her again, she was suddenly nervous, anxious for approval, and nearly curtsied to the frail old lady. After the young couple had returned to London in that dangerous-looking little green machine, Lady Fane picked up the telephone, clamped the receiver to her ear, and spoke into the mouthpiece as if shouting from a high mountain. She told Toby that she strongly objected to her only grandson marrying at the age of nineteen. It was irresponsible, Lady Fane insisted, conveniently forgetting that when she had married Sir Octavius she had been eighteen years old. Lady Fane added crossly that Fizz was a young upstart from nowhere. Why couldn't Max marry that nice Albery girl instead? Toby must do something about it, *immediately*!

All three parents agreed that Max and Fizz were too young to marry. To try to dissuade their offspring they asked them not to see each other outside the theatre, for a couple of months, as proof that their love could endure. *That* would be no problem, Fizz sniffed. Max carefully promised nothing. After that, when Max phoned Fizz, he always used a false, fishy name. The Allen maid would announce, 'Lord Whitebait on the telephone, miss,' or 'Mr Cod called, miss,' or 'Viscount Plaice has sent a basket of roses, miss.' If Jessie heard, she tried to look severe, but could not help giggling.

Jessie did not giggle when Fizz told her mother that she was pregnant.

Monday 6 June 1927. London

After hurried parental consultation, the young couple were married three weeks later at St Paul's, Covent Garden, traditionally the church of actors. Fizz wore a simple white chiffon dress, with the pearl-embroidered cap that she had worn on stage when playing Juliet.

On their wedding day, Max looked up at the early June sky and realized that it was the exact blue of Fizz's eyes, but lacked their sparkle. Toby looked his lean grey-haired best, immaculate in a pale-grey morning suit, cream cravat and grey top hat. Mimi had wanted to wear the same outfit, but Toby had been scandalized, and reminded the bridegroom's mother that she must on no account divert press attention from the bride with what would be seen as a publicity stunt. So Mimi wore demure rose, generally considered a great mistake with red hair.

As the Fane family waited on their doorstep for the hired Daimler, Mimi hopped up and down impatiently in the fine warm wind that bounced down the street – good drying weather, Mimi's mam would have said ... Impatiently, Mimi started to bawl:

'There was I – waiting at the church,
Never realized – he'd leave me in the lurch ...
Then came the note – the very words he wrote ...
"Can't get away, to marry you today,
For my wife ... won't let me!" '

As neighbouring windows were thrust up, and angry heads poked out, Toby hissed, 'If you *must* sing, can't you pick something quieter, or more cheerful?'

Mimi grinned as she switched to 'The Bells are Ringing for Me and my Gal!'

At the same time, Fizz was hollering to Jessie, 'I should have thought you'd given up by now! *Of course* I'm sure I want to marry him! I know *you'd* like me to marry the Prince of Wales, but *I love Max*!'

That evening, the newly weds just tumbled into the train before it pulled away from Victoria Station: they were headed for their honeymoon in Paris. Fizz had been allowed a week off; her disbelieving understudy was almost as delirious with joy as the bride.

* * *

'Fizz, d'you know why a man will never tell a girl his sexual fantasy?' Max hung down from the top berth on the following morning, after the young Fanes had woken to weak sunshine raying through the portholes above the usual choppy, grey sea of the English Channel.

'Why not? Tell me!' Fizz yawned happily, and blew a kiss up to him.

'Too shy,' teased the bridegroom. 'To discover a man's sexual fantasies, a woman has to act them *all* out – and see which one arouses him.'

'You're fibbing!'

'I'm not!'

'You're fishing!'

'I am, indeed!' Max snaked down into Fizz's berth.

'Be grateful you aren't a male salticet spider.'

'Why?'

Fizz giggled. 'If the male salticet spider's ritual courtship dance doesn't sexually arouse his female . . . she eats him!'

'Is that supposed to stimulate the bridegroom?'

It seemed only two minutes after they had left Victoria Station that the bridal couple arrived at Paris Gare du Nord.

Under a huge glass roof, the train halted among lines of other trains, all sending up clouds of steam. Fizz hung out of the window to watch blue-clad porters, with carrying straps slung over their shoulders, awaiting the descending passengers and calculating which were likely to be best tippers.

Fizz quickly suspected that once you fell in love with Paris, you never fell *out* of love with this exciting, fun-loving city and its sensual offers of high fashion and high living, the beautiful, the erotic, and the delicious.

However, Max and Fizz did not see much of Paris.

* * *

The young Fanes returned from their honeymoon to a small pretty rented house in Colville Place, off Charlotte Street in Soho: built in 1760, it had only one room on each of its four floors. Lady Fane scornfully called it the Mouse House.

Max and Fizz were both only children, not accustomed to sharing life and possessions with brothers or sisters, not resigned to being pushed around by older siblings or maddened by younger ones: both found it difficult to live with – actually *live* as opposed to being with – somebody else. Clothes or towels that were flung on the floor stayed there; unmade beds were no longer magically made by evening; the morning cleaner did not wash the dishes or shop, so they constantly ran out of everything, from marmalade to lavatory paper. Max thought that shopping was a woman's responsibility; Fizz, studying hard, thought that as Max was not working, he might at least wash the dirty crockery, or walk down the street to buy a light bulb or a tin of toothpaste.

It had long been arranged that Fizz would play Eliza in Shaw's *Pygmalion*, so the day after she returned from Paris she had gone straight into rehearsal at the Old Vic. As Fizz studied her part, she discussed her research with Max and used him as a bouncing board for her tentative ideas, as well as for reassurance on every other decision, whether choosing food or fashion: she then made up her own mind. One night, before attending the First Night of the Minerva's new revue, *So What?*, Fizz looked critically in the bedroom mirror at her silver, backless sheath, and murmured, 'Is this too overdressed? Or underdressed? Do I look like a mermaid?'

'No, a mackerel,' Max grinned, and dodged his first flying hairbrush.

Despite Fizz's strong, self-assured personality, she strained for perfection and never felt that she reached it. She lived in constant self-doubt about her work and her performance was never good enough to please *her*, no matter how much others admired it: no reassurance was possible, even from Max: she always felt inadequate. Yet at rehearsals she seemed completely confident when playing the impudent Eliza, so similar to her own personality.

There was no part for Max in *Pygmalion*, nor was he asked to audition for the Vic's next production – or any other production. Grimly, he reminded himself that over 80 per cent of all British actors were out of work at any given time: now he was one of them.

Max worried more about his being out of work than Fizz, who found his anxiety perplexing: they were not going to starve, and being out of work – 'resting' as it was called – was part of theatre life. All resting actors needed tough egos, to survive constant rejection.

When working, most actors expected life to revolve around them, and they demanded a lot of attention: their smallest need took priority over those of other people. Mercurial mood swings – up one minute, down the next – could make an actor or actress seem irrational, difficult to understand, and hard to live with. Max knew this intellectually, but he did not accept it emotionally, as he and Fizz started to discover the exhausting demands of running a two-career marriage.

Repeatedly, when Fizz returned home later than expected (and exhausted), Max became irritable. Fizz found that the easiest way to cure sulky Max, who felt neglected, was simply to lure him into bed. Unfortunately, she was sometimes so tired that upon touching the pillow she instantly fell asleep.

* * *

Outwardly an ideal pair, seemingly destined to be one of the British theatre's leading couples, both Max and Fizz were larger-than-life people with larger-than-life passions: both were strong willed; both were used to adoration; both were used to getting their own way. Max was reckless and stubborn. So was Fizz. Fizz was restless, impatient, tart tongued. So was Max, who had never expected to play second fiddle in his marriage.

Two months after Max and Fizz married, it had already become apparent to friends, although not to them (at the eye of the storm), that theirs was a tempestuous relationship between a traditional, masculine man and a woman who insisted on being a person in her own right and refused to play the habitual appeasing female role. Pointedly, Fizz turned down the female lead Katherina – Kate – in *The Taming of the Shrew*.

Sunday 26 June 1927. Hollywood

Almost immediately after Max's marriage, Mimi had felt abandoned and forlorn. Her beloved was under the control of another woman, whom he adored: he wished to see nobody else. A fortnight after the young Fanes returned from honeymoon, Max had only once popped in to Fitzroy Square, to say hello and borrow a frying pan.

For months, Tudor had been suggesting that Mimi visit him in Hollywood, where he had had an unexpected success, although not as an actor. Prompted by a short letter from Toby that hinted at Mimi's feelings of loss, Tudor now sent a set of undated first-class return tickets to the generous friend who had made his success possible. Although Toby could not accompany her, because he had to look after the Fane theatres, Mimi decided to take time off and go to Hollywood.

* * *

When the impeccably dressed Tudor had first arrived in Hollywood, he found it impossible to get work, although he sometimes earned $15 a day as a Best Dress extra, which meant wearing your own clothes on some ritzy set.

He spent much of his spare time with the ladies of the British Colony, who quickly realized that Tudor was as authentic a British toff as C. Aubrey Smith but more approachable; they started to ask his advice on matters of good taste and social etiquette. Where could you buy the best fish forks? Should the water in finger bowls be warm? How did you answer an invitation in the third person – who the hell *was* the third person?

The amiable, tactful Tudor, who had good taste and decorative judgement, was always ready to help choose tablecloths, decide on a menu, or advise on the correct ensemble for a visit to Pickfair. Quickly, the wives of new stars also started to consult him when their photogenic husbands were overnight transformed from soldier, sailor, cowboy or former gas-pump attendant into stars with a position to keep up. Former hoofers, waitresses and shop assistants, suddenly expected to transmogrify into society hostesses, were terrified of disgracing their husbands.

A leading decorator asked Tudor to become his social consultant, on a commission basis. Once the decorator had finished the lucrative work on a new house, he did not want the aggravation of choosing sheets or bath towels, and wanted to cut off the constant telephonic problems of his anxious, erstwhile clients. So the client was passed on to 'my Society Consultant'. Tudor was amazed that someone should actually *pay* him to give his opinion on, what was to him, the obvious, but he metamorphosed cheerfully into a male Emily Post, tactfully taught worried women how the nobs lived, and transformed nouveau riche with Old Money touches.

Studios recommended Tudor to give that touch of class to their new stars: you could trust this guy with your money, as well as your wife. Gradually, the female stars monopolized him, and then the studio heads' wives beckoned; Tudor hired a secretary and two former butlers to help him advise how to treat servants and what to expect of them; how to keep – or check – household accounts; how to organize a charity ball and stay sane. In a letter to Mimi, he wrote, 'I feel like a cross between a psychiatrist and the principal of a finishing school that runs personalized courses.'

Soon Tudor was able to buy a smart pale-grey Stutz Bear Cat, the car of his dreams. He replenished his threadbare wardrobe, so was even better dressed than formerly, in clothes from London's Savile Row; on the occasional chilly day, Tudor wore a Chesterfield coat and Homburg hat with suede spats and chamois gloves; on hot days, he wore immaculately tailored linen suits and a straw boater. Lobb of London, who had his last, crafted Tudor's handmade shoes; his shirts, ties and handkerchiefs came from Sulka in Paris, and he always smelled slightly of sandalwood.

Tudor now had no spare time during the day to accompany Betsy, whenever she needed a good-looking, well-dressed escort, although he still saw her regularly in the evening. Before Mimi's arrival, Tudor had secretly planned to arrange a sunny reconciliation between the two women, but when he had tentatively suggested that they meet for luncheon Betsy had thrown him a stare that would have frozen vodka, as she quietly said, 'I think *not*,' a vocal trick picked up from Mrs Patrick Campbell.

* * *

The post-war European movie industry had staggered back to its feet, but Hollywood was now the undisputed reigning world champion: there was an almost tangible feeling of triumphant excitement that Mimi sensed as soon as she had carefully descended from the train, flung herself into Tudor's arms, and sniffed the fresh, flower-scented air of success.

That evening, they sat on the veranda of Tudor's

Spanish-style miniature hacienda, from which fuchsia-coloured bougainvillaea drooped luxuriously over the pink-washed walls. As the two of them knocked back White Ladies, Mimi happily said, 'I *know* I'm going to love it here, so long as your friends realize I ain't high society.'

Tudor laughed. '*Nobody* in Hollywood is. Nobody here was raised by nannies, so nobody *knows* how to behave in polite society – except Greta Garbo, who avoids it.'

As Mimi giggled, Tudor added, 'To enjoy Hollywood, you need to understand in advance why everyone behaves as they do. You need not just to be prepared for – but to expect – terror, treachery, lies and humiliation.'

'You make it sound like a Bolshevik prison,' jeered Mimi as she inhaled the flower-scented warm breeze.

'Not a bad comparison,' Tudor said seriously. 'It's sunnier here than in Siberia, but there are four things to remember if you want to avoid trouble and heartbreak!' He ticked them off on his fingers, 'Rule *one* of the Dream Factory: never trust anyone about anything, particularly if he says he'll do you a favour: everyone in this town is a mercenary – only for hire, only at the right price.'

Tudor tapped his second finger. 'Realize that everyone in Hollywood is terrified, and acts hard at not showing it: a person's true state of mind – at any time of the day or night – is as if every evening were a theatre First Night.'

Mimi shivered.

'What are they all terrified of? *Failure!* Nobody wants to be associated with failure, so if you fall from power, suddenly nobody knows you.' Tudor grabbed his new chrome cocktail shaker, shook it violently, like a pair of maracas, and refilled Mimi's glass, as he started the fourth part of his diatribe. Successful actors were never as charming as they appeared: they were, after all, actors. Like politicians, successful actors were shrewd, tough and ruthless, otherwise they could not possibly have achieved success and hung on to it. It was no use coming to Hollywood if you were not prepared to be equally tough, to smile, flatter and charm, to believe nothing and trust *nobody* – not your mother, your lover or the hat-check girl.

To succeed in Hollywood you needed the ruthless social instinct of a French duchess, a skin as tough as tortoiseshell, and so great a longing for success that you would do *anything* for it: be prepared to sell your arse or your grandmother; be prepared to find that you weren't paid for either of them. Tudor finished, 'Don't laugh, Mimi, I'm serious.'

'You can't frighten me,' Mimi said dreamily, 'I know *I'm* going to love Hollywood.'

'Yes, if you remember what I've told you. *You* can get out after a month, Mimi, but most people can't afford to leave: so they cling to their dreams and end up in a different place than they started from, but still as waitresses or gas-pump attendants.'

* * *

Tudor introduced Mimi to the Hollywood British Colony; this now included Claude Rains, the beautifully mannered Ronald Coleman and Basil Rathbone, all of whom had met Mimi before, in London. Moving from the quietly genteel to the extravagantly sumptuous, Tudor took Mimi to an evening fancy dress party at Pickfair, the Tudor mansion, complete with footmen in plush breeches and powdered wigs, that Mary Pickford and Doug Fairbanks had built near the Beverly Hills Hotel.

Tudor worked during the day; Mimi enjoyed lazing by

the pool in the shade of a banana tree, out of earshot of the noisy study, where Tudor allocated work to his two dignified assistants and made decisions about placecard-holders and matters of precedence, while his secretaries answered the frantic telephones and pounded their Underwoods.

On Mimi's second weekend Tudor drove her over the Mexican border to Agua Caliente; it took six hours to get there on Saturday, but eight hours to return on Sunday evening, because of the usual two-hour bottleneck wait at the Mexican border. Stars, executives, lawyers, doctors and screenwriters felt it worth the journey to be able to let their hair down over the weekend with noisy abandon and no snoopers. There was no Prohibition in Mexico, Tudor explained, so there was plenty of booze and drugs, plus whores for anyone who had the energy after betting at the racetrack, the dog track or the casino.

Mimi spent the second week with various hospitable new friends, and was exhausted by Saturday. For a restful weekend, they drove in Tudor's pale-grey Stutz to stay with Marion Davies, the lisping, platinum-blonde mistress of William Randolph Hearst, one of America's richest newspaper owners. Their many-columned ante-bellum mansion was on the ocean at Santa Monica, where a crammed quarter-mile of sandy shore was Hollywood's smartest summer resort.

Tudor was delighted by his guest's social success; her outrageousness and energy, her independent outlook and sense of fun made her welcome – especially when she sang to entertain her fellow guests.

'You know, you could easily get in the movies yourself, as a singing character actress,' Tudor suggested.

Mimi considered this for about thirty seconds. She was

still the same weight as she had been at seventeen; her upturned nose, bright green eyes and luxuriant red hair (her hairdresser allowed no streak of grey to show) still attracted admiring looks. But sitting on the beach, Mimi drew a star in the sand with her forefinger. 'Start again at forty? On the other side of the world?' With one decisive swipe, she deleted the sandy star. 'No, thanks. Toby would hate it here – no books, no poetry, no clubs, no theatre life. Besides, audiences still love me back in Britain. And I hope I stay at Fitzroy Square until I die. For me, that's *home*, which is more important than all this money and sunshine.'

'I understand, darling,' Tudor sympathized. 'You'd miss those deliciously draughty, backstage rat-warrens. You'd be homesick for the rain, the fog and the snowy slush. You'd long for overcooked roast beef.'

Mimi scooped up a handful of sand and shoved it down the front of Tudor's bathing suit, confident that good-tempered Tudor would not similarly retaliate. She added, 'Besides, I've already told you I'm worried about Max and Fizz: they was too young to get married. Max's out of work. How's that going to affect his manly pride? I shouldn't be surprised if one of these days he won't be able to you-know-what any more – and then they'll have yet another problem.' Mimi looked up at the blue sky above the even bluer Pacific, as she thought of this little cloud on her own horizon. 'So I don't want to be away too long. I want to get back and keep me eye on 'em both.'

Tudor was astonished to hear this confidence from Mimi, who always shied away from any mention of sex.

Mimi yawned, stretched her arms towards the sky, then jerked her head backwards, towards a little group of cigar-smoking executives in slacks and open-necked shirts, behind the columns of Marion's porch; they constantly pushed bills into the middle of the table or snatched them out. 'That lot been sitting there since we arrived,' Mimi commented, 'is that their only idea of fun?'

Tudor shrugged. 'Those big boys get very little time for relaxation, and they gamble heavily: it's reckoned to be a measure of your nerves, ability and potency. *Everybody* out here gambles, from the moguls to the shoeshine boys.'

'On cards?'

Tudor nodded. 'There are plenty of all-night private poker and bridge parties, or illicit gambling clubs where the bouncers carry guns. But they bet on anything: football, prize fights, horses, elections, how far up on the beach a wave might fling itself.'

'What do they do when they're not gambling?' Mimi asked, still gazing at the little group of card players around the shaded table.

Tudor flopped back on the sand. 'Wake at nine and telephone the office. Skip through plot summaries during breakfast – studio heads don't have time to read books or plays so they hire someone else to do it. Then they go to the office, where they eat lunch with their executives, after which they head for the projection room to watch the dailies – all the unedited footage shot on the previous day.'

'Why are you grinning, Tudor?'

'Because then it's the starlet time, with the office door locked. After a shower, a massage and a nap, they're driven to some distant suburban cinema to check audience reaction on one of their new movies, then it's home to bed.' Tudor yawned. 'In other words, they never stop working.'

'Sounds a worse life than a Number Three tour, even if it *is* spent in limousines and sunshine,' Mimi commented.

'Except for the afternoon coffee break, perhaps?'

Mimi shoved another handful of sand down Tudor's bathing suit, and fled into the ocean, where he pursued her, and splashed her until her cream muu-muu was soaked.

* * *

Just before Mimi's return to Britain, Tudor planned to throw a big party for her, to return all the generous hospitality that they had received. Together, they decided on a peppermint-pink striped marquee with imported dance floor, dance band and a really delicious seafood buffet, served amidst sculpted-ice mermaids. Mimi had been to enough parties to last a lifetime in the previous twenty years, but this one was a non-business party, with no ulterior motive. As the day approached, she became as excited as a child.

Tudor had scribbled Betsy's name on the invitation list. He had received a brusque, typed refusal in the third person: 'Mr and Mrs J. O'Brien already have appointments for that evening.'

'You wouldn't think Betsy would bother to hold a grudge about something that happened over twenty years ago,' Mimi sniffed, when Tudor silently handed her the O'Brien refusal.

'You do, darling,' Tudor gently pointed out.

'With good reason,' Mimi snapped.

Once again faced with Mimi's now unconcealed hatred of Betsy, Tudor prudently said nothing. Except for her fixation about Betsy, Mimi was an easy character who forgave and forgot quickly, so Tudor did not understand why Betsy was the exceptional thorn in Mimi's side, which she seemed unable to pluck out: he did not realize that the injustice of her burns still rankled whenever she glimpsed herself, half-dressed, in a mirror or remembered her rat-bites. But she had not crossed out Betsy's name on the proffered invitation list, so Mimi must have secretly hoped that Betsy would appear at the party.

Try as she might, Mimi had not been so close to any other woman since her rupture with Betsy, and she still missed the close companionship, which once she had expected to last for the rest of their lives: this tender side of Mimi still longed to see her old friend again, although her proud, unforgiving side tried to conceal this yearning.

Saturday 9 July 1927. Hollywood

Unusually, that morning had seen a nursery uproar in the O'Brien household.

Nick thought his mother the prettiest lady in the whole world, and was fascinated by her fragile lingerie, her frail, silk stockings and the satin garters that held them in place. Most of all, Nick loved his mother's smell, loved the moment when she leaned over him in a cloud of flower-scented fragrance to kiss him goodnight.

That morning, while Betsy was taking a shower, Nick had tiptoed into her bedroom, taken the bottle of amber fragrance from his mother's dressing table and dabbed the glass top behind his ears, as Betsy did.

At that moment, Nick's father came out of his bathroom,

naked except for a towel slung over his hairy chest. Black Jack went berserk and gave a harsh beating to his bewildered three-year-old son.

Hearing Nick's howls, and the screams of the astonished nanny who stood in the open doorway, Betsy rushed in, a towel wrapped around her body.

Behind the nanny, Nick's sisters appeared and started to bellow in sympathy – which brought Mrs Bridges running in, as six-year-old Tess hurled herself forward and bit her father's leg.

'No need to worry, Jack.' Mrs Bridges saw the spilled scent bottle, and guessed what had happened. 'Nick's a manly little boy, and he don't want to smell of flowers: he just adores his mummy.'

Two hours later, all was calm and back to normal. Out on the shaded back porch Betsy was rocking gently on the new striped lounger as she drank fresh lemonade. Black Jack, in his shirtsleeves, sipped a mint julep. Stella and Tess had not yet returned from their Saturday morning dancing lesson, but three-year-old Nick was being bounced hard on his father's knee. Black Jack was a strict father, who intended to raise his son to be tough and competitive: no soft Le Rosey school in Switzerland for his son! Nick was strictly disciplined and punished when he was a bad boy. Black Jack repeatedly told Nick that only softies cry, and that he didn't expect a son of his to whine; he told Nick's nurse that if she kept the three-year-old at it for long enough, he would learn not to drop a ball, but to catch it.

Quiet, shy Nick, who had the same gentle temperament as his elder sister Stella, had already started to feel inadequate, and therefore insecure. Nick's expensive paediatrician had assured Betsy that he was not backward, despite the bedwetting, but he had added that without healthy self-esteem, no child can feel confident of his right to a place on this earth, and so Nick could not yet feel truly self-confident. Perhaps Mr O'Brien might remember that his son was only three years old: there would be plenty of time later for strict discipline.

Mrs Bridges now stomped out on the back porch, waving an invitation card. 'Blooming cheek,' she snorted. 'Has that Tudor had the nerve to invite *you*, dearest?'

'I refused it last week,' Betsy said with *grande dame* dignity. 'Your card must have been delayed in the post.'

For the previous two weeks Black Jack had noticed that Betsy, reading the newspapers as she breakfasted in bed, occasionally jerked upright and bit her bottom lip: he knew that she had just read some juicy gossip-column account of Mimi Fane's latest successful appearance.

Black Jack now stretched luxuriously. 'Maybe you shouldn't have refused that invitation,' he suggested lazily. 'Never dismiss any option until you've decided what you're going to do.'

Betsy looked puzzled. 'What *do* you mean, honey?'

Black Jack laughed, 'This dame has given you a lot of aggravation, hasn't she, sugar? Now's *your* chance for a bit of fun.'

'I still don't understand.' Betsy wrinkled her pretty forehead.

Mrs Bridges smiled. 'Jack means that now's the time for you to get your own back, dearest. Stop frowning!'

Black Jack nodded. He took precautions to ensure that he never lost a battle. He believed that the Lord helped those who helped themselves. He thought that he had taught his wife to understand those simple laws of nature.

'Now's the time to bite back,' Black Jack said sharply.

'*Always* avenge yourself, sugar, then other folks'll keep well away from you and treat you with respect.' Black Jack believed in rough justice applied by those who, like himself, did not believe in leaving vengeance to the Lord, thus overburdening Him. Black Jack did not waste time in legal battles to determine what was fair. Black Jack had observed that life was often unfair, and so was justice.

Chapter Fourteen

Sunday 24 July 1927. Hollywood

From the rear of Tudor's hacienda, a band softly alternated 'It had to be You' and 'Who's Sorry Now?' with 'Among my Souvenirs'. Tudor was sending Mimi off in style, before her ten-day trip back to Britain.

Tudor's home, considered gnome-sized for Hollywood, had a splendid entrance hall in which a lone violinist swayed, a classy touch. The hall led right through the house to a carefully tended lawn, where the peppermint-pink striped marquee had been proudly planted; inside this, rows of glasses shone, polished silver gleamed and dishes of naked salmon with bits of parsley stuck in their dead mouths waited for the guests, as did dark-green bottles of champagne in bucket after silver bucket of ice: beneath the white linen tablecloths, zinc washtubs contained further supplies.

Just inside the entrance door (rusty-nailed, Spanish Colonial, eighteen months old), Tudor and Mimi waited to receive their guests. Mimi wore a formal long-sleeved chalk crêpe pyjama suit made for her by Vionnet, with acid-green shoes and suede purse in one white-gloved hand. Tudor was casual, in cream flannel pants and immaculate navy blazer.

They waited.

At half-past six – the invitations had been for 6 p.m. – Tudor casually strolled into his study, dashed to the desk and checked the date and time on a spare invitation card: both were correct. The band had come, the caterers had come, all his hired glass and crockery had come according to plan . . . so what had happened to the guests?

Well . . . nobody in Hollywood was ever early.

Tudor sauntered back to the hall, where Mimi, looking puzzled, talked to an elegantly dressed woman in a jade-green pleated georgette outfit, and a cute jade-feathered suede hat pulled over to one side: Tudor immediately knew that she was a gatecrasher.

Half an hour later, five more gatecrashers had been politely turned away, but eventually three genuine guests arrived together, all smelling strongly of *déjà-bu* Martinis. After their greetings (as ecstatic as if hosts and guests were lovers who hadn't touched each other for six months) the three arrivals drifted through the hall into the soft, rosy light of the marquee: when they saw that the tent was empty, they all paused, then immediately made for the bar where, over breast-shaped glasses of champagne, they surreptitiously checked the time of arrival on their invitation cards. Upon realizing that the whoopee should have started an hour earlier, the three guests immediately knocked back their champagne and fled from the marquee; they sped through the hall, gaily waved bye-bye at Mimi and Tudor, then scrambled into their autos.

'Are they afraid I'll give 'em the pox?' Mimi asked crossly.

'No, darling, they've probably got that already.' Tudor gave a shaky laugh. 'What they're scared of is something that's considered a much worse fate, and even easier to catch.'

'Eh?'

'Failure. They think they smell failure.'

'But *you're* not a failure!'

'No . . .'

'So . . . they think I am?'

'For some reason that they don't yet understand.' Tudor put his arm around Mimi. 'Don't take it personally, darling, they're behaving like lemmings leaping after each other over a cliff: they're just doing what the rest of the herd is doing – and the rest of the herd is clearly elsewhere. Someone, somewhere is obviously making *big* whoopee tonight.'

'Well, at least we'll have all that champagne to ourselves.' Mimi realized that Tudor was in the middle of every host's nightmare, and decided to make a joke of it.

The band played on. The slick-haired waiters tactfully lowered their eyes to their trays of flattening champagne. The caterer wondered if he could serve those untouched poached salmons at the Flugelheim Silver Wedding tomorrow, if he sprinkled them with water and put fresh parsley sprigs in their mouth.

Slowly a cream Rolls-Royce drew up to the entrance. Slowly, the monocled Aubrey Smith, dressed as if for a royal wedding, stepped forward, followed in a similar stately manner by several of the British contingent. Another ancient Rolls now turned through the gates. Eventually, eleven of the British Colony had arrived and, in their genteel, British way, were behaving as if nothing extraordinary were happening: in the middle of the otherwise deserted marquee, they all stood deep in apparently silent conversation, like secondary action extras on a movie set.

Then, like the Bad Fairy at a christening, in the

entrance appeared a small, wizened woman, in rust-coloured silk with matching pumps and a hat like a giant chrysanthemum. Tudor immediately recognized the gossip journalist of the *Hollywood Chronicle*; Rita the Ripper also had her own radio show.

Staring through the hallway to the almost-empty marquee, a malevolent grin slowly stretched across Rita's sunburnt face, which was as lined as a map of the Nile delta. She purred, 'Tudor, you must be nuts to pick the same date Betsy chose for her surprise Cloth-of-Gold Evening!'

Tudor's face showed only polite interest, but Mimi could not hide her dismay, as she remembered, yes, some journalist called Rita *had* requested the guest list for her farewell party; which was normal, if the newspaper intended to cover it.

According to Rita, Western Union had delivered Betsy's telegraphed invitations only that morning. Betsy's secretary had then telephoned everyone on the O'Brien guest list to check acceptances and casually mention that party favours of solid gold, straight from Cartier, would be distributed to every guest – powder compacts for the ladies, cigarette cases for the men. Upon receiving their invitations, Betsy's chosen guests had immediately changed their plans for that evening: they dared not risk offending Mrs Jack O'Brien, who was on every A-list in Hollywood.

So all the people on Tudor's guest list must be at Betsy's party, which rusty-coloured Rita had just left, in order 'To say Hi-Bye to swell celeb Mimi Fane, the toast of Hollywood.'

Tudor immediately realized what had happened. Betsy, used to having her own way, had already made it icily clear to him that she did not approve of his inviting 'that woman' on Betsy's turf. No doubt, Betsy had daily read of the enthusiasm with which Hollywood society had welcomed Mimi, which had split open her old wound of shattered self-esteem. So she was upstaging Mimi's exit, making sure that Mimi left town with her tail between her legs.

Malicious Rita, delighted by Mimi's reaction to her ostracism, cooed her sympathy. '*Was* Betsy Bridges invited? . . . Too bad, she musta forgot.'

Many a woman finding herself in such a humiliating situation would have been struck dumb, but not Mimi. 'Betsy ain't got a bad memory,' she spat, 'her ma made her memorize the name of every eligible titled gent in *Burke's Peerage*!'

'That's a bit like the Four Hundred List, in New York,' Tudor interrupted, throwing a warning glance at Mimi, whose indignation was clearly about to overcome her caution.

Mimi ignored Tudor's warning glance as hot fury turned to cold rage, and with a taut smile she gave Rita the Ripper an exclusive interview on the early life of Betsy O'Brien.

Cooing sympathetically, Rita scribbled happily; how *right* she had been to take in Betsy's party beforehand, and claim her gold compact *plus* that diamond pin: her reward for handing over Tudor's guest list.

After the eleven British guests had politely faded away; after the caterers had folded their tents and disappeared; after the trucks had moved off with the catering supplies, Tudor looked gravely at Mimi. 'You'd better tell me what you did to upset Betsy Bridges.'

'*Nothing* to deserve this! . . . Well, hardly anything . . .

Look at it this way – if Ziegfeld had hired Betsy, she'd probably still be bouncing her bosom in the chorus ... And anyway, that was nearly twenty years ago ...' Slowly, diffidently, feeling unaccountably ashamed, Mimi told her story.

'You, my darling, are a permanent social success in Britain – and if you weren't, you wouldn't care.' He waved his arm toward the empty tent and said, 'Everyone here cares! Every day I teach stars who are adored all round the world – and they're all terrified of failure, of being a has-been. They all behave nervously, like someone at a party who doesn't know when it's time to leave, doesn't realize when the party's over.'

'They seemed to realize that this one was over before it started.'

'Mimi, you simply must understand that in Hollywood, failure can move mountains: one accidental stumble can escalate into a plunge as ruthless as a Santa Monica mountain mud-slide: there's no such thing as slightly bad news in Hollywood. If you're in you're *in*, and if you're not – you're *out*.'

Mimi finished her champagne. She twanged in the local accent, 'I guess it's time I moseyed on home.' She up-ended her glass on a chrome side table, and morosely watched the dregs drain down.

Monday 25 July 1927. Hollywood

Betsy sat up against her scrolled satin bedhead in a bedroom that looked as if everything in it had been instantly turned to beige by a studio spray gun. Sipping orange juice from the breakfast tray balanced on her knees, she briskly picked up the first of a pile of newspapers at her bedside and turned the switch of the bedside radio to catch the *Last Night in Hollywood* half-hour.

After listening to the cooing, eulogistic report of her 'Cloth-of-Gold Party' Betsy flipped through the newspapers. Not a word about Mimi: suddenly Mimi had social leprosy. Too bad. Betsy turned to Rita's 'Hollywood Hot News' column and her self-satisfied little smile abruptly disappeared.

Disbelieving, she read Mimi's exclusive interview. Spread over half a page was Betsy's early life, with descriptions of the dreary digs, the cheap seats on train trips, observations on Betsy's minimal vocal talent, paragraph after paragraph about Mrs Bridges' early training of her daughter: the walking downstairs with a book on her head, the copy of *Burke's Peerage* that was her bedside reading ... Betsy read on and on and on about the intimate little secrets of years of friendship. The interview ended with a bracketed titbit ('*Friendship Finishes in Flames*, see this column tomorrow').

The sound of smashing glass and another strong whiff of Chanel No. 5 brought Black Jack dashing in from his dressing room. He stepped forward and immediately trod on a shard of shattered dressing-table mirror. Trailing blood from his big toe over the beige carpet, Black Jack hurried towards Betsy, now sitting up in bed, her hands on her ears, her eyes shut: she was screaming with rage.

Protectively, Black Jack pulled his wife to his grey-haired chest, so that she had to chose between screaming and breathing.

'What the fuck's going on?' he demanded.

Betsy wept tears of rage. 'It's that awful woman Mimi! She's given an *outrageous* interview about me to— I guess it's Rita Rogers, although the goddamned article isn't signed.'

'I'll buy the paper and fire the bitch,' Black Jack offered.

Betsy wept. 'Thanks, honey. I knew I could rely on you . . . I know you'll say I'm silly but I swear if Mimi was still in town, I'd seriously consider asking the price of a knee-cap job. I'm almost more scared of what *I* might do to her than what *she* might do to me next!'

'Crush a wasp and it can't sting you.' Black Jack tore the gossip column out of the newspaper and stormed into his bathroom, pulling Betsy by the wrist. He threw Rita's frenzied prose into the empty black marble bath, picked up the enormous Queen Anne silver lighter that stood by the john, and set fire to the scrap of newsprint, which swiftly turned to black wisps. Black Jack grimly advised her: 'That Fane dame's a real snake. So what do you do with a snake? Slice its head off!'

* * *

Hollywood news tended to surface immediately after the weekend, when stars were not working, so had time to misbehave. But on the morning after Betsy's party there was little local gossip. As they spooned their breakfast grapefruit, those with nothing better to do gleefully gobbled up the embarrassingly, pathetically pretentious early life of 'Gold-Digger' Betsy O'Brien (as if there were no other gold-diggers in Hollywood) and of the cruel way in which she had arranged for her old friend's visit to end. Hands swiftly stretched to telephones and all Hollywood laughed. Imagine! She walked downstairs with a book on her head for years! No wonder the snooty bitch wears her goddamn tiara with such fucking arrogance.

From that morning, the feud between Betsy and Mimi became public, gossip-column fodder. Soon, everyone in town who had not been invited to Betsy's fabulous Cloth-of-Gold party saw it from a different viewpoint. Everyone who had envied or resented the powerful Betsy Bridges sided with Mimi against everyone who dared not offend Betsy. It was no dramatic sex scandal, but deliberately, blatantly and so expensively to wreck a former friend's farewell party was a cold-blooded demonstration of power used for vengeance: a glimpse of Hollywood with its claws out.

* * *

After Mimi had departed on her ten-day return trip to Britain, Tudor sat at his desk, unscrewed his gold-tipped fountain pen and, in a neat, slanting script, he wrote to Betsy: politely he told her that her action could not be described as ladylike, and he regretted that a friend of his should have behaved in such a fashion.

Upon reading this, Betsy winced, for Tudor was her idea of a gentleman.

Betsy's secretary subsequently telephoned Tudor, to ask him to visit, but Tudor did not see Betsy for six months, after which time, slowly and carefully, their friendship was resumed, for the good-natured Tudor knew that everyone occasionally behaves badly.

Sunday 14 August 1927. London

As the boat train from Southampton arrived at Waterloo station, travellers leaned from the windows; in high, strangulated British voices, accustomed to command, they called, 'Portah! Portah!' Obediently, porters rushed forward with luggage trolleys. Mimi walked slowly up the platform, for although it was mid-August, the Atlantic crossing had been rough, and she had spent most of four days being seasick.

Toby dashed forward and hugged the flame-haired little figure in the navy silk travelling suit. The house in Fitzroy Square had been uneasily quiet without Mimi's voice belting out some old music hall favourite.

'Mind me titfer,' Mimi remonstrated, but did not really care that her smart navy hat had been knocked sideways: she was delighted and relieved to see Toby, and be home.

On their return to Fitzroy Square, Toby told Mimi what she had to be warned about: the popular British press had picked up news of the Fane–O'Brien feud: gossip columns had been headlined, 'FAMOUS STARS CLASH IN HOLLYWOOD', 'FANE FLOPS', 'MIMI'S TINY, TINY PARTY!', 'BATTLE OF THE WITCHES!' Mimi wept.

'I got me own back, see?' Mimi uneasily pointed out later. 'Revenge is a dish best eaten cold.'

'Revenge is a poisonous dish best not tasted at all.'

Mimi hid her face on Toby's shirt-front, and snuffled, 'I felt as low as dirt when nobody turned up!'

Toby was usually sympathetic to Mimi, but felt obliged to suggest, even if by doing so he risked an underhand uppercut to his jaw, 'Perhaps it was no worse than her humiliation when you deliberately sabotaged her chance with Ziegfeld.'

Burning with indignation, Mimi stiffened. 'I'd like to murder that cow!'

'No, you wouldn't, Mimi.'

The snuffles stopped. Because Mimi loved and trusted

Toby, she was prepared to consider that he might be correct, although she did not feel it.

Toby pulled another newspaper clipping from his pocket and handed it to her. Aloud, she read that the daughter of the recently assassinated Irish Minister of Justice had said, 'The only way to deal with the unforgivable is to forget it. You then free yourself of murdering hate.'

Toby said, '*That's* what I've been telling you for years, my love. Forget it.'

Mimi looked up, red-eyed. 'Easier said than done.'

* * *

Fizz had laughed at the press coverage of Mimi's Hollywood humiliation, for she thought the enduring feud between the two women was absurd; as Fizz had not yet encountered personal treachery, she did not know how difficult it was to ignore. Max warned his wife not to mention the matter when they walked round to Fitzroy Square to welcome Mimi home.

As it was a warm evening, they took their drinks to the small rear garden. Because the little patch of earth faced north and was surrounded by high walls, nothing much grew in the acid soil (which was liberally and regularly sprinkled by neighbourhood cats' piss) except Toby's white rhododendrons and blue hydrangeas.

Mimi's family listened to her account of the jolly time she'd had in Hollywood and the strangeness and excitement of New York, which she had explored for the first time on her homeward trip.

'What was Broadway like, Mummy?'

'Hot as hell, ducky. Tar melted in the streets and stuck

to me shoes. Even in the evening, it was too hot to go to a show.'

'Didn't you even visit the Theater Guild?' Max could not believe that his mother had missed such an opportunity to see exciting experimental work. 'It started with one-act plays at the back of a Greenwich Village store, and now has its own acting school and a subscription audience. The Guild *makes money* with Shaw, and new American playwrights such as Eugene O'Neill and Maxwell Anderson.'

'That Guild Place was closed for the summer, Max. Pity I couldn't stay longer. The Lunts invited me to the country for the weekend, but I had to catch the boat back.'

'Gosh, I'd love to visit New York!' Max said, wistfully.

'Well, why don't you?' Toby suggested; he managed to stop himself saying. 'You've nothing much else to do at the moment.' Then he remembered. 'Of course you can't leave Fizz *now*!'

'I'm sorry, but that was a fib.' Red-faced, Fizz grabbed her opportunity.

'I bloody thought as much!' Mimi burst out. 'Too bleeding convenient, I said to Jessie, when I saw her knitting bootees!' Mimi threw the dregs of her champagne into her son's face. 'Don't you *never* lie to your pa or me again!'

'No, Mummy,' Max said meekly.

Toby was furious. Max looked furtive.

'Perhaps we'd better leave.' Fizz broke the angry silence.

'No, sit down,' Mimi said ungraciously. 'I suppose it really would have happened sooner or later, the way you was both carrying on.'

Give her twenty minutes, thought Max.

'We *hope* it will.' Fizz gently kissed Mimi's cheek.

Give it five, Max thought.

Half an hour later, after they had finished a second bottle of bubbly, at a prearranged glance from Max, Fizz took Toby's arm and firmly marched him into the house, saying that she wanted him to lend her the Abrahams book on Sarah Siddons.

Left alone with his mother, Max earnestly said, 'We didn't only ... that is, Fizz and I talked a lot in Paris ... Stop laughing, Mummy. It was marvellous to have so much time to ourselves, with nobody else around! ... Stop teasing, Mummy!' Max tried to look serious.

'So what did you and Fizz discuss in gay Paree? Lindbergh's Atlantic solo flight? The total eclipse of the sun?'

'Among other things, we talked about this feud of yours with Betsy Bridges. It's upset you for years, and now the press has got hold of it. Fizz and I would like you to *seriously* consider forgetting it.'

'You been talking to your dad? Is this a set-up, as they say in Hollywood?'

Max looked at his mother with the pleading dark blue eyes that had bewitched every girl at the Vic. 'You're not a Sicilian peasant, Mummy. So why not leave revenge to the gods. *Hubris* is on your side.'

'Who the hell's Hubert?'

'The ancient Greeks believed that someone who is excessively self-confident attracts punishment from the gods; so if a chap gets away with some dirty deed, he becomes more arrogant, until he gets careless, goes too far and the gods send appropriate punishment.'

'Like the Scottish King?' Theatre people tried to avoid

mentioning the word 'Macbeth', for it was considered unlucky.

'Exactly, Mummy.'

'You know that's fairy tale stuff. Is that all you got from that high-falutin' classical education?'

Max persisted. 'Why not leave it to the gods, Mummy, why not finally put this behind you? Why not let go of it?'

Max was still a child, Mimi crossly reminded herself, as yet untouched by hard human struggles and sorrow. Max was also in love, and living on rosy clouds, floating far above the real world that he was so anxious to put right.

Mimi looked down at her navy-gloved hands. Not until someone had made Max really suffer would he be able to understand his mother's rage and indignation. Since leaving Hollywood, Mimi's hellish nightmares and daymares had returned, so whatever her family felt or advised, she had no intention of forgiving or forgetting. She was hell-bent on revenge.

* * *

Fizz played Eliza in *Pygmalion* as a delightfully funny yet sad adolescent. It was a Suffragist interpretation, the slow realization that a woman's true position in history (to date) had been one of servitude to men. This provocative interpretation was a howling success; Virginia Woolf herself – tall, stooped, vague and beautiful – had come backstage to say so, and present Fizz with a signed copy of *Mrs Dalloway*.

After Mrs Woolf's departure, Max opened the inscribed book, raised his eyebrows and read aloud, ' "Life is a luminous halo, a semi-transparent envelope surrounding us from the beginning of consciousness to the end" ... But of *course*!'

'No need to sneer,' Fizz snapped, as she snatched back her precious book.

Although Max seemed unaware, it was becoming increasingly clear to friends of the young Fanes that he was becoming jealous of Fizz's career. *He* was still out of work. *She* was the principal wage earner, and as such, like a man, seemed to feel entitled to take centre-stage position in their marriage. Max (still accepting an allowance from Toby) was unfairly resentful, but would not admit to feelings of rivalry, although he visibly stiffened when addressed by a new stage-door keeper as 'Mr Allen'. One evening, when Fizz rushed off stage, flushed with success, into Lilian Baylis's study, where her husband waited to drive her home, Max muttered bitterly, 'Just *once* I'd like to feel that I wasn't just your bloody chauffeur! Just *once* I'd like to feel that I held the whole stage in the palm of *my* hand, and had the audience eating out of it.'

Fizz was silent. On stage, on the rare occasions when she didn't feel as if she was flying, she felt as if she were wading through mud. She knew that Max had always had to sweat over his small roles, and was understandably envious of Fizz's natural, seemingly effortless ability.

Outside the open door, Miss Baylis heard Max's frustration. The next day, she looked warningly over her new tortoiseshell spectacles. 'I want to warn you, Fizz. I've known that lad all his life. Max's used to being the centre of attention and he can't help being jealous of your talent, dear – so watch out. And never listen to his criticism, dear – because he'll always try to belittle you, and find mistakes in your work . . . Now don't interrupt me, I know you love him, dear, but if he ever wants to direct you – say no, because you can't trust his judgement.'

Fizz laughed off this warning, but she had to admit to herself that marriage was far stormier than she had expected, although whenever she and Max had a mild clash or a blazing row, it was quickly followed by a tearfully erotic reconciliation. But to add to Max's unrealized resentment, Fizz now seemed to be losing her enthusiasm for sex, although she clearly enjoyed a tumble on Sunday morning. If the young Fanes got out of bed in time, they then walked up the road to lunch in Fitzroy Square.

Mimi's Christmas lunch was particularly lively. Everyone drank more than usual – even the sour-faced Lady Fane, her majestic daughter Cassandra and the mild little husband that she could easily have hidden in her cleavage.

Mimi, about to open on the following day as the lead in *Dick Whittington* at the Minerva, wore a scarlet Santa Claus outfit with red tights and high-heeled thigh boots. As the Christmas pudding was carried in, aflame with brandy, she blasted everyone's eardrums off with 'Auld Lang Syne', and they all joined in. Afterwards, still wearing ridiculous paper hats, everyone opened the gifts piled beneath the Christmas tree in the drawing room, after which Mimi had invited further friends for a slap-up, old-fashioned Christmas tea.

When Max and Fizz eventually returned to their bay-fronted dream house, Fizz staggered up the stairs towards their bedroom, longing for a nap.

Max had a different aim in mind as they dived into the rat's nest of a bed that they had left unmade that morning.

Yawning, Fizz brushed his hand from her breast. 'Not now, Max, I really need to sleep.'

'That's all you ever say these days!'

Fizz knew it was true. To her surprise, she found that

sex sapped her theatrical energy: the vitality and animal magnetism required to play an important lead part well simply drained her, leaving no leftover energy for a rollicking bedroom performance afterwards. Sometimes the highly sexed Max (who had never known the demands of a lead part) found it hard to believe that his wife really loved him.

'I don't know what's the matter with you these days,' the frustrated Max complained. He added sarcastically, 'That is, assuming there's nobody else.'

Wearily, Fizz propped herself on one elbow. 'You don't really believe there is, do you? You're too bloody arrogant to think that for one minute!'

'Am I in bed with Eliza Doolittle or Mrs Fane?' Max demanded, only half in fun.

'You're in bed with me, myself, I, Fizz – and I've had just about enough of your sulking! One more word from you and I'm going to jump into Mimi's Christmas present and go back to Fitzroy Square!'

Mimi's Christmas gift to Fizz had been a pale-grey suede coat with a silver-fox collar. For one moment, Max fantasized Fizz naked beneath this fabulous garment, and then he jumped out of bed. 'One more word from you, and I'm going to New York with Dad's gift to me!' He waved the cheque in his hand.

'Sod off!' Grabbing the eiderdown, Fizz ran out of the room and downstairs to their living room. She locked the door, cocooned herself in the eiderdown, climbed on the sofa and immediately fell asleep.

On the following day, Max booked a ticket to New York in the *Corinthea*: perhaps if he disappeared for a month, Fizz might change her selfish attitude.

* * *

On the afternoon of his arrival in Manhattan, Max headed for the theatre district, in the midtown section of Broadway. Times Square was far more cheap and tawdry than its London equivalent, Shaftesbury Avenue: not even *square*, but wedge-shaped, like a slice of sponge cake, it was grubby, garish and small. Max gazed at huge crude advertisements which disfigured the buildings around which they were slapped; he gazed down at discarded candy bar wrappings, empty squashed cigarette packs and torn newspaper that fluttered under the hurrying feet of harassed-looking people, dodging the slumped, rag-clad drunks on the sidewalk. He sniffed the reek of frying oil and stale beer: the steam swirled up from underground conduits seemed appropriate. It was hellish. Max was childishly disappointed . . . until sundown, when the Great White Way lit up. Suddenly that sleazy garbage bin was transformed by twinkling stars, flung not at random as into the universe, but grouped in neat, geometrical arrangements, above each brilliantly lit theatre marquee.

Ignoring his father's introductions to the established, famous theatre people he knew in Manhattan, Max sought out actors of his own age: every morning, he breakfasted at one of the small restaurants or cafés around 41st Street and Broadway, where young hopefuls congregated; quickly he made friends; one of his new pals arranged a sub-let in a two-room apartment in a new building on 57th Street East.

For the next two weeks, Max enjoyed the hospitable and energizing atmosphere of New York, as he was rushed from one new pleasure to the next. He saw all the Broadway shows, but scorned the musicals, with the exception of the stunning *Show Boat*. He goggled at the agile black dancers and exquisite showgirls up in the nightclubs of Harlem and sampled many illicit speakeasies, where bathtub-brewed gin was drunk in thick teacups. It was nearly ten years since Prohibition had started, and even politicians were becoming concerned at the increasing health risks, lawlessness, violence and gangsterism that the law had generated.

Max's friends laughed indulgently at his enthusiasm for the city and warned him not to judge the States by Manhattan, to which he always replied that it seemed a wonderful place to start. He had never before been in a country where an individual was allowed to do pretty much as he pleased, and make damn sure no one was going to stop him. He was impressed by this refreshing assurance in the group of young actors with whom he now hung out; this included several Theater Guild members. One fledgeling director, small and shabby, whey-faced and intense, described to Max the impact of the Moscow Arts Theatre, when the famous Russian Ensemble, trained by Stanislavsky, had visited New York in 1923. Although the Russian costumes had been tatty and the scenic effects dull, Lee and his friends had been astonished by the reality produced on stage; minor parts had been played as brilliantly as star parts: Lee had felt as though he were eavesdropping on friends, rather than watching a performance of *The Cherry Orchard*.

Max quickly heard of the American Laboratory Theater, started in New York by two ex-members of the Moscow Arts Theatre: the Lab was not only a production company, but also a training school for actors and directors, where Lee had acquired the ideas for which he was developing his own theories of teaching and directing. Why didn't Max visit?

Within two days, Max had visited the Laboratory, been

interviewed by Richard Boleslavsky, and had enrolled himself for six months.

Two days before the date of Max's return to London, Fizz eagerly tore open an egg-yellow envelope and read:

EXTENDING STAY SIX MONTHS TO ATTEND AMERICAN LABORATORY THEATER STOP LETTER FOLLOWS STOP LOVISSIMUS STOP MAX.

Furious, Fizz cabled back WHAT'S HER NAME? and an acrimonious cable correspondence ensued, until Max's six-page, excited and explanatory letter arrived in London.

At least Max sounds enthusiastic about life once again, Fizz thought thankfully. Lying in bed, she swiftly scribbled a one-page reply before returning to her notes on *The Importance of Being Ernest*. She had decided to play Cecily, the female lead, as adorable and deliciously feminine, but also as a practical, down-to-earth young woman who knew exactly what she wanted.

* * *

Max continued to be elated by the purposeful air of New York; the city seemed silently to promise success if you were prepared to do all that was required for it. Every weekday morning Max sat with the rest of the cast around the big table in the rehearsal room of the Laboratory Theater, where all productions started. Every single line of the play was analysed for meaning and so was the aim that motivated each character ('What do I want and why?') as well as the specific contribution of each actor's part to the entire production. Before Max had finished his first week of training he could see the importance of table-work, for it slowly welded all the actors into one interactive ensemble, rather than a group of actors, each hell-bent on attracting the maximum attention to himself.

Max still found it hard to believe that before Stanislavsky there had been no systematic training procedure for actors and no exercises to practise technique, as in music. Every morning when he woke he practised his relaxation exercises (in order to control his nervous system) and then did his memory exercises, searching for some personal emotional experience that would help him understand the feelings of the character he played on stage. These new disciplines would help him be as good an actor as his wife.

Sunday 27 May 1928. New York

Max stood in the doorway and gazed around at the chic intellectual crowd gathered at the fund-raising party of New York's theatre heroine: Eva La Gallienne had been a Broadway star for five years before founding New York's only repertory theatre, where she taught drama, gave work in her productions to young American actors and coaxed stars to appear with them for a nominal salary, so providing her audiences with cheap seats for classical plays. Tonight, obedient stars were lavishly sprinkled to lure money from rich potential patrons and thus fund Eva's future productions.

Max immediately noticed a beautiful blonde with her hair pulled back in a classical twist – what the Yanks called a class act. Was she a star or a patron?

Carefully dressed in primrose crêpe with a classically draped Grecian top and a narrow belt buckle of genuine diamonds at pelvis level, Betsy intended to look what she was: a major patron of the intellectually OK West

Coast Little Theater Movement. She noticed Jack surreptitiously peek at his watch and knew it was time to leave. He was an old darling to appear because he hated these occasions and longed to leave: the earlier he was let off the hook, the larger his donation cheque. Betsy could sometimes understand Jack's impatience, she thought, as idly she listened to three earnest, bespectacled young men, whom she suspected of showing off on her behalf.

'Why not promote Pirandello's disillusion with the state of things as they seem?' suggested one of them. 'Acknowledge the illusion of life, and the hopelessness of our attempts to recognize reality . . .'

Betsy was wondering how fast she and Jack could get away when she noticed in the entrance a tall dark, good-looking young man, with a droopy haircut. Betsy peremptorily interrupted the conversation. 'Excuse me, who's that guy who's just come in?'

One glanced towards the door. 'Lee Strasberg.'

'No, the guy with him, the dark one.'

'Max Fane. English student at American Lab.'

Suddenly, Betsy's evening became more interesting as she watched the unsuspecting Max. She pointed him out to Black Jack: together, they stared at the animated dark-blue eyes and dark hair, easily seen above the crowd.

Black Jack gave a slow, grim smile. 'A child is a parent's hostage to fortune, Betsy. The best way to hurt a mother is by hurting her child.'

Betsy smiled broadly at that thought, and started to move purposefully through the crowd. 'Hello, Lee,' she cooed, butterfly kissing the pale cheek.

Strasberg turned to Max. 'You probably know Betsy, Patron of the Arts and Goddess of Mammon . . .'

Betsy turned her violet eyes, hypnotically, upon Max. Lee drifted away.

'What did Lee say your name was?' Max asked politely.

'Betsy.'

'Betsy who?'

Bumped from behind, Betsy used the opportunity to silence Max by spilling her champagne down the front of his trousers. She gasped theatrically, '*Now* what will everyone think?'

Max grinned as his new friend put an apologetic hand to her mouth, and giggled deliciously.

Chapter Fifteen

June 1928

Fizz snuggled up against Max. 'Did you *really* miss me, Max?'

'Constantly.'

'Were you unfaithful?'

'Not once,' Max said truthfully, if misleadingly.

'Not once in six months?'

'No, darling.'

'It shows, darling.' Fizz sighed happily.

'After beating Napoleon at the Battle of Waterloo, the Duke of Wellington's wife reported to a friend, "Three times . . . before he took his boots off." '

'Thank God you're not the Duke of Wellington,' Fizz murmured.

* * *

In June 1928 Max had just returned to Britain, where he found himself still out of work. Having invited half of New York to drop in, should they be in London, Max was astonished when his new American acquaintances immediately started to do so: invariably, these were impoverished students, actors or a combination of both, bumming their way around Europe, and hoping that Max would not mind putting them up overnight in London, on a lounge couch.

'Overnight' invariably meant a week or two. Once, Fizz crossly told Max that she had quite forgotten what the pattern on their sofa looked like, and was tired of seeing it surrounded by shabby suitcases and rucksacks, while strange sponge bags hung on the hook behind the bathroom door.

Max enjoyed his guests, for they behaved exactly as if they were still in New York; they were astonished to find that pubs closed so early, and that you couldn't get a drink or a meal in London at four in the morning. Every day, he laid in plenty of beer, so that every evening they could argue for half the night over the value of a lavishly mounted, traditional production versus an acting area in the round which provided close audience contact and required minimal costumes and props, or whether it was possible, with clever lighting, to totally eliminate scenery; or whether actors should acknowledge the presence of an audience, or behave as if it were not there. And naturally, who was sleeping with whom.

During one of these discussions, while Max was waiting for Fizz to return from the theatre, he enviously heard that some Princeton and Harvard theatre club members, including Josh Logan and Jimmy Stewart, had decided to take over a movie house at Falmouth, on Cape Cod, to start their own summer theatre, the University Players' Guild.

Max found himself wondering why he could not similarly kick-start his own directing career. He decided to talk it over with his father.

On the following Sunday afternoon, in Toby's study, having carefully mentally rehearsed their dialogue, Max prudently started the conversation by saying how grateful he was to his father for the financial support that he had been providing, but that he had to think of some way to earn his own money, because he couldn't live on his wife for much longer, and anyway, the Vic only paid Fizz ten pounds a week.

Toby, who had realized that professionally Max was getting nowhere, listened carefully.

'I want to work in the theatre, but with plays that explore social problems and encourage people to solve them.'

Toby looked sceptical. 'A few theatrical performances can't wipe out small-town corruption, slum landlords, prostitution – or any other basic evils of the human heart.'

'Bernard Shaw says people can't condemn what they don't know about.'

'But will audiences call that entertainment?'

'You must admit that Mr Shaw is successful.'

Ah, so Max intended to write plays.

Max continued, 'And audiences like the way Shaw's plays are presented.'

Toby sniffed. 'Bare boards, costumes made of sheet or sacking, lighting that makes you feel in the middle of a thunder storm, with the electricity about to cut out.'

'Simple stage settings with nothing to distract from the text. Like Gordon Craig.' Craig, the illegitimate son of Ellen Terry, had revolutionized theatre design with abstract, minimal sets and effective, experimental lighting.

Toby's face lost its puzzled look. 'Are you trying to tell me that you want to design sets?'

'No, Daddy, I want to be a director; what we call a producer over here.'

Toby thoughtfully drummed his fingers on the arm of his chair: that might be the way ahead for Max. As an actor, he was in competition with Gielgud, Olivier and that talented bunch. But there weren't many promising young producers in Britain.

* * *

That evening, after the curtain had fallen, Lilian Baylis entered her office to see Fizz sitting on the Hamlet chair, her elbows propped on the roll-top desk, snuffling unattractively into a handkerchief. She coughed. Fizz did not notice. She gingerly touched Fizz on the back. The startled Fizz shrieked, whipped round, saw who it was and continued to weep. 'I can't stand much more marriage, Miss Baylis. I go home to find the living room littered with beer bottles and American men – all called Guy – in crumpled shirts, all talking about Constructivism and the importance of social realism . . .'

'In a theatre marriage, dear, it's always more difficult, the out-of-work person can't *help* feeling jealous.'

'But it's *my* money that's paying for their food and all the beer they drink!'

'I know how you feel,' Miss Baylis said drily, 'I've noticed a husband can accept his wife *having* more money than he does: marrying an heiress never seems to worry a man. But if a wife *earns* more than her husband, that's blamed for destroying his self-esteem.'

'But doesn't stop him spending it, I've noticed!' Fizz turned and sobbed into Miss Baylis's beige-silk bosom. 'Damn Max's self-esteem! He used to be so encouraging, but now he'll say, "Of *course* you must take that part" – and then make it as difficult as possible for me to get to the theatre – which, by the way, he hardly ever visits. If he can spare the time to watch my performance then he falls asleep in the middle and snores . . . it's so insulting! . . . Everyone in the Company notices.'

Miss Baylis cautiously patted the disarrayed flaxen hair and shrugged her shoulders. 'Some theatre husbands are experts at what's called personality erosion; they do it a quiet way, drip by drip. That sort of bounder is jealous of his wife's work and her success because then it ain't possible for him to control her in the traditional way: Me brave, you squaw. You do as I tell you.'

'Not *me*!' wept Fizz defiantly. 'Me *not* squaw!'

Miss Baylis looked sceptical.

Monday 3 September 1928

With Toby's blessing (and his promise of continued monthly cheques) Max drove across Hammersmith Bridge to the unfashionable London suburb of Barnes. A couple of years before, in the tiny converted cinema, on a stage only ten foot wide, Max had admired two Chekhov plays produced by Theodore Komisarjevsky, a pupil of Stanislavsky. The inhabitants of Barnes were not interested in such plays; until the First World War, 80 per cent of the productions of the famous nineteenth-century actor-managers had been of Shakespeare, so post-war theatre audiences considered the Bard old-fashioned. Instead, they wanted modern realism as written by Somerset Maugham and acted by Sir Gerald Du Maurier, who was so realistic on stage that he appeared *not* to act. However, many serious theatregoers were prepared to trek south of the River Thames to see the exciting interpretations presented by the Barnes Theatre.

Outside the theatre Max jumped out of his green sports car without bothering to open the door, mentally preparing to make a good impression on Mr Komisarjevsky, who, he hoped, would accept him as an unpaid assistant.

He found himself facing a balding man in a tweed jacket and crumpled, grey flannel trousers; he looked a bit like Lenin, without the beard.

'You are Mr Fane, the letter writer? It is good you have this car, it will be useful.'

Max looked respectfully into slanting green eyes, sharp, sly and humorous, set in a typically flat Slav face.

Mr Komisarjevsky twitched his pointed little nose. 'You understand we can pay you nothing? But if you have talent, you *may* learn to be a producer. Follow me.' He waddled towards the main theatre entrance.

Max nodded, with relief. He could now continue the analytical, methodical training he had started in America. He followed his new master into the darkened theatre, where the cast were sitting on stage, assembled around a table.

By the end of the day, Max realized – as clearly as if God had pointed a huge index finger down from some overhead cloud – that he had found his Master.

* * *

Within days, Fizz had noticed the change in Max's entire outlook. Once again he was the ebullient, energetic young man she had married. There was only one drawback to the born-again Max: he could not stop talking about Komis.

Two weeks after Max joined the Barnes Theatre Company, over midday spaghetti at Bertorelli (the Fanes' favourite restaurant in Charlotte Street), Max continued to enthuse about his new Master. 'Fizz, I've never met anyone like him before: he's an architect, a brilliant lighting designer, a set designer, a costume designer, a musician . . . and you should hear him improvising tunes on the piano. He also writes books!'

Fizz leaned across the table and lovingly twitched the tip of Max's nose. 'Max, I'm sick of hearing about this fellow's brilliant, mad, inventiveness and impish, mercurial humour. In future, for every word you say about that balding little genius, I shall drool about Lilian Baylis!'

'Legggo by dose,' Max called nasally. Laughing, he shook his nose free of her grip.

* * *

The year that followed was the most exciting year of Max's life. Komisarjevsky radiated enthusiasm and energy, which excited and exhilarated Max, who felt a new tingling awareness of being alive.

Max carefully noticed that Komis – as everyone called him – was a perfectionist, but like all good producers he allowed his actors sufficient creative freedom, once the cast understood his concept of the play: Komis was controlled, quiet, never shouted, and he directed like a conductor interpreting a symphony, binding all parts together, so that they formed a rhythmic whole.

Max quickly found that his new job at the Barnes Theatre also involved assisting the elfin business manager, Mr Beaumont, known as Binkie. Max spent his lunch hour in the box office and did the bookkeeping on non-matinée afternoons. On Friday nights he toured the dressing rooms with Mr Binkie, carrying the actors' buff pay packets, which were handed back for reuse. If Binkie was unable to do so, Max donned smart black evening clothes to greet the audience as it entered the foyer. Helping to paint the sets and even make the clothes also taught Max how to stretch a shoestring budget. He also assisted with advertising and publicity; like his father he filled any spare five minutes with a wheedling telephone call to a newspaper critic, many of whom were difficult to lure to Barnes. He helped to negotiate contracts ('Mr Beaumont regrets that he can only pay . . .'). He unlocked the door to the cleaners at seven in the morning, always stayed at the theatre until well after the performance, and learned a great deal during this split-personality existence.

* * *

In March 1929, Fizz played Nora in Ibsen's *A Doll's House*.

On the First Night the stalls were lined with white bow ties, stiffly starched shirts, naked powdered shoulders, ropes of pearls and tiaras; the audience provided a show as well as watching one and often seemed more interested in who was in the stalls than what was happening on stage, Fizz thought crossly, as she took off her make-up after the show. The next morning she was interviewed, not by theatre critics, but by feature writers.

Still exhausted from the performance, she breakfasted with a smelly-socked reporter from the *Evening News*, sipped coffee with a shabby, clever man from the *Daily Globe*, then poured more coffee for a motherly, plump and endearingly untidy woman who represented the more intellectual (and bitchy) *Weekly Review*.

After sympathetically discussing Fizz's interpretation of Nora for half an hour, the interviewer said casually, 'Of course, your own private life is the reverse of Nora's.'

Fizz looked puzzled. 'What do you mean?'

Helpfully, the cosy woman explained. 'You're the principal wage earner. Doesn't your husband feel humiliated to be kept by you? Doesn't he feel inadequate?'

'Not that I've noticed,' Fizz said icily.

'Can I take it that your husband is never jealous, bossy or aggressive?' The woman's voice sharpened. 'He never behaves in private like Othello or Petruchio?'

Fizz gave a false trill of laughter. 'Good heavens, no!'

'But he *is* unemployed? Surely that must make married life difficult.'

'Not at all. Max is an assistant producer to Mr Komisarjevsky, at the Barnes Theatre.'

'Hardly Drury Lane?'

'You don't start learning tennis on the centre court at Wimbledon,' Fizz said sharply. 'Can we please talk about something other than my personal life?'

The woman smiled understandingly. 'I suppose everyone asks you what it feels like to be so successful, so young?'

'Some do,' Fizz admitted, relieved by this change of subject.

'Do you find that success creates more success? Do people come to *you* with the best plays, the best parts, the best projects?'

'Sometimes they do, but I'm well aware that I'm young and still learning my craft, and I'm very lucky to be doing this at the Vic.'

'One more thing,' the woman purred. 'That feud. Your mother-in-law and the O'Briens. Whose side are you on?'

Fizz gave a silvery laugh. 'That old affair keeps being resurrected by the media. At home, we never discuss it.' Smiling, she stood up. 'Please excuse me, I mustn't be late for my next appointment.'

On the following Friday, two articles appeared juxtaposed in the *Weekly Review*, under a photograph of Max looking surly, and one of Fizz, looking worried.

The first article – headed THE FEUDING FANES – said very little about Fizz's performance as Nora, and everything that the writer could scrounge from the *Review*'s cuttings library about the vendetta between Mimi and Betsy.

The adjoining article, headed, WHO'S BOSS, was unsigned. Titled PIN MONEY? it started:

Felicity Allen, lucky to be one of the few high-earning women in Britain, may be having other problems . . . at home, this brilliant queen of the stage turns into Mrs Max Fane . . . Or does she?

As wise as she is lovely, Felicity Allen laughed merrily at the idea of 'wearing the pants' and denied that fame and money have brought misery to her marriage. 'I never threaten Max's self-respect, or hurt his masculine pride,' she explained, 'Max understands how important acting is to me, but at home, Max expects to be boss.'

Does husband Max ever feel small because Felicity is such a big success? No, she says. Is Max ever called 'Mr Allen?' If so, does he hate it? No, she says.

Although home-loving Felicity admits that Max likes to be King of the Castle, she vows that at home he never behaves like Petruchio. Luckily, Mr Allen – oops, sorry, Mr Fane – is never physically violent, although Felicity knows that some less fortunate wives are abused for showing sign of independence. In many a home, the husband still packs a decisive punch!

The final paragraph was headed NAGGING.

Lovely star Felicity Allen insisted that she and her attractive husband, Max, never even argue. Can this be true? If so, perhaps the gifted actress is not so lucky, after all. Many a husband who would never dream of hitting a woman has other hurtful ways of avoiding confrontation. A husband who refuses to discuss a subject with his so-called nagging wife fears losing the argument. By refusing to talk – there is no argument for him to lose! . . . Luckily, there are no such problems in the happy home life of Felicity Fane.

Pushing his plate of eggs and bacon aside, Max read both articles. He looked up, red in the face. 'Fizz, did you *really* say I behaved like Petruchio around the house?'

'Of course I didn't, darling. And the clever bitch doesn't *say* I did. Can't you see this bloody woman wrote both these articles? Can't you see she's using *me* to air her own views? Surely she doesn't really think that ten pounds a week makes me one of Britain's highest-earning women!'

'Aha! So you did talk about money! How dare you discuss our private life with this suffragette lesbian bitch!'

'First she's twisted *my* words, and now you're twisting *her* words!' As it was nearly noon, she stormed into Berto-relli's, and drank far too much Chianti.

* * *

That evening, Fizz and Max went to Fifty-Fifty, a dimly lit supper club where it was not necessary to dress up as it was for the Ivy or the Savoy. Here actors relaxed over a drink, ate spaghetti or scrambled eggs, talked shop with other actors and wound down after a performance. As they entered, both Max and Fizz heard titters, then a girl giggled, 'Watch out! Here come the feuding Fanes!'

A jeering baritone called, 'Yoohoo, Petruuuuuuchio!' The entire restaurant broke into friendly laughter. Max's face reddened as he followed Fizz to their table.

The damage had been done. All over London, Max was now teased.

Partly to repair the rift between them, in bed one night, Fizz tentatively suggested in the dark, 'Why don't we have a little working fun together? Why not present something ourselves? In some little theatre, or on some town-hall stage? Something that wouldn't be expensive to put on ... How about ... Would you consider ... directing me in *Romeo and Juliet*?'

Astonished and delighted, Max sat up and switched on his bedside light. 'Would the Vic let you?'

'I think I could talk Miss Baylis into it, if it were only for a few performances, perhaps in aid of charity ...'

'I'll see if I can hire the Barnes theatre,' Max beamed, 'I'll have a word with Komis.' He switched off the light, and took Fizz in his arms.

* * *

Komis considered it too early for Max to direct, and also cautioned that when he did, he should entirely separate himself from any connection with Komisarjevsky, to avoid giving mischievous troublemakers an opportunity to imply that he was Komisarjevsky's puppet.

Undeterred, Max borrowed £200 from his father and hired the Hampstead Little Theatre, a flimsy, one-storey hall used for civic gatherings, by producers for rehearsals and by struggling actors able to scrape up enough money to showcase themselves in experimental, one-man shows.

Max decided to keep the lighting low, even as the audience entered, otherwise they would immediately notice that the Hampstead Little Theatre looked like a shrunken aircraft hangar.

Fizz suggested that any profit be donated to the Red Cross organization, which agreed to sell tickets through supporters. At this point, Max became more excited than nervous, for now he really had a chance to show what he had learned, and what he could do with a leading lady considered one of the best young actresses in London.

Monday 23 September 1929

In the ineradicable church-hall gloom, Max's First Night audience gossiped with the usual lack of concern: now that all British women were to have the vote, perhaps those silly old lesbians would stop chaining themselves to the railings ... The Prince of Wales had fallen in love with *another* married woman, the beautiful twin sister of Gloria Vanderbilt ... Lord Tilverton had purchased a flying boat with only one month's gains on the stock market...

Backstage, peering through the curtain, Max wished he could feel as sure as they did that a smooth performance was about to take place. He was now more nervous than excited, although he strained to appear calmly in control. He hoped he had remembered all that Komis had taught him, particularly that musical structure was the basis of a good play, good direction and good acting: he hoped he had correctly judged the rhythm and pace of each scene and speech. He knew the importance of sudden, unexpected variations in the tempo, which kept the audience alert; he hoped he had achieved the power of the pause, the crescendo and the climax – whether violently loud or still and almost silent.

Romeo was in a tizzy and showing signs of panic: he tossed his hair, kicked out his legs, rolled his eyeballs and generally behaved like a horse surprised by a motor bus. Waiting quietly in the wings, Fizz realized that such temperament came from insecurity and anxiety: suddenly, Romeo was not sure of his lines, his moves, or himself. Fizz enjoyed the familiar, blissful terror. She gave a happy little shiver of anticipation: once on that stage, she would feel relaxed and comfortable, fulfilled and delighted. She knew that there was a little bit of every feeling in every person; emotionally, all people were similar. At the moment when the entire audience recognized what a character on stage was feeling, then the empathy bounced back to the actor. Once again, Fizz crossed her fingers and hoped for that emotional identification which she always sought.

* * *

Fizz's Juliet was very different from her previous, tremulous performance at the Old Vic. Fizz played Juliet as a sex-mad little teenager; Fizz knew that girls of fourteen were not made of sugar and spice; they were touchingly hopeful but frightened, confused bundles of uncontrollable hormones. This was why, in Juliet's situation, lust swamped all her other emotions, a truth that parents never wanted to admit or accept.

On the following morning, Max threw *The Times* to the

floor and snatched up the *Daily Telegraph*. Again, he slowly shook his head from side to side, like a stunned boxer. The few critics persuaded by the senior Fanes to attend the First Night had praised Fizz's modern interpretation of Juliet, but were dismissive of the 'muddled production'.

Fizz poured more coffee into Max's breakfast cup. 'Miss Baylis is right. She says critics shouldn't be allowed in her theatre, they only upset the actors.'

* * *

As the telephone rang, Max wearily picked it up, and heard his mother's loyal outburst, 'Those that can, do; those that can't, criticize . . . This is exactly what your dad said would happen . . .'

At the other end of the line, Toby grabbed the phone from his wife. 'I warned you they wouldn't like newfangled direction. They're teaching you a lesson, son,' he explained to Max. 'Because you're a Fane, you can't expect to get off lightly, is their message.'

That morning, Max drank coffee until he twanged. Slowly he allowed into his heart from his head the knowledge that he had been a public failure. All that hard work, all his energy expended on analysis, all his concentration and care, all his ruthless cutting and attention to detail, all his little experiments . . . His poor little show had been strangled at birth by those uncaring bastards: the reviews were not damning – they were worse: nearly all conveyed a genuine disinterest and boredom.

* * *

'Trying to run before he can walk! That young pup is too big for his boots!' Lady Fane looked over her spectacles at her daughter as they took afternoon tea. 'Of course, I

expected that little trollop to be as bad as she was ...
Seemed to think that she was playing Sadie Thompson,
or some East End tart ... not the divine Juliet. Would
you pass me the walnut cake, my dear?'

* * *

Shortly before Christmas, Lady Fane, aged eighty-nine,
died in her sleep.

What was left of the Fane family gathered in the
sepulchral office of Bennett & Hopkins to hear the will
read.

As Lady Fane's only grandchild, Max listened hopefully as from behind his large desk. Mr Bennett droned
on ... 'It was our privilege to add to theatrical tradition
with the Fane Theatre Company, which I bequeath in its
entirety to my only surviving daughter Cassandra Alexandra Leopoldina Smythe, who is in my opinion the only
responsible and reliable Fane, who considers expenditure
as carefully as her mother, is prudently guided in financial
matters and who will not dissipate her inheritance on
unpopular experimentation.'

After Mr Bennett ceased to read, Max's Aunt Cassandra
(who had clearly known in advance of the contents of the
will) immediately let it be known that she and her husband intended to sell all the theatres: they were both
sixty-five years old, had no children and didn't want the
responsibility of a business. Clearly, what they did want
was the money, Max thought grimly.

'Further to my wife's decision,' the no longer meek Mr
Smythe firmly added, 'anyone who wishes to bid for any
or all of the theatres may do so from this moment. A pre-
emptive bid before auction by a family member would be
most carefully considered.'

'But is unlikely to be made,' Toby said quietly, as he stood to leave.

Thursday 24 October 1929

Across the Atlantic, the most prosperous nation in the world crashed to its knees. An unprecedented wave of panic, fear and confusion on Wall Street meant heavy selling of stock, which in turn precipitated further selling in a faster and faster downward spiral, as stocks were sold for whatever they would fetch. Police riot squads were called out to disperse the hysterical crowd in Wall Street. Many small investors lost all their savings. Ripples of insecurity washed outward from Wall Street, taking waves of panic to world trade. Theatre owners were left with near-empty cinemas. Black Jack, who had sold his cinemas and refused to invest in publicly owned companies, was still worth sixteen million dollars.

Tuesday 31 December 1929

There were not many parties to usher in the New Year of 1930, because the mood of the movie industry was sombre. Mr Lasky had been wiped out, other studio heads had also lost fortunes on Wall Street, so had many stars and celebrities. Few financiers had funds. Suddenly, the movie business was in as much trouble as almost every other business.

So Betsy's New Year's Eve party did not have much competition, in fact it was the hot ticket that year; everyone was there: Doug and Mary, Joan Crawford (recently married to nineteen-year-old Doug Junior, to disapproval from the occupants of Pickfair), Irving and Norma, plus the first Academy Award winner, Janet Gaynor. Everyone was determined to enjoy themselves and forget that Godawful Crash for one evening.

At ten minutes before midnight, Betsy checked with her butler that everything was in place. Yes, the balloons and streamers were poised above the dance floor in the ballroom (a recent home extension) ready to be released at midnight.

Betsy nodded at Black Jack, who nodded to the band leader, who immediately cut the music. After the dance floor emptied, a single trumpet sounded as Black Jack confidently walked out to stand alone in the spotlight before the band. He made a short speech in which he said that it had sure been a sad year for many, but that maybe the New Year would bring a fresh start to those who needed it, and he sure wished good luck to everyone present. As instructed, the band then started to play Black Jack's favourite tune, 'Alexander's Rag Time Band'. Black Jack bowed to Betsy, and held his arms out to his wife. Betsy's clinging white crêpe evening dress had diamanté shoulder straps, and a hem of white fox fur that swung out as Black Jack twirled his elegant and still-beautiful wife around the dance floor. Everybody clapped and cheered as the spotlight followed their host and hostess, alone on the dance floor.

Black Jack stumbled, and gave a little cough. Abruptly, he stopped dancing.

Black Jack coughed harder; he bent over and clutched his chest, but he clearly could not stop coughing. His face turned red, then the crimson-purple of a ripe plum. Waiters rushed for glasses of water. Black Jack slowly fell on his knees.

As everyone was very merry by this time, guests all clapped and cheered, assuming that old Black Jack had knocked back a few too many ... until blood started to trickle from their host's mouth; it dripped down his white shirtfront, and onto the dance floor.

Everyone hurriedly backed away from the man who lay in the spotlight.

Someone screamed.

The band faltered, and stopped playing.

Betsy fell on her knees beside Black Jack and tore at his white tie, to ease his breathing. As Black Jack's blood stained her white crêpe dress, Betsy looked up and screamed, 'Tudor, get an ambulance!'

Sunday 5 January 1930

At the Cedars of Lebanon Hospital, the doctor in the Emergency Room had listened to Black Jack's chest; even without an X-ray, he could detect a solid tumour in his left lung, and the condition of the right lung was not much better. He had been a heavy cigar smoker until 1927, when (at his doctor's suggestion), he was hypnotized and had immediately stopped smoking, after only one session. Betsy had expected her husband to put on weight – everyone did when they stopped smoking. Black Jack seemed to shrink. Betsy had also anxiously noticed his increasing breathlessness, his constant cough, and the chest pains that he tried to hide from her. There was no such thing as growing old gracefully, he had snapped, but there was no need for him to see a damn doctor, he felt fine, except he couldn't shake off this cold.

Black Jack, on his austere metal hospital bed, with an effort whispered to Betsy that he didn't want the kids to see him like this, he didn't want his kids to remember him this way.

'Stop that, honey,' Betsy cried in an unconvincing wail.

'Listen, Betsy. I'm going soon, so listen hard . . .' Black Jack, who had co-existed with movie millionaires and the Mafia, with his last breath warned Betsy to be always on her guard. Never trust anyone. Be unforgiving, ruthless. *Never* show vulnerability.

At this point, coughing cut off his words. Black Jack waved aside Betsy's shaking glass of water. When he could again speak, he gasped, 'Betsy, when a puppy craps on the carpet, you don't say your prayers. You rub the little bugger's nose in it, so he don't do it again. Never forget that.' He slumped backwards against the pillow, motionless.

Betsy screamed. Nurses came running . . .

Black Jack was not dead. He had terminal pneumonia.

For the next few days, Betsy sat by her husband's bedside, sometimes dozing in her armchair, until she felt an almost imperceptible change in the hand that she held . . . and knew that her husband was dead.

* * *

In London, Mimi and Toby were drinking a cup of coffee before setting out for the Minerva. Flicking through the evening paper, Toby commented, 'It's now two years since Joe Stalin collectivized all Russian farms. Funny way to increase grain yield, don't you think? Take away everything those farmers produce? You'd have thought the country that produced Pavlov could have worked out a better motivation to increase production . . .'

As he spoke the telephone rang. Mimi answered it. The British operator sang out, 'Hollywood on the line . . . Oh dear, I've lost them . . . Hang on . . .'

Mimi heard a harsh voice say, 'Louella Parsons speaking . . .'

* * *

On the following day, Betsy angrily read the column, headed WIDOW'S WADS.

> 'She wed Black Jack for his dough. Now she's got his stash,' claimed Mimi Fane, British vaudeville star and old friend of Betsy O'Brien. Friends were saddened yesterday by the death of Betsy's husband, Jack . . .

Betsy's disbelieving, reddened eyes reread the item. Her lips tightened. She did not ask herself whether Mimi used words such as *wed*, *dough* or *stash*. Her anger against Fate for removing her protector was immediately diverted towards Mimi. What had Black Jack once said, about squashing a wasp? Or was it a gadfly?

At Black Jack's Forest Lawn funeral, Betsy guiltily caught herself sobbing tears of anguish and regret not so much for her mate as for her protector, status symbol, solid emblem of family life and enviable escort. At the graveside she looked across at Jack's dragon of a head secretary – God, her face was a mess. To Betsy's surprise, the old girl had a quite presentable husband who now put both arms comfortingly around his grieving wife: it was suddenly clear that they were not two people but one loving couple. This made Betsy weep harder for she knew that she and Jack had never been real sweethearts, had never held hands in the park or snatched a kiss behind a tree. For Betsy it had been a straight swap – sex for security – and both of them secretly knew it. Jack got an enviable wife, kids and the society style of life that he'd never dreamed of when barefoot in that Irish bog. Betsy's ma – at last – had gotten security. She'd never been able to get over the fact that she'd never again have to run to catch a tram. Almost daily, Mrs Bridges shook her head as if waking from a dream and gazed with joy at some small object such as the silver cream jug, or stroked her frilled pillow and murmured, 'Jack's such a good provider.'

But Jack had not provided love, not the lovey-dovey, cuddling-in-the-firelight sort of love for which Betsy had always yearned, a love that warmed the cockles of your heart with just a glance; a warm, concerned, simple-pleasure-in-each-other's-silent-company sort of love. She had never been able to open her heart to Jack. It was for this that Betsy wept so hard at the graveside as she mourned the loss of what she had never possessed.

After the funeral, Betsy was informed by lawyers that her husband's fortune was held in a family trust. Apart from small legacies and allowances, the entire interest from the estate was willed to Betsy during her lifetime; after her death, it was to be shared equally among their three children. Upon the marriage or thirtieth birthday of each child, that child would immediately be granted one million dollars by the Trust.

* * *

Mrs Bridges, once again protecting her daughter, was determined that she should not risk remarriage. 'Later on you might feel like having . . . a bit of fun,' she advised.

'But so long as *you* control your money, you'll keep the whip hand, dearest: you can do as you please for the rest of your life . . . so long as you don't remarry.'

'Ma, Jack's hardly cold in his grave, and you're talking of remarriage,' Betsy sadly remonstrated. She did not need her mother's warning. Betsy – almost forty-three and getting a little heavy – trusted no man.

Although Betsy had been surrounded by suitors from the moment she left the graveyard, they only made her feel more vulnerable. She knew that older men really preferred young girls, and so did those young men who claimed to prefer a sophisticated older woman. She knew these suitors were aware of her financial position because it was general knowledge that Black Jack was one of the few rich men in Hollywood not to have invested on Wall Street.

Unacknowledged, in the back of her head, was the floating thought that should she ever remarry, then it would be only to someone safe . . . like Tudor.

Chapter Sixteen

Saturday 15 February 1930. Fitzroy Square

'I'm sick of listening to your explanations of *why* your production wasn't *entirely* successful,' Fizz shouted. 'What's the phrase your mother uses? Ah, yes. "An explanation ain't an excuse." ' After nearly three years of married target practice, Fizz's hairbrush did not miss Max.

'It's hardly an excuse to point out that theatres are closing daily.' Max rubbed his temple. Theatre jobs had dwindled as theatre audiences dwindled, partly because of the movies, partly because of the worldwide Depression, and partly because the British Broadcasting Corporation – the BBC – now entertained people for nothing, every evening, in their own homes.

The hairbrush was followed by a silver-backed hand-mirror, which flew over Max's head, crashed against a picture frame, and shattered both glass and mirror.

Max rubbed his ear. 'That bloody brush hurt!' These days, neither Fizz nor Max hurt the other accidentally. Often, Max addressed Fizz in an offhand way that sounded dismissive and wounding. Fizz, who resented Max's deliberately uncharming attitude, and the sharp-barbed comments that he addressed to the ceiling, found it easy to counterattack. Max then had an excuse for his churlish behaviour, and told himself that she had asked for it. Fizz paid him back simply by being famous and adored.

Now Fizz yelled, 'I'm *also* sick of hearing how stupid and misguided every London producer is, simply because he hasn't hired you!'

'It's not as if I do nothing! Those amateurs are bloody hard work.' For a pittance, Max produced alternatively for two suburban theatre clubs. He flung up his elbow to protect his face as Fizz hurled her powder bowl; it missed her husband and rebounded off the wall, scattering powder over him.

* * *

At lunchtime, the young Fanes celebrated their lusty reunion at Bertorelli, where Max extravagantly ordered a bottle of Spanish champagne. As he raised his glass, he felt a playful slap, and turned to see Komisarjevsky who, by secret arrangement with Fizz, had also decided to lunch at Bert's. Fizz hastily excused herself to 'powder her nose'.

Komis sat at the Fane table, taking Fizz's fork to pick at Max's linguine, before giving his fox grin and saying, 'Max, it might have been a mistake to force everything you've ever learned into your first play . . . Might easily have resulted in an overcluttered production.'

By the time Fizz returned to their table, Max had agreed to resume his duties as unpaid Assistant to the Producer, at the Barnes Theatre.

Quickly, Max again became happy and enthusiastic about life; no longer was he grateful to produce for suburban amateur groups – although he had enjoyed their enthusiasm, he told Komis.

Komis looked at him with twinkling eyes. 'You know

why your amateurs in Streatham pay subscriptions to an acting club that you can't afford and why your Hampstead intellectuals sweat to learn their lines? They're doing it to feel free, to feel they can do as they wish and be whom they choose.'

Max grinned. 'Is that why the Streatham lot always wanted to do upper-class dramas and the Hampstead Players voted for daring plays about adultery, divorce, drugs . . .'

'And homosexuality?' Komis prodded with interest.

'Good heavens, no. They'd never get an audience!'

* * *

The saucy title of the Minerva's current intimate revue was *Bottoms Up!*. In Mimi's dressing room, Daisy was buttoning her boss into an aviator's suit, while Mimi pulled on her leather helmet.

Hesitantly, Daisy said, 'Ever strike you there's something odd about the way Max can't even get a walk-on? Even though times is bad, they ain't never *that* bad, when you got a bit of influence.'

Mimi was not really listening, as she lifted her head to button the chinstrap above her neck.

Daisy yanked at Mimi's leather belt as she lugubriously insisted, 'There's some reason behind it – I feel it in me bones.'

Mimi immediately tensed: Daisy's bones were never wrong.

'After the show I'll go straight round to the King William.'

'Won't it wait till morning?'

'No. I won't be able to sleep.'

From the stage box of the King William, Toby had just

watched the fifth performance of *The Mystery of Marsden Manor*. He always watched every night for the first two weeks of every run, scribbling notes on a businesslike stenographer's pad. He noticed how each actor's performance varied from night to night; how each actor coped with a late entrance, a fluffed line, a dry or some similar problem; he wrote down every wrong sound cue, every missing or malfunctioning prop – tonight the all-important poisoned bottle of 'whisky' (cold tea) had been empty and the revolver had failed to fire *again*.

After two weeks, Toby would only monitor occasionally but it was important (particularly during a long run when actors became bored) to check the performance occasionally, for this maintained discipline and stopped the gradual deterioration of the production. Toby's prim, reproving notes were much mimicked by his Company: 'I was so *disappointed* to hear that last week certain persons arrived late at the stage door' ... 'I *do wish* everyone would remember that backstage visitors must leave after the half is called' ... 'I *regret to say* that last night's audience could clearly hear laughter from the wings during the death scene...' However, Toby's mimickers quickly learned that the milder the note, the more serious the actor's situation.

Mimi found Toby still in the stage box, finishing off. The message of Daisy's bones was not new to Toby. Reluctantly he told Max's insistent mother why her son could not get an acting job.

'Considered disruptive!' Mimi repeated indignantly. 'What nonsense! Max just won't let people push him around, that's all!'

'Quite.'

'Well *we're* going to give our boy a chance, if no one else will! We can afford it, can't we? – Don't look as if the cat's been sick on your slippers! A person has to use whatever comes his way in this life! The only really deadly sin is to waste what you're given.' She looked challengingly at Toby. 'Why don't we put Max and Fizz on together, at the Minerva? Old Come-and-seduce me can direct them.'

'Because Fizz is contracted to the Vic. She's already been allowed time off to play Juliet.'

'I'll have a chat with Lilian. That place needs a repaint.'

Hurriedly Toby added, 'Perhaps, before that, I should have a little chat with Fizz ... If those two turn up next Sunday.'

* * *

Fizz – growing more famous by the week – had recently been taken up by London hostess Sibyl Colefax, who collected celebrities and was addicted to entertaining in her pretty eighteenth-century house on the King's Road.

Eventually, after several uncomfortable meals there, and twice being addressed as 'Mr Allen', Max refused to accept Lady Colefax's invitations. 'I always get landed with her husband, who's the biggest bore in Britain. Sybil doesn't really want me: she just puts up with me, as she'd put up with your poodle, if you had one.'

'But you'll sulk if I go alone.'

'No, I bloody *won't*! I'll go out on my own!'

From such mundane matters a thousand rows developed. If Max deliberately goaded Fizz, then she neatly diverted the conversation to acting theory and always managed to say, 'Huh! All Stanislavsky did was sort out and write down everything a good, sensitive actor does *naturally*.'

Rushing to champion his hero, Max always lost his temper.

Just as their discussions generally ended in argument, their arguments ended in hurtful accusations, followed by plaintive complaints and snapped counter-complaints; maddeningly half-finished sentences; brooding resentment or loud doubts of loyalty. These two now understood each other so well that they knew exactly where to slide the dagger between the ribs, straight up to the heart. Now, instead of sexy tussles that always ended lustily in bed and afterwards at Bert's, they had angry, bitter battles that ended in cold silence which endured into the following morning.

Sunday 23 February 1930

In Toby's study, Fizz settled into a worn red-leather armchair. Once again, a depressed Fizz sought Toby's advice, for she did not want to alarm her mother, and she knew it was useless to criticize Max to Mimi, who would immediately defend her darling. Toby was the ideal person to ask for psychological help. As theatre manager, Toby needed to be part nanny, part dictator, but above all a diplomat who would placate a star, soothe the rest of the cast and sort out dressing-room squabbles. He was particularly careful with his treatment of female stars; he never praised another actress in their presence, always noticed what they wore, remembered what they liked to eat and drink and the name of their yappy little lapdog. Sympathetically, Toby would listen to complaints about their costumes. 'Doesn't fit, hard to move in, *beastly* colour, unflattering cut' – meaning fattening – 'not nearly as becoming as so-and-so's!' He was equally diplomatic during the never-ending arguments over photograph retouching (most actresses wanted flat, white, lineless faces and big black eyes with touched-up lashes) and star billing – above or below play title, letter size in relation to other performers, and so on.

Slowly, stumbling, Fizz asked Toby if he could understand why Max – who certainly loved Fizz – resented her success, although she was *glad* for any success of his.

Toby, as he poured sherry, tried to sound comfortably reassuring. 'Men are still afraid of being thought weak and powerless, dependent on some woman, as they were when they were little and had to obey their mother.'

'That's right, blame everything on the woman!'

Toby laughed. 'Who raises boys to think of women as weak and dependent, obedient and submissive?'

Fizz did not laugh. 'That's no reason for Max to make me look small in public.'

Toby refilled her glass. 'Max's unconsciously showing people that he *can* dominate you if he wants to. Men like to think they're powerful and independent. That means not being ordered around.'

'I *don't* order Max around!' Fizz objected.

'No, but you earn more than he does.'

'I'm sick of hearing that explanation for all Max's bad behaviour! Would he like it if I earned *less* than he did?'

'Yes, probably. Money's a symbol of power. The richest chap has most power, so he gets most respect. Because everyone knows you earn more than Max, he's unconsciously frightened that people respect you more than him.'

Fizz was silent; although ludicrous, she sensed that what Toby had said was true.

Toby added, 'Perhaps it would improve your relationship if you and Max had equal billing.'

'Oh, sure! But that's impossible . . .'

'No, it isn't.' Toby again refilled his daughter-in-law's glass.

Fizz hesitated. 'But why *should* Max get equal billing with me?'

Toby sighed. This was familiar ground for him. He hoped that Fizz wasn't about to turn into a Star Turn, as opposed to a Star Actress. Off stage, Star Turns liked to surround themselves with a reassuringly adulatory retinue, and on stage they liked to surround themselves with inferior actresses so that they looked better by comparison and attracted *all* the applause. They demanded their own way in everything and were prepared to fight for it with arguments (called 'suggestions'), criticisms (called 'helpful') and wilful obstinacy (called 'making a point'). They all had dozens of tricks to divert attention away from other performers to themselves. Toby, who needed good performers in all parts, had to tactfully stop such behaviour, carefully judging when to defer and when to be firm. Endlessly patient, he appeased the tantrums of his stars (often as tightly strung as violins and just as capable of screeching as a First Night loomed) or solved the emotional problems they caused with the rest of his cast.

Toby refilled his own glass and smiled gently at Fizz. 'Do you want to be a lonely star or a happily married star?'

* * *

Toby's next step was to approach Komisarjevsky and ask him to produce, but Komis shrugged his refusal. 'I have too much on my plate. I'm booked up to my eyebrows. Why don't *you* produce it, Toby? Make it a neat family package – very commercial! All the Fanes in their own little theatre! What are you going to put on?'

'We haven't decided yet.'

Komis grinned complicity. 'If you decide on *Much Ado*, then I'll help Max.'

'Perfect.' Toby brightened. Both he and Komis understood that Max and Fizz were a real-life Beatrice and Benedick. Both men hoped that their real-life drama would also have a happy ending.

* * *

The first readings were held in a Soho studio complex. As Fizz hurried down a long, dim corridor, she could hear a children's dancing class on her lift. *Clack! clack! clack!* went steel-based tap-shoes, as winsome tots in satin shorts and sequin-studded tops kicked hard, watched by hopeful mothers seated on a line of bentwood chairs against the wall.

Toby's cast was relieved when they moved to the Minerva for onstage rehearsals, and were no longer distracted by the sound of dancing – not yet *quite* in rhythm – from the adjoining studio.

Max's self-confidence had been badly damaged by the failure of his *Romeo and Juliet*; consequently he had never felt so alone and frightened as he did at the first rehearsal onstage. He stood on the dusty boards in the hard beam of a working light, and as he heard his voice echo through the indifferent, dark theatre, he tried to project the strength, excitement and passion needed for the strong-willed Benedick, but only succeeded in thinking, 'What on earth am I doing here?'

Fizz was able to coax the best possible performance from him; because of their natural rapport (and much private rehearsal) they attempted to act together with a Lunt-like naturalism that involved overlapping each other's speeches and (when acting a quarrel) sometimes shouting simultaneously at each other, as real lovers do.

The day before the First Night, when interviewed by feature writers, Fizz neatly sidestepped each veiled (and reasonable) question about nepotism.

'Yes, it permeates the acting profession – and many others, no doubt.'

Fizz had been told by Jessie that an ambitious, successful person will always attract jealousy and spite, and that the best way to deal with this was either to take it as a compliment, or ignore it. However, this was hard to do when the negative feelings were projected from the person lying next to you in bed.

The trouble was that Max realized that he was not nearly as good an actor as Fizz. Useless to tell himself that he never wanted to be the world's *best* actor. Useless for Fizz to lie about Max's ability, for this immediately led to a row. 'You *don't* really mean that, Fizz.'

'Calm down, darling.'

'Don't bloody tell me to *calm down*!'

'*All right!* You're a *rotten* actor! Now can I get to sleep?'

'Aha, the truth at last, you *rotten* liar.'

* * *

For Max, on opening night, a minor miracle occurred.

As he strode on stage, cocksure and self-confident, Max actually felt as Benedick must have felt: once more he experienced the powerful attraction that had originally yanked him to Fizz. Suddenly the two were equals:

strong-willed, passionate lovers fighting for power and enjoying it, as they tried to hide their strong sexual attraction to each other when – unwillingly – Benedick and Beatrice (or was it Max and Fizz?) again experienced their strong, unequivocal love.

Max no longer saw Fizz as a younger sister, who had the audacity to dart up the ladder of success before he had placed his foot upon the first rung. He insisted that Fizz take the final curtain call: he wanted everyone to applaud his beloved. Their new, onstage relationship lingered long after the curtain had fallen, as the young Fanes rediscovered what had attracted them to one another in the first place.

Friday 4 April 1930

The reviews were mixed: Fizz was deservedly praised; the critics noted Max's star debut at his family theatre. Nepotism was not mentioned, although one critic wrote that while much was expected of a Fane, the family talent was not yet evident in the youngest generation.

Max immediately lost his new self-confidence.

That evening, as they drove down the Strand in his open sports car, Fizz urged: 'Forget the bastards, darling. I choose my *own* critics, people I have known for ages, whose judgement I trust: I'm guided by them and nobody else. I don't read my good notices or my bad ones, so I don't get overconfident or depressed.'

'Easy enough to say.'

'Why not play lighter?' Fizz suggested. 'Have a bit more fun on stage.'

Later, on the stage, Fizz came close to Max and –

unseen by the audience – lightly stroked Benedick's groin. To Max's horror, he felt an impending erection swell the crotch of his canary yellow tights. Quickly he twisted his lower torso away from the audience.

Max had to finish the scene with his back to the audience. The rest of the cast thought this a huge joke. His subsequent stormy exit was greeted by backstage sniggers, 'That's the trouble with tights,' and 'It's happened to all of us, ducky.'

The critics might have been lukewarm, but the public loved *Much Ado*: sparks flew between Max and Fizz, as the strong-minded woman who won't be pushed around by a man until she falls into his arms in the end. Max and Fizz were a perfect theatrical married couple for that period when women (only just realizing that they had potential, and groping for some way to use it), did not yet realize that men – however charming – were determined to stop them. Benedick and Beatrice epitomized modern woman's clash of will with her man. The offstage relationship of the young Fanes added to the sexual tension of their performance. Everyone watching knew that the onstage battle of wills reflected the stormy private lives of Max and Fizz.

Monday 14 April 1930. Hollywood

Feisty heroines with platinum hair and snappy one-liners, plus a strong sense of their own worth, were also emerging on celluloid: no longer a helpless victim, a cute screen blonde might well have a swing at any suitor who tried to take advantage of her, although she, too, eventually melted into his arms, just before final fade-out.

As the Jazz Age of the twenties tailed off into the Depression, gangster movies became popular. Real organized crime was also visible in Hollywood: Al Capone's mob was infiltrating the motion picture unions, planning to demand protection money in return for no union trouble at the studios.

Female movie stars were often attracted by such gangsters: hoodlums exuded ruthless control and an easy ability 'to take care of everything' – whether that meant paying for a white fox coat or disposing of a competitor. Clearly above the law, it was in the power of these modern outlaws to provide security so actresses often married a small, ugly chilling gangster or studio executive.

At this time, Hollywood was also crawling with confidence tricksters, many of whom zeroed in on Betsy immediately after Black Jack's death (Mrs Bridges had counted five contenders at the funeral service). Luckily Betsy was well guarded by her mother. When people were astonished and offended, Betsy hurriedly apologized for her mother's overprotective behaviour. New gentlemen acquaintances who were *not* offended by Mrs Bridges' rudeness were immediately dropped by Betsy, for she remembered her husband's warning, '*You* can't hurt a conman's feelings, because the guy ain't got no feelings for you. He don't give a damn what you think of him – he's play-acting his friendliness, and he'll stick to his act, no matter how bad you insult him. He don't care.'

Betsy had fewer well-dressed suitors when it became generally known – as Black Jack had intended – that one of the stipulations of his will was that should his widow remarry she forfeited all income from the Trust, except for $50,000 a year, during the duration of the marriage: this was enough to keep her in comfort, but not enough to tempt a fortune hunter. However, Betsy also attracted genuine admiration. Nearly forty-two, she was still beautiful, although women thought she carried a little too much weight.

Betsy now turned to her children for comfort; she hated to be seen alone in public (she felt that men saw her as easy prey, and women saw her as a pathetic creature who couldn't get a man), so she generally had at least one child in tow when she left home. She preferred Stella's company, for six-year-old Nick fidgeted, and nine-year-old Tess was a load of trouble. After her father's death, Tess had become so uncontrollable that her governess had left; her mother and grandmother despaired of controlling the family show-off. Reckless, wilful, headstrong and determined to be the centre of attention, Tess was bundled off to the fourth grade at Brentwood Town and Country School, which Stella attended; Tess much preferred school to her dull life at home with a governess.

Temperamentally, Tess was clearly Black Jack's daughter. Hyperenergetic, she had inherited her father's Irish fizz (he had called her a vitamin pill on legs); she also had his endurance, and inner Rottweiler core: the spoilt little Hollywood princess was as tough as they come; when angry, her little-girl voice deepened and sharpened. Tess had missed her mother's astonishing beauty, but she was cute and pretty, with small features, navy blue eyes and dark, waving hair.

In contrast, ten-year-old Stella was quiet and gentle, an obedient and unassuming child, who could behave herself and sit quietly or be trusted to run errands if required to do so: she hated being in the limelight, as did Nick, who had a similar temperament and the same slow, hesitant voice. They had both inherited their father's dark hair, blue eyes, pale skin and large-boned frame, which made Stella look gawky and awkward, whereas it was already clear that Nick was going to be a big, strong man. Because he looked so like Black Jack, Nick was the apple, orange and banana of his mother's eye, and after his father's death, she clung to her only son.

For an evening escort, Betsy could always count on Tudor, who had changed his lucrative but exasperating job for one that paid even better.

Two years after Tudor arrived in Hollywood, the 'talkies' also arrived. All the studio heads who had thought – hoped – that sound would never catch on (for 95 per cent of their world audience did not speak English) quickly realized that there was no alternative.

Early sound equipment tended to make voices sound higher and thinner: deep voices sounded slightly different, but high voices were sometimes comically shrill. Stars who spoke with a strong regional accent or a foreign accent, which made their voices incomprehensible to most of America, were suddenly out of work. Behind the locked doors of their Beverly Hills mansions, such stars sought oblivion in cases of booze delivered by bootleggers to the back door.

Every other actor sought voice training. Gary Cooper, who had once been a fellow-guest with Tudor on a deep-sea fishing trip, remembered the Englishman's deep, pleasant voice, trained to project clearly. When Tudor amiably agreed to give him lessons, young Coop had asked if $100 an hour was OK. Tudor hurriedly agreed ... and suddenly found that he had a new and agreeable career. Now, as a diction coach, he taught important Hollywood movie stars to recite, 'Around the rock the rugged rascal ran,' 'Peter Piper picked a peck of pickled peppers,' and other tongue-twisting vocal clarifiers. Tudor quickly found that he preferred voice teaching to giving advice on fish forks and precedent. Shortly afterwards he sold half his Social Consultancy to the two ex-butlers, who ran it smoothly and never stole more than an acceptable percentage.

* * *

Betsy occupied her spare time by spending more of it with the Brentwood Players, who were grateful for her increased attention, and the cheque she sent after each visit. Because of her Little Theater involvement and the flattery which this brought, Betsy's opinion of her theatrical ability started to swell until eventually she decided that she might get involved in production herself, instead of merely contributing money and encouragement. Naturally, such ventures would be capitalized by the family Trust that Black Jack had set up, and it would not be the end of the world if Betsy's productions lost money.

Mrs Bridges agreed that Betsy needed something to occupy her attention. Was Betsy thinking of putting on just one production, or leasing a theatre?

Betsy did not decide ... until she read in the 'News from Europe' weekly column in the *Los Angeles Times* of the West End success of the Fane family's hilarious production of *Much Ado About Nothing*.

Remembering Mimi's ascribed 'gold-digger' quotation immediately after Black Jack's death, Betsy thoughtfully put aside the newspaper, and picked up her ivory bedside telephone.

Monday 14 April 1930

Luigi Carati, a competent, guaranteed-to-fix-it lawyer, had been recommended to Black Jack. Mr Carati was built like a football player, and nattily dressed, although his jacket was always unbuttoned, for easy access to the Colt that he carried in a shoulder holster for personal protection, after his Japanese gardener had been found crucified on his Judas tree.

When his secretary announced a client, Mr Carati left his desk to check his appearance in the mirror fixed to the back of the door to his office. He wore a brown chalk-stripe suit, dark brown shirt, cream necktie and elaborate two-tone cream and brown shoes: he pulled out his pocket comb and hastily slicked back his hair, as he heard heels clicking towards the door.

As soon as Betsy entered, she sensed an air of impermanence to Mr Carati's office. The walls were covered by simulated walnut, upon which hung cheaply framed photographs of boxers with their dukes up, and signed, glossy 8 x 10s of blonde film stars, easily acquired from some fan club or studio publicity guy. Mr Carati's black desk was the size of a nightclub bandstand; apart from this, the room was furnished only with a beige couch that might easily have been a Murphy bed, upon which Betsy sat as she charmingly confided her wish to become a theatre manager.

In silence, Mr Carati listened to Mrs O'Brien's ambition, strange only in that the theatre on which Black Jack's widow had set her heart was on the other side of the world. As soon as she told him that the King William theatre belonged to the Fane family, Mr Carati understood his client's motive; he made it his business to follow the gossip columns, summarized daily for him by his secretary on a single sheet of paper. To act, he needed merely to know 'what', but often in the past, the 'why' had helped his strategy.

'All you wish, Mrs O'Brien, is to acquire this theatre for yourself?'

Betsy nodded. 'Legally,' she said firmly.

'I'll get my people in Europe to start working on it.'

Monday 21 April 1930

The following week, Betsy returned to Mr Carati's office. She was gradually discarding her unattractive widow's weeds (black had never suited her), and wore a cream-spotted black silk frock and a big cream straw hat with a black rose on the brim.

'Morning, Mrs O'Brien.' Mr Carati stood up and waved his hand hospitably towards the Murphy bed. 'We got some news for you. Tobias Fane owns the King William Theatre, in King William Square – but he don't own it outright. There's a mortgage held by a young guy, name of Bill Silver, who inherited it two years ago from his pa, Sidney Silver. We start by acquiring that mortgage, right? Gives us a little leverage.'

'Right,' nodded the black rose on Betsy's hat.

'Are you sure, Mrs O'Brien, that you want to own that mortgage yourself? I would suggest ownership through a third and then a fourth party, guaranteed untraceable.'

Betsy shook her head. She wanted Mimi to know.

* * *

Six weeks later, Betsy was growing impatient, but Mr Carati assured her that those Limey lawyer searches to establish ownership always seemed to take for ever ... and always cost an arm and a leg, he warned her.

* * *

After the mortgage had been acquired, Mr Carati's European associates then ran into a little local difficulty. Mr Tobias Fane proved unreasonable; he refused to sell the King William Theatre – even when offered 50 per cent more than the value of the property. Clearly Mr Fane did not understand the importance of Mr Carati's London business associates, not even after a small fire, a small flood, and unusual trouble with the Lord Chamberlain's censorship office over a King William play in which the detective hero says, 'I can't get it up,' as he tries to open a library window.

These minor problems were not seen as hints by the insensitive Mr Fane. Despite many cups of limy tea consumed by Mr Carati's associates in Mr Fane's over-crowded little office at the rear of the theatre, he seemed not to realize the personal foolishness of his persistently negative replies to the very reasonable offers of Mr Carati's European associates.

'So what do you propose?' Betsy had often heard Jack ask this, in a quiet, dangerous voice.

'Guy needs a little more persuasion. That OK by you, Mrs O'Brien?'

'I won't be personally involved?'

'In what?' Mr Carati held out both hands and looked up as if to check that rain was not falling from his ceiling.

* * *

At that next meeting, Mr Carati stared thoughtfully at Betsy's little black veiled scrap of a hat. 'I have to report we're still having difficulties. It ain't as easy over there as it would be over here.' As the smile vanished from Betsy's face, 'But don't worry, Mrs O'Brien, it *can* be done. *Anything* can be done. But it won't be cheap, you understand?'

'If it can be done, then do it,' Betsy said sharply. It was now early September, and she was not used to such a long delay, when she wished to acquire something and had cash in the bank with which to do so.

'Can do, Mrs O'Brien,' Mr Carati hesitated. 'But if you insist on being registered as the owner of this theatre, it will have to be a two-step deal; they might not want to sell to you, Mrs O'Brien. So, my business associates will acquire the property from Mr Fane. You will then be at liberty to purchase the theatre from them.' Unspoken were the words, 'At a price.'

'Sure, I insist.' Betsy wanted Mimi to know as soon as possible that the most beautiful theatre in London belonged to Betsy. Didn't this jerk understand that was the *whole point*?

* * *

The transatlantic telephone line crackled indistinctly. Mr Carati (who had not identified himself as the caller) suggested, 'Can't you put it about he's a fag? ... *Then he'd be forced to deny it, that's why.* We can then publicize his denial nationwide, no expense spared. That'd fix him ... Oh, he *is*? ... Hang on a minute, lemme think again ...'

A good idea swiftly occurred to Mr Carati. 'You still there? ... Listen, there's only one thing the public'll *never* accept ... You know how Joe plans to acquire the Pantage cinema chain over here? . . . Well, why not work up some version of that, using a boy instead of a girl? . . . OK, let me know as soon as you have something to report.'

Monday 8 September 1930. The manager's office, backstage at the Minerva Theatre, London

At the Minerva, Mimi's new intimate revue, *What's New?*, was playing to a sparse matinée house: it was unusually hot weather in September, which had dissuaded the usual stream of sedate day trippers from the provinces.

Upstairs in his small office, behind a desk piled with ledgers and trays of neatly piled bills, Toby sat in his shirtsleeves and despondently studied the box-office takings for that afternoon.

Suddenly his office door was thrown open. Loudly it slammed behind a youth whom Toby vaguely recognized as someone he had recently auditioned – Bertram the Boy Acrobat – and turned down.

Because of this audition, the boy knew the exact location of Toby's office. He had bypassed the formidable stage-door keeper by buying a theatre ticket; he had then simply walked through the pass door marked PRIVATE. NO ENTRY at the left of the stage, which led to the back of house. He had hurriedly climbed the stairs to Toby's office, swiftly unbuttoning his clothes on the way; he did not unbutton his shirt, but roughly tore it open. Once in the manager's office, before the startled Toby had time to stand up, let alone work out what was happening, he started swiftly to pull off his clothes.

'What the *hell* do you think you're doing?' Toby asked astonished, as the boy removed a ripped undergarment and, naked, dodged around Toby's desk, diving for Toby's shirt, and with both hands ripping it open.

Alarmed, Toby tried to push the boy away: was the lad drunk, or mad? He'd get a secretary to call the boy's agent, tell him to get round fast, and remove this little idiot.

'Hey, I say . . .' Toby spluttered, then screamed as the boy bit him hard on the left ear. Toby's chair fell backwards and so did Toby, with the boy on top of him, grubby, naked buttocks bouncing up and down.

With blood running into his left eye, Toby tried to thrust the boy away. 'Help!' he roared – and so did Bertram the Boy Acrobat.

Miss Jenkins, the senior secretary, nervously opened the door a crack, as there had been no response to her knock. Then she gasped, threw the door wide open, advanced two steps. She retreated, her *pince-nez* falling from her nose. Shocked, she gasped, 'Mr Fane!'

Once the office door had opened, and Bertram sensed that a witness was present, he scrambled back from Toby, dodged under Miss Jenkins's arm, stepping on her *pince-nez* as he did so. He then ran naked down the stairs, screaming, 'Don't let that evil beast attack me again!'

The astonished Toby scrambled awkwardly to his feet. 'Thank God you're here, Miss Jenkins.'

Horrified, Miss Jenkins gazed at the blood on Toby's empurpled face, his mussed hair, his torn collar, his ripped shirt, the scattered papers over the floor, the broken chair, the discarded clothes, the grubby underwear.

'Oh dear, what will poor Mrs Fane say?' quavered Miss Jenkins.

Suddenly, Toby saw the scene through the eyes of Miss Jenkins.

* * *

Meanwhile, the boy tore down the stairs, pushing one or two startled people out of his way, screaming, 'Someone save me! Help! Don't let that monster get at me!'

On stage, Mimi, wearing jodhpurs, riding boots and a polo-neck sweater, strutted up and down in the middle of her Prince of Wales impression.

Suddenly the audience sensed a commotion to the left as the pass door was thrown violently open. They saw a naked figure silhouetted against the lighted corridor beyond.

The figure hesitated, then screamed, 'Help! He tried to rape me!' He ran towards the orchestra pit.

Opulently majestic in white tie and tails, the conductor jerked his head to the left, then dropped his baton.

The orchestra stopped playing. Mimi stopped singing. Chocolate missed mouths. Someone started to choke. There were cries of 'What's up?' and 'Get a doctor!'

Upon reaching the conductor, who backed away nervously, Bertram turned sharply to his right – everything dangling and visible to the fascinated matrons in the audience; he ran up the centre aisle, wildly waving his arms towards the Dress Circle, as he screamed for help.

From the back of the theatre the manager dashed through the pit, followed by several usherettes, trying to stop the youth's escape. However, the naked Bertram willingly hurled himself at the manager, who staggered backwards, bumping into the usherettes, who dropped their torches.

'Call the police!' he shouted as Bertram wound hairy little legs around his pin-striped thighs; nobody was going to get him out of here.

At the mention of the police, chocolate boxes slithered from matronly laps to the floor and seats flipped up noisily, as everyone in the stalls stood up and turned to get a better view. The audience, now with their backs to the stage, watched this alternative performance in fascinated silence.

Mimi strode forward and peered over the footlights; what the hell was going on at the back of the stalls?

A few minutes later, the head usherette hurried in from the front lobby, followed by a burly policeman. The usherette shone her torch on the manager, now on his feet, but still trying to disengage himself.

The policeman yanked the two men apart. Showing a brilliant sense of public propriety, he quickly unbuttoned his tunic and threw it back to front around the shoulders of the naked lad.

The manager hurried the policeman and the half-clad boy down the aisle towards the orchestra, then back through the pass door. As they went through, the boy screamed once again, 'No! No! Don't let that monster get at me!'

In the orchestra pit, the conductor tapped his baton and frantically started the introduction to Mimi's Prince of Wales song. Mimi used every ounce of her personality to force the audience's attention back upon her. She would find out later what all that had been about.

Once backstage, the lad snivelled as he told his story. Two days ago he had auditioned for Mr Fane, who had asked him to return for another audition. Bertram Bates (as he now identified himself) had duly reported, as requested, to Mr Fane's private office. Upon seeing him, Bertram claimed, Mr Fane had torn Bertram's clothes off and attacked him sexually, pressing his hand over Bertram's mouth to stop him yelling for help, as the Fane genitalia went into action.

'What the hell is this noise about?' A dishevelled, shaken Toby still wore his torn shirt as he pushed through the little crowd at the bottom of the backstage staircase.

Bertram immediately threw another screaming fit, pointed a trembling, grubby finger at Toby and yelled, 'Don't let that devil get me! Don't let him touch me!'

The police constable looked at the dishevelled middle-aged man in his torn shirt and said, sharply, 'I think you'd better come along to the station, sir.'

* * *

At the police station, Bertram Bates, snivelling, reiterated his claim that Toby had tried to rape him.

Toby claimed that Bates had no appointment to see him that afternoon. He explained exactly what happened, angrily adding what everyone present knew: sex of any sort was available easily enough in London; he carefully implied that even if he *were* a pervert there would be no need for him to molest an unwilling boy when it was a simple matter to pay for one. Furthermore, was the eminent Mr Fane likely to perform such a horrific and illegal action in broad daylight, in his *own* office, in his *own* theatre with a trio of secretaries in the next office, while his *own* wife was downstairs performing on stage? This young man must be mentally deranged.

At that point, Bates asked the police in a whine to telephone his agent, who'd tell 'em all as how Mr Fane *had* made an appointment in Mr Fane's private office, for that afternoon.

His agent – a small, nervous-looking, neatly dressed man – arrived shortly afterwards at the police station. He looked suitably astonished at seeing Bertram, and even more shocked when he heard his story. The agent confirmed that Mr Fane had indeed requested an appointment with Bertram for that afternoon, a matter that could easily be proven by the appointments book in the agent's office. He was deeply shocked that Mr Fane should have taken advantage of his position to illegally sexually assault his young client.

Shortly afterwards, Toby found himself, once again, behind bars in the basement cell of a police station.

When Mimi – still in her Prince of Wales polo outfit – turned up with a smoothly sceptical young partner from Bennett & Hopkins, she indignantly argued for Toby. There were plenty of people in the next office, surely an athletic young acrobat could have fought off a fifty-year-old, middle-aged man?

Police records revealed that Bertram had two previous convictions, one for soliciting in Hyde Park, and one for sodomy in St James's Park.

'You never told me!' hissed his manager. 'You let me think *I* was the first one . . .'

''Ere, 'ere! Stop that!' said the sergeant, sharply. He wanted no blooming fairy fights in his station.

Eventually, Toby was allowed out on bail.

* * *

Once home, Toby went to his study, saying that he needed to think. He poured himself a large whisky.

Mimi snatched the decanter. '*That* ain't going to help you think!' Only Mimi believed him. Even Daisy had avoided Mimi's eyes, when Mimi asked her if she thought it was a set-up, and if so, what was the point?

Toby gently pushed Mimi out of the door, and locked it.

Toby, who had been asked to audition Bertram Bates during that lunch at the Savoy Grill, could make a good guess as to what was happening. If he sold the King William, the lad would withdraw his accusation, and the lad's agent would confirm that Bertram was a little weak in the head, or something to that effect.

While sitting in his cell Toby had also realized the significance of that fire and that flood at the King William, each 'accident' following one of those quiet but insistent offers to purchase the theatre made to Toby by a respectable partner of a reputable firm of London lawyers, who represented 'a private client'. Clearly, if Toby did not agree to sell the King William, sooner or later, another Oscar Wilde type scandal would be splashed across the newspapers, and Toby Fane would be crucified by publicity.

Toby knew that he had to make a quick decision. It was not a question of what was right, or what was wrong, but what was best for his family. Either Toby sold the King William, or his family would be humiliated, despised and ostracized. For the first time, Toby was glad that his parents were dead.

He considered the effect that such a scandal would have on Mimi, Max, Fizz and all their friends. Toby knew, without being told, that the entire jury would be biased against him, before the trial started. He buried his face in his hands as he imagined the lawyers hammering it out, day after day, day after day, to the delight of the newspapers and the titillation of the public. He shuddered as he thought of the judge's summing up. A reporter had already phoned the theatre to ask for details of that afternoon's disturbance. With great presence of mind, the imperturbable senior secretary, who had taken the call, explained that she had not been present, but the manager had been in a scuffle with a mentally deranged young man.

Mimi hammered on the door of his study. 'Toby, if you don't unlock this door, I'm going to break it down.'

Wearily, Toby opened the door. Normally fastidious, he still wore the torn shirt, and now smelt of stale sweat and whisky, like some down-the-bill comic on a Number Three tour.

Mimi, still in greasepaint and costume, stood on tiptoe and put her arms around his neck. 'Listen, I'm *for* you, Toby! Understand that? I don't understand what the hell's going on, but whatever it is, I'm on your side.'

'I think I understand what's going on.' Toby told Mimi of his suspicions.

'That's blackmail!' Mimi said immediately. 'Whoever this "private person" is, he reckons if you're kicked low enough, you'll give up the King William without a fight so as to avoid a scandal! What a dirty trick!'

The indignation in her green eyes switched to thoughtfulness. 'Toby ... Why should anyone want to pay you fifty per cent more than the value of the King William, when we're in a middle of a slump? Who the hell would want to do that?'

Toby shrugged his shoulders wearily. 'I'm going upstairs to clean up.'

As soon as he left the room, Mimi phoned Jessie, and asked her to hop in a cab and come round fast.

When Jessie arrived, hatless and anxious, she immediately confirmed that nobody seemed interested in buying theatres at the moment – in fact, the opposite. However you looked at it, such a huge offer for the King William did not make commercial sense, not unless an undiscovered gold mine was under the theatre. And Jessie could think of no reason why any potential buyer should want to remain anonymous.

'Don't it sound fishy to you?' Mimi asked.

Jessie turned to Toby. 'Do you have any enemies, Toby?'

Toby gave a short laugh. 'Everyone in the Business has enemies.'

Jessie persisted. 'Is there anyone who hates you so much that he would be prepared to pay *fifty per cent* more than the value of the King William, to persuade you to sell the theatre?'

'*I* can't think of anyone,' said Toby, puzzled. 'Young Silver recently inherited the mortgage, but if he wanted to buy the theatre, I'm sure he'd have come to me direct. And anyway, why should a property dealer want to operate a theatre?'

'Let's check,' Mimi said grimly. 'What's his telephone number?'

Within a couple of hours she had located young Mr Silver, who informed them that he *had* recently sold the mortgage ... No, he did not personally know the man – some nightclub owner, who had clearly overvalued the property: Mr Silver had been advised that he would be foolish to refuse such an offer, so he had accepted. Mr Silver thought that Mr Fane had already been informed, but clearly the lawyers were dragging their feet over the paperwork.

Jessie, Toby and Mimi sat silently in Toby's little study: now they realized that this matter was more sinister than it seemed.

'What about you, Mimi?' Jessie suddenly asked.

All three friends simultaneously realized who might be

the 'private client': the one person whose involvement would make such events as logical as they now seemed illogical.

'Betsy!' all three cried.

Furious, Mimi exclaimed, 'I'm damned if we're going to let Betsy get her hands on our theatre! We'll fight the bitch in court!'

Sadly Toby said, 'But don't you see, just by going to court, we shall have ruined our family.' He added softly, 'Betsy is very rich. She can ruin us. I'm afraid, Mimi, that I *shall* be obliged to sell the King William.'

Toby watched as Mimi buried her face in her hands. All her fighting spirit vanished as she suddenly realized that this disaster was her responsibility. For years, Toby, who was so amiable and so kind, had tried to persuade her to stop being vindictive and to forget her grievance against Betsy. Now he was being made to suffer for her actions. For the first time, she *was* frightened of Betsy.

'Why can't that bitch let go of me? Hasn't she done *enough* to me?' Trembling, Mimi stripped off her gloves, threw them to the floor, and thrust her hands towards Jessie and Toby. 'OK, I tease Betsy from time to time, but *look what she done to me*!'

Mimi's angry resentment of Betsy was still mixed with a sense of sadness and regret, for the friendship that might have continued. Mimi had many friends, but never since her close relationship with Betsy had she known a woman that she had so completely loved and trusted. Betsy had been the first person that she had *chosen*. After her childhood of poverty, misery and emotional pain, Betsy had been such an important part of her new, hopeful and happy life. Once again, Mimi felt not only hurt and anger, but also the sorrow of her loss.

Jessie left. Exhausted, Toby and Mimi climbed wearily upstairs to their separate bedrooms.

* * *

At one o'clock in the morning, Toby tucked a pillow under his arm, and crept downstairs; he had decided how to escape his dilemma. He tiptoed down to the kitchen at the back of the basement and pushed the sisal mat up against the garden door, which otherwise let in a draught. He opened the door to the oven, carefully placed his pillow inside and turned on the gas. Then he lay on the floor, with his head resting inside.

Half an hour later, Mimi – unable to sleep, as she worried about Betsy's venom – decided to go downstairs and boil herself a cup of milk. As she reached the basement, she smelled a vile, unmistakable smell that made her pull in her breath.

Screaming, she threw open the kitchen door and saw the scene she dreaded. She leaped forward and turned off the gas, choking and coughing. She pulled the mat away from the garden door, tugged at the bolts and unlocked it. Toby lay on his back, limp as a rag doll left in the rain; his eyes were closed, his face a bright cherry red; his breathing was fast and uneven. He looked a goner.

A sleepy Daisy appeared in curlers and dressing gown.

'Get an ambulance! Get a blanket! *Fast!*' screamed Mimi. Daisy dashed upstairs to the telephone.

Alone with Toby, Mimi tugged Toby's limp body across the kitchen and out into the damp, dark night. She snatched off her own flimsy silk wrap and tenderly placed it under his head; it wasn't much of a pillow, but she couldn't bring herself to use that cursed thing that Toby had put in the oven for his head.

Yet again, she felt conflicting emotions: helplessness and tenderness, fear and rage. Toby was her best friend, her dear, dear friend. She cried fiercely, 'I won't let you go, Toby! Not now, not like this!' Whether or not Toby could hear, Mimi wanted to tell him her gratitude for the life he had given her.

Woken by Daisy, Cook puffed downstairs with a blanket. In the yellow shaft of light that streamed from the kitchen into the backyard she could see Mr Fane, his head in Madam's lap; he was barely breathing. Madam was crooning under her breath . . . 'If you were the only boy in the world . . .' Madam didn't notice Cook's proffered blanket, so Cook tucked it around Toby's body herself.

Daisy, who had remained upstairs to wait for the ambulance, clattered down the narrow basement stairs, followed by two men. Shadows moved in the darkened yard; the younger man carried a canvas stretcher; the older, heavier man gripped a black satchel.

The older man bent over Toby and did not bother to open his satchel. He muttered to his companion, 'Let's get him to the ambulance. He needs oxygen, fast.'

Mimi was too terrified to loosen her hold on Toby's hand: she wasn't going to let them take her Toby away from her. She'd kept him from prison all those years ago, and she wasn't going to let him out of her sight with any blokes in uniform, ever again.

No manoeuvring could get the stretcher and its nearly lifeless burden round the sharp corner at the top of the narrow steps. The stretcher-bearers had to slowly back down the stairs, unstrap Toby from the stretcher, then carry him up to the street. Mimi sweated with anxiety as these extra minutes were stolen from his life. In the ambulance, she still clung to his hand, terrified that if she let go, she would lose him. If he was saved, she would do anything, *anything*, she vowed, just in case anyone was listening, up there.

Eventually, the older attendant bellowed, 'Madam, if you don't bloody well get out of my way, I can't give him oxygen!'

As the ambulance hurtled towards the hospital, siren wailing, Mimi trembled. She looked down at Toby, wanting to yell angrily at him for what he had done, although she knew that he'd only done it for her and Max, and the bloody stupid family honour.

Not until Toby's chest began to rise and fall regularly did Mimi also start to breathe normally. The ambulance attendant relaxed slightly; it was bad enough having a near-terminal, without a hysterical wife.

* * *

By the time Mimi knew that he was out of danger, it was seven in the morning. She asked for a hospital telephone, and dialled the private number of the proprietor of a London evening paper.

'Max? Sorry to wake you ... No, I thought I wouldn't ... I wonder whether you could help me out of a bit of a pickle?' she explained.

'Sure, Mimi, we'll run a spoiler in the next edition.'

That afternoon, Mimi turned to the gossip column. Under the sub-heading NAKED she read:

A disruptive influence seems to be at work amongst the famous theatrical Fane family. In a recent shocking episode, a young degenerate ran naked through the Minerva Theatre in the Strand, to the astonishment and disgust of the audience. This episode is now believed to be an unamusing 'jape', possibly instigated by an envious theatrical rival.

The next paragraph, headed UNSEEMLY, stated:

Mrs Tobias Fane, whose husband was unavailable for comment due to bronchial problems, yesterday announced that the Fane family is treating the episode of the unclad youth in their theatre, 'with the contempt it deserves'. Let us hope this unseemly incident does not start a trend.

* * *

It was not difficult for Toby's lawyer to persuade the police to turn a blind eye to the whole affair: it was nothing new for an important person to be the victim of a blackmail attempt. Generally the victim preferred to pay rather than face the resultant shame and fear, but sometimes a victim committed suicide: this one had been lucky – if that was what you called it.

* * *

Three days later Mimi stood with Fizz, Max and Jessie around Toby's hospital bed. Toby, now fully recovered, had just promised Mimi – word of honour – that he would never, never, *never* attempt such a thing again.

Apologetically, he explained, 'At the time it seemed the only answer. I knew they'd continue to try to blackmail me until they *did* get me. The police couldn't prosecute me if I were dead, so they would close the case, and a scandal could be prevented by our lawyers. Nobody could blackmail *Mimi* into selling the King William.'

He whispered, 'I'm so glad to be alive. But this has got to stop, Mimi. If you can't forgive Betsy, for God's sake make peace with her and act as if you've forgiven her.' From his pillow, he looked pleadingly at the four unforgiving faces around his bedside. But like war drums slowly working towards a crescendo, the resentment felt by the group around Toby's bed now darkened into hatred. Toby's entire family had now been drawn into the feud between Mimi and Betsy: it had developed into a matter of family revenge.

Chapter Seventeen

Saturday 27 September 1930. Hollywood

Mrs Bridges stood waiting in the hall as Betsy trailed dolefully down the circular stairway, looking drained of energy.

'I wish you'd stop wasting your time worrying about that woman, Mimi!' Mrs Bridges called up sharply. 'That nancy boy husband of hers must be one of these histrionics – mind you, if I was married to that vulgar creature, I might feel like putting my head in the gas oven ... Can you see where I've put my new gloves, dearest?'

When Betsy had heard from her London contacts what had happened at the Minerva matinée, she immediately called for her chauffeur and drove to Mr Carati's office, where she asked angrily what the hell had been going on. Carati had shrugged his shoulders; he did not have 'complete control over the London end of the operation'. If Betsy had wanted this affair handled with kid gloves, she should not have come to him. Immediately Betsy called off her bid for the King William, and even attempted to tell Mimi of her regret, but whenever she telephoned – and it took hours to put a call through to London – Mimi slammed the phone down.

Betsy could not shake off her remorse. She never intended to go that far, she told herself – although if she had cared to probe her conscience a little deeper, she would have admitted that she realized Mr Carati's methods must be tough and unorthodox in order to be so invariably effective, which was why Black Jack had used him. Once again, Betsy preferred to wriggle out of the responsibility for her actions, by throwing all the blame for goading Toby to the point of suicide on Mr Carati.

Mrs Bridges sighed. '*Do* pull yourself together, dearest, or we'll be late for rehearsal . . . although Tudor will make them wait for us . . . Do you really want to wear that Chanel outfit? You've had that tan leather jacket with the checked skirt since last year. They've seen it at Brentwood before. Better go up and change.'

Betsy loved to change into a new outfit: it always cheered her up and distracted her. Mrs Bridges puffed up the stairs to follow Betsy into her dressing room (recently fitted with new rose-tinged mirrors) and watch her choose an alternative outfit with the concentration of Einstein at his calculations.

Once settled in the back of Betsy's cream Packard, Mrs Bridges smugly congratulated herself on diverting her attention from that wretched Mimi. Brentwood was a long way from Hancock Park, but it was the nearest serious Little Theater in the area and very, very prestigious. And as there weren't many other autos on the road, Betsy's chauffeur always whisked them there in no time it seemed, especially if one of the children accompanied them. Nine-year-old Tess loved attending Brentwood rehearsals, loved the flattering respect with which her mother was greeted and listened to. Normally a self-willed, disobedient child, Tess always behaved like an angel when Betsy took her there. Today Betsy had protested that her white organdie flounced party frock was far too formal for a rehearsal. But Tess already knew how to dress like a star.

* * *

Later that afternoon (without Mrs Bridges' knowledge), Betsy managed to talk quietly to Tudor about her feelings of guilt and remorse. How would she *ever* find Inner Peace?

Tudor realized that despite all that had happened, Betsy had not meant to harm her old friend and was at last willing to make the first step towards reconciliation. She also wanted a clear conscience but wasn't yet willing to come out in the open herself and risk a sharp-tongued rebuke from Mimi.

Eventually, the soft-hearted Tudor agreed to make the exhausting twenty-day return journey to London in order to act as peacemaker. Tudor told himself that this might compensate Mimi for being made to look such a fool while his guest. Naturally, Betsy would foot the bill. She immediately made reservations at the Ritz, in Piccadilly, before he could change his mind.

Sunday 12 October 1930. Fitzroy Square

London was in the middle of an Indian summer, so Tudor, Toby and Mimi took their pre-luncheon drinks to the stone-flagged terrace behind the house in Fitzroy Square.

Toby protested mildly as Mimi tucked a fur car-rug around his knees, but she insisted. 'I nearly lost you, and I ain't going to see you snuff it because you caught pneumonia in our backyard.'

Tudor had already conveyed Betsy's sorrow, contrition and apologies to both the Fanes.

'Oh, I *know* she's sorry,' Mimi had sniffed. 'She kept sending bloody great baskets of flowers to the hospital, and finally we got a dinky little orange tree! I threw them all out, immediately!'

Tudor tried again, knowing that Toby shared his wish to end this destructive impasse between the two women. 'Darling Mimi . . .'

'Don't darling Mimi me! *I* know what Betsy's really like! What you two boys both need to remember is that Betsy has *continued* with her evil tricks for twenty-six years! You're such an old sweetie-pie, Tudor! You don't understand some people are *just wicked*. Some people are born cunning and calculating, shrewd and heartless; some people deliberately hurt you, just because they like it, or because they're going to make money from it.' Mimi drained her glass then plonked it back on the wrought-iron table with such force that she broke the stem.

Both men looked astonished at Mimi's outburst. Toby hastily poured another glass of Moët & Chandon as he pointed out softly, 'But Betsy has made a friendly approach, with Tudor as an olive branch, darling . . .'

'I don't give a damn about any olive branch! You can damn well stick it . . . back on the olive tree! A friend who deliberately betrays you – *never was a true friend!*'

Mimi was not only angry, but clearly frightened of what Betsy might try next, and this was what prevented her forgiveness, Toby realized, as he said, 'Darling, wouldn't you do it for *me*? If I can forgive her, surely you can?'

'Bloody orange trees don't make up for what that bitch has done! If Betsy's genuine, why don't the dratted woman come here herself to say sorry?' Mimi added, 'I know Max feels exactly as I do!'

'But *I* don't,' Toby said, quite crossly.

There was an angry silence, as both remembered that Mimi had started this ball rolling.

Tudor said, 'Well, I've given it my best try.' He could see that to continue persuasion might include him in Mimi's distrust.

'We've both tried,' Toby agreed. 'Now shall we go inside? It's getting a little chilly out here.'

Saturday 1 November 1930. Hollywood

Betsy was disappointed when Tudor returned unsuccessful from his month-long odyssey. Her feelings now became more complicated than before his departure. She felt angry and misunderstood: she had never intended to hurt Toby, had she? She had intended to do a straightforward deal ... Well ... *practically* straightforward. Hadn't she offered 50 per cent more than that theatre was worth? Toby must be a fool not to have grabbed that wonderful opportunity.

Sunday 2 November 1930. Fitzroy Square

Max was no longer a four-letter word in theatrical management, but he had turned down all acting offers he received after the *Much Ado* season ended: he was determined to produce. Should he allow himself to be sidetracked by acting it would take him far longer, he told Komis, who said thoughtfully, 'You are the opposite of those stars who long to produce, you will be a producer who sometimes acts if he feels that he's right for the part and the production. So first, find your theatre, plan a definite project, then go out searching for backers.'

On a drizzly day in early November, Max found his theatre. He and Fizz turned up late for lunch at Fitzroy Square because he had been inspecting the dusty interior of an old disused music hall at the junction of Euston Road and Tottenham Court Road: called the Titania, and known in the Business as the Old Tit, the theatre could seat four hundred. It was here he planned to produce serious plays that could transfer to the West End, if successful.

When Max told his parents of his plans, Mimi and Toby looked up in astonishment, their knives and forks frozen in mid-air above the roast beef.

'Why shouldn't I give it a try?' Max urged. 'All you can watch in the West End is trousers-falling-down farces, drawing-room comedies, or country mansion whodunits! I see *nothing* that reflects the lives of *real* people in the *real* world of today.' As the parlour maid placed a silver dish of grapes before him upon the antique mahogany table, Max elaborated, 'No plays about unemployment, or the threat of inflation if Britain is forced off the gold standard. Nothing about the Fascist threat or the Republican fight in Spain.'

'I should hope not,' Mimi snorted. 'An audience pays to be amused, not lectured!'

Toby quietly disagreed. 'Mimi, Max is serious. So let's listen to what he has to say.'

'I want to offer Shakespeare as a popular playwright, not a scholar's intellectual exercise. Then I'll put on the best post-war American playwrights.'

'You mean Sherwood, Anderson, O'Neill?' Toby asked.

Max nodded. 'Not only serious stuff, but light comedies, so long as they're witty and sophisticated. As nobody has this production policy, it'll be newsworthy, so I should get plenty of free publicity. If I make money, then I'll use it to direct unknown British playwrights.'

Silence round the table as the Wedgwood plates were cleared away.

'Don't get me wrong, Dad. I know if I can't make money, I won't be in business long. I need long runs in the West End but I want a fresh dynamic approach with energy and passion!' Persuasively, he added, 'I can't afford a permanent company, but I want to use the same young actors as often as possible, so they get used to each other, as if in a company.' Max intended to cast almost-star actors, who would settle for a small salary to play lead parts; modern sets that relied on lighting effects would mean inexpensive productions.

Hesitantly, Mimi said, 'I know it ain't exactly up my alley, but ain't there some plan to start a National British Theatre to do something like that – like the Vic, but properly funded, by the state?'

'There's always some such plan, Mummy, but as we're in the middle of a depression, it seems unlikely to get off the drawing-board.'

'What would you first put on?' Toby asked cautiously.

'*Alice*!' Everyone turned to look at Mimi.

'*Alice in Wonderland*.' Mimi beamed. 'This Christmas at the Minerva, not at the Old Tit.'

'The critics will scream nepotism and savage Max,' Toby warned. 'So will everyone else.'

'He's our son, and he done well in *Much Ado*, didn't he?' Mimi growled. 'You give him this chance.'

Intimate revue was still running well at the Minerva, but the tiny theatre had few seats, so did not need the big audiences that the King William so successfully pulled in. The larger theatre – which presented and represented everything Max hated – would subsidize Max's production, if necessary. Toby considered the cost of this. There was no rent to cover at the King William. Labour was cheap and so were actors. The Equity West End minimum was £3, an ingénue was paid £25 and a lead actor £50 a week. *Alice* would cost under £1,000 to mount if they did it well with a cast of twenty and about six changes of set. A good production would gross £1,500 a week.

Eventually, Toby reluctantly agreed that Max could direct at the Minerva for a six-month trial period – provided his father continued to manage the theatre, for Max was only twenty-two years old.

'So *Alice* it is.' Mimi beamed. 'I've always wanted to play the Mad Hatter; fancied meself in them black-and-white-checked trousers with the top hat. It's out of copyright, ducky, so there'll be no royalties to pay. Who'll be your Alice?'

All three looked at Fizz.

'I've already agreed to leave the Vic and join Max,' Fizz said quietly. It had been a sacrifice, for she loved the Vic and had been there for nine years. But Max came first: despite their stormy relationship, he always would.

Toby relaxed a little. 'What are you going to call your company?'

'New Ideas,' Max said firmly.

* * *

Alice in Wonderland opened the day after Christmas, to some of the caustic critical notices that Toby had warned

Max to expect. Fizz just laughed at them . . . especially at the heading that said FAMILY ENTERTAINMENT – OR FAMILY EMPLOYMENT?. Most of the reviews were favourable.

Before *Alice* closed (after respectable takings), Max started to rehearse Fizz as the lead in Bernard Shaw's *Saint Joan*, which had a small cast so would be easy and inexpensive to stage. Fizz secretly smiled as she remembered Max's earlier reluctance to let her share the spotlight: now that they had, Max intended to fully exploit his major asset.

Komis advised him to take an iron grip from the first rehearsal. 'Aim to create a relaxed, yet disciplined atmosphere,' he said. 'Because actors then feel like a united group and if they feel secure, they'll trust you. It's a bit like riding a horse, you need to let the animal know that the rider's the one in control.' Whether Max intimidated them or charmed them, he was always to behave as if he knew exactly what he was doing, otherwise they would lose confidence in him, then make his life hell.

Max successfully hid his nervousness behind an assumed, quiet authority. When every word had been analysed at table-work Max plotted the onstage moves, work which he loved: this was when he started to build up the closely patterned rhythm behind the movements of each character, constantly shifting the focus of attention from one part of the stage to another.

Fizz was careful to seem always to defer to him at rehearsals, saving any arguments for the breakfast table. Max knew he wanted lots of laughter (which always relaxed people) as well as tight discipline. He wanted to stimulate his actors, keep them excited, happy, enthusiastic, and in this way lure the best performance out of them.

Max worked hard and expected his actors to work equally hard, although they were allowed their histrionics at the early rehearsals – the correct time to release their anxieties. He had decided never to rehearse for more than six hours, as he would then have an exhausted Company the next day: he remembered a couple of Basil Dean's rehearsals that had lasted over thirty hours, and resulted in a cast of zombies on the following evening.

Max's favourite moment was the delightful day when everyone was 'off the book'; without this crutch, the actors were at first more nervous, but when their fluidity and confidence returned, the movement of the play started to flow. Like an orchestral conductor, Max seemed to know instinctively where to place each pause and acceleration: his timing was better than it had been as an actor. He cut the anticlimatic Epilogue, which deals with the Catholic Church's later decision to switch Joan's image from heretic to saint. Max's production ended with Joan's agonizing screams, as she burns to death at the stake, off stage.

On the First Night, the curtain fell to horrified silence. Then, backstage, an exhausted Fizz heard the thunder of applause.

* * *

After that came fame. Twenty-four-year-old Max suddenly was no longer a spoilt brat but a wunderkind. He was photographed, interviewed and caricatured; his portrait in oils was painted by Sir James Lavery and hung in the Royal Academy's Summer Exhibition. He received fan mail and begging letters at every post; little gifts were delivered daily to his dressing room. After a matinée, the alley outside the stage door was crowded with giggling schoolgirls waving autograph books.

At first Max enjoyed this taste of success, but quickly became harassed by the feeling that he was constantly under observation. Fame had its drawbacks.

* * *

In search of Inner Peace, Betsy had started to sneak off to those in the vanguard of the new spiritual and self-improvement movement that was sweeping California. Mrs Bridges was scornful of these crank outfits and particularly disapproved of astronomers, mediums and that Blavatsky woman. Out for your cash, all of them! Betsy always wore a raincoat and a slouch hat when she disappeared on one of her 'private' trips so nobody she met could guess she was rich, although after only one glance almost anyone could tell she had a chauffeur hidden around the corner. Sharp as nails when protecting her worldly goods, Betsy was curiously naïve in spiritual matters.

Introduced to a yogi who promised serenity, Betsy asked the price of serenity.

'Two fifty an hour. Pay at the end of the month.' This one certainly wasn't out for her cash!

After Betsy's third session spent trying to tie her body in knots while staring at a candle flame in order to achieve bliss Mrs Bridges asked why she had placed a candlestick in the centre of her bedroom carpet. Was there something wrong with the electricity supply? If so, why wasn't it on the mantelpiece?

Betsy felt alarmed: her mother was getting dangerously inquisitive. Maybe the best way to relax was at the hairdresser.

After she cricked her neck when not-quite standing on her head, Betsy finally decided to give up yoga, and asked for her monthly account. She yelped when she read: *personal tuition for twenty hours . . . five thousand dollars.*

'I thought you told me two fifty an hour,' she gasped to her serene, white-robed instructor.

'Yes, that's what I've charged you.'

* * *

'You obviously didn't vibrate on the same frequencies,' sympathized Betsy's hairdresser on the following morning, as she energetically lathered Betsy's hair into meringue peaks.

The manicurist, painting Betsy's toes the colour of dried blood, looked up and said, 'I swear by Bright Cloud.'

At first Betsy thought this was the name of the new nail varnish, but it turned out to be a Red Indian shaman in the Ojai Valley who would, for five bucks (payment in advance), tell you how to restore basic harmony whether you were sick of body or sick of heart. The manicurist casually added, 'This guy has so much compassion and understanding, he can make even hatred disappear.'

Betsy looked thoughtful.

Two days later, her chauffeur was steering along bumpy dirt tracks until they finally lurched to a halt before not a picturesque wigwam but a forlorn shack with corrugated metal roof, from which an ancient skinny brown figure emerged.

From a filthy leather pouch, he produced what looked like dried plants, stones, and the dirty bones of some small animal.

The old shaman crouched down, scattered the little bones here and there, crumbled the herbs, threw a yellow powder on the earth, then blew, so that it flew up in the air. Still crouching, he looked up at Betsy and grunted,

'*You* make your own troubles.' He stood up, turned his back on her and shuffled into the hut.

* * *

Two weeks later Betsy's masseuse told her what had changed *her* life was the Better Being Group. The Introductory Evening was free, but after that, a session cost $95, which might sound a lot at first, but not for changing your life.

After the third evening meeting of the Better Being Group – which took place in a second-rate hotel ballroom – Betsy (carefully disguised as a normal person) left exhausted after two hours sitting cross-legged and chanting, 'For Better Being the Mighty Mind must always think Positive.' She turned the corner to find her chauffeur saluting nervously as he opened the door of her Packard: inside sat a furious Mrs Bridges, with a face as welcoming as a bristling bulldog. 'Just how long has *this* been going on, my girl?' she demanded.

'Why, however did *you* get here, Ma?' Betsy stammered guiltily, trying to evade her mother's question.

'I *knew* something was up, my girl!' Mrs Bridges snapped triumphantly. 'Then a friend of mine happened to notice you enter this dump, and thought he'd better call me, as it seemed a little strange. I called a cab and came right down.'

Betsy was furious. Mrs Bridges had clearly been up to her old effective trick of hiring a detective. Betsy quickly wound up the glass screen that separated the chauffeur in the front seat from the passenger seats. She then screamed at her mother, 'How dare you spy on me, Ma! Just how long has this being going on? I *won't have it*, do you understand, Ma? If I catch you doing this *once more*, you'll be out on your ear – and I mean it!'

Mrs Bridges stood her ground. 'It's my duty to protect you,' she said firmly. 'And the kiddies as well. And the Dead. What would Jack think of you? Consorting with conmen!' Mrs Bridges managed to make the word 'consorting' sound the type of verb used only in pornographic magazines. She then switched on the interior light, and consulted some typed notes. 'My friend says the speaker's aim is to hook into the basic emotional needs of the audience – for love, money or whatever. That Van Geldstrop person uses a form of mass hypnosis to emotionally seduce his entire audience … Apparently, this makes people go off and *do whatever the speaker has suggested*!' She peered again at her crumpled notes. 'My friend says Hitler and Mussolini use basically similar methods … See what a nasty pack you're running with, my girl?'

Keeping her voice quiet but unable to disguise the animosity in it, Betsy snapped, 'I won't have this, Ma! Van is a magnetic personality. He's explained to me that he's a human transmitter, someone who allows others to draw magnetic energy from his own body – *that's* why everyone feels revitalized after the meetings!'

'Human transmitter, my arse!' snorted Mrs Bridges. 'The only thing that *he* intends to transmit is cash from your account to his, one way or another.'

Betsy was suddenly silent. She had already agreed to 'contributions' of $200 an hour, for Van's personal tuition: Van had told Betsy that she, too, had a special magnetic field, but that Betsy's energy had been repeatedly drained from by someone else. Luckily, Van could – in time – counteract that negative force.

Betsy burst into tears. 'I won't have you interfering in my life, Ma! Why *shouldn't* I balance my yin and yang and heal my negative part with positive vibrations? My own mother, a dirty spy!'

Mrs Bridges paled, then realized what the problem was. She snapped, 'You know whose fault this is? That awful – *creature*!'

Astonished, Betsy ceased her snivelling and stared open-mouthed at her mother, who spat, 'If Mimi hadn't married that pansy, he couldn't have put his head in the gas oven, could he? Then he wouldn't have upset you; I know how sensitive you are, dearest.' As usual Mrs Bridges' response to accusations and anger had been quickly to distort the facts, so that her own guilt became minimal and someone else's minimal involvement became a major factor, thus blame could be diverted.

Betsy tore off her slouch hat and spectacles; she wiped her eyes on her raincoat sleeve, as she looked with gratitude at her mother, and echoed, 'You're right, Ma. It's all *Mimi's* fault, when you look at it that way.'

* * *

However, Betsy rebelliously continued to sneak out and search for Inner Peace. The mere presence of Van made shivers run up and down her spine – and elsewhere, she had to admit, when he lightly touched the tips of her fingers as he passed her a glass of orange juice. She allowed a small seed of hope to settle in her hopeful heart.

Only doing her duty to the Dead, Betsy's mother continued to have Betsy followed by a skilful soft-shoe. Betsy only became aware of this because a normally sober and upright citizen, the proprietor of a menswear store off Vine, had had a little too much bathtub gin on a balmy moonlit Saturday night in May. Just before 11 p.m., no longer sober and only just upright, he came driving hell for leather out of a side street and then mistook his accelerator for the brake. His Oldsmobile leaped across the street like a lion at a gazelle, and rammed the discreet Model T in which Mrs Bridges sat in unaccustomed discomfort, next to her detective. The Ford was hit with such force that the auto slammed sideways into the glass shopfront of a hardware store. '*Sue him!*' Mrs Bridges cried, just before her right temple smashed against the frame of the Model T and it was hurled into an artistic display of orange garden rakes. Mrs Bridges was instantly killed.

Sunday 17 July 1932. Hollywood

Real life already seemed distant and dreamlike to Fizz as she leaned out of her turreted window, feeling like Rapunzel. Or was it that real life *always* seemed distant at the Chateau Marmont? She looked down the almost vertical garden to what should, of course, be a moat but in fact was Sunset Boulevard.

Her suite was large and comfortable, with a pale green tiled bathroom; the kitchenette contained a streamlined refrigerator; all other furniture was reproduction French antique. Between Fizz's sitting room and her dinette were high wrought-iron gates, like those of a public park.

Fizz wandered back to the Louis XIII writing table (flimsy as cardboard) and finished her letter to Max. In her generous, looped handwriting she wrote:

Everybody looks as if about to break into a tap-dance, there are Shirley Temple doll displays in every toyshop window, the only subject of conversation is movies and the parts played in them by the speaker. Incidentally, every studio seems to be churning out Broadway musicals, hoping to cheer up people. Apparently, there are thirteen million Americans out of work. So how can they afford to go to the movies? The Industry is discovering that they can't.

Every unmarried blonde starlet seems to have a gangster escort, it's the latest chic accessory. Every waitress and gas-pump attendant has their own agent. This morning I was served breakfast in bed by a handsome young waiter, who then furtively whipped out his . . . guess what? . . . acting résumé sheet. He smiled winningly. 'I also tap-dance and speak Japanese.'

I'm just off for a drive with Tudor, who's been perfectly sweet to me. By silent mutual agreement, we never mention Madame O'B. General opinion among the British set is that Tudor is getting tired of courting her after two years of her *not* making up her mind whether or not she wants to marry him. I assume your mother has no idea of this possible Machiavellian twist to her long-running serial . . .

* * *

'Fizz, you must be the only faithful wife in Hollywood!' Tudor shouted. 'But I'm forgetting, you've only been here two days.' He drove his roadster far too fast, taking a right and swinging the car dangerously close to the edge of the road. A warm breeze stirred Fizz's hair as the car headed north; she gazed at the Santa Monica Mountains, ahead to the right, then left to the dazzling blue stretch of Pacific Ocean.

She tried to forget that tomorrow she would start on her movie debut. Or she might not, if Tudor's driving didn't improve.

* * *

Two weeks later, in her turret at the Chateau Marmont, Fizz finished her Sunday letter-writing with a scribble to Mimi.

Darling, I already know I *hate* movie acting!!! Studio routine is bewildering and unsettling. I find it hard to play my part in non-chronological order. There I sit, crying my heart out because my Pirate's been unfaithful, before we've even kissed!

If you're a star you get the money and adulation, hundreds of fan letters and people behave obsequiously to you on the set (my Pirate's entourage is bigger than the director's), but our beloved theatre offers me warmth and love, plus that tingling excitement for a couple of hours after every performance! For me, there's no comparison between stage and set. I'm ambitious but I'm also a realist. In future I'll stick to theatre work, and the international fame can go to hell! I've decided *never* to make another movie, no matter how much money they offer – it doesn't seem worth it. You can't realize that until you see the time and cynical effort that goes into manufacturing these untrue myths about the stars, and the enormous pressure that they really live under. Thank goodness I'll soon be back in England. Big kiss, darling Mimi. Love, Fizz.

* * *

Surrounded by frilly pillows, Mimi finished the letter she had been reading aloud to Toby, who sat in her bedroom fireside chair, drinking black coffee.

Toby shook his head. 'It was a pity Fizz decided to go. Max gets restless when she's away ... Foxtop, have you read this bit in *The Times* about Lilian's first ballet season at Sadler's Wells?' Again, he shook his head. 'This time she's bitten off more than she can chew.'

Mimi snapped, 'Lilian has teeth like a tiger, and a digestion to match!'

Toby looked over his spectacles. 'She's not the only one ... No, I didn't mean you ... Chap at the Garrick, just returned from Berlin, says the Huns talk about nothing but the power and importance of youth. Only other subject of conversation is politics: all their political parties share the same idea – to forget Germany's past humiliation and show her present strength ... which probably means the Huns are about to put us through Hell again.'

Mimi licked marmalade from her finger. 'The moment war is declared, every politician should be lined up by the army, and shot. Maybe that'd make 'em do their jobs a bit better.'

Friday 7 October 1932. Colville Place, London

Just before midday, at the entrance of Colville Place, a blackened chimney sweep whistled cheekily as Fizz, in her new navy slacks outfit, stepped from a taxi.

Fizz's first Hollywood movie, *The Lady and the Pirate*, promised to be a flopperoo, as they said out there. Everything had ground to a halt after the sneak preview. The reshoot had then taken an arduous extra four weeks. Max had sent her a grumpy cable about that, so when they'd wrapped an astonishing four days early, Fizz decided to give him a pleasant surprise, and arrive home early.

As soon as she stepped inside her own yellow front door she sensed the emptiness of her home ... Husbands! Never around when you needed them! she thought, as the cab driver heaved her two trunks into the hall passage and held out his hand.

Fizz hurriedly paid him, then gaily called, 'Max,' up the stairs.

No reply.

She called again, questioningly, 'Max?'

Silence.

She ran quickly up the narrow stairs to the living room, and then to their bedroom, but no, Max was not still asleep.

She sat on the edge of the neat bed to telephone both theatres. Neither had seen him. Nor had the Garrick club, although that's what those damned hall porters *always* said. Slowly, Fizz returned to the hall. She realized what was strange. Mrs Pomfret, her daily cleaner, was not in the house either. She traced the word *Max* in the dust on the hall table. Who would know where Max was? Obviously Mimi or Toby.

Because she was thirsty – she had eaten and drunk nothing on the boat train from Southampton to London – Fizz decided to make tea in her own kitchen once again: that would feel cosy and wifely. It really was good to be home!

No fresh milk.

Fizz carried a cup of black coffee upstairs into the sitting room, unstrapped her high heels and kicked them off. As she flopped into the arms of Max's favourite easy chair, she sniffed the lingering fragrance of his Bay Rum cologne. She longed to see her husband and happily looked forward to a catch-up chat: Max's letters, although loving, had been hurried and scrappy, with none of the naughty gossip that actors love to hear – so long as it concerns somebody else. While you could get a lot of Hollywood news in Britain, you heard nothing about Britain in the USA: American newspapers and radio assumed that anything outside the good ol' USA simply did not exist; if you took ten steps away from New York or Hollywood, you fell off the edge of the world.

Mimi answered the phone herself. 'Blimey, Fizz, when did you get back?'

'Just now. Four days early. It's a surprise for Max – but sadly he's not here to surprise,' Fizz laughed. 'How's Toby? ... Good, I'll speak to him in a minute, then ... Tudor sends his love, by the way ... Listen, d'you know where Max is? He's not at either of the theatres.'

'Max?' said Mimi, as if she'd never heard of him.

Instant red alert.

Mimi was playing for time. Something was up.

'Mimi, is Max all right? He hasn't been in a motor accident, anything like that? ... There's no money problem? No problems at the theatre? ... Oh, well, I'll go out and buy some food and milk, then just wait here until he turns up ... Now I'd like a word with Toby, please ... No, darling, nothing special, just to say hello.' Toby would be an easier nut to crack.

But Mimi said that he didn't seem to be around. He must have slipped out.

'Huh!' Fizz slammed down the telephone.

So Max wasn't away, he wasn't ill, there were no

business problems, and Mimi was acting like an uneasy cat who smells a dog just around the corner and Toby wasn't allowed to speak to her. Who could Fizz rely on to give her the bad news, whatever it was?

But Jessie hedged.

Fizz cried angrily down the telephone. 'Listen, Mummy, I *know* Max hasn't been sleeping here! . . . Don't know how, but as soon as I stepped inside the door, this place felt empty . . . No, *emptier* than normal empty. Straightaway, I felt something was wrong . . . I simply don't *believe* you, Mummy! . . . Let's say I'm psychic! I just *know* these things . . . I also know Max isn't in business trouble, and he hasn't had an accident, but you and Mimi are both acting in the weirdest way! Holy Moly, what's up? . . . Yes, Mummy, I may have picked up a few American expressions, after all I've been there for months. Now will you please stop trying to red-herring me and *tell me what's happened to Max?*'

Fizz's voice started to quaver. 'You don't think I haven't guessed, do you Mummy? I'm phoning you because I don't want some vicious, smiling bitch to tell me face to face, with everyone watching – which will happen about five minutes after I've set foot in the Minerva . . . I don't care! I want the truth from *my mother*, who I *know* doesn't want to hurt me.'

At the other end of the telephone, Jessie slowly and reluctantly admitted that there had been one or two rumours.

'What's her *name*? Come on, Mummy, out with it! . . . Oh no! *Not* Wendy! . . . How *could* he? . . . That nose. That condescending why don't-you-kneel-and-kiss-the-hem-of-my-gown attitude!'

Jessie was silent.

'And I'm told she isn't *that* good in the sack,' Fizz yelled, 'although goodness knows she's had enough practice!'

Once Max's absence had been explained, the angry Fizz became brisk, matter-of-fact. 'Has this reached the newspapers yet, Mummy? ... What do you mean *only* the gossip columns? ... No, of course I'm not going to judge my husband on any printed rubbish ... *Has* any paper printed photographs of them? ... Look, Mummy, you *know* I'll find out in the end, so *please* tell me! I'd *rather* be told by my own mother than anyone else. Honest, cross my heart...

'So when did this photo appear? ... Only *yesterday*! ... Did the two of them know they were being photographed, or was it a candid? ... How can *you* tell they didn't know? ... So what exactly were they doing? *Kissing!* What sort of kissing? ... You know perfectly well what I mean, Mummy! Did his tongue seem to be halfway down her throat? ... *Sort of?* ... Have you kept the newspaper clipping? ... Right, I'm coming straight over ... Don't you *dare* burn it before I arrive.

'Max, Max, you bastard,' she wailed, as she put down the phone longing for the husband, lover, brother and fellow professional to whom she waved goodbye as the liner pulled away from Southampton dock, only four months before. Couldn't he have tied a knot in it – for only four months?

* * *

Max denied any wrongdoing. He looked his wife straight in the eyes and said, in a wounded voice, that he did not understand *how* Fizz could suspect him of such a thing. Certainly, he admitted to the odd flirting glance. Possibly a snatched kiss, here and there . . . but on a stack of bibles, he would swear that since his marriage he had only made love to Fizz, his darling wife.

'Oh, Max, I *know* you've been unfaithful to me. The whole of bloody London knows! Even my *mother* knew!'

'Never . . . in my *heart*!'

Big mistake. He dodged a cut-glass vase of hastily sent hothouse roses; it hit the wall. The bed, now strewn with roses and shards of glass and drenched with water, was clearly unsuitable for the purpose he had intended, and counted on.

'Fizz, you shouldn't have done that,' he said, quietly and reproachfully.

'*You* shouldn't have given Mrs Pomfret a holiday – obviously so she couldn't tell *me* that *you* hadn't been sleeping at home! *I'm* not going to clear that mess up!'

When Fizz had first realized that Max had been unfaithful, and furthermore had lied to her, she had indulged in a little self-pitying, destructive self-criticism. What had she done to deserve this? What had she done to lose him? This mood had not lasted long. Accustomed to adoration, Fizz now felt empty, hurt, humiliated and scorned. She was also furious that Max believed he could lie to her and get away with it: he had betrayed not only her body, but her trust and their love. Not to mention insulting her intelligence.

Fizz now discovered that she had an uncontrolled side to her as she felt the barely suppressed violence of her sexual jealousy. She could not rid herself of the vision of Max making love to some anonymous woman: she could only see her rival's hands around Max's neck, her long scarlet predatory nails caressing his hairline; she could only see the woman's body from the knees down to her scarlet toenails – matching colour, of course, and unchipped.

Now, Max and Fizz looked across the dripping bed at each other with guarded surprise. Fizz, bewildered, wondered fleetingly whether she would ever be able to trust him – or anyone else – again. Max, in a hurt, quiet voice, accused Fizz of unreasonable jealousy. Was she not ashamed of herself?

Fizz stamped out of their bedroom.

In the days that followed, Fizz bitterly felt the loss of that intimate, carefree attachment which she had taken for granted, something she never realized how much she valued – until now she'd lost it.

She discovered that jealousy was as crazy and unbalanced an emotion as being in love, but that it was a more violently dangerous state. At times she wondered if there were any clear line between sanity and madness where jealousy was concerned, for, obsessed, she could think about nothing else.

Friday 7 October 1932. London

Herb Hoffman had produced *Danger in the Night*, one of the West End's longest-running domestic comedies. For his luncheon party at Claridges, Fizz dressed carefully in her new Schiaparelli; this dress, the most expensive and unconventional one she had ever possessed, was guaranteed to draw attention to the wearer as soon as she entered any room. Everyone was currently crazy about Surrealism. The dress was made of shocking-pink silk; it was daubed with bright yellow brushstrokes, and worn with a little palette-shaped straw hat with miniature paintbrush attached. The outfit was witty, chic, adventurous and certainly sexy, thought Fizz as she moved, laughing and joking, from group to group, deciding on a likely prospect.

* * *

By the time they parted, Fizz knew that he had a hairy back and was called Nigel.

He had given an efficient but detached performance. Because her heart and mind were not involved, in some strange way she had not felt at all involved, not even unfaithful. Afterwards, hairy-backed Nigel had not even escorted her home. He had yawned, theatrically told her that she was wonderful, telephoned for a taxi, pulled on a Noël Coward-type silk dressing gown to see her to the door of his mews house, kissed her hand, then pressed the taxi fare into it. The astonished Fizz had never felt so humiliated by three shillings, and took the money only to make a fast exit.

As soon as she reached home she ripped off her dress, crumpled it into a pink and yellow ball, flung it into the dustbin and banged the metal lid back with unnecessary force. She then asked herself, 'Why? Why?' It was *not* to understand how Max had been able to – which was the excuse she had originally offered herself . . . before she'd even *met* the man! No, her aim had been much simpler. She had wanted to hurt Max. She had wanted to *really hurt him* in that most sensitive area of a man – his masculine pride.

Instead, she had only hurt herself. Now she understood why the phrase 'she felt cheap' was a cliché: the phrase had been used so often because it was so true. After all, the tarts in Shepherd's Market were probably pushed off with more than three shillings.

Fizz felt guilty, and disgusted by herself; she wished she hadn't done it. She hoped that Max would not find out.

Now she had two people whom she could not bring herself to forgive: Max . . . and herself.

Max did not find out. Ultimately, she resented this. Her love and affection had been transformed overnight into pain and betrayal because of his perfidy, so she wanted him to feel similar bitterness, pain and misery – and to know that she was responsible for it. But she could not bring herself to tell him of her payback infidelity, for she felt such shame and humiliation. Why the hell didn't Max feel like that when he did it with other women?

*   *   *

As Jessie swiftly beat eggs for a cheese soufflé Fizz sat in her mother's tiny kitchen to confide in her. She wanted to be absolved.

Jessie, not taken by surprise, had decided in advance what to say, should her opinion be asked. So she carefully started, 'Max has always been very much a masculine man – and you know why.'

'Max is masterful, selfish and arrogant!'

'Yes, that's what I said. He also has a habit of falling in love – and you also knew about that, before you married him.'

'Well, he'd better cure the habit fast if he wants to stay married to me!'

'It's a difficult habit to drop,' Jessie sighed. After all, adultery was not exactly unknown in the theatre world.

'What do you mean, darling?'

'Having a secret little adventure adds spice to life, it makes you feel as you do when you're standing in the spotlight, your dad said; it gives you that top-of-the-world feeling that floods through you after a good performance. That's why some people get hooked on being in love, is how he always explained it!'

'Oh, darling, I'd no idea! I thought you were happy!'

'I was. Except now and then,' Jessie said sadly.

Fizz flew to her mother and hugged her.

Eventually, Jessie started to beat the eggs into submission again. 'Couldn't you turn a blind eye to this, darling?' She waited for the hurricane, but it did not follow.

Instead Fizz put her elbows on the kitchen table, propped her chin on the palm of her hands, looked seriously at her mother through swollen reddened eyes and said, almost timidly, 'I've tried, Mummy, but suddenly, for no reason, I remember and in a flash I'm simmering with fury.' She sighed. 'Now that I understand the pain which can be inflicted by someone you love, I understand how difficult it can be even to *try* to forgive ... Now I understand what Mimi feels for Betsy: black rage.'

* * *

Viscount Plaice and the Earl of Whitebait obligingly came to Max's rescue once more, and what eventually made Fizz laugh so hard that she forgave him was a note from His Grace the Duke of Haddock; attached to a cream marabou bedjacket, it read, 'I long to see you wearing this on Christmas morning. Passionately yours, Haddock.'

* * *

Jessie and Mimi breathed a sigh of relief; backstage tension eased at the Minerva.

However, at home, Fizz continually heard her sharp tongue make sarcastic references to Max's treachery, and veiled threats of retaliation. Max had often wondered why his mother and Betsy O'Brien continued to thrust at each other like blindfolded fighting cocks: revenge, like love, was clearly blind, deaf, dumb and certainly beyond reason.

Eventually, he decided to demonstrate the dangers of revenge to both his wife and mother. He suggested to his father that they present at the Minerva A SEASON OF REVENGE, to demonstrate that the inevitable result of revenge was destruction.

Toby looked doubtful. The Fane vs. O'Brien kettle had seemed to have gone off the boil. Following Toby's suicide attempt, newspaper gossip columnists had from time to time tried to fan the embers of the feud, but both Mimi and Betsy had managed to hide their mutual animosity.

Toby also had another reason for looking dubious. 'Do you think you're really ready for Hamlet?'

'No. I want to offer that to Johnnie, with Fizz as Ophelia, then pair the two of them again in *The Merchant* the following month. In future, I don't want to act when I'm producing: that way madness lies.' When Max directed himself, he did so from the front, with his understudy standing in on stage; he only actually acted on stage during the last week of rehearsal. Max further explained, 'It causes me far too much doubt and anxiety, as a producer, to criticize myself as an actor.'

Toby hoped that his relief did not show on his face.

Tuesday 14 February 1933

Max crossed his fingers as he looked across the road at the electrically brilliant words above the theatre entrance:

THE MINERVA THEATRE
PRESENTS
A SEASON OF REVENGE

He had decided to present Hamlet as an insecure, indecisive, fatherless adolescent, heir presumptive to the throne of Denmark and fearful of this huge responsibility.

'A psychological interpretation, in modern dress,' he had enthused to Fizz one Sunday afternoon, as he lay on their sitting-room sofa, a frequent source of inspiration. 'Hamlet undergoes a tremendously *sudden* pubescent initiation rite when the ghost of his dead father tells him that he didn't die naturally, but was murdered. In fact, I'm thinking of dressing the ghost as a psychiatrist, to make my point.' Listening only to himself, he continued, 'I'm emphasizing the Oedipal subtext, of course.' He swung his legs to the floor, and paced the room. 'And you see, the poor lad can't even trust his girlfriend, Ophelia, because her father is using her for *his* own ambition – wants her to be Queen of Denmark, one day.'

'Poor girl.'

'Eh? I'd prefer you to think through Hamlet's mind. Wouldn't *you* feel bewildered, hurt, and *desperately* lonely, even ... er ... impotent, if suddenly you felt you couldn't even trust the person you were in love with?'

'I'd feel bloody furious,' Fizz agreed as she viciously stabbed her needle into her embroidery. 'Betrayal is the *ultimate* sin,' she added as she snipped a thread with unnecessary vehemence.

'Exactly. Now take your average rich-kid college student of today – what would *he* do if he were told by a ghost to commit a murder? He'd head for the nearest Freudian analyst, of course.'

'Of course,' Fizz had said thoughtfully.

* * *

Waiting opposite the Minerva, Max shivered, turned up his overcoat collar, glanced at his watch and hurriedly crossed the road: the First Night audience was about to stream out. He had arranged to meet his parents up the road, in the Savoy Grill, but he wanted, unobserved, to watch his mother's face as she left the theatre. He hoped to see an unusually subdued Mimi, which might well mean that Max – with a little help from Mr W. Shakespeare – had led her to reconsider her attitude to vengeance. As much as his father, Max was now exasperated by the Fane–O'Brien feud, particularly because, as neither Betsy nor Mimi now responded to their teasing, gossip writers found the feud a useful peg for the occasional invented paragraph, when they had a bit of empty space to fill.

Arguing hard, Mimi and Toby swept past Max without noticing him. He followed them, and heard his mother say, 'You silly old buggins, the whole point of *Hamlet* is the *importance* of revenge, the *importance* of a person's honour.'

'Honour has made people do terrible things – to me among others,' Toby said bitterly. 'The point of the play, for me, is that Hamlet ends up dead.' As they waited at the kerb for a gap in the traffic, Toby continued, 'Why would a loving father come back from the dead to wreck his son's life by telling him it was his duty to murder his father's murderer? I always thought it was a most unloving, unfatherly action of the ghost.'

Mimi had to agree: the unmarried Danish Prince's revenge had brought down the whole royal House of Denmark and left the stage littered with corpses.

* * *

The reviews could not have been better, Max thought, as eagerly he read: 'The best Hamlet of his generation' ... What could be better than that? ... Why, 'this gifted producer with a fresh viewpoint'.

* * *

In *The Merchant of Venice*, the following month, Fizz played Portia. As anti-Semitism swept over Europe, Max presented a sympathetic Shylock – not a monster, but a respectable modern banker, a successful businessman who had pulled himself up from the gutter by hard work, and then found himself treated with contempt.

This *Merchant of Venice* was a play about the resentment of someone made to feel an outsider, which was why Shylock grasped his opportunity for revenge on his bullying oppressors.

Emotions do not date. Max's simple, sparsely designed productions felt exciting and modern to the fashionable audience, who did not feel like schoolboys being forced to watch something incomprehensible because it was good for them. Once again, Max had made Shakespeare a commercial West End success.

Now, Max slowly realized that he, too, had a gift. As

well as casting flair, he had inherited Toby's good taste, so Max's design choices were always spectacularly theatrical without being vulgar. He had a natural authority, he was amiable, tough, calm in emergencies (acting calm, in fact), he knew the business backwards and – unlike many people in theatrical management – he did not surreptitiously regard actors as an exasperating necessity.

Tuesday 30 May 1933. Paris

After the success of the Minerva's 'Season of Revenge', Toby had handed Max an envelope which contained a generous cheque and two tickets to Paris. As the young Fanes sat in their low-slung Parisian taxi they heard the honk of horns, the sharp whistles of gendarmes directing traffic, the fat old flower 'girls' calling their wares that overspilled large baskets; once again they giggled at the open *pissoirs*, which allowed men to piss unobserved in the street, only their heads and lower legs visible.

The smells, the noise, the elegance and the sensuality of Paris were unmistakable, thought Fizz. Unlike London, Paris was rational, easy to understand: the city had twenty districts – *arrondissements* – but you could cross central Paris, starting from the Louvre, on foot, in only one afternoon. Fizz loved wandering along the banks of the Seine as it meandered through the city, occasionally winding round some pretty island in the middle. Fizz enjoyed the Right Bank as much as the Left, the Latin Quarter. In fact, she loved every part of Paris, including the old areas, still a medieval network of dark courtyards and forbidding gates that led to culs-de-sac, worn stone stairs or passageways only wide enough to allow two donkeys to pass.

Max always enjoyed being with Fizz in Paris because here, on holiday, she seemed a different person. When working, she switched masks without realizing it. When talking about her work, even her voice changed, becoming more brisk, objective and firm: she seemed to shed her femininity.

Had she known of her husband's thoughts, Fizz would have snorted that she needed such femininity like a hole in the head. 'Feminine' to her meant fluffy bedjackets and spiteful gossip, obsession with fashion, being hopeless about money, frequent tears and fluttering eyelashes to reassure men that they really were big Tarzan, and you really were little Jane. 'Being feminine' meant confessing your secrets to your hairdresser, and assuming that they were safe and he was genuinely interested.

After unpacking in the Hôtel Jacob on the Left Bank, Fizz and Max spent their first sunny day wandering around the city; as evening approached, they sat outside a Montparnasse café, each sipping a *bock*, crunching peanuts and enjoying the Frenchness of the passers-by. That evening the young Fanes walked hand in hand past the deserted dark-green stalls of the Left Bank. Fizz stopped suddenly. She pulled Max towards the embankment and leaned against it, with her back to the darkened river. 'Max, I've something to tell you. Something serious.'

For one nasty moment, Max thought she had found out about Louise. Although possessively jealous of his wife, Max always told himself that *his* occasional lapses couldn't possibly damage their marriage.

Fizz said sadly, 'I can't help being jealous of you. All

the time. I've truly tried, but my feelings seem to be beyond my control. *My* jealousy is destroying me, and *your* infidelity is eroding my love of you and my trust in you.' She caught both her husband's hands in hers. 'So this is a warning, Max. I want you to know that when something wears away, eventually, there's nothing left to repair.'

'Why spoil our first night like this, Fizz?' Max tried to steer the conversation away from such dangerous waters.

'Whenever I confront you, you're always defensive. At first you deny it. Then you try to make it *my* fault, which *enrages* me! For the last time, I'm telling you that I always feel deceived and humiliated by your treachery, your blatant lying, and your uncontrite attitude. It's got to stop, Max. I'm not giving you an ultimatum. I'm just pointing out what's inevitable, unless one of us changes. And I *can't* change my attitude – not for want of trying.'

* * *

They walked back to the hotel in silence, and that night they did not make love. Max lay turned away from Fizz, pretending to be asleep. Did she really mean it?

* * *

Of course, by morning when the smiling maid appeared with a tray of fragrant coffee and hot croissants, the Duke of Haddock (an excellent lover) had been forgiven.

After a delightful sojourn in Paris, the Fanes spent their last evening with Fred Astaire's favourite composer, Cole Porter, and his wife Linda who, at fifty-one, was still considered one of the world's most beautiful women. Money was not a problem for the Porters. Apart from his huge earnings, in 1923 Cole had inherited a fortune from his rich, domineering grandfather; unlike his fellow heirs

Cole lost nothing in the Wall Street crash . . . because he had already spent all of it. An almost non-stop ebullient party was held in the Porters' exquisite home; everyone in the international set dropped in when they visited Paris, Linda explained, and added that she hoped to see lots more of Max and Fizz on their next trip.

* * *

Fizz and Max were now equally celebrated, Fizz for her charm and acting ability, Max for popularizing Shakespeare among those who normally only watched drawing-room comedies and musicals.

Mimi sometimes caught herself thinking of the forbidden, wishing that her mam could see the two young 'uns as they were whisked off to a Buckingham Palace garden party (it was chic to consider these rather dull) or a weekend at Fort Belvedere with the Prince of Wales and his new companion, Mrs Simpson, who Fizz duly reported 'looks like a governess, is equally efficient, and has him right under her thumb'.

Both of the young Fanes thoroughly enjoyed their now hectic social life; nearly always, after the theatre, they would dash on to some party: they went to bed later, rose *much* later and loved every minute of their lives. The '30s were arguably the best time in the history of the world to be young. Max told Toby as much: he drily commented, 'Provided you're not living under some dictator's jackboot, and are not one of the millions of jobless.'

Luckily for actors, everyone who could afford to do so still went to the theatre as often as possible: it was considered an essential part of social life. The battle still ranged between supporters of the legitimate stage and those of the cinema, but the movies were winning new territory, for they had such beautiful women gliding around such luxurious sets in such elegant clothes that they distracted your attention from the truly terrible scripts.

Chapter Eighteen

Sunday 29 December 1935. Hollywood

Nick lurked among the shadowed cypresses to watch Betsy's guests, the men in tuxedos, the women showing off their suntans in white backless dresses which emphasized their diamonds and décolletés. They had drunk cocktails in the newly decorated lounge (where the walls had been painted the beige of Betsy's face powder, to ensure a flattering backdrop for its owner), and then eaten a buffet supper in the oak-panelled dining hall; now they drifted across the darkened lawn to dance in the new floodlit miniature pantheon that glistened like an enormous shelled egg against the midnight-blue Californian sky. The dance floor was supported by Corinthian columns, with mirrored walls between each one; if you twirled alone there, you could see yourself reflected to Eternity: Tess often did.

Nick hated the ostentatious ballroom, especially when his mother gave a dance, for then she always expected him to dance the opening waltz with her. He felt an idiot in his white tux and bow tie with his hair slicked back, among such an ancient bunch – although he enjoyed wearing grown-up clothes among kids of his own age. Next month, he would be twelve years old, but he already pretended to be thirteen to girls who didn't know him.

With them, he also pretended that he smoked and drank alcohol.

'Nick, Nick, where are you hiding?'

Nick sighed. 'Coming, Mom.'

As insecure as he was lonely, Nick tried to shield himself from hurt and humiliation by avoiding other people. When he was alone he felt at ease with himself and relaxed. However, the more he withdrew from adult social activities where he felt he might behave like an idiot, the more Betsy pushed him into acting as her escort – and the more he was left alone by people of his own age: eventually he was rarely invited out. That suited him fine.

Still glamorous at forty-eight, Betsy stood on the crazy pavement before the ballroom and proudly watched her son hurry over the damp lawn towards her. As he grew older, his big-boned, tall frame looked increasingly like that of Black Jack, tidied up. Nick was skinny, but when his face filled out his features would not be so prominent; now he seemed to have knuckle-bones everywhere; his wrists were already too long for his tuxedo and knobbly ankles were visible beneath dark pants that had only been purchased last June. Like Stella, Nick always looked as if he had just outgrown whatever he was wearing. It was a pity that her son needed to wear spectacles, but Nick was too short-sighted to see clearly further than ten inches without them; Betsy thought he must have strained his eyes, reading. Like Stella, his nose was always buried in a book. He was equally hopeless with his hands: if your automobile went wrong on the chauffeur's day off, he couldn't even raise the hood. If you were uncertain how to spell Agamemnon, then Nick was your man. But who did, in Hollywood?

Nick wished that they could dance alone in the garden,

because he was as tall as Betsy and enjoyed dancing; she didn't make him feel nervous or clumsy; he never stepped on her feet, if they danced when no one was watching.

As he approached, Nick saw the customary adoration in his mother's eyes, which he found a worrying burden. Too often, he had been told that he was now the man of the house. He wished he was older, more sophisticated. He wished he could drive a Bugatti, ski like a fiend, and always know what to say. He wished he didn't need to wear glasses. Most of all, he wished that he did not feel so inadequate, helpless to look after his own mother and make her truly happy.

Only his sister, Stella, understood this anxious responsibility that Nick felt for their mother. She could always calm her down when she had one of her 'upsets', as had happened that morning when some silly old columnist had referred to 'Battling Betsy O'Brien' as if she was some boxing heavyweight. Nick hated to see his mother derailed by that stupid old vendetta; apart from anything else, Betsy seemed unable to realize that as long as she allowed everyone to see how much it annoyed her, columnists would continue to tease her with it. As they danced the opening waltz, Nick was conscious of his mother holding her head high and sucking her stomach in. Betsy was proudly conscious of the fatuous smiles and little cries of 'Oh, isn't he *cute*!'

Tess pulled a face at Nick as he waltzed past. She and Stella wore identical blue net dresses, like bridesmaids; Tess was furious when their mother dressed the sisters the same, even though Stella's gawkiness emphasized Tess's trim little figure and perky, mature breasts. Because Tess was a brazen flirt, she was unpopular with her classmates, but Tess didn't care; she hated school dances or teenage dances given by her mother's friends, for they seemed so childish and tacky: the boys sat around and talked about who could drink the most, and which girls went all the way, when it was clear that nobody did. The girls, in their pastel frocks, exchanged shrill giggles and whispered news: who was dating whom; which couple had exchanged pins. How gauche could you get?

Nick didn't mind going to teenage dances but Tess hated her little brother to accompany her; he was so gauche, she objected. ('Gauche' was her latest adjective of displeasure: the reverse was 'suave'.) She only agreed to have him along after being secretly bribed by Betsy; Tess took out her displeasure on her brother. A tattle-tale, Tess had immediately reported to their mother when she saw her brother necking – or attempting to neck – with one of her classmates, who (supposedly) had then complained to Tess that Nick was rough and clumsy; he had ruined her lipstick line, and mussed her hair. Mom had not punished Nick, but merely told him that a boy should approach a girl gently, if he didn't want to frighten her away.

As soon as he could escape, Nick hurried from the dance floor, back to the buffet, which the caterers were now clearing; he filled a plate with slices of apple pie, marshmallow pie, pecan pie and strawberry shortcake topped with ice cream. He hurried up to his bedroom, where he threw himself on the white polar-bear skin that lay stretched submissively on the floor of his bedroom. Lying on his stomach, Nick steadily ate through his plate of desserts as he listened to Benny Goodman on the radio. As usual he wished that he was old enough to go and fight with the International Brigade, in the Spanish Civil War. College guys were answering the call for action, ready to fight alongside George Orwell and Ernest Hemingway for the democratically voted Republican Left. Nick wished he found foreign politics less confusing; why were Democrats called Republicans, and Republicans called Nationalists, in Spain?

Tuesday 8 September 1936. Hollywood

Two days later, as the early morning sun streamed through her bathroom window, Betsy sank into her tub until the bubbles touched her chin. Normally she was easily able to relax in scented suds, like Claudette Colbert as Cleopatra, except Claudette had been up to her neck in *real* ass's milk: Mr De Mille never economized where it really mattered.

Outside, she heard Nick's surprised shout from the tennis court. 'Hey Tess, that was out by a million miles!'

'It wasn't!' Tess squawked. 'It was just inside the line! You're blind as a bat, that's your trouble.'

Those kids! Never-ending problems!

Since the death of her mother Betsy had felt alone, abandoned and unprotected. Despite her lifebelt of money she felt vulnerable and afraid, especially of making a wrong decision, for the possible consequences terrified her. Although they were growing up, she still cosseted all three children. She did not want them to feel responsible for their mother, as she had been. She did not see that she was making the same mistake, in a different way.

She was also terrified of losing her money in some unforeseeable way, although she knew perfectly well that her income was safe – provided she did not marry – for then she completely controlled it, and was herself not controlled by a husband. Jack had inserted that clause in the Trust which specified that if she *did* remarry and regretted it, then she could divorce and revert to her original financial position, and her divorced husband wouldn't be able to get one cent of Jack's fortune.

Betsy still missed her husband, not only for the man that he was, but also for the security that she had always felt with him; if she had wakened in the night, she put out her hand, knowing that she would feel his warm, strong sleeping body beside her. Now, if she woke with a start in the night, she felt nauseous, as if she were falling, falling, falling ... with nobody to catch her. Perhaps ... one day ... Tudor? Everybody liked Tudor, and furthermore – a big plus – he was considered the only man in Hollywood not particularly interested in money, so long as he had enough to pay his shirt bills. But until Betsy finally made up her mind about him, she had only herself to deal with her children. Nevertheless, she could ask his advice. Betsy pulled the telephone from its tubside hook on the wall ... 'Tudor, I hope I'm not disturbing you,' she trilled.

'Of course not, Betsy.' Tudor knew that she did not care a bit about disturbing him. He yawned silently, and punched his pillow into a more comfortable position. He had become leaner; his face was lined, but his hair had not gone grey (he had a little help, but so what?) and even quite young women threw themselves at the distinguished, handsome, and *unmarried* Tudor Perkins.

A month before he had regretfully decided that Betsy was obviously not interested in marrying him. Not one hint had been noticed, let alone taken. According to his code of behaviour, such a rich woman had first to make it clear that she would welcome his advances, but Betsy had never once encouraged him as a suitor. On the contrary, she made it clear at every opportunity that *nobody* could ever replace Black Jack, about whom she never stopped talking; every time she asked Tudor to help her make a decision, she sighed, 'If only Jack was still alive.' No, she treated Tudor as a close family friend, a sort of uncle whom Betsy assumed to be interested in all the minutiae of her family life.

Monday 14 September, 1936. Hollywood

It was nearly time for Tess to leave for her high school. Betsy pulled her cinnamon satin negligée closer to her body. She felt like a stupid idiot, and hoped her butler wouldn't catch her, hiding inside her own hall closet.

Betsy heard Tess slam her bedroom door, bang noisily down the stairs, yank at the elaborate medieval-type front-door latch.

Betsy jumped out from the closet, rushed forward, pulled the surprised Tess away from the door, stood with her back to it. '*Now* young lady! You and I are going to have a little talk.'

'I'll be late for school,' Tess said, nervous as a little girl caught with her finger in the honey pot.

'Since when do girls dress for school in dark glasses, headscarf and a low-cut cocktail frock? You look set for a secret rendezvous at the Chateau Marmont!'

'I'll dress as I please!' Tess was suddenly defiant. 'You want to know something, Mom? I am *never* going back to that school!'

'You're not *what*?' Betsy stared with disbelief and mounting rage.

'Mom, you look like a B movie, you talk like a B movie,

but do we need the dialogue? *I AM NOT GOING BACK TO THAT STUPID SCHOOL!*

'Stop screaming!' Betsy shouted. Two startled maids appeared from the kitchen; doors opened all the way up the house.

'Mom, I *know* you never listen, but I've told you often enough *why* I hate school! They don't teach me what I want to learn.'

'And just what's that, miss?'

'How many more times do I have to tell you, Mom? I . . . am . . . going . . . to . . . be . . . an . . . *actress*! Studs says I don't look like anyone else on the screen. I'm a *new face*, Mom. New Faces don't go to school! New Faces don't learn Latin or Domestic Science or how to find a book in the library, that ain't the road to stardom, Mom.'

'Don't say "ain't",' Betsy automatically corrected.

'Why not? The kids at school do.'

'The most expensive school in California, and they teach you to say "ain't"? Your granny would have rapped my knuckles!'

'You always forget, you're *not* my granny, and I am *definitely* not *you*! I'm not Mommy's good little girl, like Stella! Holy Cripes – I know Pop would have understood!'

'Your father would never, *ever*, *ever*, *ever* have let you be an actress. You have no *need* to be an actress, honey . . . Do you know what sort of lives those young stars really lead? They're fed on chicken soup and amphetamines to stop them feeling hungry, and those pills affect their nervous systems: they have nervous breakdowns while they're still in their teens, and their only permanent relationships are with their psychiatrists. Your daddy would turn in his urn at the very idea.'

'No! Daddy would have helped me to have a career!'

Betsy sighed, and switched to pleading. '*Please*, Tess, *please* finish high school before you go into the movies. You know how fast a girl grows up once she's in show business!'

'Rubbish!' Tess stamped her foot. 'I'm *already* grown up!'

'But I don't want you to feel...' Betsy remembered her years of constant sexual pressure, her anxiety about her looks and her consequent insecurity. Perhaps it was just as well that Tess wasn't a great beauty, for at least she'd never feel that she'd been accepted for her looks alone, and that once her chin started to blur she'd be shown the door. But Tess was *very* pretty and her personality was already well developed.

'But you don't *need* to work,' Betsy wailed again.

Again, Tess stamped her foot. 'How would *you* know what I need? *I'm* the one that knows what I need and what I want – *and* I know how to get it!' As she suddenly darted towards the kitchen quarters the fascinated maids hurriedly retreated. Over her shoulder, she called, 'OK, Mom, if you won't let me out the front door, I'll leave by the back door! But if you can bring yourself to open the goddam front door and look out, you'll see a limo. It's waiting for *me*.'

'Don't say "goddam",' Betsy whispered automatically. Disbelieving, she opened the front door. Tess turned, skipped neatly under her mother's arm, and darted towards the waiting dove-grey limousine, where a chauffeur stood respectfully by the open door. Before Betsy realized what was happening, the limo was off in a spray of gravel.

In response to Betsy's telephonic despair, Tudor firmly reminded her, 'Tess is Jack's daughter. Tess is showing guts and gumption. You'll have to give her her head for a bit, or you'll never tame her.'

'But this is her graduation year!'

'Tess will either tire of studio life or she'll make a success of it. If she tires of it, she still won't return to school. Use all your influence to help establish a movie career for Tess, before she gets into mischief by trying to do it on her own.'

There was no need for Betsy to pull strings. Tess was accepted by Planet as a student at its Charm School. As Tess was a minor, a smouldering Betsy, prodded by Tudor, signed all the necessary contract papers. After that, Tess was briskly collected at dawn every morning and taken to be groomed as an actress in the new studio at Culver City. After six months of this programme, if she passed her tests, she would be given a seven-year contract, to work in musicals.

Tess now took acting lessons, voice lessons, speech lessons and grooming lessons, at which she excelled. She had a thin but carefully trained soprano voice, just good enough for musical comedy. An extremely promising dancer, she was an exuberant, pert performer who bubbled with enthusiasm; when she tap-danced, her hips seemed no longer attached to her spine. As an actress, she projected a determined and perky optimism, winsome and sassy.

At home, Tess refused to talk about her day at the Studio. When Betsy asked questions, she snapped, 'Gee, you're such a Nosy Parker, Mom! Stop pestering me!' She was determined to keep her home life totally separate from the Studio; she never brought any new friends home, or invited any of her family – especially her interfering mom – to the Studio.

With the help of nepotism, Tess intended to stretch a little talent a long way, and her determination made her professional. She was always polite, never late, and never gave any problems: her mother and grandmother would never have recognized her at the Charm School. She shared a small dressing room with two other starlets – as the 'potentials' were described to the public. While waiting to be called for a make-up lesson or tap-dance classes the three girls smoked as if it were a profession, inhaling as on an oxygen mask, exhaling like dragons, blowing insolent smoke rings, and generally behaving like Bette Davis in something stormy.

Monday 16 November 1936. Los Angeles

Eventually, Betsy was invited by the Studio chief executive – known as 'Chief' – to visit the Charm School, and then lunch with him at the commissary table. Although Tess (correctly) suspected that this invitation was not entirely coincidental, she dared not object to it. At the Studio, she was considered a hard worker, who gave no trouble; she projected the same cute determined perky optimism, when she was (apparently) not acting; Tess wanted nobody to see the reckless, wilful side of her character.

Hollywood had recently rallied from its worst slump of the Depression and musicals were all the rage again. The Studio also specialized in extravagant and romantic operettas produced to an impressive high-gloss standard. At the very least, there should be start work for Tess, in walk-ons or bit parts, Betsy thought as she gazed to her left, at the all-white streamlined office block, and ahead where rows of buildings stood, big as aircraft hangars: the sound stages.

She walked up the steps of the office block to the chrome-plated reception hall, with its horseshoe staircase and black glass floor, on which she nearly skidded. At the desk she faced a smiling platinum-blonde receptionist, who looked as if she might break into a tap-dance at any moment.

The Charm School was on the back lot; Betsy had a long walk, for the back lot was huge, as big as a farm it seemed to her as she tottered across on her flimsy Florentine heels. She passed a village square with homes, shops and a church; a row of New York brownstones; a block of city slums; a tropical jungle with rivers and Tarzan-type waterfalls; beyond these was the noisy cottage, where the kids under contract obtained their obligatory minimal education. She was then ushered into a bungalow, set within a photogenic white picket fence: the Charm School.

In the doorway stood Tess, who greeted her mother with the brilliant winning smile that she always wore to the Studio. Politely, she showed her mother round the classrooms and rehearsal room. Betsy, dazed, then charmed by Tess's saccharine behaviour, actually said, 'Honey, I wish you could be more like this at home.'

Immediately the winsome mask dropped. Tess looked behind her, to check no one could hear, then hissed, 'Get out of here! Keep away from me!! I won't have you treat me like a child! *One more bit of snooping* and I'm leaving home! You're as bad as Granny was!'

'How dare you—' Betsy snapped indignantly, but Tess interrupted.

'I know what you're trying to do! You're trying to stop

us all growing up, so *we* stay at home and *you* have company, as if we were pet poodles. Can't you see that just makes us all want to leave you? You don't like to believe that, do you? Yes, even Stella and your darling Nick! They'll leave as fast they can, as soon as they can!'

'Keep your voice down, Tess,' Betsy whispered, hoping that the bunch of girls standing nearby in tight, white satin shorts and tap-dance shoes could not hear. 'It's just that sometimes I get lonely since I've been on my own. I find it difficult to make decisions.'

'You can't make up your mind about anything, can you, Mom? You even keep Tudor on a string! He's a nifty guy, and he won't wait for ever, you know. Can't you see that if you hang on to us, and don't hang on to Tudor, you can look forward to a lonely time in your old age?'

Thursday 17 December 1936. New York

In her dressing room, Fizz shut her eyes to powder her face. This was to be her last performance of *Flirt* in New York, so many famous faces would be in the audience tonight, invited by Noël and the producer. Outside the entrance to the theatre, Fizz had noticed the sort of crowd attracted by First Nights: drably dressed onlookers stared at the top-hatted, white-scarved men and their immaculately groomed, daintily shod, exquisitely gowned women who glittered in jewellery and moved in a miasma of Arpège; ignoring onlookers, they stepped from their limos, smiled graciously and froze for ten seconds: this was long enough for the waiting photographers, press cards stuck in hatbands, raincoats tightly belted, flashbulbs at the ready.

Fizz applied her lip brush. Her limited Broadway run

contract had specified an early release date, before Christmas; Tallulah would take over for the last few Broadway performances, and continue in the lead when the show went on the road.

Whilst Paris was elegant and London was luxurious, the only adjective for New York was glamorous, Fizz thought as she spat on her cake of mascara, rubbed the brush on it, then applied the blackened bristles to her eyelashes. As she did so, she remembered her arrival, in mid-August, to star in *The Eternal Flirt*, especially written for her by Noël Coward. New cabin trunks had been delivered from Harrods the week before she sailed; Max had accompanied her on the boat train from Waterloo to Southampton, where they were taken in a tender out to the *Queen Mary*; Fizz had found her cabin filled with flowers, champagne, telegrams, books, boxes of chocolates, invitations and a note from Captain Watts, inviting her to sit at his table. Liveried page-boys had trundled in her luggage and constantly delivered messages from other passengers already aboard, inviting her to drinks in their stateroom, or to dine with them.

After a restful voyage, press men and radio interviewers boarded the ship at quarantine when Fizz, with other celebrities, was steered towards a special little interview cabin, blue with cigarette smoke and crammed with journalists juggling drinks and notebooks.

From the upper deck she watched the Statue of Liberty slowly advance, and gazed at the famous view of New York's skyscraper skyline. There was increasing chaos as they neared the island of Manhattan; ferryboats hooted and sturdy tugs nuzzled and shoved the ship alongside the dock, where a crowd waited at the gangway to greet the arrivals.

To her astonishment, among the people hopping up and down at the bottom of the gangway, waving, was Tudor! Fizz had recognized him immediately, although he was thinner and leaner; as usual, he looked like one of the drawings that advertised men's clothing in the *New Yorker*. Fizz threw her arms around him. 'Darling! What are *you* doing here?'

'I was to visit in September, then I read in *Variety* that you were coming over, so I thought I'd give you a surprise. I hoped I might steer you round New York, when you weren't rehearsing.'

As their limousine moved through the crowded, noisy streets, Fizz peered out at New York: the elevated railway, perched on elaborate iron-pillared supports, clanked up the middle of Third Avenue; smarter avenues, lined with shops, disappeared towards distant Central Park; under dark-green or navy canopies that stretched across the sidewalk smartly uniformed attendants guarded the entrances to apartment blocks, hotels and restaurants. Leading off the big avenues Fizz glimpsed smaller roads, lined by brownstone houses with railings and wide steps that led up to front doors poised above the sidewalks, which were covered by a restless surge of people, black, white and all shades between; the working girls who hurried by had attempted, with the help of make-up and peroxide, to look as much as possible like their idols, Garbo, Dietrich or Crawford.

Fizz was booked in at the St Regis Hotel, conveniently close to the Belasco Theater; waiting by her bedside were books by Damon Runyon and Dorothy Parker, chosen by Tudor because they imparted the wit, speed and chutzpah of New York. Flowers welcomed her from every flat surface; her suite was a modern dream of luxury, with air-conditioning that made it hard to leave the hotel and step into the sultry city heat of August.

On her first evening, Tudor took Fizz for dinner to El Morocco, where they sat on zebra-striped banquettes and drank lethal cocktails in triangular glasses on stems. Thirteen years of Prohibition had ended three years earlier so alcohol was lawfully consumed in the restaurants and nightclubs that had replaced the speakeasies. Tudor ordered a delicious meal that started with long drinks of cranberry juice, crammed with ice; next came refreshing chilled pink watermelon, squeezed with lime juice, followed by crab salad served on a bed of crushed ice; they finished with passion fruit ice cream.

'Now I know what it's like to feel frigid,' Fizz murmured.

* * *

On the following morning Fizz reported to the rehearsal hall, a small studio on West 57th Street, and the hard preparation work began. In the evening, if she was not too tired, the charming and attentive Tudor often took her out on the town; a glamorous pair, both were frequently asked for their autographs by people who had no idea to whom they were offering their autograph albums.

During the three weeks of rehearsal, Fizz hardly ever felt tired. Tudor said that the air was exhilarating, like champagne, and that no New Yorker would dream of admitting to going to bed early with a good book, for fear of being considered out of the swing. Together they took in a Fred and Ginger movie; they spent the following evening watching *Idiot's Delight*; afterwards, they visited the Lunts in their dressing room, where Lynn and Alfred charmed their visitors while exchanging ideas on the performance, as they changed costumes. Watching the companionship of the Lunts, Fizz realized that she was becoming similarly close to Tudor. Sadly she wished that she and Max still had such a trusting relationship.

One morning when Fizz was not needed at rehearsals Tudor took her to the airy new Whitney Museum of American Art, an ideal setting for modern pictures. Afterwards they met Prince Serge Obolensky and the beautiful Mona Harrison Williams, at a luncheon to which you bought a ticket because the party was held on behalf of the unemployed. Fizz, who was being paid £500 a week with a twelve-weeks-guarantee contract, felt guilty.

* * *

By the time *The Eternal Flirt* tried out in Philadelphia Fizz felt she deserved every penny of her salary.

The First Night audience laughed at all the right places in the first act; as the curtain fell the producer hurried to a private bar to meet the press, for their notices needed to be phoned in to their newspapers before the play finished, in order to be printed in the last edition, so that the reviews appeared on the morning after the opening.

After a no-big-problems second act (that nevertheless still needed a bit of work), and a triumphant third act, the audience applauded enthusiastically. Smiling as she bowed, the sweating, trembling, exhausted Fizz had finally been able to relax. After the final curtain came euphoric backstage congratulations and everyone's almost visible relief. Fizz had then been called to the producer's hotel suite, where a post-mortem was to be held. In a haze of grey cigarette smoke the telephone rang and champagne corks popped non-stop: the atmosphere was one of delirious happiness.

They opened to good reviews in Philadelphia and similar ones in Boston, before moving to Broadway, where Brooks Atkinson of the *New York Times* cheerfully approved it . . . 'Fizzing with fun!' Before the end of that day, the show had been booked solid for a successful autumn run.

Fizz was delighted by this success. After the flop of *Pirate* she had feared she was not as attuned to American audiences as to British. Now that *Flirt* was a smash she felt she had redeemed her earlier failure.

Tudor flew back to New York for Fizz's last week. He arrived looking haggard and pale after the nineteen-hour trip by air, but he brightened considerably after a couple of triangular glasses in El Morocco.

'Shall you be sorry to leave?' Tudor asked Fizz.

'Of course, darling.' But Fizz had quickly found that behind its glittering façade, New York was an unfeeling and unforgiving place. She was homesick for shabby old London, and for Max, also as familiar as a comfortable pair of bedroom slippers.

'Max'll be pleased to have you back.'

'I hope so,' Fizz joked, as yet again she wondered what was happening in her absence. Her mother had reluctantly promised to keep an eye on Max, via the grapevine, but Fizz didn't feel that you could rely on a mother to transmit bad news with speed. Yet again, she wondered if Max was really as happy with her as he appeared to be. There had been a couple of odd moments on the telephone . . . nothing she could put her finger on, just a hurried glibness. Outwardly, the two of them seemed such a well-suited couple, but she felt in her heart they were growing apart. She did not know whether Max had abandoned his flirtations or whether he was merely more careful: she suspected the latter. Perhaps it was because her husband was deceiving her – and he knew it, even if she didn't – that the closeness and trust that had once been between them was vanishing like mist in early morning sunlight.

Fizz enjoyed that week even more than the rest of her triumphant sojourn in New York. A round of farewell lunches was given for her, and on her last free afternoon Tudor took her to a matinée performance of Clare Boothe Luce's *The Women*. Tudor was the perfect escort and the perfect friend, who clearly admired, appreciated and respected Fizz. She would miss him, Fizz thought, as she heard a knock on her dressing-room door, and for the last time an adenoidal adolescent voice chirped, 'Overture and beginners, Miss Fane.'

* * *

Fizz made the most of the last applause she would hear from a New York audience. 'Even more curtain calls than we had on the First Night!' she murmured to Noël as they bowed.

She returned to a dressing room filled as full of flowers as a funeral parlour; a baby's zinc bath was crammed with ice, from which poked dark-green necks of champagne bottles, looking like strange Antarctic creatures, struggling to emerge.

Friday 18 December 1936

New Yorkers made a great fuss of departing guests. It might take the entire voyage to recover from their last goodbye party, Fizz thought, as, swathed in Tudor's chinchilla Christmas gift (he must be doing well), she leaned over the deck rail and waved her new friends out of sight. She pulled back, sighing with happiness. It certainly was nicer to leave on the crest of success, rather than after a flopperoo. She looked up and picked out what seemed to be the brightest star in the dark sky . . . *that* must be the Wishing Star. 'Please no more surprises like last time,' Fizz murmured, then hurried from the chilly deck to her snug stateroom.

As she closed the heavy door behind her she stared at a big gilded basket of bright-yellow chrysanthemums, which had been placed in front of her other pretty flowers. Why would anyone send chrysanthemums? Cemetery flowers. The chrysanthemums had a strong smell, fusty and mournful. Fizz looked at the card attached to the basket; a typed message, unsigned, read, 'When the cat's away, the rat will play . . .'

'That's a hell of way to say "Bon Voyage",' muttered Fizz, as she rang the bell. When the steward arrived, she asked him to get rid of the vulgar basket. She also asked him who had sent the evil-smelling chrysanthemums.

The steward shrugged. 'Madam, if it don't say on the card then I can't tell you. When we leave New York, we get more flowers than a state funeral.' He backed out, hidden behind the huge basket of flowers.

Fizz looked again at the card. (Why had she kept it?) The rat reference was obviously to Max. She felt apprehension root.

Some jealous rival had sent this card. Jessie had warned her never, never to pay any attention to anonymous notes: they were deliberately written to cause trouble.

The trouble was, they did.

Damn it, she was going to have a good time on the

Queen – and she deserved it! She tore up the card and threw it away.

She retrieved the pieces.

By the time the *Queen Mary* docked in Southampton, Fizz had been telling herself for four days that she wasn't going to say *one word* to Max about those damned chrysanthemums.

Wednesday 23 December 1936

As soon as Max closed the yellow front door of the house in Colville Place, Fizz blurted out, 'I hear you've been misbehaving.' She had meant to say it lightly in an amused voice (in fact, she had meant not to say it at all), but her words came out as harsh accusation.

'Ain't misbehaving,' Max hummed, hugging her.

Fizz was torn between wanting his love and wanting to find out what had been going on while she had been away. Of course she had expected Max to have flirtations (he always did) but that big basket of chrysanthemums must have meant something.

She twisted away. 'Who've you been seeing? You might as well tell me now, because everyone else will, before lunch tomorrow.'

'Fizz,' said Max, in his injured voice. She could tell that he was not hurt, and that he did not want to hurt her, but she could also tell that there was certainly something for her to be hurt about. 'You're so suspicious, Fizz. I've only been seeing the usual crowd.'

As she still looked disbelieving, he added casually, 'You go away and leave me for months at a time. You knew very well I couldn't leave the Minerva to pop over to New York for a few days, when I had a play to put on and then a panto. What do you expect me to do? Sit at home and knit?'

'I've as much right as you have to use my talents! I've as much right as you have to a career! And if that means we can't always be in the exact geographical spot that you wish, Max, then that's a pity, but it's no excuse for bad behaviour.'

'*You* are the one who is behaving badly, with no reason.'

'You mean, not a shred of evidence!'

'You see? As soon as you get home, you start on me! Have *I* complained that you left me? No!'

Fizz snapped, 'You wouldn't expect *me* to complain if *your* career meant that you had to go to the States! Kindly remember those years when you were out of work, and my career paid your bills!'

'Typical of a woman to shove *that* in my face! Don't I remember something about "for better, for worse"?'

'It should be "for worse and for worse". My experience of the give-and-take of marriage is that the woman gives and the man takes!'

'Typical of you to twist my words out of shape!'

'I'll twist something else out of shape, if you're not straight with me! *Who have you been seeing?*'

Max looked her straight in the eyes and said, 'Honestly, there has been *nobody* else, darling. I've been longing for you to return.'

He knew that the first rule of adultery is learn to look your wife in the eyes ... and lie.

* * *

Fizz knew before evening.

When Max appeared with half a gallon of Schiaparelli perfume in a big, witty bottle shaped like a dressmaker's dummy, Fizz said icily, 'The phone hasn't stopped ringing. I hear it's Gertie.'

'Oh, God, you're so possessive! And so suspicious! I've seen Gertie a couple of times ... maybe three ... just lunches ... maybe one dinner. It's nothing.'

'What do you mean, *it's nothing*?' Fizz glared. 'What is *it*?'

Max gave a would-be sophisticated laugh. 'You know perfectly well that Gertie doesn't count.'

'By now, Gertie's *lost* count.'

Max shouted with deflective fury, 'Who do you think made sure you heard about it, darling? Have you wondered why? No, as I suspected, you simply assumed the obvious. So let me give you a script précis: Gertie resents Noël writing a play for Fizz. Noël's play for Fizz is huge success. Gertie is jealous. Gertie winks at Max, Gertie flirts with Max. Gertie stirs up gossip. Gertie then sends bouquet with anonymous mischievous message to Fizz. Fizz, stuck on *Queen Mary* for four days, starts brooding, gets madder and madder. Fizz has major row with Max upon landing. Fizz ends up miserable. Darling, you're reacting just as Gertie planned! She'll be *so* pleased!'

'You've forgotten something, darling. After Gertie flirts with Max, Gertie *fucks* Max!'

'So what?' Max snapped, finally losing his temper.

Fizz wailed, 'Max, why do we have this problem every time I go away?'

'You've just answered your own question,' Max

snapped. 'Gertie was *there*. What's the use of a wife who's away half the time, and too tired the rest of the time?'

'How would *you* feel if I had an affair with . . . Michael Redgrave?' Fizz angrily demanded.

Max laughed. 'Darling, I'd bet against it.'

Fizz wailed again, 'But why do you always want me to find out? – I know you do, I can sense it.'

'Don't be ridiculous!' Max truly loved Fizz, but since he was fourteen he had put a high value on being a man who was attracted to – and attractive to – women. Plus, he liked the excitement of the chase, the thrill of romance and secrecy. And although he would never admit it, he did like Fizz to find out: he enjoyed the explosive, dramatic scenes that followed, and the equally explosive and passionate reconciliations.

Tuesday 29 December 1936. The Ivy Restaurant, London

'Darling, you were wonderful.' In the crowded Ivy restaurant, full of famous theatre faces, Noël raised his glass of champagne to Fizz. 'And now we must think of what to do next . . . Order, perhaps,' he teased for menus as large as playbills were whisked before them. 'You *must* try the hot bull-shot . . . be careful how you pronounce it to the waiter, my darling Fizz . . . it's consommé with *more* than a dash of vodka – one of young Margot's favourites . . . Oh, look, she's over there!' He waved.

Obediently, everyone smiled and waved back, except for the man at whom Noël waved; he left his companion, a pretty woman in a black velvet hat, and headed towards Noël's table, which no one else had dared approach.

Over the happy buzz of gossip, Noël waved towards

the newcomer and asked Fizz, 'Of course you two know each other?'

'Of course,' Fizz smiled.

'Not well enough, perhaps?' The man bowed.

Thoughtfully, Fizz looked at him. Larry's profile really belonged on some ancient Greek coin ... Like the girls in the gods, Fizz felt weak at the knees as she stared up at him and thought, I wonder if ...

Noël turned; one lifted eyebrow brought three waiters running. Larry looked down at Fizz with slightly closed, come-to-bed eyes beneath what she could only describe as winged eyebrows; he took her hand, turned it over, swiftly kissed the palm, then seemed to vanish.

In the middle of his crème brûlée, Noël was summoned to solve a rehearsal problem.

'Don't worry about me, darling.' Fizz blew him a kiss. 'The doorman can call a taxi.'

Two minutes later she glanced furtively towards Larry's table. He and the pretty woman had vanished, and waiters were whisking away the tablecloth, which meant that she was *not* upstairs, powdering her nose.

* * *

Hesitating in the entrance of the Ivy before stepping out into the rain, Fizz heard (as so often when she hesitated) the small voice in the back of her head. 'Here's your chance. Don't muff it. Don't think for one minute that he happened to be *accidentally* driving past the door as you walked out of the Ivy. He's been parked up the road, watching and waiting for you. He tipped the doorman, and that's probably why, mysteriously, the doorman can't procure a taxi. If you really want to give Max a taste of his own medicine, then administer the mixture in the very best teaspoon: the finest British actor of his day – except, maybe, Johnnie Gielgud – but Max would never believe you lured *him* into bed.'

Fizz looked speculatively down as black-fringed dark eyes looked soulfully up into hers. 'I'll take you anywhere you want,' Larry offered, pushing open the door of the silver sports car.

'Thank you,' Fizz said demurely, bending down to corkscrew into the silver car, 'I know exactly where I want to go.' She directed him to Colville Place.

* * *

Two hours later, a dazed Fizz respectfully had to admit to herself that Larry certainly knew his geography. She also thanked heavens that Mrs Pomfret didn't clean in the afternoon.

Wednesday 30 December 1936

Max did not notice the faint, lingering scent of lime eau de Cologne in their bedroom. But on the following morning, he noticed that his razor had been used, and that the blade had not been replaced with a fresh one: he *always* changed the blade after using it.

He crashed into the bedroom. 'Who's been using my razor?'

Sleepily, Fizz turned to face him. Slowly she propped her left elbow on the pillow, fitted her jaw into the palm of her left hand, then yawned. 'Well it wouldn't be Mother Bear, would it?'

Max stamped forward and stood threateningly over her.

'You've got your own bloody little razor for your legs. *Who's been using my razor?*'

Fizz wondered, What's the big difference between using another man's bed, using another man's wife, and using another man's razor? How come they have this intimate relationship with their razors? 'I forget which one it was,' Fizz yawned again. 'Was it the cat burglar who gave me that kiss, I saw that look in his eye . . . Or was it the postman, the milkman, or the upstairs maid . . . ?'

Max hurled his razor at the window which, luckily, was open. The shining razor soared in a graceful arc, out of Max's life and into that of somebody else: there was an angry shout from the street below.

Still naked, Max leaped towards the dressing table, upon which lay Fizz's scarlet suede handbag. With one mighty twist, he undid the catch, hurled the contents on the floor and pounced on her navy blue Smythson's diary.

'I use a code for lovers,' Fizz offered, 'you'll never guess it. Look for the circles around the dates.'

'Those are your bloody periods.'

'I love your choice of adjective. But count how many circles there are in one month . . .'

Max turned dusky pink, but said nothing as he rustled through the diary until he reached the entry for the previous day.

'Try the address section at the back, they're all listed under X for kisses,' Fizz helpfully explained, 'and when that page was full, I switched to V for vice.'

'Ha! You had lunch with Noël at the Ivy . . . and there's no entry for the afternoon!'

'Nevertheless, I played a matinée. And gave a *very* good performance, if I say so myself.'

Max flipped a glance at his wristwatch. Eleven o'clock ... he grabbed the telephone as if he loathed it, and dialled as if he were stabbing it, but when he spoke, it was with a suave and charming voice. 'Luigi ... helloooo ... I wonder whether you could *possibly* find me a table for two for lunch? ... Couldn't you *possibly* squeeze us in somewhere?'

Max lowered his voice. 'But, you see, today, is a *very* special day for my wife and me ... Terrific! Thank you so much, Luigi, we'll see you around oneish ... Might I offer you a couple of complimentary tickets for next week? ... Whichever evening you care to choose, Luigi ... Fizz will be in the lead ... Yes, I know she was in yesterday, she adores the Ivy, she says it was *very* glamorous, *packed* with celebrities ... Yes, yes, I know, she was having lunch with him ... Miss Matthews as well, eh? ... and Mr Mason ... and ...' he flashed a look at Fizz with a triumphant glitter in his eye, 'I haven't seen Larry for ages ... Cheerio, see you soon.'

He turned and flung the heavy Bakelite telephone at Fizz's head.

She ducked, then leaned over to the floor and picked up the phone, the blanket sliding from her naked rump.

Back in bed, she pulled the blankets up and glared at Max. 'Thank you for passing the phone, darling. I'm now going to call a journalist – the one who wrote I was so lucky not to have a violent husband.'

'Larry, of all people! That vain, arrogant . . .'

'Handsome, sensual, successful . . .'

'*Have* you, you bitch?'

Fizz smirked.

Max stood over Fizz, shook her shoulders and snarled, 'And how was it?'

Fizz gave a reminiscent smile. 'I think it was good for him too.'

'You're not very selective, my darling.'

'But I *am* appreciative, my darling. And so was he.'

'You double-crossing slut!'

'What *is* the male equivalent of the slut? I've often wondered.'

'How dare you do this to *me*!' Max shouted.

'What you mean, darling, is how dare I do it with a marvellous actor ... Don't you wish you could act like Larry? Such a wonderful performer, such stamina for the heavy parts.'

His anger totally out of control, Max yanked up his arm, and made a threatening fist. Just in time, he realized that if he hit Fizz's purring face, then he might seriously hurt her. He remembered what his father had told him when he started school, 'When you feel like smashing someone's jaw, turn your back on trouble and get away as fast as possible. Don't walk – run.'

Breathing heavily, Max stamped to the bedroom door, yanked it open, remembered that he was naked, stood still, remembered he had to cancel that table at the Ivy.

'You'd better use the hall telephone to cancel our special lunch,' Fizz suggested, 'this one doesn't appear to be working.'

Max could hear someone treading slowly and heavily up the stairs: it might be Mrs Pomfret or it might be Jessie.

He ran to the bathroom, angrily pulled on a white towelling dressing gown and stalked out of the door. Immediately, he bumped into Mrs Pomfret, and knocked over madam's breakfast tray.

Max pushed past the astonished Mrs Pomfret and hurled himself downstairs towards the hall telephone. Fizz then heard a yell, a crash and an angry stream of foul language. Max had slipped on her boiled egg.

* * *

'Fizz? First the good news, it's Noël ... Well, even your smoky contralto might sound a trifle *castrato* if you'd just observed your hunk of a husband leaping on Larry ... Do let me *finish*, darling! ... I'm at my club, it's like being an alcoholic in a brewery ... No, I was *lunching* with Larry, when we were amazed to see Max *leaping* ahead up that sumptuous stairway. Then, to my surprise, Larry started ... well not exactly running, but walking very fast towards the Gents. I thought he'd been taken short ...

'No, Fizz, he didn't make it. Before he got to the door, Max yanked him back by the collar and shook him like a terrier shaking a rat ... or a rat shaking a terrier, depends which side you're on ... Before I could *scrrrrream* for help, Max and Larry were rolling around on the carpet – banging into other Members, at *heavy* risk to their own, with Max yelling gynaecological obscenities ...

'No, Fizz, of *course* I didn't, a flock of club servants tried to pull Max off. Max hit a couple of them: one tumbled backwards down the stairs; the other suddenly embraced a marble bust of Sarah Siddons, rather hard ... Eventually a couple of menials held Max down. No, Larry had somehow managed to protect the famous profile ... that nose is probably insured at Lloyd's for *slightly* more than Gainsborough's *Blue Boy* ... Larry had *just* scrambled to his feet – when Max broke loose and went for him again ... Larry was able to dodge rather well – he's more of a fencer than a boxer after all ...

'No, *of course* Larry didn't try to hit back. He just fled, very sensibly: after all he has a matinée this afternoon ...

show must go on and all that ... The reason I felt *you* should know, darling, is because one *cannot* have such vulgar histrionics in one's club: it disturbs old gentlemen in the library, who have been snoozing for thirty years behind *The Times* ...

'... So that you can *stop* him, darling, why else? Well, after all, he *is* your husband ... Not for long? ... *You've definitely decided?* ... Darling I hope you're using Withers, they squeezed a wonderful settlement out of Hugh for Brenda ...'

* * *

From then on, at the back of Fizz's mind, ran a sort of adult nursery rhyme, an updated version of 'Ring Around the Roses'. Gertie avenges herself on Fizz by having an affair with Max; Fizz avenges herself on Max by having an affair with Larry; Max avenges himself on Larry ... and Fizz files for divorce. Was Fizz allowing herself to be sucked into a stupidly destructive spiral of revenge?

Friday 29 January 1937

No matter how hard the strong-minded Fizz tried to deny it to herself, to her fury, her own heartstrings could be casually tugged by Max whenever he felt it was the correct time.

After a month, Max tugged.

They met, at his suggestion, to discuss whether it was possible to circumvent the lawyers and work out the Fane divorce between themselves (a practice that generally leads to more violent rows and larger lawyers' bills).

Fizz looked sadly across the table of the cheaply

cheerful Italian restaurant: each hoped that the other might perhaps be a little better behaved and not throw things, in public. Bianchi's was public, without being too public.

'What's happened to us, Max?' Fizz whispered, miserably. 'We used to be in love. Now we seem to be in hate.' She did not understand how she could still be attracted and emotionally bound to her mate, but simultaneously feel hostility, hatred and a violent wish to be avenged.

As if reading her thoughts, Max warned, 'Hatred and revenge lead to violence and war.'

'Are we in hate and at war?'

Solemnly, Max pulled out his white handkerchief and waved it. 'I've come to discuss a truce. I'll do anything you want. Just give me one more chance, if you'll forgive the clichés.'

This was what Fizz had expected, and she had thought about it a great deal.

She coldly replied, 'There really is no point in us going through this little scene, over and over again, is there? So I don't want any more excuses. An explanation is not an excuse, as you've so often told me. I don't want to hear, "I was drunk", or "You were away".'

Under the table, Max leaned forward; theatrically furtive, he groped for her knee. 'I love going through some little scenes with you, over and over again.'

'Stop,' gasped Fizz, determined not to capitulate. Or at any rate, not that easily.

Good Friday, 26 March 1937

On Fizz's birthday, which fell that year on Good Friday, they left at six in the morning because Max thought traffic might block the road later. He collected Fizz from Colville Place and in the little red open MG they sped out of London. After an hour, they passed through the small Berkshire village of Kintbury. A few miles beyond it, they reached forest land. They drove through a green tunnel of rustling leaves, until Max turned off the road, to an overgrown rutted track, along which they bumped for a further ten minutes.

The trees suddenly ended. In the clearing ahead of them stood a white-and-black-timbered thatched Tudor cottage, subsiding slightly to the left. Diamond-shaped window panes reflected the early morning sunlight; smoke climbed from a twisted chimney.

'Let me guess,' said Fizz, 'we're visiting Hansel and Gretel?'

'It's supposed to be one of Henry the Eighth's hunting lodges,' Max said, clearly very pleased with himself, as he handed Fizz a key. 'But now it's yours, darling. And it looks as if the cleaner is in, so coffee should be ready for us.'

The scarred heavy oak door opened to a central dining hall, with French windows on the far side: outside, Fizz could see white roses. She ran across the small, empty room to the window and saw that beyond the white roses was a stone-paved terrace, bordered by boxy yew hedges; beyond it, an old herringbone brick path, lined by lavender bushes, divided the lawn, at the end of which fruit trees sloped down to a wide stream, edged by willows on the opposite bank.

Fizz turned on her heels and flung her arms around Max. Together they explored the rest of the miniature house. On one side of the hall was a sitting room, on the other was the kitchen; upstairs were two small bedrooms and one bathroom.

'It's our own hideaway house,' Max said in a muffled voice, as Fizz hugged him again.

'Only room for the two us?' she asked hopefully.

'I promise.'

Chapter Nineteen

Two years later, Betsy took her annual trip to Europe earlier than usual, for she also planned to take Stella, who was to spend the year at finishing school, in Paris.

'Do I *have* to go, Mom?' Stella begged.

Betsy looked exasperated. 'You'd think I was forcing you to go to a Bolshevik prison camp in Siberia! How many more times do we need to go through this? Plenty of girls would *love* to spend a year at finishing school in Paris! Now take my hatboxes and let's have no more of this nonsense, or we'll be late for the plane.' Her butler bowed her out of her front door, and her chauffeur bowed her into her new maroon Lincoln Brougham.

For the last time, Stella hugged Nick. He yanked off his gold bifocals (how Betsy wished he need not wear them) and, unashamedly tearful, gave Stella one last hug. Although Nick was almost sixteen, four years younger than Stella, they had the same quiet temperament, but whereas Stella was shy and immature for her age, Nick was old for his and outwardly sophisticated, having been dragged as an escort by his mother to various grown-up functions, when no more suitable beau was available.

Stella and Nick also shared the same interests; they liked walking and swimming in the ocean; Stella showed

Nick her poetry and he showed his writing to her. Their mother complained, 'You're never around when I need you: Stella always has her nose stuck in a book, and Nick locks himself in his bathroom for hours on end, scribbling. It's just as well he told me, because I was about to dose him with castor oil.' She looked pleadingly at Stella. 'Why can't you be like other girls and go off dancing or to swimming parties or beach parties? Why do you two *both* like to hide yourselves away?'

'Mom, I like reading, and I don't like constantly moving around in a giggling gaggle of girls who always have one eye on the boys, who always have one eye on them. And Nick's the same. There's nothing *wrong* with us.' Here Stella had an inspiration and added, 'We're both creative, I guess!'

Creative. That sounded better than 'bookworm' and 'scribbler' to Betsy. Creative, eh?

Stella, who felt decidedly uncomfortable with other boys, felt fine with Nick; he was not threatening and she did not feel he was assessing her on points: Nick wasn't deciding she was too tall or too big, and not pretty enough. Stella had straight black hair and handsome, pronounced features, rather than waving golden hair, cute, retroussé nose and the giggling air of awe that was essential if you were to be chosen as cheerleader, swamped with invitations to the Prom, asked to swap pins, or any other of the strange bobby-soxer, girl-grading and courtship rituals.

Betsy was determined that finishing school in Paris would change *all that*! She envisaged Stella in a year's time: neat and sleek, mysteriously shrunken by six inches in all directions, wearing some witty hat from Schiaparelli, the centre of a laughing circle of eager, eligible Ivy

League swains. She was expecting a lot from Paris, but then she was paying a lot for Paris.

'Hurry *up*, Stella!'

Stella hurried towards her mother, already sitting primly in the limousine, her maroon crocodile jewel box on her knees.

The O'Briens caught the night plane to Chicago because Betsy had to sign some business papers for one of Black Jack's former associates. They then caught the Twentieth Century train to New York. Betsy loved walking across the red carpet rolled over the platform; she loved sinking into one of the deep armchairs in the club car and being attended by obsequious coloured porters in white coats; she loved the meals, perfectly served and always delicious; she loved the commodious three-quarter-width beds with fluffy down pillows, the iced water on tap, the private toilet.

She had considered flying coast to coast, but thought she might find the long trip too exhausting. Stella had asked if they could fly across the Atlantic on the new Pan-American Airways Clipper, which had beds, served five-course meals, and was just as comfortable as a train, but Betsy was frightened of all that ocean down there, and those transatlantic flights had only just started. Betsy preferred to cross the Atlantic in a super-de-luxe ocean liner, which gave her an excuse to wear plenty of frivolous, delicious clothes: she had booked one of the best suites in the *Normandie* and looked forward to four days of cosseted opulence, in dining rooms, cocktail bars, massage rooms, steam bath, gymnasium and swimming pool, followed by a trip to the hairdresser; the elegant liner was a floating hotel that only lacked a tennis court.

The trip, although cold on deck, was very comfortable. Betsy's Deauville suite of *bois de rose* and gilded splendour consisted of two big bedrooms, each with a marble bathroom; an oval salon with Aubusson tapestries hanging against the walls; a circular dining room and a private sun deck. Portholes? Not on your life! The suite had floor-to-ceiling French windows.

From Cherbourg, mother and daughter caught the train to Paris, where two automobiles waited to take them to the Ritz: one car was for their luggage. Betsy had two days before she was due to deliver Stella to Mme Boué's Finishing School for Young Ladies, a time during which she intended to shop around the clock – for one thing, they had all Stella's clothes to buy. Betsy would wait until Stella was at school before visiting the couturiers, to order outfits for herself.

Betsy sighed happily as she walked from the Place Vendôme into the Ritz; she never did this without remembering those gruesome digs of her youth: the smell of boiled fish or cabbage that hung around the hall; the sweet, dusty bedroom smell, with sometimes the added unmistakable odour of mice . . .

Betsy shuddered, then sniffed the erotic odour of Parisian luxury: expensive fragrances mingled with the fusty, slightly rusty smell of French central heating. As she listened to the gentle hum of international chatter she gazed contentedly at the elegant people sitting in the Ritz foyer, the uniformed page-boys scurrying past with umbrellas, the men bending to kiss the hand of some exquisitely *maquillée*, *coiffée*, *parfumée* and *habillée* lady, as well turned out as one of the Aga Khan's horses, and often accessorized by a little yapping poodle, dachshund, or the sort of fluffy dog that looked as if it unzipped to hide pyjamas.

Betsy loved the chi-chi atmosphere, the *flan-flan*, the gossip; the unmistakably rich East Coast Americans; the unmistakable haughty air of the British aristocracy. She confined her activities to the small area formed by the Ritz at the Place Vendôme and the Palais Royal: the area where glamorous women glided along beautiful streets with suitably elegant male escorts, chose jewelled collars for the fluffy dogs, wonderful diamond folderols, sequinned gowns, outsize bottles of amber perfume and glamorous fox furs. Betsy rarely strayed far from the Ritz, except perhaps to visit the jewellers and Mlle Chanel in the Place Vendôme, or on a longer excursion to other major couture houses or the Rue du Faubourg-St-Honoré, where she purchased quantities of fragile underwear, painstakingly embroidered by peasants in Madeira, until their eyesight failed.

On the first evening of her stay, Betsy dressed carefully in a bias-cut eau-de-Nil satin frock with which she wore her emeralds, for she had arranged to meet Maisie, the stick insect from Jolly Joe's troupe, who often joined her for a trip to Paris, when their conversation always started complacently with 'Who would have imagined that *us* two would be the ones to make it big-time . . .' Mimi was never mentioned.

As she entered Betsy's drawing room, Maisie looked extremely elegant (it was so unfair that some people were naturally skinny) in a little black frock that simply shrieked Vionnet, with a small dead animal draped over one shoulder, fake glass eyes staring from its own eye sockets, and a ridiculous little hat with black veiling cocked over one eye; Maisie now had a skin like an overripe peach: dusty crimson and rather hairy.

She lifted her scrap of black net to beam at Betsy. 'Betsy! Fancy *us* being *here*! Don'cha wish Jolly Joe could see us now?' After their embraces – a rite performed without actually touching each other's carefully arranged face – Betsy politely said, 'I was sorry to hear about Gus.'

Maisie's face immediately fell. 'Two months ago, ducky, and I still miss him so bad. Can't believe he's dead. Feel lost without me old darling. Don't like going anywhere by meself, so I've really been looking forward to this trip.'

Betsy nodded, for she too felt nervous and vulnerable when obliged to enter a public place alone, as if that immediately told every male in sight that she was easy prey; she felt all the women looked at her with pity: alone, unprotected . . . unable to get a man.

Maisie accepted a glass of champagne. 'Poor Gus was a diabetic with classic symptoms, but the bloody doctor who'd always looked after him never noticed the brain tumour for a whole year. After Gus died, the specialist I'd paid thousands of pounds said' – Maisie mimicked a haughty toff voice – ' "I categorically refuse to accept responsibility. This was an act of God." '

Maisie held out her glass for more bubbly then continued sorrowfully, 'But the second specialist – the one who diagnosed that tumour – looked me *straight in the eye*, and said, "It should not have happened, madam, and I hope I have learnt by this mistake." '

'Fat lot of help that was!' Betsy sympathized.

Maisie shook her head. 'No, I was able to forgive him *immediately*. Because he was straight with me, and I could see he meant it. One Sawbones had the guts to admit his mistake, the other didn't. Soon as I forgave the second specialist, all the rage I felt for him *immediately* left my heart.'

'But didn't you complain to some doctors' organization?'

'No fear! *Their* first duty is to protect doctors, ducky.'

Betsy wondered what Jack would have advised Maisie to do. Briskly she decided aloud, 'You should have sued 'em both, Maisie.'

'That wouldn't have brought my Gustav back to me, would it? I did visit a medical negligence lawyer. He told me nearly all his clients who sue really only want what he called "acknowledgement of the responsibility", wiv an apology. "A person cannot *stand* a cover up," he told me. "You want acknowledgement of the truth, and regret duly expressed."'

Maisie lifted her veil and dabbed at her eyes with a tiny scrap of handkerchief. 'Never mind, ducky. I looked after Gus to the end. He had everything possible, and lots of love. There are worse ways of dying, you got to admit ... Did you read Florence Lawrence, that Biograph Girl, committed suicide last year? After that studio fire, she was never able to work again ... Oh, Lord, now I've put me foot in it, haven't I, ducky.'

As Betsy's face reddened, once again she experienced the old sinking feeling of guilt and unease.

* * *

Betsy presented Stella with a pretty little diamond wristwatch before delivering her to Mme Boué's Finishing School for Young Ladies.

Mme Boué was a typical Frenchwoman, bird-boned and small, with carefully tinted black hair around a pale, lined face. She was not smartly dressed, for that would not be appropriate, but she had good clothes, beautiful manners and a kindly disposition. She 'received' between twenty and twenty-five girls a year in her large airy apartment, in a pale-grey *belle époque* block. The rooms were elegantly furnished, with nineteenth-century copies of eighteenth-century French furniture; upholstered in pale-grey satin, and with legs bowed like dachshunds, low-slung gilded armchairs awaited corseted behinds.

Betsy had been told that unlike the gyp-joint finishing schools in Switzerland, where girls learnt to ski and apply make-up but little else, Mme Boué's Finishing School provided far more: her girls were given a frivolous, exciting time and yet when they left they were all reasonably well educated in French history, literature, art and music, and knew exactly how to comport themselves in good society.

After studying during the morning, the girls spent their afternoons in outings to museums, dancing classes and little bridge parties, after which English-speaking girls could never remember the English for *trefle*.

All pupils – or guests, as Mme Boué preferred to call them – were expected to read French newspapers daily – *Le Figaro*, *Le Figaro Littéraire*, *France-Soir* – and then discuss what they had read, at meals – in French. Stella found that she was not permitted to remain silent: Mme Boué always sat newcomers next to her.

At the evening meal, Mme Boué was always seated in the middle of the table, with the most important guest opposite her. Stella quickly learnt French table manners to eat meals that took a long time for one parlourmaid to serve; by the time everyone started eating their invariably delicious food, it was also invariably cold.

After dinner, there was often an etiquette lecture. Stella

had never imagined lessons on how to dress! Mme Boué taught restraint in all things. To overdress was vulgar. If in doubt about what to wear, always ask your hostess what *she* will be wearing. When you had dressed, and were ready to depart, you regarded yourself in the mirror – and *removed* some adornment; to wear too much jewellery was *très vulgaire*, and it was *très, très vulgaire* to wear a diamond necklace or tiara before evening. Stella blushed, for this was clearly not realized by her mother.

Girls also learned to be careful. Stella learned that this did not mean what it did back in Hollywood. Mme Boué meant that her girls were always to look up some newly introduced acquaintance in the *Bottin Mondain*, the snob's bible and the bedside book of every French society hostess: any handsome young stranger was immediately checked out in the *Bottin* to ensure he was not an impostor. To belong to one of the forty thousand families listed in the *Bottin* often meant you had a *particule* – a *de* before your name. To her surprise, Stella found that to get in the *Bottin* you need not have money! Neither need you be well educated. All that mattered was that you were 'one of us'. All listed mothers of eligible daughters belonged to a suitable *rallye* – a group of up to a hundred mothers, who took it in turns to organize monthly parties for their daughters, from the age of twelve. Mme Boué was astonished to learn that there were no *rallyes* in Los Angeles.

The two high points of the lecture on savoir faire were delicate matters that worried not only Stella but every pupil: knowing the way to a restaurant's ladies' cloakroom (Mme Boué provided a guide) and the problem of what a *jeune fille* should do if, in public, her knickers fell to the ground, should the waistband elastic sag or the button drop off her unmentionables. In this horrific situation, the *jeune fille* simply stepped out of the garment, picked it up *without* looking at it and stuffed it in her purse or pocket. Should this happen on the dance floor, a girl should step away from the garment and ignore it; like retrievers, good waiters had been trained to dart forward and pick up *les panties*. If a girl's stocking fell around her ankle, she sat on the nearest chair, removed it, replaced her shoe and then headed for the cloakroom, a maid and a safety pin. The girls all looked relieved. Now they knew the Done Thing.

After dinner Mme Boué often shepherded her pupils to the ballet. Stella eventually learned not to confuse *Giselle* with *Swan Lake*, but preferred to spend an evening at the theatre. Mme Boué liked her guests to see the classics: Corneille, Racine, Molière, Voltaire, so they trooped off to the ultra-conservative Théâtre-Français to listen to the perfect French pronunciation of the actors: Stella found this declamatory grandiloquence almost hypnotic, and sometimes dozed off.

The girls never went out in one huge bunch, but in a group of half a dozen or so: Mme Boué detested the thought of walking *en crocodile*, preferring people to think that perhaps she was shepherding a group of goddaughters to some fashionable couture collection, or one of the speciality shops, or the best restaurants and cafés in Paris, of which the girls preferred the Suchard café in the Champs-Élysées, which specialized in gooey frivolities made of chocolate.

Like all the other guests, Stella was only allowed to go out unescorted if she was visiting friends of her mother, approved by Mme Boué. Mme Boué asked each mother for a list of such friends. As she scanned the O'Brien list, Stella had heard her murmur approvingly, 'Ah, *les Cole Porteurs . . . tellement chic.*'

For the first few days, Stella felt homesick, abandoned, deprived of her life. Shyly, she made friends with the other girls: they all giggled at each other's grammatical mistakes at meals; they all appreciated Mme Boué's efforts to make them feel guests, and not a bunch of schoolgirls; they all enjoyed their comparative freedom to enjoy the frivolous side of Paris; they all loved Mme Boué, who considered both Josephine Baker and Schiaparelli to be serious artists, who ordered delicious food for them and considered it essential that her guests be able to discriminate between various grades of foie gras; who had a weakness for chocolate and haute couture, and wangled invitations for her girls to all the best collections.

Stella quickly realized that she would enjoy her year in Paris, after all.

Saturday 1 July 1939. London

During the previous year, Fizz had enjoyed further success, playing Lady Macbeth opposite Raymond Massey at the Minerva. The entire play had been performed in Nazi uniform, with Fizz made up as Hitler's mistress, Eva Braun, uncharacteristically ambitious and willing to do any dirty deed to keep her lover in power. The consequence was ... in Berlin, Max and Felicity Fane were typed on the Führer's special Black List of Britishers to be exterminated as soon as Adolf set foot in Buckingham Palace.

In fact, the young Fanes seemed doomed for different reasons. Max's romantic adventures put a heavy strain on his relationship with his wife. Latterly, he had at times almost hated Fizz: he resented the necessity for lying to her, and felt slightly contemptuous of her because it never seemed to occur to her to question his lies. His consequent guilt made him want to find fault with her, as an excuse for his bad behaviour: naturally, she snapped when he tried to blame her for something which she felt she did not merit, and it was easy for her to retaliate, for she knew Max's sensitive spots. In particular, he had been jealous of Johnnie Gielgud since he had started to produce. 'I hear Johnnie's hell to work with,' Max would say casually to Fizz. 'It's all trial and error, he changes his mind about everything all the time, apparently. Must be very confusing and exhausting.'

'Yes, but look at the result,' Fizz would not be able to resist pointing out, and another verbal boxing match would start.

Often, these barbed arrows concerned other actresses, for she now realized that a Watercress Man never changes his spots.

After twelve years of marriage, she could tell when Max had started a new affair by one simple, give-away action that demonstrated his new elation and excited intensity: he whistled when he showered.

As Max's hot love affairs were always with theatre stars, they provided gossip fodder to mischievous newspapers, which was further humiliation. She felt deceived by his treachery, each demonstration of which shattered her trust of him; no sooner had her confidence been built up again than once again he shattered it.

Fizz's jealousy always built up slowly; first she felt defenceless, miserable and without energy. But, inevitably, the moment came when, in bed, she looked up at Max and wondered who he was making love to. Just how many people *were* there in their bed? Then she felt angry, and all sexual feelings vanished. Max never understood what had suddenly switched her off.

When she confronted him he always started by denying that he had been unfaithful, and swiftly turned the blame on her for her admitted jealousy, which he said was unprofessional: this only enraged her further, almost as much as his uncontrite attitude.

When she consulted her mother, Jessie had looked uneasy and said, 'I suppose most people mean to keep their marriage vows when they make 'em, but then they're in love – although *that* rarely lasts longer than a couple of years.'

'Surely for some people love lasts for ever?' Fizz asked, miserably.

'Very few. Far more women say, "I love you" to get security.'

'What Bernard Shaw calls respectable whores,' Fizz nodded glumly. 'But at least they don't feel jealous!'

'Not sexually jealous, but that sort of woman's violently jealous of any other female who threatens her security. Men are different.'

'In what way?'

'Men are jealous of losing their power, their position or their possessions,' Jessie said with unusual force.

'Sometimes I suspect Max thinks of me as his possession, and that's part of our problem.'

* * *

On a sunny Saturday morning in early July Fizz had just dressed and was sitting before her dressing table – a frou-frou of white organdie – when Mrs Pomfret knocked and entered. In the mirror, Fizz could see her, standing red-faced in the doorway, a pile of sheets in her arms. 'These sheets were in the laundry basket this morning, madam, should I send them to the laundry? Usually I don't change the bed till Monday.'

'Yes, please.' Fizz unthinkingly bent forward towards the mirror, crimson lipstick in hand. Mrs Pomfret did not move; there was a strange disapproving air about her.

Suddenly Fizz realized why. She swung and stared at the purple lipstick stains carefully exposed on the crumpled sheets. One look at Mrs Pomfret's sour face and Fizz knew that she had already sniffed them.

'Put them back in the laundry basket,' Fizz said angrily. Satisfied, Mrs Pomfret left the room.

*　*　*

'Get out!' A hand-mirror flew across the bedroom; Max expertly ducked, and it shattered against the wall behind him.

'Some people get lots of toasters as wedding presents. *You* should have been given hand-mirrors.' Max ducked the hairbrush.

'This time, *I mean it*!' *Crack* went a cut-crystal candlestick as it broke against the pale-blue ribbons of the wallpaper. 'There comes a time in every woman's life when she has *had enough*!'

'You're not going to leave again?' Max pleaded.

'No. This is *my house*! *I* paid for it with *my* earnings!' Fizz yelled. '*You* are going to leave!' As she spoke, she sprang to his wardrobe and started to pull out his clothes. Astonished, Max watched his wife leap to the open window and hurl them down to the cobbled street below.

He tried to stop Fizz throwing out her second armful. He turned to the window as a thought occurred to him and he peered down ... yes, someone was picking up *his* clothes! He dashed downstairs to the cellar and grabbed the suitcases. Clearly, his entire wardrobe was about to be hurled out. If he replaced his clothes in the cupboards, Fizz would only throw them out of the window again ... Best if he and his wardrobe stayed at his club for a couple of days, as usual.

That afternoon, Fizz had the locks changed.

That night, she hid her head under the pillows to avoid hearing Max's roars of protest and eventual threats from the street outside.

Eventually Max cooled down by walking back to the Garrick thinking, as usual: She'll come round, given time.

Upstairs in bed, Fizz wept into the pillows. She had never before felt so low-spirited, lethargic and lacking in energy. She felt ill with anger.

* * *

During the next few weeks, Max pestered Fizz for a reconciliation. Once again, baskets of flowers arrived from Lord Lobster; Viscount Plaice once again sent exquisitely wrapped gifts from Bond Street; Mr Cod sent pleading yellow telegrams. This time, Fizz was not piscatorially tempted to yield.

Much to her fury, she found herself unable to stop loving the husband who had so constantly betrayed her. Miserably, she asked herself how much of her feeling was genuine love, and how much was possessiveness, plus determination that no one else should have him.

She noticed now that when she entered the theatre or the Ivy, restaurant conversation stopped and people looked up speculatively at her. It did not occur to her that many of the glances she saw were admiring ones; everyone in the theatre world knew of Max's wandering, and most of them admired Fizz's public disdain of it.

Fizz loathed feeling despised, pitied, the object of mockery and ridicule. She hurt. She felt deceived, cheated, betrayed, angry, and humiliated. She no longer knew whether it was hurt pride or black rage that swirled in her chest, a previously unexperienced force that now erupted dangerously fast when Fizz was least expecting it. Once again, she told herself that she had had ENOUGH!

* * *

Two weeks later, Fizz still refused to talk to Max and, backstage at the theatre, people were becoming uneasy in their presence, Max tried to talk privately, but she had changed her dressing-room lock.

The following week, at 3 a.m., when Fizz had just dropped off to sleep, she was suddenly woken by curious noises. She dragged herself to the window and peered out. In the narrow cobbled street below stood a group of dance-band musicians, wearing white satin tuxedos; as the saxophonist started to warble, a crooner burbled, 'I'll be loving you . . . *always*, alllllllwaaaaaaays . . .'

Upon seeing Fizz's sleepy face at the window, Max grabbed the megaphone from the crooner and yelled through it, '*I love you!* I'll do anything you want. *Please, darling, give me one more chance* . . . I'm *so* sorry, darling . . . *Please* forgive me . . . I *promise* it won't happen again . . .'

'I should bloody well hope not!' roared an angry neighbour as, all around, windows were flung up and sleepy people in pyjamas and hair curlers peered out.

'Please, please darling!' Max's amplified words rang

through the narrow street. 'Please, please . . . *Ouch!*' From an upper window, someone had thrown over Max's head from an old-fashioned chamber pot what Fizz hoped was not water.

Instantly, the musicians stopped playing. They peered anxiously at their instruments. The band leader started to argue with Max, but their discussion was cut short by another deluge. Hurriedly, the musicians retreated to the end of the narrow street.

Fizz felt her way back to bed, now in tears. How many times had she heard Max say he was sorry? She could no longer afford to believe him. Her heart could not take another beating. She was no longer prepared to risk it. And she certainly didn't believe that it wouldn't happen again.

Friday 28 July 1939

Eventually, Fizz sought sleeping pills from her doctor, who wormed her troubles out of her, gave her a bottle of placebos and sent her to a colleague in Harley Street, a specialist in marital problems. Had her doctor told her that his friend was a psychiatrist, she would have indignantly refused to go. She was not mad. There was nothing wrong with her head. Trouble reared its ugly head in Max's cocksure penis.

Sitting in the standard, sawn-off Harley Street consulting room (once the north-west corner of a ballroom, as revealed by the elaborate ceiling cornices topping two walls only), Fizz apprehensively looked at Dr Dawson on the other side of the Dickensian desk. He wore a black jacket and pin-striped trousers, so Fizz felt uncomfortably as if she were talking to her banker, rather than a specialist in marital problems. She explained that she did not necessarily want to get her husband back. 'I simply want to understand why he acts as he does and what he gets out of it!' That might help her to overcome her rage at being humiliated by Max, now as big a success as she (particularly after last year's *Macbeth*). But still, in some weird way, he was jealous of her and she couldn't put up with that, either. 'It's so hard to know if Max genuinely wants a reconciliation. He doesn't understand that I've had as much as I can take.' She had forgiven him on so many occasions, so how could she make him understand that she was seriously serious this time? Max knew, better than anyone, that Fizz could seemingly switch on love, hate, regret and remorse, to order: he could no longer tell a crocodile tear from the real thing.

* * *

Afterwards, Fizz walked slowly up Harley Street, remembering snatches of what Dr Dawson had explained. 'Women want to be liked, they value trust and intimacy. Men want to be respected. Many men fear intimacy, which might lead to becoming emotionally dependent on a woman, and therefore at her mercy – in her power. A man keeps his feelings safely under lock and key in a secret inner core, a sort of psychic bank vault, where no one – man or woman – is allowed lest someone else discover his vulnerability, his fears, his loneliness ... and his weaknesses. Few men can allow that.'

'You mean some men don't trust their wives?'

'Most men don't trust *anyone*,' Dr Dawson had said firmly. 'Most men see a relationship as a pyramid with only one seat at the top, a throne ordained by Nature for

the man. Women don't need to feel on top in a relationship to establish their female identity to themselves and
to the rest of the world. When a woman senses that a man
is holding back a part of himself, she starts to distrust
him!'

'But why does Max need to humiliate me *in secret*?'
Fizz had then asked painfully. 'Why does he make love to
another woman in *our* bed, where he and I make love?'

'That's *why* he does it.'

Fizz had stared in dismay as Dr Dawson continued,
'Loss of face is important in the Orient because it *is* so
important to humans. Your husband wants to humiliate
you – and don't assume he didn't intend you to discover
it – because *he* feels that you have humiliated him.'

'But I *haven't*!' Fizz protested.

'Yes, you have. You have not allowed your husband to
dominate you,' Dr Dawson said smugly. 'Revenge restores
his self-esteem and superiority.'

'What do you mean by "dominate"?' Fizz puzzled. Max
had never shown any horrid sexual tendencies.

'Max wants to be obeyed without being questioned.'

'Like Hitler,' Fizz snorted.

'Yes, Hitler is seeking revenge on behalf of Germany
for the humiliation that they inflicted on themselves by
losing the Great War. That's why Germans love him.'

* * *

In Cavendish Square Fizz bought an *Evening Standard*
from a ragged urchin, hailed a taxi, settled back and
opened the newspaper. She read the usual gloomy war
rumours, and skipped through the Leader, which
explained why Hitler might attack Poland. In the next
column, politician Winston Churchill made it clear that if

Poland had to use force to keep Hitler out, then Britain would keep its pact to go to Poland's aid.

When she flipped open the gossip page, Fizz sat up abruptly. She stared at a large photograph of Max captioned: NEARLY ELIGIBLE BACHELOR?

The writer started by lightly skimming over Max's most recent successes, particularly his season opener, the provocative *All God's Chillun Got Wings*, which dealt with racial intermarriage in a fairly sentimental way; this had been followed by *Marco's Millions*, a bitter satire about an aggressive businessman who had lost touch with Beauty and Eternal Truth.

As who has not? Fizz wondered, then angrily read that Max sorrowfully admitted that his wife had left him. He wanted to make it absolutely clear that he did not entirely blame her. Fizz and he had once been very much in love – she was, after all, a wonderful woman as well as a wonderful actress. But when their careers began to collide ... Naturally, Max could not expect Fizz to turn down plum parts in order to stay with him, at the little Minerva ... 'Yes, I suppose I felt a little lonely, when my darling stayed so long in Hollywood – that was in 1932, and then she was off again to New York, in 1936. Of course, by then, we had been married many years, so it's understandable that Fizz might have felt bored by me ...

'After that, we just seemed to drift apart. After she returned from New York, Fizz was offered Juliet in Edinburgh – a marvellous production, by the way. Fizz was thirty-one, so I realized it was probably her last chance to play a fourteen-year-old with any conviction. I knew I must not selfishly stand in her way, but of course I missed her. Still do. Sadly, the success rate of theatre marriages isn't very high.'

Sitting upright in the beetle-black taxi, Fizz angrily crumpled the newspaper, threw it to the floor and stamped on those words of treachery.

Once again, Fizz felt the same pain that Mimi must feel about Betsy O'Brien's actions: Fizz was sorry she had ever thought their feud absurd. Fizz could now understand wanting to *kill* the person you loved, after being treacherous.

* * *

A week later, Max received a recorded-delivery packet, which contained two letters. The first informed him that Withers' client, Mrs Felicity Eloise Fane, born Allen, intended to sue him for divorce. The second announced that as their client, Mrs Felicity Eloise Fane, born Allen, had no formal contractual relationship with Fane Productions Limited, their client had instructed them to inform said Fane Productions Limited that upon the termination of the current West End production, their client no longer wished to work for Fane Productions Limited.

This time, she did mean it!

Although Fizz and Max spoke about this matter to nobody at the Minerva, within two minutes everybody backstage knew that at last it was all up for the Watercress Man, and about time too; officially, everyone carefully avoided noticing the frost zone between Max and Fizz, who now – if obliged to speak to one another in public – addressed each other as 'you', in order to avoid mentioning the other's now-hated name.

Sunday 30 July 1939. Fitzroy Square

It was a warm morning and delightfully quiet, as always in central London on Sunday, so Max and Toby took their drinks to the garden terrace, while Mimi had a hurried conference with the cook, who did not like to confess to Toby that she had burned the roast – a leg of lamb – in the new electric cooker. Cook didn't know why they'd had to switch from good old-fashioned gas, where you could see the flames.

In the garden, Max stretched out luxuriously in his striped deckchair. 'I'm off to Paris tomorrow. Fizz can't come.'

Toby looked startled. 'Is that wise – at this time?'

'Most people don't believe the Nazis'll invade Poland, but I do. So I'm taking one last quick trip to Paris – because after that, I probably won't get a holiday until the war's over.'

Toby sighed. 'What do you intend to do when get back? RNVR?' Eighteen months beforehand, Max had joined the Royal Naval Volunteer Reserve, when the Admiralty wished to enlarge this with yachtsmen who had had some experience of the sea.

'When the war starts, I'll be called up and trained as a temporary acting sub-lieutenant.'

'Here we go again! I suppose I'll have to patrol the Embankment at night again, instead of going to sleep. We might as well not have won the bloody war! It only took the Huns twelve years to start up again.' Toby had been deeply suspicious of Hitler since September of the previous year, when the British Prime Minister, Neville Chamberlain, had returned from a Munich conference with Hitler, waving a piece of paper, a so-called Promise of Peace, signed by the German Führer. Despite wide condemnation of Mr Chamberlain's gullibility, his little bit of paper had given Britain an extra year in which to prepare for war. From the moment it was signed, the British army – though not the British Government – had immediately started to plan for war.

'I suppose Hitler's got to be stopped at some point,' Toby added gloomily. 'Of course he's using the Jews as a whipping boy for the problems of Nazi Germany.'

'An updated witch hunt,' Max agreed. He remembered his research for *Joan of Arc*. 'Eight million women were burned as witches in medieval Europe. And now it's starting again. Here.' He added hastily, 'I mean the anti-Jewish mob violence stirred up by the damned British Union of Fascists.'

Toby looked down at his mint-sprigged drink, so emblematic of peaceful summer days in an English garden. Suddenly angry, he said, 'It's so easy to use mob violence to get rid of people you envy. It's so easy for some charismatic, power-hungry man to make rabble-rousing speeches that incite people to behave in a way they wouldn't normally, then hide behind the mob conscience, while everyone in the mob feels, "Well, if I'm told by the leader to beat up Jews, and if everyone around me is beating up Jews, then clearly it's the right thing to do, so I won't be punished for it."

'You know where those damned dictators learn their rabble-rousing techniques?' Toby asked.

Max laughed wryly. 'At the theatre, of course.'

* * *

Mimi appeared, looking flustered. 'As it's such a warm day, Cook thought we'd prefer cold salmon-trout with mayonnaise.'

Toby looked surprised. 'But I ordered trout for this evening.'

'I thought we'd go round to Maisie's for dinner this evening,' Mimi said firmly. Maisie had recently hired Sybil Colefax to redecorate the Earls Court Theatrical Hotel; the new dining-room decor was based on the interior of the Brighton Pavilion. Each bedroom now had its own bathroom, and there wasn't a mousetrap in sight: few actors could afford to stay there, these days.

Chapter Twenty

Max checked into the Scribe, a quietly luxurious hotel in the centre of Paris. It was late afternoon; tar melted on the roads, fat concierges fanned themselves with concertinaed sheets of paper and the whole of central Paris still smelt of luncheon. When he saw the pretty girls in their short summer skirts, and smelled the odour of cheap scent, cheap cigarettes, stale perspiration and garlic-scented hot air that wafted up from the Métro exits, Max felt happy, for the first time since he had realized that Fizz really, definitely never wanted to see him again.

This evening, he would call on Linda and Cole, at cocktail time, and then see what happened; if nothing did, he would dine by himself in some little bistro near the Rue Jacob, then visit Natalie. He phoned to check that the Porters were still in Paris, in this sweltering August heat, and would welcome him.

In the oppressive heat of the low-slung taxi, Max realized how pleasant it would be to see the Porters and afterwards walk once more in the quiet, dark garden of American heiress Natalie Barney. Since Napoleon, brilliant women had held salons in Paris, each famous hostess on a different day, so that salons did not clash. The famous, the creative, the rich and the decadent met *chez*

Natalie, who was what was called an Amazon; she had once told Max, '*You're* interested in women only from the waist down, *I'm* interested in men only from the neck up.' There were always beautiful women, Amazons and otherwise, at her parties; Max was unlikely to finish the evening alone, he thought to himself, as he paid off his taxi in the Rue Monsieur.

Because of the energy-sapping city heat that bounced back from the cobblestones, most Parisians had already left the city to holiday in the mountains or at the seaside; nevertheless, there were many guests in the Porters' music room, a stunning, long salon large enough to dance in, with walls lacquered silver, zebra skins on the parquet floor, white-leather sofas, cream suede chairs and a piano.

Linda Porter wore a cunningly cut sea-green dress from Nina Ricci which rippled and changed colour when she moved, as if made of waves. 'Be a darling and talk to Stella O'Brien,' she whispered to Max, 'she's so very shy and gauche. Over there with M. Fixit.'

M. Fixit was Jacques Joyeux, who worked in the Ministère d'Information; he was well known for his perfect English, his tact and his swift ability to cut through the bureaucratic red tape that wound around French life. The girl he was talking to was tall, dark and dazzled. Although accustomed to meeting celebrities, Stella felt as if she had walked into the society pages of *Vogue*, as she watched Grace Moore flirt with Maurice Chevalier, Coco Chanel chat guardedly to Lucien Lelong, Serge Lifar smirk at former tennis champion Suzanne Lenglen and Elsa Maxwell, who had rescued herself from unemployment by converting party-giving into a job.

'No, she's not an Amazon, darling,' Linda smiled. 'It's simply that Stella's strongly built and doesn't know how to dress yet. I promised her mother I'd keep an eye on her till Christmas, when Stella returns to Hollywood.'

Suddenly alert, Max asked, 'O'Brien?'

'Yes. Black Jack's daughter. I'll take you over to meet her.'

Max was immediately intrigued. He looked at Stella with new eyes; he now noticed her lovely dark blue eyes and pale skin. 'Don't bother, Linda. I'll introduce myself.' Drink in hand, Max moved towards the couple standing by the window, greeted Jacques Joyeux, then turned to Stella. 'You're Stella, aren't you? I'm Max.' Deliberately, he omitted his surname.

Stella was always grateful when talking to a man taller than she. As she stared into Max's eyes (almost the same colour as her own), as Max intended, she was intrigued by his quiet charm and air of reassurance, as well as his handsome face. She blushed, furious with herself for doing so. Max noticed, and so did M. Joyeux, who could see that the Englishman had scored another hit.

'How are you enjoying Paris?' Max asked Stella.

'Very much indeed,' stuttered Stella, tongue-tied.

'I'm surprised to find an American still here.'

'There won't be a war,' M. Joyeux quickly reassured them.

Max joked, 'If the Ministère d'Information says there will not be any war, then there assuredly will be.'

'My mom's friends in Washington say that Hitler can't attack on two fronts at once,' Stella volunteered. 'The German troops are tied up on the Eastern Front.'

'In Washington they don't think there'll be a war, and neither does anyone in Paris,' M. Joyeux added smoothly. 'The politicians will work something out. Nobody wants a repeat of the Great War.'

'Except the Germans,' Max politely contradicted him. 'What will you all do if Hitler *does* suddenly march into Paris?'

Stella tried to sound self-assured, well informed. 'The USA isn't going to get involved, this time. Mom says it's none of our business. The Germans are so efficient, it'll probably be finished by Christmas.'

'The Germans are efficient, eh?' Max gave a little grin. 'So are the French, come to that. Haven't you noticed how they love to keep everything tidy? Their women, their homes, their poodles – everything is always *très soigné*; even their gardens look unnaturally neat, like sprouting Persian carpets.'

For a few minutes the three discussed the French impulse towards order, which fought an equally strong French impulse to noisily disputed authority. Few large union negotiations took place in France without a preliminary disruptive strike, to flex and display muscle. M. Joyeux had frequently seen university students riot: they overturned little cars and incited the gendarmes to rough treatment, with a thwacking of batons and flourishing of the heavy lead-lined capes that all *flics* considered an auxiliary weapon.

M. Joyeux melted away, leaving the field to the Englishman, for clearly the tall girl was already mesmerized by him, and the sophisticated Frenchman had just discovered that Stella was still at school. So he had lost interest, as he remembered the need always to return early, the ridiculously elaborate lies for the teachers, the girl's constant anxiety and lack of experience: young married women had no such problems.

Max then enquired which parts of Paris Stella had visited. After her reply, he exclaimed, 'But you only know the smart parts of Paris, the parts reserved for tourists and politicians!'

'Where else should I go?'

'Have you been up the river on a *bateau-mouche*? . . . You *haven't*! But it's a *must* – like those cliché horse-drawn fiacres in Central Park! Every American in Paris takes his girl on a *bateau-mouche* up the Seine to St Cloud. Would you like to try it? It's so hot in Paris.' But he obviously couldn't take this little virgin to Natalie: she would be scared stiff by the Amazons.

* * *

By the time the large tour boat had glided back to central Paris it was dusk, and Stella had already fallen in love with Max, as he had half intended. Together they leaned over the side and watched the glittering lights reflected in the water, sniffed the beguiling cooking smells that wafted from buildings on either side of the river, and gazed dreamily at the deep violet-purple of the water as their boat slid beneath the blue-grey haze of some bridge.

Max had been careful not to touch Stella, in order to make her want him to. Now, as he guided her towards the gangway to disembark, he put his hand under her elbow; she shivered with electric delight and immediately dropped her purse, which fell open, throwing the contents on deck.

Helping to pick them up, Max stared at an old studio portrait of a beautiful woman in a pale, draped Grecian-style dress. Max instantly recognized her.

'That's my mom,' Stella said proudly. Max moved beneath a deck lamp to examine the photograph. Yes, he clearly remembered flirting with this lovely creature . . . Where was it? . . . At some fund-raiser in New York; he'd gone with Lee Strasberg. Only now did he realize the identity of that classically featured beauty, although he clearly remembered his regret at having to refuse her invitation to dinner because Lee had already organized their dates for the evening.

Silhouetted in the circle of yellow light thrown by the deck lamp, he coldly wondered whether Betsy had known his identity; whether Betsy had attempted to play the same game that he was now playing with her daughter. Momentarily, Max remembered his father in hospital after the suicide attempt. He tightened his lips with anger. 'Don't be emotional, be reasonable,' Max told himself; this sweet, gawky girl had *nothing* to do with that horrific incident . . . But wouldn't her mother be furious if she could see the two of them now, holding hands in the twilight, on a *bateau-mouche*? Max felt an illicit thrill of power.

When they had disembarked, Max steered Stella into a quiet place of shadows on the quay. Taking plenty of time to do it, he gently, tenderly, kissed her.

Stella quivered with what she did not yet recognize as lust. She felt Max's hand slide up her blouse across her naked back, and thought she might faint; her excitement mounted as Max's fingers swiftly unhooked her bra; his hand slipped round to the front of her body. Stella trembled so violently that Max wondered whether he should perhaps stop . . . it was just too easy . . . but he was enjoying the thrill of revenge, and his mounting sexual excitement quickly wiped everything else from his mind as he felt the soft, soft skin of her breast, felt her jump as he touched her pointed nipple. As Stella clung to him, weak-kneed, both knew that they had passed the point of stopping.

At which point, Max pulled away. Stella groaned.

'We mustn't do this,' he lied, fully intending to, 'I must do the decent thing and get you back to school.'

Stella peered at her diamond watch. She gave a horrified gasp. 'Oh! I do *hope* that Mme Boué hasn't telephoned Linda Porter! We're supposed to be back by eleven o'clock, at the latest.'

'Linda knows you're with me. She'll cover for you,' Max said confidently. Everyone covered for everyone else in Paris, and then immediately telephoned all their friends.

In the taxi, Max again kissed Stella until she could feel only the urgent insistence of her body. When the Citroën stopped, Stella reluctantly grabbed her bag, pulled out her compact and quickly combed her hair with an agitated hand.

As she rang the outside bell for the concierge she turned to look at Max, but the Citroën had pulled away from the kerb, and disappeared.

Later, lying in bed, Stella could not sleep. Over and over again she relived every passionate moment of the most important evening of her life: not only had she met the man of her dreams (in fact, *Max was better* than the man of her dreams) but he had actually *liked* her! A sophisticated *real* man of thirty-one who had not thought her dull or quiet or stupid. Stella knew she was unable to chatter prettily like other girls, but Max had carefully listened to what she said. He had not behaved in a provocatively flirtatious manner, but had simply . . . behaved as if he had known all his life that one day Stella would enter it and stay there.

Blissfully happy, Stella once again remembered the first moment that she had gazed into Max's sincere dark blue eyes. Yes, it had been love at first sight, for both of them.

* * *

On the following day, Stella skipped her dancing class, and told Mme Boué that Mme Porter had asked her to a tea party that afternoon, and had also wondered if Stella might stay for supper.

'But of course.' Mme Boué approved. Such sophisticated, concerned friends could only help the quiet, retiring Stella to blossom as eagerly and charmingly as her other pupils.

* * *

By arrangement, Stella descended from Mme Boué's limousine in the Rue Monsieur, hopped in to tell Linda how much she had enjoyed the previous evening, found that the Porters were not at home. Perfect!

Stella then hurried back into the street, hailed a taxi and shortly afterwards stood in the dignified marble entrance of the Scribe, a few minutes before her rendezvous with Max.

* * *

Max was surprised at the ease with which he lured Stella into his bed, not realizing that for her there had never been a question of 'yes' or 'no', but only 'when'. She knew that Max was, and always would be, the only man in her life, and she could not wait to be in bed with him, to feel his naked body warm against hers. Max was her destiny. Only with her brother Nick had she felt such trust, such loving reassurance, such tender affection; she had always been a little frightened of her father, although

Stella knew she was expected to marry a man like him, and lead a life exactly like that of her mother.

When she told this to Max (as a way of introducing the word 'marriage'), he kissed the top of her head and murmured that a meaningless life was an empty one, whether led by a slum child or a rich woman with nothing better to do. Genuine pleasure and satisfaction, he assured Stella, stemmed from a sense of purpose and achievement, whether that resulted from ... er ... baking a cake or writing one of those poems she had told him about.

'No, Nick wrote the poems,' Stella murmured happily, snuggling closer to his lean, hairy chest.

Max said hastily, 'But you read them, darling.'

* * *

Stella could not bear the waiting. She counted the minutes. She could not concentrate on her lessons. She could concentrate on nothing, except that it was so many minutes since she had last seen Max, and that it would be so many minutes until she next saw him.

For the rest of that week, Stella briskly lied to Mme Boué with a facility and invention that surprised her. On the rare occasions when they left Max's bedroom at the Scribe, he took her away from the Right Bank, where she was nervous that she might be seen and recognized by one of her schoolfriends or one of her mother's friends, and instead they spent their time on the Left Bank. Stella especially liked to linger in the Jardin du Luxembourg, which seemed far from the noisy bustle of the Latin Quarter. Happily they strolled hand in hand in the afternoon sunshine, passing other young couples similarly entwined, little children with bored nursemaids and old men contentedly playing chess in the sun. They always visited the pretty rectangular pond surmounted by a three-tiered fountain, against which flirted a couple of stone lovers. Beneath plane trees, golden carp flirted around the pond, darting away whenever a leaf fluttered into the water.

A frog leaped from the pond: on attenuated hind legs, it sailed through the air, landed and disappeared. 'There goes your fairy prince in disguise,' said Max.

'You're my prince, and you need no disguise, and you aren't going to disappear.'

Suddenly, Max felt a toad. So much so, that he felt obliged to tell Stella that he was a married man.

All Stella's dreams smashed into a thousand pieces.

She felt as if this idyllic scene had been cut into shards and whirled in the air, as if inside a kaleidoscope twirled by an overexcited child.

Max belonged to another woman.

Too shocked to cry, numbed and silenced by this news, Stella threw her arms around Max's chest and hugged him tightly to her, as if for the last time. It had never occurred to her for *one minute* that Max was married. He didn't behave, or talk or move like a married man! Why, why had he deceived her?

'Hey, wait a minute, I'm not such a monster,' Max gently disentangled Stella's arms, cupped her chin in both his hands, looked into her staring, frightened eyes and told her that he and Fizz were about to divorce.

Stella jerked her head back. 'Fizz? . . . Are you *Max Fane*?' Part of the thrill of their love affair had been the anonymity of it. She had not wanted to think of Max as having friends or family elsewhere. She wanted him to be only hers, for the short time he was in Paris. There would be time enough later to meet the rest of his world. She knew Max was a theatre director . . . that was the sort of person one met at the Porters', but when she and Max were together, Stella had preferred simply to forget everything and see only herself and Max together in Paris, as if the spirit of the city sheltered their love with some invisible barrier that real life could not penetrate. The ecstasy she always felt when with him made her feel more alive than she had ever felt before, as if she were in tune – at last – with the music of the planets. One loving look from Max could make her feel as if her heart would burst with joy. That happiness had now exploded.

'Yes, I'm Max Fane,' Max looked winningly contrite. 'Darling Stella, I hated to keep it from you, but I was so afraid that you wouldn't . . . that I'd lose you.'

Stella felt even more mortified than she had a few minutes before. When Max pulled her to him, she tried to struggle away, but his strong arms made him irresistible. He whispered, with erotic warm breath, into her ear, 'Surely you're not going to let that stupid feud come between *us* – some senseless quarrel that our mothers had over thirty years ago.'

Stella stared silently. Quietly, she leaned against him and started to cry. Max stroked her hair comfortingly, and kissed the top of her head from time to time, until Stella snuffled and looked up with red-blotched face, 'Max, why didn't you tell me?'

'Because I knew you would react as you've just done! So I wanted to put it off for as long as possible. But I leave tomorrow . . .'

Stella jumped. Another blow!

'. . . And I wanted to be honest with you, darling.'

Stella clung to Max's excuse, and twisted it into a message of hope. Afterwards she would analyse for hours each word he had said. Max had been honest with her. As he had repeatedly told her, he had been unable to resist her: something invisible within her had made him treasure her, as she treasured him. Of course, Max had not wanted to smash their wonderful, enchanted world by telling her that he was the one man in it with whom she must not fall in love.

'Romeo and Juliet,' Max's warm breath reminded in her ear.

Once this thought had been implanted in Stella's mind, she saw their love affair as a romantic, forbidden passion. She flung back her head and looked into those reassuring eyes. 'Let's go back to your room. Now.'

Once back in bed, all thoughts of ever being separated from Max were forgotten.

* * *

Afterwards, Max sensitively explained the tragedy of his marriage. Apart from the inevitable stresses put upon it by Fizz's greater success, they were often apart for long periods. Men flocked around Fizz, so Max felt not only jealous but also lonely. They had gradually drifted apart.

At last Stella brought herself to ask the question she dreaded.

Sorrowfully, Max shook his head. He had always regretted being an only child, he had always wanted to have a real family, always longed for his own children. But Fizz refused to have babies, because of course they would disrupt her career ... When you thought of it that way, he supposed that he could not blame her ... but he had never ceased to long for his own children. It might have made all the difference to their marriage.

He did not mention infidelity until Stella asked about it.

'Once or twice, I'm afraid. We both did. I was unhappy and lonely . . . Can you understand that sort of loneliness? The loneliness of living with someone who . . . doesn't particularly want you to be there?'

Between passionate kisses, Stella confided to Max that she did indeed understand loneliness. She had felt the loneliness of responsibility ever since her father died, for as the eldest it was her duty to make her mother happy, but she could not help her mom. She didn't know what to do. Ever since Pop's death, she had felt separated from the life she wanted to lead: a quiet life with books and cats and dogs. She had been shy and lonely until the moment she met Max, and still could hardly believe that Max really liked her for *herself*, for he was the only person – apart from Nick – with whom she felt herself.

Max felt a twinge of guilt, but then resented Stella for making him feel guilty. He had intended a light-hearted affair in Paris, and a minor revenge on behalf of his father. He had not intended Stella to become his psychological burden. But now he knew he would feel a shit when he ended it.

* * *

Stella could not explain her absence to Mme Boué for long enough to see Max to the airport and get back to the centre of Paris. But there was time for a steamy farewell at the Scribe.

After Max had rushed off, late, Stella slowly took a tub in the pale marble bathroom. As she was dressing, a nimble, dark chambermaid entered the bedroom, her arms full of clean sheets. Upon seeing Stella in tears, the chambermaid hesitated. When she had first seen the American girl in that bedroom, she had blushed, and the chambermaid had winked. By the time Max departed, Stella and the chambermaid were exchanging complicit smiles whenever they passed each other in the corridor, or when Rachel – for that was her name – briskly turned down Max's bed for the evening, in theory: in fact, she had to remake it.

When Rachel looked beyond Stella's heaving shoulders to the cupboards with their doors hanging open, the emptied drawers, Rachel immediately realized what was wrong. This girl, of roughly her own age, had just said goodbye to her elderly lover, *le lord anglais*.

Rachel dumped the clean sheets on the tousled bed, moved across the room and put her arms around Stella. '*Il reviendra bientôt*,' she reassured her. '*J'en suis sûr*.'

Sadly Stella nodded. She, too, was certain that she would see Max again. But when?

The chambermaid stayed until Stella's tears subsided to snuffles. She led Stella to the bathroom and carefully washed her face. Cheered by this comfort from a relative stranger, Stella sadly left her lover's bedroom for the last time.

* * *

In mid-air, Max found that he could not concentrate on his book; every time he tried, he saw Stella's hopeful young face, and her tremulous dark blue eyes, tender, devoted, never reproachful.

So why did he feel that he *had* just been reproached? He was genuinely fond of the touchingly forlorn creature; she reminded him of his boyhood beagle puppy, who grew too large, and had to be given to a friend in the country. He had promised to return to Paris – and he would. More than that he could not promise . . . After all, he was not yet an *un*married man. So would his conscience please shut up and let him get on with the latest Hemingway?

* * *

After saying goodbye to Max, Stella sat in a nearby café sipping a *citron pressé*. Her familiar exultation, mixed with quiet triumph, slowly faded into sorrow: for there was no disguising the fact that Max was married. That Max was a Fane. That Max had left her.

Humiliation, pain and sadness momentarily squeezed her young, untested heart.

Had it been worth it? *Yes!* Because for that short time, Max had been *hers*! . . . and Max could *still* be hers. Swiftly, her imagination painted an idyllic picture of what their life together might be. The irrational adoration which she felt for Max – and wrongly believed that he felt for her – had provided so powerful a boost to her low self-esteem that the threat of losing his love had now become dangerously alarming. Stella no longer wanted to be an individual, but half of a pair.

By the time she had finished her *citron pressé* she had persuaded herself that Max was in love with her, that he intended to marry her and that they were going to buy some simple little farm near Paris where they would lead a simple, quiet life with at least four beautiful children. Why, she might even be pregnant now! Stella hoped that she was. How did you feel if you were pregnant? You were sick in the morning and your stomach swelled, that was all she knew. By the end of her second *citron pressé*,

Stella had convinced herself that she felt nauseated, and that her stomach was definitely larger than it had been an hour earlier.

For better, for worse, Stella knew that she was Max's for ever and he had promised to return. Stella wondered whether, when she and Max married, this would reconcile their mothers – or further distance them?

* * *

Mme Boué swiftly noted the change in Stella. It was a pity *les Porteurs* had returned to America, for Mme Porteur had clearly had a good influence on Stella, in only one week. Those walks in the park had brought colour to her cheeks. The girl had also lost her forlorn air, and now seemed more alive, more determined to enjoy life. She spoke up more at mealtimes, and seemed genuinely happy. In class, she paid more attention to the subjunctive, and had mastered her irregular verbs, while her written French was now as good as that of a French girl of her age – which was not, however, much of a compliment. But her mother would be pleased.

Chapter Twenty-One

Sunday 27 August 1939. London

Max returned from Paris to his club, where his room was furnished like a bachelor bedroom in an English country house: bed, wardrobe, small table, upright chair; a bedside light the only concession to comfort. Ten minutes after Max's arrival, Freeby the door porter handed him a yellow telegram. 'Sorry, sir. It's been here for three days but we didn't know where to send it on, seeing as how you said you're ... temporarily not at home.' The porter gave a discreet cough.

Max whipped open the telegram and read:

DARLING IMPORTANT NEWS TELEPHONE FASTEST
LOVE AND KISSES FIZZ.

Max thought, Ha! He *knew* she'd come round, although he hadn't expected a reunion before Christmas. Max grabbed the telephone, and dialled his home number. There was a click, then he heard a recorded upper-class drone, 'We regret that your numbah is temporarrrrily out of orderrrr.'

He quickly changed, washed and shaved, then hurried out of the club, the exterior of which was now heavily sandbagged to ten feet above ground. As there were no cabs in sight, he walked round to Colville Place. After his plane trip, he was glad to stretch his legs.

The yellow front door at Colville Place was opened by Fizz. Laughing with joy and surprise, she threw herself into Max's arms and covered his face with kisses, eager and loving as a puppy. Max prudently decided merely to assume that he was forgiven and not comment on this astonishing volte-face, as Fizz dragged him into the narrow hall, shut the door, leaned against it and looked up at her husband with blue eyes sparkling like a June sky after summer rain. 'You'll never believe it . . . I don't know how to tell you . . . *we're pregnant*!' Again, she flung herself into Max's arms. 'Oh, darling Max, I've missed you so much . . .'

'When?'

'Next February, the doctor thinks.'

'You're sure?' Max asked cautiously. They had been married for over twelve years.

Fizz nodded, too excited to speak. Max pulled her into his arms and kissed her hard. Then he drew back. 'Oh . . . I mean . . . that's . . . are we allowed to . . . ?'

Laughing, Fizz nodded, took him by the hand, and tugged him upstairs. Outside their bedroom door, she turned to him, stood on tiptoe and kissed him once again. 'I've been so broody, darling. As soon as I realized *why* I had been feeling ill, I didn't mind. Jessie and Daisy have already started knitting little white vests and shawls . . . I've tried, but knitting isn't my sort of thing, darling . . . Oh, I can't *believe* how much I long for this baby! I never, never, never would have thought it of myself.'

Suddenly, Fizz seemed once more the laughing, happy and loveable girl that Max had married; tenderly he took her in his arms, pushed open the bedroom door with one foot, and carried her to bed.

* * *

The next morning, Max returned to the Garrick, ostensibly to collect his clothes, but also to write a difficult letter to Stella.

He knew that for him their love affair had been an enjoyable holiday flirtation, but he also acknowledged that the virginal Stella had fallen in love.

Having tried several times to write his letter, Max again crumpled up the paper and screwed the cap back on his fountain pen. It was no use, he would be obliged to return to Paris and tell her, face to face. Heaven knew why, but that would be easier than writing a letter, for he imagined Stella's joy at receiving a letter with a London postmark, then her shock upon reading it. Max clearly could not telephone, or Mme Boué would smell a rat as big as a cat, and perhaps check all those visits to the Cole Porters. He would fly over, Max decided. On his way out, he asked a club servant to telephone Cooks and arrange a seat on the first aircraft to Le Bourget on September the fourth, returning on the following morning by the first plane.

Sunday 3 September 1939. Fitzroy Square

Nobody spoke. It was a pleasant sunny day, the Sunday peace broken only by a lone plane droning overhead, the *clackety-clackety-clack* of a lawnmower in a nearby garden and the gentle buzzing of bees among the flowers in Toby's small herbaceous border.

'Isn't it exciting, Toby?' Mimi's eyes were bright with anticipation. 'Don't you look forward to being a grandfather?'

Toby gave a sly grin. 'Most men of my age look forward to having a grandchild, but they don't look forward to being a grandfather, and still less do they like the idea of sleeping with somebody's grandmother.'

Mimi laughed. She heaved herself out of her deckchair. 'I'm going to crack open a bottle of champagne, maybe that will cheer us all up.' Max, Fizz and Toby nodded in silence. When Hitler invaded Poland, Britishers knew that war was inevitable, but it had nevertheless been a shock to be told so, over the wireless, by the grave, tired voice of the Prime Minister.

Max's first thought was that he would be unable to travel to Paris to see Stella. His second concern was what would happen to Fizz. Max would be called up immediately, and he did not want the pregnant Fizz to live on her own.

Toby turned to Max. 'I suppose you'll be reporting to the RNVR?'

'Tomorrow. I'll probably be posted immediately to HMS *King Alfred*, that's the big place on the seafront, in the middle of Brighton. After one month's training, hopefully I'll pass out as a temporary acting sub-lieutenant: apparently the training's going to be fairly sketchy, with lots of examinations.'

'I've already joined the ARP.' Toby sounded resigned. 'Another few years of lost sleep because of some damned Hun's greed.'

Max threw a glance at Fizz. 'Fizz doesn't really like the idea but I would be so grateful if she could move in with you. She could sleep in my old bedroom.'

'No, no,' Toby remonstrated. Max looked surprised, until his father added, 'We must look after Fizz carefully now, mustn't we? She can't climb up and down those stairs. We'll put her in the drawing room and make it a really comfortable bedsitter for her. Your mother and I can sit in my study in the evening, and Fizz can join us in there if she feels like it.'

Mimi returned with the glasses and a bottle of Moët. 'Cook's just told me she's joining up tomorrow. Daisy and I will have to manage on our own, because the rest of 'em are going as well.'

In silence, they considered this gloomy prospect as they drank champagne.

* * *

By October Max had discovered that the war was harder work than being on tour – and he couldn't say worse than that.

Having been commissioned into the RNVR, Temporary Acting Sub-Lieutenant Fane had been posted, not to sea, as he had expected, but to a stone frigate – a desk job – in Portsmouth Dockyard; he was to be part of the efficient naval administration ashore that supplied the fighting ships and kept them in repair: the Supply and Secretariat Branch of the Royal Navy.

When Max first arrived, he had immediately spotted the unmistakable outline of the *Queen Elizabeth* liner, which was being converted into a troop transporter. Apart from grey warships, the Harbour was crammed with various other craft, including tugs which assisted with berthing; fleet tenders to carry stores and equipment; specialist crafts to ferry fuel and ammunition out to the ships; and a fleet of lighters, manned by civilian crews, which was responsible for the movement of ships, men and assorted materials.

Literally a town within a town, Portsmouth Dockyard was a thriving community with factories, stores, houses, schools and a church. It had its own police force, fire brigade and railway to haul heavy loads from ships to workshops, or to the slipways. The Yard had been immediately reorganized for war, and was now extremely busy; workers toiled around the clock, seven days a week, nonstop. Few were lucky enough to work only what was then the standard ten-hour day, six days a week. No time could be wasted, for Pompey (as the city was affectionately known to its inhabitants) was Britain's premier naval city. The Yard serviced destroyer flotillas, and was packed with ships in for refit, for battle repairs or to take on fresh supplies. It was a dangerously dark place at night, for there was nothing to stop people falling into the water – and they often did, especially after a pint or two of bottled sunshine, which was inclined to get you horizontal, stitched up or shot to ribbons, a state of mind that could only be improved by time, aspirin and a hot cup of char the next morning.

Max had been appointed personal assistant to elderly Lieutenant Commander Higginson, who had been hurriedly recalled from a leisurely retirement spent playing golf and sipping pink gins to be responsible for general administration concerned with supplying men and ships with everything they needed, from armaments and fuel to sausages, rum and dried pease-pudding, a Mess favourite.

Max worked in a long, narrow office, filled with clerks, which ran the full width of the building; from the back window he could see the masts, spars and rigging of

Nelson's flagship, HMS *Victory*, which had beaten the French and Spanish at Trafalgar; from the front window, he could see – through a chink between two large buildings – the narrow Harbour entrance. When he felt bored and depressed he described his job as 'a clerk's job at a desk in the Supplies Office', but he knew that although it was tedious, his was as necessary as all other wartime jobs. He had been billeted in a once-gracious Georgian house in St Thomas's Street, a slum area not far from the Dockyard entrance, to which he bicycled every morning. He was lucky to have a room to himself for although it only contained a single bed, it meant that Fizz could visit him. When she did, Max actually slept on the floor, on the landlady's sunoil-stained pre-war beach mattress, formerly used by children to float upon the sea.

Max occasionally groped his way through the blackout down to the Star and Garter on the Point of Old Portsmouth, where he drank a pint of watery, wartime beer; otherwise, his evenings were spent in the officers' Wardroom, opposite the Victorian red-brick Victory Barracks, where he yarned with officers attached to the Torpedo School at HMS *Vernon*, and those doing the gunnery course in HMS *Excellent* on Whale Island, a genuine little island in the Harbour, known as 'Whaley'. At night, after he returned to his billet, Max did not often leave it, for the whole city was blacked out; every night, all buses were driven out into fields, so they were not bombed; the citizens of Portsmouth could shelter in several large air-raid shelters, which could accommodate thousands, built under Portsdown Hill, at the rear of the town.

Everyone's life was disrupted as the city waited for the Hun to attack. Sometimes Max remembered Stella. He still felt guilty about her, but knew there was no point in writing, for the censors would not allow the letter to leave Britain.

* * *

'Everyone in Britain wants to win the war but hardly anyone seems to understand why we're fighting,' Mimi remarked one morning when Toby brought up her breakfast tray.

Toby looked grim. '*Somebody's* got to stop the Germans, once and for all.'

'You'd have thought they'd remember what hell it was for their poor lads in the last war.' Mimi thought sadly of Baz.

'That's the problem! The root cause of this war is injured German pride and resentment because they were beaten last time.'

Mimi scraped the bottom of the marmalade jar. 'Well, *you're* doing your bit to stop Hitler.'

Having taken a refresher first aid course, Toby reported every night to his shelter on the Embankment, where he manned the telephone, drank cups of strong tea and learned to play poker while waiting for Luftwaffe gas attacks – a real anxiety, for thousands of still-living gas-crippled pitiable ex-servicemen reminded every Britisher of such horror and gas had again been used by the Italians to invade Ethiopia in 1935.

While waiting to be called up by His Majesty, many actors now worked as relief porters or nursing auxiliaries at big London hospitals. Basil Dean, however, had landed a plum job in a cosy office in the Theatre Royal, Drury Lane, organizing entertainment for the troops. No menial work or bloody battlefields for Bastard Basil! Actors too old to fight in the services joined the Home Guard, a stay-at-home fighting force for the defence of the civilian population against invasion, with a vanguard of Nazi paratroopers posing as nuns, canisters of gas and machine-guns cunningly hidden beneath their voluminous habits.

Jessie alternated between wanting to evacuate Fizz to countryside safety and wanting to keep her daughter right under her eye. Fizz, who wanted to stay in London, and not be sent alone to the middle of Wales (far from Max and among teetotaller lipstick-disapproving Chapel congregations), pointed out that the government had plans to evacuate pregnant women if necessary – which it clearly wasn't, or they would have done it. She also reminded her mother of the chaos already caused by the evacuation of city children to the countryside; many were now returning, preferring to risk being bombed than face rural terrors, such as cows, and live with strangers who had strange habits, such as washing daily and crapping on a seat with a hole in it.

Besides, Felicity could shelter from bombs with the rest of the household in their Anderson air-raid shelter in a deep pit at the end of the garden. To accommodate it Toby had uprooted his beloved rhododendrons. About six foot square, it was basically an arch of corrugated iron, which householders then covered with eighteen inches of earth. Toby had planted vegetables on the protective curve; Daisy had done her best to cheer up the inside, with a wind-up gramophone, cushions that soon went mouldy and had to be constantly re-covered, and an array of bottles and glasses, corkscrews and can openers. Ice was unnecessary: it was always freezing cold in the Anderson, where six to eight people could crouch in great discomfort, often with damp feet. As there was no drainage system, the acid London clay beneath the shallow topsoil was quickly reduced to sticky mud.

Toby held Home Shelter Rehearsals, miserably failing in an attempt to be as bossy as an ARP Warden should. When he blew his whistle in the middle of the night, his womenfolk were supposed to hurl themselves into action. But they all yawned and complained as they stumbled downstairs in their dressing gowns and slippers, each grabbing a rug from the pile by the back door before staggering twenty feet to the Anderson and hurling themselves through the small, low opening.

Agile Mimi was always the first to dive into the shelter, so she kept the precious stock of matches in the pocket of her dressing gown, ready to light the hurricane lamp. The next one in was always Jessie, who now occupied Max's bedroom, to help look after Fizz and everyone else. This meant another mouth to feed, but an extra pair of hands to help feed them, for now the Fanes had no staff. Daisy (now extremely stout) always puffed last into the Anderson, before pulling the blackout curtain across the entrance so that Mimi could light the lamp.

Mimi often pointed out that as they were supposed to have enough imagination to conjure up bleeding Hun bombers, could they not hold the rehearsals in the afternoon, and *imagine* it was four in the sodding morning? Then a person might not risk breaking her bloody neck on a blinking cabbage, only to be ticked off for wasting food.

One night, as they sat sheltering from non-existent bombs, trying to pretend that it was all an exciting adventure, Toby said sorrowfully, 'I shall really miss the Cunningham Whites.'

'Do we know them?' Mimi puzzled.

'Cunningham White is the name of a variety of rhododendron – the ones I had to uproot to make way for this blasted thing!'

* * *

When Britain declared war on Germany, so did France. The French immediately blamed their politicians for bringing them into a fresh war.

From Hollywood, Betsy hurriedly telephoned influential friends in Washington, who all agreed that there was no point in the Germans fighting the French, so some sort of Armistice arrangement would undoubtedly be reached before Christmas. In the meantime, the USA was firmly keeping out of other people's quarrel.

Betsy then telephoned Mme Boué, who said that so far there had been no cause for alarm, although naturally she would do whatever madame required.

Betsy subsequently called all her Parisian friends, who reported that there was no sign of the Germans, except for occasional swastika-bearing photo-reconnaissance planes. She was reminded that the French government had spent a fortune protecting France from the Germans with the French equivalent of the Great Wall of China. The supposedly impenetrable Maginot Line ran along the northern border, a huge complex of concrete emplacements and deep bunkers; it was intended to channel German invaders onto a killing ground of French choosing.

She was relieved to hear that all was tranquil in France, for clearly Stella was determined to stay in Paris.

* * *

By early October, Betsy was still able to telephone Paris with ease, and when she did so, Stella always reassured her by explaining that everything was exactly the same as usual, except for the blackout. No one had seen a German – in fact, any Germans in Paris had quickly scuttled back to Germany. There was really no need for her mother to worry. Nobody else did. What Stella really wanted was to finish her school course, as planned, then return home at Christmas. Why not? There was clearly no danger. Stella was not worried.

Although her fears were lulled, Betsy continued to check by telephone with her Parisian friends, who cheerfully informed her that after a little understandable confusion when war was declared, life was now back to normal; the newspapers assured everyone that the politicians would soon settle their squabble and it would all be over by Christmas. Meanwhile, there was no shortage of food or wine, although a good *pâtisserie* was becoming hard to find, for instead of cakes, bakers had been ordered to produce bread, made with the new, rough, Government-approved, unpopular, wholemeal flour.

Parisians tried to make the war as chic as possible, Betsy was told. Society hostesses kept their *sang froid* and threw glittering charity balls for the army, the navy and the Red Cross. For 'sheltering in the Ritz' French *Vogue* featured satin pyjamas with colour-coordinated hoods or one-piece trouser suits; your maid should be instructed to put an air-raid ensemble on a chair when she turned down your bed in the evening. In apartment blocks there was much competition between concierges to run the best cellar, and these old girls soared in social importance, almost to the heights of society hostesses. The atmosphere the concierges intended to create during the as yet non-existent air raids was half-café, half-speakeasy: dark, warm, smoky, naughty.

* * *

However, by the end of October, Stella was certainly worried, for she had realized that she really *was* pregnant. Although she felt elation, she also felt fear. She was frightened to tell anyone that she was pregnant. She was frightened to go home and face her mother. She was frightened of the day when Mme Boué would discover that her 'guest' was *enceinte*. What to do? Stella longed to be told . . . by Max, naturally.

She was only mildly worried that she had not heard from him. The post had stopped abruptly when the war started, so she might not hear from him until Christmas. From a nearby post office, she tried to telephone him at his club, but this was very difficult, for a London call had to be booked hours ahead, and if the line at the other end was busy, a repeat call could take further hours. The telephone at the Garrick club seemed constantly engaged.

After two afternoons of further uneasy lying to Mme Boué in order to get to the post office, Stella finally managed to get through to a Garrick porter, who told her that Mr Fane was not staying at the club and neither was he staying at his home address. The porter suggested that madam send a letter, which Mr Fane would collect the next time he visited.

That evening Stella wrote a halting, loving letter telling Max of her love for him, of her trust . . . and of her joyous news. Slowly, she sealed the envelope before writing her name and address on the back, in the American fashion. Tenderly, she kissed the envelope before slipping it into the postbox.

Stella – after all, her father's child – now found herself, for the first time, doing something that she really wanted to do, and the fact that it was shocking and forbidden concerned her only briefly, for she had achieved what she wanted in life, which was to get away from home, find out who she really was, and what she really wanted to do – and then be it and do it. She now knew that she was the love of Max's life, and she wanted to give her adored lover the child that his wife refused to bear. And surely the baby that Max longed for would be a greater inducement to return to Stella rather than to a wife who was always busy with her own affairs somewhere else?

* * *

By mid-November – the second month of what the British now called the Phoney War – Mimi was almost disappointed that nothing seemed to have happened on land. The expected gas bombing had not come.

The Phoney War seemed to be run by Government civil servants, rather than admirals and generals. In some way, perhaps this was just as well: the Air Minister, Sir Kingsley Wood, when asked if RAF aeroplanes might bomb the industrial factories of the Ruhr, had explained that this was *quite* out of the question, because the Ruhr factories were private property. Furthermore, interdepartmental communication was not good. For instance, the Ministry of Health's psychological experts had warned of two wartime dangers. Citizens might develop a 'deep shelter' mentality and so quiver underground in their thousands, fearfully refusing to come to the surface like frightened voles. The second was that civilian morale would shatter under air bombardment; mad with panic,

Londoners would then flee their ruined city to the countryside.

Should this happen, the mad evacuees might well be mowed down in their thousands by friendly fire, for the Home Office experts had advised that it would be prudent to turn back any hysterical urban mobs – with machine-gun fire, if necessary. Luckily, Londoners were unaware that they should perhaps worry more about the dangers of extermination by their own government than by Nazi bombers.

The absence of the enemy also disappointed Daisy, for the Anderson was clearly not about to be used for the purpose for which she had intended it – a jolly family nightclub, from which to defy the Hun. Everyone was losing interest in it. Toby had even suggested that they really didn't need the gramophone in the Anderson, where it was rusting, and could not be wound up without some-body's elbow putting out somebody else's eye. Grumbling, Daisy moved it into Fizz's bedsitter; the wireless was kept in the kitchen, where they could all sit round the battered central wooden table and solemnly listen to the BBC nine o'clock news – always deeply depressing.

Gradually, life returned to normal; cinemas and theatres reopened to record business. Nonetheless, despite the absence of Nazis, life was more difficult and perilous for Britishers. Mimi complained that apart from the dangers of catching pneumonia during midnight air-raid rehearsals there was also the peril of the blackout: lampposts, post-boxes and Government sand bins (in case of fire) seemed cunningly to alter position after dark, as she groped her way, inch by inch, around Fitzroy Square and other streets that she thought she knew well.

Mimi, Betsy and Jessie all joined the Women's Voluntary Service, ready to serve a cup of tea to anyone who had just had her house bombed to the ground. They practised bandaging each other; everyone enjoyed practising being in shock, because the patient got a hot cup of tea. They all looked after Fizz; having happily vomited every morning, she lay on a sofa for the rest of the day, scribbling letters to Max, or reading what Mimi referred to as 'Toby's dreary books'. Whenever she saw Fizz standing up, Mimi ordered her to 'Get back on that sofa and put them feet up!' Mimi spent a lot of time standing in line – queuing for food – because Toby, still managing the theatres, had no time and Daisy's bunions always played up after five minutes on her feet.

Mimi had been relieved when Jessie joined the household and took over the kitchen, for Daisy's ability to prepare a meal was limited to efficiently opening a can, making tea and burning porridge; her own culinary experience was even more limited. Jessie scorned vile recipes issued by the Ministry of Health for fatless pastry and crustless pies that ingeniously stretched your vile-tasting margarine ration. Instead, she and Toby held a weekly food meeting, when they would prowl around the end of the garden, and peer at the top of the air-raid shelter to see what was 'coming up'. Toby had sternly forbidden any black market contact; morality apart, the penalties were draconian. Jessie's dexterity in stretching their rations depended in part on an enormous number of friends with country estates who seemed happy to provide her with unrationed rabbits and game (she made a delicious Italian recipe for hare with chocolate, although chocolate could not be shot in the country). Had Jessie been one of the sixteen-year-old chorus girls from the

Minerva's current non-stop revue (*Whistle Stop*), then Mimi could have understood the butcher slipping her a couple of kidneys now and again. But Jessie had never been what they now called 'glamorous'; usually she pottered around in a porridge-coloured twin-set and baggy tweed skirt, topped by a balding old squirrel-fur coat that she wore inside out because it felt warmer that way; her feet were hidden in a pair of fleece-lined sheepskin boots that made her legs look like tree-trunks.

Once reorganized, the occupants all agreed that the house in Fitzroy Square was now a bit like being in digs, but without the dreary smell of cabbage in the hall and, of course, no lino in the bedrooms.

Mimi was relatively happy, especially as she knew that Max had a safe desk job. She would move around the house singing snatches of music-hall songs, and bursting into Forces' favourites from the Great War: the house shook with 'After You've Gone', 'For Me And My Gal' or 'Keep The Home Fires Burning'. The only time she was quiet was when she was working with Max's old school paintbox. Thanks to bloody Hitler, Mimi was producing homemade greetings cards to send at Christmas instead of her usual hampers of goodies dispatched from Fortnum & Mason, the King's own grocer, to a long list of old performers that included everyone left alive from Jolly Joe's old troupe, with the exception of That Bitch.

Friday 17 November 1939

One chilly autumn morning Mimi waited on her doorstep to the tinny strains of 'The St Louis Blues' from Fizz's room. As the antediluvian postman swung off his bicycle (only one delivery a day – don't you know there's a war on?), she eagerly snatched her post before he had time to push it through the front-door letter box. There were only three letters: a Ministry of Food leaflet, a flimsy from Max for Fizz, and ... Mimi peered with interest at an official buff envelope with the address of the American Embassy on it: it was addressed to Max and had been forwarded from his club, to his wartime civvy address.

Puzzled, Mimi slit open the envelope and pulled out another pale-blue envelope which bore no stamp. Mimi turned this over and, to her surprise and instant suspicion, saw a childish scrawl on the back, a forward-slanting handwriting with many loops. Mimi read the words 'From Stella O'Brien' followed by a fashionable address in Paris. Clearly, as the pale-blue envelope had no stamp, it had been sent by diplomatic bag, from the American Embassy in Paris to the American Embassy in London.

Mimi could not resist.

As soon as Jessie left the kitchen to trot off on her morning round of shopping, she sneaked back, heated the kettle, quickly steamed open the envelope. She whisked the envelope out of the kitchen and upstairs to her bedroom, where she settled herself on the uncomfortable, inter-ribbed Hamlet chair that formerly had stood in poor Lilian's office before she died in 1937. Mimi clutched its arms, and, as always, felt Lilian's strength and comfort.

Mimi did not want to open the Embassy-hopping pale-blue envelope that she held in her hand, intuitively feeling that it brought bad news; but she also knew that she had to act fast, before the envelope glue hardened again. Eventually, she sighed, carefully slid the pale-blue letter from the pale-blue envelope, and opened it. She blinked in disbelief as she read Stella's outpouring of her love for Max. On the fourth page, she shared with Max the wonderful news that Stella was now pregnant, and expected her child – *their* child – in mid-April 1940.

At this point the horrified Mimi – usually not backward in coming forward where reading other people's letters was concerned – felt it would be unfair to continue to read these eager, childish words of love. The pale-blue sheets of paper fluttered from her hand to the carpet as she realized that she and Betsy were about to share an illegitimate grandchild.

Mimi eventually decided not to forward the letter to Max, but to hand it over when next she saw him, so that she could see the reaction on his face. She didn't want to give him time to think up any convincing whoppers.

When Mimi broke the news to him, Toby looked equally aghast. 'Hubris!'

Sorrowfully, Mimi said, 'This time our Max's gone too far and shoved his own firework up his own arse.'

'That's what I said.'

Chapter Twenty-Two

Thursday 30 November 1939. Fitzroy Square

In the middle of the night, Fizz snapped on the light in Jessie's bedroom. She did not need to say a word; she simply stared at her mother, her eyes a blue flash in her white face, her distended stomach clearly visible through her baby-pink flannel nightgown.

In bed, Jessie shot upright. 'Why aren't you in your dressing gown?'

'Mummy, it's started.' Fizz looked down and Jessie saw water dripping onto the carpet.

'But it's only six months!'

'I know,' said Fizz, frightened. She was convinced that her baby was dead: she couldn't feel it moving.

Hurriedly Jessie wrapped her own dressing gown around Fizz, told her to start getting dressed, and rushed to shake Mimi, then Toby, awake.

Fizz felt too disheartened and depressed to dress, so she simply pulled on Jessie's fleece-lined boots. Toby eventually obtained a cab, and the three women hurried to the Soho Hospital for Women.

About a year after her marriage, Fizz had experienced an early miscarriage: it had been a bit like a violent, painful period; after they'd vacuumed it all out in the hospital the gynaecologist told her that having had a miscarriage would not affect her chances of a future normal pregnancy. Twenty-year-old Fizz did not tell him that she had not realized that she was pregnant, and was deeply relieved to have had a miscarriage. Speeding in the taxi towards the hospital, Fizz remembered her relief, and bitterly contrasted it with her present distress.

Upon arrival at the hospital, she was immediately rushed into the premature labour ward, and her child – alive, a boy – was born very shortly afterwards. After daylight, the hospital authorities hurried a priest round, who baptized the 1lb 12oz baby Patrick.

Nobody needed to tell Fizz that Patrick had very little chance of survival. Immediately after birth he was wrapped in a blanket and placed on a trolley in a celluloid oxygen tent, in a very warm recovery room, into which oxygen was pumped. He lay, naked.

Toby did not know of the birth, for after delivering Jessie, Fizz and Mimi to the hospital, Fizz had begged him to get Max. Obediently he had puffed to Piccadilly Circus, where even in wartime you could find a taxi. At Waterloo Station, he caught the first train to Portsmouth.

All trains, especially night trains, were now slow, crowded and grubby; they ran only with the blinds drawn, each compartment illuminated only by one dim blue central bulb, by the light of which Toby could hardly see the ghostly passengers wedged on the opposite banquette. Naturally there was no restaurant car, and because the corridors were crowded with sailors (as were the compartments), once the train was moving it was difficult for anyone in it to move. Toby, painfully thirsty, set out to climb over the kitbags, suitcases and crumpled, curled-up figures sleeping in the corridor. When he arrived at the lavatory, he found a line of milk-pale hungover sailors jiggling impatiently. He had to wait for twenty minutes before he could enter the stinking, swaying cubicle, within which the motion of the train had not helped accuracy of aim; he was then able to drink water which dribbled slowly from the tap into his cupped hands. It tasted of soot.

* * *

Toby travelled in person to Portsmouth because he was determined to make quite sure that Max knew what was happening to Fizz as soon as possible. Wartime messages had an odd habit of getting mislaid.

After leaving the station, he stopped a battered Austin Seven driven by a civilian. When he explained that he had to get to St Thomas's Street, a matter of life and death, the driver agreed to take him, and hurtled towards the Harbour Point at a speed far beyond the legal limit. When Toby hammered on the door, everyone in the house appeared at such sounds of emergency; the narrow entrance passage was crowded with yawning young men in pyjamas. The only occupant who did not appear was Max, who slept in the top-floor back room.

Toby shook him awake and told him what had happened. Max shot out of bed and jumped into his clothes, shooting questions at his father and fumbling with his shirt buttons. 'There's no phone here, Daddy, so I'll have to cycle to the Dockyard and ask for a forty-eight-hour compassionate. I daren't go AWOL or I'll be clapped in irons.' He suddenly stopped. 'I wonder whether Guy Findlay would lend me his bike? You never know how long those bloody trains are going to take . . .'

He left Toby, who, suddenly exhausted, slumped on the edge of his son's rumpled bed. Max reappeared looking pleased. 'The tank's full and the lads had a whip-round to give me their petrol coupons.'

Guy's motorbike was a Triumph Twin Speed 500, with an advanced engine and smooth power delivery, a dream of a bike to ride. Once in his office Max was able to telephone his commander, who hurried in, scribbled the necessary paperwork and handed Max his pass: forty-eight hours' leave, on compassionate grounds.

Toby, who had already caught the 7.20 train to London, had to stand in the corridor for the entire journey. By the time he reached Waterloo, he was feeling and looking his age. Sixty years had changed him only slightly, but he had begun to resemble his own father; his eyes were watery, he stooped more, and, undeniably, he had a little pot belly about which Mimi teased him.

* * *

Max arrived in London well before Toby, and immediately rushed to the hospital. Fizz lay in a dimly lit ward. Screens with green pleated curtains had been drawn around her bed.

She was not sobbing, but lay silent and limp, tears trickling slowly down her face. Mimi tenderly swabbed them with a red-checked tea towel she had grabbed from the kitchen as they hurried from house to cab – just in case . . .

Max crouched by his wife's side and kissed her limp hand.

'Have you seen the baby?' she whispered.

'Not yet. I came to see *you* first, then they're taking me to see Patrick.' They had long ago decided on his name.

'I'm so sorry, darling,' Fizz whispered. 'I had so longed for you to see our son in my arms.' Those lazy, happy, pregnant months had been spent lying with her feet up under a tartan rug in Mimi's drawing room, sleeping in a single bed, which soon became surrounded by little tables, as by Mimi's bedside, and with almost as much mess on them: pills for this and that, a bottle of thick concentrated wartime orange juice, thanks to the Yanks; some grubby white knitting (a matinée jacket clearly destined never to be finished), reassuring books on the joys of childbirth, and all of which, Fizz now realized, had lied through their teeth.

Max again kissed her hand, then straightened up. 'Now I'm going to visit *our son*, *Patrick*. I'll tell him that his mother sends her love.'

He was shown into the hot, small room that contained three oxygen tents, but only one occupant. He looked at the small red living creature; even his tiny fingernails were perfectly formed, and his pinched little face looked exactly like Toby: his body was thin, but his thighs were chubby. His eyes were closed, and he was sleeping; as Max anxiously watched him he seemed to shrug his shoulders and wriggle his tiny arms and legs.

'Hello, Patrick,' Max whispered. He put his hands to his face and did not try to stifle his sobs.

* * *

Patrick died at 6 a.m. on Friday 1 December 1939. His heart had probably failed to develop fully, a doctor told Max. As was the custom, the child was immediately taken to his mother, who, for the first and last time, could hold her baby in her arms.

Mimi and Jessie disappeared, leaving the parents to sorrow together. Although Patrick was now wrapped in a blanket, Max felt beneath it to stroke those fragile little toes that he had so longed to touch as his baby lay in the oxygen tent.

Fizz rubbed her cheek softly against the top of the baby's head. 'I had no idea I could feel so sad. I'm too sad to cry. My heart feels as if it's being squeezed by some monster's fist.'

Max could not speak, for he did not want Fizz to see him cry; he had to be strong at this moment for he understood that emotionally she was at this point completely dependent on him. Wordlessly he shook his head as a nurse popped her head around the screen and brightly asked if they would like a cup of tea.

Beyond the screen the ward was waking up; women were washed, there was a clatter of trolleys, a fuggy smell of hot porridge.

With his index finger Max softly touched Patrick's head; the child was already cooler.

He whispered, 'You are our son. No one else can understand how we feel about you, Patrick. No one else can understand that you are now part of our life, and always will be. We promise you that you will always be with us, you will always live in our hearts and we shall always remember you with a love that is for you alone.'

'He never saw a tree or a flower,' Fizz said sorrowfully.

'As long as he was alive, Patrick was loved. He had all our love for all of his life,' Max said firmly. 'And he still does. And he always will. And I'm sure that he knows that.'

Fizz looked at Max with gratitude and knew that she would never love him more than at that moment. The three of them had been a family, just for a few hours.

Sadly she said, 'People think that when a newborn baby dies, it doesn't count. But goodness, it does. I couldn't love Patrick more if he were twenty-one.'

'I know what you mean.' Max kissed his son's head. 'I loved Patrick the moment I saw him. Like falling in love, only firm and for ever.'

'I could do nothing for him. I felt so helpless,' Fizz sobbed.

'So did I.'

'We *will* always love him, won't we?'

'Always.'

For two hours Max stayed with Fizz, until a silently sympathetic nurse came for the baby.

For the last time, his parents kissed Patrick's fragile little ears, his delicate blue-veined eyelids. Fizz handed him to the nurse, who moved away behind the screen.

Max sat on the side of the bed, took Fizz in his arms, and stroked her head, which lay shuddering against his chest. He whispered sorrowfully, 'Poor Patrick ... Poor Fizz ... Poor us ...'

Eventually Fizz cried herself to sleep. Max gently settled her on the pillow, tucked her blanket around her shoulders, tiptoed into the uninterested corridor, leaned against the pale-green wall tiles and wept. When he felt able, he found a sluice room, with rows of shiny metal bedpans. He stuck his head under a cold tap, and wiped himself dry as best he could.

Inconsolable, he walked through dreary drizzle to Fitzroy Square, where he squeezed round the precious Triumph motorbike (parked in the hall for safety), and stepped slowly downstairs towards the basement kitchen.

Mimi, Jessie and Toby, glumly drinking tea around the

scrubbed kitchen table, heard Max's heavy tread on the stairs.

Max stood in the doorway and silently shook his head.

Eventually Jessie pulled herself upright, took a plate from the kitchen dresser and, moving like a sleepwalker, started to prepare breakfast. Fat spat. An egg cracked. Bacon crinkled.

'Kidneys and bacon,' Max said, surprised, 'egg and fried bread! How did you manage *this*, Jessie!'

'We think she's having it off with the butcher,' Toby said. Nobody laughed.

After his meal, Max took a short sleep. He was in the hall, about to depart, when Mimi called down from her bedroom, 'Max, I want to see you in my bedroom, just for a couple of minutes.'

'I don't want to talk about the baby.'

'Of course not.'

Catching the grave insistence of his mother's voice, Max followed her, wondering what he had or had not done, as he trudged up the stairs.

Once they were together, Mimi shut the door and locked it. Without saying a word, she opened the top drawer of her dressing table, drew out the buff envelope from the American Embassy and handed it to him.

'Why did you open my letter?' Max asked, puzzled.

'Take a look at it. It looked bloody official, bloody mysterious – and you weren't here. I thought it might well be something important – and it bloody well was.'

Max looked at the envelope as his mother added, 'It was sent from the American Embassy in Paris to the American Embassy here. They posted it, as instructed, to the Garrick. As you didn't turn up, your club eventually sent it here; you'd given Fitzroy Square as your forwarding address for the duration.'

This carefully explanatory, clearly rehearsed speech was so odd coming from his mother that Max immediately knew what he had, and had not, done. 'Oh, God!' he muttered.

When he read Stella's loving, happy, trusting letter – which referred frequently to their lovemaking in Paris – he understood why his mother looked so sour. When he reached the last page he murmured, 'Oh, no!'

He finished the letter, but still did not look up. He did not want to look his mother in the face. Sensing women ganging up against him, he felt guilty, but also a little resentful. He had intended to have a light-hearted affair in Paris, and God knew she had been willing enough. He had nothing to reproach himself about, Stella knew that.

But nobody else did, and nobody else would: he was thirty-one years old, not a star-struck nineteen-year-old girl in love for the first time, when you always believe that this is the one and only time. Stella had been easy prey, others would assume.

Hesitantly, Mimi said, 'I suppose it is . . . ?'

'She's in love with me,' Max said, unwillingly.

'But why didn't you . . . ?'

'For God's sake, Mummy, do you think I don't wish I had?' Max had not realized Stella was a virgin. After that first time he had been 'careful'.

'I suppose this happened while you and Fizz were separated?'

Max said defensively, 'I really thought Fizz had left for ever.'

'Clearly, so did this young lady,' Mimi sighed. Eventually she broke the silence. 'Well, son, what are we going to do about it?'

Max sank into the fat rosebuds of the overstuffed fireside armchair; he buried his face in his hands. 'I don't know what the hell I should do. Mum, please help me.'

'What you're *not* going to do,' Mimi said firmly, 'is tell Fizz. Don't unload your guilty conscience onto her.'

'The honourable thing to do is to go straight back to Paris and sort things out with Stella.' Max started to pace the room. 'But I've no hope of getting to Paris in wartime. I can't even get a letter to Stella . . . although perhaps . . . via the American Embassy bag? . . . Yes. That's what I'll do.'

'Sounds too late to "sort things out",' said Mimi quietly. 'And it sounds to me as if this young lady don't want to be sorted out. She's clearly longing to have your baby.'

'But what can I do about that?'

'I think *you* should do nothing,' Mimi said, 'until we know more.' She didn't want Max going AWOL, then being clapped in irons by the navy or captured by the Nazis; most of all, she did not want to worry Fizz.

'One thing more, son. Her name. On the back of the envelope, Stella O'Brien it says. Is your lady friend . . . ?'

'Yes. She's Betsy's daughter.'

On a rising note of wrath, Mimi growled, 'May I ask why, of all the bleeding women in the world, you had to choose the one that would give me grief?'

'Hush, Mummy, they'll hear downstairs.'

'Don't you dare hush me, you wicked young pup! How did this happen?'

Max suddenly remembered that there *had* been an

ulterior motive for his interest in Stella. 'Don't think I'm not ashamed of myself, Mummy. Don't rub it in.'

'No, son, I won't. Because I'll tell you who will: Stella's mam. Betsy O'Brien.'

Max, who had thought his predicament could not get worse, now looked as horrified and defensive as if a paratrooping nun had leaped through the window. 'How does Mrs O'Brien know about this?'

'She don't, son. You're going to tell her. The right person to look after that girl at this moment is her own mother. Unlike us, Betsy'll have no problem getting to Paris because the States ain't at war with France or Germany.'

Max looked aghast. 'How can I telephone Stella's mother? She'd suspect some ulterior motive. She'd think of a thousand convoluted reasons for my call. She'd decide that I'd done it deliberately, because I was after Stella's money . . . or . . . or . . .'

'That's enough, son. You *will* phone Stella's mother, because this kid's only nineteen. You will phone her because I've raised you to be a responsible adult, and she's *your* responsibility,' Mimi added sternly. 'And you will phone Betsy *because I say so*.'

'But as soon as Betsy knows who's speaking she'll slam down the phone!'

'Then phone again until she listens. If she won't, then I don't care how you do it, but Betsy *must* be told as soon as possible, so she can get over to Paris and take care of her daughter. For all we know, this kid's trapped in Paris – this letter was written over a month ago.'

Somebody tried to open the door to Mimi's bedroom, then shook the handle so that the door rattled. Toby called, 'Are you all right, Mimi?'

'Right as rain,' she agreed. She moved forward to unlock the door.

Max looked pleadingly at his mother. Looking at his exhausted face, she remembered that he had just lost his first-born child.

She sighed. 'OK, OK. I'll phone her. You get to the hospital, Max, and I'll look after this. Better leave that letter with me. I'll give it back to you later, after I've phoned.'

'Phoned who?' Toby asked as the door opened.

'The florist. Flowers for Fizz.'

'Good idea if they've got any, Foxtop.'

As Mimi kissed Max goodbye, she whispered in his ear, so that Toby could not hear, 'I'll phone Betsy from the American Embassy. Useless to use our phone, they'd never put me through to bleeding Hollywood in wartime.'

Friday 1 December 1939. Hollywood

'You did!'

'I didn't, so!'

'*Yes*, you did, Tess. You're a little *liar*! Do you think your own *mother* doesn't know when you're lying through your teeth?' Angrily Betsy waved the newspaper clipping, headed O'BRIAN–FANE FIGHT – ROUND 89, which reported an entirely fictitious account of how eighteen-year-old Tess O'Brien had repeatedly urged her mother to stop this painful vendetta, and then gave a short rundown on Tess's career to date.

It was eleven o'clock on Friday morning, and Tess, who was not needed at the Studio that day, was waiting to be picked up for drinks in the Polo Lounge and lunch afterwards in the adjoining palm-shaded courtyard restaurant. Standing in her bedroom (now spray-gunned peach), Betsy still wore her housecoat, a peach organdie marabou-trimmed affair. She stamped her marabou-trimmed slipper. 'I will *not* stand this sort of behaviour, Tess.'

'Come off it, Mom, *you* know that any publicity is good publicity,' Tess whined. Inside info on the powerful meant first, no attacks from the people to whom Tess gave her information; second, that they repaid her with free publicity.

'Rubbish! I know damn well that neither Hedda nor Louella invented that nasty stuff in "Confidential" last week – that bit about hatred keeping me young . . . Those awful candid shots of me with my mouth hanging open.' Again Betsy stamped her slipper. Thank God, the war had cut off Mimi's bitchy humiliating memories and comments on Betsy's behaviour and appearance. But Tess was pitching tiny poisoned darts at her own mother! She leaked inside stories about Betsy and her friends to either Hedda or Louella. The Deadly Duo, as the pair of gossip columnists were called, had the power to destroy reputations, careers and marriages. Of the two, Hedda was considered the more vindictive, but Louella's husband, a specialist in venereal diseases, had been house doctor to a top Hollywood bordello; his contacts had provided his wife with some of Hollywood's most intimate secrets. Although a known alcoholic, he was paid a substantial retainer by Paramount, which wanted to shelter from Louella's spite, and if an alcoholic's shaking hands performed possibly dangerous abortions – well, that was just too bad.

Tess was not a fool, and she was very efficient in her efforts to further her career; she realized that she needed all the help she could get and had an instinctive understanding of the delicate obligations of favour swapping, so cooperated carefully with her Studio publicity department. She never complained about doing interviews or the resulting stories. Although she had now been working before the cameras for two years (in Technicolor musicals), her career had not moved upwards as fast as she had hoped, because of hot competition from other young actresses: Rita at Columbia; young Judy and Lana at MGM; Susan and Paulette at Paramount; Anne Sheridan at Warner; and Deanna at Universal. Which was why Tess still played younger sister parts.

Tess was impatient but not downhearted. Although a daddy's darling, a spoilt child who had hardly ever been frustrated or disappointed, she both worked and lived in the land of Make Believe, and with the tenacity inherited from Black Jack she simply would not accept that she was never going to be a star, or that the story of her life might have an unhappy ending.

Betsy pulled her peach negligée around her and stamped her foot again. 'I hate the stupid gossip that's printed about you, Tess. I don't know *what* to do with you.'

'Try doing nothing,' Tess advised from her mother's dressing table as she applied another unnecessary crimson layer to her mouth.

Betsy said, half pleadingly, 'Why do you always have to dress as if you were some twice-divorced woman, Tess? Why can't you wear a plaid skirt or pedal pushers with saddle-Oxfords, like other teenagers?' Thank God Stella was safely in Paris, having a great time with Mme Boué, according to her aerogrammes. Darling Nick never gave any trouble, either. But Tess . . .

'I may still be a teenager,' snapped Tess, as she licked her forefinger and readjusted her left eyebrow, 'but I don't *feel* like one, and I'm certainly not going to act like one.'

'That's *another* thing we have to discuss, young lady.' Betsy now bravely said what she had long wanted to. 'Tess, I don't like you going out with older men.'

'I like older men and so did you, Mom,' Tess said belligerently. 'What's wrong with that?'

Betsy persevered. 'We both know why actresses go out with older men.' Hopefuls were obliged to provide sexual favours to appropriately selected Studio personnel. 'But *you don't have to do that*, Tess!'

Tess stuck out her chin. 'Older men look after a girl.' There was a surprisingly large number of fatherless girls in Hollywood, forlornly seeking a father substitute with whom they could – finally – feel safe.

'But you know that's just part of the Studio system!' Betsy cried. Starlets were encouraged to see the Studio as a stern but protective father; so long as the girls worked hard, never complained and were successful, they were generously rewarded – trained by the best teachers, coddled by the best masseurs, hairdressers and fashion designers.

Tess scowled. 'Older men are more sophisticated, less demanding.'

'Not . . . sexually,' Betsy stuttered. There, she'd said it! She tried to lower her voice. 'It's not right, honey. You're still so young – only eighteen, after all. How will you feel on the day you get married to someone you *really* love?'

Betsy shivered as she remembered her own wedding night. 'How will your *husband* feel?'

'Oh, Mom. You're so old-fashioned. After sixteen, everybody does it, not just starlets.'

'I don't care about everybody. I care about *my daughter*! It's not only that you go with older men, it's the awful ones you choose! Nightclub owners! Types like that horrible Stompanato, and the other underworld hoodlums he goes around with.'

'Oh, Mom! You know as well as I do that for the last ten years nobody's been able to be in show business in America without being involved with hoods!' Organized crime had controlled the speakeasies in the twenties and when Prohibition ended they had gone legal, first becoming nightclub owners, then infiltrating other areas of show business, which was why performers automatically knew gangsters.

Betsy tried to sound reasonable. 'Some stars like to be seen with hoodlums,' she agreed. You had nothing to fear around town if you were seen with one of these protective panthers, but then a girl left herself wide open to other dangers. 'Suppose something happened to you?' Betsy wailed, meaning drugs, as she pulled her housecoat protectively around her. She longed to ask Tess if she had been 'fitted' (with a contraceptive diaphragm) but could not bring herself to.

'Yes, of course I've been fitted.' Tess scornfully guessed what her mother was dying to know. 'Two years ago, as a matter of fact.'

Betsy did not know whether to be relieved or furious. 'Can't you understand?' she screamed. 'I'm *worried* about you!' She bit back the words, 'I have no one I can talk to about it,' for Tess would wrongly assume that her mother was trying to steer her back to the kid-shrink, as she contemptuously referred to him.

Betsy had been told that Tess's problems stemmed from Black Jack's death. Pop's little princess now expected other people to make her happy, as her father had – but he had been snatched away. Since he died Tess emotionally refused to accept what had happened. 'Insecurity sometimes leads a child to make unreasonable and constant demands on other people, in order to test their affection,' the expensive expert had explained. 'But it also means she is incapable of accepting such assurance. So little . . . er' – he consulted his notes – 'Tess will never be satisfied, will never get enough praise, recognition or gratitude. Eventually, only self-pity will comfort her, so she might unconsciously seek out trouble to justify this self-pity!'

'But nobody will put up with her! She'll run out of friends!'

'And exhaust her husbands.' Sorrowful shake of the head. 'Unless, of course, she is treated.' He threw Betsy his famously reassuring twinkling smile.

'And if she isn't?' Betsy asked doubtfully.

'Her emotional security will depend on the . . . ah . . . unreliable opinions of other people, who will reassure her so long as she makes it worth their while.'

'*Spongers?*'

Sorrowful nod. 'And little Tess will be an easy target for confidence tricksters who flatter her into forgetting her insecurity.'

'How much?' Betsy firmly opened her purse.

After her first visit, Tess had refused to return to the conman kid-shrink. Now, she twisted on her heel and snapped at her mother, 'And another thing! I reckon I'm old enough to look after the money I earn. It's too bad I have to turn to you for every cent! It's *not fair* the Studio pays my salary to you!' Tess's contract specified that as a minor her salary was paid to her mother, acting as her manager, until she reached the age of twenty-one.

Betsy ruthlessly used her control of Tess's purse strings: retrospectively, she had always been glad that Mrs Bridges had regularly put by part of her salary, and had taught her to save. Had she not done so, the Bridges would have been unable to afford tickets to America, unable to afford to eat while Betsy was out of work for months. So she now paid Tess's monthly salary into a bank deposit account, except for 20 per cent – quite enough allowance for a young girl, Betsy considered.

Tess saw herself as a thwarted heiress, and hated this arrangement. Not only was her *own* money kept from her, but her beloved father had, for some reason (no doubt arranged by her stingy mother), arranged that none of his children should inherit their money from his Trust fund until their thirtieth birthday or until they married, which-ever came earlier. Sometimes Tess was tempted to elope to Mexico, get married, come back, claim her million dollars and then get a quickie divorce. However, caution told her that she didn't want to inherit a pile just to see some husband walk off with a percentage. Or hang around to cause trouble, unless she paid him off with a regular allowance until he died. (Goodness, some people simply asked to be bumped off.)

Betsy and Tess continued to quarrel, their voices grow-ing louder and angrier, until Betsy's bedside telephone rang.

Without stopping her angry tirade, Betsy automatically

moved to the telephone and lifted the receiver. Tess took this opportunity to whisk out of the room, for she had just heard the crunch of tyres on gravel. Johnny had arrived to collect her.

Surprised, Betsy heard, 'Good day, ma'am. This is the US Embassy in London, England. I have an important call for you.'

* * *

It was eleven in the morning, Pacific time, eight hours behind London time. Mimi had managed to get a message passed to Avrell, who had immediately arranged for a transatlantic line at the Embassy in London to be put at her disposal at 7 p.m. London time, for the purpose of speaking to Mrs Betsy O'Brien, on the west coast.

When Betsy heard Mimi's voice she almost slammed down the phone ... but the Embassy had said it was an important call. What the hell was Mimi doing in the US Embassy? Her curiosity won. She snapped, 'You've got a nerve calling me!'

'Please, Betsy, *listen*! ... Stella needs your help.'

'Rubbish! How would *you* know? If Stella had a problem, she would call *me*.'

'Not with this problem,' Mimi said quietly.

Immediately, Betsy knew what the problem was.

Numb with shock, she listened in silence as slowly, carefully, Mimi told her that her elder daughter was pregnant. Hesitantly, she added that the father of Stella's baby was her own married son, Max.

Betsy, stunned to silence when she heard that Stella was pregnant, became incoherent with rage when she heard by whom.

In London, Mimi held the telephone away from her ear until Betsy had calmed down. Once again, Mimi tried to explain that she wanted only to help, to do what was best for Stella and (deep breath) their grandchild.

'How do I know this fantastic story isn't some other cunning way to humiliate me? How do I know Hedda or Louella aren't listening on some telephone extension at this very moment? You realize this is *libel*? Or slander. Maybe both!'

'Why don't you check with Stella? You can phone Paris, Betsy – but I can't. That's the trouble. There's a war on over here, remember? If there wasn't, Max and me could handle this ourselves.' Mimi again held the telephone from her ear. The torrent of abuse finally exasperated her. 'Don't blame *me*, Betsy! I wasn't even in the same bloody country when it happened!'

'Why didn't you raise your son to know that a married man shouldn't—'

'I never met a married man that didn't!'

'Thank God *I* don't know *that* sort of man.'

'The sort of man who goes whoring?'

'That's exactly what I mean! . . . How *dare* you twist my words! *My daughter is not a whore!*'

'Looks as if she behaved like one,' Mimi said quietly.

That shut her up. Eventually Betsy made a tearful, half-hearted counter-attack, 'If it hadn't been for *you*, Mimi, they'd never have met.'

' "If wishes were horses, beggars would own their own stables",' Mimi said tartly. 'You can't blame me for a string of coincidences . . . Or if you must, then blame Baz for nicking a sandwich nearly forty years ago. If I'd let Baz be arrested at Crewe Station, then I'd never have met you, I'd never have met Toby, we'd never have had Max and your Stella would never have pulled her knickers down for him in Paris!'

'How dare you be so crude! How typical of you, Mimi!'

'Betsy, *you* can't change what's happened! If you want to blame someone, blame Fate, blame God. But I'm not having you blame me for it. I'm sorry my Max was ... involved. But I'll be damned if that was *my* fault.'

Mimi heard sobs. Conciliatory, she said, 'I'm sorry, Betsy, I'm really sorry. But this is an emergency, too serious for quarrels. That's why I'm phoning you. Won't you telephone Stella and ask her – gently, mind – whether she really is pregnant? You can say I told you, then she'll know how I found out.' Her voice hardened. 'And if she is, Betsy, then it's your job to look after your daughter and get her out of a war zone.'

'I've been assured by several *very* knowledgeable, important politicians that everything in France will calm down by Christmas.'

'Supposing your smart contacts are wrong, Betsy?' Mimi asked gently. She understood Betsy's pain and mortification: the daughter who had, at enormous expense, been groomed to be a lady had clearly behaved in a most unladylike manner. The responsibility of Stella's pregnancy was clearly that of Max and Stella. But Mimi could hear that if something went wrong with Betsy's life she still blamed somebody else, and if the fault lay within someone she loved then she managed to redirect the blame. So, as Betsy loved Stella, then Betsy would lay the entire blame on Max.

Mimi was wrong.

Chapter Twenty-Three

Friday 1 December 1939. Los Angeles

Before checking with her travel agent, Betsy had telephoned a friend in Washington, to get his perspective on
the European war danger. Since the beginning of September 1939, nothing had happened in France or England:
everyone was relaxing in the anticlimax of the Phoney
War. From Washington, the conservative viewpoint was
still expressed over the telephone. 'Let them get on with
it over there, it's none of our business.'

What clearly *was* Betsy's business was Stella's condition. Mme Boué had been her usual charming self and
(among other matters) had reassured Betsy that her daughter was in the best of health. Betsy had twice spoken to
Stella, who sounded her usual self, in fact happier than
usual and not at all in the state of terror that an unwanted
pregnancy produced. On the first call she had asked Stella
if she was seeing a boy and Stella had laughed and said
that none of the girls yet spoke French well enough to
flirt and anyway they weren't allowed to date. On the
second call, Betsy had managed to ask, 'You haven't done
anything foolish, have you? You aren't pregnant?'

'*Whatever* makes you ask that, Mom?' Stella had
sounded astonished.

Immediately Betsy had been vexed with herself. 'Just

the usual vicious gossip, honey. I should never had paid any attention to it.' Then they had chatted about Stella's return home at Christmas.

However, for the next two days, Betsy had continued to worry. She told herself that Stella would be flying home in a few weeks. Had her daughter been pregnant surely someone in a girls' school would have noticed? Had Stella been pregnant she would not have sounded so cheerfully excited, she told herself. But her small, inner voice kept telling her that something was wrong. Somehow, Stella had sounded different. Eventually, she had decided to catch her daughter unaware and take her straight to a gynaecologist, upon some pretext. Then perhaps she would be able to sleep at night again.

At least, Betsy consoled herself, she could order new clothes, it might be her last chance for some time: Parisian society women were now ordering voluntary-work uniforms from their couturiers. Chanel had closed down, and her seamstresses were now stitching gloves for soldiers. Other couturiers were defiantly producing new collections with flippant names: 'False Alarm' was an ermine coat, 'Offensive' a jacket, skirt, blouse and gas-mask bag of matching materials. The new shoes had thick cork soles; hats remained tiny, frivolous and cockeyed.

With trepidation, Betsy decided that she would just have to grit her teeth and fly to Paris, where she would organize the operation for her poor child: she had the address of an English-speaking doctor.

Betsy once again spoke to her private string-puller in Washington, who managed to procure a reservation on the Clipper, due to leave four days later.

Betsy had been exhausted by the time she eventually

arrived in New York; thankfully, she had flopped into bed at the Plaza, hoping she never had to take that frightening flight again.

Wednesday 6 December 1939. New York

The Clipper sat complacently on tranquil water, like some enormous ungainly marsupial. There were airfield rumours of delay: she would be three hours late taking off, she would be six hours late; there was engine trouble; the entire flight might be cancelled; the plane was not going to take off at all.

After a two-hour delay the passengers were herded into a launch, which conveyed them to the Clipper. As Betsy climbed on board, she turned to look back towards the grey smudge of land: was she seeing it for the last time? Was it too late to turn back? She felt a sinking feeling in the pit of her stomach as she forced herself to climb on board; there, she accepted a cocktail (a rare occurrence) before a simple, delicious dinner: clear soup was followed by grilled sole, after which she ate lamb chops and a heap of French fries (which normally she would never touch); crisp salad proceeded a large slice of cheesecake, after which she knocked back a double brandy. Shortly afterwards, she saw two stewardesses bending over her, to ask if she was feeling all right.

'Absholutely shpiffing.' Betsy gave a ladylike hiccup, held her hand to her mouth, and giggled.

There were several Frenchmen on board, who looked fairly miserable; the rest of the plane was filled with men in assorted uniforms. The atmosphere was similar to that in the lounge of a genteel hotel, Betsy thought, just before she dozed off, despite being thousands of feet above the Atlantic.

On the following day, she sat, rigid with fear, until they arrived at Lisbon, at 7.30 p.m. She stayed at the Braganza Hotel, and on the following day caught the luxurious Sud-Express train, which left Lisbon at 12.30 p.m. She arrived in Paris the day after that, on the 9th of December, feeling very modern: the twelve-day journey from Los Angeles to Paris had now been cut to four days.

Weary Betsy now saw that – as Stella had reported – the Place Vendôme looked just the same, the people strolling around as elegant as ever, although there were many uniforms. Betsy hobbled into the Ritz on painful, swollen feet, her shoes in her hand, too tired to feel ashamed of herself. Thankfully, she sank into a swan-soft bed and, to her astonishment and dismay, she stayed there for over twenty-four hours, completely exhausted not only by travelling, but by her anxieties over a possible plane crash at sea.

Monday 11 December 1939. Paris

When Betsy woke up, to her surprise, several envelopes were delivered with her fragrant coffee and croissants, mouth-wateringly crisp as usual. Her Washington friend had contacted the American Embassy in Paris and asked them to take care of Mrs O'Brien. The Embassy had sent notes to various influential Americans in Paris, announcing Betsy's impending arrival.

When she opened her envelopes, it was clear that the social life in Paris was again in full swing. Lady Mendl had invited her for luncheon to her famous Villa Trianon in Versailles, once the home of the Empress Josephine; Mlle Chanel was giving *un cocktail*. Betsy shuffled through her invitations to luncheon parties, drinks parties, dinner parties, supper parties, and one theatre First Night: in Paris, war and peace seemed pretty much the same. In fact, there were even more functions and entertainments than usual, in aid of various charities, the Red Cross and the army. The maid who unpacked Betsy's clothes warned madame that it was no longer considered chic to wear evening dress. Ignoring her invitations, Betsy called for a taxi and went immediately to Mme Boué's apartment.

She found Mme Boué in a state of great distress, with half her usual complement of young guests, the other half having been hurriedly recalled to their various countries by their parents. In addition, two days before, Stella had disappeared.

Mme Boué had immediately telephoned Madame O'Brien *à 'Olleewood*, and had been told she was on her way to Paris. Mme Boué then alerted the police; no avenue, no bridge over the Seine had been left unexplored in their efforts to locate Stella. The gendarmes had already checked with all hotels, the hire-car firms, the travel agencies, the airports, the hospitals. Also – Mme Boué lowered her voice – the morgues.

It was clear that Stella's disappearance had been planned, for she had taken her jewel box. According to the *femme de chambre*, Stella had not taken all her clothes: oddly enough, her ankle-length ermine evening cloak had disappeared, and also all her sweaters and blouses – but no skirts, no lingerie, and none of her evening gowns. Wherever she was, Stella must look a *drôle de spectacle*.

Mme Boué hesitated to say to Mme O'Brien, but Stella's clothes must have been cunningly removed a few at a time, in smart shopping bags, for if any servant had seen her leave with a suitcase (none of which were missing), it would have been reported immediately to Mme Boué.

Mme Boué had already telephone les Cole Porteurs, but their house had now been closed for the duration and was occupied by a caretaker.

By the time Mme Boué had finished her story the police officer in charge of the search for Stella had arrived at the front door. Loathing every minute, Betsy accompanied him to the Préfecture de Police, a shabby, noisy clump of grey-painted offices that stank of Gauloise cigarettes, other people's armpits and stale wine. There, the horrified Betsy was shown photographs of dead girls: they had recently been discovered either drowned in the Seine, raped and strangled in some dark place at night or dumped in the street, after a drug overdose. Betsy's eyes filled with tears as she looked at the crude photographs of sad, dead, once-hopeful faces.

Thank God, none of them were Stella.

The police officer tactfully said that as Mlle O'Brien appeared to have had no accident, and as her departure had been planned, she might well be visiting a friend. Did Mme O'Brien know of any such close friend, male or female? Betsy, white and shaking, was shown courteously from the police station by the gendarme who had brought her there. On the doorsteps, he murmured in her ear . . . might he suggest, a discreet investigation . . . more time . . . more facilities . . . The gendarme then slipped Betsy a card with the name and address of a private detective, who would doubtless hand the *flic* a commission on whatever Betsy paid him.

Betsy went right back to the Ritz, locked her bedroom and wept a little. She was too ashamed to telephone the American Embassy, but ten minutes later she told herself that this was ridiculous when Stella's life might be at stake. But what good could the Embassy do? Contact the French police, is all, and that had already been done. What Betsy needed was indeed a French detective. Here, in her hand, was a bit of pasteboard bearing the name of one recommended by the police.

Betsy bathed her face in cold water, then telephoned the detective. Luckily, he spoke a little English. No, no. Madame was not to disturb herself, it would not be a problem for himself to voyage to the Ritz, without doubt in half an hour.

With a sigh of relief, Betsy replaced the peculiarly heavy French telephone on its black cradle. She decided to go down to the lounge. That glass of brandy in the Clipper had certainly had a reviving effect when she felt exhausted.

* * *

For a month, Betsy fruitlessly searched Paris for Stella, with the half-hearted help of the French police who had far more important things to worry about than a missing rich American girl who had clearly run off *avec son petit ami pour un peu de batifolage quelque part*.

* * *

It was reported that a Mlle O'Brien had checked into the Negresco, a smart hotel in Nice, but she had only stayed one night. Betsy and the detective immediately caught the train to Nice. With the aid of the local police and a colleague of the detective, Nice was then thoroughly searched for Stella, without success. 'She has clearly arrived in the south of France,' repeated the Parisian detective, for a couple of the staff at the Negresco had nodded upon seeing Stella's photograph, and had agreed that they remembered this eccentric *mademoiselle américaine*. The receptionist remembered her face and her American accent, the floor-service waiter recalled her because she had ordered for *petit déjeuner* two portions of chocolate ice cream with one portion of pickled herrings.

Betsy stayed at the Negresco. Although the hotel staff spoke a little English, Betsy felt out of place. Disconsolately, she gazed from her balcony at the brilliant blue Mediterranean sky above the darker blue sea; even though it was nearly Christmas, a couple of little sailboats floated lazily on the water. Betsy could not enjoy the pale December sunshine: she felt disorientated, and emotionally exhausted. She had been through difficult times, but never alone. She could not become accustomed to coping on her own. She had no travelling companion, not even a secretary; there was no really close friend in Paris in whom she could confide. She should have asked Tudor to accompany her on this long, alarming and fruitless journey to search for Stella. Oh, how she wished that dear Tudor were here to look after all this for her, deal with these officials, look at the latest batch of photographs of sad, dead girls.

Betsy suddenly felt an old woman. Her shoulders sagged. Quickly, she straightened her back. She was damned if, on top of everything else, she was going to allow herself to feel old! She turned on her heels, went to the bathroom, redid her make-up, adjusted her purple nest of feathers jauntily over one eye and headed for the bar.

* * *

After spending a great deal of money for nothing, Betsy heard from Paris that Stella had written to Madame Boué. Relieved, but extremely depressed, Betsy now agreed with the detective that Stella must be somewhere in the south of France, staying with friends. 'Possibly the father of her child?' the detective discreetly hinted. Grimly, Betsy shook her head. 'Not possible.'

Betsy returned to the Ritz to find that a cable had arrived for her on the previous day. She ripped it open and saw it was from Acapulco. Puzzled, Betsy read:

GUESS WHAT TUDOR AND I MARRIED HERE TODAY STOP GAVE EXCLUSIVE TO LOUELLA STOP PLEASE BE HAPPY FOR US STOP WE SEND OUR LOVE STOP TESS PERKINS

Crossly, Betsy wondered whether sending such a silly cable was Tess's idea of a joke. But the cable definitely had been sent from Acapulco. Should she phone Louella to check? That would mean admitting that she had not been told in advance ... Then the enormity hit her. *Tudor!* Surely Tess could not have married Tudor? Why should she? Why should he? Surely Tudor would have not done something so underhand? She looked again at the cable. Suddenly, she furiously realized that 'please be happy for us' *did* sound like Tudor. How *could* her beau have done this behind her back? To think she had thought that streak of a slime a gentleman! Huh! It was disgusting! Incestuous! Tudor must be nearly fifty, old enough to be

Tess's . . . so *that* was the attraction, she realized bitterly: Tudor was Tess's stand-in for Black Jack. And with marriage came a million dollars for Tess, according to her father's will.

Bitterly, Betsy asked herself why she hadn't seen this danger before? It should have been obvious. Tess had made it clear she'd had enough of egocentric, predatory young fellows, all of whom knew that Tess was an heiress. Tudor was everything that Tess had insisted she was looking for in a man. Tudor was considerate, discreet, charming, amusing; Tudor was loveable, a teddy bear, the perfect escort. Tudor didn't gamble; Tudor earned a respectable living as a voice coach and so did not have an actor's habitual feeling of insecurity; Tudor was one of the few men in Hollywood who wasn't particularly interested in money, so Tudor was unlikely to be a fortune-hunting conman.

Betsy had thought she could trust her beau. She knew that Tudor had discreet liaisons, but then he was a man with a man's needs, and Betsy had been careful to give him no encouragement, for she had not wanted to commit herself, to get into something that she could not easily get out of. Well now, she couldn't get in it! And she couldn't get out of it! Tudor was part of the family. No longer her beau, but her son-in-law. She could spit.

What made this elopement even more galling was her suspicion that it was no accident that Tess had eloped with her mother's long-established beau: Tess was getting her revenge for Betsy not having handed over Tess's entire salary for the previous two years. In a temper, Betsy yanked the telephone towards her, broke a nail and burst into tears. She had to admit that there was a hard streak in Tess; although she hated to admit it about her own daughter, Tess was wilful, impetuous and headstrong, as well as vengeful.

Wearily, Betsy telephoned the America Embassy. Perhaps it was not too late to annul the marriage, if she returned immediately. There was no point in staying in Paris for Stella had clearly left the city. Betsy, who spoke no French, could be of no help in the expensive search for her that was now taking place in the south of France. And she had another crisis to deal with back home.

Where had she gone wrong with her daughters? They had both had the best nannies that money could buy. Thank Heaven Nick was tucked safely away in his hoity-toity East Coast academy.

Betsy once again headed for the Ritz bar, where she brooded over the snifter of brandy, and ordered another. By the time she downed her third, she realized that this was all Mimi's fault. Had Mimi not sent Tudor to Hollywood, this could never had happened! If Mimi had never given birth by immaculate conception to that oversexed tom cat, Stella would not be pregnant.

One day, Betsy would avenge herself.

* * *

Stella's disappearance had been surprisingly easy to arrange. After Max had left Paris, she had lived in a mist of elation. But as the mist dissolved, she saw reality more clearly. Then she started to slide towards a gorge of despair: would she ever see him again? One afternoon, she sneaked off to the hotel Scribe, where she calmly walked into the elevator and casually asked for the third floor as if she was a hotel guest.

Once on the third floor, she slowly walked along the carpeted corridor, feeling calmer every minute; she was positively happy when she reached the doorknob of the door to 'their' bedroom. At least she could touch something that her lover had touched: the round brass doorknob seemed a link between them, and Stella held it until it felt warm in her hand. She lingered as long as she dared, then went to a nearby café where she always ordered a *citron pressé*; as she slowly drank it, she once again relived every hour that she had spent with Max.

Stella repeatedly returned to stroke the doorknob fondly, wishing that a twist was able to magically whisk her back to relive those days with her lover.

One day the bedroom door suddenly opened, and Stella found herself facing the little dark chambermaid, who hugged a pile of crumpled sheets.

'Hello, Rachel,' Stella blushed.

The chambermaid instantly realized why Stella was there. 'You can come in while I clean the room, if you like,' she offered.

Stella moved around surreptitiously touching the bedhead, the stiff little armchair, the window frame against which she remembered Max silhouetted. By the time that Rachel had finished making the bed, Stella had told her (in fairly good French) everything that she had been forced until now to keep hidden in her heart. How wonderful Max was ... No (in response to Rachel's dubious question), Stella's mother knew his family: *ce n'est pas un de ces je-ne-sais-qui de je-ne-sais-où*. On the contrary, Max was *un serieux* and socially acceptable. He had promised to return to Stella, but this wretched war had prevented their reunion. Max longed for a child, he had told her. So she had written to tell him she was pregnant.

Stella had told nobody about that letter. But now,

Stella's mother knew she had written it. Although the telephone line had crackled badly, it was clear that her mother was very angry to hear of Stella's pregnancy. Stella was frightened. What should she do?

'Your mother has to be told some time.' Rachel gave a philosophical, Gallic shrug.

'But she'll make me have an abortion!'

'It's too late, I think.'

'You don't know my mom! She can fix anything she wants! And if it is too late, then she'll force me to give my baby to some adoption society! I don't know *how* she'll fix it, but she'll tell me that she won't be able to hold up her head at home if her daughter gives birth to a ... She would call our baby a bastard ... She'd be right, but I don't care!' Stella pulled her sloppy-joe sweater tight around the bulge that was still hardly visible, although her waistline had disappeared. 'But I don't want to go back home! I want to have our baby, and marry Max as soon as this war's over, then have more babies. If I'm married, I inherit money from my pop. Mom can't stop that. So we could easily afford to live in Europe.'

'Why did Max phone your *maman*?'

'He didn't. He must have told his mother, because she contacted my mom.'

'Why did he not call *you*?'

'He was sort of in the navy. Maybe he's at sea, already in some battleship. Maybe he can send aerogrammes to Britain, but not use the phone. Maybe people can't phone France from Britain any more: it took hours for me to book a call, weeks ago. This war!'

'Console yourself, Stella. Max must be concerned about you, if he got a message through to your mother.'

'Yes, but she'll be so mad I'm going to marry Max!' Tearfully, the Romeo and Juliet story came tumbling out. 'She'll come to Paris!'

Rachel sat in the Louis XVI armchair and scratched her ear thoughtfully. 'You say your *maman* always stays at the Ritz? So we telephone to see if she has reserved accommodation.' She flipped through the Parisian telephone directory, and scribbled the number of the Ritz on the bedside pad. 'Stella, telephone from the *cabine* in the lobby. If we use this telephone, the operator would immediately report it, and I will lose my job, *pouf!*'

Twenty minutes later Stella burst back into the bedroom. 'You were right, Rachel! Mom's expected on the ninth of December, she's reserved a suite.'

'But when she arrives . . . you, my little bird, will have flown away.'

'Where to? Can I stay here?' Stella asked.

'If you wish to stay hidden, you cannot stay in a French hotel,' Rachel advised. 'Every guest is recorded for the police, together with identification details. So if your maman asks the police to find you, you will be discovered within hours if you are here.'

Stella's face fell. 'I could take a flat for you,' Rachel offered. 'A little cheap flat, maybe on the Left Bank, where I live. If you give me money, I can pay a month in advance and book it in my name. As nobody knows we are acquainted, you will be safe, so long as you don't stick your nose outside the door until your *maman* has returned home. She cannot stay in Paris for ever.'

Stella's face brightened. She rushed off to the American Express office, and returned to give Rachel the necessary cash. That evening, Rachel rented a cold-water walk-up sixth-floor two-roomed apartment in an alley between the

Rue de l'Université and the Boulevard St-Germain: it had been taken in Rachel's name for a deposit and cash in advance; no one had asked any questions.

It was Rachel who had thought of smuggling out a few of the clothes that Stella could still get into in smart shopping bags, a few at a time, rather than in one giveaway suitcase. Then she had another bright idea.

On the day Betsy arrived in Paris, Stella walked out of Mme Boué's Finishing School for the last time: this was not difficult, because Saturday afternoon was free time for the pupils. She walked to the cheap hairdresser recommended by Rachel and two hours later emerged with crudely dyed short red hair, parted on the side and pinched into waves. She looked dolefully in the mirror. Never before had she been so ugly.

'What's wrong?' Rachel demanded. 'Now nobody will bother to look at you. This is exactly what we want! Now we check daily with the reception clerks at the Ritz to ask if Mme O'Brien is still in residence. When she departs, then you will be free to have your beautiful baby in Paris.'

* * *

That evening, Stella caught the Train Bleu, the express from Paris to the south of France. Just before arriving at Nice, Stella had pushed back her hideous red hair and hidden it beneath a headscarf; she then made a conspicuous overnight stay at an expensive hotel. Stella did not care to think of Mme Boué facing her mom. On Sunday evening, on hotel stationery, she wrote a contrite and truthful letter of apology to Mme Boué; the old darling trusted and respected her pupils: these were major factors of a pupil's success and enjoyment of her finishing school; you weren't pushed around like a kid.

On Monday night, Stella returned to Paris. She immediately went into hiding in her two attic rooms; tucked under the eaves, the ceilings sloped downwards from the centre of the room: it was a bit uncomfortable, but very romantic, she told herself.

'Only the rich find poverty romantic,' Rachel commented.

Friday 15 March 1940

Now in the eighth month of her pregnancy, Stella listened to her new radio as she pulled on her boots before going on her morning walk; incongruously, she wore several sweaters over a pair of man's trousers, with the fly buttons undone, suspended from her shoulders by a man's pair of braces; over this ensemble, she wore her now-grubby floor-length once-white ermine evening cape.

French military brains had still not realized that while the Maginot Line might stop intruders from the north, the Germans might invade from another direction than that which had been planned for them, but there had been no sign in Paris of the threatened Nazi storm troopers, the radio reassured its listeners. The exiled Polish Government had published documents revealing German plans to invade Russia, and surely Hitler would not be so foolish as to attack simultaneously on two fronts? Stella did not take much notice of this discussion: her world, like that of any mother to be for the first time, was bound only by what was likely to affect her baby. Why did the radio go on and on about the war? Stella wondered, as she switched off. Who cared about the war? Very few people in Paris, except those who did not approve of the new restrictions on what could be eaten and drunk: ration cards were to be distributed, while pastries and chocolates would be restricted, perhaps even banned.

The doctor to whom Rachel had shepherded Stella had not even asked whether or not she was married. A jovial, kindly chap, he was proud of his English, which he insisted upon speaking, although he knew very few words. Stella hoped that she interpreted correctly: she understood far better when they spoke in French.

The doctor had told her to walk in the morning, and again in the afternoon, despite the cold. That winter, all Europe had experienced one of the severest frosts on record: in Hungary, the River Danube had frozen and hundreds of ships were unable to move because of the ice. The unusually cold weather might have been one of the reasons that the expected German attack on the Western Front had not materialized.

It was a cold but beautiful day. Stella's body was kept warm by the grubby ermine cape, but her face numbed with cold as soon as she stepped on the street. As usual, Stella went down the Métro steps, pressed the light-up map, shut her eyes and pointed at the map, then opened her eyes: wherever her finger pointed, she travelled to that station, and then walked back towards the Boulevard St-Germain until she was tired, when she trudged to the nearest Métro and returned home. Stella loved seeing so many new sides of the city. Everyone always seemed so cheerful and full of joie de vivre, even when it was freezing, and the Germans might appear at any moment.

One morning in mid-March, Stella plodded up the freezing Boulevard des Capucines to a street café, glassed in for the winter. In the steamy warmth, she ordered coffee (only one lump of sugar now served) and watched

Frenchmen sipping an early-morning *bock* or eating a leisurely breakfast as they watched shop girls trotting off to their jobs, red cheeked and blue legged in enticingly short skirts.

Stella walked slowly until she came to the Arc de Triomphe, turned into the Champs Élysées – glamorous as ever – and walked down to the Place de la Concorde, still grey and gracious beneath a bird's egg blue sky. She trudged into the Jardin des Tuileries, where the rose bushes had been so ruthlessly pruned that the rose beds looked like some miniaturized forlorn Great War battlefield; with skinny witch-fingers, trees reached to grasp the sky; pools wore sheets of ice; nude statues looked chilly.

When she reached home, before attempting the six flights of stairs, Stella sat in another glassed-in café, to warm herself with a hot milk-and-honey with a shot of rum in it. She rubbed clear a patch of steamed-up window and gazed out at the rosy-nosed people hurrying cheerfully about their business: working men and women, young lovers walking hand in hand, mothers trundling purple-cheeked babies in perambulators piled with shopping.

That reminded her, she must buy a perambulator. She looked forward to the joy of the day when her baby would join her in Paris, the city she loved: she had no money problems (as yet), and when this stupid war was over, she would marry the man she loved. She knew that she was happier than she had ever been before, except during those days spent with Max.

Chapter Twenty-Four

Tuesday 9 April 1940. Paris

Stella went into labour at two o'clock in the morning, on the day Hitler occupied Denmark, invaded Norway, and the Second World War suddenly came to life.

Unaware of this, and the disastrous effect that it was to have on her, Stella lay in her bed, feeling her insides flutter like a butterfly. The baby had stopped kicking, and this fluttering was a new feeling. Stella felt elated and excited. *It was starting!* She was about to meet her baby.

Half an hour later, she started to feel a cramping sensation. An hour later, the contractions were growing steadily stronger and more frequent. She lay there still enjoying this secret moment, hugging it to herself.

Suddenly the bed was flooded with fluid. The amniotic sac had burst: her waters had broken. Cautiously, she sat up in bed and urgently whispered, '*Rachel!*'

Lying on the floor beside her bed, a sleeping bag moved and mumbled. Rachel had been staying, in great discomfort, in Stella's apartment for the past two weeks, so that somebody would be present when the baby decided to appear.

Stella put out one hand, located Rachel's shoulder, and shook it. 'Quick! It's started!'

Rachel sat up sharply. 'You're *sure?*' She did a horizontal rumba out of her sleeping bag.

Quickly, she helped Stella to dress, then draped the top bed blanket around her, for now neither of Stella's coats would meet around her stomach. Carefully holding hands, the two girls very slowly crept down the unlit stairs, groping their way by the flame of Stella's cigarette lighter. Rachel carried a shopping bag filled with things that the nurses had said Stella would need after the birth.

Once outside in the chilled, dark street, the two girls could find no taxi, so slowly they walked the quarter of a mile to the hospital of St Pierre. Every few minutes they had to stop while Stella bent over, hugging her stomach until her contraction ceased. Gasping with the pain, she welcomed every one because it meant her baby would soon be born.

At the hospital, Stella was hurried into the labour ward. Rachel sat downstairs in the bleak waiting room, with the brown shopping bag of baby clothes and sanitary towels.

Twelve hours later, at four in the afternoon, after only an hour of second-stage contractions, and with very little inconvenience to her mother, Caroline was born; she weighed a little over three kilos.

The doctor checked the baby, then handed her to the nurse to clean up a bit; after he had attended to Stella, still lying on the delivery table, the nurse placed Caroline in her mother's arms.

Stella had never known such delight. At last, after years of dutiful obedience, she had someone of her own to love, and to love her. Never in her life had she been so happy; she nuzzled the soft, fair down of her own baby's head, she smelled the milky smell of the baby's skin. Caroline casually wriggled against her mother, as if she did not realize what a little miracle she was.

* * *

When Rachel eventually took the new mother and baby home, it was clear that Stella was still very weak. They had to stop to rest five times on the landings between each staircase.

Stella had hired an old, quiet, sad woman, who had lost two sons in the Great War, both at the Battle of the Marne. Stella dared not ask the age of Mme la Grange, who spoke very rarely, but carefully looked after Stella and her baby and never once complained about the stairs that she had to climb up with the shopping, and down with the refuse bin.

Tuesday 28 May 1940. US Embassy, Paris

In a stuffy anteroom, the uneasy young man behind the desk told Stella, in his flat, Boston accent, 'I can only repeat my advice. Leave Paris as fast as possible. Most Americans in Paris left after May tenth.' The Germans had attacked Holland and Belgium and were deep into France: clearly, their next objective would be Paris.

Stella clutched the swaddled Caroline closer to her. M. Fixit had assured her that she could rely on M. Drexel to help, as he was acquainted with Betsy. Stella made another attempt. 'My baby isn't two months old. We've tried to buy tickets to the States for the three of us, but there are none to be had, on boats *or* planes. We tried to buy train tickets to Portugal, because that's neutral and closest to Britain. But there were none left.'

Rachel leaned forward and murmured in French to Stella.

'Ah yes, we've also got to think about money, because my bank can't transfer funds from America ... I don't really understand why.'

'Americans caught in Paris in the Great War had a tough time because all the banks closed immediately. The black market charged a hundred per cent to change dollars into francs. Your bank is being cautious, Miss O'Brien.'

'Could you at least phone my mom?' Stella begged. 'I'm sure she'll think of something. She always does.'

'Things are getting chaotic here,' the young man said. 'I don't think your mother can help. Unless she's Eleanor Roosevelt, that is. But if you can wait another hour, M. Drexel will be back from lunch. If, as you say, he's a friend of your mother, then he may be able to assist you.'

Half an hour later, a bell pinged. The young man shot from his desk, opened the door behind him a crack, and slid obsequiously in. Ten minutes later the young man shot out as if propelled by a kick. Before he hastily closed the door, Rachel heard an American male voice growl, 'That's the best I can do! Don't put any more calls through and get rid of that girl.'

The young man smoothed his hair and reassumed his air of languor. 'We'll arrange three tickets on the *Reliant*. She sails from Bordeaux on June third, and arrives at Portsmouth, England on June fourth. She's a British-owned cross-Channel ferry boat, normally operating between Folkestone and Calais. These boats are making a fortune for their owners by ferrying refugees from Bordeaux to Portsmouth, at thirty times the normal price. Cash deals only, handled from their Paris office.'

Stella handed over the amount required to purchase three tickets.

'I'm afraid we can't help you get to Bordeaux,' the young man added as Stella opened her purse. 'But no doubt you'll be able to make your own way there.'

Rachel, who had not understood this conversation in English, whispered a question to Stella, who answered her in French. Rachel nodded and looked relieved. 'I know how to get to Bordeaux.'

As Caroline had just dirtied her nappy, evident to anyone in the room, the young man hurriedly checked that Stella, her baby and nursemaid had valid passports. Rachel Stein did not, and neither did Caroline. The young man sighed, and once again sidled into his boss's office. Again Stella heard a rumble of thunder from within. Five minutes later, the young man emerged looking more harassed. 'We can easily arrange a temporary passport for your baby, especially as you are ... er ... unmarried ... so there's no French husband to complicate things.' He hesitated and looked at Rachel.

'My nursemaid is Jewish and so she *must* come with us. Her parents are both dead.'

'I'm sorry...' The young man shook his head, with genuine regret.

With her father's obstinacy, Stella said, 'I'm not leaving here until you've arranged a passport for Miss Stein.'

The two women sat in silence as the unpleasant smell in the room became stronger. Feeling treacherous, Stella surreptitiously pinched her baby on the thigh. The indignant Caroline immediately started to scream.

The young man clapped both hands to his ears, and once more slid into his boss's office.

He reappeared, now looking outraged and indignant as if he had dodged a book thrown at his head. 'It will be arranged. But for Heaven's sake, don't tell anyone else or we'll be mobbed by every . . . er . . . other refugee wanting a passport. Oh, by the way, M. Drexel thought you'd like us to send a cable to your mother.'

'No, not my mother,' Stella said firmly. 'Please cable Max Fane, the Garrick Club, London.'

After the girls had left with the still-screaming Caroline, the young man rushed to open the windows. As he did so, he thought he'd better cover his ass and do as his boss had said. He would also send a cable to that tough little monster's mother.

Thursday 30 May 1940. Fitzroy Square

Pale spring sunshine fell through those bits of the basement windows not criss-crossed by beige sticky tape onto the kitchen table, where it highlighted the *Daily Express* headline B.E.F. FIGHTS DOWN NARROW CORRIDOR TO DUN-KIRK. Mimi started the chorus of 'Hold Your Hand Up, Naughty Boy'. Fizz, sitting next to her, raucously joined in, as did Phyllis and Joyce, two new chorus girls at the Minerva, reopened to dish up what the troops wanted, which was non-stop intimate revue. The Minerva performances ran from 2.30 in the afternoon to eleven o'clock in the evening, and the theatre was always packed with servicemen, making the most of their leave.

Mimi thanked her stars that Max was relatively safe in a desk job at Portsmouth, as the whole of Britain waited grimly for the expected invasion by a million German soldiers from Belgium and Holland. Toby was becoming increasingly exhausted by running both theatres (the King William had reopened with Ivor Novello's romantic operetta *White Tulips*), plus waiting for bloody Hitler to turn up. Once again, he was nightly patrolling the Embankment in an ARP helmet.

Normally Mimi avoided her kitchen as much as possible, but since fuel rationing had started this was the only warm room in Fitzroy Square. Four women sat round one end of the wooden table, while at the other Jessie prepared vegetable soup; she was surrounded by enamel jugs, worn saucepans and a chipped colander, which was filling with chopped cabbage as she swiftly wielded her favourite old knife, its yellowing bone handle and blackened blade worn uneven by constant sharpening.

Like every other Britisher now, Jessie never threw anything away: all bones were boiled for soup; any leftovers were fed to the Rhode Island Reds (recommended by the Ministry of Food) that Toby now kept in the backyard hen-run; he dared not let the chickens roam free in the garden, or they would immediately move into the Anderson shelter, and as Mimi had said, the last thing she wanted in the middle of the night with bombs raining down, compliments of Adolf, was to fling herself onto squawking chickens in a watery cave.

Everyone round the kitchen table, except Jessie, was wolfing lunch; sugarless milkless hot cocoa and Spam sandwiches, the grey bread smeared thinly with margarine. They all wore wartime ensembles. Jessie was enveloped by a crossover flower-printed pinafore; Mimi wore a workman's faded blue boiler suit with the bottoms rolled up; Fizz wore one of Max's darned naval sweaters over slacks, her hair hidden in a pink turban, which saved trips to the hairdresser's. One of the chorus girls wore a skimpy maroon utility overcoat; her friend nestled in a moth-eaten wide-shouldered fur coat. Both wore saucy hats, because you never knew who you might meet on your way back to the theatre.

Still white-faced and fizz-less, Fizz now had little time to be depressed, and firmly tried not to think about Patrick: she would do so only when she could manage it without the awful inner turmoil that overcame her whenever she remembered holding his limp, dead body to her breast. Fizz now worked for ENSA – the Entertainments National Service Association – in a touring revue that played before and after night shifts in factories which, as she had just explained to Mimi, was teaching her to give a good performance under *any* conditions.

'Don't sound like much fun,' said Mimi.

'The only moments I enjoy are those when Bastard Basil has to publicly admit yet another mistake,' sighed Fizz. Basil Dean, who had organized entertainment for the troops during the last war, was the director of ENSA, and so was Fizz's boss. His dictatorial and despotic manner had not mellowed with time, although perhaps Mr Dean gave Fizz a hard time because – elephantine in his memory of insults – he clearly remembered Max's Farewell Performance at the Liverpool Rep. Performers were delighted that Bastard Basil was making such a balls-up of running ENSA – Every Night Something Awful, as it was known in the business.

'He's offloading on you because of the mess he's made in France,' a junior secretary had whispered to Fizz. 'Nearly all the dance bands missed their concerts – even the Christmas Day one with Gracie Fields – because when they arrived in *la belle* bloody Frogland, no one at the port

– 618 –

had been told they were coming, so nobody had arranged transportation!'

'*Quel dommage!*' Fizz had grinned.

Jessie called across Mimi's kitchen, 'Anyone want more cocoa? If not, I'll use what's left to flavour tomorrow's rice pudding.' Everyone passed their mugs up the table. Joyce asked Mimi for another song.

Mimi was in the middle of 'Boiled Beef and Carrots' – which she sang at terrific speed and with great zest – when Fizz stuck her fingers in both ears and nodded upwards, meaning that she thought she heard the doorbell.

The doorbell rang again.

Mimi gave a theatrical sneer. 'It's probably one of Jessie's influential friends.'

All the women shrieked with laughter, for Mimi had just uncovered Jessie's crafty cookery secret. Many of the Minerva chorus girls, who liked a sing-song and a plate of home-made stew around Mimi's kitchen table, had been giving comps (free tickets) to Jessie, who quietly slipped them to the butcher, the baker, and the greengrocer, who somehow found time to visit the naughty afternoon shows at the Minerva without their wives finding out.

Mimi, who was the nearest to the kitchen door, hurried up the stone stairs to the hall and opened the front door. Outside stood a lad who must just have left school, for he couldn't have been older than fourteen; he wore a Garrick page-boy uniform, originally made for somebody shorter and fatter, so his bony wrists stuck out from his sleeves, and his trousers didn't reach his ankles.

'Compliments of the Head Porter at the Garrick, madam,' the lad said, saluting smartly.

Mimi looked at the cable. It had been forwarded from the US Embassy in London and (as a cable merited priority) had been smartly dispatched to Fitzroy Square.

Mimi tipped the lad with a sixpence and tore open the cable. After reading it, she thoughtfully slipped it into the breast pocket of her boiler suit, and carefully buttoned up the pocket. Very slowly, she walked downstairs and rejoined the noisy, cheerful group around the kitchen table.

'Who was it?' Fizz asked, casually.

'Some lad wanting to know if we had any spare pig swill,' Mimi said, casually, 'I told him if we had, Jessie would be making it into soup at this very moment.'

Everybody laughed.

Friday 29 May 1940. Dunkirk

After Hitler had occupied Denmark and invaded Norway, on the 10th of May – the day upon which Winston Churchill became Prime Minister of a Coalition Government – Germany attacked Holland, Belgium and Luxembourg with tanks and infantry, supported by Stuka dive-bombers. It was not difficult, even for the British top brass, to guess that the Germans would now overflow France, and prepare to invade Britain. With German forces speeding towards France, Churchill flew to Paris; he found the French Government about to flee the city.

However, before the Germans marched triumphantly into Paris, Hitler was anxious to wipe out the British and French armies which, surrounded by Nazi troops on all sides except the sea, had been forced back into a thirty-mile stretch of coastland that surrounded France's northernmost port of Dunkirk. This seashore pocket that contained the only port of evacuation left open to the Allies was now protected by the remainder of the French army who bravely held off the Germans (the Panzer corps were only ten miles east of Dunkirk), and so enabled the evacuation of Allied troops to take place.

The Royal Navy was in charge of the entire operation including the Dunkirk beaches. At Dover (the nearest British port, forty-five miles across the sea) a fleet of small boats had been hurriedly assembled by the Royal Navy, who had requisitioned (confiscated, stolen) anything over thirty feet long that could get across the Channel: smaller boats could not carry enough men. Pleasure steamers, coasters, yachts, barges and fishing boats had been commandeered; they looked a jolly, cheerful sight as they bobbed across the waters of the Channel, as if to some enormous regatta.

The Flag Officer at Dover had a difficult job, for there had been little time in which to organize this vast armada of small craft. Half of the hurriedly enlarged Royal Navy had never been to sea before, so many owners who best knew how to handle their precious boats volunteered to crew them. It was because of this that there were civilians at Dunkirk.

Eventually, eight hundred and forty-eight civilian 'little ships' and over two hundred naval vessels took part in Operation Dynamo – the code word for the Dunkirk Evacuation, hopefully intended to rescue 45,000 men. Never before in the history of the Royal Navy had such a strange fleet gone into action: many of the skippers, who had no protective metal helmets, wore bowler hats instead.

As well as rescuing the British Expeditionary Force, the Royal Navy's job was also to drive away U-boats and keep the Channel clear of mines – a constant menace. Although these British vessels were being constantly bombed and machine-gunned by the Luftwaffe they also fired on the German shore batteries behind Dunkirk.

On the afternoon of Wednesday 29th May 1940, Max left Portsmouth Harbour, having been appointed a Liaison Officer on one of the map-numbered sections of Dunkirk beach, with nine boats under his command; they ranged from a 35-foot-long open cutter that could (just) carry twenty, to a 70-foot-long narrow wooden motor launch. Max's flotilla crossed the Channel in convoy, for mutual protection, with big fleet tugs 200-foot-long and packed with volunteer seamen: RNVR officers, chief petty officers and Dockyard workers, sardined with civilian yachtsmen and dinghy sailors.

Crammed in a Dockyard tug, Max tried to look calm; the same anxieties brought a family closeness to his group of men who had known each other only since that morning, but were now laughing and joking, like old pals. It was a bit like theatre life, he decided. Actors were perverse and difficult only when things were going well; in trouble, actors all pulled together.

As he neared Dunkirk the distant but ominous rumble became gradually louder; when he could make out the shore line, the noise was ear-splitting and relentless. Ahead, through the drifting fog of gun-smoke that hung above the coast, billowing clouds of black rose lazily to the sky from the battered town; orange and scarlet streaks of flame shot up through yellow-grey fog.

The town and port of Dunkirk had been under continuous Nazi air attack, and many ships in the harbour had been hit. Max had already heard that while Allied stretcher patients were being removed from trains at Dunkirk station German fighter planes had machine-gunned them, obeying Hitler's orders to attack relentlessly. The rescuers on board Max's tug knew they could expect no mercy from that enemy.

* * *

Max's job was to take his boats to their designated section of the beach, then ferry exhausted or wounded soldiers back to the destroyers and other big ships waiting out of range of the German shore guns, to carry survivors back to Blighty.

While waiting for their human cargo these big ships would anchor, but hover offshore, where they would follow a zigzag course to avoid a constant barrage of Nazi bombs. Consequently, it was extremely difficult for the small, slow boats returning from the beaches to try to recognize and then reach their designated ships. Because of this, the Shore Liaisons and their signals officers were vital.

As Max's vessels headed for the beach, he travelled as a passenger, accompanied by his young signals officer, Sub-Lieutenant Browning, not yet twenty-one. Max was to liaise between the commanding officers on the beach and those on the destroyers; Sub-Lieutenant Browning's hand-held flags would signal the landing spot to Max's boats, as they headed for the beach.

As they drew nearer to the terrifying sandy scene ahead, Max wished that he could tear off his protective tin helmet to relieve his throbbing headache, brought on by the gunfire: the constant, sinister percussion of noise was deafening. He glanced around at the other vessels under his command, now facing the enemy gunfire. Most of the seamen stared straight ahead, their faces blank.

Max wondered if they, too, had headaches because of the hellish noise; if they, too, were as scared as he was.

Nearer the beach, the air became misted with dust and grit. The skipper coughed, then spat with more force than necessary to clear his mouth. They could all smell the stink of cordite. Silent, as most of them prepared themselves to go into a battle zone for the first time, the men wondered whether submerged defensive mines lay in the shallow water ahead.

Max could see that sand dunes, some tufted with sparse grass, lay to the rear of the flat sandy beaches. Along their entire length ran a dark litter of discarded equipment. The retreating army waited between this and the sea. Covered by rain-capes, overcoats or only ragged battle-dress, exhausted soldiers limped and stumbled forward, their only aim to reach one of those rescue boats and be heaved over the side. It would then – thank God – be up to the Royal Navy to decide what to do with them.

Above the helpless soldiers, swastika-decorated Stukas bombed the beaches; the Ju-87s were fitted with de-moralizing attack sirens – *Jericho-Trompeten* – which were activated by the fast near-vertical dive and terrified the exhausted troops, who were also under a constant barrage of long-range enemy artillery fire from the rear of the beach. Paralysed with fright, some men huddled against the sparse shelter of the sand dunes. Many helped wounded companions, staggering under their weight as they dragged them towards safety. The badly wounded lay on the pale, damp sand; dying in agony, men screamed for their mothers.

When the small boats neared the beach, the disciplined khaki lines broke as terrified men hurled themselves towards the sea and their rescuers. Soldiers swayed up to their necks in freezing water; over-eager frightened men, suddenly finding themselves out of their depth, floundered and thrashed around in the waves: some who could not swim drowned. From the line of little boats, helmeted rescuers leaned swiftly over the side, ready to heave the survivors aboard.

Max, momentarily frozen in horrified pity, stared down at the blackened faces, the blood-stained khaki uniforms, the filthy bandages of these soldiers, all looking hopefully upwards, praying to be taken to safety.

Quickly, he and Sub-Lieutenant Browning lowered themselves over the side and waded with their signalling equipment towards the beach, pushing their way through panicking men who threatened to sweep them back to the cutter.

When each rescue boat was full, it turned and headed out to sea – far too slowly, it seemed to the exhausted passengers – back to the waiting tugs and destroyers. Scrambling-nets hung from the deck of the larger vessels, so that men could climb up from the sea. The little craft pitched dangerously towards the sides of the big ships, as those soldiers able to do so climbed the scrambling-nets. The walking wounded were helped on board; ropes were tied under the armpits of the seriously injured, who were hauled up to deck by the crew: often, by the time they reached safety, they had died.

Monday 3 June 1940. Dunkirk

Five days later, the almost empty Dunkirk beaches were littered with abandoned equipment, crumpled khaki blankets and bloody corpses. Max had worked as hard as all other rescuers, pausing only to sleep whenever he could, wherever he could, and to cram into his mouth whatever he was offered. He had forgotten what it felt like not to be tired; like everyone else he kept going only because the job had to be done. Max had lost three boats and four men.

The Dunkirk retreat had not been entirely controlled: noise, chaos, and fear had literally driven some men mad; deliberately, they had swum out until they reached a depth deep enough to escape the noise and Nazi bombs, and quietly drowned. Some British officers deliberately shot their own men if they were endangering others: once, when it was falsely rumoured that this was the last departure, waiting survivors had panicked, had tried to heave themselves up into overloaded boats. Max had seen an officer in charge of a motor-boat pull out his pistol and shoot a desperate hanger-on who threatened to capsize the boat.

Max had been sombrely grateful that so far he needed to take no such decision, as in the dimming evening light he watched one of his launches heading for the beach. She nosed in, bow first, and stopped about thirty yards away, in order to avoid catching her propellers on the bottom. The survivors, waiting up to their necks in water, hurled themselves at the scrambling-nets that hung over the side, and heaved themselves aboard.

A Luftwaffe dive-bomber came screaming down from the sky. The Stuka flicked over Max's overloaded launch. Above the thunderous noise of battle, he heard agonized screams as men fell in all directions, some overboard. Someone yelled, 'All the bloody sailors have been killed! Who can drive this fucking thing?'

Surely not all six of the crew? Max swiftly turned to his

signalman. 'Stay here, Browning, I'll investigate.' A stationary launch would be a sitting duck for the Stuka's next dive.

Max waded then swam to the launch and climbed aboard; he forced his way through dead, dying and frightened men to the empty wheelhouse. The skipper, who had been hit in the ribs, was slumped on deck and bleeding badly; he confirmed there were no able-bodied seamen. Max immediately took the helm.

As he did so, he suddenly caught a glimpse to starboard of someone he recognized, floundering in the grey chopping water. It was Freeby, an obliging young porter at the Garrick; an accomplice and alibi-provider, he had often covered up for Max.

At that moment, Freeby recognized Max. 'Mr Fane!' he yelled, pleading for his life. '*Please*, Mr Fane,' he sobbed.

Max glanced at the wounded skipper. 'Think you can hold her steady for a tick?'

The grey-faced man nodded without speaking.

Max forced his way to the side through injured men. He snatched up a mooring rope, coiled it, and hurled it towards Freeby. Unfortunately, the rope was too heavy to reach him. Max suddenly felt an overwhelming and unreasonable sense of his own failure. This was followed by a determination to succeed. Back at the wheelhouse, knowing that he would have to reverse the launch and turn through 180 degrees to get the craft offshore, Max swiftly decided to steer within a few feet of young Freeby (not too close, he didn't want to run him down), stop engines and pick him up.

Having performed these manoeuvres, Max again handed over to the injured skipper and pushed his way back to the side where he watched Freeby – clearly exhausted – heave himself slowly up the scrambling-net. Then Max heard an eerie banshee wail, glanced up at the sky dark with shrapnel and saw another Jerry Stuka heading down, the oddly angular wings, the black-and-white identification crosses blurring into a streak of grey above him.

Impatient and anxious, Max leaned over the guard rail, seized Freeby by the back of his battledress blouse, and strained to haul him aboard. But he had miscalculated the speed of the Stuka.

Then Freeby jerked, his mouth stretched in a rictus of horror: there was too much noise to hear his scream.

Max also convulsed as he was hit in the left thigh. He lost his balance on the guard rail, which was acting as a fulcrum, balancing his weight.

For a hideously slow moment his instinct told him to hold on with his toes, but his boots were stiff and unyielding.

Slowly Max toppled over into the dark-grey choppy waves.

Only as he went under did he realize that he should not have left the wheel; his mistake had been to try to do too much. His job was on the beach, and he should have stayed there. 'Act first, think second,' his mother would have criticized, tightening her lips; no doubt the Royal Navy would agree, although Max had also been instructed to use his initiative, and the order had been to evacuate every living man from Dunkirk.

When the two men surfaced, Max still clutched Freeby's blouse. The young man just gasped, 'Thanks, Mr Fane,' before he died.

Not realizing Freeby was dead, Max headed for the launch as best he could, doing a one-armed backstroke while, with his left arm, he held the man against his chest. So he clearly saw the German fighter pilot's goggled face as he flew low for a third attack.

Max saw many men blown off the launch into the water: some surfaced and wearily struck out again for the boat; others stayed slumped in the sea, swaying sluggishly in the rhythm of the waves.

Although only a few seconds, it seemed to Max a long time after the Nazi plane had flashed past that he felt a stab of pain in his left shoulder. Then his mind was overwhelmed by agony. He screamed, and salt water slopped into his mouth. Unable to use his left leg, he could not swim; hampered by his heavy clothes and boots, he started to go under; unable to think clearly because of his pain, he still clung to the corpse he was determined to rescue. Though yelling hoarsely for help, he could not be heard in the racket. He was just another body in the dark grey water.

In the general mayhem, the wounded skipper did what Max should have done: he pushed the throttle forward, to get the hell away from the beach, and headed for the nearest big ship.

Swaying in the water, Max continued to protectively hold the man he had rescued, until they both sank slowly beneath the disinterested waves.

* * *

Early on the morning of Thursday 4th June, a British major-general in a fast motor-boat travelled at full speed along the shoreline, to ensure that no live soldiers remained to be lifted off the beaches.

At sea, the last big ships headed for their final journey home – all crammed tight with men, even down in the stokehold, even in the engine room: the only place forbidden to the rescued was near the guns.

All little boats now headed for home separately, as best they could, to the nearest port they could reach in southeast England.

The vast majority of Dunkirk survivors were rescued by the British Navy. Dunkirk was a colossal naval achievement, a remarkable example of impromptu, determined, efficient organization. Six destroyers and 243 other British vessels had been sunk, including clearly marked hospital carriers. The Luftwaffe had lost 150 planes in seven days. The tiny force of RAF Fighter Command had lost 106 planes, which it could ill afford from the pitifully small array with which it prepared to fight the Battle of Britain. For although there were still 140,000 British troops in France, together with most of the French army, now France would fall, and there definitely would be a Battle for Britain.

The British Prime Minister, Churchill, correctly described the Dunkirk evacuation as a colossal military disaster, but also, he added rousingly, a miracle of deliverance.

Certainly Dunkirk was a miracle of official public-relations doublespeak, which instantly persuaded the British public that being ignominiously kicked out of France by the Nazis had been a major moral victory.

Once allowed a carefully worded description of the event, the British public obediently echoed it. 'The Dunkirk Miracle' was a phrase that conjured up a romantic picture of tiny fishing smacks sailing gallantly through the moonlit waters to evacuate our brave boys.

Chapter Twenty-Five

Friday 31 May 1940

The cable, sent from the American Embassy in Paris, arrived at Betsy's home in Los Angeles when she was in New York having taken Nick to visit a world-famous eye surgeon about his alarming double vision noted at his annual test for new eyeglasses.

After examining Nick, the jovial eye surgeon had announced that he *might* need an operation to rectify the problem, but before taking this decision, he wished Nick to stop wearing his eyeglasses for six months.

'But I won't be able to see!' Nick protested.

'You won't be able to *read* for a while,' said the specialist firmly.

Much relieved, Betsy decided to spend a week in the Big Apple and have a little fun. However, at midday on Friday the telephone rang in her suite at the Plaza. From Los Angeles Betsy's butler read her the cable.

YOUR DAUGHTER STELLA O'BRIEN PLUS BABY CARO-
LINE PLUS FRIEND RACHEL STEIN CATCHING FERRY
BOAT NAME RELIANT FROM BORDEAUX FRANCE 3RD
JUNE 1940 ARRIVING PORTSMOUTH DOCKYARD BRIT-
AIN 4TH JUNE WHERE FANE WILL MEET YOUR PARTY.

Betsy could hardly believe her ears. She thrust the telephone to Nick, asking him to write down the cable, and then collapsed into a chair.

Stella had been found! Stella's baby had been born!

Betsy snatched the pad from Nick's hand and stared at the last words of the cable, 'Fane will meet your party.'

Could it be an error? Could the post office have made a mistake? Assuredly that was 'friend' rather than 'Fane'.

Whatever it was, the cable meant that Betsy had little time to get to Portsmouth.

Grimly, she put through a call to the American Embassy in London, but was told that now such calls could only be routed through an official department in the British Embassy, Washington. So Betsy phoned one of Jack's old friends who worked for the State Department. She was put straight through; she explained her predicament, and asked for help as a very great personal favour.

Within twenty minutes, Betsy's call had been returned from Washington. Did Mrs O'Brien and her son have their passports with them? Good. Valid? Excellent. They were to drive to La Guardia immediately; arrangements had been made for them to fly to London. In London, they had been booked into the Dorchester Hotel where a car would be at their disposal, waiting at the airport to take them first to the Dorchester and the following day to Portsmouth. The driver had been issued with special petrol coupons, ration cards for food, and a loan of one hundred British pounds in cash until Betsy had time to make further financial arrangements. In Portsmouth, the O'Briens had been booked into the royal suite at the Queen Alexandra Hotel, Southsea, from June 3rd, indefinitely.

Betsy telephoned the Plaza housekeeper. Within a minute, three maids were packing her suitcases.

'Shall I get out of the way and wait in the car, Mom?' Nick asked. It had taken him five minutes to pack his few casual clothes and the couple of sweaters that he had brought, plus his tux (Mom insisted) and a dark brown suede jacket of which he was real proud.

'Do you *really* need me along, Mom?' he asked once again. He looked much older than sixteen, for he was tall and broadly built, like his father. Privately, Nick thought he looked nineteen; quiet, shy, and unassuming, he practised being masterful before his mirror, and longed to shave twice a day.

Betsy looked at Nick sharply. 'Of course I need you, Nick. I need someone to look after me.' She hated to be alone and needed someone to fetch and carry for her.

'Shouldn't we tell Tess we're going?'

'Certainly not!' Betsy was still not speaking to the newly-weds.

Nick ran his hand through his fashionable crew-cut and looked at his mother frantically issuing instructions. He thought he'd better get out of the way. 'I'll check the car's waiting.' He hurried to the elevator with the gangling, loose-limbed, self-conscious walk of an adolescent.

* * *

The Pan-American Clipper arrived in Lisbon on the following evening and the morning after that the O'Briens boarded another aeroplane, destination London.

After landing for a refuelling stop in Bordeaux, the O'Briens stiffly tottered down the steps that had been trundled out to the plane, then walked in brilliant sunshine to the airport restaurant, where they sat and ordered large cups of black coffee and croissants. The place was crammed with noisy refugees: many men and women were in tears, others looked hopeless and depressed; nearly everybody carried bundles tied with string, cardboard boxes, anything they thought they might manage to get on the plane. Betsy did not understand the hysteria until someone explained to her in broken English that on the radio that morning the Germans had announced they were about to enter Paris.

Immediately, Betsy was anxious for Stella. She wondered whether her daughter was perhaps only a few miles from her. Hurriedly, she purchased three bottles of champagne and two bottles of cognac before the passengers were ordered back to the aircraft: Betsy rarely drank herself, but she had no idea what the situation might be for her friends in Britain.

Back on the runway, their plane was surrounded by gendarmes, to prevent refugees without tickets from attempting to stowaway. The plane had left Lisbon at nine that morning with only a few passengers. Now, when the O'Briens climbed back into the aircraft, they found that every seat was occupied.

Ten minutes later, the aeroplane lumbered along the runway and turned slowly into the wind. Betsy pressed her forehead against the small window and watched the beautiful green orchards and vineyards of Bordeaux slowly become hazy, then vanish as the plane flew higher.

When the plane flew low over the Channel Islands, Betsy could see fishing boats and people lolling on the sand while their children played, as if on a normal summer holiday. The plane continued to fly low as it reached the Hampshire coast, and then headed towards London. The aerial view of the countryside was just as green and beautiful as that over Bordeaux had been. As they finally glided towards London, Betsy had an eerie impression of calm, of eighteenth-century tranquillity and remoteness from any unpleasant events.

When the plane bumped down at Hendon aerodrome, Betsy realized that not once had she been frightened during the trip. She had certainly been anxious, but only for Stella and the baby – the granddaughter whom she had not yet seen. She was now excited as she always was when arriving in Britain. 'Yah-boo sucks, I made it *anyway*! So now roll out the red carpet, you guys!'

Waiting at the airport stood an ancient black Daimler; Betsy had seen nothing like it since before the Great War. Standing by it was a man who looked older than a Dickens novel. He had a benevolent expression and drooping white moustache, yellowed from nicotine around his mouth; his black chauffeur's uniform was far too large: either he had shrunk, or it belonged to somebody else. As Betsy approached, he saluted her with a quivering arm, then deferentially removed his peaked cap before he spoke.

Betsy stared at the car, then back at the watery, pale blue eyes. 'There must be some mistake.'

A bleating voice said, 'If you are Mrs O'Brien, I am Sutton, your driver: I usually only do funerals, madam, following the hearse with the bereaved. However, the American Embassy has retained my services for the duration of this unpleasantness. They kindly provide the petrol coupons for my journeys. A lucky thing for me, madam. Although it may seem odd in wartime, there ain't many people dying, leastways not in my area. Trade has dropped off badly since the men joined up, and now the women are working in munitions factories: nobody has time for the full panoply, even at reduced rates.'

When Betsy was seated in the car, although it was June, Sutton tucked a fur rug around her; then with the grave air of a verger offering a prayer book he handed her several envelopes. 'Arrangements have been made direct with the Dorchester, madam, but you will need to hand the ration books over to the hotel manager, when you arrive in Portsmouth; a person can go to prison for breaking food regulations.'

'*Food regulations?*'

'All food is rationed,' Sutton said in a voice perfectly suited to condolence as he drove at funeral speed. Occasionally, some man on the street removed his hat and bowed, to show proper respect for the dead.

Betsy noticed no children ('Evacuated last September, madam') and that all pedestrians had a cardboard box slung around their backs. 'Gas masks,' Sutton laconically explained. 'The Government expected over a hundred thousand casualties in the first weeks of war: they cleared the hospitals, stacked the mortuaries with piles of cardboard coffins, and dug lime-pits to cope with the dead. I know this, because I'm in the business, you see.'

All houses had beige tape criss-crossed over the windows to prevent broken glass blowing inwards; dirty sandbags were piled high around the doorways of public buildings. Betsy shivered at the gloomy sight and turned to the glossy magazines in the car; instead of debutantes at balls or peers on yachts, the photographs featured heiresses driving ambulances and debutantes lugging fire hoses. *Vogue* urged readers to spend the war learning to knit or cook and continue to dress for dinner; it featured fashionable housecoats for air-raid-shelter wear and recommended Elizabeth Arden's 'Burnt Sugar' as *the* lipstick colour to go with khaki.

As the Daimler turned into Park Lane, Betsy saw that the pretty wrought-iron railings had disappeared from Hyde Park, as had the splendid gates. The park was now a military area, dotted with barbed wire and air-raid shelters. High above what was left of the grass floated pale-grey barrage balloons – like bloated silver whales when the sun shone – ready to snarl any enemy aircraft foolish enough to fly beneath them and become entangled in the stays that anchored the ungainly balloons to the ground.

They drew up to the doors of the Dorchester. The chauffeur slowly creaked from his seat to open the door for Betsy, again saluting as he did so. 'The Dorchester is considered the safest place in London, madam. Bombproof, prestressed concrete construction,' he announced, suddenly as proud as if he'd done it all himself.

Inside, to Betsy's surprise, she and Nick were not led up to a suite, but down to the basement where the air-raid shelter was situated in what had been the hotel's Turkish baths. Betsy stopped abruptly as she stared at the rows of hospital beds, spaced about two feet apart, covered by pale-pink or blue silk eiderdowns. Slippers had been placed by each bed; a dressing gown and night wear were carefully draped over each eiderdown. Some beds were hidden behind curtains: a sign pinned to one of them read RESERVED FOR LORD HALIFAX. Betsy stopped abruptly.

'Mom,' Nick urged, 'I don't care if I sleep in a coal hole, I just want to lie flat.'

Betsy was shown to a bed where she immediately fell, fully dressed, beneath the pink silk eiderdown and slept until 9 p.m. When she woke, she found that her suitcases had been unpacked; she changed into a black taffeta cocktail frock, which had been immaculately ironed while she slept.

Because Nick was (as always) hungry, they went upstairs to the crowded restaurant. By law, nobody could be charged more than five shillings – one dollar – for a meal, but for that sum the Dorchester offered native oysters, cold lobster, smoked salmon, boiled ham in Madeira sauce and other delicacies. How did the hotel manage to achieve this astounding miracle of wartime housekeeping? By charging a fortune for the drinks. Nobody queried the prices. Everyone around was bent on having a good time while they could and to hell with the expense.

* * *

On the following morning Betsy was woken by something scrabbling at her feet. Aaaaagh! Rats! She shot upright, and opened her eyes to see a woman wearing a Schiaparelli-pink satin dressing gown and a tin helmet on her head. As she whipped away a newspaper from the foot of Betsy's bed, she boomed in an autocratic, upper-class bray, 'Sew sari.' Clearly not sorry at all, she graciously explained, 'My ass of a maid mistakenly put my *Times* on your bed.'

Outside the revolving doors, Sutton waited with the Daimler. 'Had a good sleep, madam? Most of Mr Churchill's War Cabinet have rooms at the Dorchester, and so do all the famous society hostesses: I expect you saw some of them last night.'

Betsy wondered whether the odd figures seen that morning in dressing gowns and curlers, shuffling between the beds with their sponge bags, could be so described, as the driver explained, 'They can't run their houses no more, with no staff.'

Leaving London, the Daimler was obliged to travel even slower than usual, in a slow-moving stream of vehicles, bound for indefinite exile in the country; coaches were full of children; cars and beetle-black London taxis were piled with luggage, even on the roofs.

'I expect you've wondered why I'm not in the Home Guard, madam,' Sutton volunteered. 'You wouldn't believe it, but I'm nearly seventy.'

Betsy ostentatiously picked up the copy of *Vogue* and hid behind photographs of a dozen different ways to tie a turban, and the most chic overalls you could wear to work in an armaments factory. She read with her eyes, but her mind continued to worry about Stella. Why hadn't the US Embassy in Paris warned her earlier? she wondered yet again. Perhaps Stella had only just come out of hiding? What had the birth been like? How was the baby doing? Was Stella breastfeeding little Caroline? Did the baby have sufficient diapers?

The drive to Portsmouth, Sutton assured them, normally took two hours at the most. He added with a chuckle that they were lucky it was a daytime trip on a straight road; all signposts – especially those at road junctions – had been either removed, painted out or deliberately pointed in the wrong direction, in order to confuse paratrooping Nazi nuns. Naturally, this led to chaos on the roads, especially at night-time.

To reach Portsmouth took nearly six hours. Luckily the Dorchester had provided a wicker picnic hamper with food, china and glass. Due to her anxiety for Stella, Betsy had little appetite, but for an adolescent mealtime is any time. Nick dived into the hamper and read the menu card as if he were a reciting waiter. 'Sandwiches of foie gras, individual rabbit pies, individual treacle tarts, *petits fours*.

Red wine, ginger beer, vacuum flask of coffee.' Nick ate it all, then hunched up in a leather corner, and slept soundly.

They drove through little Georgian towns and charming villages with thatched cottages. Betsy dozed fitfully, waking occasionally to see a tapestry of quiet green fields, trees, sheep, cows and horses standing quietly, as if in a Constable painting.

Betsy finally woke when the car stopped. 'What's wrong?'

The chauffeur half-turned to announce, 'We have arrived at the crest of Portsdown Hill, madam, the best view of the city.' He waved to the panorama before them. His passengers slowly eased their tired bodies from the ancient vehicle. The chauffeur proudly pointed to the horizon, as if he owned it. 'That grey strip, madam, is the sea. From here, you can see the Harbour quite clearly – to your right: the original town was built around the Harbour mouth, the narrow opening. From there, the seafront – closed of course – runs six miles to the Royal Marine barracks at Eastney, on your left.'

'Do *all* those ships belong to the Royal Navy?' Nick asked.

'No, some of them battleships belong to the French Navy, but we threw off the Frogs, sir, and requisitioned their boats.'

Betsy sighed. 'Where's our hotel?'

'About an inch to the left of the Harbour mouth, madam, in Southsea, a superior neighbourhood, madam.'

When Betsy next woke, she saw the Daimler had stopped in the forecourt of a red-brick Edwardian Gothic castle with turrets and cream-framed windows, all crisscrossed with beige paper.

Inside the Queen Alexandra Hotel the O'Briens trailed through a hall lounge that clearly established the hotel's gentility, with potted palms, chintz sofas and hunting scenes of men in red coats leaping over hedges on exquisitely groomed horses with bulging, goitrous eyes.

Nick noticed that everyone in this lounge spoke in a funereal whisper, as if conversation was forbidden. Beyond the lounge, the reception area was on the left, with the elevator beyond it. The wall opposite was plastered with patriotic posters that urged, MEND AND MAKE DO!, DIG FOR VICTORY!, WORK!, SAVE! BUY WAR BONDS! Large cartoons featured Hitler, comically drawn beneath the sofa of a courting couple (both in uniform), crouching under their restaurant table, and so on: the caption always read CARELESS TALK COSTS LIVES! This joke wore thin fairly quickly, as the O'Briens waited and waited for the elevator.

'So sorry, madam,' explained the harassed, matronly receptionist. 'Our lift is a little temperamental. It must be stuck on an upper floor.' She added, apologetically, 'The engineer's been posted to a munitions factory in Aberdeen.'

Naturally, the porters had also been called up, so Sutton and Nick staggered upstairs with the O'Brien luggage. The Embassy had booked the royal suite for them; more flowered-chintz chairs, potted palms, hunting prints and heavy mahogany furniture in each room.

With a sigh of relief, Betsy turned to her son. 'Here we are at *last*, honey . . .' She stopped abruptly. She had never seen Nick look so pale. He stood in the doorway, looking queasy. Alarmed, Betsy hurried to him and cupped his chin in her hand. She stared into his tired eyes. 'What is it, honey?'

'My head feels funny. I feel like heaving. Now.'

Car sickness? The ginger beer? That fois gras?

Nick barked, 'Quick, where's the john?' But it was too late: he threw up over his mother's beige jersey Chanel suit.

It was the fois gras, Betsy noticed with relief, then she ran to the bedside phone. There wasn't one. Betsy stuck her finger on the bell and kept it there until an ancient maid waddled in. 'Please have the manager get the best doctor in town! Quick! My son is ill! And get me a basin . . .' As she spoke, Betsy beckoned Nick to her and started to unbutton his shirt.

'Oh, Mom,' protested the embarrassed sixteen-year-old, but he was clearly too weak to stop her. Betsy guided his arms into his pyjama jacket, helped him into bed, smoothed the covers over him, then tenderly sponged her son's face.

The maid returned with a zinc bucket. 'This is all we can spare, madam. Doctor will call when he's finished his surgery.'

'How long will *that* be?'

'Can't say, madam. There *is* a war on, you know.'

Nick muttered, 'I don't want to see anybody, I just want to die.'

This alarmed his mother so, that she temporarily forgot her nagging anxiety for Stella.

By the time the doctor arrived, Betsy had taken a bath and slipped into a fresh dress.

The doctor examined Nick slowly. He's just being thorough, Betsy assured herself, nervously holding two fingers crossed.

The doctor turned to Betsy. 'What's he been eating?'

'Fois gras and ginger beer.'

The doctor shuddered. 'Food poisoning, but there's no

need to worry, he seems a healthy lad.' He straightened up, scribbled in what looked like ancient Hebrew on a little prescription pad, tore off the top sheet and handed it to Betsy. 'Keep him in bed for a day or two. The more he vomits, the better.'

By early evening, Nick had recovered enough to sit up against his pillows, although he continued to feel boneless, gutless, and grateful for the bucket at his bedside. Betsy stamped downstairs to see why Nick's medicine had not yet arrived.

* * *

Nick was dozing when the door crashed open. His mother stormed into his bedroom, her face red and angry. 'Can you believe it? *That woman's here!*'

'What woman?' Nick made an effort to pull himself upright.

'Mimi Fane! Dressed like a governess: navy coat, black stockings, lace-up shoes,' Betsy exploded.

'Maybe the woman *was* a governess. How can you be sure it was her?'

'We recognized each other instantly. I cut her dead. Ha!'

'Why, Mom? After all, Mrs Fane took the trouble to telephone you with news of Stella,' Nick reminded her.

'Exactly! I haven't forgotten that it was *her* son who shamed our family.' As the tirade continued, Nick slid slowly down until his body lay flat, turned his face to the wall and closed his eyes.

Betsy hesitated. Obviously her son was still feeling ill: Nick was usually so sympathetic.

She rang the bell, ordered consommé and plain white rice for Nick, then asked for the menu as she wished her meal to be sent up to the suite: she was damned if she was going to eat in the same dining room as Mimi Fane.

The maid hesitated. 'We don't usually serve meals out of the dining room, madam, for we haven't the staff. And we don't have a menu: there's only the one set meal.'

'I know. I know! There's a war on! Could you *try* to get the manager here?' Half the people in Britain acted as if there were no war, while the other half used it as a convenient excuse for slow, sloppy service, saying no and doing nothing.

Eventually Betsy was served with a tin tray with thick, dark brown soup, grey mince and a bowl of tinned prunes and custard, made from powder mixed with water: it tasted disgusting and she did not eat it.

* * *

Four floors above the Royal Suite, in a small room with a single bed, Mimi, seething, paced three yards of carpet. Although she had risked humiliation to warn Betsy that her daughter was in trouble, that cow had snubbed her – right in the middle of the crowded lobby, right in front of the reception desk, where Mimi had been wearily waiting for her room key.

Mimi's journey had also taken three times longer than expected. She had arrived at Waterloo Station half an hour early, to ensure a seat. As there were no longer any porters, a nice young seaman had heaved her suitcase up on the luggage rack. An hour after the scheduled time of departure, the guard's whistle had eventually shrilled. Everyone saying goodbye on the platform had looked relieved, then guilty: uniformed sailors scuffed out their cigarettes, then crushed their girls to their chests. Doors banged. Everyone switched on bright, brave smiles. Men leaned out, waving from the windows, as the train pulled away. Mimi's compartment was packed with uniformed men in various stages of hangover, some standing in the small space between the seats; the corridors were stuffed with more men, kitbags, battered suitcases, gas masks, overcoats and curiously shaped brown paper parcels.

The train stopped frequently for no apparent reason in the middle of fields that contained surprised cows; at one point it shunted backwards for half a mile, snorted and came to a standstill. Whenever this happened, the troops within started singing the same song, until Mimi felt like throwing herself on the track if 'We'll Meet Again' was bawled once more by admiring male imitators of Vera Lynn.

Eventually, the train arrived. 'Portsmouth Town!' the guard called. When the heavy train doors slowly swung open, half the occupants of the train burst out as if shot from a popgun.

Mimi dragged her once-elegant crocodile suitcase to the steps, then pushed it, so that it slithered like a toboggan to the underpass. There, another strange young sailor kindly grabbed it and carried it to the taxi stand. Mimi waited nearly an hour until a taxi appeared.

'St Thomas's Street, Old Portsmouth,' she instructed, brightening at the thought of being so near Max. Mimi had often been in her son's billet, although she was not allowed in the Dockyard, where he worked. She had half-hoped that Max would be there, but there was no answer when she hammered at his door: he was obviously still working in his office, she thought, disappointed. However, she would have another chance of seeing him as he entered or left the Dockyard gates, she told herself as she clambered back into the taxi, glad once again that her son was safely installed in the best-defended town in Britain. It did not occur to her that Portsmouth was so heavily guarded because it was so irresistibly attractive to the Luftwaffe.

At the Queen Alexandra Hotel Mimi waited patiently, daydreaming. How she longed to cuddle that little scrap! Did the baby look like Max? She *might* look like Mimi? ... She would look after Stella as Stella's *real* mother bloody should! Had she eaten any food on the boat? Was Stella breastfeeding? Had she been so frightened that she'd lost her milk? Maybe she should pop to a chemist, first thing in the morning, to get a tin of powdered milk and a bottle; and some nappies, if there were any: how many bloody coupons did you need for a baby's nappy?

Mimi was just about to be handed her room key when she smelled Arpège and heard behind her an American voice asking what the hell had happened to her son's medicine.

The receptionist hastily turned to the wooden pigeon-holes behind her; from one she grabbed a bottle of red medicine, and thrust it over Mimi's shoulder. Irritated by this queue jumping (already considered the worst possible wartime behaviour), Mimi turned around. Her mouth opened in surprise as she found herself face to face with Betsy O'Brien.

Betsy glared at Mimi, then ostentatiously whirled in the opposite direction, on ridiculously high heels. Mimi, left speechless, white and shaking, was unable to move. What was Betsy doing at the Queen Alexandra?

Meeting Stella and the baby, of course.

Blast!

Away flew her dream of outstretched gloved hands

taking her adorable grandchild from the weary devoted young mother.

Despite her shock, Mimi had been determined not to be forced out of the best hotel by the hated Betsy, when there were no free rooms to be had in Pompey, now bursting with extra naval personnel and thousands of imported Dockyard workers. Once in her tiny bedroom she decided that she might have to stay in the same hotel but she certainly wasn't going to eat in the same dining room as the odious O'Brien cow. Angrily, she rang the bell. When the maid eventually appeared, Mimi asked for her meal to be sent up to her room.

'Sorry, madam, there's a war on. No room service.'

For a second, Mimi considered going out to a fish 'n' chip shop: wistfully, she dreamed of gold potato chips sprinkled with vinegar, crispy, fried cod eaten straight from the newspaper in which it was wrapped. Delicious! But she didn't want to stumble around in the blackout and risk breaking her nose on some unyielding lamppost, so she searched in her shoulder bag for an emergency packet of chocolate – her confectionery ration for the month. Having nibbled half of it, she sauntered downstairs to the crowded bar and ordered a gin and tonic, with ice.

'Sorry, no ice, madam.'

Of course.

Mimi slid behind a small table as two teenage air force officers vacated it; an aged waiter removed their dirty glasses and ashtray with flouncing disdain, then placed before Mimi two bowls containing unidentifiable dried bits that might have been stolen from an ethnographical museum.

'The *amuse-gueules* are raw carrot-shavings and dried

turnip slices, madam ... No need to look like *that*, madam! Moses didn't come down from the Mount saying, "He'll have it with a twist of lemon plus olives and peanuts." '

'Resting, are you?' Mimi guessed.

'How did you guess I'm in the Business?' The aged fairy looked delighted. 'ENSA wouldn't have me ... arthritis.' He gave a roguish wink. 'For you, madam, I think I can find a packet of crisps behind the bar.'

Everyone was talking about the leaflets that the Germans had just dropped on Paris, warning that they were about to take the city. The bar was also buzzing with rumours about the British Expeditionary Force. They had been surrounded by Nazis. All our lads had been trapped, slaughtered in their thousands on the beaches. Our lads had all escaped on special rafts, parachuted down by the RAF. It was a pity, Mimi thought, that Hitler wasn't hiding beneath some table to tell them all exactly what was going on.

* * *

Later that evening, Mimi dialled Max's billet at St Thomas's Street, but yet again the phone only rang and rang. So she telephoned Toby in London. 'No, old man, I'm not bloody comfortable,' she growled. Like every other hotel in wartime, the Queen Alexandra operated with minimal heating and ice-cold bedrooms in which hot water taps produced only a bronchitic cough. Even in summer, war seemed endlessly uncomfortable, which added to the exhaustion clearly felt by everyone, particularly the octogenarian waitress who had served Mimi. 'A bland, bloody Windsor soup then what they had the cheek to call shepherd's pie: grey mince covered by that powdered potato you add water to. Tinned prunes for afters. War or no war, they intend to keep our bowels regular.'

'Haven't you any newsier news, Foxtop?'

'Yes, I have. You'll *never* guess what happened, Toby.'

'You've enlisted in the Wrens?'

'You'd like that, then I'd be out of your way.'

'I've grown accustomed to having you in my way.'

Normally, Mimi enjoyed such banter, but she only had three minutes of a long-distance call before the pips went, after which she would be automatically cut off, so without wasting further time, she said casually, 'I bumped into Betsy O'Brien at the reception desk. She's here with her son.'

After a long pause, Toby said encouragingly, 'Then now's your chance.'

'What do you mean?' Mimi knew perfectly well what Toby was going to say. She knew exactly what Toby thought of the feud. He had told her so, often enough.

'Mimi, you've been secretly hoping for this opportunity, on and off, for over thirty years. Think what it will mean to that baby if her grandmothers aren't at each other's throats all the time. Don't waste this opportunity, Foxtop!'

'It ain't that easy, Toby. Maybe I could forgive but it ain't that easy to forget.' Every time she removed her gloves, Mimi remembered.

Toby knew that. 'Listen carefully, Foxtop. "I can forgive but I can't forget" does nothing to heal emotional scars; that only proves that the wronged person has *not* forgiven and is never going to let the other person forget it! So don't use pretended forgiveness as a weapon of revenge and forget your moral superiority. Genuine forgiveness *always* includes forgetting because that's the only way to heal hurt feelings or damaged relationships. It's the only kind of forgiveness that really works. It will make *you* happier, darling.'

'You reading off a script?'

'No need. I know it by heart, I've been saying it for years.'

Pip! Pip! Pip!

Before Mimi could reply, the line went dead.

In London, Toby wondered, How can I get them together when I'm over seventy miles away?

Toby knew that Mimi was an easygoing sort, although she was quick to resent injustice, which was why this stupid feud had gone on for years. Surely he could do *something*.

Sitting anxiously at Nick's bedside, Betsy eventually spooned some consommé into his mouth, but he would not touch the rice. She wanted to hold his hand, but he was still smarting from the humiliation of being undressed by his mom, at the age of . . . well . . . *practically* nineteen. So she merely stroked his forehead, which seemed to be permitted. She was also allowed to empty his bucket.

Nick stirred restlessly, 'Maybe I have appendicitis?'

'No, honey. The doctor checked that.' Betsy went to remove the two pillows from her own bed to prop Nick up more comfortably.

Now, when Mom was being so soft and tender, she *might* listen. *Now* was his chance! Now, when Mrs Fane was actually in the same hotel! So many times Nick had rehearsed what to say, if ever he had the chance to tell his mother firmly to dump her self-justifications.

Apprehensive, he plunged into planned battle. 'I heard you say something about her when you thought I was asleep. You called her Mimi, not "that awful creature!"

Mom, when are you going to stop your game with Mrs Fane?'

'What game?' asked Betsy, sharply, sensing attack.

'You whack her, she whacks you. You hurt her. She hurts you.'

'That awful creature tried to wreck my career!'

'If you'd been a Ziegfeld dancer, you might not have married Pop, and had Stella, Tess and me.'

Betsy counterattacked, 'And Stella wouldn't have become pregnant!' *Ratatatatatat!*

'Mom, Mrs Fane wasn't in bed with the two of them.' He blushed. He had never discussed sex with his mother.

Betsy's lips tightened in silence.

Nick shifted to a flank attack. 'Mom, how would you react if Mrs Fane knocked on our door right now, and asked you to forgive her?'

'*You must be sicker than I thought!*'

After an uneasy lull, Nick tried again. 'Mom, why not stop making excuses to yourself?' he urged. 'Go downstairs to the lobby, find out what room she's in and simply knock on her door. She'll know why you're there. You needn't apologize, just tell Mrs Fane you *regret* what's happened – that's true, isn't it?'

'Of course! Truly, I didn't realize Mimi was still in the theatre that night – that's why I told the fireman she'd left the building.'

'Mom, you're not *entirely* to blame, but I understand why Mrs Fane feels as she does: she has those terrible injuries. You didn't intend to hurt her – but you *did* intend to humiliate her at Tudor's party. You *did* intend to get that theatre away from the Fanes. Mr Fane felt so bad, he *did* try to kill himself.'

'*How do you know that?*' Betsy hid her face in her hands.

'Mom, back home the servants know everything before it happens. I hear them talking in the kitchen.' Nick reloaded. 'Mom, do you think it was maybe wrong of you to humiliate Mrs Fane and then hire Mr Carati?'

'That awful creature deserved it!'

'If your enemy behaves badly, that's no excuse for you to behave badly: that's what we were taught at school.' Nick offered temptation. 'Mom, this whole thing might be resolved in two minutes – and that would certainly be to your advantage.'

Betsy found it difficult to believe that her gentle, quiet son, her adored Nick, was ticking her off. She again donned her armour, was lowered onto her charger, yanked down her visor, and firmly grasped her lance. 'You know what your father always said – *get them, before they get you!*'

'But Pop was an unemotional fighter, and he knew when to stop: when he was losing. *You* don't understand when you're losing, Mom.'

'Me? *Losing?*'

'Mom, I know you're not entirely to blame for everything that's happened – but if you look back far enough you can *always* blame your present problem on somebody else until you reach the point when you can say, "Well, it wouldn't have happened if I hadn't been born" – because *that* sure wasn't your responsibility!'

'I can't believe I'm hearing this!' Betsy cried, as exasperated as she was indignant.

Nick quietly persisted, 'You even blamed Mimi for the death of Granny Bridges, but if you hadn't been seeking Inner Peace with that phoney Van in the Better Being sect, then Granny Bridges wouldn't have been killed.'

'She was killed because she put a detective on *me* – her own daughter!'

'Put yourself in her place, Mom,' Nick coaxed. 'Grandma was worried. She had no one to talk to, no one to help her. What else could she have done, to check whether her daughter was in danger?'

Betsy was silent, but Nick sensed that she had lifted her visor, and was listening, at last. He pushed home his advantage. 'Whoever was indirectly responsible for Granny's death, it sure wasn't Mrs Fane.'

Betsy burst into tears and Nick nearly capitulated, but stuck to his guns. 'Crying doesn't work as evasive action, Mom – but it shows how bad you feel.'

'How dare you tell me how *I* feel! How dare you tell me not to cry!'

'If only you faced up to your responsibilities like you're always telling me to, then maybe you wouldn't cry so much, Mom. Apologize. Make amends if possible. Then forget it. Please, Mom, stop pretending to be a little girl who needs to be looked after, and *grow up*!'

There, he'd finally said it.

Betsy, tears arrested, stared open-mouthed. Nick knew he was being hard on her but he also knew that there was no one else to do it, and he might never get another chance.

'Why should *you* care about Mimi Fane?'

'Because I care about *you*,' said Nick, love in his eyes. 'Can't you see you're just as scarred inside as Mrs Fane? Everyone else can see what that theatre fire did to her, but *I* can see what damage it did to you, Mom. You have a bad conscience about *something* to do with Mrs Fane, and only an apology will clear your conscience.'

Betsy hesitated. 'Is that the only way?'

He leaned forward and took his mother's hand. 'Mom, the real cure is: one, action; two, words.'

'What do you mean?'

'Go to Mrs Fane. Say, "I'm sorry." '

Betsy suddenly looked as pale and drawn as Nick. '*If* I spoke to Mimi, how could I be sure she wouldn't turn on me?'

'You can't.' Nick added persuasively, 'Remember how much fun you had with her before the fire, how close you were?' He slipped sleepily beneath the covers. 'Don't waste any more of your life on this stupid vendetta.' Physically and emotionally exhausted, he mumbled a few more sentences, then Betsy heard a small snore.

In her imposing but pillowless bed Betsy found it harder to go to sleep. She felt guilty. She felt resentful about feeling guilty. Every time she told herself it was Nick's fault for making her feel so bad, she remembered Nick saying that all his life he had seen her duck the consequences of her actions, and dump them on somebody else.

She remembered his final mumbled sentences before he fell asleep. 'You've spent years being unforgiving, so you know *that* hurts. Why not try forgiveness? I'm told it takes practice, so why not start now?'

'I've missed you all these years, Mimi,' Betsy murmured; half-conscious, she drifted into a nightmare, in which she was trapped in the flaming Daimler in the middle of a bomb crater. She screamed for help to the chauffeur, who wore a ballet tutu, but he shook his head, simpered, 'Make up and mend,' then flew away, fluttering diaphanous wings.

Chapter Twenty-Six

On the following morning, Nick hopped out of bed. 'When's breakfast?' he hollered as he nipped into the bathroom.

'Whenever you want, honey.' Relieved, Betsy walked to the bay-fronted window, looked out and shivered. It was a typically grey British summer's day. Beyond the neglected gardens and some balding parkland she could see the seafront, and beyond that the cold, grey waters of the Solent. The hotel manager had explained that the whole of the seafront was closed, and Southsea Promenade was also out of bounds to the public. Regretfully, madam could not visit the canoe lake, the rock garden, the miniature golf course, or either of the piers, as all these pleasure grounds had been declared a defence area.

Betsy could see barbed wire coiled all along the beach; the entire British coastline apparently bristled with dense, thorny metal; the beaches were also mined, if the authorities thought them a suitable place for enemy invasion. Beyond the wire she could see enormous blocks of cement, apparently thrown at random by some Almighty hand but in fact deliberately placed erratically, to stop enemy amphibious craft from landing.

As she looked at the depressing scene, she remembered

how cold England could be in June. She had packed only a few summer clothes for the quick trip to New York, mainly smart stuff ordered last January from Balanciaga, that new Spanish man in Paris. Now she needed a warm coat, a few frocks and at least a dozen pairs of silk stockings.

Her sartorial train of thought was interrupted by the delivery of a telegram. Astonished, she read:

THE POET LONGFELLOW WROTE QUOTE IF WE COULD READ THE SECRET HISTORY OF OUR ENEMIES WE WOULD FIND IN EACH MAN'S LIFE A SORROW AND SUFFERING ENOUGH TO DISARM ALL HOSTILITY UNQUOTE TRUST YOU AND MIMI WILL CONSIDER THIS WITH CARE STOP SINCERELY TOBY FANE

'Holy Mackerel,' she squawked.

Nick, wearing a towel as a sarong, appeared from the bathroom, streaked across to his mother and grabbed the telegraph from her hand. What had happened now?

Relieved not to be reading bad news from Stella, Nick looked up at his mother. 'This guy sounds like a sensible fellow.'

'He's got a nerve!'

* * *

Mimi's morning routine was similarly interrupted by a tap on the door, around which a young lad's hand appeared holding a telegram. It read:

DARLING REMEMBER FORGIVENESS IS A LUXURY FOR THE FORGIVER AS WELL AS THE FORGIVEN STOP LOVE TOBY

Mimi, who had not yet pulled on her gloves, glanced at the hand with which she held the telegraph; her lips tightened as she looked at the unnaturally white puckered skin. She sniffed.

* * *

The O'Briens breakfasted on reconstituted scrambled eggs, strangely speckled grey bread and a dab of margarine about the size of Betsy's diamond wristwatch. Toast? Silly question. Betsy did not mention the previous night's conversation.

After breakfast, Sutton drove Betsy to Handleys, the smartest local department store, where she discovered to her irritation that clothes had just been rationed, and unless she could produce fourteen coupons for a woman's overcoat, a further eleven for a warm dress and two for each pair of stockings – if you could find a pair – no money in the world could buy them.

On her subsequent short trip to the Dockyard Gate, Betsy noticed that the city was full of hurrying people. Every man not supported by a stick wore some sort of uniform or a Home Guard armband. Without stockings, slacks for women were clearly a necessity. Any woman with hips narrow enough to do so (and many not so qualified) wore a battledress waist-length jacket, and the rest were in knee-length coats cut like a skimpy tent. A cardboard gas-mask box was slung across every back.

Sutton turned his head as the Daimler slowed to a walking pace. 'We are now in the Hard, madam, with the Dockyard Gate ahead.' On Betsy's left the street sloped to the water; the right side seemed composed entirely of old-fashioned pubs leaning drunkenly against each other.

Majestically, the Daimler approached the Dockyard

Gate, which was surmounted by a wrought-iron arch with a central suspended lantern; set in the wall on the right was a small heavily guarded door for pedestrians, overseen by a seventeenth-century coat of arms, carved in stone. A mass of uniformed young people strode purposefully in and out. 'The building just inside the Gate, to the right, that's the Old Porters' Lodge,' Sutton announced. 'The one on the left is the old Police Cell Block, built to house naval defaulters.'

Suddenly, a crowd of bicycles debouched from the Dockyard Gate, pedalled by men wearing scruffy blue overalls, greasy flat peaked caps and old tweed jackets; they were Dockyard workers, coming off a shift. Everyone on foot hastily jumped out of the way.

Betsy leaned forward. 'Sutton, please go and ask when the *Reliant* is due to dock.'

After twenty minutes, he returned, regretfully shaking his head. He gave his trembling salute, then opened the back door of the Daimler. 'They won't give me any information, madam. It's all exceedingly hush-hush.'

Nick – who had insisted on accompanying his mother – offered to try to get news but Betsy impatiently shook her head, 'You stay out of the wind. I'll go.'

Shivering in her rose-silk suit, but with the self-confident air of the rich and powerful, Betsy clicked on her high-heeled peep-toe shoes over the cobbles towards the armed soldiers, policemen and uniformed sailors who guarded both the outside and inside of the Gate. Unexpectedly, she found herself repeating the same phrases over and over again, to these expressionless men. 'A ship from Bordeaux, the *Reliant*? . . .' 'My daughter, Stella O'Brien . . .' 'My granddaughter, Caroline O'Brien . . . a two-month-old baby . . .' The men shook their heads. One said, 'Sorry, lady.'

Betsy had started her enquiries with a faintly arrogant attitude, which quickly changed to an aggressive, slightly bullying one. She then tried tears and pleading, like Pickford in an early movie. The sentries on duty continued to ignore her.

In exasperation, she stopped a man in dungarees, carrying a tool bag. Amiably he listened, then replied, 'Don't know nothing, lady. Twenty-five thousand men are trying to work in there, and the refugee boats keep pouring in. The Yard's packed with ships, in for refit, in for repairs, in to take on fresh supplies. Best thing you can do, lady, is keep waiting here till your party turns up.' As he spoke, another burst of bicycles spewed from the Dockyard Gate. Betsy waited until they had passed and then hobbled back to the Daimler. Grimly she said to Nick, 'I won't give up until I see them! I'm going to *sit here twenty-four hours a day* until I see Stella.'

No matter what she had to do to manage it, Betsy would get Stella and her grandchild back to the safety of Los Angeles and quickly circulate some story about a hasty wartime marriage to a sadly now-dead hero. Two calls to Heda and Louella plus a call to Cartier would fix that.

'What about . . . ?' Nick nodded towards Sutton.

'He can go off when he needs to eat and sleep. But *I'm* going to stay here. I mustn't take my eyes off the Gate.'

Suddenly, Betsy's head jerked forward. With a perfectly varnished, blood-red nail, she pointed ahead, and gasped, 'I don't believe it!'

Having clambered off the back of a motorbike, Mimi

kissed the driver on the cheek, then sauntered towards the Dockyard Gate.

For the first time, Nick gazed, fascinated, at the mysterious devil that haunted his mother. The trim little figure wore a blue wool suit with a short skirt, black stockings and black laced low-heeled shoes. She had clearly come prepared to wait for hours, for she also carried a heavy overcoat and what looked like a man's pre-war opera cape – black with white satin lining – slung over one shoulder. Her unnaturally bright red hair was caught back in a snood, a resurrected medieval hairnet.

After waiting outside the Gate for over an hour, Nick saw Mimi dart towards a naval officer as he came out of the Gate; she was clearly asking him for information, and equally clearly he gave it to her. Mimi scribbled a note, walked up to one of the policemen standing by the Gate, handed him the note. The policeman immediately took it to the Porters' Lodge.

A few minutes later, a naval sub-lieutenant hurriedly appeared, shook Mimi's hand and smiled. He talked for several minutes, clearly answering Mimi's questions. The officer then kissed Mimi on the cheek and returned to the Porters' Lodge.

What did that officer tell Mimi? Betsy wondered, frustrated.

Mimi turned and trotted purposefully up the Hard. Almost without thinking, Betsy wrenched open the door of the Daimler and clattered quickly in pursuit on her Hollywood heels. Almost immediately she tripped on the cobbles, managed to regain her balance and urgently beckoned to Nick, who ran to his mother.

'Quick! Follow her, Nick, before she disappears! Find out what she knows!'

Nick hurried after Mimi and caught up with her as she was about to enter a red telephone cabin.

'Mrs Fane,' Nick gasped, short of breath.

Mimi swung around. She looked puzzled. This young man's face was familiar, but she couldn't place it.

'I'm Nick O'Brien, Betsy's son.' Nick gravely extended his hand.

Mimi shook his hand, as if in a dream.

'Mom and I haven't been able to find out when Stella's boat's due. Do you know?'

Mimi hesitated. So that explained it. Hah! Betsy needn't think that she would get any news from Mimi about . . . *their* granddaughter.

Reluctantly, she scowled, 'The *Reliant* was supposed to leave Bordeaux on the third of June but she's been delayed. Nobody knows why. They've had several false alarms. She'll be steering a zigzag course, undisclosed for security reasons. I'm just going to phone my husband, to tell him I won't be home yet.'

'How can you be so sure that the *Reliant* has been delayed?' Nick said politely.

'My son's stationed in the Dockyard, and I've just spoken to one of his mates.'

'Thank you.' Nick repeatedly shook Mimi's gloved hand. The two hesitated. Each felt something more should be said, but neither knew what.

Mimi nodded brightly and dived into the phone box. Almost immediately she came out muttering, 'Out of bloody order! I'll phone Toby from one of them pubs.'

'The *Reliant* has been delayed,' Nick reported as he scrambled back into the Daimler and repeated what Mrs Fane had told him.

'Ha!' Betsy snorted. 'How do we know that's true? Maybe she wants us to leave! I'm staying right *here*!'

However by midday there was no sign of the *Reliant* and they had brought nothing to eat. Nick needed a warm, easy-to-digest meal at midday, not a packet of greasy crisps from a pub. Betsy had eaten practically nothing yesterday, and at breakfast had only taken one mouthful of scrambled egg, pulled a face and put down her fork. Now she leaned forward and rapped on the glass partition. 'Back to the hotel.'

As they turned the first corner, Nick saw Mimi, obviously heading on foot for their hotel. He nudged his mother. Betsy defiantly shook her head. She wasn't going to share her car with that woman. The Daimler glided past.

After making a few purchases (newspaper, indigestion tablets and a thermos flask) the O'Briens headed for their hotel suite to freshen up. With difficulty, Nick pulled open the creaking iron-grille doors of the elevator. Standing inside, he heaved the doors together. He had almost closed them when they were yanked apart again from outside by a breathless intruder who tumbled into the elevator.

Intent on slipping through the closing doors, Mimi did not realize the identity of her companions until they were moving upwards. Betsy gave her a cold stare, then looked straight ahead. Mimi's face flooded with colour; she turned her back to Betsy and faced the iron-grille doors as the elevator jerked slowly upwards. Nick could not think what to say or do.

The lift slowly shuddered to a halt when its occupants were at chest level with the next floor.

In thunderous silence, the two women waited as Nick

fiddled with the elevator buttons. Why had he been so self-possessed last night, when talking to his mother, yet now behaved like a tongue-tied, clumsy kid who couldn't even open an elevator door?

Impatient, Mimi rattled the grille-work doors and bawled, '*Help! We're stuck! Get us out of here, somebody! Where the hell is everybody.*'

Betsy jumped in shock as, once again, she heard the Black Velvet voice at full blast.

As nobody appeared, Mimi boomed even louder in the voice that so easily filled a theatre, '*Stop molesting me, you evil brute!*'

Within minutes, the elevator was surrounded by a strange assortment of people – some half dressed; some defensively holding hairbrushes; an officer in khaki carried a drawn pistol. Behind these, a few ancient hotel servants tottered nervously down the corridor.

Eventually, the balding manager (called out of retirement to resume his duties) creaked up the stairs. With difficulty he knelt on the worn crimson carpet and whispered apologetically to the heads of the trapped passengers, 'I'm *so* sorry, ladies. This machine plays us up something shocking, but we'll have you out in no time.'

'No time' proved to be fifteen minutes of tight-mouthed heavy breathing inside the lift and distant clanking and cursing outside, followed by jerking and several false starts. Eventually, slowly, the lift shuddered back to the main floor, where the manager was waiting to apologize: it was the war.

'What excuse do they use in peacetime?' Betsy angrily asked Nick, as they trudged up the wide staircase that wound around the elevator.

'He was displacing responsibility,' Nick said smugly, as

he opened the door to their suite. Betsy sank into a flowered armchair and pulled off her shoes. 'The minute I see Stella, we're out of this dump!' She was tense and furiously angry following her encounter with Mimi.

When Nick reckoned she had simmered down, he asked tentatively, 'Couldn't you be a bit more friendly the next time we come across Mrs Fane? She clearly has good contacts, and we know nobody. She gave us that information this morning. If it wasn't for her, we'd still be sitting there, waiting.'

'I'll think about it, honey,' Betsy spat, making it clear that she intended to do no such thing.

Nick again wished that while they had been trapped in that elevator he could have defrosted the two women in some way. But what could a sixteen-year-old do? Mr Roosevelt himself couldn't have raised the icy temperatures in that elevator.

For lunch, they ate an unappetizing dish called Woolton pie, which smelled of armpits and tasted as if someone had already eaten it; this was followed by stewed figs covered in a glistening, oleaginous yellow liquid. When the O'Briens returned to the Daimler, Sutton said brightly, 'Looks like rain, madam.' Betsy glanced up; the afternoon air had suddenly grown sullen.

The drive back to the Dockyard was unexpectedly long and suddenly the city seemed one big traffic jam. Sutton had considerable trouble in parking near the Dockyard Gate and was only allowed to do so after a muttered conversation with a harassed young policeman on point duty, during which Nick repeatedly heard the words 'VIP' and 'Admiral's wife.' Once again, Mimi was already in position at the Gate, talking to the same young sub-lieutenant, who kissed her again before he disappeared.

As the rain grew more persistent, Mimi briskly shook out her black white-satin-lined Dracula cape and clamped it round her throat; it almost reached pavement level.

Steadily, the rain fell heavier.

'Why don't we invite Mrs Fane in here?' Nick suggested. 'If she's getting information that we can't, it's a sensible move, Mom!'

Betsy hesitated. She was used to having her own way, but this morning, as she sat for hours in the unheated Daimler, her thoughts had returned to what Nick said on the previous evening. In particular, she remembered Nick describing her angry vendetta with Mimi as a lethal ping-pong game. *What was the point of it?* Nick had asked. Betsy now began to wonder as she reluctantly reconsidered, from Nick's perspective, the history of her vengeful, long-running quarrel with Mimi.

Certainly Mimi had been badly burned in the theatre fire, and blamed Betsy for *accidentally* telling the fireman that she had already left the building. But Mimi had *deliberately* prevented Betsy from getting a job with the Ziegfeld follies. Betsy had paid her out for that when she publicly humiliated Mimi on her trip to Hollywood. Mimi had spitefully retaliated with the interview which had made Betsy a laughing stock of Los Angeles ... Agreed, Betsy had deliberately intended to hurt Mimi with her attempt to purchase the King William but Betsy had certainly *not* intended to force Mimi's husband to attempt suicide and she refused to take the blame. Of course, between those events there had been constant sniping, the occasional hand grenade and one or two hidden land-mines, all gleefully reported by gossip columnists whose mischievous comments had goaded both Betsy and Mimi to further retaliatory action ... which of course had attracted yet more gossip-column inches. Of course, you had to blame a lot of it on the press.

But not all of it.

What *was* the point of all that angry bitterness? Suddenly, Betsy found herself unable to give herself a true and reasonable answer. Suddenly, she, too, could not see the point of the vendetta. She pulled Toby's telegram from her purse and reread it. Almost unwillingly she found herself wondering whether there was a remote possibility that there *might* be two viewpoints of their long-running feud. Eventually, she considered that Mimi might not be *entirely* in the wrong. She found herself admitting that Mimi was not responsible for Stella becoming pregnant. Stella had clearly hidden herself in Paris so that she could have her baby. Whether or not Max had seduced her, it was obvious that Stella did not regret it. Stella had a child that she welcomed, and now that daughter was what mattered, for she was Betsy's first grandchild.

Mimi was also about to meet *her* first grandchild; she must be standing in for her miserable cowardly son! Hang on, review that . . . perhaps he wanted to meet Stella, but was unable to do so, for some genuine wartime reason. If so, Stella might be pleased to see Mimi. Stella could be quietly obstinate, or she would not have insisted on having this man's child. Betsy guessed that Stella would just as obstinately wish to retain all possible contact with Caroline's father, and his family. Should Betsy attempt to sabotage such a relationship, Stella (as she had already demonstrated) was clearly capable of cutting away from her mother, so her priority was also clear: on no account would she cause or be goaded into having a fight with Mimi. Reluctantly she said to Nick, 'You're right. It would make sense to invite her in here. Just until this rain stops.

But I warn you, she'll probably refuse. *You* talk to her, honey, she certainly won't come if I ask her.'

Nick opened the door, put one foot on the running board, then drew back. 'Mom, this is your responsibility. *Please* do it yourself.' As Betsy shook her head, he added, 'For Stella's sake, Mom.'

Betsy hesitated . . .

She felt ridiculously self-conscious as, head down, she ran through the rain, kicking her high heels sideways, as if her knees were tied together. As she neared the uniformed people massed outside the Dockyard Gate, she wondered how she should invite Mimi into her automobile. Casually? Gravely? With a smile . . . Not on your life!

At that moment Mimi casually turned her head. She gazed disbelievingly at Betsy. Her enemy wore a short-skirted rose silk suit covered by a rose linen coat; her peep-toed cream pumps had perky bows. Her hair – the grey streaks carefully blonded – was piled on top of her head, *à la* Betty Grable, which made her look charmingly, nostalgically Edwardian; a small pancake covered by pink rosebuds was pinned over one eye. Looking at her, Mimi remembered Betsy's girlhood excitement when she was allowed to put up her hair for the first time.

Suddenly, like a flock of starlings, a cloud of bicycles flew out of the Dockyard Gate as a shift of Dockyard workers came off duty. Unfortunately, Betsy was running directly in their path. Bewildered, she stopped abruptly and then hesitated, wondering whether escape lay to left or right. She hopped a step in one direction and then another, doing a little hesitant two-step on the spot as do two strangers trying to avoid colliding headlong on the street. A bicyclist heading straight for her yanked his handlebars to match her actions, then roared, 'Make up your mind, missus!' as he just managed to avoid her.

As she flung herself out of the bicyclist's path she lost her footing and fell heavily to the ground, in the middle of the tangle of bicycles, all of which miraculously circumnavigated her with a twist of the handlebars before charging onwards. They disappeared as fast as they had arrived, leaving her sprawled on the muddy cobbles. Winded and shocked, dazed and instinctive, Betsy's reaction was to tell herself, 'This is entirely *Nick's* fault! If he hadn't pushed me into approaching Mimi . . .' Suddenly she realized that she was doing exactly what Nick said she did; dumping on somebody else, like a child whining to its mother, '*Now* look what you made me do!'

Mimi hurried towards her enemy, who no longer looked like Betty Grable: Betsy sat sprawled on the filthy cobblestones, feet wide apart; one cream pump had fallen from her foot, both silk stockings were torn, her face was muddy, her knees were skinned; her clothes were spattered by dirty water; her little rosebud hat hung ludicrously from one ear.

Mimi, who had intended to help Betsy to her feet, suddenly stopped. A memory as evocative as that summoned by Proust's *madeleine* had just floated into her mind. She remembered the blustery, rainy day in Wigan High Street, just after Betsy had given her that wonderful crimson umbrella. They had both nearly ruined their new spring coats in the mud, but neither girl had been able to stop laughing.

Mimi started to giggle.

From the dirty cobblestones, the ludicrously overdressed and mud-splattered Betsy screamed, 'Take that grin off your face, Mimi! What's so darn funny?'

Helpless with laughter, Mimi pointed a shaking finger at Betsy. 'Oh . . . Oh . . . Who's the golliwog now?'

For a second, Betsy appeared puzzled and then her face softened as she shared Mimi's memory. She gazed at the tiny figure of her girl-friend, swathed in a sodden black opera cloak that reached her schoolgirl-laced shoes; a yellow oilskin sou'wester covered that ludicrously red hair.

Slowly, very slowly, Betsy smiled, '*You* don't look so hot yourself, ducky. Certainly not a sweetly pretty doll, dearest.' Sharing that happy girlhood memory, Betsy sat in the dirt, feet wide apart, laughing her head off.

From the Daimler window, the incredulous Nick saw Mimi bend down to help Betsy to her feet. Betsy kicked off her remaining shoe and discarded it. With arms around each other, both women staggered off the cobbles and leaned against the Dockyard brick wall, where they giggled like schoolgirls. Whenever one managed to stop, she caught the other's eye – and they were off again.

Finally, the two bedraggled, laughing women staggered towards the Daimler. Imperturbable, Sutton opened the door for them, saluting as he did so. Once both women were seated, the laughing slowly subsided, but they looked at each other like a courting couple, thought Sutton as he peered in the windscreen mirror; he saw his lady reach out for the other one's hand and both women exchange a poignantly sad and loving look.

'I've missed you, my gal,' Mimi said quietly.

'So have I. You'll never, never know how much.'

Both women silently acknowledged that their affection for each other had been rekindled.

'Let's just remember Wigan High Street and that binge we had at the whelk stall after we ruined our coats.'

'Yes, Mimi, let's forget *everything* that's happened since

then.' Tears of emotion fell on Betsy's cheek and her mascara dribbled two black rivulets down to her chin.

Unnoticed, Nick tactfully nipped in front and sat beside the chauffeur, on the other side of the glass partition (Nick called it 'the class partition'). With no intention of wasting this second opportunity, Nick told Sutton to drive back to the hotel. Slowly.

'You haven't changed much, old girl,' Betsy lied.

Mimi thought, She's put on weight. She said, 'Neither have you, old dear.'

'I know what you're thinking, but after Jack died, I just couldn't stop eating comfort food, practically overdosed on Hershey bars, would you believe it? But I'm going on a diet . . . next week.'

'*You* don't need to diet, Betsy.' Mimi knew the First Rule of Female Friendship. 'If you have put a bit on, then it suits you.' Here she told the truth. Betsy's complexion had a few faint lines, but was unwrinkled.

Mimi asked curiously, 'Still clean your face with olive oil?'

Betsy nodded. Mimi was clearly as vibrantly energetic as ever but her face was now pinched, her cheeks were hollow and her eyes slightly puffy. Of course that hair must be dyed, for it was still an outrageous foxy-red. Her body seemed thinner.

'No, I still don't need to diet,' Mimi said smugly. She looked carefully at Betsy: that jaw line was certainly blurred, but Betsy's eyes were still beautiful: the whites were still startlingly white; the violet irises and double row of thick black lashes remained as fascinating as ever.

'You still have lovely eyes, Betsy.'

'They say there's always one part of a woman that

Time leaves untouched: her legs or shoulders, maybe her hands or bosom.'

'With me, it's the ears, ducky.'

They were still holding hands. Gently, Betsy disentangled their fingers and deliberately peeled off one of Mimi's gloves. Mimi did not snatch her hand away as she would have done had anyone else attempted this. Betsy looked sadly at the puckered skin, the ugly discoloration. Gently she lifted Mimi's hand and kissed it. 'I'm sorry, Mimi.'

Mimi was silent. At last she'd said it. Mimi sighed, then felt at peace.

Betsy said huskily, 'I never thought I'd get the chance to do that.' Her heart thumped faster. Quickly, before having second thoughts, Betsy gabbled, 'I don't want to waste the next thirty years, Mimi. So I guess . . . I'm sorry . . . It *was* my fault . . . But not entirely, of course.'

'Not entirely,' Mimi slowly agreed, with more tact than conviction; she then realized that what she had just said was *the truth*. In her heart, she had known that Betsy noticed nothing else when seated before the dressing-room mirror; certainly she had not deliberately tried to trap Mimi in that burning building. But Mimi had *deliberately* prevented Betsy from getting the Ziegfeld job, which was what had really started that spiral of hatred and revenge.

Mimi felt unexpectedly cleansed, freed by her own generosity, as her deliberate exaggeration of Betsy's responsibility became clear to her. Happily, she added aloud, 'After all, Betsy, *you* didn't set the Angel on fire!'

'Indeed I didn't,' said Betsy, acidly.

Suddenly recalling a long-forgotten memory, Mimi

laughed. 'And Jolly Joe was wrong! The old troublemaker always said it was you as locked me in me digs that night, when we both hoped Cockie would discover us ... You remember, surely? That night I sprained me ankle, jumping out of the window, to get to the theatre on time ... Never, for one minute, did I believe Jolly Joe!'

Betsy jerked her head and stared, unseeing, from the Daimler window. Then she turned back to face her newly found friend. If they were to be as genuinely close as they had been before, then she would need to be truthful with Mimi from now on.

Betsy disengaged her hand. She looked straight ahead. 'I hate to admit this, Mimi, but Jolly Joe was right. I *did* lock you in.' There. She'd said it. Immediately, she felt relieved, even her body felt lighter.

Mimi tensed and inhaled deeply but managed to keep her lips firmly together. Eventually, with some difficulty, she muttered, 'We just agreed to put all unpleasantness behind us. So let's forget it.'

As the Daimler moved regally forward, to Betsy's surprise she found herself saying, 'I've been such a fool, Mimi. I care too much about what other people might think. I didn't care enough about my daughter's feelings. If only I'd been ... *motherly* ... Stella might now be in California, not Heaven knows where!'

'No use hitting yourself over the head, ducky,' Mimi soothed. 'What's done can't be undone, as the Bard said, so don't fret.' She squeezed Betsy's hand, too moved to speak.

Betsy whispered, 'We were girls the last time we held hands – and now we're grandmothers.'

'You, me and Gloria Swanson,' Mimi muttered.

Betsy smiled warmly at her feeble joke. Mimi felt her

old affection for Betsy flood through her body as contrition replaced indignation, anger and vengeful retribution. Both women gazed fondly at each other. Once again, each knew what the other was thinking; of their lost friendship, of when they had been eager, young girls. Every day, they had shared their lives, each anxiety, disappointment, hope and triumph; they had giggled, and hugged, and borrowed each other's ribbons, hats and hair tongs: they had been closer than sisters, for each had chosen the other.

'We punished ourselves, you know,' Mimi said, crossly. During the many lost years each woman had missed and grieved for the other as if she was dead; each had felt sorrow and loss and directly denied any such feeling. Each had encouraged hatred to simmer in her heart as she sought destruction of the other until hatred had boiled over and spilled into the rest of their lives. Each woman had damaged herself more than the other and they had squandered their time, energy, talent and money in that stupid search for revenge. 'Each time one of us tried to get her own back, the situation got worse, not better,' Mimi added.

'Damn right,' Betsy said regretfully. 'I'm sorry it took me so long to see it.'

'What a waste,' Mimi said quietly.

Betsy again squeezed Mimi's hand. 'How I've missed you.'

'Me, too.'

Silently they sat holding hands.

Sutton was glad that madam had forgotten to wind up the glass partition. That had been as good as a play on the wireless.

It was only as they reached the Queen Alexandra grounds that Mimi remembered, 'I swear I'll forget me own name next! That young sub-lieutenant just told me that the *Reliant* won't dock until tomorrow. Probably in the afternoon. Tomorrow morning, they may be able to give us a more definite time. Apparently things are a little unsettled at Bordeaux. So there's no need to hang around the Dockyard today. You needn't worry. You won't miss Stella and the baby.'

'How do you know about Stella and the baby?'

Mimi dug into her shoulder bag and produced a cable. Betsy took it. 'Hey, this is addressed to Max Fane, at the Garrick Club! How did *you* get it?'

'Max's club sent it by messenger to my house,' Mimi explained. 'Cables are always urgent. So I opened it.'

'Why, yours is almost the same wording as my cable,' Betsy said as she scanned it. 'I didn't realize the Paris embassy *asked* your son to meet the boat.'

'I expect Stella wanted that.'

Betsy winced to hear her old enemy talk so casually of Stella. Both women fell silent. Old wounds did not immediately disappear after one shared fit of the giggles; hurt feelings needed time to recover.

Eventually, Mimi squeezed Betsy's hand. 'I'm so happy that we're friends again, Betsy. I never had another pal like you.'

'Neither did I.' More than Mimi, Betsy had felt that lack: she had never felt such open, happy affection for any other woman and she knew that no other woman had felt it for her; at first Betsy had been too beautiful, and then she had been too rich.

Sadly, Mimi said, 'I know you can feel how happy I am to be sitting here with you, the both of us holding hands again. But before we can forget all that's happened, there's something that you and I need to sort out.' She hesitated then said in a rush, 'You see, my Max don't know that Stella's about to arrive. I couldn't get hold of him.'

'That doesn't matter. They'll see each other later,' Betsy said forgivingly. Clearly there was now no need for her to invent for Stella a war-hero husband who had been killed in action. Instead, morality would be appeased when divorced Max married Stella.

Mimi shook her head. 'Max and his wife were reconciled before he knew that Stella was expecting ... Then Max's wife had a baby that died ...' She added bleakly, 'Fizz was told she probably won't be able to have another baby, so it looks as if little Caroline will be my only grandchild—'

Betsy angrily interrupted, 'You mean that Max *isn't going to marry Stella*?'

For the first time since her arrival in Portsmouth, Mimi ardently hoped that Max would *not* suddenly appear around a corner, out of the Dockyard Gate or into the bar at the Queen Alexandra. With quiet determination, Mimi shook her head. 'Max ain't going to abandon his wife, and to be honest, he don't want to. He ain't even told Fizz about Stella. When we talked it over I told him there was no point in upsetting his wife.' She took a deep breath. 'But he wants Stella to know that he'll take full responsibility; he's the father of her child and he knows it. He'll do whatever Stella wants, so long as it don't hurt Fizz.'

Betsy's pride had already taken a hard beating and now her humiliation was kindled fast as a match thrown on oil. Her daughter, Stella, pregnant by a man who had a simultaneously pregnant wife, the two-timing dirty rat! If Jack were alive he'd pulp that bastard!

Mimi said timidly, 'In your place I'd feel the same.' Hard though it was for her to admit it, Max had certainly been a very naughty boy.

With an almost visible effort, the trembling Betsy pushed her turbulent thoughts from her mind. With difficulty, she said, 'We'll just have to work it all out, somehow.'

Mimi sensed what an effort those words had cost and saw clear proof of Betsy's true intention to rebuild their former, treasured friendship. Silently, she lifted Betsy's manicured white hand to her lips and kissed it.

As the Daimler drew up to the hotel steps, Betsy gave a determined smile. Each woman knew that if they were to share a happy future, rather than one of continued venom, they had to abandon the if-onlys of the past and together do their best for the future.

Mimi hadn't known such blessed relief since she'd had her wisdom teeth out.

* * *

At ten o'clock that night Mimi made yet another attempt to telephone Toby. Earlier she had left a message at his ARP station, 'Had a good giggle with Betsy over lunch.' The girl at the other end had said crossly, 'This doesn't sound like a war message!'

'It most certainly *is*,' Mimi assured her. She still felt light-hearted so she hummed an old music-hall song as she skipped towards the bar; she was too excited to sleep, so she'd knock back a nightcap, if she could wheedle that old waiter to find a snort of brandy.

Betsy had refused to eat ('I've lost five pounds since I arrived in Britain'), but had sipped French champagne (you could still buy a bottle of good wine if you were prepared to take out a mortgage to pay for it) while the ebullient Mimi entertained Nick with spirited stories of his mother's larks when she was young. The two women laughed and talked so merrily that other diners turned to stare at them; Nick's ears turned red as he demolished all three portions of watery mashed potatoes, three thin slices of tinned Spam followed by three slices of carrot tart with dried-egg custard. Afterwards, still shaken by her fall, Betsy decided to have an early night, but Mimi had been too elated to sleep. After her unsuccessful telephone call to Toby, she decided to have a drink in the bar before trying again.

A blast of noise made her blink as she opened the door to the bar, which was even more crowded with uniforms than on the previous evening. She immediately noticed the excited, feverish atmosphere. She caught stray phrases above the din – 'Dunkirk' . . . 'flotilla' . . . 'that God-awful dive-bombing' . . . 'Never thought I'd get out alive' . . . 'Never heard such a bloody noise . . .'

Mimi nudged the nearest naval uniform. 'What's up, mate?'

The officer turned and grinned. 'Nothing much. The Royal Navy's just rescued the British army from the Jerries in France. Where would those boys in khaki be without us?' Smiling, he turned back to his uniformed girlfriend.

Mimi dreamily enjoyed the noisy buzz of talk and laughter in this bar where strangers spoke to each other.

A couple of females not in uniform wore a scrap of frivolous veiled nonsense perched over one eye, to remind themselves (and everyone else) that deep down they were still ridiculously adorable women; they also showed a lot of leg, regarded almost as a patriotic duty, to boost the men's morale and remind them that they were also fighting for the erogenous zones. A uniformed group hung over the baby grand piano, noisily and tunelessly bawling 'We'll meet again, don't know where, don't know wheeeeen. But I *know* we'll meet again some sunny day . . .'

In peacetime Toby had once brought Mimi to the Queen Alexandra for a weekend by the sea and this bar in the evening had been as gloomy as a funeral parlour, with a thin old girl in a black satin gown who had played soft classical mush on that piano. Waiters had obsequiously whispered to couples in evening dress who murmured to each other . . . The British used to be such a quiet, mousy lot but now they were all in the same uncomfortable boat – united by the common enemy, as Winnie Churchill put it. Now they all shared a common goal – to boot the Nazis back where they belonged – now all of them knew that they might die tomorrow, why, the British behaved just like a troupe of theatre folk on tour. This reminded Mimi to peer around unsuccessfully for her waiter. Still standing just inside the door, she wondered whether she could ever make it to the bar without a cattle prod. The white-jacketed ancient gnome behind the counter was doing his wartime best: beer handles were pulled, tops snapped off bottles, exotic coloured drinks were theatrically stirred with a long spoon, change was given and tips accepted with archducal condescension.

Mimi decided that it really wasn't worth the trouble for a small brown puddle in a balloon glass. She turned to leave the bar and nearly bumped into Guy, the naval lieutenant who owned that noisy motorbike Max so often borrowed (and parked in her clean hall) in return for a couple of comps for the Minerva.

'Why, look what the cat brought in!' Mimi beamed. 'I need a big chap like you to get me a . . .' She stopped in mid-sentence. Open-mouthed, the man was looking at her with a mixture of horror and embarrassment. 'Hello,' he stammered.

Mimi peered at his white face. How odd he sounded. How peculiar he looked. Was he ill or . . .

'What's happened to Max?'

'Please don't ask me, Mrs Fane.' The strangled, over-polite voice trailed away. Guy stretched out two big cold hands and clasped her gloved ones. He almost pushed her against the wall. 'You must be brave,' he said with difficulty. 'Oh, Hell.'

'Tell me!' Mimi whispered fiercely, not wanting to be told.

Eventually Guy looked down, swallowed and mumbled, 'Max and I were at Dunkirk together, pulling soldiers off the beach . . . Max was working the boat next to mine . . . We were under constant dive-bomb attacks – for the Jerries it was like shooting fish in a barrel . . . Max left the helm, that's what caught my attention.' He looked up straight at Mimi. 'Oh, God, I'm sorry, Mrs Fane . . . I saw Max hit. He was covered in blood. I saw him fall. I saw him go under . . .' There, he'd got it out. He added, almost pleadingly, 'There was nothing I could do. Men were screaming for help in my own boat.'

Frozen-faced, Mimi stared at him.

Guy added, 'Someone else grabbed the helm of Max's boat and she headed out to sea, so I knew straightaway that there was no hope for him.'

Mimi tried to think. *'How can you be so sure it was Max?'*

'He'd called across to me, shortly before it happened, when there was a sudden lull in the bombing.'

'*What did he say?*'

Guy hesitated. 'Max said, "Do you come here often, you old bastard?"' he blurted out.

Mimi felt helplessly in pain and bereft as if an arm had suddenly been torn from its socket. How could she continue to breathe when her heart was being so painfully, remorselessly squeezed and her blood was pounding so hard that she felt it would burst out of her eardrums at any moment? How could she survive this awful moment? Not that she wanted to survive in a world without Max. It wasn't fair, it just wasn't fair that her only child should be removed from her so swiftly, easily and brutally when there were plenty of other mothers with a flock of children still intact. *It wasn't fair!* Why, the bloody war had only just started! And what had Max been doing in France when she had thought him safe in a desk job? Mimi had felt so sorry for mothers whose sons had been posted overseas, for anxiety had then become a permanent part of their lives, something they got up with every morning: they made the toast with it, they made munitions with it, they knitted with it and oh, how they listened with it to the news on the wireless . . . But it had never occurred to her that her own son might be killed.

She turned her face and stared hard but sightlessly at the antics of the old bartender. His every movement seemed to have slowed down, like a dance tune on an old-fashioned gramophone that needed rewinding. Nothing in the room had altered but everything was now different. The determinedly cheerful crowd seemed two-dimensional and their happy chatter one violent, humming noise that threatened to engulf her, as did the grey miasma of cigarette smoke that whorled under the ceiling lamps and mingled with the suddenly sickly smell of whisky fumes, stale beer and too many bodies squashed into an airless room.

'I say, Mrs Fane, do you feel all right?'

'No,' Mimi breathed with difficulty. 'I'm not all right *and I never will be.*' A vital force had left her life. She felt emptied, drained and knew that she would feel like this for the rest of her life.

'Oh, God, I shouldn't have told you!'

'I saw it in your eyes,' Mimi said dully. Dazed, she wondered how one look from this young man could change her life for ever.

Someone was standing at her side, proffering a large brandy. Mimi shook her head: she could hardly breathe, let alone swallow.

'You need fresh air, madam.' The old waiter firmly steered her out of the bar and onto an empty terrace that faced the moon above a grey, glittering, ruthless sea. Every step Mimi took used far more effort than usual, as if she were moving under water. There was a singing noise in her ears as if she had dived too deep too fast, and the waiter's voice sounded distant.

'Will you be all right, madam? I have to go back to the bar.'

Mimi nodded as she leaned against the wall. She wanted to be left alone in this indifferent, black and silver night.

Why had she not sensed Max's death? How could she have laughed and joked when the child to whom she had given life, whom she had carried in her body for nine months, whom she had thought of as part of her . . . how could she not have noticed that this part of her had suddenly vanished?

She could not believe that Max would never again

charge into the house in Fitzroy Square, instantly untidy-ing everything and energizing everyone. She did not want to believe that Max would never again put his hands around his mother's waist and lift her high in the air while she squawked and pretended to be annoyed but was secretly proud that out of her body had come this strong, muscular creature, larger than herself.

Eventually, the waiter returned and, holding her firmly by the arm, he steered her through the now-deserted, dimly lit hotel. Once inside her room, he sat her on the chair, unlaced and removed her shoes, whisked off her jacket and skirt, pulled back the blankets, gently pushed her into bed and tucked the bedclothes under her chin. 'I lost both my brothers in the last war,' he said softly as he switched off the light, then left the room.

Mimi stared into the blackness that surrounded her. When Max was a child, if he had a nightmare he used to stumble downstairs to her bedroom and climb into her big, soft bed. Half-conscious, she would turn towards him and pull his chilled little body to her warm one, listening sleepily to her son's frightened voice. 'Mummy, it was *horrible*! I dreamed I was being pushed down something wet, down a long, dark, squidgy tunnel – small as a drainpipe. I tried to call but I couldn't make a sound. So you couldn't hear me and you didn't come to me . . . was . . . so . . . frightened . . .' Slowly his voice would trail off until she heard regular soft breathing as he fell asleep, pillowed in the reassuring, warm arms of his mother, who sleepily inhaled the beloved fragrance of her child's silken hair until she, too, drifted to a far land.

Now into her mind floated a painful picture of his body swaying limply in bloodied water inexorably sucked by a black tide, deeper, deeper, into the far darkness and silence of the waters of the ocean, endlessly drifting further and further from his mother.

She was absolutely certain that as her child sank below that bloodied water he had called for her. For her, his frightened cries would continue to echo faintly through eternity. Hopelessly longing to pull her child to her and comfort him with her own body warmth, Mimi felt fretful, agonized impuissance. How could she bear this anguish for the rest of her life?

Eventually she fell asleep, briefly. She found herself struggling through a thick grey fog, hopelessly following the faint echo of a frightened, childish voice which repeatedly called to her, urgently and trustingly, 'Mummy, where are you? . . . I'm so frightened . . .'

She woke with a start. The cold bedroom felt oppressive, so she stumbled to the blackout curtains, yanked them back and opened the window. The chill night air that seeped into the room matched her emotion. Deep in her body, radiating chill, was a ball of ice and her tear ducts seemed to be frozen. As usual, she couldn't even have a good cry, although the stuffing had been knocked out of her. She felt like a Christmas turkey the morning after.

She would never forgive those murdering Nazis for invading France and killing her only son. Killed by some Hun who'd never even met him! Killed to satisfy Hitler's megalomania which had built on Germany's wounded pride at having lost the First World War, as Toby had explained. Toby had also pointed out that France's previous war with Prussia had occurred because France had attacked Prussia and had been humiliatingly defeated, with the result that the thirst for revenge had dominated the itchy French military between 1871 and 1914. So perhaps Max had been killed in 1940 as the result of some greedy French general's unrealistic ambition, nearly seventy years before. Once again, Mimi bitterly wondered whether God, Fate, Chance . . . or Vengeance had casually twisted her destiny and changed her entire life.

As a grey dawn lightened her room, Mimi leaned from her window. There was a turgid swell on the sea with a leaden sky above it. How could she bear this awful ache that was to be part of her life for ever? She now had no reason to live.

She glanced down at the stone terrace, fifty feet below.

When Baz died in the last war, Toby had told her that the Swiss analyst chap he was always quoting said there was no proof that anything of us is preserved for eternity but there is a definite probability that something of our soul continues beyond physical death. Jung's words had comforted Toby but not Mimi, who cared only for the brutality of death as it affected *her*. Baz had been torn from them. In one second their happy, loving friendship had been smashed. Mimi had mourned the loss of this precious relationship that of course she had taken for granted. Eventually Toby consoled her with the thought that the relationship existed in its own right and had not been severed; she could still think about and talk to Baz but for reasons beyond their control it would in future be a one-sided communication. No telephones in heaven.

Whenever Toby had attempted to *seriously* discuss with Mimi the three eternal mysteries of life – Where do we come from? Why are we here? Where will we go? – Mimi had brushed aside these questions and chirped, 'I came from Liverpool. I'm a performer. After the show I go home.' Now, as she looked out at the bleak, grey, disinterested seascape and realized the casual cruelty of death, she had one urgent question: *Where was her Max?* Was life just snuffed out like a candle flame or was death really the release of a soul, like a white dove from a cage, to heights of eternal bliss? She tried hard to imagine that Max now knew only joy but she was hampered by childish religious memories and sadly found it impossible to imagine him in a white nightgown, perched on a cloud, happily strumming a harp for ever. He wasn't that fond of music.

Wherever he was, she had to accept the pain of knowing that she would never again see her son and could not even kiss his dead face farewell.

Never again, never again ... Mimi remembered the dolorous toll of the village church bell at the funeral of Sir Octavius, that mournful repetition: Never again, never again. The solemn rhythm had been matched by the slow, shuffling steps of the pallbearers, at which sound Toby had started to weep uncontrollably.

She suddenly remembered that Toby did not yet know of his son's death.

She must get back to Toby as fast as possible, before the official telegram from the War Office arrived, he mustn't be alone to open it. She might try to hide the telegram and let Toby live happily for just a bit longer, put off telling him for as long as possible.

But before returning to Fitzroy Square, she had to meet the girl who would be carrying in her arms all that was left of Max. Neither must she let Stella know of Max's death because it would be too much of a shock; she might lose her milk and that would upset the baby too.

So that meant she mustn't tell Betsy what had happened.

That was going to be difficult. Of course, she could leave some cheerful, lying note and simply catch the next London train but ... Oh, how she wanted to see Max's baby! Betsy would take them back to America and away from the war as fast as possible but Mimi wanted to make sure that Toby saw his grandchild before they left ... They would have to make sure that poor Fizz didn't know, of course.

Mimi wished her head wasn't in such a muddle when she needed to think clearly. Thank Heaven the *Reliant* wouldn't dock until this afternoon. She would send Betsy a note to say she had a headache, so would see her after lunch; that would give her a breathing space. She couldn't bear to face anyone yet. She just wanted to sit here quietly and hold the living memory of Max in her heart for just a little longer. She now realized that the cost of love is anxiety and sorrow. She now knew that the only thing that really matters in life is death.

* * *

An hour later, the need to think and act had activated Mimi's pragmatic spirit. She went to the washbasin, pinned back her fringe, splashed her face with cold water, then coaxed her hair as usual, so that it hid the puckered scar on the upper left side of her face. She peered in the mirror above the washbasin. To her surprise, she looked the same as she had yesterday, a bit paler perhaps; but her face wasn't red and swollen because there had been no tears. 'So pull yourself together, my girl,' she admonished herself in the mirror.

She had clear duties: to see Max's child safe and then to look after Toby. She would sorrow later, with Toby. Until then, she was professional, wasn't she, she was a performer, wasn't she? 'So get out there and perform!' she sternly told her reflection.

* * *

Over the newly installed wireless loudspeaker in the hotel dining room Victor Sylvester was conducting an invigorating foxtrot; the BBC was orchestrating the entire war with ruthlessly cheerful, hum-along music.

Betsy, who had just finished nibbling at her lunch, jumped up as Mimi approached. 'Isn't it exciting, honey! They'll be here in only a few hours! I've already reserved the Churchill suite for Stella.'

Mimi did her best to stretch a smile across her face. Her friend's happy, excited expression reminded her of what it had been like to greet one of the luxury liners before the war, when bands played, coloured streamers whirled and confetti fluttered through the air. Those on board leaned over the side to wave enthusiastically to people below with whom they were about to be reunited, while cries rang out, 'There she is!' . . . 'Look, he's hanging over the rail!' . . . 'Yoohoo!'

Betsy was so joyful in anticipation that she failed to notice the strain on Mimi's face, or her subdued mood. 'Nick's been hanging around that Dockyard Gate since early morning. Sutton says there's an enormous crowd and we haven't a hope of parking anywhere near the Gate. It's this Dunkirk business, survivors are still coming ashore, he said. The newspapers are full of it, of course. Exciting to think that *we're* here when it's all happening, isn't it?' As she spoke, Betsy signed her bill, picked up her purse and swept from the dining room, a radiant figure in cornflower-blue silk with matching silk shoes.

Once seated in the Daimler, Betsy wound up the partition and turned to Mimi, whose mouth was firmly in the closed-lips-half-smile position. Clearly Betsy was about to deliver a speech.

'I've had all morning to think things over, honey, and

there are a couple of things I want to tell you.' Betsy sighed. 'I know I'm not considered a good actress but, by golly, I certainly am! I've acted all my life! When I was eight years old I was the family wage-earner but I had to act being a good, obedient kid.' She paused as she remembered her secret resentment of that regimented early life. Painfully she said, 'Then I acted being in love with Jack ... After that I acted being a rich guy's wife and society hostess ... But we didn't have the sort of marriage a girl dreams of. We had all the *things* but we was never love-birds, me and Jack. It was sort of ... convenient ... for both of us. Jack was exactly what Ma had always wanted. He knew it was time to settle down if he wanted kids and a family. I was right for the part of society dame ... In fact we was ... were ... *both* on stage, always.'

'Plenty of women live like that.' Mimi tried to sound reassuring. 'It doesn't matter now.' Nothing mattered now.

'Of course I *really* love my kids but again I acted being the perfect mom and I expected them to be real neat and act cute as if we were all in some MGM family musical – and that wasn't always good for them.' Betsy sighed again. Her violet eyes looked directly into Mimi's green ones. 'But one thing I never acted was my affection for you, Mimi: that was real and that was important to me. You burst into my life like one of them ... those ... sparkler fireworks and you lit up my life, you really did. You were all I had of a girlhood, Mimi.'

'We *did* have fun,' Mimi agreed bleakly.

Humbly, Betsy continued, 'And then I lost you, through my own self-obsession and vanity, that you always kidded me about. It was my own fault I lost you, and it was my fault that horrible thing happened to you; but you wasn't ... weren't ... the only one hurt. I lost my happiness and my girlhood when I lost you, Mimi, and it was a horrible punishment.' Betsy beamed. 'I want you to understand how much it means to me that we're friends again.'

'It means a lot to me, too.' It was ironic that Betsy should confess to having lived a faked life just when Mimi was trying her best to fake normality.

Betsy continued, clearly determined to play this scene as she had planned it, right to the self-abnegating end. 'I'm real sorry I've been so stubborn, such a darned mule.'

It will be sackcloth and ashes next, Mimi thought, if they could be bought without coupons. She gave a brief nod. 'Pride is expensive. We've both discovered that.'

Sutton turned to tap on the glass partition. 'I can't get any closer, madam.' Ahead, the road to the Dockyard Gate was jammed by military and naval vehicles. Dazed, bandaged men in torn khaki or naval greatcoats were being helped into ambulances and the back of trucks by sailors and nurses.

'Oh, those poor boys!' exclaimed Betsy.

'They *are* alive, madam,' Sutton pointed out.

Mimi's lips tightened, she mustn't give way now. 'I'll find out what's happening.' She jumped out of the door.

It took her over thirty minutes to thread her way through the crowd to the Dockyard Gate and back to Betsy who, with Nick and Sutton, stood at the back of the crowd.

'The *Reliant*'s just docked but they can't say when the refugees'll be through.'

Upon hearing this news, Betsy suddenly looked younger, eager, hopeful. She felt a flood of relief followed by an adrenaline-surge of excitement. This nerve-shredding waiting was nearly over!

Ten minutes later, unexpectedly, Betsy thought she saw Stella – but she was mistaken. Her sudden excitement evaporated, and she collapsed in tears. Silently, comfortingly, Mimi reached up and put her arm around Betsy's shoulder. 'Don't cry old girl.' Shrewdly, she added, 'You'll ruin your make-up.'

From the rear, Nick watched the two women, his mother in smart bright-blue silk and little redheaded Mrs Fane in her shabby navy suit and governess shoes. Clasping hands, they stood on tiptoe to search the crowd; his mother jumped up and down, as excited as a child. Nick hoped to God that Stella was on that boat.

Three hours later, there was a sudden stir of excitement around the Gate. Although the day was now sunny, two women wearing headscarves and fur coats burst through the crowd; both carried crocodile jewel boxes. They were followed by a thin middle-aged man wearing a raincoat with the collar stylishly turned up and a black beret on his head *à la* Borotra; he lugged two burgundy crocodile suitcases. They moved towards Nick.

Betsy screamed 'Ask that guy what boat he arrived on!'

Nick leaped forward. 'Please sir, did you arrive on the *Reliant*?'

'*Excusez-moi. Je ne parle pas l'anglais.*'

Carefully, Nick said, '*Vous êtes de Bordeaux?*'

'*Oui. Où sont les taxis?*'

'*Vous êtes venu sur le bateau* Reliant, *monsieur?*' Nick persisted.

'*Oui. Où se trouve le train pour Londres?*'

Nick's shoulders hunched in an apologetic Gallic shrug. Carefully, he said in schoolboy French, '*Je regrette, monsieur, mais non taxis, non trains.*' He turned to his mother with triumphant thumbs-up and a big grin.

Joyful, hopeful, Betsy clutched Mimi and squealed: 'I'm about to become a grandmother!'

To hide her own emotion, Mimi nodded at Betsy's cornflower-blue silk suit, with matching coat and shoes. Gruffly she joked, 'I can't see you in *that* part. You're not the grey-haired old granny type.'

'Grannies no longer go grey, they go blonde,' Betsy said firmly. Suddenly serious, she asked wistfully, 'But *do* they grow older and wiser?'

Mimi nodded firmly. 'You're never too old to grow up.'

Acknowledgements

Every author knows that sending your manuscript to an editor feels like watching your teenage daughter go off to babysit for Fred and Rosemary West but working with my meticulous freelance editor, Fanny Blake, was as enjoyable as a shopping spree at Harrods on someone else's credit card. I am similarly grateful to Clare Alexander for her thoughtful, helpful and concise criticism, which I found stimulating. I would also like to thank my agents, Anne Sibbald and Morton Janklow, who supported and encouraged me during the writing of this book.

Fellow writers who have been particularly generous with their time and expertise include: Cyra McFadden, who was thorough and explicit in her criticism, and gave my manuscript a red tick whenever she laughed (occasionally at something intentionally funny). Business journalist Lois Bolton criticized my first draft over candlelit breakfasts. Felicity Green Hill, Malcolm Brown and Angela Lambert tactfully criticized my theme; Dr Dennis Friedman shared his medical expertise; medical TV journalist Vivienne Parry generously advised me on sources of research; Alan Brien improved my Noël Coward; Cynthia Heimel helped Fizz to define her femininity; and Venetia

Murray, daughter of the Duke of Haddock, provided piscatorial detail.

Suzanne Baboneau's early criticism of my synopsis was most helpful, as was that of Geraldine Cooke. I am also particularly grateful to actress and author Ann Queensberry, my painstaking technical editor.

I am indebted to Kristina de Linares for her patience and shrewd but supportive criticism, right through from first synopsis to final manuscript. David Solomon also criticized my synopsis, and couriered my drafts around the world. At very short notice business consultant Paula Whittam proofed the final m.s.s. Barbro Eklund then waited at London airport until four in the morning to meet it. Carbon Secretarial Services of Brighton typed the final corrections.

As usual, I am grateful to my sons Sebastian Conran and Jasper Conran and my daughter-in-law Georgina Godley Conran for much discussion of my theme, as well as for their usual advice and benevolent tolerance. For helping me to research my theme – the difficulties of forgiveness and the dangers of revenge – I would like to thank two Roman Catholic priests, who prefer to remain anonymous, for their help and support during my early work, as well as the Reverend Murray Grant, Sally Fear and Elizabeth Chatwin. I also discussed forgiveness and revenge at great length with the Earl and Countess of Longford; Lord Longford kindly sent me his (regrettably out of print) book on forgiveness, which helped fill the yawning cavern in my religious knowledge.

From the theatre world, Sîan Phillips taught me much about early theatrical make-up, trusted me with a suitcaseful of rare books from her theatrical library and also told me many theatrical anecdotes ('At the age of five, my grandmother, Kate Bishop, and Ellen Terry played together as fairies in *The Dream*'). John Wells instructed me on the responsibilities of a director; director Robert Carson allowed me to rehearsals of his opera, *Cinderella*, and director Anne Batt allowed me to rehearsals of her pantomime, *Cinderella*. Playwright David Campton gave me much biographical information about Vesta Tilley; actress Bettina Culham also shared her theatrical knowledge with me, as did Julia de Bierre.

In Hollywood, movie producer Joanne Brough kindly gave me much sociological information; the management of the Château Marmont and the Beverly Hills Hotel, Hollywood, allowed me access to their archives, as well as their accommodation. In London, I would like to thank Enid Chanelle and the management of the Theatre Royal as well as Linda Bellingham and the management of the Old Vic for kindly allowing me backstage during performances, and also for access to all parts of their theatre.

This book has also benefited from the learning and experience of the authors who wrote the 157 preparatory books I read, which sadly did not always agree as to facts and dates, particularly those concerning the early history of Hollywood; where different dates were given, I'm afraid I chose what seemed to me the most likely.

In order to establish authenticity, I have occasionally used the names of real people, real places and real organizations, such as the Old Vic and Lilian Baylis. As all my characters are imaginary, no scenes in which they participated actually took place. When my imaginary characters interact with real characters, places or events, the scenes are, obviously, fictitious.

As usual, my research secret weapon was Charlotte Abrahams Siddons, who did an astonishing amount of

work in only one day. Jane Ashley gave me in   P
concerning the House of Commons and Steven
kindly checked my anthropological deduction
Packer, Lady Iliffe and Lady Peake generously
their debutante recollections with me; Tom Johns
Dr Peter Jones were thorough in their clarificati
hubris.

Mimi's voice coach was Chuck Mallett; her finan
and property problems were swiftly solved by David Ki
Roger Seelig, Maria Boyle of Westminster City Coun
Information Department and Roger Bloom of the City o
Westminster Planning Office.

Charles Chatwin, RNVR retired, generously shared his
wartime recollections with me, as did many present residents of Portsmouth. My aunt, Dorothy Spittle, and my
god-daughter, Zenna Atkins, also helped to locate Portsmouth background material.

As a child, Brian Patterson, a Director of the Portsmouth Royal Dockyard Historical Trust and the Curator
of Portsmouth Naval Base Property Trust, spent the
Second World War unpleasantly close to Portsmouth
Dockyard, and (thanks to the Luftwaffe) was finally
obliged to leave the rubble of his home and live briefly in
the comfort of St Agatha's Church. I much appreciate his
information and criticism, and I would also like to thank
Annabelle Boyes, Commercial Manager, and her secretary,
Simone Friswell, of Portsmouth Historic Dockyard Ltd.

I am equally indebted to Dr Chris Howard Bailey,
Head of Oral History and Director of Publications at the
Royal Naval Museum, Portsmouth, Sarah Quail of the
Museums and Records Officer for the City of Portsmouth
(which includes the D-Day Museum), and Diana Gregg,
Senior Searchroom Assistant to the Record Services at the

ortsmouth City Museums. David Ware, Ian Frazer and Jikki Fraser also clarified details. Maggi Thomson kindly visited my home in the evening, whenever my fringe obstructed my vision.

Finally, after a year and half spent on research, then two years spent on four drafts, each of half a million words, having eventually typed the words THE END, I would like to Thank God.

THE END